IN LIMBO

A.D. ALIWAT

ALTAIR
PRESS

Published by Altair Press
New York, NY

This is a work of fiction. Names, characters, locales, and events are either the product of the author's imagination or are used fictitiously. Any resemblance to actual persons, living or dead, corporations, institutions, organizations, incidents, or places is entirely coincidental.

ISBN: 978-0-578-72589-5

And the LORD God commanded the man, saying, Of every tree of
the garden thou mayest freely eat:
But of the tree of the knowledge of good and evil, thou shalt not eat of
it: for in the day that thou eatest thereof thou shalt surely die.
> *Genesis 2:16-17*

Think different.
> TBWA\Chiat\Day
> *Advertising Campaign for Apple Inc.*

To be, or not to be, that is the question:
Whether 'tis nobler in the mind to suffer
The slings and arrows of outrageous fortune,
Or to take Arms against a Sea of troubles,
And by opposing end them…
> William Shakespeare
> *Hamlet*

IN LIMBO

There's something in the air, but it isn't love. "I ♥ NY," he reads over and over again, staring at stacks of T-shirts in the gift shops that line the Crossroads of the World, the Great White Way. He's on Broadway and 49th, straddling a cheap gray road bike, waiting for the light to change or the stream of cars running by to slow to a trickle. Anticipation, muscle fatigue, a tepid breeze: besides these, Raymond Gonzales is not sure what he feels, but bold, bighearted love for New York wouldn't be on any list.

Although he can't be sure, he figures he died at some point during the summer of 2007. His best guess is that it was shortly after the release of the first iPhone, that a few weeks later he had probably been struck by a car while walking across a street or something, lost in his brand-new little God Machine. He does not remember floating above himself or going to a white light or any similar metaphysical process that would have been informed by his quasi-Catholic upbringing or ideas of transcending worlds from reading or television or movies, but all the same, he was no longer living, this he now knew, and had not been for quite some time.

The light changes and he moves fast. One with his bike, dressed in a black sweatshirt and jeans, the right leg rolled up, with a thick chain wrapped around his trim waist, he flies through the crowd like a concrete-camouflaged phantom. His helmet—also black, multisport-style in shape—is angled low, his hazel eyes busy beneath. His fight is against all of them, them everywhere, them every type, moving every direction, every speed—fast, slow, fat, thin, white, black, brown, beige, men, women, children, fashion-forward, fanny-packed, happy, sad, vacant, shouting, speaking, silent; then more cars, honking cabs, empty pedicab operators preying, a few other cyclists zipping and creeping, less immediate than the pedestrians but every bit as bothersome: all contributing to the blare and clang, all adding to this entanglement illuminated by the lurid digital glow of a flashing red, green, blue corporate ideography. Times Square—loud and bright twenty-four hours a day, bearing a more stunning light than the Statue of Liberty ever could, a Disneyfied Lucifer leading New York's damned to a fire ever-building, ever-burning. As he tears across 43rd Street down Broadway, headphones playing Modeselektor to help drown out the cacophony of the streets, Ray thinks more about the "I ♥ NY" on white and black and multicolored tees and sweatshirts there countless in their surrounding of him. *I have to be dead,* he reassures himself. *This isn't real. It would be too much.*

He had just delivered a commercial for an advertising agency to MTV, and every aspect of this was almost as silly as it was sad to him. He's on his way downtown, to SoHo, where the dispatcher from the courier service he works for has instructed him via text on his iPhone 4S to pick up some candles to deliver to *Good Housekeeping*, in the Hearst Building, back up on 57th and Eighth. Depending on the Sixth Avenue rush-hour traffic he may end up cutting through part of Times Square again when he returns. On the good weeks he takes home around four hundred dollars as a bike messenger, his salary almost purely commission-based, and this his current only source of income. He holds a B.A. in anthropology from Columbia University, Class of '08, and celebrated his twenty-sixth birthday a few weeks ago, back in February, in this, the year of our Lord 2012.

Riding to beat the dying light of a now fast-setting sun Ray glides across the 59th Street Bridge. Up ahead, the shared bike and footpath climbs 130 feet above the East River; the UES, Roosevelt Island with its tram, and some red-orange sky make up the left; to the right the bridge's bi-level lanes of hurtling automobiles in bi-directional traffic partially obstruct jagged Midtown East beyond. All is covered in the warm blanket of partly cloudy dusk that makes most everything that was blue or gray a half hour before matte violet. He's pedaling quickly, but not without the joy that accompanies a leisure activity. Work is over for the day. A gentle breeze is coming from the southwest and the air smells good for city air, vague traces of perfumed trees blooming somewhere below cutting through the abundant exhaust left by the nine lanes of traffic to his immediate and above right. There are only a few pedestrians and fellow cyclists using the path and, his headphones now pumping in Mozart's *Requiem*, he's for the most part aloof to what's going on beyond the southern guardrail. This is well earned after spending the last eight hours caring very, very much about what the cars were doing beside and all around him. Today—with temperatures in the low sixties—was warmer than it had been so far in March, or the year to date. It now seems like spring. For a moment, there's a strange pang of recognition, déjà vu, and then for a few flickering split seconds afterwards he feels very happy and strong and free on his bike, almost majestic, soaring through the soft air, the wind at his back, returning home. Something quite different from the anhedonia that has become his default. When all of this eventually flutters away in the breeze, he is relieved.

A little while longer and he's there. Brian has beaten him home. He knows this because the hallway smells like weed. Good weed, their weed, not the neighbor's schwag. Unlocking the door and rolling in his bike, he's greeted first by a fuller expression of the aroma—distinct citrus overtones in this batch, definitely sativa-dominant, Ray's preference—and then by the man himself, on the couch next to the entranceway, with a "Hey." After a very short silence, not long enough to say "What's up?" or even "Hey" back, Brian continues: "Just missed EJ. Got you an eighth, you owe me sixty."

"Smells good."

"Yeah, it's some new high-quality Lemon Haze. Treating me well so far."

Ray rests his bike under the window against the opposite wall of the living room. A chief perk of Queens habitation, especially in an older building like theirs, is that they have a nice amount of space. Everything is oriented toward a 42-inch Samsung flat-panel LCD television—currently playing the *NBC Nightly News*, on mute—and the slightly broader, bench-like dark brown entertainment center supporting it. Powerful speakers and a surge protector where the electronics plug in share the surface behind the TV, between it and the wall. The stand has two shelves in the middle. A collection of DVDs and Blu-Rays, most unwatched for at least two years, are stacked on the top shelf; the bottom is home to an Xbox 360 and PS3 along with their controllers and a few favored games, everything but the consoles heaped in careless order, but its own order it is. Inside of the stand's cabinets, next to the shelves on either side, are more games and movies. The apartment's modem and wifi router take up the floor space to the right of the entertainment center, between it and the hallway, little chartreuse dots dancing, flashing on and off side by side and with still ones. The rest of the room is a hodgepodge of twentieth-century furniture collected from thrift stores, Craigslist, and the curbside—a well-worn tawny-colored couch across from the TV; a scratched-up oak end table to its left with an old lamp shaped like a soldier on top; a green armchair in the corner catawampus, perfectly angled toward the TV, after that; a mid-sized dusty bookshelf on the other side of the chair, perpendicular to the couch and next to the window; and a frayed Persian rug in the room's center covering the old hardwood floor. In an attempt to bring together the contemporary aesthetic of the TV wall and emphatically noncontemporary one of everything opposite it, the perimeter is decorated with a few large Bob Ross-style oil paintings that Ray modified to feature popular Nintendo, Sega, and PlayStation franchise characters living in trees and coming out from behind mountains, their images reflected in smooth hyaline lakes in the two of these paintings that have lakes. Ray got high and made them one day and Brian never complained after he put them up, so there they remain. There are also some newer books on the shelf, but not many, mostly nonfiction. The room is helped somewhat, too, by anybody leaving or using a laptop or tablet on the couch, Brian nose-down right then reading something on the latter—a more even spread of the machines that signify a comfortable twenty-first-century environment.

There's a window that gets a good amount of natural light and features a dramatic view of the Midtown skyline, including the Empire State Building. Throughout the week, the colors of its tower lights may change from night to night, marking different occasions. Ray likes to play a guessing game most days, where he picks what colors they'll be before they come on. Usually it's just classic white. Inasmuch as the apartment's located on 21st Street in Long Island City across from the open and airy Murray Playground, the view really is something, and depending on the weather, weed, or whatever, it can occasionally take a visiting friend's or acquaintance's breath away, literally. Brian and Ray are a bit jaded though, especially Brian, whose own room is off of this one and has an almost identical view, his doorway to the left of the TV. Ray goes down a hall to the other end of the apartment, through the eat-in kitchen, past the bathroom, to his room—which does not have a view of anything anyone would describe as breathtaking, unless someone was really stricken by brick walls five feet away—and brings back sixty dollars after dropping his gear. He hands it over and Brian, between tokes, slips it into his pocket.

"Thanks," still holding the smoke in, he hands Ray the joint, then a sandwich bag containing his supply for the next two or so weeks. Ray sits down next to him and takes a hit. Brian, a light-eyed, brown-haired Irish-Italian, is wearing a white button-up shirt, red tie loosened at the neck, and slacks, meaning he didn't have enough time to dress down for the evening before he was supposed to receive their dealer, or that he's decided to subtly fuck with Ray. The area around the blurry gray-blue circumference of his irises is on its way to matching his tie in a dullish pink. Ray's have had a similar tint for the past four hours because of wind and overstimulation. Brian places his iPad on the table beside him and exhales. "How 'bout this weather?"

"Fuckin' beautiful."

"Titties are comin' out."

Ray nods, still inhaling.

"Goddam, I wish I had your gig on a day like today," Brian says through a smile. He speaks with the fast tongue and the sort of gravel-throated whine of someone who grew up on Long Island, which he did.

Not done holding it in—"No you don't."

"I saw the sun for like ten minutes all day. That's it. Five on the way to work. Zero at lunch. Five coming out. And now it's on its way to Japan. You, you're a free man."

"I'm a prisoner of my situation," Ray exhales, a plume rising then fading above.

Brian laughs, harsh and derisive. "Your situation?"

"Yeah."

"What's that?"

"Bad luck, mostly, I guess." He takes another. They look ahead at the news. It's the end of a story on obesity: large round bodies walking the streets without faces, a doctor's brief testimony. Then Brian Williams teases a couple of segments coming up later in the broadcast—Romney and Obama trading barbs on the campaign trail, then the kicker, which seems to involve an inspirational soup kitchen somewhere—and the commercials roll.

Brian shakes his head. "Riding a bike all day for a living and you're the prisoner, damn."

Ray hands the joint back and raises his index finger in a just-one-moment gesture. He exhales, "You say that like I'm getting ready for the Tour de France, selling Wheaties. Or that riding a bike for more than an hour isn't hard fucking work. It's not much of a living." Not much of a living… the words don't get far before they fly back in through his ears and echo all across his mind.

"How much do you pull in again?" Brian knows exactly how much he makes.

"You know what I make."

"I forgot."

"Usually a little less than a hundred a day." The THC is really start-ing to settle in and Ray appreciates how nice it is to sit on something as wide as the couch.

"Maybe I could make it work." Brian grins, bringing the joint, now almost gone, to his lips. Its ember glows. The apartment, a two-bedroom walkup, is his turf. It was his uncle who bought the building back when LIC was a moldering eighties hellhole and who lets them live in it on the cheap. Brian has been here since graduating from Columbia alongside Ray, through his time at NYU Law immediately after, and in the nearly two years since that he's worked as a tax lawyer. He does not normally get home so early, usually putting in something like fourteen-hour days. But he leaves early from time to time depending on the weather or a shortage of weed. His plan is to live here, meagerly enough—marijuana, the random night out with his colleagues, and takeout twice a month his only real indulgences—until he's close to thirty-five. This is because he's playing the long game. At twenty-six, he has a 401k, IRA, and some cash he messes around with almost daily in the stock market. By 2020, he'd like to buy his own large three- or four-bedroom house, he's told Ray, back on Long Island. Ray, on the other hand, who has now lived here for almost two years, needs the rent break desperately. His early-twen-ties-until-recently were spent in various journalism and media jobs, mostly stopgap contract or freelance roles for well-meaning rinky-dink online outfits that eventually fell victim to the Great Recession and its obdurate half-life… though there was also the occasional larger com-pany, all of which still paid like shit because they could. When Occupy Wall Street hit last fall, he was already too tired to join in on any protest. He knows there's really no good reason he should be living in a place that is one stop and five minutes away from the heart of Manhattan, with a dramatic view of the Art Deco masterpiece and quintessential New York emblem that is the Empire State Building, for only five hun-dred bucks a month. To Brian, the place is a compromise, another in-vestment—hence the furniture—to Ray, it's the best thing he has going for him. And this is well known to the benefactor. But while there is some weirdness to their dynamic as a result of this, Brian needs Ray in his own way—that way being few people he went to college or high school with actually enjoy or even tolerate his company—and respect and shit are generally doled out in equal measure by both parties.

"You couldn't last a second in my world."

"I couldn't last a second riding a bike on a beautiful day… Jesus, I've ridden a bike here, Ray. It's not that crazy."

"Where'd you ride? Central Park?" Ray imagines more deliveries somehow bringing him through Central Park, how happy that would make him as more and more plants germinate and trees bud with bright flowers and virid little leaves in the next month. This feeling inverts on itself once he realizes how truly improbable that is. In the three and a half weeks he's worked as a messenger, he's had, like, one delivery above 59th.

"I rode around." Brian takes one last hit and stubs the joint out in a coconut shell ashtray that rests on the end table.

"Around."

"I've ridden in the city. Shit."

"The Central Park loop is a six-mile pleasure cruise, my dude." It is such a pleasure cruise that it's one of the reasons Ray, about a month ago, when the last real job interview didn't pan out, at that point almost five weeks without even a one-off gig, decided on becoming a courier. Riding his bike used to be a favorite activity, a love; now whatever fun can be had soon fades.

"I wouldn't know." Brian stares at the news, back from break, watching the other Brian's lead-in followed by footage of people manufacturing something, jobless claim statistics on a chyron beside them.

"I almost get hit *at least* twice daily. Like really hit. Like hospital-trip hit. I can't control anybody else on the road and besides my helmet I'm totally unprotected. And I have my dispatcher constantly on my ass for not being fast enough. It's terrifying." Ray scratches his head. It feels weird because he is officially high now. Meaning: he can actually feel his nails scrape off bits of scalp, and it's louder than it should be. His body feels nice—very nice—however, like he hadn't spent the last eight hours tearing it down, the last three days before doing the same, the last three and a half weeks save the weekends before that. When he takes hits, he holds them down at length, but still: it only took two, and he smokes a few times a week. This is indeed a good strain, though there's probably a little more indica in it than previously guessed.

"Well, whatever, get a better job or sue when it happens. Shut the fuck up until then."

"Maybe Chris would take the case pro bono." Mentioning Chris, a former classmate who's now a trial attorney, is always fun because he's a more successful lawyer than Brian.

"Why don't you sell weed? You're Mexican. You must know somebody."

"I might be already. Most of the time I have no idea what's in these packages. Also, fuck you."

Brian laughs, very pleased with himself. "MaRaya Full of Grace over here carrying around heroin and coke for three hundred bucks a week. You're right. Raw deal. I *wouldn't* last a second in your world. Disbarment is one thing, but I'm too pretty for Rikers." He laughs more, harder. Ray's now grimacing, and though he had turned to Brian when he first heard his own name and some excitability in tone, he had since turned back to the TV. It gave him something to do while trying to wrap his head around the MaRaya Full of Grace comment, attempting to avoid its spikes and sting, to little avail. Brian, bothered enough by the silence, adds, "But hey, you're already in a prison, right?"

Chapfallen, thick, mustached men and wild-haired women in Middle America complain about how they still don't have enough or meaningful work, their eyes moist and mouths trembling, speaking without a sound. Oh, hey, I know that guy, thinks Ray, and it helps him forget about the train he was on… transgressive faux-racism and gender roles, how he shouldn't be at all offended he was called a Colombian teenage girl, but a part of him is… how that same part also wanted to clarify that he was only half Mexican, which Brian damn well knew anyway, and how shameful that urge was… how he should be more bothered by the careless and weird joke at the expense of terrified people who are actually made to ingest and poop out dozens of drug-filled balloons… everything Brian was able to unearth in one not-even-good pun following a relatively lighthearted jab about an oft-belittled ethnic background he happens to share and its vilified role in the American drug trade… how the whole point of going to a school like the one they went to, ultrabright futures aside, was to not say shit like that, and to think your way around it when it is said, unfazed because you have truth to support you… Then he feels bad about himself for caring so much. It's not that big a fucking deal. Brian's just kind of a shithead and always has been. That's why nobody likes him. Also, he isn't even real. None of this is. He's just a psychospiritual projection of the guy he roomed with freshman year in Carman, a few years before he got run over or whatever. "It's a hard knock life," comes out about three seconds later than it should've.

"Don't call me if you get locked up."

"I won't. I'll call Chris." Ray smiles.

"Yeah, if you want the max sentence. But I wouldn't have time for your ass, anyway. Work's crazy right now. I only came home early today because we were running low and it's nice out, and they know I've been working till ten every night this week. Shit is brutal."

"I bet." Ray's still staring ahead and Brian turns back to the screen, too. Now something's happening in the Middle East.

"Can you deliver me, like, an eight ball tomorrow at lunch? Sixteen-hour days are coming soon. You'd be a real hit with my division."

Ray gets up. "I need to shower."

"I think I'm gonna check out the Gantry. What's it, like high fifties still?"

"Something fifties."

"Call of Duty later?"

"Yeah, maybe." Ray's mind is elsewhere, in the shower already, trying to feel each individual drop as it hits his flesh. It's overwhelming, entirely, and he can't wash his hair.

Two minutes later, by the time he's actually there, steam rising, hot water rinsing the film of dried sweat from his mostly hairless body, he has moved on again. He's plotting the rest of the night—dressing himself in basketball shorts and a brushed cotton T-shirt; smoking a little more, alone, with the vaporizer; eating a big dinner before Brian's return and avoiding him as much as possible, only playing Xbox if he really has to; drinking a couple of the Trader Joe's Simpler Times beers he has left in the fridge while he plays some PS3 on the small TV from college in his room; opening up the silver MacBook and browsing Facebook, joking around with old friends or subtly flirting, via likes, with girls he wanted to have sex with in college but never did; texting one or both of the two girls he's currently occasionally actually having sex with; jerking off to Pornhub; watching something on Netflix drowsily. He shampoos his hair twice without realizing it. He moves on to bedtime, quiet comfort under warm covers in a cool dark room. A deep sleep. He suds up his body with a loofah. And though he tries to deflect it, limit everything to the meager, superficial forgiveness allowed in this place he calls home, it's made its way in and he's back there again, riding on, back and forth, up and down the rectilinear grid, on and on, crural muscles tearing, brain on fire, on and on and on.

▲▽

This is nowhere. These words flash across her mind. Only once, nano-second fast. She isn't sure what they're referring to. It could mean a lot of things. Or absolutely nothing. So she ignores it. Forgets. She is aware, but not. The only thing she wants to do is move on.

She is in the middle of three text conversations. She is gchatting in one more. She is playing two games. It is her turn in one, Words With Friends. It is her friend's turn in the other. She forgot what game that was. All she knows is that it is not also Words With Friends. She did not forget what friend it was, though; it was Kim. There is music playing in the background. She does not know who it is, or care, not enough to Shazam it, anyway. Though, she does notice she likes it, but also notices she does not care enough to Shazam it. She is in a little restaurant. It is very white. It smells more sterile than it should considering all the Asian fusion being cooked in the back. She likes this. She has already checked in here on Foursquare. She is drinking a bubble tea. She remembers a homework assignment due tomorrow. It is for English class. She has not started yet. She had just seconds ago got a new alert on Facebook. She checks it. A friend has tagged her in a photo. She looks cute in it, so she is happy. This friend, Maeve, has tagged her before where she has looked not so cute. She likes Maeve a little more now. She opens the Yelp reviews for this restaurant for the third time today, the second time while here. She is kind of bored. There is a nineteen-year-old boy sitting in front of her. She is on a date.

Haruka Kidokoro is herself eighteen, and at least twice as many hours of her day are spent looking at some sort of screen than not. A freshman at NYU, she is from San Francisco, is of half-Japanese and half-Chinese descent, and has lived in New York for seven months. Her major is undecided. Most things about her are, except for the way she dresses—outfits completely in black, shades of gray, or, in the summer-time, white—and her dream: one day, she will work for a major tech company. Her top picks: Facebook, Google, and Apple.

"How's the tea?" asks the boy, Pete. She met him on OkCupid, like the rest.

She reads a new tweet from *Time Out New York*. It is a promotion for some Yoga class. Then another one from *The Huffington Post*. It is about a celebrity she has never heard of adopting a dog. About five seconds pass. She looks up: "Pretty good." She looks back down.

They go through the rest of the motions involved in a date. The kinds of dates worth going on, anyway.

After the act she always washes. It's like brushing teeth, though not her teeth. A gesture of nurture. Her Little Kaiju very well can't brush its own teeth. That's what she calls it, Little Kaiju. Boys name theirs all the time, but she's never heard of a girl naming hers, besides herself. But she doesn't share this with anyone, the name. Maybe that's why she's never heard of another girl naming hers. Girls know the value of a good secret. She feels happy.

It's not a shower; it only requires the sink, a cupped hand, and a bit of water. She dries and again puts on the black shorts and T-shirt she had dressed herself in immediately after the act, before she crossed the suite to the bathroom. She has to be safe even though none of the Three Witches are here right now. It's Thursday and they all like to go out on Thursdays. But that doesn't mean they couldn't walk in at any moment. She's been yelled at for walking through the common area naked once already.

He's still there when she returns. She's had a few that were not. She'd be fine with them doing that if it didn't end up complicating the sign-out process down with security. She wonders where he'll fall on the spectrum. It starts with the ones that leave while she washes and ends with the ones she has to almost physically remove from the bed.

Hers is a double room: dressers and desks and beds line both sides, a window in the middle. Witch One, Lauren, shares it with her. It's decorated not unlike a Target dorm room-type advertisement. He's leaning on one arm, propped up, smiling earnestly, following her with his eyes. She can't remember their color. He's still nude, at least from the torso up, where she can see. Thin and pale. He and the room are cast in blue light. She grabs her phone, left unattended for twenty minutes, and looks at her alerts. There are eleven notifications more deserving of her attention than him but she'll do what she has to do first.

"Hey there," he says.

"Hey…" She sits at the foot of the bed, which is extra long and narrow, the standard dorm room bed. She twists to face him, her eyes wide and brow raised.

He smiles. His eyes are blue, she guesses. He's blonde so that would make sense. But maybe they're green and it's just the light. Everything is blue right now except her. She is black. "What's going on, stranger? Why so far away?"

"I like to be alone after," she says.

"Oh…" He sits up. He scratches his face. "Okay…"

"And my roommate will probably be back any second."

He laughs to himself. "Right, gotcha." He sits on the side of the bed and finds his underwear and pants on the floor nearby. They go on. She checks her alerts—four emails, five Facebook notifications, two from games. His T-shirt is inside his sweater, so he can put both on simultaneously. That's good. She stands up when he is fully clothed. "Oh, almost forgot this." Without noticing, she had been sitting on his fedora. She had worn it while riding him.

"I'll sign you out," she says.

She had made it a point to sign him in before 10:00. They got there at 9:53, she read then on the paper. Sign-out was no big deal. It was now 10:45. He tries to kiss her goodnight in the lobby and she does not let him. She takes an Adderall and does her English homework.

This had been Haruka and Pete's first date. She goes on several of these a week—first dates—what is a nerve-racking experience for many her favorite leisure activity. All of her dates take place with boys, or sometimes real men. A few even more than double her age. For the most part, except for the older ones who wholeheartedly own what they're doing, these encounters are introduced as an invitation to "hang out." But she knows they are not all that casual. They're real dates, even if they're just going to see some friends' band or grab a cup of coffee. And this is because she knows what they're all really after—her Little Kaiju.

She lets them meet Little Kaiju at the end of every one of these if the male hasn't messed up too badly. Most don't. She is forgiving of almost everything, especially saying something "dumb." A lot of dumb guys are good at sex. She only draws the line at "dorky." This shouldn't be confused with nerdy or geeky. Those things are a turn-on. She loves talking tech, geeky stuff. But dorky guys, she learned after two or three experiences, were bad at sex… did not sate her Little Kaiju… and so those nights would end with a peck on the cheek, followed, maybe, by a demure giggle as she turned down a New York City street and quickly vanished.

Otherwise, she would introduce them to Little Kaiju, and it would eat them whole. It would take them in, all of them, and after a little fight, spit them out, drained of their souls and life essences. She had them then. And they empowered her. But beyond the neurochemical reactions tied up in this little boost, they didn't get to her at all. She's smart enough to know that material objects don't ever actually touch, that sensation is just electron fields overlapping and repelling each other, and all they're feeling are resultant rushes of dopamine, serotonin, oxytocin, and endorphins. Connection is in the mind.

They're not so smart, though. They think it might mean something weightier and so many soon want a second date. They want more time with Little Kaiju… but it never eats the same meal twice. In her seven months in New York, she'd been on thirty-six first dates and zero second ones.

She's usually less than half present during these dates, and tonight was no exception. It drives most of them a little crazy, she can tell, when she glances up every now and again. Men like to be the ones who ignore. But she does not care. She barely knows when she's doing it anymore; it's just what she does. And in the end, most, unless they're dorks, and she rejects them—or the secret dorks that tell her at the end of the night they want to take it slow, the kinds that likely couldn't please her, anyway—will accept her invitation to come back and "hang out" more in her dorm room. Some of the older ones insist on showing her their fancy apartments, but others like going to the dorm room for the thrill. She loved the look on the security guard's face after the third of those she signed in. If Witch One happens to be in the room on these nights, Haruka will ask for forty-five minutes alone. Witch One hates her because of this, but still agrees. She mostly just goes across the suite to Witch Two and Witch Three's room, where they complain and cackle. She hears them sometimes. The worst is with the older men—"Prostitute!," "Whore!," once even "Keep the happy endings in Chinatown!" from high-pitched Witch Two. Racist bitch. They're trying to shame her, but she knows they are just jealous, jealous of her and her Little Kaiju. It's not her fault she's prettier than they are, or that her hypothalamus is more active. Those three have little sex. And they don't go out to eat nearly as often as she does. They're stuck eating gross cafeteria food all the time, while she and Little Kaiju have so many nice meals, eat so much that is tasty.

She collects these boys and men. Their souls. She knows they will think about her, love her again in their minds. Blood courses from the head back to the heart. Then it is done. They are hers forever.

▲ ▲

Oh, what the devil? Hunched over a mahogany writing desk, the large white-haired man nearly knocks over the prasinous-glassed banker's lamp next to the computer monitor as he pulls at the page stuck in the printer. He had all but given up twenty minutes ago when the thing had jammed for the second time tonight. Now the third, he wishes he just had, but the two pages that are supposed to print have needs unfortunately far more important than another of his piddling wants. "Goddammit," he says.

Emerson Towers is seventy-two years old and, when completely vertical, a mountain of a man, standing a broad, lumpy six-three, with low shoulders and stocky, somewhat bowed legs. Decades of deep thought have carved thick wrinkles spanning his broad forehead, while dread and laughter account for the many finer ones spreading from his gaunt blue eyes and thin-lipped mouth like crags. Conversely, from just as many decades of eating exactly as he pleases, ample heft rounds out his cheeks and chins. His hair is always kept somewhere between tousled and wild, a signature part of his look. He dresses well in the tweedy way professors, which he is, do, even now, and projects a patrician mien at all times.

Of course, really, it *was* physically possible to just edit them on the computer. But this is not how it's done. His job is to judge works on the page, and so in this way he must judge his own. Words of any importance, of any real worth, appear on a page, not screen.

With a grunt, he rises from his tufted brown leather office chair, which, like most chairs, is far too small for him, its casters swiveling then rolling backwards across hardwood flooring until they catch the short side edge of an antique oriental rug. Like always. He moves toward the other end of the office, the hardwood covered only by the rug in the center of the room, creaking beneath his considerable weight with each step. Immaculately organized bookshelves line the walls on either side from floor to ceiling, and a section of the wall he's facing. Nine of these books were written by him, on the highest shelf in the literary criticism section. Even though he's not in the best of moods, he makes sure to wink as he passes, something he does anytime he catches them. The shelves to his right end at the doorway, which leads to the living room, this office making up the larger of the two bedrooms in his resplendent apartment. A stately eighteenth-century mahogany armoire shares the wall with the shelving on the far end, where he has now arrived. He opens the doors, gingerly, gazing up at the Royal HH typewriter he had used to write his first book, as well as the following six.

It has its own special place, up above, on its own shelf, of course. He reaches for it and carries it back across the room with a firm grip and gentle gait.

Approaching the desk, he sees his image reflected in the window directly above it, a lucent, ghostlike figure one with the night. If he were in a better mood, he might've winked at himself, too. That damn printer! This west-facing window has a notable view of the Hudson River and the Palisades escarpment above during the day, a view where Emerson sees the rest of the world opening up before him, waiting to receive him, particularly during the glorious gleams of twilight. But now it is pitch dark. Almost pure black, like the soul of whichever quality control inspector let that useless thing get past! No, no. Maybe it's just acting its age. He's had it for over ten years now. These office apparatuses aren't people, after all… He sets the Royal HH down, gracefully, and removes its cover. Shunting the computer monitor and keyboard to the side of the desk, he slides the typewriter to cover the dust-ridden spaces they had occupied. Yes, that's more like it! Isn't that nice? He runs the fingers of his right hand over the cool, rounded, gray surface directly above the machine's ROYAL lettering, then back the other way across the QWERTY row of green and white keys. Be still! Be still, old heart! He wipes it with a cloth and begins his preparation ritual, at once familiar and frightening. Dare he? Yes. He sits.

Emerson looks to the computer monitor for the words already written. The keys clank. The bell rings. He pushes the carriage lever to the right. The keys clank some more. The bell rings again. He pushes the lever to the right once more, and it feels as natural and effortless as pecking at the keys. In these moments, he is young again. Truly. Soon enough, he has his pages. Then after that, what he's been waiting for, the red pen.

Three drafts and about two hours later, it's done. He looks at his finished pages. They are beautiful. They are perfect. He has found the right word in every instance and each punctuation mark serves the organization of his thoughts in the best possible manner. It would not, could not fit in any other configuration. He makes the necessary changes to the Word document he began with and saves it. He drafts a short email and attaches the file, quickly double-checks this message for grammar and flow, finding that it too is perfect, requiring no editing whatsoever, and adds his friend Sam from *The New York Times Book Review* to the recipient line. He sends it off.

There was a time when Emerson wrote exclusively about the Western Canon. These days, on the rare occasions he produces work, he writes mostly about others writing about the Western Canon. That was the case this evening, in his brief review of a new book about William Wordsworth's love life.

It's a little after 1:00 a.m. now. But Emerson's always been a creature of the night, and he does not have to teach class until noon. He pours another glass of cabernet, grabs *Lyrical Ballads* from the shelf, and begins to read. It has been decades since he's read and the aesthetic purity of the words alone was more important than the concerns of his role as a preeminent literary scholar. He doesn't know when this transition happened exactly, but also doesn't care. For you see, it is literature that exists for him, not the other way around.

The *Times* piece will be the first thing he's published in nearly three years. Alone in his bed a couple of hours later, he dreams he's frolicking nude along a hilly English countryside, wildflowers everywhere, and he awakes upon producing a nocturnal emission. It's something he didn't know he was still capable of doing at his age, especially after such a period of desuetude, and while a little messy, it's not an entirely unwelcome surprise. It seems he's still got it.

▲▽▽

Fifth Avenue isn't so bad in the mornings, really. Ray uses the bus lane for the most part, and though there are a lot of buses and they're all in a rush, there aren't so many cars in the next lanes over that they can't go around him, so everybody's able to get where they need to go without too much trouble. Plus, he keeps up. Ray runs every red light he can when the threat of getting run over isn't imminent, and except for the obstinate, thunderous inter-borough express buses, the buses stop a lot. This is hours before tourists flock to the Midtown stretch he's riding down—the drag between 59th Street and 27th—to window-shop or make their way to Central Park or the Apple Store or MoMA or Rockefeller Center or St. Patrick's Cathedral or the New York Public Library or Empire State Building, before the sidewalks overflow and they bleed into the street and make things harder on everyone, including themselves. During those hours, Fifth is an all-around shitshow. If he were to try to use the bus lane then, the buses would probably parp at him unremittingly, and the cops might actually give him a ticket, and for an amount that would not only forfeit his day's earnings, but also dip into his very limited savings.

Ray's courier office is in the Flatiron District. Most days he reports there around 8:30, before receiving his first assignment. Occasionally there are days where he wakes up to a text or gets one while wolfing down breakfast—something protein-and-carb-packed that always involves eggs but features a rotating source when it comes to the carbs, including bread, oats, and whole grain cereal, today being cereal—with the details of a run he's already supposed to make. The dispatcher knows where the couriers live, and will send them rush jobs accordingly in the mornings. Ray's one of two people who cover Midtown East. The other guy—coming from Astoria—has seniority, so he gets first dibs. While they can be disruptive to a morning routine, these early rush jobs are nice because they allow the couriers to get out there and start a route. Otherwise, they have to report to the office first and wait.

He rolls his bike into dispatch at 8:28. The front room is small and cluttered, and mostly looks and smells like a bicycle repair shop, with bikes lined up in rows in the center of the room—some belonging to the couriers, some extras—and parts and other accoutrements hanging all over the walls—the metal, rubber, and bike cleaning supplies accounting for the slight though not unpleasant olfactory sting. There's a desk in a back corner where a counter might typically be in a bike shop. The dispatcher, Jeff, also a co-owner, is sitting there thumbing through a bike catalog while he waits for the phone to ring or an order to pop up on his computer monitor. "Mornin' Sunshine," he says. Ray's nickname here is "Sunshine." Jeff came up with it. He's not sure if it's meant to be ironic because his name is Ray or if it has something to do with him wearing a lot of black and often looking unhappy, or a combination of these things. In any event, it was a sobriquet quick to catch on and now over half the fleet also calls him "Sunshine." It is not a coincidence that these are the fellow couriers he does not really like.

"Hey Jeff." The chimes hanging from the door clink together as it shuts. Jeff does not look up.

A few of the other riders are already here, talking and cachinnating in the back, which is separated by a little hallway just wide enough for a single bike to pass through. "Yeah, but that motherfucker don't know shit!" It's a booming male's voice, undoubtedly Deion's, Ray hears, followed by laughs, then Amanda waiting for it to wane just enough to come in with, "What do you mean he doesn't know shit? That's all he knows! He's got shit for brains! He's Mister Shit-for-Brains!" More laughter, though Deion's boom is notably absent this time. Ray parks his bike in the front room, in line with everybody else's, in front of Jeff's desk. He hangs his messenger backpack over the handles and retrieves a silver thermos from the inside. "Hold up, hold up, hold up! If you got shit for brains, you still don't know shit. You need a brain, a mind, to know anything. Even shit. Miss Shit-for-Brains!" Everybody laughs; Deion, too, who laughs loudest at his own jokes. Always. People only bring their bikes to the back if they need a repair or tune-up, which they all usually do themselves. Aside from the workstation, there are a couple of chairs back there, a table, mini-fridge, water cooler, coffee machine, sink, and the door to a bathroom that is the saving grace for many of the couriers throughout the day while passing through the Flatiron; the detour to the office usually takes less time than waiting to pop into a Starbucks bathroom, which are considered by many locals to be New York City's default public restrooms. Nobody really sits at the table, but sometimes people turn the chairs away from it and sit facing the others standing or leaning against the walls. Generally speaking, everybody stays upright for the first ten or so minutes. Resting is bad for people who thrive on inertia; the majority of the couriers seem like they consider the chairs to be a bit of a tease. "Oh, don't be so literal, D! You don't have to be a bitch about it." Amanda, a proud lesbian, is always trying to one-up Deion, and Ray thinks it's because he is often the largest and loudest man in the room, and knows he's not just being ignorant or reductive in thinking this. Some lesbians are actually like that. Ray enters the room. Deion's tall, mostly muscle, black, in his mid-thirties; Amanda's about five-seven, white, late-twenties, and with a haircut that screams to the world she lives off the L train or wants to, her brown hair long and ratty but with the left half of it shaved off from the temple to behind her ear; Eli looks a lot like Amanda, in a strange way, except he wears glasses and his hair, while longer for a man's at shoulder-length, is not shaved in any peculiar or otherwise ridiculous-looking way; and Bill's about Ray's height, blonde, pasty white, hallowed eyes. Everybody else pretty much wears earth tones. "A bitch about it? I ain't bein' a bitch about shit!" Deion, who doesn't drink coffee, has an open thermos full of tea cooling in his hand. Eli's eating an egg sandwich. Amanda's clutching a half-eaten bagel, a little cream cheese smudged on her lip. A lot of the couriers like to just grab street food on their way in and eat it while they wait for their first run. "Hey Sunshine! Sunshine's here everybody!" Amanda calls out as she sees Ray, her mouth full, probably just trying to change the subject since Deion actually seems to be getting pissed. Ray has to eat at home because of how expensive it would be otherwise, and has no idea how these people can afford to get breakfast every day like this, even if it is only like three bucks for a sandwich, donut, and coffee or whatever at some bodegas and street carts. He knows not everybody has his student loans, but still; they, like him, only get paid five bucks a run. NYC rent alone should make this impossible. Usually Ray has to bring his own lunch and any other victuals he might need, and the days he doesn't, it's a real treat.

"What's up, guys?" Ray goes straight for the coffee machine. Rarely, if ever, is "What's up?" or any of its variants an actual question here.

"Hey Sunshine," says Bill.

Eli nods in Ray's general direction, chewing. The bells chime from the door opening up front, meaning another courier's walking in. There are currently eight people making up the fleet, and typically everyone's in by 8:35; that is, unless they're on one of those early-morning runs. Ray figures Scottie, the guy from Astoria, got one this morning.

" 'Sup Ray," says Deion.

"How's that piece of shit bike of yours?" asks Amanda. She takes a bite of her bagel. Eli and Bill chuckle. Deion smiles.

"Well, it got me here this morning. I think it'll get me around today. And I'm pretty sure it'll bring me home in the evening," says Ray, pouring coffee into his thermos. The room offers him slight pity smiles, which he notes before his eyes get lost in the blackness filling up the inside of the thermos. Dry humor rarely goes over well with this particular crowd, with the exception of Eli, and only sometimes.

Deion's been waiting for Ray to turn toward them, and when he does, says, "I think he means 'Still shitty!' " This is followed by uproarious laughter from the room, mostly Deion's own. Ray receives this with his own pity smile, though he's not sure if it's directed at them or himself.

The phone rings up front and it takes exactly two seconds for the back to go completely silent. Like the dogs they are, Jeff has used Pavlovian conditioning to train the couriers to become quiet and very still at the sound of the office phone ringing. He has an acute sense of hearing and will deny runs to anyone he perceives as talking or moving around too much during a call. Client calls never take long—everyone's in a hurry in this business—and they're what they're all here for, so the couriers are happy to settle down. They can faintly discern Jeff picking up the phone; he's directly on the other side of the very wall Bill and Eli are leaning against, but most of what they hear comes snaking down through the hallway connecting the two rooms; it sounds pretty strange, simultaneously hearing something through vibrations in a close-by wall and better from a distance over the air. "Gotham," he says. This is the short name of the courier company, Gotham Courier Service. As they stand around waiting—Ray blowing on his coffee, Deion smirking to himself, Amanda chewing, Bill staring at the floor, Eli taking the last bite of his sandwich—Victor walks in. It's 8:34. Karen, another veteran, coming from Sunset Park, likely got a route this morning, since she does most mornings, being the closest to FiDi. "Hey Dan. How's it going?" continues Jeff. Victor is Ray's favorite person on the fleet. A New York native and the son of Dominican immigrants, he's the only other Hispanic on the crew, but much more than that, Ray thinks he's a natural showman—as opposed to Deion, who's mostly just loud—a guy you can laugh with and at. He's on the shorter side, broad-shouldered, closely cropped hair; he wears a red hoodie and gray pants, and carries a thermos. His free hand in the shape of a gun, he points at Eli and Bill, firing two shots. He approaches Ray, who's the closest, and gives him a fist bump. Deion receives the same. His hand is still in a fist when he turns to face Amanda, and at first he fakes her out by making his hand into a gun again, but then instead of firing any shots he closes it back into a fist and gives her a fist bump, too. She's beside herself because of this, nearly blushing, finding herself on the receiving end of a greeting normally reserved not only for the guys on the fleet but the ones with a certain prerequisite amount of melanin. "All right, we'll have someone there within a half hour." Jeff hangs up the phone. "D! You're up!"

"About time!" Deion has the most seniority of the couriers currently in the office. "Excuse me, Sunshine." He brushes by Ray and heads toward the hallway.

"What it do, what it do, what it do? Happy Friday, motherfuckers! Y'all ready for this shit?" Victor asks the room. He moves into the spot Deion had occupied.

"Hell yeah," says Amanda.

"What are you ready for Mandy?"

"Friday, man. Tearin' shit up." Bells clank against the front door behind Deion.

"Tearin' shit up! Uh-oh! What are you ready for, Ray?"

"Payday."

"Oh, I hear that! Pay-fuckin'-day, today! Gotta love Fridays! Finna invite some people over... you know, some girls... cop a few forties... and chi-l-l-l-l tonight. You guys down?" Amanda's eyes go wide. "Just kidding. None of you are invited. Private party. Eli, what are you ready for, my dude?"

"A run."

"A run! I want a run. I am ready for a motherfuckin' run!"

"Bill! You ready for a run?"

Bill nods.

"Hey Jeff!" Victor stares intently at the wall, the spot where Jeff is sitting on the other side. There's no reply. "Jeff! I'm speaking to you!"

"What?!"

"The white boys want a run!"

"Huh?"

Victor grins. After a second, his lower lip widens, his neck stretching below so you can see the contours of its many cords, especially those on either side of his Adam's apple, and then just as quickly the grin snaps back into place. It's a little pop of an expression commonly used by someone who's about to say or has just said something insolent, but who knows they're being insolent. He waits another second. "You know what it is!"

"Shut up, Victor."

Bill and Eli kind of glare at Victor, who reassuringly smiles back. "Jeff! I said the white boys are ready for some fun!"

"And I said shut up!"

"Yeah, all right!" He looks toward Eli and Bill and waves, shaking his head. "You guys are fine. Ray! That coffee still warm?" What's especially funny about this, to Ray, is that Eli has been working here longer than Victor. The phone rings. Silence. Ray nods, and Victor starts filling his thermos.

"Gotham," they hear. "Sure, let me pull that up... We'll have someone there by noon, Steve." After Jeff hangs up, they wait. The next person in seniority is in fact Eli, who Jeff calls "Specs," but instead of hearing "Specs!" there's a click then the fuzz of a two-way radio. "Scottie, come in." Jeff must believe Scottie's already near the pickup site. If he is, Scottie's got himself a route. They can't hear Scottie's response, but Ray figures it's "Roger" or something similar. Scottie's older, and old-school. A haggard-looking and inexplicably tan functioning alcoholic, he's been a messenger for around twenty years or something horrible like that, and still uses a two-way radio. Amanda once tried it for a week the previous year, Ray learned from Eli, but hated it. These conversations between Jeff and Scottie are always heavy in radio transmission lingo, to the point that they sound almost cartoonish. The rest of the fleet receive their pickups and drop-offs through texts. "You still downtown?"

Since it doesn't seem like anyone here's closer to a run, and talking would be a bad idea, they all start pulling out their phones and sort of tuning out, except Victor, who's adding milk and sugar to his coffee. Ray opens up Gmail. Scrolling down his inbox, there isn't anything that important from when he last checked right after waking up this morning. Mostly, it's just messages from Groupon, LivingSocial, and other companies offering discounted goods and experiences. He tells himself nearly every day that he should unsubscribe from these—they're just noise, and he probably can't afford what's being offered anyway—but a part of him also doesn't want to miss out on a truly great coupon or opportunity. He's bought a handful in the past, after all. He opens one. It's for a place selling fancy fries.

"Some riding yesterday, huh," whispers Victor.

Ray looks up. He smiles and nods. Victor's stirring his coffee. Ray looks back down.

"Finally gettin' to be that time of year."

The two-way radio business is still going on, but it seems to be winding down. "Roger. That's the drop-off," says Jeff.

Ray offers Victor a "Yeah, man," quietly and out of the corner of his mouth, like Jeff would somehow be able to see it, too. He's reticent the way a boy in grade school might be, trying not to be disrespectful to the guy in charge or get himself in trouble, while also not outright ignoring the friend who's attempting to speak to him. Victor does his best to drag him into this susurration routine sometimes. Ray thinks it's because he has ADD and doesn't own a smartphone. Victor has a flip phone, or "burner," as he calls it.

A muffled, somewhat low-speaking Jeff says, "Roger and out." He sounds so serious it seems particularly stilted and absurd this time. "Specs!" Jeff continues down the list.

Eli's head pops up from his phone, also an iPhone. "Yeah?!"

"Got something over the wire for you." The wire is what Jeff calls all web orders for some reason. Scottie aside, web orders are easier for everyone because Jeff can just forward all of the information over text through some email-to-text system.

Eli throws away the wrapping from his egg sandwich and steps toward the hallway. His phone makes a buzzing sound in his hand as he leaves, probably with the details of the run.

"We're gonna miss you, Eli," says Victor.

The phone rings up front. There's another one of the "Gotham" deals with Jeff and a client. Ray pays attention to the first two or three but after that only listens for when his name is called. He shifts his focus quarterwise from Victor, who he had politely smiled at after he said what he said to Eli, back down to his phone. It's still the french fry coupon. He navigates back to his inbox and deletes the other offers. Victor puts his coffee down on the counter. Amanda and Bill have been on their phones since Jeff had used the two-way, both Android-based phones, Amanda's a Samsung and Bill's a Motorola, Ray thinks.

When Jeff hangs up, Victor keeps his watch on the wall. About ten seconds pass. "Hey Jeff!"

"Yeah?"

"What's up?"

Jeff takes his time. "Gave that one to Karen."

Victor shakes his head, frowning to one side of his face, "Yeah, but I'm faster than her!"

"She's already downtown. Also, you're not that fast!"

"Oh well," says Victor. "Fuck it."

But in another five minutes, he's gone. Then Amanda ten minutes after that. Then Bill, who started a week before Ray, a few more after that. Ray sits down after everyone else clears out. He stares into his phone, waiting. The turnover rate at Gotham is high in the bottom two slots; the rewards for sticking it out aren't that great—Scottie might get six bucks a run—and there are other companies a motivated young courier can work for. But Ray wasn't really motivated to do this in the first place, so he's even less motivated to do it somewhere else. The phone continues to ring throughout, most of these orders getting routed to the fleet already on the road. It's 9:11, fifteen minutes after Bill left, almost forty-five since he got in, by the time Ray hears "Sunshine!" called from down the hall and through the wall.

▲ ▽ ▲

He is just so big. Everything about him is big. He is tall. He is fat. His voice is loud. His name even sounds like something big. His eyes get big when he talks. And everything he talks about is big. Life. Death. Love. Hate. Only big things. What a big man. Just listen to him now: "And so we continue along. Polonius hears Hamlet coming toward them, and he and Claudius hide from view. Enter Hamlet, and what is probably the best-known line from all of drama or literature…" The best-known line. So famous. So big. "To be or not to be?" he says, "That is the question."

Haruka's seated in a classroom surrounded by two dozen other students. There's a notebook in front of her, a black pen in her hand. The pages are filled with notes in impeccable handwriting. So neat and consistent it actually looks fake. Like one of those handwriting fonts. She watches Professor Towers more than she listens—What a big question… To be or not to be? Of course it is better to be. Hmm. It sounds like a big question, but maybe it's actually stupid. Shakespeare's a little boring. Was in high school, still is now… Is Hamlet supposed to be sexy? Like, deep? Or is he a dork?

Haruka writes this last thought down.

Professor Towers' class is the only one where she actually uses a pen to write notes. This is because he does not allow laptops in his classroom, and anyone who claims to be using a phone to take notes is met with a huge laugh followed by a prompt order to leave.

"I must admit, I feel a little trite reciting it… me, the old man, up here in my sports jacket, speaking the way I speak…" Professor Towers over-enunciates a lot. He always sounds theatrical, not just when quoting Shakespearean soliloquies. "It might seem as if I'm a living cliché, a character from the movies, a hoary caricature of an old English professor." There's a sly smile as he says this. Several students chuckle. Haruka does not. "But recite it I must! Because it is one of the best-known lines in the English language for a reason. What is Shakespeare doing here?" He looks around the classroom, which is structured in three stadium-style rows, lit overhead by fluorescent lighting. The students seem to either keep their noses down in their notebooks or vacantly stare away, their eyes looking toward various walls. Haruka, whose eyes drift between him and the class and the wall behind him, sits in the back. "What does Hamlet mean?" A male student with reddish hair in the second row raises his hand. "Yes?" It seems that Professor Towers doesn't bother to learn any of the students' names. Haruka's never heard him use one. The wrinkles in his forehead deepen as he leans forward, preparing to listen.

"Hamlet's contemplating suicide."

His eyes wide and forehead still crumpled, Professor Towers waits for some elaboration. But it does not come. "Yes, but why?"

The student shifts in his seat. "Because he thinks life is painful. It's about how hard it is to be alive."

Professor Towers repeats the student, each word sounding longer: "It's… about… how… hard… it… is… to… be… alive." He nods.

"So maybe he should end it. But then he goes on to say he's afraid because death might be worse."

"Good. Good. So what is Shakespeare doing then?"

"Ummm… I don't know." The young man shrugs. "Offering food for thought."

"Shakespeare is meditating on the very nature of the human experience!" Professor Towers centers himself in front of the classroom and projects. So loud. Heads snap toward him, joining her own. "Life is suffering! It is painful—'the slings and arrows, the heartache, the thousand *natural* shocks!' But it is also all that we know and all that we can know. And this is why we endure it. We would rather 'bear those ills we have than fly to others that we know not of.' At best death is something utterly unknowable, and at worst, it is something plausibly more painful than life. Hamlet believes that if he were to take his own life, it could very well lead to damnation. Hellfire! Agonies upon agonies upon agonies! Life, then, for all truly sentient beings, is lived out of a fear of death, not because of love for life itself." Professor Towers scans the room. "Thoughts?"

A blonde girl with a ponytail sitting in the front row raises her hand. Professor Towers nods towards her. "I disagree. I think that's a very bleak way of looking at things."

"Define bleak."

"Grim, depressing."

"Yes, my apologies, it was not my intention to adjure you to function as a dictionary or thesaurus. I'm asking what do *you mean* by bleak?"

"I mean it's the wrong way of looking at things. There's a lot of beauty in life."

"What is beauty?"

"A feeling," she says, tapping the tip of her pencil. "Like love. Kindness. You know, warm things."

"I doubt Shakespeare would disagree that love is beautiful. But what is its function? How are these things making your life worth living?"

"The answer to both of those questions is the same. Because it's there."

"There doing what?"

"I… I… it's a feeling. It's there to be felt. I don't care if it sounds cheesy." Professor Towers winces. It's like he thinks the word "cheesy" has no place in his classroom or something. You can tell that's what he's thinking. "But I know the good things are there to make our lives beautiful, and this is the basis of life. It's why we're here. Life is simply beautiful."

He takes a breath. "We gravitate toward the beautiful, we chase these, as you call them, 'warm' feelings, because life, by its *very nature*, is cold, difficult. This is what Hamlet and Shakespeare are driving at. The natural state of the human is not a happy one."

"Yeah, but that's just so emo."

"Emo?"

"Emotional. Shakespeare just sounds like a downer here."

Professor Towers laughs uncontrollably. "Well, I guess that's why they call it the ugly truth. You're young still, dear, you'll see. The truth hurts. And much more than love, kindness, or any of these warm feelings you're so fond of, *truth* is beauty, and the thing that will set you free."

Before this moment Haruka had not much liked Emerson Towers' English 101 class. His phone policy alone was enough of a reason, but she also didn't very much care for English as a subject. Never has. The rules of the English language, its building blocks, barely make any sense. English is not logical, it's expressive. And expression is nothing compared to logic. She'd read growing up, of course, but it was mostly whatever was assigned in school or manga. The best stories were interactive, in video games or on Facebook or other forms of social media. Hers was a mind more interested in math and the sciences. Real things. Logical things. All this "serious" literature stuff was boring and mostly seemed designed to speak to the soul, and she was not so sure she had a soul. She knew God didn't exist, and for someone to have a soul, surely they would need to believe in something like that. Faith is what creates a soul. That's why her Little Kaiju was so effective. Men believed in it, believed that it would heal them, and for the time she was with them, she was a goddess, a ruler. Additionally, she found Emerson's size and loud voice offensive;

he was little more than this grotesque figure teaching a mostly useless class. But as he laughed at the young white woman with the ponytail, his mouth wide, with pink gums under curled lips and very sharp-looking teeth she could see even from all the way in the back, something clicked. She saw a little bit of herself in that mouth, and thought maybe she just might have a soul, after all.

▲ ▲ ▽

Whoa, there it is again. Like on the bridge the evening before, Ray, without having made any kind of conscious association, ever so briefly becomes taken over by something that seems very familiar, followed by a sense of happiness, strength, and freedom as he rides up Lafayette, passing Bond. For a few blinkering moments, he is not sorrowful or confused or lost; it's as if he has been found.

But unlike the evening before, this time he stops. Two blocks ahead near East 4th Street, he pulls to the left of the bike lane, one foot resting on the curb, and turns to look behind. Cabs and SUVs with inimical-looking grills and other assorted automobiles barrel up the street; a few trailing cyclists ride up the lane. He maneuvers his bike up onto the curb and slowly makes his way back to the intersection at Bond. There aren't many pedestrians along this stretch, but enough that he can't take the sidewalk at full bore. Also, by creeping, any cops happening by would be less inclined to give him a ticket; riding on the sidewalks is illegal, and going at a measured pace makes it look more like he's just trying to find somewhere to park his bike. When he's made it back to Bond, the feeling does not return. He's stationary, straddling the bike on the northwest corner, next to a small parking lot, cars stacked on cars in a blue-and-yellow-painted hydraulic lift system, a mostly white billboard overhead featuring a slender model Photoshopped to look even more slender selling women's clothes. He looks west. Cabs, people, the end of Bond at Broadway, low-rise buildings, the cobblestone of the street interrupted by the more arterial Lafayette's black pavement at the intersection. He looks east. The return of the cobblestone, more pedestrians and low-rises, some barren Gallery pear trees in the distance. Nothing invites the strange familiarity. He crosses Bond and continues along on the sidewalk, going down another block and a half. He descends the curb and gets on Lafayette again, then tries to recreate the moment, riding at a similar pace, his eyes seeing what he thinks they saw the first time. But still nothing. Halfway up the block, he turns back yet again. His mind races as he makes his way down the sidewalk—What was that? Why does this keep happening? I almost, in these moments, feel like I'm where I should be. But that makes no sense. I am dead—this I know—and death has clearly brought me to some strange purgatory or limbo, a constant state of unease and flux—not quite hell but far from heaven—and nobody really belongs in purgatory. It's not a destination point, it's a waiting room. So what else, then? Is it a warning? A clue? Both? Something to help me along? Could this possibly be the spot where I was run over, all those years ago, lost in my first-generation iPhone? Then what would that have been on the bridge? Did I not die looking into my phone? Did I jump off a fucking bridge? Or am I really even dead at all? Is this something I just like to tell myself to justify why my life is so shitty? Should I jump off a fucking bridge? Am I just fucking nuts?

When he makes it back to the corner of Lafayette and Bond, he pulls out his phone and takes a photo. He makes sure to catch the crossing of the street signs. Then he's back on Lafayette, riding uptown at a frantic pace, making up for lost time.

▲▲▲

There's not much of a point to going out, but you can't always stay in. Sometimes, on a Friday night, when the temperature outside is agreeable and he's primed for a laugh—a night like tonight—Emerson will take in a movie. He'll stroll over to the neighborhood theater close to his apartment on 85th and Riverside, or, for more options, he'll catch a cab and go to one of the cinemas down around Lincoln Center, where he'll sit in a dark room, a tub of popcorn resting on his lap, a large cup of Coca-Cola in hand, and delight in the images dancing up on the screen. The silly, stupid images. Whoop-de-doo! Derivative of the drama he knows so well, yet so far removed that they're really nothing like it. All traces of the original art are gone; botched simulacrum, deformed clones birthed by deformed clones—here there is only kitsch. Some say there are thirty-six dramatic situations. Emerson figures Hollywood uses about five. Everything eventually leads back to his dear Shakespeare, of course, or the Greeks, he well knows. The scripts. The action. The humor. The pathos. The payoff. Even what's modern and rumored to be edgy barely holds a candle to *Titus Andronicus* or *Oedipus Rex*. Occasionally the theatergoers among him laugh. They laugh at the jokes. An actor's clownish contortion of face. A thrill of the plot. They've momentarily forgotten their troubles, themselves. And they are open. Present. Transfixed by movie magic. But not Emerson. His laughter never occurs with theirs. It is a bawdier laugh, one that accompanies the unadulterated joy of a person at their purpose; his laugh signals not the mere deconstruction of the scene or situation—the slight, wry smile covers this—the laugh comes with evisceration, complete and gory destruction, of what's before his eyes.

And so, already in a good mood, keyed up from the laughs he had in his class earlier—gainsaying students never disappoint, but the girl up front today was one for the ages—and feeling like he should reward himself for writing such a beautiful book review the previous evening, this is what Emerson does. He goes to a picture. It's a maudlin affair that's little more than a love letter to the cinema itself, one of several idiotic offerings with the same theme out this season, something called *The Artist*. It's even racked up some awards, Emerson remembers reading in *The Times* and *New Yorker*. So, of course he loves it. Loves how horrible, otiose, bad it is. Loves how it makes him feel. The power. These people that make films, they just don't know. The masses, they just don't know. He laughs like he's alone. Eventually some imbecile even shushes him, during a scene that's supposed to be an emotional high point, that's trying oh so hard to mean something, to impart some truth. But he cares not. He just laughs and laughs and laughs. So abjectly puerile, hilarious. He laughs like he's alone because, really, he is.

▲▽▽▽

It's not a real party. Just a dorm room party. Haruka's here with Allison and Maeve. She doesn't know anybody else. There aren't that many people to know; only eleven people in total occupy the common area of the suite. Haruka feels duped.

Sure, it's one of the more apartment-like dorms at NYU, but it's hardly the "apartment party" Maeve sold her on. Haruka had imagined she was going to an East Village loft full of young, interesting people celebrating the night. Dancing to a tribal beat, pulling off to corners to hold stimulating conversation. Finding even darker corners to do even more stimulating drugs; having sex in the bathroom. She's been to stuff like this before, with Maeve, back in the fall. In Alphabet City and in Brooklyn. What we have here is eleven college students in a bright room listening to a dull Pandora station through tinny MacBook speakers. This is often cited as the number one dream school in the country, located in the cultural capital of the world and populated by some of tomorrow's brightest and most creative minds, and there are high school kids in the middle of nowhere having way better parties than this.

She's near the window, and some guy's standing next to her, talking at her. She thinks his name is Campbell, but it might be something more like James. He's tall and handsome in the way nonthreatening thin white boys with wavy brown hair are. If she had met him over OkCupid, she would definitely have sex with him. But since they go to the same school and know the same people, she will not. And this is a big part of what makes him standing there talking at her hella dumb and totally insufferable. She sets her red Dixie cup down on the window sill and reaches for her phone.

"I mean, I'm from Boston and our subway system stops at around midnight. Or maybe it's 1:00 now? Whatever, something like that." He's still looking into her eyes as they begin to drift downward toward the screen. "People like to talk a lot of shit about the MTA, but it's really an amazing system, when you think about it. The trains run twenty-four hours. It serves something like four million people daily. Over a billion rides a year. And it does a pretty good job staying on schedule. Yeah, it could be a little cleaner, but it's not so bad. What's the BART like?"

Haruka flinches. It's not because of something she sees on the screen; she's been scrolling through texts so if he were to absently catch a glimpse or try to sneak a peek at what's on her phone, he'd see something less offensive than, say, Facebook. This is the courtesy she gives him as a friend of a friend of a friend. She flinches because she's forgotten she told him where she was from. Sometimes when she drinks, she lets her guard down. It's not an uncommon question—"Where are you from?" is second only to "What's your major?" here, and probably at every college ever. But she feels like he knows too much about her now. Usually she lies, even to friends of friends. Especially friends of friends of friends. People are very trusting. They're wired that way through evolution; human babies depend on their parents longer than any other primate, members of the tribe need to be able to rely on one another to survive. She looks up from the last text she received—How r u? How is NYC in springtime? It's from one of her best friends from high school, Cindy. "The same. Cleaner than here. Stops around midnight," she says.

He smiles. "So... how did you and Maeve meet?"

"Class."

He nods. She stares at him, waiting for more words to come at her. A return of the smile. It's a nice smile. What a shame I didn't meet him over OkCupid, she thinks. "You're shy, aren't you?"

She reaches for her drink. "No." She sips. He waits, the smile now close-mouthed and only to one side. There's a little too much vodka for the amount of cranberry juice in her drink. "Why do you say that?"

"Class?"

"That's where we met."

"Care to elaborate?"

"It was microbiology. We were lab partners." It was actually a statistics class, but Haruka doesn't want him to know anything else about her.

He touches her shoulder. She doesn't like this. Touch connotes ownership. "There you go." He laughs.

"There I go, what?"

"That's all I wanted. Just, you know..." He motions with his hands, pushing and pulling. "Something to work with."

Haruka nods. She's uncomfortable and very badly wants to look at her phone again, but knows this would only make the conversation even more awkward. Also, it would probably reveal something else about her that she would not want him to know. "Sorry, I've just been a little distracted tonight."

"Why's that?"

"I don't know."

"Aren't we all?" he says. Haruka smiles and shrugs. "So, she's been hanging out in our suite a lot." Campbell-or-James is looking across the room now at Maeve and Willie, who are standing next to the door. Willie's nodding as Maeve talks excitedly, slinking toward him. Maeve has dark blonde hair and deep blue eyes. Her lips are enviable for a white girl's, but Haruka's are better. More pillowlike. Haruka is also slightly thinner. Maeve's breasts are larger, though. Haruka's never understood why men make such a big deal out of breasts. Milk comes out of them. Like a cow. They're kind of gross. "You should come with her sometime." Haruka thought she was actually in their suite. She doesn't know whose suite this is. It must be the two boys' who Allison's talking to over there on the couch. Or maybe just one of theirs. The boy right next to her has too many muscles and the one next to him looks short and kind of fat. Allison is too pretty to be talking to either of them. She could do much better with her long brown hair and soft features. She must just be bored, Haruka thinks. Like her.

"Maybe I will." The boy is smiling at her and looking her up and down like he thinks he's going to meet Little Kaiju. Moron. She pulls out her phone and looks at it. "Yikes! Looks like I have to go."

The boy smiles, as if to himself. "Well that's too bad."

"Oh, no, no, no, no… Did you just say you have to go?" Allison's chiming in from the couch.

Haruka finishes her drink. The vodka's especially harsh at the bottom. "Yeah, I have that thing in the morning."

"That thing?" Allison's mouth is open. Her forehead is scrunched a bit in the center. The muscular boy sits there with one eyebrow raised looking at her and the pudgy one scratches his head, looking away, then at his phone.

"Yes. I thought I told you. I'm volunteering."

"Where?"

"The cat shelter." Haruka used to volunteer with the SPCA back in San Francisco, which is probably why this came out so fast.

"You volunteer with cats?"

"Sometimes."

"Since when?"

"High school." Really, it was all animals in high school. But she liked the cats the best.

"It's only 11:30."

Haruka has become aware that now everyone in the room except Maeve and Willie is listening to their conversation and looking at her. This kind of attention makes her unhappy. "I have to be there at 7:00."

Allison's head tilts. "No, you don't."

"Yes, I do."

"That's way too early for a Saturday."

"Cats wake up early," Haruka says.

"No, I'm pretty sure they're most active at night. My cat growing up slept all day."

"Not these ones."

"Okaaaaay," says Allison. Haruka figures Allison is just upset because now she is stuck with the ugly strangers and has no buffer. Maeve is obviously too preoccupied to be depended on in any way. She can't believe Maeve. She just wanted to use her and Allison; to show off that she had hot friends to Willie, so that he'd like her more. Allison turns to the boy with too many muscles. "Maybe she's not lying. I mean, my cat *was* a lazy piece of shit. His name was Rufus."

"It was nice meeting you," Haruka says to Campbell-or-James.

"You too. Have fun with the cats."

Haruka grins in a very strange way. "I always do." She waves at the boy in an even stranger way and crosses the room. She does not say goodbye to anyone else at the party even though she's met them all. She also does not acknowledge Allison in any way. She reaches for the door.

"Where are you going?" Maeve peeks around Willie's shoulder, his back to the door. Willie turns and twists his neck toward Haruka.

Haruka's opened the door. It's cracked slightly as she holds it with her foot. "You didn't hear any of that?"

"Any of what?"

"Me and Allison."

"Oh, no. Sorry. Willie and I were discussing—"

"I have to volunteer with cats early in the morning."

Willie's eyes narrow, his head sort of zags. Allison nods. Both seem confused. "Oh. Okay then. Goodnight…"

"Bye." The door closes loudly behind her. Dorm suite doors are too loud.

Haruka makes her way down the hall toward the elevator. The party sounds a lot more fun from the outside than in, like most parties. She hears a muffled Maeve say, "God, I love that girl. She is so fucking random," followed by Willie laughing. This kind of attention makes her happy. Waiting for the elevator, she passes the time by looking at cute pictures of cats on her phone. She decides that's what she'll do with the rest of her night. Back in her room, she'll lie in bed, looking at more cats. It's going to be a much better party, the after-party. A private party with just her, her phone, and the cats. All night long. Tomorrow, she'll sleep in. Yes, that'll be so, so much better.

▲ ▽ ▽ ▲

Well, fuck, as if this couldn't get any more frustrating… Now they gotta get into pragmatics and semantics, all that stupid shit. He wishes he could blame it on the wine, but neither of them really got drunk. If it had been two bottles, or one of those magnum bad boys, that would've been something else, but they just had the one regular bottle; two and a half glasses each. Not enough to make them sloppy, just enough to make them honest. "You know I didn't mean it like that," Ray says. But they both know he really did.

They're twenty-five minutes into the fight. Fernanda sits on the opposite end of his bed, against the wall. "Saying 'You don't have to be so bitchy' is the same as calling me a bitch."

"But that's not even what I said. What I said was, 'Wow, that's kinda bitchy.' "

"Whatever. Still the same. It's all just you calling me a bitch." Ray's known Fernanda for six years. They met in college, where they became friends, and also had sex on two separate occasions. Three months ago, they reconnected and began casually seeing each other, which mostly amounts to her coming over to Ray's place once a weekend or every other weekend and on the occasional weeknight to drink or smoke weed and, ultimately, have sex.

"No, it's not."

"Yes, it is. You don't have to be so *assholey*, Ray. It is."

Ray smiles to himself. He's a few feet away from her at the head of the bed, leaning against the same wall, his legs stretched out. Hers are folded Indian-style. "You know how I took that? You know what I just heard? A comment on my behavior. Not a comment on my character."

"Yeah, but in the moments that you are behaving like an asshole, it's because you are an asshole! So if I'm acting bitchy, that must make me a bitch." Fernanda's Brazilian, and actually from there—pretty, her face unconventionally so, with big, almost bug-like eyes and a round nose, everything balanced out by a wide mouth and wild, loosely coiled hair; but her long, lean brown body is the stuff of any red-blooded male's dreams. In college, Ray literally once wrote a poem about the curvature of her ass. He still has it memorized:

If you could only see
Tonight's moonrise over Rio
Then you would understand
Just why my heart aches so

Christ the Redeemer
Can't even compare
To the spectacular wonder
Climbing high over there

So far above me
So out of reach
Lighting the city
Lighting the beach

With a heavenly glow
With God only knows
Endless beauty to behold
Moonrise over Rio

He stares off as he thinks about the poem, then snaps back. She probably thought she really got him with her last point. "That's not the same as character. Character's something you are. What you're talking about is temporary, fleeting. People behave a lot of different ways."

"I don't think of myself in these maxims, Ray. Nothing about me just is. I grow. I change."

"You know what I mean. There's a difference."

"Maybe for you, but not for me. I am my actions. I'm accountable."

"Also, let's not forget I used 'kinda.' " The argument started when Fernanda suggested they go to one of the bars over on Vernon Boulevard after they finished their bottle of Shiraz, which she brought over. Ray, disinterested in paying a disgustingly high premium to drink among strangers, especially since he isn't making that much money at the moment and she technically isn't even his girlfriend, politely declined. That's when Fernanda said, "I should have known. We never do anything actually fun," and Ray made the comment that brought them to this.

"Oh, yeah... sorry... I forgot about 'kinda.' You think that actually makes it better? Dressing it up only makes it worse, Ray. It's like, 'Hey, here's a present. *Kinda*'s the bow on top. The *y* at the end of *bitch-y*'s the wrapping paper. But you know what's inside? The only thing in there is you calling me a bitch."

"Jesus, Fernanda, can we please stop? You know I don't think you're a bitch." He doesn't. She's right; that was his way of calling her that in that moment, but it's not because he actually thinks she is. Her "no fun" comment hurt, and saying that was his way of making himself feel better, to let her know that that wasn't cool. Their arrangement is supposed to be low-maintenance. "What can I do to make you happy?"

She sighs. "It's just… Oh, fuck, Ray. I don't know."

"Well, we definitely don't need to fight. That's what's nice about this. It's supposed to be fun. We keep it light. You know?"

"That's the thing, though. That's why I said what I said. I don't think I'm having fun anymore." When she's done speaking, Fernanda's mouth settles into a frown. Her eyes are giant dewy saucers below an upturned brow, searching his. The room's lit low by a solitary lamp on the nightstand and the air now seems thick and sad.

Ray's nervous. "And I guess that's why I said what I said. I didn't appreciate that. I think we still have a good thing going."

"Look, I'm twenty-six now." Her birthday was earlier this month, a week and some change after his. Ray did not celebrate it with her; she didn't ask him to, and since she didn't really do anything for his, it would have seemed weird to put forth more effort. "I can't give up my Friday nights when I actually might meet someone so I can come over here and get drunk or high or both and watch movies and have sex with you. It's good sex, Ray, don't get me wrong. But that can't be everything."

"I understand," says Ray. This is bad news. He likes Fernanda; he cares about her in his way, as a friend, and feels better when she's around. And the sex has indeed been good. For a while, back during the nascent phase of this, it seemed like she might have been interested in more. That changed when he lost his last media gig and started working as a bike messenger, and things have been strained since, especially after the big two-six. Ray's more than well aware his current market value with women is low, in particular with someone like Fernanda—successful enough for her age, a TV producer working at CBS—but he hasn't felt exceptionally lucky or anything to be sleeping with her or the other girl he sees from time to time; it just sort of made sense because most of his waking moments are so flat or dysphoric. It seems fair that he still gets to have sex; otherwise, this wouldn't be purgatory, it really would be more like hell. "But I don't think I've been holding you back. We connect when we're both available, you know?"

"Yeah, but I make plans with you. And I don't break plans with people I care about."

"You can break them."

"Look, Ray, I—I can't. I don't think we can really give each other what we want. Eventually I want to build a life. And we both know that's not what this is about." Fernanda looks down, seemingly at the space between her lap and where her ankles cross, then up, her eyes soon lost in the ceiling of Ray's small bedroom. She's wearing jeans and a white T-shirt, no socks.

"Obviously I want that for you. I want you to meet someone and fall in love and be happy. But in the meantime, you can still come over here when you're free and chill, and—"

"No, Ray. I can't." She smiles, shakes her head. Those weird gibbous eyes shift their focus back to him. "It's getting late so I'll stay tonight. But we can't do this anymore."

Ray nods and tries to swallow his disappointment, to no avail. "Okay, Fernanda. Come here..." He reaches for her. She hesitates briefly, staring still, then scoots toward him. Slowly leaning over, she rests her head on his chest, which moves up and down with his breath, her limbs folding under her at odd angles. His heart thuds. He kisses her softly, makes it a point to smell her hair. She always smelled good, that Fernanda. He knows this one isn't real, because he isn't real, but the smell, like hibiscus and vanilla, is the same as it was those six years ago. He lays her down, her long, brown legs wrapping around him, undresses her, and moves inside her, one last time. Then the gift he gave himself in this strange place is taken back, the lovely little light of this rekindled college flame extinguished, and the darkness of night surrounds him.

When it's morning, he walks her to the train. Ray does this for himself as much as her; there's a certain quiet dignity to it, the chivalrous gesture by the dumpee. He's with her, but also on his own walk, down the high road. He may be a loser with a shitty job; he may have never lived up to his promise, that of the cool, bright guy who focused on sociocultural anthropology with his degree and wrote for *Spec*, the guy Fernanda had a crush on back at Columbia, but he does the right thing. He walks the girl to the train. It's a short walk, and she seems ambivalent throughout. She didn't really want it in the first place, he could tell: "You don't have to," she had said, putting her jacket on after breakfast. "But I want to," Ray replied. But now he can tell she's glad they're doing it together.

It's chilly out, overcast. They're both groggy and have heavy hearts, but adrenaline propels their feet along, one in front of the other. It's not so much "Let's get this over with" as it is "Let's get over this." He tries to cut the tension by making the situation self-aware. "Don't forget about Queens," he says.

"I really like Long Island City. I'll be back." Twenty-first Street is nice and still, like it usually is on Saturday mornings. She looks very pretty in the early argent light—no makeup; her dark hair a little wind-swept—doing her best to appear positive, despite her big eyes still carrying a tender sadness.

"Maybe I'll run into you at one of those Warm Up parties this summer. You know, over at PS1?"

She flinches. And suddenly she doesn't seem so soft. In that flash he sees her remembering how fun the Warm Up parties are supposed to be, recognizing them as Ray's turf because he lives, like, a block from the museum, and realizing how awkward it would be to run into him there. It was actually something they were looking forward to going to together. He knew just as soon as the words came out that she probably wouldn't want to run into him as early as the summer; he just said that because it seemed like something to say. "Yeah, maybe." She kind of laughs.

"What?"

"So you'll go to that but not the bars around here?"

Ray doesn't appreciate the dig. Giving a callback to something as unpleasant as last night's fight in their final moments of whatever-they-had-together isn't cool. But the high road is not always evenly paved. "They're different. More like concerts. Plus Long Island City residents get in free, so…"

"Gotcha." She's at ease again, vindicated by the notion of Ray as a broke-ass, cheap motherfucker not worth her time. This is what he sees on Ghost-Fernanda's visage as they approach the subway entrance. He's happy to take the hit, to play into her narrative—if this were real life, he would have wanted Fernanda to know that she was doing the right thing. Because she would have been. It's not that Real-Ray wouldn't have been good enough for her, but he wouldn't have been right for her. He would've wanted her to follow her heart. They stop in front of the stairs that go down to the E/M line.

"Okay," he says. "Take care of yourself."

"You too." They hug, kiss one last time. He tries not to smell her hair. Retracting, they look into each other's eyes. Hers are slightly vitreous, his doing their best to smile, to be reassuring. Her hand slides down his arm, letting go at the wrist. She turns from him and begins her descent down the subway steps. He looks at those long legs as they walk away. While she was never really his, she at least was in the times they were here in Long Island City together, and this is indeed a sad sight for Ray. What an ass, he thinks. What an ass.

Then he walks back.

In the five or so minutes that Ray's been gone, Brian's gotten up, poured himself some cereal, and stationed himself in the living room, watching Saturday morning cartoons over Netflix—vintage *Looney Tunes*-type ones that aren't actually *Looney Tunes*. "Back so soon?" he says. It's a sugar cereal with a lot of red, blue, and purple artificial berries that look especially lurid surrounded by the pure white of the milk. Ray didn't even know that he was here this morning.

"Oh, hey. What time'd you get in?"

"Late. Avenue with the broworkers, man. Models and bottles. I shouldn't even be awake now but you and, who was that, Fernanda?"—Ray nods—"I heard you guys making breakfast and talking out here and that was it for me. You're lucky all the alcohol I had was already metabolizing in my system as a stimulant, or else I would've been pissed."

"Models and bottles, huh?"

"Work hard, play hard." He takes a bite of cereal. Ray watches him and smiles, amused by Brian's silly lifestyle slogans, phrases that seem to have been sold to him by liquor companies and the Las Vegas Tourism Board. One cartoon ends and another begins. He turns toward the screen, partly in interest and partly to seem less conspicuous. A dog chases a cat chasing a mouse clutching some cheese. This one's more like a *Tom and Jerry* knockoff, but with creepier animation. All of these old generic cartoons seem to have been drawn by even more disturbed hands than those at Warner. Brian chews. "How the fuck are you still pulling that off, by the way?" he asks, his mouth full.

"What?"

"Fernanda."

"Oh." Ray reaches across and scratches his other arm, sort of holding himself. "I'm not."

"What's that mean?" The mouse runs into a hole, and the cat and dog slam into the surrounding wall, the dog landing on top of the cat. Brian chuckles, some milk running down his chin in rills. Ray smirks.

He's mostly laughing at Brian, but it's partially also for the scene itself. A bump grows on top of the dog's head.

"We decided last night that we shouldn't hang out anymore." The cat bolts out from under the dog.

"Oh, shit." Brian plays with his spoon in the bowl, absently sifting through the bright fake berries. The clinking is as obscene as the berries' candy-colored glare. Brian allows himself sugar cereal on the weekends, but the rest of the week eats oatmeal.

"She's got that Twenty-six syndrome now. You know? Biological clock's telling her to do all kinds of crazy shit."

"You mean she dumped you for being a loser." Brian looks over and grins. "It doesn't take a biological clock to tell her not to fuck a bike messenger anymore, Ray. Just common fucking sense." He takes a bite. "Shit. I'd plant a seed in there. Have some pretty little beige babies."

"Go fuck yourself."

"Seriously, though, can I get her number?"

"Seriously, though, go fuck yourself," says Ray.

Brian laughs. Mashed up blue and red and purple amidst pink tongue and yellow-tinted teeth. "Just kidding." More milk trickles down the chin. "I know I can do better. Like the *fuckin' models* from last night."

The dog, hackles up, resumes its chase of the cat, and Ray's struck with a vision of Brian and Fernanda lounging together on a beach, a small curly-haired boy building a sandcastle before them, between them and the surf. Then, like they're being pulled into a black hole, Brian and the boy sort of get sucked into each other, and morph into Ray himself, who stands in the halfway point between where Brian and the boy had been. Fernanda's wearing a bright cerulean bathing suit that contrasts strikingly with her radiant brown skin. Realizing it's him, she stands up, then circles him, making her way between him and the water. She stops. One foot's stuck in the sandcastle, or rather its remains. Her toes poke out from the wreckage—sand scattered on top in patches of grains and granules—the nails painted red. The mid-afternoon sun hangs in the sky behind her, and she smiles big in its warm glow. Ray's never been to a beach with her. The vision only lasts a couple of seconds, though the scene feels much longer, like in a dream, and Ray does not skip a beat when he says, "Yeah, you keep holding out for the models, Brian. They love tax lawyers. Rock stars and tax lawyers."

"This is just one part of my journey, Ray. I've got some stuff in the works." He taps the side of his head. "I'm a businessman, really, an entrepreneur. You know this. And models love businessmen. They're always dating old-ass businessmen."

Ray makes a conscious effort not to think about Fernanda, and while his eyes never left the screen, he starts actually paying attention again. The mouse is in its own little house inside the wall, surrounded by hoarded cheese. It adds the block it was carrying to the pile. "Tell me one of your ideas."

"Okay. But only because I know you won't ever have the resources to try to rip me off. I have one called The Rolodex. It's Facebook for people with jobs."

Fernanda pulls him into the water. She gets her hair wet. "You mean LinkedIn?"

"LinkedIn's for desperate people with shitty jobs." Brian takes another bite. "Remember back in the early days how Facebook was cool because it was exclusive? Like you needed a college email address to sign up? Well, it's gonna be like that, except you have to have a business email address. From a good company."

"I still don't see how it's that different." Ray's carrying Fernanda around piggyback-style, their bodies bobbing slowly in the gentle, circumfluent waves. Her legs feel like butter. He tries to stop. The mouse pokes its head out from inside the wall, making sure the coast is clear.

"Then you're an idiot. I already said it. Exclusivity. It's a rolodex. High-power people connecting with other high-power people. Not a poorly designed networking tool for underemployed retards."

"Tell me another one."

Brian drinks the milk and the last of his horrible cereal, his little larval fingers curling around the bowl. Thank God it's gone. "Atlas. It's a gym powered by the workout equipment. This one will take a lot of R&D. You know what R&D is right?"

"I went to college, Brian."

"And look at you now."

"I know what R&D is, man."

"Well, I didn't know. You spend your days outside, playing. Your education couldn't have been that great." Ray half listens. The other half hears lapping waves, seagulls. The girl is still on his back. He's trying to make her morph as they bob in the waves, like Brian and the boy had. "I would need to develop the equipment, but basically it would be a fully sustainable gym." On the TV there's a loud crash—the dog's flank has collided into the refrigerator, chasing the cat and mouse, the mouse now riding on the cat's back clutching another block of cheese, grinning from big annular ear to big annular ear—and Ray snaps back from his place on the beach. "Like everything is powered by solar panels and the equipment itself, the energy people generate by lifting with machines, running on a treadmill, riding a stationary bike, whatever." Ray returns, and the girl's been shaken from his back. Standing in front of him, she no longer resembles Fernanda. She no longer resembles anybody. She's stuck midmorph: her face devoid of features, completely blank. Her limbs are shorter, skin lighter; the bathing suit has become a pale blue-gray; her hair is still dark, but it's a bit shorter. These are the things that are discernible. Otherwise she's nobody. A terrifying nobody.

Ray lets the beach fade into his living room and turns toward Brian. "That one actually isn't bad."

"I knew you'd like it. It's all green and shit, and you're a pussy, and pussies love stuff that's all green and shit."

"We do."

"Smart people like it because it leads to the other green, the real green." On the screen, the mouse now rides the dog, holding its collar with one paw like it was holding the reins of a horse, the block of cheese under the other, both chasing the cat. They jump up onto a couch and run across its top.

"It does?"

"And you know what that leads to?"

"I can't even begin to imagine." The chase leads them back to the kitchen.

"Models, motherfucker."

"Ah," says Ray. Brian smirks as the dog bites the cat's tail, causing it to screech and rocket upward, its head getting caught in the ceiling.

"Every model's favorite color is green, even if they say it's orange or purple or fucking periwinkle. Their second favorite color is black because it makes them look skinnier." The mouse pulls on the dog's collar, causing it to stop in its tracks and catapult the mouse forward through the air. It lands near its hole and runs inside. "Third is probably white."

"All right, man. I've got some shit to do."

"Call of Duty later?" asks Brian.

The mouse adds this last block of cheese to its pile, winking at the viewer as the cartoon ends with orchestral accompaniment. The opening credits for the next cartoon play in a fade-in-fade-out slideshow. "Yeah, maybe."

▲▽▲▽

It's the weekend and the phone hasn't rung in over three weeks; that must be her. About once a month Claire will call, usually on a Sunday, though this time it's a Saturday. Peter never calls anymore. He's his mother's son, and while Claire is hardly what one could call a daddy's girl, she's at least… diplomatic. Emerson, settled in his favorite living room chair, had been absorbed in *The Times*—reading his own review for the seventh time this morning—when the phone first started ringing. On the occasions when something he's written appears in the paper, he'll read it first thing, then bounce around the other sections while periodically coming back to it, taking great satisfaction in how much better his writing is than any of the other contributors to the paper or its staff writers. He was extremely irritated by the sound and interruption at first, but now, realizing who it probably is, has become quite pleased. He folds the *Book Review* neatly, the paper crepitating ever so slightly, and places it on the table next to his chair. Then he lumbers over to the nearby kitchen, picks up the phone, his only phone, a black rotary-style landline with a squiggly cord that rests on the counter, and says, "Hellllo…"

"Hi Daddy." He smiles. Half of the smile is for Claire, the other half for being right.

"My darling Claire. How are you?"

"I'm well. And you?" Her voice is mild, measured. He wonders if she's called to congratulate him on his tremendous review, or just to say hello. He misses his daughter deeply.

"I'm fine, thank you. I went to the pictures last night and had such a great time."

"What did you see?"

"Naming it would give it attention it does not deserve, my love." He lowers himself onto a stool, the closest to the phone of the two situated under the counter, which separates the kitchen from the living room. The stools are metal and have seats topped with large black leather pads, and while they're big, he's much more so; he's always imagined he looked something like a polar bear doing a balancing gag in the circus sitting here, but these stools are the best, no, the only conceivable option for this space. "All you need to know is that it was dreadful."

"Oh, Daddy. You and the movies."

"The best way for a critic to fight against bad art is to keep it a secret."

"So you've said before." Emerson likes that his daughter admits to paying close attention to the things he says. Claire hasn't always done this; it took her well into adulthood before she showed she cared. He waits. If she's called about the review, this would be the moment for her to take a breath and segue. His eyes wander around the small kitchen, his black-and-white-checkered flooring and dark maple cabinets. He makes note of the sink. He's neglected doing the dishes for a couple of days and they're piling up. Her throat clears, then, "Hello?"

"I'm sorry, Claire. I'm here."

"Thought I lost you there."

"I'm very much here. I must apologize again. Me and my old age." He smirks.

"Oh, stop!"

The way she says "Oh, stop!" always does a number on him. Palpitations are standard, but this time his stomach sinks, too. It's one of the only things apart from her good looks that she inherited from her mother, and boy, is it ever a doozy. He tries not to dwell. "How's Marc? How are the kids?"

"Doing very well. We're thinking about taking a trip this summer. Mexico. Maybe Belize, also." Any image of his ex-wife forty years ago— the perfect bone structure, the conspiratorial smile—are replaced immediately by the red cast of fear upon his very own flesh and blood, and, more importantly, pale skin. While Claire did indeed receive Diana's stunning features, they're under a layer of Emerson's lily-white skin. Unfortunately, her own children suffered the same fate, despite their father being a swarthy Italian. Emerson's predominantly Anglo-Saxon heritage is just too strong, the hint of Russian Jew in there from a few generations back never made much of a difference; it seems his clade is destined for permanent pastiness.

"My goodness, why would you ever want to go *there*? With the children, no less?"

"It's practically their idea. Well, Jonathan's anyway. He's been very interested in the Mayans lately, what with their calendar coming to an end this year and all that silly doomsday stuff." That Jonathan is going to be a troublemaker, Emerson thinks. No. Red pen. Wite-out. Correction: that Jonathan *is* a troublemaker. "You know how kids are. And Kate, well, she's pretty much up for anything. It's a lovely trait and I know it won't last, not once she becomes a teenager next year. You remember how I was at that age."

"You've always been a peach, Claire."

"I have not. But I appreciate that." Claire was an absolute terror from twelve to seventeen, another thing Emerson is pleased she's willing to admit. He doesn't hold a grudge—it was long ago, and she was not fully formed yet—but still, the truth is the truth.

"If you want to leave the country, why not take them to Europe?" He shakes his head. Really, it should go without saying.

"This will be good for us, Daddy."

"You're actually going to enjoy walking around in that heat just to look at those temples? The morbid cutesiness of all this end-of-the-world flapdoodle aside, it sounds like a complete waste of time. There's no real cultural value there. Take them to Europe."

"They'll get there eventually, Daddy. Everybody does. They should be old enough to properly appreciate it, anyway. Mexico will just be fun." Her voice has not risen once; there's been no edge to it like there almost always was during those terrible teen years. Claire is calm, self-assured... as if she's just telling him what she plans on making the family for dinner tonight. He knows he cannot win. Oh well, it's her life. Her time, trouble, and sunburnt skin. So be it.

"If you say so, darling."

"And how is your class?"

"Oh, let's not talk about that." It's an innocuous enough question on the surface, sure. But she knows the answer, and she knows it's not a good one. This is a ploy, payback for the vacation comments; passive-aggression is her weapon of choice these days, which while ugly, is still highly preferential to the bold animal aggression of the old, restive Claire. Two can play at that game. Also, she doesn't use it nearly as often.

"That bad?"

"I start out each semester optimistically. One must." He says this thoughtfully, staring out at the point where the farthermost cabinet meets the ceiling, giving his words more room. They need to breathe, join the air. "But soon the reality of the situation crushes the spirit. And every batch seems to be getting worse and worse, Claire. I do my best. But I fear for the future. I really do."

"Oh, Daddy. There's still Kate and Jonathan. They'll lead the way."

"If anyone can, I believe it's them." And he does, mostly because they're *his* grandchildren. It will take a true cultural shift, however, one where critical thinking and actual art are valued more than distraction and simple entertainments, to stand any kind of chance. "Are you keeping them away from the gadgets?"

"Not exactly. But we're trying to teach them to view them as useful tools."

Emerson laughs boisterously, his body shaking on top of the stool. "I laugh, darling, but this makes me more afraid than I've ever been before—My own flesh and blood! My own flesh and blood!"

"They're everywhere, Daddy. And it's inevitable." Claire's voice climbs a bit, all sympathy erased. She seems to mean business as she argues her point: "For the children to remain competitive with their classmates, both academically and socially, they need to keep up with these things. They're even being integrated into curriculums at some kindergartens, preschools."

"Nightmare. An incomprehensible, petrifying nightmare. Please don't say another word about it."

"I'm sorry, Daddy. Let's talk about something else."

And so they do. They talk about what else Claire's been up to these past few weeks, how her painting is coming along, the show she has lined up later this year. They talk about watercolors, her newfound interest in experimenting with them, and how spring is the perfect time to view them. They move on to the weather in general, the subtle differences between March in the city and up in Connecticut, where she lives in the tumulous Fairfield County countryside. They both say they miss each other. They bemoan their busy lives, the hectic schedules and countless important commitments that keep them from seeing one another more often. But Emerson knows she could easily remedy this, the onus more on her as his daughter. Once the conversation has gone on for about thirty-five minutes, they each begin to keep their questions short, tight, and exhale more at the end of their answers, their words leaving long trails. Emerson has turned around on the stool and is staring across the room, through the living room window, which also has a very nice view, though not quite as impressive as the one from his office, to the world outside, his son and ex-wife out there somewhere, too. Soon he and Claire will say goodbye and get off the phone, but not before Emerson has suggested she pick up tomorrow's *Times*. If she were still a subscriber, she would've gotten the *Book Review* today just as he did—receiving certain sections of the Sunday paper on Saturday being one of the key perks of the at-home-delivery subscription system—and surely she would have mentioned his review back near the top of their conversation, her congratulations from the heart and very enthusiastic.

The week leading into spring marks the start of the hunt. After a rainy Sunday afternoon mostly spent getting high, watching whatever episodes of *The Daily Show* and *Colbert Report* he missed the week before on Hulu, and browsing Reddit, mainly r/todayilearned and r/pareidolia, Ray decides to look at the photo he took of the intersection at Lafayette and Bond. It's the first time he's seen it; Friday afternoon following the incident kept him busy with rushed end-of-week runs, and he basically just had time to shower, get dressed, and shovel something down his gullet for dinner before Fernanda came over that evening. Then Saturday was sort of a pity party, mourning the loss of the girl he never took all that seriously until she left, so far gone in the throes of self-loathing that he actually spent six hours well into the night playing Call of Duty with Brian. Fuckin' Call of Duty. Older generations actually went off to war and fought shit worth fighting for, meeting and overcoming horrors that made them into men; now less than 1 percent of Americans enlist and your average guy in his twenties, Ray included, would probably have a helluva lot more pride in their performance playing that particular, stupid franchise… Anyway, some might consider his choice of activities on Sunday a continuation of the pity party, but it's actually a normal enough Sunday for Ray. It's the most recent photo on his camera roll, and he notices something strange immediately.

The first thing he sees is the clusterfuck of intersection markers—the green LAFAYETTE and BOND signs crisscrossing below two perpendicular traffic lights that stick out parallel to the LAFAYETTE sign, sandwiched between these and stark black-and-white ONE WAY signs themselves crisscrossing in the reverse order, so that the Bond one-way sign is above the Lafayette one, directly below the Bond Street sign, followed by a white and red NO PARKING sign and perpendicular pedestrian crossing signals at the very bottom—but right behind it, there's a small mural, a simplistic replica of The Creation of Adam. It registers as something very, very important. But he still might be a little too high to figure out exactly why just yet, outside of the obvious surface-level thing of it being an iconic religious image, some symbol that would easily play into the narrative of all the weird existential shit he's been going through lately.

He studies it, squinting, holding his phone closer to his face: While hardly the masterpiece on the ceiling of the Sistine Chapel, the mural's not unpretty, the light blue, black, white, and flesh tones of the composition blend together nicely, weather-beaten and sort of burnt-looking in parts to reveal what looks like a wooden or metal canvas underneath. The wall behind it is brick, the bottom painted oxblood and top black, the mural dividing these sections with areas of bare, gray brick on either lateral side, indicating the wall was probably painted after the mural was placed. Even though it's kind of crudely done and more than likely meant to be blasphemous down over there in the formerly hip East Village, the mural still shines with a certain purity and hope against the moody black and red wall; the whole thing has an air of paradoxical downtown beauty. He hadn't noticed any of this while there in the flesh—his eyes fixed on the intersecting street signs, feeling uneasy still and hurried, he really only took the photo as a reminder of where he was when the déjà vu occurred. And it also wasn't anything he would've seen during the actual onset of the strange feeling, since he was riding due north on Lafayette then and the mural's west-facing—so if anything, it would've only been there peripherally. He emails the photo to himself and looks at it on his computer, larger. It's a little blurry, but examining it on a bigger screen helps. The small screen of the iPhone didn't do justice to how big and meaningful this thing here must be.

Now instead of being self-conscious about trying to figure out what's going on with the picture while still a little high, he leans into it, the overanalysis it might yield: An interesting thing about the way he framed his photo, he really appreciates now, is that on the right side of the mural, just next to God reaching out to Adam, the jumble of intersection signage is partially obstructing His legs and many of the cherubs who should be surrounding Him. The traffic light in front of this portion of the mural is lit orange and Bond's one-way sign is pointing in His direction. The specificity of the legs and cherubs is beside the point; all that matters is that the street signs and traffic signal are leading Ray toward Him. What the photo's saying, Ray decides, is that if he wants to advance in the afterlife, to leave behind purgatory or limbo or whatever and enter heaven, he must truly *bond* with God, must go to Him, and that this is the only way, the *one way* to advance. This picture is actual confirmation that he is indeed dead, a bona fide clue. The déjà vu thing is ephemeral, but this, this right here he can reference. He thought the photo would lead him back to the déjà vu, but now he thinks the déjà vu has led him to this photo. The traffic light is orange because it's the best way for God to communicate to him that he is in fact in purgatory. Red would've been hell, green the go sign for ascension. But here, in purgatory, not limbo, he still has work to do. Atonement. The fate of his very soul hangs in the balance. Déjà vu will lead him toward more steganographic pictures, which will lead him back to his death, where he'll understand what he did wrong during his life and what he must do to rectify it. He'll do whatever that is and then move on to the next phase of his afterlife! Out on the streets, déjà vu is what he must chase.

So with the scent, he hits the trail. Monday's a gray day, low fifties. Sporadic sprinkling. Through hectic, hyperreal New York City streets he searches for something within himself. Before, he thought being a bike messenger was simply a product of his circumstance; now he knows there is no circumstance: exploring Manhattan's grid is exactly what he's supposed to be doing. The pickup and drop-off points of his route are guideposts pointing him to the places where he will gather what he should be gathering. He scans, sniffs, feels, tastes, and, his earbuds left at home, listens to the city streets, noting everything acutely: large buildings looming in muted light; the chilling winds tearing down avenues; a few ghost bikes, both ominous and reassuring in this world; grit, spit, petrichor; clamorous horns in relentless Monday traffic. Every block more people, pigeons, and cabs, people, pigeons, and cabs. He keeps the mission at the front of his mind, constantly conscious of it, analyzing it while carrying it out. Religious symbols are everywhere—churches hardly lacking on Manhattan Island; some graffiti referencing the Bible, with more than one "John 3:16"—but he experiences nothing but the sensory. The reaction is never triggered. At one point late in the afternoon he stares into an iridescent oil slick, thinking he might have found an acheiropoieton of Jesus. Nothing. When he rolls his bike back into his Long Island City living room that evening, he knows he's tried too hard, and was trying too hard then to understand the ins and outs of how he tried too hard. The vigor with which he embraced his newfound purpose defeated the purpose.

Tuesday he's more relaxed, and there's a glint of something, over in Murray Hill, mid-afternoon. In a yin to yesterday's yang, he rides like he's not looking for anything at all, only the pickup and drop-off sites of his route, like he rode before, letting his mind drift. And while he feels something similar to déjà vu followed by a disconcerting sense of strength and freedom and happiness riding uptown on First Avenue past 37th Street—the sun warming the back of his neck and lighting the way ahead toward the U.N., his drop-off, earbuds back in and pumping party rap, Das Racist's *Shut Up, Dude*—it's missing the pop of disassociated recognition and the decompression back into the mind and body that accompany real déjà vu. It's just slightly familiar, oddly familiar, and he can only chalk it up as being nothing more than nostalgia. Déjà vu is something you know when you feel. It's a nice day, and it should feel good to ride a bike on a nice day; these positive vibes make him uncomfortable because they remind him of simpler and better times during years past when he would almost exclusively ride on nice days, and sometimes on a loop that would take him past the U.N., way back before he knew he was really dead.

By mid-week, he's ready. He sees things more broadly than he did with Monday's purpose blinders while not being so wide-eyed that he'll fall victim to Tuesday's bullshit form of Zen. Caring so much made him too aware; not caring made him unaware. Wednesday he wants to just be aware. His eyes survey the streets while his mind goes where it wants—sometimes to what he's looking at, often not. Riding down the vale that is Broadway during his fourth run of the day, it drifts—like a lot of guys who are no longer having sex with someone they were recently having sex with—down to his pants. It also makes its way inside the pants of the more attractive scantily clad young ladies there on Broadway on this partly cloudy, warm late March morning, or up their skirts if that's what they're wearing instead. Enter another thing Ray hunts for this week: someone else to have sex with. While there has indeed been another girl besides Fernanda who he's met up with in a friends-with-benefits-type arrangement this year, it isn't half as consistent. Plus, he knows this girl, Emily, is also regularly having sex with another guy or two, and probably random dudes from bars and parties on occasion. The nice thing about Fernanda was that she wasn't really like that; their arrangement was loose but she wasn't, at heart she was a good girl. If there had been a guy in her life besides him at the time, he would have been surprised. Maybe at the very end... but that would have made some sense, unfortunately. He wouldn't feel right only fucking Emily. And Emily probably wouldn't like it either if she were able to figure it out; it would probably scare her off. Then he'd be fucking no one.

Of course on the street, Ray just looks. He can't imagine a world where catcalls and pick-up lines would actually work. Not that he would want to try, but still. Engaging beautiful strangers who are minding their own business and achieving any kind of a positive result seems like a lie told by twentieth-century entertainment. This is the twenty-first century. He's able to interact with other pretty girls, ones he's already met; girls he can call on with some semblance of trust, where there are references, mutual acquaintances tying them; girls he's been keeping tabs on without really trying to for years: He's able to interact with girls on Facebook. And since Fernanda decided to go her own way, he's been perusing more and more of his female friends' profiles, as a new vesperal habit or while waiting for his first run of the day in the mornings back at dispatch, forming a list of possible girls to reach out to in the back of his mind. So here he just looks, just rides.

The looks are always split-second fast. They have to be. Anything more would be too dangerous. In fact, he can't look at anything directly for all that long. A couple of cars pass on the left, one a dirty, red sedan, dried mud on its bumper, the other a cab. He crosses 20th. Then there's one by the Loews on 19th and Broadway—an ethnically ambiguous brunette with an hourglass body. Tight cobalt dress, pale pink heels. Highly bangable. He wonders if there are any movies worth seeing right now. Probably not. Another cyclist to pass up ahead, a white stick figure depicting a cyclist painted on the green below. Like cartoon versions of the ghost bikes he occasionally passes but with their ghost riders still on top, flattened like in *Who Framed Roger Rabbit?*, floating along a barranca. They're everywhere—two or three each block—though he rarely notices them anymore. Except for right now. He usually sees them the way he does red lights, absently, reflexively. The real ghost bikes, the ones that mark the fellow dead, have always been quick to catch his attention, but this is actually more frightening. Eighteenth then retail and delis on both sides. The bike lane ahead now gray instead of green, bare except for the outline of the lane. Three more stick figures below before the bike lane turns off to the left at the end of this block. A conscious decision to pay less attention to them; to accept them as traffic symbols and avoid thoughts about how menacing they really are, creepier than the memorials. Crossing the intersection at 17th where Broadway turns into Union Square West. Restaurants and shit on the right, the park and too many people on the left. Nevermind the too many: another two. They momentarily get the blood purling away from his legs, up, but not too far—lissome blondes with big tits in a group of four or five, a brunette and another less attractive blonde among them. Sort of stringy hair, all of them. Probably tourists from some semi-sad place in Eastern Europe like

Serbia or Hungary or the Czech Republic, countries that export a lot of hardcore porn. A guy starts walking out leading with coffee in hand and doesn't stop till Ray yells "Hey! Hey! Hey!" Nearly got hit because of his own idiocy and the mamón still shoots him a censorious look and throws his free hand up. His face is dumb, the features sharp but flesh fatty, designer sunglasses perched just above an undoubtedly receding hairline. Yuppie piece of shit. Case in point about the looks needing to be quick. If he had studied the Eastern European blondes more that shithead would've gotten smashed. He himself would've been all right, though. Probably. He's the predator in this situation. So why not look? That motherfucker would've deserved it. With his dumbass fat face and bad, stupid haircut on his square-shaped head. The bike would've probably gotten fucked up, that's why. Speaking of, the asphalt's been broken by cobblestone. Can't be good for the wheels. Some people to weave around close to 14th. They misjudged his speed or didn't see him or didn't care. Nothing compared to Times Square. It's okay. Everything's okay comparatively. Everything. Except him. He's not okay, really. Really, really. If he were okay then he wouldn't be here. The other side of 14th. Down University Place, riding against traffic. NYU territory now… Fuck these kids. It's weird to feel superior to them because he's dead and has a shitty job and a frustrating quest to free himself in the afterlife, but he went to a better school, so he does. Some of the people here aren't students. They're just people. Some seem like they could even be native New Yorkers. Whatever the fuck that means. The poor Indians that sold the isle of Manhattan for twenty-four bucks are the only real native New Yorkers. Oh, shit… another one. Tall, black jeans, a small leather jacket. Her hair pulled back in a ponytail, light brown and gleaming in the golden light. Callipygian but with legs like a gazelle. Her body's like Fernanda's from behind, which is saying a lot for a white girl… Fernanda. Fuckin' Fernanda… This one actually could be a model; she's dressed like one. Maybe on her way to or coming back from a go-see. They actually walk around downtown. Sometimes together. Flocks of models. What he wouldn't give for a night in one of those model apartments. They stack them in there like they're in dorms, he's heard. A flash of Brian eating cereal. Models and bottles. Brian in a club sitting with a bunch of other guys in suits, their ties loose, talking amongst themselves, all scared. Brian laughing with milk running down his chin. Conscious rejection of any notion of Brian. Passing her. He wants to look at her face, but doesn't. Shame for caring about whether or not she's a model. Some models are actually very weird-looking.

Comfort in this, something that diminishes the impulse, still lingering, to look back. Fernanda was in all truth prettier than some weird-looking models. Conscious rejection of the thought of Fernanda. A new reflex, rejecting Fernanda, discovered right here. Cars coming as he's going the wrong way. None that fast. Not too fast. A delivery guy also going the wrong way, but on the other side of the street. Also Hispanic. But short. A lot darker than he himself. He's wearing a reflective orange vest. The type most imagine when they hear "Mexican" in New York City. Especially other Hispanics. Might be some other type of Central American— Guatemalan, Honduran, Nicaraguan—but maybe not. They could actually be related. Fuck, that's weird. Or maybe kind of cool. Mostly just weird. Passing 9th. A covey of three or four Asian girls up ahead on the right, walking along the sidewalk in front of a CVS, a sign that reads PHOTO in red letters above them. Who the fuck processes photos at a drugstore in New York City in 2012? Maybe tourists from the heartland. The nineties wouldn't be such a bad place to be stuck. Those halcyon days, much better than bullshit early-twenty-first-century purgatory. Last century we looked out, this one just in. We went to the moon, for Christ's sake. But wait, wasn't the moon landing just conceived to frighten the Soviets with our missile power as part of the arms race? Kind of wack. That is, if it even happened. If Stanley Kubrick didn't direct it. Nevermind that. That was the sixties, which were still fucked, not the nineties. The nineties were great. There are so many Asians at NYU. There were a lot at Columbia, but goddam, NYU. That's not racist. "So many" is not the same as "too many." Also, Asians in America seem to have it a helluva lot better than Mexicans, mostly. Isn't that how racism's supposed to work? Like, in the sociological sense? Something about the power structure in society regarding the different races. You can't be racist if you're among a more oppressed minority or some shit? That sounds stupid—a bigot is a bigot by any name, whether sociology likes it or not—but he'll take what he can get. It doesn't matter that he's only half Mexican. Half is enough. He's never had sex with an Asian girl. He'd like to. Though not with any of the ones he's passing now. Childlike clothes and dispositions, not enough attitude. There was an Asian girl back in college during freshman year who said he "had a body like Diego Luna and eyes almost as nice as Gael García Bernal's." It was flattering and insulting and she looked good and he almost fucked her that night but didn't.

Then it happens again.

He had just passed the intersection at 8th Street. He pulls over to the sidewalk. Stops. Thinks… His mind was in college, thinking about sex, his body here. There were Asian girls. A cloud had just blocked the sun and he's by NYU. It's 11:08 a.m. No God iconography as far as he can see. Just another intersection on a downtown Manhattan street.

He takes a photo, the CVS and fading Asian girls in the background, then, utilizing his iPhone 4S' front-facing camera, one of himself. He looks at the camera roll. The photo of the intersection is a little blurry. A flick of the thumb. Himself: he's too large in it, his helmeted head blocking most everything contextual. But his blank expression rings true; the quality of seeming neither here nor there. Inside he's still buzzing with strength and freedom and happiness, but these feelings wane as he continues to shrink back into his body. Soon a strange mixture of pride—for having found a clue—and fear—also for having found a clue—makes its way in and takes over everything. Embarrassment would have been a part of it, too, for taking a "selfie," not because any-one on the street would have known—the beauty of the front-facing camera is discretion—but because *he* would have known; however, the photo as evidence would've been very stupid to pass up. He understands the value of proper due diligence. There are things that can't be ignored, no matter how ridiculous they may seem.

▲ ▲ ▽ ▽

Certain jokes are always funny, others get old. Then there are those that aren't funny anymore not because of the joke itself but because the per-son who hears it has changed. The joke about Professor Towers is that he'll let you get away with plagiarism as long as you're plagiarizing him. She read it on a website called RateMyProfessors, right after she got placed in his class. It didn't take long once the course was underway to really get the joke. She used to think it was very funny. Now Haruka gets why it would be funny but doesn't still actually believe that it's funny.

He's been her favorite professor since last week, Professor Towers. English isn't her favorite class or anything, but he is her favorite profes-sor. She even changed her mind about his size. He reminds her of To-toro now, but old: white hair instead of brown. Totally kawaii. Last year she read a WordPress post about how Totoro is the god of death. It was a conspiracy theory saying that the story in the cartoon was based on the Sayama Incident, a famous murder case in Japan, where two sisters died: one murdered, one by suicide because of the grief over her sister. The two girls only see Totoro because one is dead and the other has opened up death's door to find her. At the end neither of the girls have shadows. She liked the theory.

Professor Towers is not quite the god of death but he could certainly be a prophet. He's obsessed with it. Of all the heavy things they talk about here, death is number one. Like right now. They're wrapping up *Hamlet*, Act V, Scene ii… "Understanding he has not long to live, Hamlet turns to Claudius and proclaims, 'The point!—envenom'd too! Then, venom, to thy work,' stabbing him with the poison-tipped sword. The people cry, 'Treason!' The king asks for their help in his defense, but it does not come—there is only Hamlet, forcing him now to drink from the goblet of poison that had killed his mother, commanding him to follow her…" He revels in it. Emanates it. Can't wait to share it. Death. Eighteen- and nineteen-year-olds think they're invincible. He's here to remind them that they're not. Through these books he loves, written by dead men, mostly about death… "Here Laertes remarks that the king has received his just deserts and begs that he and Hamlet 'exchange forgiveness' before they expire as well. 'Mine and my father's death come not upon thee, nor thine on me,' he declares. Then Laertes, too, dies." Sometimes it feels like more than a reminder. It feels like being surrounded by it. Death. "How did you feel reading this, class? What were your thoughts as the bodies began to fall, then pile up?" His eyes scan the room. The only black girl in the class raises her hand. She sits a few seats away from Haruka near the end of the back row and wears glasses. "Yes. Please."

"It almost made me dizzy. The different revenge plots being realized, Gertrude and Laertes dying on top of that pretty much by accident, everything happening as fast as it did. It was a lot."

Professor Towers smiles at her. "Yes. Yes, it sure was *a lot*." He nods. The girl nods back. "Anyone else?" He stares at the boy with the reddish hair in the second row, the boy who talks more than most. Nobody really seems to like talking, but some do more than most, and this boy the most of all. Class discussions are never actually class discussions. Nobody else's thoughts matter. Professor Towers will guide the class till someone says the thoughts that are his, and if no one does, he'll just say them. His thoughts, mostly about death. "There are no wrong answers," he says, stringing the boy along. But of course there are.

"I guess I thought everybody sort of got what they deserved."

"Hmmm… did they deserve to die?" The reddish-headed boy shrugs then shakes his head up and down a couple of times. A little gesture of wishy-washy affirmation that matches his wishy-washy language. Professor Towers turns to the black girl. "Do you think they deserved it?"

She hesitates. "That's not my question to answer. Morally."

He paces a little, scratches his chin. The real one, the top one, not the second, larger one that's actually part of his neck. "Anyone else? Can anyone make that call, morally?" They remain silent. He stops. Looks the room over. "Well, I asked you your thoughts. I asked you how you felt. Both of those answers were fine ones." He smiles at the two students who participated. "It's a shame the rest of you have no thoughts or feelings." He laughs to himself; it lasts almost ten seconds and at one point he slaps his thigh. Parts of his body, face bounce and wobble. He gradually regains composure. "I myself am comfortable saying, morally, that it's all a bit gray." His eyes remain smiling. "And so on to Hamlet's death…" Last week when he laughed at the blonde girl with the ponytail, Haruka saw they were the same. Both contemptuous. Both truth-tellers. That's why her mirror neurons lit up like they did. But there is a difference in how they go about it. He's more upfront with his truth. He will tell it to you, to your face, celebrating his honesty, laughing. She's sneaky. She will only reveal it to the recipient through the recipient. Any celebration is private. She likes it that way. Overall, it's better. But sometimes she wonders if the recipient even recognizes the truth. Some might be too dumb to see their own worthlessness. This might be why Professor Towers carries on the way he does. Maybe there's room for both, telling as well as showing. It's something to think about.

The thing about truth is that it's not the same as fact. They're synonyms but shouldn't be, Haruka's realized. Facts just are. Everything adds up, check out. Truth requires faith. It's personal. It can change. Like with love. One day someone knows they love you—they feel it, they know it's there—then the next day they don't. They felt it then they didn't. It happens. Most people trust truth more than they do facts. This is because people are stupid. They want to feel so badly. So much. All these different feelings. So many feels. Haruka never thought she'd take English seriously as a subject. She never got it: its function. Now she does. It's a purveyor of truth. A spreader of feels. Mostly about the futility of life, the inevitability of death.

Death always triumphs in the end. Over everything: even love. She's learned from him. The professor. He helped her recognize these truths, the faith she must have in herself to rise above them, use them to her advantage, like he does. There is a spiritual element to her contempt of everyone, she knows now, especially the men she takes home. What she does when she makes them think she loves them until they realize she doesn't. She will continue on. Little Kaiju will be like the well of poison the sword is dipped in in *Hamlet*, the men's penises swords. They will take them back into the world and do what men do. Her mouth will be the poisoned goblet. They will drink from it when they kiss. So much death to spread. Haruka sits there listening intently as Professor Towers goes on about Hamlet's death, how it was "neither heroic nor shameful, it just was," drawing her favorite professor as Totoro, little hearts around him everywhere, all while playing with her hair. So much truth, such a wonderful teacher.

He looks at them again when he gets home that night: the pictures. While waiting for the elevator at NYU's Bobst Library down on Washington Square South, his drop-off destination when the incident occurred, Ray had emailed the photos to himself, and now he's studying them closer. He's also looking at the one with the mural again, this time not high, everything organized in a newly created folder labeled EVIDENCE residing directly on his MacBook's desktop. They're practically full screen in Preview. His giant face in the one: hazel eyes staring dead ahead, a mesorrhine nose below, followed by his full lips, the top a little more prominent than the bottom; all surrounded by the black of the helmet, the light and dark grays of University Place's sidewalk and asphalt lining the frame along either side. A large portrait of a person not there, in neutrals. Next the CVS in all its NYU student-catering chain store glory, except a little blurry, sort of sexless Asian girls wearing hoodies in the distance, a few other people here and there, some cars parked down along University Place; a lot of asphalt, brick, stone, and glass, vague reflections of things. The CVS/pharmacy signage is intensely vivid in its imperial red under the cloud cover's caliginous shadow, but otherwise the photo is sort of bland. Lastly there's the one from the week before, which he understands and accepts on its own, but not how it would fit with today's two.

The first thing he tries to find is a pattern, and besides both of the intersection photos being a little fuzzy, there's nothing really to go off of. It's not like there's another hidden religious mural he didn't see before. The blurriness is a little weird—like he's photographed the feeling in the air, the vague strangeness of déjà vu visualized in the smear of the people and objects at the site where it occurred. He wishes he had something, anything, from the bridge to add, but is left only with his memory, which while also fuzzy, isn't quite the same. That the photo of himself is crystal clear, despite using the front-facing camera which has far fewer mega-pixels, only plays into this. But it could also just be shaky hands—due to adrenaline from biking or his reaction to feeling the déjà vu again—that caused the blurriness. Or it could be that he had zoomed in a little on both intersection photos, while the one of himself had to be zoomed out all the way in order to capture his face in full, what with the limitations of taking a photo of himself with a phone like that. Or it could be a combination of the two. Or nothing.

It's a pretty weak premise for a pattern, blurriness, so next he looks at how the two intersection photos are different and complementary. The first thing that really stuck out upon viewing the photo of Bond and Lafayette last week was the Creation of Adam mural. For this other in-tersection, it was the vivid CVS/pharmacy signage. God creating man in one. A drugstore in the other. God… then drugs? They could possibly add up to something. They're two things often thought of as being in-congruous, God and drugs—most popular religions aren't too fond of intoxicants—but there's also some evidence to suggest they can work together. For Christianity, there's water into wine, the cannabis oil Jesus was said to have used. And anyone who's ever taken an anthropology class or even just hung out for an afternoon at the Museum of Natural History would know a lot of tribal religions use hallucinogens as part of their spiritual development, including, maybe, whatever Mexican tribe he descended from.

Ray decides then it's probably a good idea for him to get high. He didn't want to. Really. He had planned on looking at all these with a clear head, forgoing his normal ritual of taking a few hits right after work to kill the day's pain and elevate his mood for the evening. He wanted to really hunker down and study, free from any type of influence. Now, weed isn't *always* bad for studying—it's especially useful for looking at all the facets of a thing, its layers; really getting and feeling it. But it can be a little trickier to find the specific thread tying separate things, as opposed to forcing one to string them together, appreciating in reality what should be most relevant in a system of interconnected parts, at least in Ray's case. He gets so caught up looking at and feeling the thing that's commanding his attention in any given moment that the thing he should be relating it to gets marginalized or even temporarily forgotten, and then if he remembers what he should have been looking for, what should have been there in the back of his mind the whole time to contextualize the thing he's currently looking at, then that thing becomes the thing commanding his attention, and he can no longer really give the other thing its due, and so on. And on the off chance he does remember, he'll just foist some retiform pattern upon them. When trying to "see the forest for the trees," you can't see the forest when completely lost in the thick of it or when stuck in one particular tree. But the word "drugs" calling out to him like it is here seems like it could be a sign, like maybe just how déjà vu had led him to the picture of God the other day, which itself is supposed to lead him to God, that the déjà vu today had led him to this photo telling him to go to drugs. His favorite drug being weed. That's what this is saying, right? It was the ONE WAY sign, under the BOND sign, that was pointing toward God before. Where's this one pointing? The one-way signs are the pattern, Ray now realizes—another example of finding what he's looking for only after he's stopped trying. "Holy shit!" he says. And this one is pointing... away from the CVS? So he's supposed to move away from drugs? Away from weed? Really? Hold on, hold on... Hold the fuck on. No, no, no... That was careless, fast and loose, silly thinking before. Sure, CVS is a "drug" store, but what kind of drugs are we talking about here? Pharmacies are mostly about pimping out man-made shit. Right? Right? Synthetics. There's the stuff that saves lives, the marvels of Western medicine, beautiful benchmarks of man's achievement and progress—penicillin and insulin and vaccines and whatnot—but more than that really there are a lot of drugs sold just to make a buck. Dangerous chemical concoctions. The types of substances that give him the heebie-jeebies; the ones Big Pharma creates instead of the cures to diseases and the ones that could easily be replaced by a good diet and some exercise, or all-natural supplements. That away-from-weed thing before, that was a gross oversimplification, the worst kind of reductive thinking. Ray doesn't even take Advil if he can help it. And why would he, when he can smoke weed instead? He learned his lesson in college. Maybe that has something to do with his death? Could he have died taking the wrong mixture of pills at Columbia, and not while crossing the street looking into his first-generation iPhone? It's possible… But first things first: it's time to get high. Weed isn't sold at this chain store pharmacy with its garish red sign; it's nothing like the type of drug you could get there. Weed's a friend, it's natural, and, as established when he first figured he should get high moments ago, it's something that's in line with getting closer to God. He most definitely should smoke some right this second.

Five minutes and a few hits from the vaporizer later, he's feeling good and vindicated, in addition, of course, to a little high. Verity and beauty prevailed in the end. He's as connected to it as he was the intersection photo with the Creation of Adam mural, this picture of a drugstore that told him to get high before telling him not to get high until it let him know it was okay to get high again. Now he's picking up on other little things. Really getting it. The one-way sign is pointing east, the same direction as the one on Bond telling him to go to God. That other intersection is actually close by, a few blocks to the southeast, and the fact that they're pointing the same way, east, seems very telling. The direction the sun rises, the direction graves face. Then there's the 8th Street sign below the ONE WAY sign, linked to it like the BOND Street sign was with its ONE WAY sign, the figure eight on the street sign looking like an infinity symbol tilted vertically. Purgatory is temporary but heaven will be infinite. To bond with God forever, to enter heaven, he needs to stay this course. Eastward ho. Vaya con Dios. This is what the street signs, the two intersection photos, are telling him. Where is east, though? It can't literally be east. That's just weird. He's from the West, west of New York City, anyway, coming from Texas; does this just mean to move further away from his birth, deeper into death? Of course he'd like to, but doesn't he have to look back toward his life first, to figure out how to do that? How to atone and transcend? Then it hits him—the east is probably the Middle East, where the God from his quasi-Catholic upbringing is from. It's all just pointing to God. So what's the significance of the CVS, really? While there is no traffic light in this photo like there was in the other one, there is a pedestrian crossing signal next to the CVS, which is showing the little white figure of the walking man: that it's okay to cross. This could be an invitation, something to do with looking back at his use of synthetic drugs. There were times when he took the easy way out sophomore year… stimulants to study more assiduously, sedatives to take the edge off, or just for plain fun. It's possible that the little pill phase could have done him in. Too much Xanax and Valium or Klonopin taken too close together; any one of them while also drinking. The crossing signal could be telling him to look at what his actions had wrought—death by drug overdose. It's a pit stop on his way east, toward God. The little pedestrian signal is even white: ghostlike. His ghost. Him. It's possible he's looking back at his own death here. This could be it.

He surveys the picture of himself again, to see if there's anything written on his face about the possibility of prescription drug involvement. It's weird looking at a picture of himself like this while a little high… too familiar. There was a lot of him in it before; now there's too much. Way too much. He doesn't like it. Most of the time he doesn't care either way about his looks. But this photo is weird. He looks weird. Kind of like a more chiseled version of a Muppet, wearing a helmet. But everyone looks funny wearing a helmet. Helmets are funny. It's just so hard to take this photo seriously. This fucking picture. So silly. Bike helmets make everyone look just so bizarre. Even the "cooler" multisport style he favors—also called "skate style" by dint of its preponderance in the always-so-cool skateboarding community—looks stupid. Soon he's succumbed to a full-on laughing fit: one that would have embarrassed him if Brian were home, too, if he weren't alone. He laughs for two straight minutes at the photo of himself before hunger pangs snap him out of it. A feeling of shame then washes over him. Not only because of the seriousness of the investigation he's disrespecting, cachinnating, but also because he's just recently eaten. It's strange that munchies are a real thing, but they are. He knows why, though. THC binds with smell receptors. So then it's not strange, actually. He can't remember what he should be looking for. Something about a drug overdose. His drug overdose. Possible overdose. He snaps back and searches his expression. But there isn't really an expression. His face is blank. Like he thought before, a portrait of a person not there. That could be it. That could be the point. Sedative cocktails kill a lot of people, why wouldn't he be one of them? People become numb on benzos: expressionless. Shells of themselves. Plus, he hasn't really aged since college, physically, no real wrinkles or anything. That could play into this. There was that one time when it got a little scary, when he almost called Poison Control because everything he said was so low and slow, and he felt like his mind was being surrounded by a gradually growing darkness. But then he drank a cup of coffee and eventually felt fine. That doesn't mean he didn't die in his sleep, though, afterwards. Another hunger pang. Yes, but can he really discount the whole iPhone theory? That he died while looking into it? I mean, it would make a lot of sense. Everything's been so different since he's had one of those things, even if he didn't realize it until recently. Or maybe they're one and the same? Maybe he was high on Xanax, dragging his heels lost in screen and thought, when he was run over. There's no way of knowing just yet. The evidence is inconclusive. "Fuck it," he says. He decides to go make a sandwich.

Everything about the sandwich is amazing.

When he comes back to his room and flips the MacBook back open, instead of clicking on the EVIDENCE folder again, he opens up Firefox and clicks on the Facebook shortcut in his Bookmarks Toolbar. As he learned on Monday, out in the field, these things can't be forced. Some good progress was made this evening, what with the one-way signs, the possibility of pharmaceutical drugs playing a role in his death; the rest requires more. Time to move on, forget about his soul for a bit and follow his heart. Or, really, his dick. There's a deep blue bar filling the top of the browser, a strange searchable and hyperorganized and highly fragmented facsimile of a social life below.

It's a fine art sending that first Facebook message to someone you'd eventually like to have sex with, Ray well knows. After all, that's how he got into Fernanda's good graces—and more—after four long years. His shortlist is down to three. Two girls from college, one he met after: Jill, Margarita, and Frances, respectively. He's at least liked some of their statuses, if not commented on them, in the past couple of months, and they some of his, which means his reaching out won't seem at all strange or creepy. Jill is one of the girls he's flirted with regularly, and she's who he'll try first. He doesn't want to do all three at once since they could all accept an invitation to hang out. Too much to juggle. He's not trying to whore around; he really just wants someone to take Fernanda's place, so that things will seem more balanced again. Less hell, more heaven, in this purgatory of his. Jill's cool like Fernanda, but doesn't look anything like her—she's another white girl, like Emily, with more tits than ass. Margarita's actually similar to Fernanda in the looks department, but that shouldn't really matter, and it'll be best to keep the path of least resistance with this. Jill works best. He's picked a good day, Wednesday. The time is right: 8:05 p.m., evening but not too late. While critical thinking is its own ballgame, writing friendly notes while a little high is not an issue for Ray. He gets high often enough: "Hey Jill- How's everything? It's been a long time since Mowsh's molecular biology. What are you up to these days? You free to grab a cup of coffee or a drink next week? Catch up away from the watchful eye of Marky Z, properly, in person?" He reads back his message: His tone is positive and casual, the sentences short and action-oriented. It's good enough. He clicks send. And it is only a few minutes later, while going through some of the recent photos she's been tagged in, that there's an alert from his inbox, and a message from her: "Sure, let's grab a drink. Would be great to see you." If only everything were so easy.

▲ ▲ ▲ ▽

This day, like always, is a truly wonderful day. Usually whenever he's done teaching *Hamlet* for a term, Emerson will celebrate by rereading it. He could recite it to himself instead, by memory, if he so wished—he has the entire thing committed there, available for instant recall, and this is all he relies upon for the class lectures—but his delivery, while grand and moving, is nothing compared to the enactments that take place in his mind with the play in hand. He understands his limitations as a thespian, and although his performances are adequate for his class, they are not for himself. More importantly, keeping things solely within his head makes it easier to honor his own words: his assessments, analyses, feelings, all integrate into the text seamlessly, in real time. Some people say Shakespeare should be experienced in the theater, not read. This is only the case for people with weak minds. It's much better to keep the words self-contained, the words in the mind not competing with those spoken aloud. So he reads.

He owns several copies of it in various formats, ranging from handsomely bound rarities to newer printings that feature strikingly vivid typesetting, but the one he'll read as part of this ritual is the same from forty-eight years ago, the very clothbound edition he used to teach his first-ever class, back before he had the play perfectly memorized in full. It's covered in notes, all of which he'll read, too, as he goes along, most of which he still agrees with… old thoughts flowing together with the new. Many of the brilliant observations and asides scribbled in the margins are actually still used during his lectures, often verbatim, his explications then largely the same as they are now. Right is right. He'd like to think this copy of *Hamlet* might go on auction one day, after his death, as an important artifact for academia. Hopefully it will go to someplace nice, maybe the Morgan.

Additionally, he'll make it a point while reading to remember the particulars of how he taught the scenes and sections in the days and weeks just past. He'll replay the amazing lectures, the riveting class discussions: his marvelous explanation of Act I, scene iii; the stupid questions some students asked about Ophelia, whether she was truly mad; his dramatic summary of the final scene right before he coaxed the class to weigh in on the play's central themes.

It is this reading that he looks forward to as he's returning home for the evening, after a nice seafood dinner alone, and sees the red light from his answering machine blinking. He presses the listen button. "You have one new message," a robotic male recording announces. The machine beeps. Then there's an old familiar voice: "Hello Emerson. It's Bob. Saw your piece in *The Times* Sunday. Good work. I'd like to get together for lunch next week if you're available. Give me a ring back when you have a moment. Thanks."

Emerson shudders. Robert Weisman is his book editor and has been for the past thirty-five years. He knows what he wants, and it's the same thing that he himself wants, but it's nothing he'd like to think about. Not yet. He wants the next book—the book Emerson has decided will be his last.

▲▲▲▲

Such a bitch. She pretended not to hear the first time. Now Haruka has to say it again. "Lauren, can I please have the room for a while?"

Lauren closes her textbook. She looks over at them, Haruka and the boy. Her chair drags loudly across the floor as she rises. "Why do I even pay for this fucking room when I have to live in the library?" She begins to gather her things.

Haruka looks over at the boy and rolls her eyes a little. He smiles reassuringly; they're on the same team. Strength in numbers. She doubts Lauren's going to go to the library. She'll either go across the hall to Witch Two's room and say mean things about her or stand outside the dorm on Washington Square West, smoking cigarettes and saying mean things about her to someone else on the phone. Haruka's seen this before when signing other boys and men out down in the lobby, on the occasions Witch Two and Witch Three aren't around. Lauren through the window, looking like she's complaining—a phone up to her ear in one hand, a cigarette in the animated other. Also, she doubts Lauren pays to live in the room. Her parents probably do, like Haruka's. Lauren storms out. Haruka locks the door behind her, shuts off the light, and guides the boy over to the bed.

Soon they are having sex.

It's okay, not the best she's had or the worst. His size is adequate but he doesn't move very well. A little too herky-jerky. But that doesn't matter. "Oh my God," she says. Normally Haruka doesn't talk in bed. She will only offer positive reinforcement in the form of soft moans and gasps. Like Little Kaiju is saying "Mmmm" or "Nom nom nom." But she needs to talk now for the sake of her soul. She needs to speak her truth. Testify. "You feel so good inside me."

The boy says nothing back. Just keeps going with his clumsy dick. He's an attractive enough boy. His name is Raj and he's of either Indian or Pakistani or Bengali descent, something along those lines. She didn't ask. A lot of the men with origins from that part of the world have very good bone structure, like they could all be models or Hollywood actors if they were white. Cheekbones to die for. He's one of those. Goes to Pace or Parsons or Pratt, one of those P schools. She can't remember. It's not his fault; she just didn't care enough about it when he told her to remember exactly which one it is now. But none of that really matters anyway. This is not even close to being about him.

She pulls herself up and pushes him down so that she is on top of him. In control. She made a note that he did not remove his socks when they began. She doesn't mind; in fact, now it's preferable because his feet are up near her pillows. It would have been gross to have to sleep on them later if his bare feet had touched them.

"You like that pussy?" she asks.

Again, nothing. Just sort of a sigh or moan.

She keeps going. She is building the pace. But not too fast. He seems like the type that could come at any time. He let her take control too easily and would be more enthusiastic about the dirty talk if that weren't the case, she's decided. He'd be charming and try to one-up her with his own porn-inspired one-liners. The dirty talk would be its own dance, like the sex. Instead, he is passive. "I asked you a question. You like that pussy?"

She grinds into him, twisting. "Yeah," he says finally.

"Something is rotten in the state of Denmark." She searches his face as she continues to ride him. There isn't much by way of reaction. Just his well-defined features bobbing up and down at the foot of her bed, his brow pulling a little. "I said there's something… rotten… in the state of Denmark."

"What?"

She tries to remember more ominous quotes from Professor Towers' class. No more *Hamlet*. A bust. She's done with that for now. Before *Hamlet*, they read the *Inferno*, then before that the *Odyssey*, then before that one *Gilgamesh*. She thinks *Gilgamesh* would be good for him. Closer to his origins. "You will never find that life… for which you are looking," she says.

He shakes his head and pulls himself up by her shoulders. Then it seems like he's trying to guide her down, but she stays put, unrelenting. They're in a lotus pose together. Now she can make sure he can hear her and will see him hearing her. "Harder," she says. He moves in and out of her with a very determined expression on his face. "You will… never find the life for which… you are looking." She stares into his eyes.

"Huh?"

"You don't… like it?"

"I don't… know what you're… talking about."

"Harder," she says.

He moves in and out of her very, very fast. It isn't harder, just faster. He is not a good listener. "I'm gonna come," he says after a short time. He takes her and moves her down to lie on her back, her head resting on the pillows. He really goes at it. Finally it's harder. He is coming in the condom he is wearing, his life essence draining into it.

"How long does… a building stand before it falls?"

"Ugggh! Uhhh!" He's still coming.

She grabs his face. "How long does a building… stand before it falls… Raj?"

"Uggggh! Ommmmm!" The animal noises eventually stop. He rolls over. His face seems content. He's orgasmed. Now his body is relaxed. He's had sex tonight. It was a good night, he must think. "Sorry. Now, what were you saying?"

She sits up against the wall at the head of the bed. "I want you to know something, Raj. That meant nothing to me."

He flinches. "Okay…"

"Also, your penis is of adequate size but you don't move very well."

He rises onto his elbow, smiling. "What the hell?"

"I just thought you should know." She reaches for her phone on the windowsill and looks at her alerts. There are two texts, three Facebook notifications, and some tweets she could read. She's more interested in having him perceive her as ignoring him than actually ignoring him: instead of reading, she watches him in her periphery, his face lit indirectly by the pale light of the phone.

"Funny girl." He laughs, trying to deflect her. He takes his condom off, leans over her, and tosses it in the bedside wastebasket.

"I don't think so."

He sits up and looks at her. "Okay…" He breaks out into more laughter. He shakes his head. "You're funny."

"No I'm not. I'm being me." She decides to look at some of the Facebook notifications. The urge is too strong and she can multitask, she's concluded. "You're the one lying to yourself. I can tell you don't know yourself very well."

He kind of tilts his head. "Whatever that was while we were having sex… this… it's the strangest dirty talk I've ever heard, Haruka. I know I move well. My people got rhythm." That was racist toward himself. Why would anybody be racist toward themselves like that? Plus, he didn't have any rhythm at all, so it also wasn't true. "But whatever floats your boat."

"It wasn't good, Raj. You can't move. The boat sunk. Titanic-style. And you should've talked back more." None of the Facebook stuff is important; a few more people liked the picture of her lunch that she posted during the afternoon and a friend from high school tagged her in a post about people she misses. She continues to watch him out of the corner of her eye.

He shakes his head. "Whatever. I know it was good. You told me so."

"I was lying."

"Right… I think I'm gonna go." He gets out of her bed.

"Good." She puts the phone down to watch him. The timing of this gesture is meant to really get him.

He starts to bend down like he's going to look for his clothes but then he pops back up. "What's with you?" The gesture worked.

"You didn't say the right things back to me, it ruined it."

"Well, shit! I'm sorry! But I had no idea what the hell you were talking about! And I still don't! Denmark? What the fuck?" His skin and the room are dark enough that it's hard for Haruka to see him now that he's not next to her and her phone is no longer lit. She can mostly just make out the whites of his eyes and his teeth.

"It's okay. It doesn't matter."

"Right." He looks down and feels around the floor for his clothes. "I gotta turn the light on."

"Don't."

"Okay…"

"We're all gonna go someday, Raj. I'm gonna die, you're gonna die."

"Of course we are." He's still looking for his clothes. "I gotta turn the light on. I'm sorry." His voice is shaking a little.

He flicks the light on. He's completely naked, like her. She sees his clothes peeking out from under Lauren's bed. Soon he sees them, too, and puts them on. Nobody says anything for a while. She wants to read the texts she's received but does not. He shakes his head. "So what you just said… what was that, like, a threat?" Raj is stupid, she's decided. Hella stupid.

"Death threatens us all. Always."

He laughs. "Right!"

"Ha-ha-ha-ha-ha!!!" She laughs back, louder. Then she stops and stares at him. This is fun, she thinks. She especially likes that he's fully clothed now and she's still naked. There is much strength in her nudity.

"Whoa, dude! Okay, you're crazy."

"Raj, you're not a good lay."

He shakes his head in response.

She smiles.

"What are you, some kind of, like, OkCupid serial killer?"

"No. I'm just a girl speaking the truth."

"Whatever. Psycho," he says this while crossing the room. Now he's got his hand on the doorknob.

"Raj! I was totally JK-ing! Come back and fuck me again!" She splays out like a kitten. He looks at her skeptically, those nice eyebrows of his upturned. The knob has been twisted halfway. "I was just testing you. You passed with flying colors. Now bring that nice big dick back to this bed this instant!" He smiles. "I just wanted to see what kind of guy you are. If you'd suffer through me acting crazy or if you'd call me names or try to reason with me. That stuff's important if we want to spend time together. I wanted to see what you'd do."

"I don't know if I should believe you."

"What you should believe is how good I can make you feel." She is a little sore but doesn't care. More work to do. "I just wanted to see how much intensity you can tolerate. You've got a high threshold. A little bit of craziness in bed is fun."

"Right…"

"You do wanna go again, right?"

"I guess…" He takes his hand off the knob and comes back over.

"This time I'll show. I won't tell." She disrobes him, kissing him softly.

Then they have sex again.

This time she says nothing; she just makes nice little noises for positive reinforcement. He takes his socks off for this one, but his feet do not come near her pillows, thankfully. She lets him do it from behind for the novelty.

She thought it would be fun to try to tell someone the truth to their face. See what it was like. Not that she thinks it's better. But it was interesting. There was something to the change in the look on his pretty face, the pitch of his voice. And now he'll really be in love with her. He already is, taking his socks off like that for the second round. That's intimacy. She's a crazy girl on an entirely different level. The most intense lay he's ever had, probably. A challenge, a surprise: the kind of girl you can't forget. They write songs about this type of girl; make her into a character in the movies. And Raj will never have her again. None of the others from before will remember her quite like he will. The girl who both showed and told him the truth. Something that will remind him of death, something that will haunt him for the remainder of his days.

▲▽▽▽▽

There's a good crowd here tonight, enough people that the place feels lively, but not so many that he can't grab a booth for the two of them. Ray chose where; not only because it seemed like the thing for the man to do, but also because he wanted to make sure they went someplace where the drinks ain't so bad. He's glad Jill chose drinks, even though it'll be a little more expensive than coffee. It's sexier.

The Subway Inn is one of the only bars Ray really likes. A dive right across from Bloomingdale's on 60th Street, it's unpretentious on the inside, weird on the outside, and fun both inside and out. The out is what first drew him to it a couple of years ago: this sort of seedy-looking place complete with a refulgent red neon sign directly across from what's known as one of the fanciest stores in the world. That kind of juxtaposition... some "Only in New York" shit. But the inside is what kept him coming back: it's one of those bars that brings in an eclectic group of people who can coexist peacefully in a shared quest for a good time— young, old, income levels and races across the board. This is a place where people can get reasonably priced drinks while listening to everything from golden oldies to filthy trap beats on the jukebox, black-and-white-checkered floors below, bright beer signs and TVs that play sports and movies on the walls all around, the smell of something dank but oddly comforting in the air. A bar speaking a universal language. He used to come here when he wasn't so broke, and feels a little wistful walking in.

He's early. She's coming from Harlem—a lot of Columbia students stay uptown after graduation, some, including her, venturing from Morningside over to real Harlem, regardless of race—so he figured he would get here first, and he's glad he did. Now he can grab a drink, get comfortable, settled... ready for showtime. He approaches the bar. Drafts and well drinks are only five bucks, and the drafts aren't just Bud Light and other variants of horse piss; they've got a seasonal or two. He orders this springtime Sam Adams thing from a strictly-business Puerto Rican bartender and settles in at one of the last remaining booths.

It's weird to just sit in a booth. He wonders how people used to do it; like, just sit and wait. Fifty, a hundred years ago. Not everybody would carry a book or some other type of reading material. What else would you do, doodle or something? Nah. You have to look cool in situations like this: meeting someone at a bar. Especially someone you eventually want to have sex with. More people would smoke back then, he guesses. That's what they would do with their hands. Cigarettes may stink, but smoking sure does look cool. To this day, still. But people can't smoke in bars anymore. Not that he would if he could. The two or three times he's smoked a cigarette didn't go so well; the smell of tobacco's just so damn acrid and gag-inducing. Weed might be all right, but that'll never happen—except for those weird e-cigarettes, the notion of smoking in a bar is a thing of the past. In the twenty-first century, it's all about the phone, so that's what he does with his hands while he sits, waiting, nursing his beer. It's a good seasonal—flavorful enough, a nice mixture of citrus and maltiness. He skipped dinner tonight so he'd feel more of a buzz. Another way to get more bang for his buck: saving on dinner *and* getting a better buzz. Six or seven minutes pass. He's checking his email when she walks in.

"Ray! So good to see you." He looks up from his phone. She saw him looking at it, saw that he didn't even notice her walk in, and that must've made him look pretty damn cool. Looking at your phone *is* the new smoking.

"I know, right? You too. Long time, no see." He slides the phone into his pocket as he stands up. And it is good to see her, too, really: she mostly looks the same as she did at twenty-one, twenty-two. Pretty, trim. Her black hair's a little shorter than it used to be and she's got a few laugh lines, but she wears it all well. A good-looking woman in her mid-twenties. They hug. "Thanks for coming out. Sit, sit."

"Maybe I should grab a drink first?"

"I got it. What do you want?"

She sits down. "What are you drinking?" Across the booth she sees his glass. "Beer?"

Ray nods. "Try it."

"Never became a fan." She looks around the place, sort of shimmies, pondering. The low-cut top revealed by removing her jacket clings to her body nicely. There's that sizable chest he remembers, a multi-strand silver necklace hanging above her cleavage, drawing his attention to it. "This looks like the type of bar where you should drink whiskey. How about a Jack and Coke?"

"You got it." Ray walks over to the bar. He can't remember if Jack and Coke counts as a well drink or not; if that's their whiskey-coke. They use a lot of decent stuff for well. If anything, it's only a buck or two more. It doesn't matter. This is a special occasion. Or, it's more like an investment. Another cool girl to have sex with sometimes. That's worth an extra buck or two here now. He orders the drink. It is indeed an extra buck. He brings it back to her.

"Thanks." She smiles. "So…" The lower lip widens. She's wearing a deep burgundy lipstick and her teeth look nice and white. "What's new?"

He might have already been dead the last time they saw each other, but his awareness of it is certainly new. That and the bike messenger thing. These are what she wouldn't know about in the broad, big-picture sense—what she couldn't glean over Facebook—but they're not things he'd particularly like to publicize, especially considering his cause. It's a hard question to answer. "In the last four years? Not much." He laughs to himself and hopes she'll join in. She offers one or two small chuckles, a smirk that lingers a little afterwards. "How about with you?"

"Well, I still haven't left uptown. For the last two years I've been working for the Clinton Foundation…" She answers the question like he didn't already know these things. While she's never told him personally, she could only assume he'd have this information; she talks about both her neighborhood and where she works often enough in status updates on Facebook—some of which he thinks he's liked—and also lists them in her "About Me" section. It's not that he's stalked her or anything; what she's giving him now is, like, common knowledge. It would be hard not to know that shit as her Facebook friend. The answer feels odd, off, like an act; a twenty-first-century girl answering a question the way a twentieth-century girl might. He nods along. "… I like it there a lot."

"What do you do specifically?"

"Oh, I'm part of the Clinton Climate Initiative. I'm a project manager."

"Wow, that's awesome." Ray takes a big sip. Her job title was something he hadn't gathered through Facebook. And while he obviously knew she would be more successful than him, he didn't know by how much. He had hoped she would be a coordinator or something lower level. Even if you're just managing projects and not people, it still sounds impressive. This might be an uphill battle.

"Yeah, I'm pretty happy. We're doing good things." She sips too, drinking through a straw. He wonders if she's nervous or thirsty. He hopes nervous.

"Where are you in Harlem? You just walk to work?"

"Actually, no, I wish. Most of the office moved. I'm in the 120s on St. Nick, but the Harlem office is pretty much just President Clinton's personal office now. My team works out of Rockefeller Center."

"That's still not too bad a commute." Of course talking about commuting isn't all that interesting or fun, and it's definitely not sexy, but one step at a time. She doesn't seem bored or anything. A little small talk at first is fine. Good, even. Keeping it cool.

"No, not at all. The D's express from 125th to 59th. Twenty-five, thirty minutes door-to-door." She looks down and takes another sip. Okay, maybe she's a little bored. But that's all right. Highs only seem higher after a low.

"Have you met ol' Slick Willie?"

She smiles. "A few times. He's nice."

"How about Hillary?"

"Not yet. But I can't wait. She's been pretty busy, you know?"

"Yeah." That went well. It was the Clintons, it was glamorous, but it was also about her. It's hard to evoke Bill Clinton without thinking of sex, strangely. Almost more than anything, that's his legacy. That shit he did with the cigar was just too fuckin' wild.

"What about you? What have you been up to?"

He takes a sip. Ray was able to deflect this question in its broader form of "What's new?" the first time, but knows it would be weird not to give more of a real answer now. He has something stock prepared. "Freelance stuff, mostly. A lot of reporting, copyediting, technical writing sometimes when I have to."

"Nice," she says.

He hasn't exactly lied to her. Up until six or so weeks ago, "freelance journalist" indeed would have been the closest thing he'd have to an occupation. And though he knows he's exactly where he should be when he's on his bike, questing, he'd still accept assignments if any actually came his way, to work on in the evenings or while waiting around at dispatch in the mornings. "Yeah, it's all right. I haven't done anything too special yet. Right after college I was writing for a local paper out in Brooklyn, which was fun, but it folded not long after. It was the closest to what I was doing at Columbia with *Spec*."

"I remember your work for the *Spectator*. It was good."

"It's nice to see your name in print. But since then I've been stuck on the web."

"I mean, I know what you're saying. But that's where everything's headed now, anyway. I wouldn't be surprised if *The New York Times* is digital-only in ten years. Or is just limited to, like, the weekend edition." Jesus Christ, what a shame it would be if the Gray Lady herself was just a fucking website in ten years. Here's hoping she's wrong. But you can never know, not these days… "So if I google your name are a bunch of cool articles gonna pop up?"

"I mean, like I said, nothing too special yet."

She takes a sip. Her lips are no great shakes, but she still looks pretty damn sensuous sipping through the straw here in the low light of the booth. Like making a little kissy face. "Yeah, but I thought you were just being modest."

"No, really, I wasn't. But I don't know what would come up. I haven't ever googled myself." He's lying, of course. Ray probably googles himself every two weeks to a month. He used to do it to find articles or blog posts he'd recently written in circumstances where the editors of the sites hadn't told him they'd gone up yet; now, having not written any-thing in some time, he does it sort of out of habit.

"Oh, come on."

"I haven't."

"Everybody has. Even me. And my name isn't on any articles."

"I don't know, it seems weird." He says this without really thinking. Googling yourself is an act rooted in either narcissism or paranoia, or both, and it seems weird because it *is* weird, but that's not why he says it. He says it, he knows, to be contrarian: to flirt.

"Well, let's do it now." She pulls out her phone, flirting back. Harder. This might not be such an uphill battle after all. Between the shirt she's wearing and the way she's acting, maybe they can start having sex tonight.

"Nah, let's not. Real-Ray's right in front of you. You don't need to look at that now."

"What are you trying to hide, Ray?"

"Nothing." He takes a sip.

"I'm sure there's some Real-Ray in your writing, just like I'm sure there's some Fake-Ray right here." She looks down and begins typing. That was a heavy thing to say. Intimate, really. He actually visualizes himself in bed with her. "We haven't seen each other in a long time, it's hard to be 100 percent authentic."

Ray laughs. "You're seriously gonna sit there and read something I wrote?"

"Not the whole thing, just a quick look. I'm having fun." She sips.

"All right, all right. But like I said, I don't think there's anything too special there."

"You can google me now if you want. Check out my LinkedIn or something…" Jill continues reading. Ray doesn't really know what to do. He wants to look at his phone, too, but has no interest in googling her; he just wants to check Facebook or scan some news headlines while he thinks more about what it would be like to fuck her. But if he did, he would appear to do what she had just told him to do, and this wouldn't do him any favors in the little flirtation dance thing they got going on. So instead, he just sits there like he's above it all, making it a point to seem like he's not just waiting for her, but committed to his "Real-Ray" idea, looking up at one of the bar's TVs behind her, watching some movie on TBS with Owen Wilson he's never seen before and sipping from time to time while he imagines himself in various sexual positions with her. Occasionally his eyes drift back down to see if she's still looking at the phone. When he can see her reading intently, engrossed by the search results, he sneaks more glances at her tits. "Do you write under Ray or Raymond? Because when I google 'Raymond' a bunch of other guys come up, obituaries, a photographer, some professors…"

"Those are all me. Even the obituaries. I faked my death a bunch of times to avoid paying off my student loans." If only that were true, if only he wasn't really dead and still saddled with exorbitant debt. She laughs. "No, I use Ray."

A few seconds pass while she modifies her search. One last glimpse at the tits before he brings his eyes back up to the weird movie, trying to seem aloof. He stops thinking about sex so he doesn't actually start to get an erection. "Okay, here we go!"

"Yeah, like I said…"

"Hey! *Vice, Bullett, Paper, Thought Catalog…* I knew you were doing cool shit!"

"Yeah, but that stuff's few and far between. And not all of it paid."

"Really?"

"Unfortunately. I just gotta keep grinding and something'll break." Ray sips. The beer's getting low.

"I hear ya, Ray. I'm finally starting to feel okay. I had to temp for a long time before the Clinton Foundation."

"Yeah."

"I don't know if I'll ever get to own an apartment here or anything, but things are good. I like my job. I like where I live. And I've got a nice boyfriend…" Ray's eyes pop. Boyfriend?! ¡Qué chingados! Of all the things she'll share on Facebook, this is the one aspect of her life she keeps hidden? Things were going so well. So fucking well. All the flirting—the I bet you're doing cool stuff and the I'll google you and you can google me. Why did she want to meet up with him? And why is she wearing a tight-fitting fucking shirt that shows off some damn good cleavage? Is she here to fuck with him? Or was she willing to explore the possibility of cheating on her boyfriend until she realized Ray was nothing but a mostly-broke guy with a stillborn career at twenty-six, someone so dumb that he'll sometimes allow himself to get wheedled into working for free? Not that he'd be into helping a girl cheat. But whatever the case, Ray's now convinced she's just a demon brought up from hell to terrorize him here in purgatory. To make him spend money he doesn't have and tease him with her tits.

"Oh, cool. How long have you and your boyfriend been together?"

"It'll be a year in June."

"That's great." Ray finishes his beer.

"Looks like I've got some catching up to do." And the bitch is still flirting. Or is she? Is Ray just an asshole, a cad? Was she simply here to meet an old friend? Talk about what's new in her life face to face with him, like he asked, maybe remember some good ol' days from college? Their genitals wouldn't have anything to do with that. She could wear what she wanted; it would have nothing to do with him. She continues to suck on her straw. There's what looks like a third of her Jack and Coke left, but it's mostly ice, so it goes down fast. Ray feels ashamed. "Here, let me get the next round." She gets up. "What are you drinking again?"

"You know what? I'll take a Corona." Corona's a comfort beer. Before, he wanted to pay for everything, or at least the first two rounds depending on how it went, but he has no problems letting her buy him a drink now. Demon, friend, whatever—it would only be fair.

▲ ▽ ▽ ▲

The welcome at the door was warm, as it customarily is here at Michael's, but it could've been warmer. Most of the time it's Michael himself there up front, and when it's not—today being one of those days—there's no guarantee that the greeting will be quite right. The host in his place seemed new. Weisman more than made up for it with his welcome, though, to the point where it almost seemed condescending. The handshake was too soft and his smile a bit too wide. He said, "Glad you could make it" as well as "Thanks for meeting with me." And he's dressed more foppishly than usual, even wearing a silken pocket square to match his lilac bow tie. All of this has Emerson on edge. He sits there with his hands folded on top of the white tablecloth, gently rubbing back and forth over the stretch between the knuckles of his right thumb.

The drinks are on their way.

"Some familiar faces here." Weisman's own face looks a little younger than Emerson's, even though he's two years older. He's got half as many lines and there's a lot more color in his cheeks still; nothing hangs. His Semitic features have remained sharp, his brown eyes limpid. The curly salt-and-pepper hair on top boasts more pepper than salt. He looks like an aging man, not an old man.

"As always."

"So Emerson, again, that was a great little review the other week."

"Thank you."

"Let's talk about it."

Emerson stops rubbing his thumb, using his hands while speaking: "What I have to say on the matter was, of course, best expressed in the review." He smiles. The hands then come back to rest on the table top, the fingers interlocking once more. "But I know we're not here to talk about Wordsworth."

"Why are we here?"

"I think we both know the answer to that." And they do. One of the things Emerson likes about Weisman is that he's direct. It's an invaluable and unfortunately all-too-elusive trait in the book business, and asking a question like "Why are we here?" is both out of character and stupid. Emerson doesn't quite know what to make of it. Three, maybe four years have passed since he's seen Weisman; perhaps the aging that should have been going on in his face has instead taken a toll on his mind. This might be a problem.

"Right. We're here to talk about you. I know you don't like to put yourself out there without a reason." There's the Weisman he knows. That shrewd man. The old devil. "So what's going on?"

Emerson smiles. Weisman smiles back. The waitress comes forward and sets down their drinks, cutting between their dueling smiles before the moment becomes overdrawn and even more uncomfortable. Emerson's ordered a glass of chardonnay—a little something for the nerves—and Weisman an iced tea. She's a pretty young thing, the waitress, strawberry blonde with light eyes. Looks a little like Claire anterior to the kids. "Are you gentlemen ready to order?" she asks.

Since she's oriented toward him, most likely out of deference for what she presumes is his advancement in age over the other man sitting there, Emerson goes first. "I'll start with the endive salad. Then the chicken paillard."

"Excellent choices." She turns to Weisman. "And for you?"

"The oysters and the steak, please. Medium rare." A strange choice for Weisman. He never used to order the more lavish fare at lunches; it's almost as if he's trying to prove something. Emerson's mildly envious of his selections, but feels, overall, that his were the more appropriate ones for a mid-day repast. However, now he just might have to have steak for dinner.

"Wonderful." The waitress leaves.

Weisman smiles again. Emerson sighs. "What's going on?" He's back to playing with the thumb. "I suppose I was stretching a muscle, you're right about that."

"Well, that's very exciting."

"But I don't know if I'm ready to run on out just yet."

"And what would that take?" Weisman sips.

"I'm not sure."

"Let's not beat around the bush here, Emerson."

"I'm not. I honestly don't know. It's certainly not money, if that's what you're driving at." Done with the thumb again, Emerson sips, too. He knew Weisman wasn't suggesting anything about money; he just figured alluding to something like that would make him uncomfortable, and making Weisman uncomfortable would make he himself less uncomfortable.

"No, of course not."

"The next one needs to be special. Not too many things have been interesting me that much lately, sadly. I really don't know what I want to write about yet."

"Well, let's figure that out." Another incredibly stupid thing for Weisman to say.

"You know I've never worked that way." Emerson laughs. Really, it's at Weisman, but he's sure Weisman will think it's at himself, something self-deprecating and mannerly, which is fine; Emerson knows the truth and that's all that matters. It's a big, hearty laugh, like one he might make in class or at the movies. People at other tables glance over.

"I'm just excited, Emerson, that's all. It's been, what, twelve, thirteen years since the last one? You write these reviews from time to time and I can't help but hope it's the start of a new work cycle for you."

"I understand your position, Robert, and I certainly appreciate your continued interest and support." Of course Emerson knows Weisman's chief motivation is his desire to share in the glory of his own magnificent writing—the unparalleled, gorgeous prose and sterling insights of his empirically correct literary criticism—but he knows there really is some genuine interest and support there, too. The man is as good a champion as anyone could hope for: he's a fan, he's got a good set of eyes, and he knows the publishing landscape well. They've enjoyed a good working relationship together and Emerson considers him a real friend. Weisman smiles—his mouth closed, the top lip disappearing, his brows arching high over bespectacled squinting eyes; the overall effect is somewhat avian. "My own daughter hasn't even said anything to me about the recent piece yet, and I've asked her personally to read it."

"I'm sorry to hear that."

And with that small token of sympathy it's time for the big reveal: "Yes, well… Anyway, another thing that bears mentioning is, full disclosure, the next thing I do will be the last."

"Will it?" Emerson tries to get a read on Weisman, but nothing holds. His countenance is more or less blank, maybe mildly curious, like the question itself would suggest, and his head is slightly atilt… that's pretty much it. A strange reaction indeed. It should hardly be shocking because of their age, but still. Emerson was hoping for a little something more.

"It'll be the tenth book. There's a certain authority to that number. Ten."

"Right." Weisman nods. "There definitely is something to that number."

"So you can see why I intend to make it count." Emerson almost plays with his thumb again but instead sups his wine.

"You've made everything count, Emerson. And now that I know where you stand, this is probably the best time for me to share something as well. We're actually on the same page. I, like you, have been thinking of things in terms of finality lately. And in another two years or so, I think it'll be time to hang up my hat."

His own big reveal! But not before the last book! This can't be! Even a mentally deteriorating Weisman would be better than no Weisman at all! Emerson is a wreck—his insides flipping about, he's almost completely lost his appetite now, incredibly—but outside, he retains his cool. "You? Retire?"

"That's right."

"And you said I was beating around the bush. My goodness. I always figured you'd die at your desk." A little humor to diffuse the situation. A joke, but only half. The other half is very serious: planting a seed that says he should see Emerson's last book through… or die trying. Emerson sups again, a second swallow this time.

"Thanks, Emerson. I'm not saying I wouldn't come back out to do one last project with you." Thank God. Oh, what a shock that was back there! What terror! The publishing house could have even considered pairing him with, oh horror of horrors, a young editor. Someone they would want to build up on his name. Someone not only less qualified but less deserving of basking in the glow of his final masterwork, whatever it will be. "We've had a good run, and I'd like yours to be one of my last. But I hope you'll start soon. I mean, let's forget about the time in between for a second: some books have taken you eight years to write."

"And others have taken eight weeks."

"I doubt this last, special book will be one of those." It absolutely won't. Emerson's best guess: three to five years. But what he said felt like the best thing to say.

"You're probably right. Look, I'll get started on something soon."

"That's music to my ears."

"But no promises as to when I'll have pages for you."

"Of course." Weisman sips his tea. This will be good, Emerson knows. As long as Weisman's still around.

"And I know you look sixty and all, but if it ends up taking me a few years, don't just retire and die. It wouldn't feel right crossing the finish line with someone else."

"I'll do my best not to." Weisman offers another birdlike smile.

"My goodness… retirement. Any plans?"

"Oh, sure. There's a lot I haven't done yet. I've never been to Africa, or Australia." Two places nobody should ever want to go: a hot, malaria and militia infested hellscape and a giant island with strange creatures everywhere mostly populated by the descendants of convicts. What's with people these days? Weisman's one thing—and he better not be in any foreign land when a draft of the last book is ready—but he can still barely believe Claire wanting to drag her family down to Central America. "Hell, there's a lot I haven't read. You edit ten titles a year for over forty-five years, where do you find the time? You know I haven't even read *Anna Karenina* yet?"

"My God. That's awful."

A food runner appears with the appetizers. He's Hispanic, like they all are these days. He places Emerson's salad down first, then Weisman's oysters. Emerson first read *Anna Karenina* at thirteen. By his late twenties he had read it in Russian. "Thank you," Weisman says. The man nods, then leaves. "Anyway, I'm glad we had this talk."

"Yes, me too." And he is. "Except now I have to get to work." Emerson smiles at Weisman, the first one he's really meant since sitting down, and digs into his salad. Weisman slurps down an oyster. He must be eating a little prettier on the company dime now that he's on his way out. Whatever that was in the past, whether good form or restraint, unnecessary at this stage. It's all about him now: his legacy. And that's why he's called on Emerson. That's why he wanted to nudge. He knows the work they did together was the best of his nearly half-century career. Will have the biggest, the longest-lasting impact. He wants now to go out with a grand closer. He wants to be remembered, ultimately, through the greatest reader, the greatest critic who ever lived and who ever shall live. He wants to be remembered through Emerson Towers.

▲▽▽▲▽

Whoa! She thought she was busy before, but now she's *really* busy. Sometimes she even finds herself saying, "There aren't enough hours in the day." That's not a phrase she's ever liked. Usually whenever somebody says it, she gets annoyed and thinks they're dumb. A day is made up of twenty-four hours. It's not too few or too many. It just is. People fill the hours however they choose. Work, school, leisure activities, sleep: those kinds of things. Then a new day starts. But in the weeks since her epiphany in Professor Towers' class, Haruka's really felt that way. So now she's been saying it, too, in those rare moments she can catch her breath.

After she decided to spread more of her truth, she's accepted more and more dates so that now it's basically double what she used to go on. It's up to five, six dates per week. That's a lot of dates!

The hardest part has been keeping up with her schoolwork. She's always been an excellent student, and that's not about to change. Companies like Google, Facebook, and Apple only hire the best. The second hardest part has been keeping up with her OkCupid inbox. It's limited to three hundred messages, which includes those going out as well as coming in, and while that might sound like a lot, it's really not. Once you get a conversation going—which is what leads up to a date—the messages can really pile up. Imagine ten or so threads taking place at once and it's pretty easy to see how quickly this could become a problem. So she has to delete older messages every day, sometimes several times a day. Not to mention, before there can even be a conversation, there are always introductory messages to weed through. First she has to determine if it's a good first message, that they read through her profile and wrote something they thought she'd like, and then she has to read through their profile and look at their pictures to see if they're worth her time. OkCupid has a lot of creeps. Those people are already corrupt—poisoned, evil—and her time would be better spent with guys not like that. She wants the good ones. Even if they're older and hitting on someone less than half their age, they can still be somewhat pure of heart. A middle-aged man looking for a thrill with her is just as hopeful and naïve and precious as a boy looking for love. These people are the ones she can really destroy. It's not worth it to try to get under the skin of some jerky creep.

The worst thing is that she doesn't have as much time for texting or Facebook anymore. She's still active with both, of course, just not as much. There's been a pretty drastic decrease in her Twitter and Tumblr usage, though, only posting once or twice a day now. Games have taken a back seat, too. And forget about Reddit. She still uses her phone a lot on the dates themselves, but now instead of doing those other things, she's mostly on OkCupid setting up more dates.

Another way the dates are different is that now most don't end in her dorm room. She just goes on too many. Kicking Lauren out a couple of times a week is one thing, and she still does, but not almost every day. Even she has her limits.

They're also a little shorter, the dates. But that's better. More efficient. It usually does not take long to get them interested in sex and then she does what she came to do.

Right now in Professor Towers' class, they're reading *Madame Bovary*. She likes it a lot. There aren't really any good one-liners for sex... it's more subtle than that... but it's still a very dark book. She's decided that telling as well as showing is the best route. Men are stupid, and a lot of them need to be told things on top of being shown. Fortunately, she still has lines from *Hamlet*, the *Inferno*, the *Odyssey*, and *Gilgamesh* fresh in her head to call upon.

And that she does. All of the men have been freaked out by it. Her strange, sexy talk of death. And all of them, of course, want more. In the days that follow, she'll wait for the first follow-up message from them, then block them. Another message thread to delete. Then on to the next one.

▲▽▽▲▲

So it's come to this: online dating. Ray never thought he'd see the day.
It's shed a lot of its stigma for people his age in recent years, but there's
still more than enough there. Time was, only middle-aged losers would
get caught up in this shit, on sites like Match.com, eHarmony,
Lavalife… He remembers the commercials from when he was growing
up and how hilarious they all were. The testimonials, the corny music.
He'd think: I know it can't be as easy as it is being young and in school,
but why don't these people just ask someone out at work? Or the grocery
store? Or if they're religious, church? Or maybe they could join one of
those recreational adult sports leagues? Or some other kind of club? Or
have a friend set them up? Or better yet, why not just go to a fucking
bar and see what happens? How socially inept or masochistic would you
have to be to want to get involved with online dating? It was something
he never got. Something to ridicule. In fact, once during sophomore year
in high school, he and a couple of his more waggish friends pranked
another friend by starting a free trial on Match and creating a fake profile for him, sending him a screenshot of it with a caption that read "Any
hot dates lately?" and telling him someone had just passed it along to
them, like it was going around. The plan was to let the guy know that it
was only a prank and no one else had actually seen it after getting his
reaction, but he was so apoplectic the next day at school they couldn't.
He threatened to kill this other guy who he suspected had made it, this
dude whose ex-girlfriend had become his girlfriend earlier that year but
was now recently his ex-girlfriend, too, without any context whatsoever,
really just going up to the guy and saying, "I know what you did and I'm
going to fucking kill you." They almost got into a fight then and there, a
little bit of shoving but no punches, and later on that night their friend
ended up going to this other guy's house and throwing a rock through
the living room window. Now here Ray is, setting up his own damn
online dating profile for real. Fuck!

But it's what he has to do. After the whole Jill debacle, he knew he
could no longer trust Facebook. The other girls on his little shortlist appeared to be single, but their relationship statuses were not explicitly
stated in their "About Me" sections, and it would be too embarrassing
to ask any mutual acquaintances what they knew, so there would be no
way he could confirm this before meeting up with them, before it was

too late. Rather than waste more time, effort, and money he doesn't really have on someone who might not be looking for anything remotely like what he's looking for, he's decided to swallow his pride and set up an account on OkCupid. The site is youth-oriented and free, and at this point it's just the most practical solution to his problem. No guesswork, everybody lists what they're after—choosing from categories that include new friends, long-term dating, short-term dating, and casual sex. Obviously those that list they're only looking for casual sex are probably just prostitutes using the site as a cover. Casual sex isn't too hard for ladies to find out in the real world, even those who aren't all that attractive. And he'll steer clear of the ones who list they're only interested in long-term dating, since he's not trying to lead anyone on who's trying to find their future husband or anything, all those other Fernandas out there, or those who say they're only looking for new friends, since that means they're either crazy or just plain weird. Listing that as the one thing you're looking for is the kind of doublespeak that would only be used by the site's real mind-gamers, or if they actually meant it by its strangest and stupidest users. Who would join a dating site just to try to make a friend? That's what Meetup's for. Short-term dating on its own isn't that great either, since he's looking for something consistent, but that listed along with another category seems to be the sweet spot, the golden mean. It's like saying you're interested in casual sex without outright saying you want casual sex; the subtle, smoother approach. There's bound to be a cool girl out there who sort of just wants someone to fuck once in a while, like him. His own profile says he's looking for short-term dating and long-term dating.

The site itself is easy to use and aesthetically pleasing; they did a good job hitting a lot of notes that resonate with a younger demographic. It's got an intuitive layout, a nice clean look featuring a lot of light blue and silver, with a little pop of pink here and there. Good font choice. Overall, a friendly, laid-back vibe. Reminiscent of the inchoate days of Facebook, back when it was all profiles and shit. Like we're all just here to hang, have fun, check each other out. Still, he can't believe he's actually doing this. Should he just go to a fucking bar and see what happens? Nah, bars cost too much money, and if he could go to bars as often as that move would suggest, he wouldn't have lost Fernanda. He's sure he'll have to go to some bars using this, but at least he'll have done some groundwork first.

His worst fear is that someone he knows will find him on it. Some old colleagues who were recent New York transplants as well as a few of his weirder friends from college have told him they've used it, and there could be others more private about it like he plans to be. While of course he knows it doesn't really matter because he's dead and all, and that even if he weren't, which he is, it also wouldn't matter because they'd be members too or lurking—that they'd be in the exact position as him or worse, wallflowers on an online dating site, which are designed for wallflowers to begin with, so wallflowers among wallflowers—it's still a terrifying prospect. An irrational fear is just as scary if not scarier than one that's justified. FDR said, "The only thing we have to fear is fear itself," yet he was actually deathly afraid of the number thirteen. It would be easier if he were younger, Ray thinks. OkCupid's a site that kids in college now or whatever use habitually and don't seem to think twice about. He's only been out of school for four years, but that's one of those things where it already seems like there's a big cultural divide. But it makes sense. Those his age are conscious of what life was like before the internet; he may have been young at the time, but he can still remember when people only socialized with those they knew already or the people physically around them. Someone born in the nineties can't do that. The internet's been a part of their lives, their consciousness from the beginning; they were born at the same time and have literally grown up together. Nothing about communicating with strangers seems weird or second-rate. Because Ray can remember what life was like before, he sees it as something less human, but they don't—their experiences as humans are intrinsically tied to the internet and the connections they make online are just as valid and meaningful as those they could make with the people sitting next to them in a class. It's at once sad and kind of enviable.

At least he isn't trying to make a human connection. That ship sailed when he died. He's doing this to restore balance, to make sure he's not descending from purgatory into hell. It's been a rough few weeks since Fernanda; on top of what happened with Jill, Emily hasn't wanted to hang out, in fact she outright ignored his last text, almost like she could smell the miasma of failure coming off him all the way from her place in Bed-Stuy. So for nearly a month it's been Pornhub and his right hand, coarse from gripping poorly taped handlebars all day. He knows things could be worse and that it would be a stretch to call what he's going through now hell—that would be more like if he got his hands chopped off or his dick chopped off or both; he's still getting the job done, after all—but if this is purgatory, it's tilting, and he's been slowly sliding downward.

The standing of his primary mission has only reinforced this. Though he rides with presence, keeping an eye out but letting his mind wander when it wants to, he hasn't experienced any more instances of déjà vu since the drugstore intersection. With each passing day, the standstill has made him feel worse and worse. And now, sitting here at his computer, browsing OkCupid profiles, he's starting to believe that sex may not just be a pleasurable physical activity to level out all the unpleasant physical activity he experiences daily, but something way more crucial than that. Having access to a vagina might be an integral part of the quest itself, like having access to heaven's gate: the only way he can ready himself to receive signs from God. His most recent déjà vu experience happened a few days after he had had sex with Fernanda for the last time; it's possible that whatever manna still in his system from his then-steady diet of sex has run out. Without it, he can no longer catch these glimpses that will lead him ultimately to enter heaven. Something like sex magick…

A moment later he realizes this is all bullshit. It's happened again.

He had just been looking at some Asian girl's profile thinking these thoughts when he briefly popped out of himself and saw and felt himself looking at an Asian girl's profile thinking these thoughts and feeling really fucking good. He settles back into his head. Focuses on the girl's photo. She's cute—great-looking skin, nice lips. They're curved in a closed-mouth, mischievous smile. She's wearing a black scoop neck that shows off her clavicle. He can't tell what her exact heritage is, but he's leaning toward Japanese. This is when he snaps back to what he was thinking before and dismisses it: sex would be nice to have and nothing more… Yeah, it would indeed make everything seem more level and fair again, but pussy is not any type of gateway to heaven and his dick is no key. Another déjà vu… Thank God… m_ss_ngp_eces/18/New York, NY. She's so young. Too young. He doesn't even know why he clicked on her in the first place. Probably because he was just sort of absently clicking on faces while envisioning vulvas as pearly gates. Eighteen, though? He remembers the EVIDENCE folder. Going into this he knew he'd prefer meeting girls a little younger than himself—like, twenty-four, maybe twenty-two the youngest—but not eighteen. He takes a screenshot of the profile and drops the image file into the folder. What he wanted was a recent college grad still coming off of her party-girl phase, someone old enough to relate to him but young enough that there would be some time before she got that Twenty-six syndrome like Fernanda, who might actually be somewhat impressed in her post-grad nascency by his bylines as a freelance journalist for publications she might read, or, if she had the disposition where he could be *all the way* real with her, perhaps even slightly thrilled in a kind of silly Brooklyn girl-type way that he was a bike messenger, like it was rebellious or antiestablishment or edgy or something. The image of the thin dude with the fixie, even though his bike has gears. Not an eighteen-year-old. He begins reaching for his iPhone then stops. Instead, he opens up Photo Booth on his computer so he can take a picture of himself. After pressing the red camera icon, there's a countdown that sounds like something out of a car racing video game, followed by a shutter noise that accompanies the flash. He has to do something, though, he knows… That déjà vu thing was clearly a sign. His picture—looking below the lens, staring at the screen—drops down to the camera roll and he saves it to the EVIDENCE folder, too. Seeing the names of the other files in the folder there he's reminded of his last déjà vu and the sort of androgynous-looking Asian girls he saw right before it. Could she have been one of them? No, that's stupid. Racist, even… if a half-Mexican can be racist, that is. He still has to look that up; like, would his white half balance out the Mexican so he and Asians would be at the same level of power socially? Is that even a question worth asking? Probably not. Not now, anyway. Probably not ever. It's actually a pretty stupid question. Enough divagating: The point is, they don't all look alike. This girl's a lot more chic than any of them were, he can tell from just the one picture. Wait a second… Now he remembers that at the exact moment of that previous déjà vu, he was thinking about college, about that one Asian girl freshman year he didn't have sex with when he could've. Those other hoodie-clad Asian girls had led him to that Asian girl. Is this here now all some kind of magical thinking to justify why he'd try to become fuck buddies with a college-aged Asian girl? Some sort of convoluted reclamation of a missed amatory conquest from his time as an undergrad? No. You can't force déjà vu. He's tried. Riding around the city, he tried and tried and tried. This thing here's the real deal. A sign from God. Truly powerful. He clicks back on Firefox and scrolls down the profile to see what she's looking for, if she'd even be open to receiving a message from someone like him. It reads: Guys who like girls, Ages 18-55—what?!?!—Near me, For new friends, long-term dating, short-term dating. That age range is a little crazy, but at least he's on the lower end of it. Hopefully she doesn't have daddy issues. Never fun. He feels like less of a letch now, and that's a good thing. They're all, you know, adults here. He won't make a habit out of hitting on teenagers or anything—he's just doing what God's telling him to do.

He reads through the "About me" section to get a better sense of who she is, or at least how she presents herself, so that he'll have some idea of how to best approach her. Everything is written in short, snappy sentences, almost like advertising copy, or in lists. It's different from the way he wrote his own "About me," which is a lot more conversational. Based on the questionnaire people take when they set up their profiles, they're actually only a 65 percent match, but judging by what she included in her profile descriptions, the two of them seem to have a good amount of things in common. *The Office* and *Parks and Rec* are indeed good shows—though, really, *The Office* only used to be. She has decent taste in music. And he also likes eating good food, coffee, and museums. But he can't just write, "Hey, what's your favorite museum? I like the Met. Wanna go sometime?" That's too banal, stupid. She probably gets ten messages like that a day. He has to do something to actually stand out, while still seeming cool and casual. Also, now that he thinks about it, it would probably be best not to actually ask her out in the first message. Going to the Met would be cool as a first date, though, since it's by donation. He could get away with, like, a two-dollar date. Hmmm... Should he practice first? Like, write some other girl? No, that wouldn't work. First of all, every girl's going to be different. To really gain the experience to do this well would take a lot more than one girl and weeks if not months of messaging, and even then the best he could hope for is that it would point to a trend; nothing would be guaranteed. Secondly, he doesn't actually want to write anyone else now. He had saved a few other profiles—the site actually lets you save people as favorites, which would seem pretty fucking weird if he were actually trying to make a real human connection—but now he feels so strongly about little miss m_ss_ngp_eces that he fears this would compromise things. It would be bad for the quest, bad for his soul. He wants to write her and her alone: an act of devotion, in part for her, but mostly for the God that pointed him to her. Maybe he should, like, research this. Read some dating site tips about intro message construction. No! That's fucking ludicrous. Joining OkCupid was one thing, but reading some geeky fucking guy's blog about how to land dates over the internet would just be too goddam much. He's overthinking this. Not even a little bit high, and overthinking this like he's ten bong rips deep. He's a good-enough-looking dude, educated, he filled out his own profile well, and he can write. So that's what he'll do. He'll write. Pitch some Grade-A woo, twenty-first-century style.

But not just yet. After all, there are still more pictures of her to see… He clicks on the photos tab, scrolls down. Below a larger version of her profile pic there are two more. The first is a full-body shot of her standing in the middle of what looks like a West Village street. If he had to guess, he'd say Minetta Lane. She's alone and wearing a slate gray dress with a collar, her hands folded just below her abdomen. The surrounding street takes up most of the frame, and while he can see that she's looking at the camera, if she's smiling, it's only the slightest hint of one, the right side of her mouth only barely upturned. It's her lithe body that's showcased here, the proportions suggested by her ballerina-like clavicle before now confirmed. In the second photo, she's framed in a close-up much like her profile shot except she's smiling big over a large round coffee mug, steam rising, looking away. She's wearing a light gray turtleneck in this one. He likes the way she dresses: simply. Pretty similar to him. He clicks back to her "About" section. He reads through it again. Everything's short, to the point, so he'll be the same. But while still being himself, conversational. Under the subsection "What I'm doing with my life" she lists "Going to school" and "Exploring the city." Something falls into place with the second one. Enough reading, time for action. He clicks on the "Send a message" button and begins typing: "I notice you also like exploring the city. Find anything cool lately? They say that Albert Einstein's eyeballs are stored somewhere here in a safety deposit box. I've been looking for those for a while now, but so far, no luck." He clicks send. In hindsight, it was kind of a strange message, but fuck it. At least it wasn't boring. It felt right at the time, for whatever reason.

▲▽▲▽▽

He holds a copy of *Madame Bovary* in one hand. The other, the left, clutches his thigh. This is no easy feat; half-submerged in water a bit too hot, the large mound enclosed in soft dimpled skin is coated with a slippery mix of soap and sweat where it surfaces and meets the thick, steamy air. I may never truly know what it's like to be a woman, Emerson thinks, but there's a little Emma Bovary in all of us.

Though he's read Flaubert's near-perfect chef-d'oeuvre many times before, the translation Emerson has here, the same he's assigned his students, is relatively new, fashioned by Lydia Davis, and he's not quite as familiar with it as he'd like to be for the sake of his lectures. He prefers reading the book in its original French, of course, but next to that, this edition really is the best thing out there. It's a little odd, since most modern translations are total shit—the English language is only deteriorating, after all—but this one really does capture the sonorous, elegant nature of the original. A decent number of his contemporaries weighed in on it upon its release a couple of years back, all more or less agreeing it was good. He wonders now why nobody approached him for a blurb. They probably thought he had better things to do, considering how he'd already written about Flaubert in some of his early books. That must be it.

He turns the page with the same hand he uses to hold the book, a technique executed with a stroke of his meaty thumb while his other fingers save the pinky keep the book in place. Sweat continues to accrete. His head and right arm have not yet met the water, but soon they'll look just like his left arm, left leg, right leg, belly… everything now peeking above the water, gleaming, that has. Moisture begins to transfer from his hand to the page. It's not enough to permanently damage the book, however, so he'll read on. Before it gets to that point, he'll have to stop for another reason. More pages turn. Two runnels of sweat streak down his face in rapid succession, the varying planes and textures from forehead to second chin providing only minimal resistance, and now it's almost time. Soon his eyes will begin to burn with salt. He races toward the end of the current paragraph. Then there's the sting: one eye, then the other. He finishes the paragraph anyway.

After placing the book on the floor next to one of the tub's claws, he tilts his head back and sinks down into the water, reflexively blowing air from his nostrils as the water spreads over his face. He's surrounded by warmth, and in this moment everything is truly lovely. The capacious vintage tub was installed almost immediately after he bought the apartment decades ago, the first and most important investment he put into it—Emerson does some of his best thinking while in the tub. And now that he's read all he can humanly read while bathing this evening, this is what he plans to do: think. He will soak—his senses practically suspended, lulled by the warm water all around—and think, about the book, mostly. Not *Madame Bovary*, but his book. He pokes his face just above the surface of the water, his head still horizontal and white hair undulating, and stares at the ceiling.

What should he write about? How does one even begin to cap off a career as tremendous as his own? The answers to these questions are like priceless treasures, and only his best thinking could guide the way. Considering he wrote so much about the Western Canon in the past that he's only been able to write about others writing about the Western Canon in the years since his last book was published, this is not going to be easy. Obviously he wouldn't dedicate an entire book, especially his final one, to evaluating the work of biographers and other critics. That would be preposterous. But the wellspring from which the text should flow must be a natural one. He can't force interest. And he also can't just return to familiar subject matter—he's already covered what's worth covering extensively; anything he included now would seem like scraps… packaged nicely with a pretty ribbon, perhaps, but one his enemies would be all too eager to unravel and reveal the disgraceful thing inside. He's already anatomized works that run from antiquity to the twentieth century, making arguments in his nine books about what's good and why, the importance of aesthetic purity, context as a double-edged sword, the inevitability of intertextuality, cultural preservation and moral obligation, the artistic supremacy of the written word, intent as frivolity, the dangers of social lenses, and modernization and the war on thought. Looking down at the copy of *Madame Bovary* on the white tiled floor, something occurs to him. Could there perhaps be an entire book in the idea of reading in original languages? It *is* something he feels strongly about. He learned Greek, Latin, French, Italian, Spanish, German, and Russian, in that order, for the sake of literature, after all. But this last book must be a sensation! Not everyone is as brilliant as him and can learn seven languages; such a book would be a dud. Oh, the irony… Here he is: an extraordinarily accomplished polyglot, and afraid he won't be understood! Because of the very nature of his accomplishment! He shakes his head. Goodness. Still, it wouldn't be enough. What he really wishes he could do is add on to the Canon, submitting newer texts he deems fit for inclusion and bringing his body of work full circle— adding to what he's drawn from for his work—but unfortunately, not enough has been written in his lifetime to warrant more than a pamphlet. Most of the writers working in the last fifty years are hacks with no talent whatsoever. He can't remember the last time he read a worthwhile newly released novel or short story or poem or drama. None have been produced in this century to date, that's for sure. Really, his last book, the one about modernization and the war on thought, is more applicable now than it was upon its release in the late nineties. It will probably only appreciate in value as time marches on. But that doesn't really help him here. He turns on his side, coming to rest on his belly, and lowers his face into the water. A different approach. He holds his breath and thinks. Wouldn't it be nice to have this final book also lean toward the future, though? His first and last book of the new millennium: something to leave humanity for the next thousand years and beyond. He could write about the Canon in terms of what the new additions *should* be, the types of things people aren't writing but ought to. Eventually, somebody's going to have to build upon the Canon and protect actual culture. Some other critic will need to fill his role; it would only be right that they'd follow the guidelines he had laid out. He's been holding his breath for a considerable length of time now, and as sometimes happens these days, at his age, when he does this in the tub, he's stricken with a frisson of fear that he could have a heart attack and die at any moment. But still, he holds his breath. Then he realizes something incredibly important: There is no future for the Culture—the real, proper Western Culture as he knows it, all he holds so dear. It's going to die with him.

▲▽▲▽▲

This one actually wanted to take her to a museum. On a Sunday. That's how wide-eyed he is. Instead, she suggested coffee during the week. She mostly goes on coffee dates now. They're quick, convenient, efficient. Plus, holding something warm makes people more trusting. Most of the guys she meets don't need that, but still, there's only an upside to it. It probably makes them fall even harder for her. She's on her way to meet him now. He's handsome but not leading-man handsome, she could tell by his pictures. She likes that. It's a good type for what she's doing. He also wrote a weird first message. Something about Albert Einstein's eyeballs. She gave it an A+. Her response was restrained, though. They always are. She responded more like she was giving it a B- or C. Her profile is intentionally a little bland—she doesn't want anyone to actually know anything about her—so to write something so quirky means he's confident. He can probably have sex well. Haruka will find out soon enough. Wide-eyed but still confident: a perfect candidate for ruin.

▲▽▲▲▽

Au Bon Pain… it's an odd choice, but he'll take it. There are more than enough quaint little spots around the Village and East Village with better coffee, ambiance, everything, so she's either got some of the strangest taste buds in New York or she's trying to keep this first date on a whole 'nother level of casual. That's cool, though. Maybe that's the OkCupid way. Or maybe just her way. It wouldn't have been his place to say "Nah, let's go somewhere better" after she countered his invitation to the Met with coffee at the Au Bon Pain on 8th and Mercer; Ray feels lucky she wanted to meet him at all, the way things have been going. And at least she didn't want to go to Starbucks—while they may have better lighting and the quality of what you can get at the two is pretty much the same, their particular vapidity and level of ubiquity would've made the suggestion more insulting than weird. Chains are one thing, but super chains are another; plus, there are far fewer affected-looking people with laptops at Au Bon Pain, and nobody really wanders off the street to try to use the bathroom like he does sometimes while working.

He's coming from his last drop-off now, riding down 8th Street, close. That she wanted to meet him literally two blocks from his most recent public déjà vu site and not far from the one before that is not lost on him. And neither is the translation of Au Bon Pain into English as "With Good Bread," what with all its Jesus and therefore godly connotations. But he's not trying to actually mull any of that over right now. Not only because he's tired as shit—the caffeine he's about to consume will be much appreciated—but also because it would probably be completely paralyzing. It's time to switch on the charm, not get lost in thought. He tears past the CVS, keeping his eyes straight ahead.

When he's about one hundred fifty feet away, he locks up the bike; this stretch of 8th has a lot of parking stations, the kind that look like upside down u's or wavy m's. He wanted to give himself about a block of distance to change his shirt and put some deodorant on in case she got there a little early, so she wouldn't see him. He can't do anything about the swass, unfortunately. Here's hoping there are some phero- mones in ass sweat. Ducking around the corner onto Greene, next to a Ricky's, he takes off his helmet and shirt, then, putting the helmet away inside his messenger backpack, reaches for his water bottle so he can use what's left in it to wet a dry section of the shirt he'd been wearing and clean his body a little with it. Ricky's slogan, to the right of their logo on the sign above, reads: "Looking good! Feeling good!" He dries as much as possible with another area of the shirt that he didn't intentionally or unintentionally get wet—quickly, since he's now only got four minutes until he's supposed to meet her—applies some Right Guard—first to his pits, then in some rushed strokes to random parts of his torso and back since it smells good and his body does not—and puts on the other shirt, a black polo. It's a little wrinkled, but oh well. The people walking by sort of look at him curiously throughout all this—without the bike and with him putting deodorant on in random spots like that, he was definitely giving off pretty strong homeless guy vibes, and this section of the Village is a little too commercial and central for that; it's not like he's on Saint Mark's—but he doesn't give a fuck. It's not about them. It's about him. And her: Haruka. He learned her name in the fifth or sixth message they exchanged. Apparently it's Japanese, meaning either "Far off, distant" or "Spring flower." He looked it up.

After checking his hair in the reflection of the Ricky's window, he rounds the corner back onto 8th and walks briskly toward the Au Bon Pain. They made the plan on Saturday; it's now Tuesday and they haven't communicated since. She never gave him her phone number, ignoring the part of the message he sent where he asked for it in case anything happened, so there've been none of those progress texts that normally go with meeting anyone anywhere these days. He appreciates that—there's a certain romance to just saying, "I will be here at this time. Meet me." It doesn't matter that the place they're meeting is a weird chain store or that she's probably only doing it for protective reasons involved with online dating and not out of reverence to a notion of old-timey romanticism… there's still something to it. That it played out this way, that it's what they're doing. He scans the corner to make sure she's not outside waiting for him as he approaches. She's not, so he goes in. Then there she is. Loose gray sweater, black pants. Shiny hair covering her face as she looks down at her phone, in line to place her order.

"Haruka?"

She looks up. "Hi."

▲▽▲▲▲

He went in for a hug. A lot of the time they do that. Haruka understands. They're on dates, after all. It's not like they're supposed to shake hands—though some of the more dorky guys have done that, too. That's a lot more awkward. Much worse. Sometimes they don't touch at all, which is nice, not until later when she wants them to. It would be great if they all just sort of nodded instead. But it's okay. The hugging. This one's vaguely Latino, so it especially makes sense. That's not racist. It's actually a part of that culture. Warmth. At least he didn't try to kiss her cheeks.

She couldn't help but notice during the hug that his back seemed a little moist through his shirt. He also smelled strongly like a concoction of sweet chemicals and body odor; it was enough to cut through the thick coffee aroma here. What's strange is it's not that hot out and he doesn't seem nervous or anything. Just calm. In any case, she doesn't really mind. He's been nice so far. Even paid for her coffee and cookie. She never knows. A lot of guys—especially those below thirty—like to go Dutch on these first dates. That's another part of why she mostly goes to places like this now. Paying half on all these dates was really starting to add up! She gets a little allowance from her parents every month, but not enough to go on that many dinner dates!

They're on their way to sit down now. It looks like he's eyeing a table in the corner, next to the window. "I'm gonna grab that table," he says, nodding toward it. His pace quickens, and she lags a few steps behind. Instead of sitting when he gets there, he stakes his claim by resting the hand that's holding his coffee on the tabletop, waiting for her to sit first. Some guys would have just sat down in that situation. Others might've pulled out her chair. He chose a good middle ground. Polite. Nothing more, nothing less.

Over the next ten minutes, she notices other things like this about him. Things that speak to his character. That tell her why he's here. What he has to gain, lose… The way he nods along intently as she talks about studying at NYU; that his voice gets a few octaves higher when he says he works as a freelance journalist; how he leans forward and clutches his coffee, black and still cooling, when she tells him she's from the Bay Area in California; the big smile and laugh that come with describing the climate where he grew up right outside of Austin, Texas;

how he watches her like a hawk when she dips pieces of her cookie into her coffee; that he takes a small sip followed by another very large one once he realizes his coffee's cooled enough; the way he scratches his head when she says she doesn't really miss driving; how he cracks a joke when he admits he's new to online dating; that his eyes haven't wavered once from hers since they sat down, no matter where she's been looking. Then she stops. She knows all she needs to know now. And this is when she reaches for the phone.

▲ ▲ ▽ ▽ ▽

For the last five minutes, he's been subject to what he can now only guess is some type of sick game. She started out by saying, "Sorry, I have to check something," and while she hasn't completely abandoned the conversation—responding briefly to his questions, asking a few back—she has pretty much altogether abandoned eye contact, and hasn't at all addressed what that "something" is or why it's requiring so much of her attention there on her fucking phone, so Ray, having ruled out an emergency, since surely she would have left already if that were the case, now suspects it's nothing at all.

He thinks he lost her either with the dumb joke about OkCupid—"I joined OkCupid only a few weeks ago after I decided to delete my offline dating profile"—or when he asked about her cookie.

The joke seemed to go over well enough at the time; she smiled, replied with, "I've never had an offline dating profile. I hear they're for old people who don't know how to meet anyone online." But maybe she was actually offended. Maybe she thought that while it was, sure, a somewhat odd and self-effacing thing for him to say, it had also taken a bit of a jab at her. It's possible that these kids today don't just look at online dating as another equally valid way to meet people; they could be sensitive about it, too. Ray didn't even really know what he meant when he made the joke. She had asked if he goes on many of these, and it just seemed like sort of a weird and funny if corny response. He started this whole thing by referencing Einstein's eyeballs in a safety deposit box, after all; the joke was in keeping with the role he cast himself in. He still doesn't really know what it means. If you deleted your offline profile, that would be, what, like killing yourself? He's already dead, of course, but for the sake of argument, that's one idea. Or it could be, like, forcing yourself to become so awkward and remote out in social settings that you would be completely undatable? Whatever the case, that response of hers could have been more defensive than playful, he's come to realize now, looking out the window, a good thirty or so seconds having passed since anybody's said anything. He had replied to it with, "They are. That's why I had to delete myself." It was a pretty good way to handle it, he thought, more self-deprecation, but without anything that could be construed as a slight to her. There's no way she couldn't have known he meant well after that. Maybe she doesn't like guys who make fun of themselves. She could be so literal or stupid that it turns her off. No, no; her response was too good the first time, too much like his own joke. She got it. It couldn't have been the joke.

Within seconds of that whole exchange, without enough time for any real lull, is when he had inquired about the cookie. "So how's the cookie?" he asked. And that's when, after simply responding, "Good," she pulled out the phone. To check the big "something." More like Facebook, Twitter, her texts, probably. He looks across to try to see, but she's holding the phone, an iPhone, up at an angle now. Maybe in the reflection of the window… Nope. Still too light out. It's entirely possible she's another demon, like Jill. Could asking about the cookie have been that boring? Or did she think he wanted some and she didn't want to give him any? Did she decide the date was over then? Or is there something from before he's not considering? Something he had said about California or NYU that could've pissed her off; he doesn't like either, but he doesn't remember saying anything that would've given anything away. No. That seems ridiculous. Actually, all of this seems ridiculous. Should he whip out his phone and fuck around on it, too? Or just get up and leave? He definitely doesn't want to use his phone—follow her lead, or stoop to some kind of pettiness—and he also doesn't really want to leave, though he doesn't know why. He should. She'd deserve it. But he can't bring himself to do it. He has to do something, though. He's been staring silently out the window and occasionally sipping coffee for something like a full minute now. Thinking this convoluted and asinine blame game shit to himself at a caffeinated ten miles a minute. It's starting to make him feel like he's the one who's weird, when in fact everything that's wrong about this situation is her fault. Wait, could this have just been part of her game, to see when he'd finally take action? When he'd prove he's assertive? A man? He had been understanding for the first thirty seconds or so, had cleared his throat around the first minute. Laughed

about it and asked her if everything was okay by two minutes, breaking
a little monologue he was offering up about Columbia's core curriculum.
Tried his best to be patient during the third and fourth as she talked into
the phone about the difference between what he had described and the
undergrad requirements at NYU. Entering the fifth or so minute is when
he shut down and stopped asking questions. Whatever. Enough thinking, enough staring, enough sipping. This girl just needs to get off her
phone. Now.

"Hey, so, what's going on over there, if you don't mind me asking?"

Her eyes stay fixed on the screen, of course. "Sorry. It's my friend.
She's going through a crisis."

"Oh?"

"Yes, boy trouble. I've been helping her through it all day." She
continues typing. "So tell me what it's like being a journalist."

"I'm sorry your friend is going through something right now, but I
can't really talk to you anymore while you're doing that." He half believes her explanation; it seems like a plausible thing for an eighteen-
year-old girl to do. But even so, it's hardly a good enough excuse for how
she's treating him on a date. This is the deciding moment.

"Okay. Sorry, sorry! I'll tell her now I'll call her later. That I'm with
someone." She looks up. Her eyes are luminous, inviting. "I can't tell
her how cute you are, though. She's thinking about breaking up with
her boyfriend and it would seem like I'm bragging." Ray's ears perk, and
he feels better about things all of a sudden. She puts the phone away,
finally. "Do you want to get out of here? My dorm is close by. We could
finish our coffee on the way there."

This is a strange turn of events. "Sure…" She goes from ignoring
him one second to inviting him back to her place? "Okay."

"Awesome sauce," she says, popping the last bit of cookie into her
mouth. A bewildered Ray stands up. Then they grab their things and
leave.

▲ ▲ ▽ ▽ ▲

Something strange happened on the way back. Well, it's not that strange
when she really thinks about it, here now signing him in. It's just never
really happened before, and that makes it strange.

They were crossing Washington Square Park when he said, "Did you know there are twenty thousand bodies buried here?"

Haruka didn't believe him. "No there aren't."

"Yes, there are. This used to be an old farm, and back at the end of the 1700s the city bought a chunk of it to use as a burial ground. Mostly for poor people, criminals, victims of epidemics."

"You're lying."

"I'm not. Google it," he said. Then he stopped in his tracks. "But don't make me regret giving you permission to break out the phone again." She glared at him, but in a fun and pretend way, and he smiled back. They were by the fountain, on the north side of the park near the big white arch. It was a weird thought: this pretty place that is practically NYU's quad as some kind of mass grave. The park that seemed so fancy, so French with its replica of the Arc de Triomphe. She pulled out the phone, googled some of the relevant terms, and he was right.

Then the strange thing happened: it made her wet. Made Little Kaiju salivate right then and there. Nobody's really done that before just with talking. Usually it takes at least a little kissing.

"You're right," she said, bringing the phone down. She linked her arm in with his and they walked back to the dorm like that.

Now she can't wait to get him upstairs.

▲ ▲ ▽ ▲ ▽

Well that escalated quickly; not that Ray's complaining—he had a pretty good run back in his day—but if this is online dating, then he could have easily slept with twice as many girls had this been a viable option while he was in college. Holy shit. It was a good thing he popped in an Altoid back in the park when he finished his coffee, because not ten seconds after Haruka kicked her roommate out she had pushed him onto the bed and her tongue into his mouth. It seemed like one balletic sequence, from closing the door behind the roommate, to turning around, forcing him down, mounting him, and kissing him. He didn't even have time to take his bag off. The lump of his helmet is now digging into his back, and what's left of the Altoid's still there, getting batted around by both of their tongues. It's all starting to be a bit much.

"Hold on." He sits up, takes the bag off, and then the mint out. She had been watching him with anticipation as he pulled away, then sort of smiled to herself when he took his bag off, proud, he was sure, but then she made a face like he was gross after she saw the little white speck of Altoid go onto his fingertips. But he doesn't care. It's not gross; it's just an Altoid. And it was getting in the way. He realizes now he could've just chewed and swallowed it, but it's too late at this point. "You got a wastebasket?" She points toward the floor under the window next to the bed. He leans over and drops it in, then climbs on top of her. They kiss each other harder. Soon he's pulling at her sweater, and it comes off, followed by his shirt, then her bra, and all the rest.

Everything's happened so fast that it's only when they're completely nude, lying there side by side kissing, one of his hands holding her breast, that he realizes how strange this situation should feel, being in a dorm room at his age, about to have sex like this. But it doesn't feel strange. It feels good. Not that it makes any sense. It doesn't, at all. But things don't have to make sense to feel good.

There must be some pheromones in swass, he thinks now, propping himself up and kissing around her nipples. Unless this really is just what OkCupid is all about. That, or she feels guilty about the phone thing and is trying to make it up to him? He's been fine, charming enough, but it's wild that she's this attracted to him after, like, fifteen minutes in a coffee shop and a ten-minute walk. All the same, he'll take it. It's been a little while since he's had sex—a while, really, since anything that nice at all has happened to him—and it's time to restore some balance. Unless this is some kind of ultimate bait and switch: like she's this particularly malignant demon come up from hell who will reveal herself to be a prostitute after, hitting him up for cash lest he want his legs broken and the money forcibly taken by her pimp, Satan in the form of the Yakuza, to be left penniless and without the means to make any sort of an income anymore. No, no. He should give himself more credit. Nothing about her intention, the passion she's displayed here really seems spurious. Everything just feels right. But why? Maybe because he died in college, when this type of thing would be normal. Is this some sort of homecoming? Nothing to cogitate on now. In fact, all this thinking's keeping his dick from getting hard. If she's to lead him to where he's supposed to go, he needs to be there for her to do that. Truly present.

He moves back over to his side and slides his hand down her torso, over her smooth, hairless pelvis, between her legs. She moans at contact, already wet. He rubs her clitoris, gently at first, kissing her softly. Little by little, he rubs harder… kisses harder. Giving makes him feel good. Not thinking makes him feel even better. Now he's just doing. Soon she reaches for his member, and she strokes it as he continues to rub around her clitoris and inner labia. Once she can tell he's fully hard, she stops. She pushes his hand away and looks into his eyes.

There's a condom in his wallet, still tucked away from his non-date with Jill a few weeks back. He hesitates; his wallet's in his jeans, which are on the floor, and he doesn't really want to bend over in front of her. It's still only around dusk now, and the room, with its open blinds, is pretty bright. "I think I have a condom in my wallet," he says. He does this sort of to explain the hesitation, but also to see if there's anything she might be able to do to help them out instead.

"I have some." She leans over him and reaches into her nightstand. He's thankful, since he probably would've given her a choice view of his asshole, or else would have had to do some really strategic jackknifing to look like he was naturally getting into his jeans, had she not acted. His view is of her slender torso hunched over him in profile, the flawless lambent skin of her flank.

She hands him a condom, then pulls back the covers, getting under, waiting. It's the same kind he uses, the NYC Condom brand given away for free around the city that's actually just a repackaged version of Lifestyles. His own supply features black wrappers with rainbow lettering, but they must have changed the design since he last picked some up. Now the wrappers, for whatever reason, prominently feature the power button symbol—the same one used on computers and various other electronics, in the shape of an incomplete circle with a vertical line at the top poking halfway in and halfway out—in gold on a maroon background. Sitting on the edge of the narrow bed, he rips open the plastic and unrolls the condom over his erection. The faint scent of latex hangs in the air, and his hands bear traces of the lubricant covering the condom. He turns to her and smiles, and she smiles back, her head tilting slightly. He moves over her, kissing her again, their lips similar in size and shape, he appreciates then. He places his member lengthwise along her vagina, pressing against it and gently grinding. In one last tease, he shakes his head against her clitoris. Then, unable to take it another second, like food placed before someone or, more accurately, something starving, she reaches out and pulls him inside.

▲ ▲ ▽ ▲ ▲

They're a couple of minutes into it now. The pace has been established, and it seems like he's very comfortable. Almost time.

He's maybe her third or fourth Latin guy, and it's true what they say: they can move. Nice, fluid hips. This one's also especially sensual. He strokes her. Kisses her. Some guys, once the sex starts, don't kiss at all. But he's still doing it a lot. Along her cheek, down her neck. The confidence he has in bed is different than how she thought it would be. It's less about him and more about them. When he's not kissing her, he's smiling down at her, like he knows he's making her feel good, like he knows he's doing a good job. The atmosphere is extremely positive. Haruka can tell he really, really likes her. That's good. More for him to lose.

She wraps her legs around his torso and squeezes his penis with her pelvic muscles, stopping him while he's all the way inside her, so that she can roll over to the side and then on top of him. It's a move that makes some guys come, but she figured it wouldn't with him since he's proven himself to be pretty sexually competent. She rides him resuming their previous rhythm. As she looks down, biting her lip, he smiles big. She grinds into him slowly, pulling her fingers through her hair. His eyelids hang low and he stretches out his legs more. She picks up the pace again then begins slamming down harder, faster. His eyes pop all the way open again. "What's my name?"

He looks at her funny, then while laughing, says, "Haruka…"

"My name is Nobody."

▲ ▲ ▲ ▽ ▽

At first he thought she was just trying to do some faux-dominatrix-type shit, but now he knows it was much more than that—the déjà vu thing happened again, right as she was telling him her name was "Nobody." He couldn't help but laugh after she said it, harder than he did when she asked him to say her name; on the surface, it was just such a startling and perfect thing for her to say considering the date they've had. She didn't seem to appreciate the laughter. Not one bit. Beyond the surface, Ray agrees with her. This here is deadly serious.

She grabs his hands and makes him squeeze her breasts, holding his outstretched arms still at his wrists while riding him hard. He wishes he could take a picture of her then one of himself in this moment for the EVIDENCE folder. But he'll just have to make do with his memory. "Your... last hour has come. You die... in blood," she says, bouncing on top of him.

"What?"

"You... heard me."

"Say it again." It's a terrifying thing to hear, especially from some-one fucking you like you're a piece of meat, even if that person is roughly half your size and speaking in strained fragments. But fear is not the reason he wants her to repeat it. Ray isn't afraid. The statement sounds familiar—not in a way that's connected to the déjà vu, the last vestiges of which are still fading, but actually familiar—and he's trying to place it.

"Your last hour... has come... You die in blood."

"Isn't that... from the *Odyssey*?" Despite the almost daily extended cardio, he, like her, can't say more than a few words in one breath while having sex at a pace like this.

"Shut up."

"It is."

"Shut up... Mister Ivy League." She pushes his hands away from her chest.

"Actually I... remember that from high school... Haruk... a."

"Nobody should... say 'actually'... while fucking."

"You're right," he says, reaching for her hips. "Sorry." Once he gets a good hold on them, he rolls her over and himself back on top.

"Nobody should say 'sorry'... while fucking... either. Not unless you bump... heads or scratch the other person with... your toenail or some-thing. It's a... turnoff."

"Right." He moves in and out with measured, unhurried move-ments, gyrating a little at the end of each.

"You're going too slow."

"Am I?"

She wraps her legs around him and rises up on her hands, propelling herself forward while his body slides underneath, almost like she was playing leapfrog. On top again, she rides him with her feet planted on the bed instead of her knees, keeping him down and herself up by pressing hard on his shoulders. "By hook or by crook this peril... too shall be something... that we remember," she says. Another one from the *Odyssey*. He feels the motion and her body weight as she crashes down on him, and little else. If it weren't for the condom, he would probably be able to feel a lot more of her from the inside, too, and this kind of sex might have made him come already. He doesn't know what to make of her. Is she one of his verisimilitudinous projections? Or is she some kind of a spiritual guide native to the afterlife? Either way, he wants to experience this like it's more on his terms.

"My safe word... is Ithaca." he jokes.

"There are no... safe words... here."

"Duly noted."

"Quit talking like... that!" One of her hands slides over his mouth while the other remains on his shoulder. She seems to be getting tired, so the pace gets slower. "Aren't you afraid?"

He extricates her hand from his mouth. "No."

"Why not?" She twists around, so that she's riding him while facing away, and speaks without looking back at him. "You don't know me. You don't know... what I'm capable of." He watches his dick go in and out of her, the lips of her vagina gripping it. Above, her anus appears and disappears as she moves up and down, back and forth. Outside the sun is finally setting and the room is gradually becoming dark. "I could have a knife... hidden near the foot of the bed here."

"I know you're not going... to kill me. I'm already dead."

She looks back at him. "What?"

"I've been dead... for years now." He grabs onto her hip with one hand and reaches across her breasts with the other, guiding her down so she's lying supine on top of him, raising his knees to support her weight as he moves in and out of her at the pace she had eased them into. Her head tilts back and jounces next to his. "Tell me where... to go... please."

"Huh?" She cranes her neck and rotates her face toward him. "Go?"

"From here... From purgatory."

She rolls onto her side, keeping him in and behind her still, then continues turning until she's hunched over on all fours. "Go deeper... into my pussy."

"Okay." His thrusts go all the way in.

"That's it, fuck me... harder." He increases the pace a little, maintaining full depth. "Fuck me until... you love me."

"I don't think I can love… anyone anymore except… for the people I knew when I… was alive."

She looks back. "So you're crazy then, huh?… You really think you're… dead?"

"I know I'm… dead."

Laughing, she looks forward again and whips her hair back, her head coming to rest at an upward tilt. He admires her slim back, the elegant curve of her spine. "Some things you will… think of yourself… some things God will… put into your mind."

"What's that… from?"

She hangs her head as he continues to move at a good, steady pace. Their bodies clap together. "It is necessity and not… pleasure that compels us."

"These sound fam… iliar."

"I can't do this position anymore." She crawls forward and away from him, near the top of the long bed. The last bit of light outside casts her faint shadow on the wall. The room is now bathed in a dull bluish hue.

"Okay."

She turns over. "Kiss me."

He does, hard, their tongues twisting and curling. Lying on her back, she reaches for his member and puts it back inside. She wraps her arms around him and pulls his head down next to hers. Whispering into his ear, she says, "Abandon all hope, ye who enter here."

"Oh shit. It's Dante." He jolts back up so he can look at her. "That last one's… pretty obvious."

"Mister Ivy League thinks he's… so smart. I'm only calling you that 'cause I… forgot your fucking name. You know that, right?" She slaps his ass as he continues moving in and out. "Where's your Pulitzer… journalist?"

"So are you a demon?"

"Do I look… like a demon?"

"No. You look more like… an angel."

"If I'm an angel, I'm the angel… of death." He recalls the view from moments before, when he was having sex with her from behind and could see her arching back. Beneath the skin at her shoulder blades, he sees her bones begin to warp and tremble, as if wings were about to tear through and spread, but the vision ends before this happens and he's unable to see if they're the wings of an angel or those of a demon. She could be a demon; she could be an angel; she could be the angel of death. She could be anything.

"Tell me where to go."

Staring up at him, she says, "Soon you will be where your… own eyes will see the source and cause… and give you their own answer… to the… mystery."

"Beautiful… that's what I've been… waiting for."

She pulls herself up by his neck, and presses him down yet again. Looming over him, she slides up and down faster and harder than she had at any point before, having seemingly caught a second, more powerful wind. "Hope not ever to… see heaven. I have come to lead you… to the other shore… into eternal darkness… into fire and into ice."

"That's not the… outcome I was hoping for."

"It's what you… deserve."

"So this is it, then? I'm going… to hell."

"You're already… there," she says.

"I didn't think there'd be… sex in hell."

"Of course there's… sex in hell."

"Not like this." He plants his feet firmly on the bed, raising his knees and pushing her forward, then grabs her hips to control the pace. "There's still… pleasure in this."

"How come you're not… freaked out?"

"Because you're a… spiritual guide… This is where… I'm supposed to be."

"I am no guide."

"Then you're just a projection from… what's left of my mind." He slides one hand behind her back and uses the other to rotate the both of them over so he's again back on top. "You're not real… None of this… is."

Pulling herself up by his neck again, they sit with their legs folded over each other, gyrating. She stares back, her hair falling over her eyes. "I'm a projection of… no man's mind. I am… my own." He inches a finger toward her anus, then circles it while the rest of the hand holds her up. The other hand feels her breast. He continues pumping in and out in long, deep strokes. She slides one of her own hands down and works her clit, holding on to his neck with the other. "I am… very real. And to you… I will be… Oh fuck!"—she starts coming—"everything."

"Bring me to God."

"I'm your God… now. Come already. Come with… me. Now."

He leans his forehead against hers and thrusts deeper, harder. Catching the end of her orgasm, there's the familiar rush from deep within his abdomen, followed by a massive release. "Aaaaaahhhhhhhh!" She pushes him down so she's on top during the final seconds. Weeks of pent-up tension flow into the condom's reservoir tip. Masturbation never comes close to this. It's like a new awakening.

"Good." She holds his face between her hands. The room is now much darker than when they began, but not so dark that he can't make out her eyes staring into his. She pulls his head next to hers, her mouth over his ear, and insufflates: "Now you're mine. Now I'll be with you always. Now you'll love me forever." He falls back and closes his eyes, trying to block everything out and wrap himself up in warm post-coital fuzz, but her face is still there, staring, matter-of-fact and chilling in that dim blue light.

▲ ▲ ▲ ▽ ▲

This is unbelievable! The motherfucker actually made her come. Goddammit! Haruka is pissed! Now she likes him. Dopamine, serotonin flooding her system! Like, she has a crush! On him! This fucking guy she barely even knows. Number fifty-whatever! It's terrible.

He only did half the work, but it's still all his fault. The way he moved and all those weird things he said back to her made her want to come, so she used her fingers and made it happen. Not good. When she orgasms, it's like Little Kaiju is throwing up.

This is not fair. It really isn't!

Nobody else besides her first boyfriend back home, Kenji, who's now at Stanford, has ever had a part in bringing her to full climax. While she said the creepy thing at the end that let this Ray guy know she owns his soul now, she's afraid he could get to her in a real way, too. Getting near her heart, or even, heaven forbid, her own recently discovered soul. That would be a major problem. And just by thinking this, she's already made things worse. The fear in and of itself has made her vulnerable: humans can subconsciously smell fear in pheromones. She needs to get rid of him fast. "Hey asshole!"

He's just lying there, like he's sleeping. What a jerk.

"Hey asshole, open your eyes!"

His eyes remain shut. "Just let me ride this out for a minute longer. I haven't felt this relaxed in a while."

"You're not supposed to feel relaxed right now."

"But I do. This feels right."

She reaches for her phone and bonks him on the head with it.

"Ouch!"

"Nope. Nap time's over." She steps down from the bed, crosses the room, and flicks the light on. The previously cool blue room is now a bright yellow. Spots and curtains dance across her vision and it takes a while to adjust.

"Okay… Okay…" Finally, he opens his eyes.

"Get out of my bed please. Time to go," she says, looming over him.

"One step at a time, Haruka. One step at a time."

"One step at a time, nothing! Don't say my name like you know me." Her phone is still in the one hand and oddly, she's had no desire to check her alerts the entire time. She's only wanted to look at him. This makes her very, very uncomfortable. "Also, one other thing, don't you ever tell a girl what she can do with her phone. 'Don't make me regret giving you permission to take out your phone again?' Excuse me? 'Permission?' Who the hell do you think you are?"

He sits up. "I thought I was just engaging in a little flirtatious banter."

"Flirtatious banter, my foot. Get out!"

"So you're really a demon then, huh? Do you know Jill? Or Brian? Is he a demon or a projection?"

"Huh? I already told you, I'm your God."

"If you're my God, you sure are a wrathful God." He rubs the spot on his head where she struck him. "So where am I exactly? Still in purgatory, but some weird part?"

"I already told you, you're in hell."

"But this can't be hell. The sex was too good." Even though he's slouching and lit very severely under the bright dorm room light, she still thinks he looks cute. Goddammit! "Also, I don't think God, my God, whatever, would be in hell. Maybe it actually is limbo? But the orange traffic signal in the picture…"

"God is everywhere. I'm everywhere. The sex was supposed to build you up so that you'll fall down even harder. The entrance of hell, the one I've made for you, is supposed to seem fun because it's a trick. It'll make your sense of loss a lot worse the lower you go."

"That would make sense for limbo, but I still don't know if this is a test. I don't know what you are. What I'm really supposed to believe."

"Come on, Mister Ivy League. I don't know what's so hard for you to understand. You came in me and I have you now. I have your soul. You're mine, and I'm everything to you. As your God, I've sentenced you to damnation. Time to accept it and get what you deserve." She grabs onto his wrists, the one hand still holding on to the phone, and pulls him off the bed, only letting go when he's up on his feet.

"But why would you tell me? Wouldn't the trick be better if I didn't know?"

She gets back on top of the bed and sits leaning against the wall, rumpled covers beneath her. "It's a part of the fun for me." Crossing her legs, one hand comes to rest on her thigh while the other slowly twirls the phone, over and over. "I used to just show guys like you, play the trick, but now I like to tell you all about it, too. There's a lot to that recognition. The knowing. It makes it hurt more and that makes me laugh."

"When can I see you again?" He's standing there staring at her, making no effort to pick up the clothes at his feet. His penis has shrunk and it looks strange. She hates it. Her eyes return to his.

"Only in your dreams."

"Seriously?"

"Yes."

"I don't believe you," he says, scratching his face. That nice-looking, interesting face. Very pretty eyes in this light. She didn't know they were hazel. Why won't he just leave already?

"The truth is the truth."

"If that's the truth, then I'm not leaving." He crosses his arms. "The signs told me to go to God. To be with God. If you're my God, then I shouldn't go anywhere."

"The longer you stay here with me, the worse it will be. Your hell."

One arm falls to brace his trim stomach. He has, like, a full six-pack. The other comes to scratch that face of his again. "This isn't a test?"

"Jesus! Not everything is a fucking test! You're pathetic!"

"Tell me about the signs you made for me. Tell me about the mural and the drugstore, the bridge."

"Huh?"

"I can't be sure you're God if you don't know what I'm talking about." His hands come to his hips, elbows out, his lean muscles stretching.

"You're in no position to make demands. Also, it would be wise not to question me."

"I was taught that faith is a journey, and doubt is a part of that journey."

"You were taught wrong. I'm done with you. I've told you everything you need to know already. Now put your clothes back on and go, you fool."

He bends over and picks up his underwear and pants. First one athletic leg, then the other. Once he's halfway dressed, he reaches down again for his shirt. Some real progress now, thank goodness. "When will it start to feel like hell?" he asks, struggling to get his head to poke out of the neck hole. It's pretty cute. Oh, no!

"It could happen the second you walk out of here. It could happen gradually... after days, weeks, maybe even longer, years. But rest assured: It will happen."

"And what did I do? What did I do to deserve this?" He's tying his shoes now.

"The short answer to that is the same as it is with everyone: You were born and then you failed. As for the long answer, well, you'll have the rest of eternity to figure that out."

"I can't accept that. I need you to tell me. I've been in purgatory or whatever this is for a while now and I still haven't been able to figure out what I've done wrong. I deserve to know."

"What vanity. What entitlement. How dare you speak to me this way... Forget what you were taught. Faith is not about you. It is about me. Now, for the last time, go."

"I don't think you're God. I think you're a demon. Sent here to lie to me. That, or you're lying to yourself."

"You can think what you want. Like I said, the truth is the truth. You'll see soon enough."

He picks up his bag from the floor then moves away from the bed. When he's at the door, he takes one last look at her. She stares back stone-faced, still nude and cross-legged with her phone in the one hand. He sort of nods at her. It's weird, this gesture. Haruka doesn't get it. Turning, he lowers his head and makes the sign of the cross. Then, finally, he opens the door and steps out. The door shuts behind him, the latch clicking. Then the door to her suite, too, the sound of the automatic lock audible through the wall. Then he's gone.

Now she can breathe for a minute. Try to assess the situation calmly.

She's not sure how much of an effect she'll have on him, but she did her best. He's obviously mentally ill or something—not as good and pure as she thought—but she has high hopes for this special case. All the more for its truly unique qualities, actually.

If he ends up believing her, he'll be tormented for the rest of his days. That would be nice. But it's also possible he'll find something else that convinces him he's going to his "God" and she was not it. You never know with nutcases. There will be a follow-up message, she is sure of that—that's the one thing she could tell was certain from that nod at the end. Hopefully she'll get a sense of what's going on then.

It was weird to talk like that with him, be so honest with him on her end, too. While she says creepy things to all of them, he's the only guy she's told exactly what she's doing. But it was the best way to deflect the absolutely crazy things he was saying... Is it strange that she felt like they were speaking the same language? Each speaking their truths? No! Fuck! That is the type of question a girl who is really falling for someone would ask. And she is not doing that. No. She can't. This fucking weird guy. Einstein eyeball guy. Fuck him. He took for-fucking-ever to leave after she had asked him to. Very rude. One of the worst ever. She had to literally pull him out of the bed. As in physically. That's never happened before, only almost. It's a surprise she didn't have to call campus security.

Speaking of, he's probably going to forget to sign out. Another damn thing for her to deal with because of him. She'll do it in a few minutes. After she washes Little Kaiju. Poor thing. Throw up everywhere. Lauren will probably be back soon, maybe she should go wash and get dressed now. She can't believe that fucking guy. Making her come like that. Kissing her, moving the way he did while they screwed, saying those weird things she liked... Making her have so much fun. Letting her actually play the role of a goddess... No, God... That fucking guy...

Haruka puts her phone down on the nightstand, alerts still unviewed, slides back under the covers, and masturbates.

▲ ▲ ▲ ▲ ▽

It's been such a treat, seeing his daughter this afternoon. When she called yesterday evening, Emerson thought something terrible must have happened. A call from Claire after 9:00 p.m. on a Tuesday? Who died? But it turned out she was coming in for a last-minute meeting today here in the city—the downtown gallery that represents her is showing some of her new work next month—and she wanted to get together. Lunch wasn't an option because of his class, so she proposed a mid-afternoon visit to the Whitney, to see the Biennial. And here they are.

This is hardly his favorite museum, and the Biennial, in particular, has never been anything he's enjoyed. Contemporary art, like contemporary literature, theater, music, everything, is almost always completely atrocious. In fact the only contemporary art he likes is Claire's, in part because she's his daughter and he sort of has to, but also because he had a large role in exposing her to good painting as a child and adolescent— in monthly trips to the Met, and abroad on vacation visits to the British Museum, Prado, Uffizi, Hermitage, Louvre, and other world-class institutions—so her aesthetic sensibility is actually quite refined. As far as the whole modern thing, only half of which Emerson can tolerate, the MoMA and Guggenheim have far better permanent collections, and he definitely would've preferred going to one of those instead. But it doesn't really matter. What's hanging from the walls or filling the rooms is entirely secondary; it's walking and talking with his daughter he cherishes. They haven't gotten together since Thanksgiving.

Starting on the fifth floor, the top, they've been casually meandering through the museum's galleries, mostly discussing her family, the kids. Unlike on the phone, Emerson has been making an effort to be affable, doing his best to offer validation and encouragement wherever he can, even when faced with something absolutely dreadful. He wants this to be a nice day, a pleasant memory for them both. It can be trying:

"So, we've gone ahead and booked our plane tickets for Mexico," she had said up on the fourth floor.

"Have you now?"

"We're leaving in late June."

"Well… I'm sure it will be very exciting." Emerson actually forced a smile.

"And here I figured you'd tell me to exchange my tickets and go to Paris. You've certainly turned a new leaf."

"Not exactly, but I've already told you what I think. It's your life. Just please be safe."

Every now and again she'll remark on the work, too. It's a lot harder to hold his tongue then. Almost all of it is far too primitive or derivative, but it would upset her if he told her how he really felt. He does his best:

"Isn't this one marvelous?" she had asked, looking at some ghastly painting on the third floor by some hack named Andrew Masullo.

He gulped, then said, "Yes, I rather like the use of Mikado yellow."

Now on the second floor, she's become particularly stricken by another artist's work, one with a small room devoted to him: a Mister Forrest Bess. His paintings are some of the most primitive he's seen all afternoon. They mostly consist of crude, oddly colored lines, shapes, and the occasional figure on small canvases framed by rough wood, like they were made by a child or some sort of whimsical caveman. Emerson had dismissed the paintings within five seconds of walking in, so to give himself something to do while Claire gets her fill, he's taken to reading about them and the artist, something he didn't really do in depth when looking around the other galleries because Claire had, thankfully, kept it moving. A little context to clue him in as to why anyone would dare champion something like this. His highest hope is for a brief chuckle. She hasn't said anything about how wonderful it all is to him yet, but he's sure it's coming.

Crossing the gallery's parquet floor, moving over to the big white wall with the main exhibition introduction, he learns that this Mister Bess actually isn't a contemporary artist at all; rather, in an unusual turn, a sculptor the Biennial curators had invited to take part in the event instead chose to honor Mister Bess, who's been dead since the 1970s, with this carefully curated room they have here. The Whitney people are giving this sculptor, a fellow by the name of Robert Gober, credit for the "installation" that is the room, and so technically, this is his piece, a work of art called "The Man That Got Away." Oh, contemporary art, contemporary everything... Always giving credit where credit's due. Emerson reads on. Apparently, this Mister Bess was a paranoid schizophrenic fisherman who lived along the Gulf Coast of Texas, and many of these paintings are supposed to be faithful representations of the visions he would have. The awful nature of the work seems to make a lot more sense after reading that. Mister Bess also had some complicated theories about his sexual identity, and performed several operations on his genitals... that turned him into... a pseudo-hermaphrodite? What the?! He wrote at length about how uniting the male and female within would increase consciousness, creativity, and eventually lead to eternal life?! And some of these writings can be found here in the display case on the opposite wall... Emerson had completely ignored that long vitrine during his initial scan of the gallery, figuring whatever was held inside would be even more painful to behold than the artwork on the walls. During his lifetime, Mister Bess had wanted to show these theories alongside his paintings, but his dealer Betty Parsons always declined… At least she had the good sense! But these writings appear here along with corresponding photographs—finally realizing Forrest Bess's wishes for the display of his work!?! This is terrible! Utter exploitation of a dead lunatic masquerading as a celebration of some kind of twentieth-century van Gogh!!! Credit where credit is due, indeed, Robert Gober! For shame! This is grotesque even by the Whitney's standards!!!

Turning sharply, Emerson finds Claire across the room. She's looking down at the display case now! The day is ruined, he thinks. His heart is frantically palpitating. It feels as if his entire face is on fire, like it must be burning a bright crimson. Why couldn't they have just gone to the Met? Like old times. This sort of thing never happens at the Met. Of course she's an adult, of course she can handle it, but to him, in a lot of ways, she'll always be his little girl. It's his job as her father to protect her. On top of that, he's her oldest and, he hopes, dearest museum buddy, not to mention one of the world's foremost critics—and although he's technically not an "art" critic, he is a well-respected guardian of even higher culture, the superior form of expression visual art has traditionally fed off the most: literature—he really should have found a way to shield her from this. He feels like he's failed her three times over. A thin layer of perspiration forms above his brow and he wipes it with a pocket handkerchief.

Just being here is saying something about himself as a critic that he can't stand, that's utterly mortifying; it's a good thing he's rarely recognized out in public. He wants to just leave the gallery, go out into the main room and look at something halfway decent—not in the artistic sense, of course, since clearly that's not going to be possible here, but at least in the moral one—or find a seat somewhere, but he knows this would upset Claire. He's suspended his ego for the last hour and a half; he can't just quit now. No, he has to put on his best poker face and rejoin her.

It's not that he isn't curious about the man. He is… but it is a shameful, macabre curiosity. That's where some of his reaction is coming from—this whole room is beyond anything even remotely resembling good taste. Perhaps if he actually liked the paintings it would be easier to rationalize why it's okay to read more about this man, to now take in his outrageous thoughts with these archival materials—become completely wrapped up in his little world. After all, Emerson greatly appreciates a good many talented writers throughout history who obviously suffered from some form of mental illness; the relationship between madness and genius has been commented on since Aristotle. This must be the case with Claire, he decides… he could sense how taken she was with the work the second they walked in. That makes his continued presence here okay. It isn't a tacit endorsement as either her father or a critic; it's just support for her as her own person. What's on the walls, filling the rooms is secondary, he reminds himself as he trundles back across the gallery to stand next to her.

It's every bit as horrific as he'd thought it would be. Looking down upon the display case, in a spot between Claire and a young couple dressed in the raggedy Bohemian fashion favored by too many of the youth these days, the first thing he sees is a photo, a Polaroid in black and white, of the man's genitalia after one of his operations. What appear to be the ends of a pair of forceps stretch open a black hole at the base of the scrotum, a finger holding the top of his penis upwards for clarity. Dark, coarse pubic hair surrounds everything as a sort of filler, contrasting dramatically with the light shade of the man's skin. "What an astonishing human being," says Claire.

"Yes, quite."

Next to the photo are pages of his writings, some with accompanying images themselves. One such page—the words typewritten, the images consisting of two illustrated cutouts from old books along with a drawing and another photo of what is presumably Mister Bess's genitals—delineates how the perineum, scrotum, and penis together make the Tree of Life. Several nearby pages expound on this. Emerson begins to read the object labels, while Claire sighs contentedly and leaves him, moving on to the remaining paintings. The bedraggled-looking young people follow her, the way idiots in museums tend to follow anyone coming to or leaving anything, though Emerson is grateful for it.

Alone now, he continues to read. He reads about the Australian Aboriginal rituals that partly inspired Bess's self-surgery, how the man thought the opening pictured above, if dilated enough, would be able to receive another penis and lead him to feminine orgasm as well as athanasia. It's all incredibly sick, and Emerson feels horrid reading it. This should be in some obscure psychological journal only read by doctors. Claire isn't even here anymore; he can stop. But he doesn't. He can't. Like he's come across a gruesome crime scene, he's fascinated in the worst way. He reads about Bess's correspondence with Carl Jung; how he even wrote President Eisenhower about his theories. He then scans the other pages on display, which are mostly correspondences with his dealer and an art historian, outlining more of his ideas. He reads the labels that relate to these; everything ties to the man's genitals: his consciousness, creativity, transcendence. Learning about his creative output after the procedure, they refer to something called the Steinach operation, something similar to what Bess did, but far less extreme, more like a vasectomy, and how other artists and thinkers believed it led to increased vitality and output. Then Emerson sees a familiar name and can hardly believe his eyes—Yeats! W.B. Yeats, the genius behind some of his favorite poems had some quack alter his genitalia for the sake of his writing?! And he also reported an increased sex drive? Calling it a "second puberty?!" How could this be? How could such a bright man do something so incredibly stupid? Or is it stupid? If these dates are correct, it led to some of his best work during his twilight years… If it's good enough for Yeats…

"You ready, Daddy?" It's Claire. He had no idea she was standing next to him, or for how long.

"Yes, of course."

They begin to make their egress from the gallery. Emerson can't help but see the abstractions hanging on the walls as more worthy, interesting. So much better. They're not primitive; they're universal. "Some Biennial, huh?"

"Yes," says Emerson. "It's been a revelation." And oh, has it ever.

▲ ▲ ▲ ▲ ▲

The time on the phone reads 4:17. Less than an hour has passed since he last looked at it, so he places it down on its face and turns away, moving the covers as far up as his ear. Just enough room to breathe. She had said he'd see her in his dreams, and she was right. Two weeks have passed since his date with Haruka and now Ray can hardly sleep.

When he wrote to her over OkCupid the day after their evening together, he was almost instantly blocked. Like, within minutes. He had sent the message, logged out, then navigated over to the PBS website to try and distract himself by watching the Fleet Foxes/Joanna Newsom episode of *Austin City Limits*, when he clicked back and logged in again to reread his message—to feel it once more, assess it after the fact—and saw her image had been deleted from her half of their conversation thread along with a message at the bottom reading: "Sorry, m_ss_ngp_eces no longer has an account." At first, Ray was flabbergasted. She wouldn't have deleted her account over him or that message, would she?

Well, no. Of course not. Ever the diligent journalist, Ray opened up Chrome in Incognito mode, confirmed he wasn't somehow logged into OkCupid on it, and typed in the web address specific to her user profile. He saw that it was there, intact, and that little image disappearing act and the business with the deleted account message were just OkCupid's ways of trying to let him down easy or something: white lies by algorithm.

Getting blocked didn't come as a complete surprise considering the strange way she threw him out of her room in the end, but still, it was far from the outcome he wanted. If she was his God now, as she so claimed to be, he thought maybe her pushing him away was a means to draw him closer. Some kind of deific reverse psychology intended to make him prove his dedication to her—his plenary devotion, faith. Because, really, what sort of a God would actually build someone up just to knock them down?

Then there was the other possibility, and one that was a lot more likely, that this Haruka wasn't "his God" in any way, shape, or form. That she was nothing close to that: no angel, no demon, no type of spiritual guide or native to the afterlife whatsoever. She could have just been a girl. A chiflada girl he made up… into some of the strangest role-playing imaginable, but a girl nonetheless.

He had approached his message with this duality in mind. On one hand, she was a girl. That she wasn't even real, that she couldn't have been anything more than a phantasm composited from some Asian co-eds he missed hooking up with in college was beside the point. A girl's a girl. And Ray always reaches out to the girl the day after they first have sex. That it was their first date didn't matter, nor that it was arranged online, fairly strange in the beginning, and beyond strange in the end; it was still an actual date, not something that was supposed to be a one-night stand, and he needed to treat it as such: with a chivalrous follow-up. It's something he learned from TV and movies as a kid. In practice, instead of doing this with the cordial telephone call so many sitcoms and romantic comedies ingrained in him as the go-to gesture, he's done it by sending texts, Facebook messages, and now, because it was the only way he could contact this Haruka, an OkCupid message. He's done it the new way, with chivalry native to the twenty-first century. Then there was the other hand. While unlikely, it was, again, *possible* she could be some kind of physical manifestation of God. God is everywhere. God can be in anything. Anyone. God is God—omnipotent, omnipresent. She sure spoke to him like she knew what was going on with him, his quest. It was hard to reconcile these two things: the girl he was checking in on the day after they had sex and God; to avoid feeling blasphemous or like a loser and strike a balance between post-coital decency, flirtatiousness, divine veneration, fear, and hope. When he wrote her, he wrote this: "Are you there God? It's me, Ray. I'm still trying to wrap my head around what happened yesterday evening. How are you doing? While it was a weird date for sure, I still felt really honest with you, like we were communicating on our own level. Do you still feel the same way as you did last night? Despite all you said then, I can't just let this go. I'd understand if you didn't want to see me again yet, but can we at least talk about it?"

Nope. Blocked.

At first he was defensive. He made it to the weekend sleeping like a baby, dismissing what had happened, her. She was relevant to his quest, sure, but she was not the point of it. There was no way she could actually be God; that encounter was not his final judgment. Instead, she was a projection that God allowed him to create for himself, and that encounter was mostly about getting laid. While it wasn't the start of something steady like he had wanted, it did feel good and had helped restore some equilibrium in his world. The weather was improving and he was riding expeditiously at work, making a lot of runs, bringing home a little more pay. Bill quit, so they hired someone new and now he wasn't dead last on the roster anymore. Things were indeed better. During the rest of that week, he'd keep an eye out for more clues as always while riding, but whenever Haruka crossed his mind, like, say, on a run downtown in NYU territory, or when he'd see someone who sort of looked and dressed like her in his periphery, he would reflexively think about something else. In the evenings it was mostly same old, same old: smoking a little and/or drinking a couple of beers, eating, checking out the journalism job boards for freelance work, maybe playing video games with Brian or by himself, showering, scrolling through Facebook for a minute, watching shit on Netflix and Hulu, reading web articles or a chapter of a book right before bed. The only new aspect to the routine, and something that played further into his defensiveness, was that he'd also occasionally get on OkCupid, looking at other girls... and while he didn't write to any of them, he did save some as favorites. Aside from that, he thought about the quest here and there—didn't try to deflect it like he did her specifically—but it had taken a back seat in a passive pursuit of normalcy.

That weekend, though, with less structure to his days, and a lot more time to just hang out and think, things changed. He couldn't deny her any longer. And she's been with him since.

Saturday was shaping up beautifully. He woke up after nine glorious hours of sleep without the slightest semblance of a hangover from the booze or weed the night before and had a nice, leisurely morning, making himself a big french toast breakfast with banana slices and syrup on top, doing laundry, and reading the online version of *The New York Times*. Brian had gone to visit his parents on Long Island for the weekend so he had the entire apartment to himself. A Grooveshark classical station played over the air from the living room speakers and the springtime sun flooded through the windows. Around 2:00, he made lunch, a hearty chicken quesadilla with brown rice and some guacamole—the avocados purchased as a small reward the evening before after having a more lucrative week—and caught up on some shows he missed from the previous few days. Feeling kind of logy from the big breakfast and lunch, what with his body conditioned to burning the first half of the day's calories off in real time, and knowing the temperature was pretty nice outside, he decided then to go for a walk down to the Long Island City waterfront.

He crossed the street from his apartment and ambled along the outer edge of Murray Playground, passing the dog run, the AstroTurf ball field, and the handball courts at the opposite end, the park alive with people and pets and play. The sun was high and warm. A few minutes and industrial blocks later and he was on the main drag of Vernon, the quaint street bustling with its restaurants, bars, and shops, an old church spire pointing skyward a short distance away. He was more present than he'd been in a long time and feeling good. Mostly he just thought about what was there in front of him, everyone in the neighborhood shaking off protracted hiemal gloom, or the articles he read that morning, the delicious food he had eaten so far that day. Soon he was in condo territory, then shortly after that his destination, Gantry Park, with the Midtown Manhattan skyline in all its glory like a postcard there in front of him.

Then, the first big shift…

It wasn't the city that did it, the panoramic view of where he spends his days, searching. It wasn't the 59th Street Bridge over to the right, the site of that first big déjà vu seven weeks before. It wasn't the Asian girl soaking up the sun in one of the park's weird-looking wave-inspired wooden recliners that, from a distance, vaguely resembled her. It was the water that led him to it. Or, rather, that led it to him… doubt.

The East River smeared the Midtown buildings, the bridge, the sky in its reflection, everything before him together, but blurred, subverted. The impression of these things in that murky gray-blue triggered the memory of Haruka staring at him in the dim blue light of her dorm room, and this time he allowed it to remain. "Hope not ever to see heaven," she had said. "I have come to lead you to the other shore; into eternal darkness; into fire and into ice." Here in Queens, he was on the shore opposite hers in Manhattan, he could see then. It was possible. She could have been God, after all.

Of course, he knew he could have just been indulging himself, going off of complete bullshit, overreaching by miles. Water? The East River, of all things? Huh? Come the fuck on, man. But maybe not. There was a case for it. Just as there was a case for her being some batshit crazy chick he had made up. The point is, there was no way he could know. About anything.

And so standing there, leaning on the guardrail, staring into that water, he let doubt take over, and it brought him closer and closer to her. Until she was there in total. Those eyes. Both staring into his and rejecting his, transfixed by her phone. The phone. As much a part of her as any physical feature of her body; what the deal was with that, really. The way she moved. In bed, almost violently, and out, gliding gently alongside him arm in arm in Washington Square Park. The tone of her voice, like a song when they first sat down at the coffee shop, then furious and piercing at the end as she condemned his soul, expelling him from her room. This little being of such range, tremendous extremes. What was that the other day? What had really happened? Had it even happened? Doubt begot more doubt, and everything came rushing back all at once, no part having been processed in his subconscious since, almost too much to bear.

He walked north along the riparian footpath, hugging the water, trudging slowly forward as he moved over the wooden planks. Other park-goers strolled by; some rode bikes. If she's God, then he could indeed be in hell, he thought. Like she said, it could take a while to *feel* it. But what is hell? This week's been pretty good. And that might not just be her building him up. Does hell have to be so bad? Hell, as he understood it, from that quasi-Catholic upbringing, wasn't about fire and brimstone. That's Middle Ages scaremongering, Dante. The shit she was quoting. From what he'd been able to figure out, hell mostly just means being separated from God. And if she's his God, then that probably isn't so bad. She *was* nuts. So maybe no unpleasantness will hit. Maybe she was talking about him recognizing this separation as being the terrible thing, because from her perspective, it would be. But from where he stands, that could be a very good thing. If his God is more like Satan, then his hell would be more like heaven. There is no more down. Just away. Up, up, and away.

Looking out at the 59th Street Bridge above in the distance, finding the section of it where his quest began, this growing notion that he was in hell hardened fast into belief. Doubt receded as quickly as it came. The reason that first déjà vu was followed by all those warm and happy feelings of freedom was that it was a precursor to this moment—this very, very happy moment! It is no coincidence that the bridge spans the body of water that led him to finally understand. The quest had come full circle. His soul was no longer in purgatory or in limbo, waiting at the edge. It was in full-blown hell. This beautiful, beautiful version of hell, where he made more money, got the apartment to himself on the weekend, and could take nice, leisurely walks in the park. Sure, he never learned the mystery surrounding the circumstances of his death, but it didn't matter; things were good now. This is enough. More than enough. He breathed deep, took one last look at the bridge, the skyline, the water, then turned down a path that would lead him back to the apartment.

There's nothing like belief. Having something to hold onto. This was much better than operating under the previous assumption—and it was only that, an assumption—that Haruka was just another piece of the puzzle. He thought he knew then, but he didn't know anything. This here, this was real. The trangram had been completed. No more missing pieces, m_ss_ngp_eces; everything was right in the world. Goodbye, Haruka.

It was a glorious ten minutes.

Because just as he walked through the front door, his phone chimed and vibrated, and looking down while the door swung shut behind him, he saw a text from Emily asking "You free tonight?" which felt eerily similar to the time he walked through the door of his apartment and the exact same thing happened at the exact same moment. Another déjà vu! Then the cerebral sense of freedom he had been enjoying was immediately replaced by the physical, tingly one that came to mark all the déjà vus on his quest so far. It was this last part that let him know it wasn't over. He tried to rationalize the sensation when he first felt it—of course he would feel déjà vu again; he had felt it before there was any quest, back when he was alive and since, and probably would after—but this thought just ended up being a part of the déjà vu and then that post-déjà vu blissful feeling did him in for good… Full circle nothing, this thing ain't close to over; hello there, again, doubt. He stopped. He took a picture of the entranceway, then himself, a little grainy in the low light, but sharp enough that you could still make out the frown he wore recognizing his mistake. That big, big mistake. A screengrab of the text. All for the EVIDENCE folder—which on the way home, in a passing thought, he had figured he could probably delete, the fool he was.

He wrote Emily back, invited her over… knew he needed to follow that sign, see where this would take him. She said she'd come by around 9:00. Then he dumped the new images in with the old ones on his computer without looking at them or any of the others again, knowing it was pointless.

Instead, he stared at pictures of Haruka. He typed her profile address into Incognito Chrome again and searched her eyes. What would they offer now? Could they be a window to her soul, in pixels? They didn't look like the eyes of God, but that didn't mean they couldn't be; she was more than just a girl, though, that was clear. The mystery they carried went deeper than that enticing playfulness present in most girls' eyes. After staring at the picture of her standing in the street for two uninterrupted minutes, he closed the browser then the computer. This wasn't healthy. No, not at all.

The rest of the afternoon was spent hanging out and passively watching TV, reading a little, then getting the place ready for Emily. He straightened up, thought of a couple of things they could watch on Netflix before having sex. There were a few Criterion Collection options on there and he knew she always liked those. After dinner, he picked up a couple of cheap bottles of wine at the liquor store near Court Square. She rang the buzzer at 9:11.

He let her up without asking if it was her. There was a knock at the door. He opened it. "Hey there," she said. She was wearing a black leather jacket over a white T-shirt featuring the name of some band Ray had heard of but never actually heard—Black Flag—and blue Levi's.

"Hey."

"You don't check your buzzer anymore?"

He closed the door behind her. "I knew it was you."

"How?"

"This is around the time you said you'd be here." They started moving into the living room, toward the couch.

"You've never done that before."

"Yeah, well, Brian's out. That's more his thing. It's his uncle's building. Territorial bullshit, insurance reasons… I don't know."

She took off her jacket and sat down. Ray remained standing. "I could've been anybody. Did you even look through the peephole?"

"No."

"What if I was a mugger or murderer?"

"It's a good thing you weren't, I guess."

She cocked her elbow out onto the armrest, bringing her hand to the side of her face, her fingernails chipped-black, and smiled big. "We'd never do that in Bed-Stuy. You're such a rebel, Ray."

"That's me. Want some wine?"

"Sure."

Then Emily's role became clear. They were around forty minutes into *The Lady Vanishes* and had gone through two-thirds of a bottle of cabernet when they started making out. It was a conservative choice on her part, the film; he thought for sure she would've gone with something foreign or very new. He had actually seen it before, in college, and tried not to dwell on the implications of this or its title when she chose it from his shortlist.

"So Brian isn't coming back?" she asked, after a particularly deep and lasting kiss.

"He said not until Sunday."

She bit her lip. "Let's fuck on the couch."

Ray laughed. He studied her eyes to see if she was serious. She was. "Okay." He kissed her again, then sucked her neck lightly.

"What if he comes home unexpectedly?" She broke away.

"Then I guess we can run to my bedroom."

"Is this your couch?"

"No, his."

"Good. I fucking hate Brian." She sat up and started taking her shirt off. "He's half the reason I haven't come over lately."

"What's the other half?"

"Just been, you know, busy." She undid her bra. Ray hung back for a moment and just looked at her, free and self-assured as the reflection of the black-and-white light from the TV danced over her torso. After a moment her eyes narrowed, head canted slightly. It seemed less like she was waiting for him to act and more like she was wondering why he was just staring at her like there was something on her.

"Nice to see you again, Emily."

"Don't be weird," she said.

He mounted her, kissed her chest for a minute, her eyes fluttering, a closed-mouthed murmur or two coming from the top of the throat. She reached for his crotch. "I'll be right back." He sat up.

Ray went to his room and grabbed a condom, and couldn't help but note the wrapper. He thought about the graphic that had been on Haruka's, the weird power sign thing, then made a conscious effort to block all that out. It was the least he could do for Emily, so easy-going and honest with him—this girl who could take her shirt off and just chill on the couch, who enjoyed with him an arrangement that carried no pretenses. Yes, it was flawed and somewhat frustrating due to its instability and her eagerness to share this part of herself with so, so many others, but still it was what it was. Not many things are like that.

But in the end, he couldn't block the experience with Haruka out: Emily lost, or really Ray lost. After more kissing and a little heavy petting, they started having sex, and Ray could feel nothing. Physically— the emotional aspect having never really been too big a factor with her. Five minutes in, he felt like he was fucking a void. An abyss. His dick weltering with taurine force in and out of a big nothing… Once, junior year in high school, when he was very new to sex and a couple of years away from coming into any real prowess with it, he used an Extended Pleasure condom to help prevent himself from prematurely ejaculating with his then-girlfriend, Daphne, who he had recently lost his virginity to. The condoms contained benzocaine and he went from coming after at most three minutes to faking an orgasm after thirty, out of consideration for her; after she complained of getting sore, he couldn't even tell if he was still in or not. What was happening now was way worse.

Ten minutes and a few couch-centric positions later, he was only able to climax after looking out the window, seeing the Empire State Building, and thinking of Haruka. I wonder if she's seen it tonight, too, he thought. It was lit up in blue. He looked down at Emily, clearly enjoying herself, eyes rolling back, the lids low, her mouth a toothy oval blowing warm wine breath at him. He shut his eyes and imagined her as Haruka. And just like that, he was no longer fucking. That's all he and Emily ever did. Instead, he was having sex. It was strange—what he and Haruka did was harder, rougher, but it still seemed more intimate; much closer to that term, that silly-sounding, mawkish expression that's always bothered him: making love. He moved just as he had with Haruka—like he was trying to save or lose himself, he didn't know which. Looking out through his mind's eye, he saw her staring back knowingly. That's when he came.

Emily fanned herself as he rolled off of her, going, "Wooo!" She shook her head. "Jesus Christ, Ray."

"Yeah, I don't know what came over me," he had said.

The next day, when he used Pornhub to try to masturbate, to see if what had happened was a fluke, nothing and no one could do it for him. No Perfect Tens, no Big Tits, no Big Asses, no Teens, no Latinas, no Blondes, no Anal, no Threesomes. Nothing with girls dirty beyond belief or the ones that could have passed for actual models, so beautiful they really had no business being in porn. Nothing in HD. No POV. Not even his last resort, dangerous for obvious reasons—Asians—had produced anything resembling endorphins or dopamine or really even sensitivity to his own touch. It wasn't until he closed his eyes and thought of her. Then he was coming in no time.

This masturbation problem persisted, until he was jerking off to the thought of Haruka two then three times a day by the middle of the next week and he stopped altogether. The day he didn't do it at all was the day he had his first dream about her, which was, of course, a wet dream. Then that Friday, Emily, still flying high on their last encounter, invited him over to her place, and he thought it would be good, that maybe the change of scenery would be all he'd need; maybe fucking in her Bed-Stuy bedroom would cure him. But it didn't. It was exactly the same as the last time. He fucked her for a good long while, feeling nothing, until he closed his eyes, thought of Haruka, and started to move with all-consuming zeal to gasps and squeals and nails digging in his back and what he assumed were several orgasms until his own. "Oh my God," said Emily. "Oh my God."

Ray's own God had him. He was right where she placed him. He knew it. Now he got it. So, this is what hell's like. That last week, the walk in the park. That was the last of the good times. "Of course there's sex in hell," Haruka had said. Ray got it.

By the end of the weekend, he still hadn't masturbated. That Sunday he dreamt he and Haruka were alone in a dark room together, a circle of pale light surrounding them from some unknowable source. They were naked and standing across from one another, some space between them. For a moment they just looked at each other. Then she pointed at his penis and laughed. He looked down and it was erect. She covered her mouth at first, but then couldn't help herself; she slapped her stomach, almost bowled over, laughing and pointing. The laughter filled the space and seemed to expand it at the same time, until it was infinite. Ray awoke with a start and his penis hard, underwear wet, semen sticking the two together. Now he was having wet dreams without any sex in them, but instead some sort of profound humiliation. It took him almost two hours to fall back asleep afterwards.

The next day he masturbated, only once, but still had a wet dream about her. In that one it started with them having sex but ended with her drowning him in a bathtub filled with his own shit.

And then, yesterday, Tuesday, two weeks to the day after the date, he bought and took some melatonin, hoping it would help him to sleep through the night. The two nights before he had only gotten around four or five hours, between the time it took to relax enough to first doze off then fall asleep again after the nightmares. Riding a bike all day is hard enough; riding one while completely exhausted had led to almost getting hit by something like eleven cars and messing up at least five orders that he had to go back for. He doesn't really know… finally, he's drifting. No, falling. Air rushing by his neck and ears and limbs, but no impact. The heart pounds and pounds. No impact. Never an impact. Just the short sucking of more air and a shot forward until he's back in his room. Another wet dream. No sex in this one, Haruka pushed him off a cliff and the feeling of falling was especially vivid because of the melatonin. He reaches for his phone and checks the time again. It's 4:54, and it hurts to be awake, but not as much as it hurts to be asleep.

▲▽▽▽▽▽

A dancer's body, neat hair, probably gay. Their waiter balances two plates on one forearm and holds the third in the other hand. She thinks that one's hers. The one alone. Yup, that's it: penne with lamb meatballs. It looks good. Haruka can't wait to take a picture of it.

And she doesn't. He places it in front of her and she begins framing the shot with her phone. She takes the first photo without the flash.

"Excuse me," says the waiter. His voice is soft. He's addressing Allison. Her phone's in the way and he can't put down her plate. That happens sometimes. But they should be able to figure it out; that's, like, their job. Waiters can be so rude. Oh well, it's his tip he's messing up.

Haruka's following this in her periphery. Her focus is mostly on taking the second photo, this time with the flash. The restaurant has a rustic-chic thing going on, lit by candles and dim orange overhead lights, and they're a little too low to successfully take a photo naturally. The table goes momentarily white.

"Another bottle, please," says Maeve as her pappardelle with oxtail ragù touches down. The wine's almost gone. That's what they're doing here, really, on this, their last "girls night out" of the school year. Allison heard this place didn't card. Maeve apparently got her fake I.D. taken away at some bar last weekend and doesn't think it's worth it to get another one until she comes back from Vermont in the fall. Next week it's going to be all about dorm and apartment parties, celebrating the end of finals and saying goodbye to everyone until the next school year. Boy, did this semester fly by. The whole year, really. Haruka can hardly believe it's May.

It actually feels good to be here. She never really liked these "girls nights" before, but tonight she's in the mood to celebrate. It doesn't have much to do with school being over or her friends. Those things are nice and all, but she has a bigger reason: This past week she learned she'd landed a paid summer internship! And now instead of going home for the summer, she gets to stay in New York in her dorm room, with her parents paying for most of it! It's all very exciting.

"Of course," says the waiter. He leaves.

The internship is at Tumblr. It wasn't her top pick, or even her second, but it'll do! It'll do! Landing an internship at Google or Facebook your first time trying is nearly impossible. You pretty much have to know somebody. But having Tumblr on her résumé will only help when she tries again next year. Especially with its cool factor. Tumblr's such a young, cool company! Hip. Since she found out, she's started using it more and more again.

Part of the reason she's been able to do that is now she's going on fewer dates—just two or so a week, like old times. School's required most of her energy with finals coming up. She really only has time to take the occasional internet break, not dedicate hours on end to going on dates in between studying. Plus, she knows she's already done a lot of damage this spring. Killed something in a great many of these boys and men.

Their requests for second dates have gotten more and more desperate since she started telling as well as showing. It's hella funny with men. How dumb they are; how much it seems they really hate themselves. There was one guy she called worthless who invited her out to a fancy dinner and a hit Broadway play in his follow-up. *Venus in Fur*. This other, older one offered to take her to Italy for a long weekend. Then there was that journalist, that weird-smelling Ray guy who made her come, which she still can't believe. Stupid chemicals. His message afterwards was *really* pathetic. He wrote it the next day and was still calling her God, and was all like "Can we talk about this?" Seriously. Like he was begging, pretty much. Ha-ha. What a loser. It was enough to make her crush go away, thankfully. Since then, she's told others that she was God, too, but they didn't react that way. They just treated it like dirty talk. She could tell she really got to that one.

This weekend she's going to write her final paper for Professor Towers' class. The last thing they read was *The Metamorphosis* by Franz Kafka. Out of everything they read the whole semester, she liked it the best, because she related to it the most—to the book itself, that is, not to Gregor Samsa. It's how she saw the men after she was through with them: disgusting bugs left to wither and die. Someone, something like her was the cause, she knew. Kafka never said, but she knew. It was like she was reading back her own words. Those are usually the best books. She just got a fresh supply of Adderall and plans on starting the paper tomorrow when she gets up. For now, it's all about the wine and the penne with lamb meatballs and her silly friends.

"Oh my God, this is sooo good," says Allison. She got the potato gnocchi.

Haruka puts down her phone and takes a bite of her food. It's really, really good, but she wonders if Allison's might be better. She hopes not.

"Oh my God, mine too," says Maeve. It would be bad if Maeve's were better than hers, also. "Wanna trade?" She and Allison take bites from each other's plates.

"Oh, wow," says Allison.

"Oh, wow," says Maeve.

They both nod at each other and make their eyes go big. White girls' eyes can get so big it's scary. Allison swallows. "How's yours, Haruka?"

"Oh my God, it's amazing."

"Really?" asks Maeve. They're well aware Haruka doesn't like to share her food. Unless it's an appetizer, she prefers to pick a thing and eat it until it's gone. But they're not like that. It's also a thing on dates.

With the older ones. A lot of them ask to try her entrees, but she never lets them. She's let Maeve and Allison a few times, begrudgingly; just because she was too curious about theirs. If she's not curious, then she doesn't let them. Tonight's a night where she's curious.

"Go ahead, try it." She pushes her plate toward Maeve. Maeve stabs a small sample with her fork and brings it to her mouth. "Here Allison." Allison does the same. Maeve pushes her plate toward Haruka and she takes a bite. The ragù is good but not as good as the meatballs. Relief.

"Oh my God, Haruka, yours might be the best. I'm a little jealous," says Allison. "Here." She nudges her plate forward and Haruka tries a bit of gnocchi. Very rich, tasty. But not quite in the same league as the penne with lamb meatballs. Haruka wins.

"I don't know," says Maeve. "I'm pretty happy with mine." Haruka knows Maeve is just saying that to save face; to try to seem better than she really is, like she had the superior judgment when ordering. Haruka's dish is clearly the best.

"I am, too. But Haruka's… just, wow!" says Allison.

"One thing I'm not happy with, though, is how long this wine is taking to get here. What the hell?" Maeve has finished her last glass, and the bottle is now empty. There's still a little bit left in Haruka's and Allison's glasses. The restaurant is very busy, since it's Friday, and there are only two servers on the floor including theirs because the space itself is pretty small, but she can see where Maeve is coming from. It was only wine. It should have just taken thirty seconds to grab and open. He shouldn't have gone on another food run first, or whatever it is he did. Haruka agrees with Maeve's sentiment, though she knows she only made it to switch the subject away from her defeat.

"I know," says Haruka. "I was just starting to write my Yelp review in my head when I thought: the slow service may cost them a star."

"Right?"

"The food is really good, though," says Allison.

They all nod in agreement, chewing. Then the waiter's back, finally, with the wine, opening it then filling their glasses. "Sorry for the wait," he says, as if he heard them. It's very possible he did. He takes away the empty bottle and leaves the new one in its place.

"Should we make another toast?" asks Allison. Their first toast was to "friendship."

"Sure."

"To the end of freshman year!" says Maeve. Their wine glasses clink. The sips go down. Maeve's a little drunk, it seems.

"Shhh!" Allison swallows, laughs. "They'll know we're not, you know…"

"Who cares? This is our city. These people are here for us. I'm sure half their business comes from nineteen-year-olds who just want a little wine! And we deserve it. We just finished our first year of college, guys. Crazy!"

The waiter glares at them from across the room, but they don't care. They go on laughing. Haruka takes a bite of lamb, pressing it against her tongue, then chews, rolls it around, tastes some more, swallows. Yes, she made the best choice of all. Like she always does. With everything. Human beings make thirty-five thousand choices a day and all of hers are perfect. It even pairs well with the wine. Probably much better than theirs does, too. Maeve and Allison laugh some more. And so does Haruka, but for reasons all her own.

▲ ▽ ▽ ▽ ▲

Take the moment, it's yours. With exactly five minutes until his class is over, not only for the day but for the term and year, he looks out at them. A sea of young faces: multifarious colors, features, shapes, but still somehow the same. A sea whose danger is belied by its calm, some monstrous thing lurking just below the misty surface at all times, ready to drag the unsuspecting captain down into depths black and bottomless. But he was always at the ready, and now he's conquered it—the sea with its leviathan. Steering the ship called the Canon, Emerson sailed intrepid to this shore.

If they truly listened, they are his: they've overcome their hideous nature to become thinking and sentient beings, scholars, and joined him here on land, ready to build their own boats and embark on their own journeys. But if they didn't, he cares not. He's done his part, shared his genius, and that's all he can do. People can change, can rise up out of their ignorance, but only if they so choose. Some terms Emerson feels like taking a bow in this moment, the moment where he looks out, marking the end of another scintillating performance, his tour de force as the fearless captain. But he never does. Instead, he smirks, produces a single clap, and says, "And that, my dears, is your introduction to *literature*. You may have thought you had met it before, but now you really have. If there is one thing I hope you take from this course, in addition, as it should be, to the proper technical training in reading that I have provided for you all, it is this: how to truly be *human*."

Today is Monday. It's the last day of instruction, with the final exam period set to begin Wednesday. There is no final exam here—only a final paper which will be handed in to his TA by 3:00 p.m. Friday. It's worth 50 percent of their grades, the other half coming from the two papers written earlier in the term. Emerson does not factor attendance into his grading. Anyone can show up. That doesn't mean a student was actually there, that they listened; it doesn't indicate that they learned from him and grew... became more human. Attendance means nothing, bodies are not minds.

Once the final papers are collected, they'll be dropped in Emerson's office mailbox, and he'll come in the late afternoon to pick them up. He will start grading them that evening, over wine. Usually the one session is all it takes.

Emerson spent the bulk of this last class going into more depth on Kafka's *The Metamorphosis*. He'd only had time to give one lecture on it, Friday, and any students wishing to choose it as the subject of their final papers would have been at a tremendous disadvantage without having heard his thoughts first. Of course these students are already at a disadvantage in that those who write about Kafka are all but guaranteed to earn at most a B. To get an A, it would not only have to be a superlative paper, but one written in German. Just because he doesn't make them sit through an exam doesn't mean Emerson isn't testing his students. And a student making that choice considering everyone else they've read wouldn't be making the best choice. Writing about Kafka in this day and age is just so easy: the world is more bizarre, senseless, surreal than ever—it would mean the student isn't really exerting themselves; today, Kafka is just too *relatable*. Plus, though Emerson likes the man, he's no Shakespeare, Dante. Truly great papers must be about truly great subjects. But still, it was only fair to spend the time today talking about Kafka.

"Now before I let you go, are there any final questions?" He scans the room from his promontory. No shift, no sea change; there isn't a hand that goes up or a head shaking yes or no, just a few shoulders adjusting weight, a wriggly bottom or two. "This is your last chance, so please don't be shy." Again, he's met with nothing. And this is what typically happens when he asks this, presents an opportunity for one last lesson, which he does at the very end. It makes sense: those who would have joined him at landfall have no more questions. They're ready. And those who haven't joined never had much curiosity to begin with; they just want to get back to flirting with their co-eds in the cafeteria and listening to pop music and playing with their horrible gadgets. Oh the things they could, should ask him. But they never do. Emerson wonders what the breakdown will be from this class… his best guess: there will be one or two A students. Usually he has three or four. He doesn't have a curve or a quota; that's just what time and heuristics have told. But this group has been particularly bad, based on their uninspired, discursive term papers and dull class discussions, so his estimate must be a conservative one. He likes to be right because he usually is.

Over the years he has gotten some questions, from either the staunchly average—those with just enough of an interest and drive to evolve, but not enough to actually do it, the amphibian—or the class clowns, the fools. The former ask well-meaning if dim questions for clarification on something that's been vexing or weighing on them from earlier in the term, some trifle that Emerson might answer briefly, while the latter, well, they just want to delight in their ignorance; they demand a spotlight to giggle and drool: "Do you have any tips to make reading more enjoyable?"; "What do the things we've read here have to do with life today?"; "How can you be so sure about everything in such a subjective medium?" and once, actually, "Do you ever regret spending all your time reading instead of having a life?" He's answered these questions honestly, assured that things would sort themselves out for the nitwits who asked.

But here, again, the response was nothing. One last look at that calm sea: Who has made it to the shore with him? That redheaded boy, maybe. Surely not the blonde girl who sits up front, this subaqueous idiot currently chumbling on her pencil eraser. Perhaps one or more of the quieter students. Probably none of the minorities. Emerson hates to admit it, but some stereotypes are true. The black students tend to be lazy, mostly manifest in their aversion to picking up proper English. The Hispanics, less intelligent: while they can express themselves decently, they rarely say anything substantive. And the Asians disinterested, laconic, which is likely deeply rooted in ancient fears; Qin Shi Huang, after all, helped build his empire by burning books and killing scholars. But, in any event, the proof is always on paper. "Then in that case, go forth! I look forward to reading your work." Emerson turns away from them, toward his TA, making idle chat while the classroom clears.

Except it doesn't. Not all the way, anyway. While everyone else is heading out the door, one student has come down to him. An Asian girl, if it can be believed. She's standing next to the podium with her hands folded over her notepad and a copy of *The Metamorphosis*—a short, slight, pretty thing. If memory serves, she uttered not a peep during the entire course. His eyes pull with concern. Surprise, always short lived for anyone of intelligence, has fast turned into irritation. This is highly unorthodox. Most students know better than to approach him after any class, let alone the last one, to try to ask a private question. His office hours are perspicuously posted in the syllabus. It's like she's trying to share in his glory. This is his time. Not hers. But then he remembers that he has no more office hours… "Yes, dear?" he asks, peering down at her.

"I just want to say, Professor Towers, that I've learned a lot from you. Thank you."

"Well," he laughs a little, tilts his head toward the TA, then back to her again. That was not what he expected. "You're very welcome."

She smiles and turns, then, like the others, leaves. Maybe this group wasn't so bad after all. Or perhaps it's just her. There's only one way he'll know… about her, about any of them: when he reads.

▲▽▽▽▲▽

Another lap won't hurt—Ray's taken to looping around certain sections of NYU during runs that bring him through the Village, searching for Haruka. Sometimes he'll do one. Sometimes he'll do two or three. Like now. He's just finished his second ride around Washington Square Park, and he thought he saw her—a petite Asian girl in understated dress approaching the northwest corner—but, after closer inspection upon turning around, it ended up being somebody else.

He doesn't know what he'll say if he finds her. That's not the point; the point is the finding. Whatever he's meant to say, he'll say. But he needs to find her soon. It's early May and he knows school will be getting out for the year here shortly. Unless she's one of those very rare students who stays for the summer, time is of the essence.

Inside his front left pants pocket his phone buzzes; the sound of the text notification cuts through the country music drifting from his ear-buds, Hank Williams, the same sad old *40 Greatest Hits* album that's been playing on repeat since last week. Probably another downtown pickup. Pulling over to the sidewalk on Washington Square South, he reads:

Dispatch: Client just called. You close? That run was a rush. Should've only taken 20 minutes tops.

"Oh, shit," says Ray. He hightails it over to Broadway and 9th. The package he has contains a hard drive or something going to AOL, a company he had sort of forgotten about when people abandoned AIM for gchat in the mid-aughts, only really remembering it last year after they bought *The Huffington Post*. He's surprised by how nice their New York office is when he gets there: Nineties money, whoa.

Riding the elevator back down to the lobby, he composes his reply to Jeff:

Just dropped it off. Hit a crack pretty hard and had a problem with my chain. Took a few minutes to fix roadside. Where to next?

This is another in a string of excuses he's made for manifold fuckups in the weeks since Haruka started haunting him. He's already used: flat tire, bad traffic, seat came loose, elevator problems, charley horse, bug in the eye, and indigestion, some of these more than once.

The phone vibrates in his hand seconds later:

Dispatch: I think we need to talk. Can you come back to the office?

Well... this should be interesting. Ray's stomach sinks. He's about to get dressed down for his poor performance in a shitty job that's barely worth doing—especially now that the streets don't seem to have any more clues for him, only Haruka—a new low. Pressure builds in his head, his heart pounds. Back outside, he unlocks his bike and rides north.

Yeah, he's made more than a few mistakes lately, but it's not like he could actually be getting fired now, could he? Nothing's gone so wrong it couldn't be fixed. And he's done all the fixing. The streets leading up to Union Square blur in his periphery; what's in front of him is dim, flat, only partly there. This is probably, like, the first of the real strikes. The first sit-down meeting... let's talk about what's going on here, what needs to change, how we can make this work. So far Jeff's just met his excuses with curt acquiescence over text—usually an "ok…"—followed by the details of a new run. There's no way he could actually be getting fired right now. Just a stern verbal warning. Right? On 14th, he makes a right up Sixth. These thoughts play on a loop until he reaches 27th.

When he's out in front of the office, he doesn't quite know how he got there. He knows riding was involved, but it hardly seemed like he was the one pedaling, and it definitely didn't seem like it had only just happened, or maybe ever happened. Space and time had been unnaturally traversed to get here. The feeling in his stomach worsens. He breathes deep, and tells himself whatever he's walking into doesn't even matter: he's already dead, and worse, he's already in hell. Compared to all that, this will be nothing.

Ray rolls his bike through the door. "Hey Ray," says Jeff. He called him "Ray" instead of "Sunshine." That's weird and probably not good.

"Hey, sorry about that back there—"

"Yeah, well…" Jeff clears his throat. "Here, I grabbed a chair from the back. Why don't you sit down?"

Ray nods, rests his bike against the wall. He moves over to the desk and sits. "What's up?"

"This is never fun." Jeff frowns then looks Ray dead in the eye. "I'm sorry to say it's not working out…" Holy shit. Holy fucking shit. Forget all that stuff about already being dead; the what's-the-worst-that-could-happen denial: yes, he's already in hell, but this, this here—Raymond Gonzales, Columbia '08, getting fired from his ridiculous, godawful bike messenger job—is descending into the next circle. Holy, holy fucking shit. This is actually happening. "It's just been too much lately, man."

"Right…" Ray nods, smiles sort of pitifully to one side.

"Nobody has as many problems as you say you've had, Ray. Especially this time of year. It should be smooth sailing out there now that the weather's good. When you started there was snow sometimes, and no problems."

"Again, I'm sorry Jeff. If you give me another shot, I won't let it happen again. I'll deliver everything on time. Early. No more mistakes. I promise. I sort of need this job right now…"

"I like you Sunshine, you're a good guy, but I just can't risk having you out there anymore. Last week, when you were a half hour late to MCB—you know, that law firm on 42nd?—that day you told me you had a stomachache or the shits or whatever, I had to do some major damage control there. Deep discount on their next few runs. We're not the only messenger service in town." Jeff plays with a pen, wiggling it between his forefinger and thumb. If Ray weren't already dead, he'd probably kill himself. "And I don't need AOL calling me asking where their package is when you picked it up from a site less than a mile away."

"I mean, if you've made up your mind then I guess that's that."

"Sorry, Sunshine. I have." The phone rings. Jeff answers "Gotham," then gives Ray the "one-minute" sign with his finger. "Hey, Stu. Yeah, yeah." He turns to the computer and begins typing. "Great, I'll have someone there then, around 4:00." He hangs up, continues typing for a few seconds, and nods back over at Ray. "Where were we? Oh yeah." He pushes over an envelope. "This is your take for your runs today, plus a little bit on top. I know I'm not giving you much notice. So think of it as severance. You might be the first bike messenger in history to get that."

Ray holds on to the envelope, looking it over, not what's inside, just the envelope. He clutches it tight in one hand and sort of shakes it at Jeff, smiling a smile he hopes can communicate a mixture of appreciation and regret, though he's not really feeling these things, just humiliation. He doesn't want to say "Thanks" because it's a weird thing to say to someone who's firing you. "Okay," he says, instead. He plants his feet firmly on the floor, about to stand up.

"And hey, try to spend it wisely, man," Jeff says, catching him before the rise.

Although Ray knows he should leave, he can't help but be interested in what Jeff has just said. He stands but stays put. Tittering, he asks, "What do you mean spend it wisely?"

"We're all the same, here, Ray: fuckups. Me, you, everyone in the fleet. This isn't a job for failed Grand Tour riders. At worst they might work in the shops. It's a job for fuckups. You can't be in this game if you're not one. Why would you? Unless you have a pathological need to ride a bike all day, it's hard, dangerous work for next to no money. But I'm sorry to say I think you're a little worse than the rest of us. That's why I say, spend it wisely."

"I still don't get it."

The phone rings again, Jeff answers—the same routine. To pass the time, Ray counts the money in the envelope; by his calculations, Jeff's given him an extra fifteen bucks. Some severance. "Mm-hmm, mm-hmm. I'll have someone there in around thirty," Jeff says hanging up. Typing the details of the run to send off to someone, he then asks: "You went to college, right? Didn't you say that when I hired you?" He hits enter and squares himself toward Ray.

"Yeah…"

"What college you go to again?"

Ray shifts his weight onto one leg. "I'd rather not say."

"That's right. Because it's embarrassing. You're embarrassed by your station in life now. I've met a lot of guys like you, Ray. Hell, I'm a lot like you. I did a couple of semesters at Brooklyn College back in my day. Sometimes it's true: the bigger they are, the harder they fall. The difference between you and me is I can handle my shit. You can't. It's so obvious I can smell it on you, Sunshine."

"Smell it?"

"I know you're not the only one. But everyone else gets their runs done no problem. So I don't care. If you do this job right, you're in and out with the client in under two minutes and it's probably only the receptionist or mail room anyway and they don't know or care. Maybe you're still sweating out the liquor from the night before. Maybe you wake and baked, or took a little hit out on the road. But still, you throw on some cologne or whatever and get your shit done. Not you. I like getting high, Ray. I like drinking. What's not to like? Sometimes I do my job a little high, too. But you, you're just so damn obvious about it."

Ray laughs. "I've never smoked or drank anything before work or on the clock, Jeff. I swear. I just haven't done laundry in a while." This is true. All of it. Back before he was only getting four hours of sleep a night, he'd at least remember to spray Febreze on whatever he was wearing the next morning. Not anymore; in spending his days going through the motions, he's apparently forgotten a few. "To be perfectly honest, I've just been having some problems with a girl and I haven't been getting much sleep."

"Come on, Sunshine. Give me a break. I don't care if you got dumped by a Victoria's Secret model, you ride one day like we do here and you sleep like a baby, let alone five a week."

"Jeff, I understand why you might have some problems believing me right now, but——"

"Right now you smell like weed and B.O., Ray. You've been forgetting shit all the time. You make up the lamest, most bogus excuses when I check in… I'm not trying to ride you here. If you need help, you should get it. You know? This is me talking to you as a friend."

"Holy shit, I can't believe this."

"That's what I said when you told me you got stuck in an elevator the day after you told me your seat broke."

"Right." Ray nods. "I get it, man. No hard feelings. I've appreciated the work." He extends his hand. Jeff does the same. They shake on it.

Ray moves over to the wall and grabs the handlebars of his bike. He starts to roll it toward the door.

"Good luck with everything, Ray. I mean that." Ray stops. It's bad enough he was fired. And he could handle being told he was a bigger fuckup than all the other degenerates that make up the fleet here; in a way, he is. But to be told "Good luck" walking out the door after all that, plus "I mean that"; it's just, it's just too much. Like a double good luck. A double insult. Jeff's never been this much of a dick before. Never been so fucking Old New York-condescending. Maybe there's something else going on here.

Turning, Ray says, "Tell me something, Jeff."

"Shoot."

"Are you a demon?"

"Huh?"

"Are you—a *demon*?"

Jeff holds his hands behind his head, fingers locked, elbows out. "Fuckin' A, man. What else are you on? Crack? PCP?"

For a moment Ray looks at Jeff. Like, really looks at him, the underside of his eyes narrowing a little. If Jeff is a demon, he probably won't admit it. This much Ray knows about Jeff. But that doesn't mean Ray can't suss out the truth. "What can you tell me about Haruka? Is she God or Satan or neither?"

"You better not be going postal on me here, kid. Fair warning: I can defend myself." Jeff lowers his hands, placing them under the desk, out of sight. Maybe he keeps a shotgun down there or something. A knife. Ray doesn't really care.

"Or is she just like, *a* god? And not *the* God?"

"I don't know what the hell you're talking about."

Ray looks him up and down one more time. Jeff's hands stay hidden. He's probably a demon, but a minor one. He's done his part. "Okay."

"Now get the fuck outta here."

"All right," says Ray. Then he's gone.

▲ ▽ ▽ ▽ ▲ ▲

Rarely does it happen this way, that such words come so easily, words that already seem there—fully formed, perfect, real. But Emerson can't know for sure now; they're still trapped in the monitor. The damn thing's doing it yet again.

Another grunt, another groan—it's no use; his fingers are just too large.

What to do now? Retrieve the typewriter? If he chose to rewrite what he had just written using the trusty Royal HH, he'd probably have to keep going with it draft after draft until the very end, abandoning the computer completely. He knows himself too well. As fun as it might be to relive his youth in such a way, bring his writing process full circle, it would be a wildly inefficient method by which to get the job done. He'd for sure run the risk of Weisman dying before he finished. Also, more importantly, this isn't supposed to be about his youth; it's about his reading life in its entirety, an ode to and a lament for all of literature, the highest of all the high arts, the best of the best in all of culture. Should he just go out and buy another printer? Perhaps. It's a thought. That would probably make the most sense. But then again, the things are heavy, and he is old.

That's something that can't be ignored: his age. He decided to put in some work on this sunny Tuesday because, with lecturing behind him, he now has a pocket of uninterrupted time before he'll have to grade papers Friday, and every single day counts. But there was no intention of actually *writing* yet. He thought it would be more of a brainstorming session—something broad, not even organizational. When he sat down at his desk, it just came out. Like he was speaking directly from the heart: a heart that had just been broken; a big, beautiful heart that had lost everything but its voice, as eloquent and fervid as ever speaking its last words. And it has! Oh, has it!

What he wrote is good, that is clear enough, but greatness is the goal here—a work canonical in and of itself. Could he have reached those heights entirely off the cuff? If only the first page hadn't jammed. The anticipation! Maybe if he prods at it with the letter opener, he can slide it out. Then reprint. It might work.

He grabs the blade, pokes inside. Grumble, grumble… a low growl. Nothing. Maybe he should hurl the thing out the window. Yes, defenestration is more than warranted now! It actually, statistically, jams more than it prints these days.

Twirling the opener and trying the other side—even though it's exactly the same—he realizes the printer problem could be symptomatic of something even greater. There simply can't be any more interruptions like this: no more hiccups, no noisy coughing as he stands at the Culture's grave and says goodbye. The work to be done is too important; it demands to be carried out with lapidary dignity. And here he is, bent over this shoddy piece of junk, trying to fix it with a tool designed for a completely different task, like a fool, like an oaf! No, worse… he's more like a hungry ape, dipping a stick into a mound of ants! His words are supposed to burn with the glory of stars, not be stuck in a hole befitting filthy ants! He shouldn't have to worry about something as stupid as fighting against technology, struggling against that which was invented to make life easier; he shouldn't have to fritter over anything remotely like this, really. No distractions. His mind, all his energy this summer must be focused solely on The Thing. He should be like God, creating the heavens. And his human concerns should be taken care of. They should be addressed the instant they arise—no, anticipated. What Emerson needs is an assistant.

He sits back down, thinks. Does he dare?

He's taken on assistants while working on books in the past, but never because he actually needed them; instead, he wanted them. And did he. With every inch of his being.

The affairs, which he also carried out with the occasional TA, weren't those of the clichéd middle-aged college professor abusing his power with nubile co-eds for the sake of carnality. Emerson's motivations resided on a much higher plane, a place of purity, one deeply rooted in the fundamentals of education itself. The inspiration behind them came from no less than those widely regarded as the chief architects of Western Culture as we know it: the Greeks. A mentorship should be no breezy thing. To provide the best education, the protégé must submit to the mentor fully. Intellectual submission isn't enough. Sexual submission is what's required. It means that the pupil has placed all of their trust in the teacher, has opened themselves up to receive them, all of them; without the meeting of bodies, there is a barrier between the minds. Only through somatic intimacy can a student be yours completely. This is what the ancient Greeks knew.

While he found certain specifics of how those early teachers carried this out incredibly disturbing, Emerson saw the principle behind it as a thing of great beauty. He likes to think that what they did was a byproduct of the times, that if education had been accessible to young women then, that the best teachers, those like he is now—Socrates, Aristotle—wouldn't have been pederasts, but instead, like him, would have picked out the best of the fully flowered females as the students to provide their most significant lessons. They were probably just making do, like brutes in prison. Because it just makes more sense, it's more logical, that the ideal form of this relationship would take place between the sexes: the passing of knowledge is, after all, an act of creation, the lesson like spermatozoa, the mind of the pupil a fecund womb, making something, a synapse, where there wasn't anything before. The knowledge, like DNA, is passed, gestates, then takes on a life of its own: growing, flourishing, perhaps creating new knowledge itself. There is no greater purpose in this world than the creation of life. And so, Emerson approached these relationships as no mere flings; they were carried out with an occupational duty and an almost spiritual intensity, as a matter of immense import.

His identity was not only defined by his enormous stature as a critic, but personally through these mentorships. His role as a professor was never as vital; the classes he taught were always a means to an end, though he did at least make it a point to learn all of his students' names then, if only as a matter of consideration: for through his writing he could reach the most people, and through these mentorships he could have the greatest effect on a single individual's life. And he did. The young ladies all went on to do great things; the knowledge they gained from working intimately with him aside, at the height of his career, the right recommendation from him would shoot them to the top of publishing or academia, whichever they chose. Through their bodies, they got to truly know his mind: it was a far from even trade, weighted heavily in their favor, of course, but still, it was an arrangement that worked.

As time went on, the more important these affairs became to him: the young women like Russian dolls, each taking up more space in his heart than the last. He became obsessive, then careless. Diana found out about the sixth one. They worked through it; eventually, she forgave him and she picked up the mantle as his assistant on the next project, helping him out here and there when she could while he worked from the family home in Westchester County, cooking for him, finding the occasional quotation. But it wasn't the same. The primary role of his assistant was always an object of desire; he, again, did not need them—he could find his own passages, order takeout, and he had all of the energy in the world to do so then—he wanted them. He wanted them to give him sponge baths, to dance for him, to reward his very loins with release after finishing a stubborn section or chapter. And Diana was his wife: he liked her best that way, cherished her in that role, uncompromised; the one time he essayed to make a move, she shirked away, asked him what he was doing, said she hadn't showered yet that day. She needed no education from him, already knew his mind. Neither party had skin in the game. Then there were the kids. It was beyond difficult working from home with the kids; writing well with children in the house is damn near impossible, even for a genius like him. So before the first draft was halfway complete he found himself staying back in their Carnegie Hill pied-à-terre, writing late into the night, working alone. That is until the temptation became too strong and opportunity too easy, and there was the seventh, who Diana also found out about, then her own affair, and the eighth, until, finally, they were done.

In addition to significantly poorer, the divorce left him an emotional wreck, and he hasn't had a romantic relationship or even a female TA since. Not to mention, the scandal forced him to resign at Columbia and move on to the far lesser NYU, where they relegated him to teaching basic 101 courses, making matters so much worse. He had a violent reaction to the whole thing, and has chosen to live the last twenty-five years with a sort of literary asceticism, devoted only to his books and himself, keeping his students at an even greater distance, which is why he no longer bothers to learn their names. For the first few years it was tough, but now he doesn't remember what he's supposed to be missing. If a commercial for Viagra comes on the television while he's in his bedroom watching the local news or *60 Minutes*, he'll change the channel; it all just seems so obscene. Old men riding motorcycles with fawning brunettes prancing about and the like. It could still be his reaction, it could be the advancement of age, or a combination of these among other things, but the entire concept of sexual intercourse just seems gross. Still, he will take on no pretty young thing as his assistant for this final project. Who knows what would happen if they got deep into the process and the memories began to rush back.

He would just hire his current TA, Kevin, the dopey-faced lad, but he vaguely recalls the boy mentioning something about how he would be spending his summer in the Catskills or Berkshires or one of those nearby mountainous regions, where he was apparently raised. While he isn't particularly fond of Kevin, he would have been fine to do things like make coffee, order lunch, and carry out the assorted research tasks that might make his life easier. Maybe he should check; maybe he would cancel his summer plans for the opportunity to work with him on a book. Lord knows the young ladies would have in the past. No, no… This is just laziness. This is just desperation on account of that obstinate first page. Honestly, he knows the boy is not worthy of working on this, his last, and what he is sure will be greatest, book. In fact, he hasn't had a TA in years that would be. No. Instead, he'll have the boy put out a job ad for him… in *The New York Times*! He'll get someone actually qualified.

Emerson turns to the computer and opens up Internet Explorer. He logs into the NYU portal and writes an email to his TA outlining what he'd like done, just one last task before dropping off the final papers, thanking him and promising a nice recommendation whenever he might need it. That should be enough. He'd like to hold interviews at the beginning of next week, to start immediately. Of course the candidates must look good on paper, must have excellent résumés, superbly written cover letters. But in addition to that, he's going to leave this page jammed here in the printer: it will be like Excalibur, and if enough worthy young men make it far enough, the one who pulls it out will be Arthur, he the God to be served.

So what to do in the meantime? He can't just waste these next three days. Should he simply keep going on the computer, no printing, no reading back? That hasn't been the way he's ever worked. The process of getting any given section or chapter to first draft has always been: write, edit on the page, rewrite, move on. Even when it was on the typewriter. No, he needs the words to be there physically. But he's already ruled out the typewriter. So what's left? Longhand? Technically, it would be on the page. But he's never much cared for writing longhand and never written anything serious that way… handwriting is just so crude, and his, though he hates to admit it, especially so. He knows the principal strength of what he did today was its emotion, how it came from the heart and all, but in the past he'd even write love letters on the typewriter. The authority of the typewritten page, that's what suits him. But… what else is there? But, but, but… This is no time to dither. No time to be picky. Longhand… it's all there is. He'll rewrite it that way then keep going until he gets access to a printer again. Maybe it won't be so bad. Most everyone who wrote anything worth a damn throughout history wrote it longhand first, after all—typewriters were only invented in the mid-1800s. And there have been few canonical works since. So, maybe this happened for a reason. Perhaps the Muses are exhorting him to write the whole thing this way. It will likely be faster than his hunt and peck method of typing; his assistant can transcribe the sections as they're completed. He'll be able to work at twice the normal click. By God! The page jamming was a blessing in disguise. Now he'll definitely complete it before Weisman dies, and what's better, it will be composed like all of the other great works it will mourn and celebrate: by a pen, a great hand guiding it.

▲▽▽▲▽▽

Halfway across the bridge he stops. It feels about right, this spot, roughly where he began his true descent. Ray looks out through the fence: there's Roosevelt Island, Astoria, the Triborough and Hell Gate Bridges a few miles north in the distance, hazy but still a little brighter, a little clearer in the mid-day May sun than they were during that mid-March dusk. The Hell Gate… right. Now he gets it—that Queens connection. He follows the shoreline. A lot of parks, projects: places for *the people* in this part of Queens. Heaven is for the holy, hell is for *the people*. From Queensboro Bridge Park, his gaze shifts back to center and the dusty rufescent brown chain link fence momentarily pops back into focus—its color not unlike that of dried blood, a darker version of the still coagulating reds covering the arches over on the Hell Gate and Roosevelt Island Bridges; except for the Triborough, which is the cool blue of a corpse in livor mortis, the paths to Queens seen here are all seemingly slathered in blood—before his eyes can adjust to their target, the slowly moving water below. Several boats travel in either direction. He looks down through the three-or so-inch crack separating the fence from the concrete at his feet. The current appears to be flowing south, though it could be north. Slight vertigo ensues. The direction of the East River's flow changes, switching up to four times a day because it's not really a river; it's a tidal strait. Its name is a lie. But so many things are.

Ray looks up, first back to the northwestern Queens panorama, then all the way to the sky, his neck craning, skin tight over his Adam's apple, his head extra heavy because of the helmet. A few fluffy cumulus clouds float from west to east. Are these clouds just clouds or teasing reminders of the heaven he'll never see? He can never know. The only thing any-one can really know for sure is that you can't really know anything for sure. If you're lucky, you can get half the truth. As a former fledgling journalist, he'd be the first to admit as much, and that's why he had always favored the gonzo approach more than anything: his namesake, that which he was born into. Experience with a thing was all that could be trusted, as close to verity as you could get. Fully objective journalism isn't really possible. Every word choice is subjective, tells one thing and ignores an alternative. A good journalist can only do the best they can do—sort of like a good person. Was he a good person? Apparently not. But he thinks he was a decent journalist. That's why, he realizes now, in the afterlife, the state of journalism has only gotten worse; it's specific to his sentence. That's why his beloved gonzo approach has been perverted so that everything is injected with opinion, but not in the pursuit of truth, instead in the pursuit of a reaction and page views, clicks, advertising revenue. Who knows where it will go now that he's actually been damned.

Another cyclist zips by. The gust of wind snaps Ray back to; he turns sharply and watches as the cyclist tears down the path toward Manhat-tan. If he were that guy, if he weren't himself, he'd hate himself right now: this dickhead standing with his bike on the wrong side of the path, *his* side of the path, partially occluding it, having just gotten lost in the sky like the dome was a giant version of his own navel. Although, he already hates himself. If he weren't already dead, he would kill himself— that was a thought as Jeff was firing him twenty minutes ago. There are some pedestrians approaching from the Manhattan side, people he must have passed before, but they probably won't hate him. Walkers walk, and can walk around; they don't have the single-mindedness, the inertia of the cyclist. The ride here was a blur. Like before, like after Jeff had told him they "needed to talk." All he was able to notice were the two ghost bikes, the one at 36th and Sixth, then the other on 58th a few minutes ago, leading up to the bridge. Fuck. That really happened. He really got fired. Still in shock, lunch-hour Manhattan streaked by. He didn't plan on stopping here. It just feels like the right place to be now.

One thing that Ray had been looking forward to in solving the mys-tery of his own death was reexperiencing the death itself through under-standing the circumstances surrounding it, since he has no recollection of it. If he had indeed gotten hit by a car while crossing the street looking into his phone, he would've gotten to relive it, feel it: staring at a text or whatever web page as it lit up the screen, a blaring horn, the car inches from him right there as he looked up in the last split second, his body flying upwards at impact, squealing brakes, the crash of his head against the windshield, some dull sensation shooting across then spreading all over his head, flight in the opposite direction, his body landing hard on the asphalt, followed by the crack of his skull right behind, the sight of the street and grit and tires of the car that hit him stationary at odd angles, never-before-felt debilitating pain, blood warm and deep and metallic on his tongue as it rises up from inside, the legs of people surrounding him, their voices, a siren in the distance, then everything dimming, receding—the street scene; the taste of blood, so much blood now; the smell of it, too, and of the exhaust and the thick urban air; and that terrible pain, thankfully, also going away. Maybe a montage in the dark, a feeling of great peace washing over him: it was short but sweet, life, I had a good run. It was beautiful. Now it's over. Goodbye… Or if it had happened by some other means, he would've experienced that. The only way he wouldn't remember it is if it happened in his sleep, like if he had died of that prescription drug cocktail he thought was possible but not plausible when he experienced the third déjà vu on 8th Street or, say, carbon monoxide poisoning. But that still wouldn't make it right. Since he was a teenager, in a sort of morbidly romantic fashion, he had always looked forward to the experience of dying someday. He hoped and figured, like most people, it would happen in old age, lying in a comfortable bed, with family at his side. He wanted that moment. Or something like it. Even serial killers get last words. To be a conscious dead being now but denied any memory of this sensation or even the circumstances surrounding his passing seems unjust, cosmically cruel.

Ray takes his helmet off, hangs it from his bike's handlebars, and looks back down to the water. A few more boats skim about here and there, it's a grayer hue than the sky. He still can't tell which way it's actually flowing. Maybe he should die another death: claim the moment that had been denied him. He's already in hell after all. Worst case scenario, he descends into yet another level. Big deal. He's probably going there eventually, anyway. Might as well get it over with. Best case scenario, his reclamation is rewarded—the derring-do demonstrated by taking what was his allows him to ascend back to the first level, maybe even back to limbo or purgatory. It's not that he'd get his shitty job back; he wouldn't want it. But something else nice could happen. Maybe he'd forget he ever met Haruka. Maybe he'd get an email from an old colleague and he'd get to work as some sort of journalist or media professional again. His fingers grip the fence. He looks in both directions.

Nobody's around. There are cars on the other side of the guardrail, but there always are, and they're moving fast enough that they shouldn't be paying attention to him. He wants to be alone for this and he is. Is this his moment? What should he think about as he climbs? His life or the first five years of death, everything since? His life. No, both. He's closing out both. Is it weird to try to manufacture your own life-passing-before-your-eyes thing? Isn't that a cliché? And if not, shouldn't it just happen? No, this act is about control. Fuck the notion of cliché. This is about him. Memories flood his mind as he ascends the four metal rungs of the guardrail buffering the bottom half of the fence, some of which he chooses, some flowing from those: his mother holding him close as a toddler while wearing his favorite shirt, his Snoopy shirt, how there could be nothing better in the whole wide world; his father teaching him to ride a bike with no training wheels, the terror when he let go, then that exhilarating first feeling of gliding, truly gliding, like he never wanted to stop; climbing the live oak in his front yard, so many other wonderful trees in those years, rough bark leading to gentle breezes whispering through the leaves; hide-and-seek with his sister and cousins, how big his tía and tío's little house could seem then, and how small he could become in those hidden dark places; Super Soaker fights with his little brother, where fast feet, cool streams, and loud screams were the only things that could beat the intense summer heat; his first kiss, Matilda, who tasted like strawberry lip gloss, feeling her face and hair with his fingertips, how much she seemed to like that; high school baseball practice, trading lighthearted barbs with all the other boys trying to act like men there kicking up dust with their cleats; Texas sunsets so orange and so vast, the desire to go out somewhere and burn as brilliantly, how life-affirming they could really be; the smiling faces of college friends and lovers surrounded by sweet, diaphanous smoke, laughing; bright New York nights where anything seemed possible and occasionally was; the covers of books he's read, all his favorites; his hands at work, writing in field notepads, typing; the mural downtown of God and Adam… then Haruka. Fuck. He's actually on the fence now, near the top, about to do it, he need only hoist himself over, and there's Haruka. Grinning. She's in the dark with her phone in her hand waving it at him. No. Think about Mom. The last time you saw her. Over a year ago. Go back to your mother for rebirth. And jump, pussy, jump. Jump! But… he'd certainly have time to think in mid-air while falling. What if Haruka comes back before he hits the water? And what if it takes him a few minutes down there to drown and die again? His last thought could be of her?

Or thinking about thinking about her? Why not think about his first love, instead? He didn't even use her name then. Just "first love." What the fuck is that saying? Why does this Haruka girl get so much fucking ownership over his soul? He can't do it. He just can't do it.

Ray descends the fence, hops down off of the rail. A cyclist en route to Queens fast approaches. Ray's hands tremble. The cyclist gives him a dirty look as he rides by—probably thinks he's just some jerk, screwing around. Little did he know. He would've seen him jump. Would've totally fucked up his day, probably. Not that it matters. The cyclist is either a phantasm or a fellow lost soul… maybe a demon. Wait, is he himself a demon now? Are all those in hell demons? Certainly they should have the potential. A demon would've jumped. A demon wouldn't have cared. He would've yanked that phone right out of Haruka's hand and stuffed it up her ass or down her throat, or both, wiping that smile clean off if she interrupted his vision. Then, flipping one last time in the air, he would've seen the Midtown Manhattan skyline and imagined a nuclear bomb going off, blowing the whole fucking thing up; no, worse: he would've seen the entire world in flames, the universe disintegrating. No, Ray's no demon yet. But maybe he should be. Maybe he should lean into this hell. Real hell. If you can't beat 'em, join 'em.

He gets back on his bike and reaches for his helmet. Instead of putting it back on, he takes it and lobs it over the fence. It spins slowly as it falls out of view. His hope is that it hits somebody passing under the bridge in a boat. But he doesn't stick around to check. He rides on to Queens.

Before he gets home, Ray stops by 5 Pointz in pursuit of spray paint. He wants to steal some. He would've done it at a neighborhood hardware store, but those are more elusive in Long Island City now that all the blocks are getting bought up to make way for more shoddily constructed condos. There's a guy on a tall ladder painting what looks like a pissed-off light bulb. He's got one can of yellow paint and another of black up with him, and a bucket full of unattended cans below. Ray goes through them looking for white.

"Hey!" the guy hollers once he realizes someone's rummaging through his shit. "What are you doing?"

Ray finds it. "I need this." He gets back on his bike.

"The fuck?!" says the guy. He starts climbing down the ladder but before he's even a third of the way down Ray's gone.

At the apartment building, Ray goes through the vestibule then down a set of stairs and out back, where the tenants all take their garbage and recycling. It smells like decaying food and other putrescible waste. A swarm of flies gyres around the trash bins on his way to the recycling receptacles, where he finds several cardboard boxes and breaks them down. He lays them on the ground away from the bins, places his bike on top of them, and begins to paint it white. All of it. Not just the frame—the wheels, the seat, the handlebars: the whole shebang. Once the left side is done, he flips it over and paints the right. Then he slides everything over to the fence separating the building from the next one over, the one his room faces, and, using makeshift newspaper gloves, he props it up on top of the cardboard, releases the kickstand, and locks it to the fence so it can dry. Now it looks like one of the ghost bikes he can't help but notice so much lately. "I shall call you Ghost Horse," he says to it. He goes inside.

The building is still. All of his neighbors are out at work. Motherfuckers. Pendejos. Inside his apartment, light pours through the windows at slanted angles. He looks out. The fluffy opalescent clouds seem to be mocking him. The Empire State Building, too. He flips it off, then the clouds.

He goes into the bathroom, opens the cabinet under the sink, and takes out his hair clipper kit. The kit was a gift given to him in college when, after a trip to a rude barber, he started cutting his own hair with scissors to mixed results. His girlfriend at the time, Hannah, gave it to him. He became very good at it very fast. The clippers were the best thing to come out of that relationship. First he buzzes his hair using the 1/2-inch comb. It falls, onto the floor, sink, toilet—in clumps and by single strands. Next he detaches the comb and uses the blade alone. A few of its teeth are missing, leaving a few patches of hair here and there in strange thin stripes, but they don't last long. He just goes back over what he missed with the good section of the trimmer. To finish his head he employs a Mach3 disposable razor—the blade part he's had for a couple of months, the handle since before he died: then he is completely bald. After this he removes all of his body hair. Well, almost all of it. He doesn't touch his eyebrows. Without them, his face wouldn't be the same, and he doesn't want that. He doesn't want to be someone else. He wants to be himself, but glabrous, better equipped to deal with his environment. Now he's starting to look like it: the demon he's become. And a baby. The baby he's always been. Part demon, part baby. A big baby demon. But everything else goes. First with the Wahl, then with the Gillette. There wasn't too much hair to begin with. The chest, arms, armpits, legs don't take long. The pubic area is a little more stubborn. And his scrotum and anus require the utmost care. But the whole operation is over within minutes. He throws the Mach3 away once he's finished, spitting on it. Then he sweeps up his hair and throws that away, too, also spitting on it. After that he showers and draws a bath, in that order. It'll be the first bath he's had in years. While the tub fills up, he goes to the kitchen, takes some of Brian's bourbon—good shit, Bulleit—and pours the equivalent of a shot in the water before taking a swig himself. The tub hasn't been cleaned in a very long time. Soaking there, he thinks about Haruka for a bit, then masturbates. But he doesn't imagine himself having sex with her; instead, he's having sex with an ungulate, winged demon woman, whose face sort of looks like Sheeva's from Mortal Kombat, on top of a pile of bones. He cuts off her head with one of the sharper bones and fucks the head and then the stump at the thrapple as she bleeds out. It works; he comes. The sperm, having no hair to get stuck to, slides down the drain with bits of grime and dirt that remained on him after the quick shower. Though he knows there's more than enough dirt still there. Baths don't really get you any cleaner. You just swim in filth. Now he's ready.

Before he leaves the bathroom, he sullies Brian's toothbrush. He sees it, grabs it, and clenches its handle between his butt cheeks for a few moments while admiring himself in the mirror, flexing his chest, arms, abs. The bristles face outward, but only because he doesn't want Brian's tartar or plaque or tongue and buccal germs touching his gleaming, beautiful skin. He unclenches and lets it fall to the floor. Turning and looking down at it, he notices a little after-ejaculate wetting the tip of his penis. He takes some onto his fingertips and, picking up Brian's toothbrush with the other hand, rubs it on the bristles before putting it back in its place. "Brian must have nice white teeth for work," he says. Then he washes his hands, dries himself off, hangs the towel up, and goes out into the hallway. He's decided to spend the rest of the afternoon nude.

Returning the bottle of bourbon to the kitchen, he takes another swig. He struts into the living room and sees the Empire State Building again, along with some more clouds. Near the window he stops and waggles his penis at them while making a foul face, mocking them this time. He erupts in obstreperous laughter then goes to his room. The room is cool and a little dark. He makes no effort to turn on any light, so it stays that way. Grabbing his MacBook off of his small desk/nightstand, he sits on top of his bed, against the wall, then places a pillow on his lap followed by the computer on top of it. He opens the computer.

In the tub he had had a revelation. He's going to use his demonic powers of duplicity to arrange a face-to-face with Haruka. If she's God, she'll see it coming and won't let it happen. If not, then she is but a demon like him, and he need not fear her. He will tell her she's not as smart and powerful as she thinks she is, and then maybe he'll steal her phone and destroy it in front of her. It will be fun. But more than that, there will be no more reason that she should haunt him.

The plan: he's going to create a fake OkCupid account using photos of this guy he's Facebook friends with who's a model, some guy from his freshman year dorm who dropped out after he started picking up steam in the fashion world. The photos will be candids pulled from Facebook, not any of the guy's professional or portfolio shots, which will not only give them an air of authenticity but will also be untraceable through Google's reverse image search. He'll fill the profile out simply, making the guy out to be a bit of a naïf, which he in fact was, and then he'll send out a jaunty introductory message intended to make Haruka see him as sweet man-meat, someone she'd undoubtedly want to go out with.

Yes, this is the plan, and sitting there in bed nude during the middle of the day, the taste of stolen whiskey on his lips, this is what Ray does.

▲▽▽▲▽▲

Really, she shouldn't be here. She's got her statistics final tomorrow, plus she wants to give her *Metamorphosis* paper one last look before she prints it out. Read it backwards so as to avoid mistake blindness. But still, here Haruka is, waiting. This one was just too hard to resist.

It's not because of his looks. He's easily one of the most handsome guys that's contacted her over OkCupid, but that's only a small part of why she wanted to meet him. Most of the best-looking guys she's been with were the worst at sex. You would think it would be the opposite because they should have more experience. But that's not the case. No one's ever made them get better from the time they first started having sex because they are too pretty, so all their experience just amounts to rote motions. She can only expect complete mediocrity from this tall, blonde, blue-eyed, oh-so-chiseled creature. No, the main draw is not about the pleasures of the flesh, but instead her greater purpose. Feeding the soul in the midst of finals. A nourishing break.

The message he sent her two days ago was just so upbeat and optimistic: "Hey there!! I see you like coffee. Ever been to Cafe Reggio downtown? It's one of my faves. I'd love to get you a cup of coffee there sometime! Are you free this week?" Those introductory exclamation points. Using one of the most humdrum parts of her profile to start the conversation—I mean, who doesn't like coffee? The familiarity implied with "faves"; how he'd "love to" do something with her. Not to mention he asked her out in the very first message. It's, it's, it's just all too much! No, she hasn't been to Cafe Reggio, but she's looked it up on Yelp now. It seems okay, even though some people call it a tourist trap. She couldn't think of a better place to meet a guy like him. Honestly. But that's not what she agreed to, where she is. No, they're going to keep it simple. On her turf.

She's meeting him at the Au Bon Pain on 8th and Mercer, where she meets most of them these days. They'll order, walk, talk, fuck. He'll be gone in an hour, but she will never leave him, of course.

He's now close to seven minutes late. Five minutes was one thing, but seven is too much. He better get here soon! Typical someone so handsome wouldn't be on time. She hasn't ordered yet: she's just sitting there, waiting, looking at her phone. He said he'd pay, after all.

He has no idea.

▲▽▽▲▲▽

Just a few more minutes and he'll approach; considering the little epiphany he's now had here, he wants to try to think this all the way through first... plus she looks up from time to time and it's been nice to see her squirm. It's nothing compared to the cold sweats, the nightmares, the horrors he's been through. God? That there's no god. She's been but a succubus all this time; what Ray's figuring out now is the extent of just what that means.

When she asked to meet at the Au Bon Pain on 8th and Mercer instead of the quainter, if a little touristy, coffee shop closer to her dorm that he suggested, he thought for sure she was onto him. That she'd stand him up, look down from on high, and laugh. Look at this chump, falling for such an obvious gag. But still he had to try. There was nothing else to do. Maybe it's where she meets all of her dates, he thought.

Maybe he really did waste all that time riding around those NYU blocks when he could have just hung out here on a weeknight. Well, it turned out she probably does and he for the most part had. Because at 6:30 on the dot she appeared on the other side of the window, wearing a short tungsten-colored dress, looking more done up than she did on their date. He watched her from the corner behind a large newspaper, occasionally sipping his coffee, like a caricature of a twentieth-century spy, vindicated.

But aside from being a demon, who was she, really? This is what he wants to know. Thankfully, he at least knows himself again. The real Ray.

There was a moment right after she walked through the door that weighed on him with a certain disorienting sadness. His stomach sank, throat rose then gulped. It was *her*. The girl he's been thinking about nonstop—awake and in dreams—for damn near a month. And there she was. He knew, really, he should have only felt anger—he'd lost so much because of her: sleep, his job, what was left of his sanity—but sadness is a funny thing. It visits a person when it wants. But he wasn't a person. He was a demon; he should have felt no sadness at all. Only insensate hatred, want. Which could only mean he wasn't actually a demon. Had never been. These past few days, he's just been playing a part. A part she, through sophisticated chicanery, tricked him into tricking himself into playing. And he went Method on that shit.

Before, in the tub, when this plan of deceiving her into meeting him appeared before him, he couldn't see what her showing up would actually mean. He had been trammeled by demon logic, which doesn't involve much real logic at all. Demons don't really think; they just do—hatred and want too hot for reason. Her coming here meant that, because she was not God, then she could not have ever condemned him to hell. Thus another reason he couldn't have been a demon. Demons can exist in purgatory or limbo, just as they exist on Earth, but they are there to test the soul of the sinner; the sinner couldn't become one himself. He was still a man, one who hadn't descended into hell after all. His sadness showed him this.

So he's still Ray, still a person. He just looks a little funny and has a few more things to atone for now. Oops. But he trusts the mix-up happened for a reason.

The current working theory is that God, the real God, put all of those déjà vus in place, the events that would lead him to believe he had gone to hell, everything, in order to guide him here right now to defeat this demon Haruka. His demon, Haruka. But who was she? If she is his demon, what does she represent? People have demons. And those demons have a meaning specific to that person. Sins, addictions, other failures and assorted traumas… sources of torment bodied forth. So what are his? This is what he's been working through as he furtively watches her wait, the thoughts broken up only by little flashes of triumphant recognition whenever the front door opens and she looks up from her phone, hopeful, anxiously awaiting her male model.

Like right now. Another entrant and she's doing it again. But it's shorter this time. Only a split second before she's back on her phone. The phone, the phone. Always the phone.

Then—bam!—another epiphany. The phone!

Haruka is Death, his death. She wasn't lying when she said, gravely, "If I'm an angel, I'm the angel of death." If he died while crossing the street looking at his phone, as he most suspected, then all signs would point to her: a creature inseparable from her phone, an iPhone, what they were calling the God Machine back in 2007. How blasphemous. Just like her. She even dresses like she's a phone. Yes, she is his Death incarnate—and now he knows he stopped really living shortly after he got his iPhone. This was his great sin: every second spent staring at the screen was a second spent rejecting life. To do it while crossing the street, out in the actual world, under something as glorious as the firmament? That's no different from suicide. The car that hit him merely carried out his will, a bullet from the phone-shaped gun in his hand.

Now, how to defeat her… Was there anything to his demonic instinct? While flawed in the "why," the "what" boasted some strokes of brilliance—bringing him here, after all. Yes, maybe there is. For what is a man but something between a demon and an angel? He will still say "You are not as smart and powerful as you think you are" and then break her phone in front of her. Yes. Sort of like Jesus cleansing the Temple—knocking over the tables of the moneychangers, driving away the merchants selling animals for sacrifice. God's authority will be his, not hers. Au Bon Pain… the place with the good bread. Indeed.

▲▽▽▲▲▲

There is someone standing over the table. Haruka looks up. It's not him; it's someone else. Someone familiar. This sort of Latino-looking guy wearing all black. How does she know him? Her fusiform gyrus is failing her. Is he in one of her classes? No, a little too old-looking. A TA? "You are not as smart and powerful as you think you are," he says. That voice. Uh-oh. She definitely remembers that voice. That stupid voice. Shit. This fucking guy. Now she can see. He's shaved his head. Bright hazel eyes even more pronounced because of it. She does not need this right now. Wait, what the fuck did he just say?

"I… I…" How can she get out of this? "I think you've mistaken me for someone else."

He snatches the phone from her hand and throws it face down hard against the tiled floor. She can't believe it. What. The. Fuck. Now he is pouring coffee over it. Ho. Ly. Shit. He empties the cup then smiles at her. She looks at him, speechless, her mouth and eyes presumably little ovals.

"He's not coming and never was. I set you up. You are not as smart and powerful as you think you are."

She screams.

His head pulls back, chin sucking into his neck; his eyebrows raise, mouth pulls down. "And here I thought you were a creature too cold for such emotion," he says. "Maybe this just means I'm free." Then he runs. The nutjob runs. Past tables of shocked onlookers. Past the guy behind the counter scrambling to get over to stop him. Out the door. Down the block outside he runs.

She can't even look at it. It will be that bad. For now, she just sits.

"Are you all right?" It's the woman at the next table over. She is a middle-aged white woman; thin, hook-nosed, curly brown hair. Statement piece jewelry dangles as she bends over to pick up Haruka's phone. The woman is ugly. Haruka hates her. She places the phone in front of Haruka—the screen shattered, colors bleeding all around the display, patches of black in certain areas—like insult to injury. Stupid white woman.

"No," she says. "No, I am not." A tear streaks down one cheek, then another down the other.

"Did you know him?"

Haruka hesitates. She wants this woman to leave her alone. Mostly, she just wants to be alone right now. What happened here was maybe the worst thing that's ever happened to her. But she can get another phone. Dad will get her another phone. "No, I didn't know him."

"Do you need help? Do you want someone to call the police?"

"No. Don't call. I... I have insurance."

"Smart. You know—" No, she doesn't know. And she doesn't want to know. But still this horrible white woman carries on: "I was born and raised here, and while it's true the city's gotten a lot safer, you still gotta watch out for the wackadoos. You always will." Haruka just stares at her. This ugly woman just wanted to say something like that, talk about herself; she didn't want to help. That was entirely inappropriate. After meeting Haruka's prolonged silence with an uncomfortable grin and sigh, this terrible woman turns back around, back to her croissant, latte, stupid old ugly PC laptop—back to minding her own business.

Haruka blots the phone with a napkin, then picks it up, cradling it in her hand. It's dying. Behind the intricate spiderweb of cracks, between the patches of warped liquid crystal, what's left of the clear part of the display is now going dark. She can't even read the time anymore; the exact time of death will be lost to the ages. Goodbye, phone. She loved you more than anything in the world. Her truly amazing iPhone 4. From the moment she opened you on her seventeenth birthday, the gift her parents gave her to replace the old 3G she had received on her fourteenth, you've been her favorite thing. You were so much better than the Honda Civic she got on her sixteenth birthday. Carried her to so much more freedom. For it was with this phone, her second smartphone, that she really found herself. Her 3G was more like a tracking device for her parents—they had even put a parental control app on it, limiting what she could download, do; monitoring her activity. But her second, this one, was just hers. With their hands off, her hands were free to do exactly as they pleased. And oh the things they did. It was a window to an unlimited world. Oh, the places both inside herself and out into the universe this phone brought her to. She loved it so much. There was nothing between them, not even a case. And until today that was just fine. Almost two years, and there was not even a single scratch on it. Is what happened here her fault for not protecting it with a case? No. That fucking crazy person would have done what he did anyway, would have found a way. What she had with it was pure. And that's how she'll remember it. Always. Just her fingers on the glass, one hand supporting it from behind, the others stroking the screen, bringing her where she wanted, when she wanted; her reflection in its luster. The two one and the same. Completing each other. She is indeed saying goodbye to a part of herself. But it is a part that can, thankfully, be regenerated.

The time for sentimentality is over. On to the next one. The 4S. Even better. At least all of her contact info, apps, etcetera are synced to the cloud. It won't be too hard to download them using her new phone. And there's another silver lining in that now she can post a status update about the death of her phone on Facebook. It will elicit much sympathy. Bring her much attention. Haruka rises.

All eyes in the place are on her. She hates this kind of attention but very much looks forward to what she is going to get digitally with that update. As she crosses the room, the guy from behind the counter earlier walks back through the front door. He apparently had given chase. He's a young black guy, wearing the standard-issue Au Bon Pain hat, apron. Out of breath, he yells "Lost him!" out to one of the ladies behind the counter, followed by a little shake of the head. Then he sees Haruka there in front of him. "You okay, miss?"

"Yes, I'm fine." And for the most part she is now. She'll go back to the dorm, borrow Lauren's phone, call her parents, tell them hers was randomly stolen, and they'll get the process going. She'll have a new one tomorrow. A better one. The man is still there. "I have to go," she says. He nods and walks away, back to the counter, his real job making coffee; he was a failure as a hero. Then Haruka leaves. But not before she drops her phone in the trash.

Without a phone to listen to music or look at while walking back to the dorm, Haruka has nothing else to do but plot. Plot her vengeance. That guy, what was his fucking name, Randy, Ramón… no, Ray. Oh, how she hates Ray. Ray must pay. Yes, Ray will pay, dearly. Dear. Ly. She will get him back somehow. Soon. But it should be done anonymously. For one, he seems actually crazy. A part of her is flattered he cared so much about her that he stalked her and destroyed her phone, but she's also frightened about what he could do next. What she's doing is working; he's the real proof, and it's nice to be validated, but she must be of sound body in order to continue doing it. If he did that to her phone, what could he do to her? Still, she must retaliate. What he did was not okay. Not. O. Kay.

But what exactly to do? Maybe she can ruin his name or credit rating somehow. Something big that can be done over the internet. She's got a hacker friend or two back home that might be able to help her out. Guys who claim to be in Anonymous. All she knows is she never wants to see

him again. That Ray. She needs his full name. Ray went to Columbia—
that she remembers because it's a better school and made her feel inad-
equate—and was a writer? No. Journalist. Looked about twenty-five,
maybe a little older. This is good enough for now, she supposes. Good
enough for a Google search. She'll see where it takes her. But not now.
Not yet. After calling her parents and what will be a truly epic Facebook
update, it'll be time to concentrate on her finals.

She will get straight A's this semester, like she did last. And one day,
perhaps when she is a big-time executive at Apple, she'll think back on
this and laugh. She'll take the power away from this terrible incident.
Whenever they release a new iPhone, she'll look down at the one in her
hand, throw it down, pour something all over it, and laugh. There will
always be something better. A new model. A much better one to grow
in its place.

▲ ▽ ▲ ▽ ▽ ▽

Evil travels—like all energy, it transfers between people and objects; it
moves, gets stored, moves again. But where did it originate? When Eve
ate the apple? Or before that, with Satan, that fallen seraph who took
the form of a snake and whispered with slithering tongue into her ear?
Did she birth it or was it thrust upon us by some insufflating malefic
serpent? Is it man-made or a supernatural force? Ray doesn't know.

What he does know is that it's not the fruit's fault it was forbidden.
An object can only be a conduit for evil; whether it is an apple in the
Garden of Eden or a smartphone which bears its image some six thousand years later. This is why Ray is keeping his phone. Two days ago,
right after defeating Haruka, blazing through the wind atop Ghost
Horse, he thought about chucking it into the East River once he reached
the midpoint of the Queensboro Bridge; that this would be some prodi-
gious symbolic event—just like when he threw his helmet over and embraced everything harum-scarum in demonhood—breaking the final
link in the chain connecting him to his great sin. He thought he need
only cast away his 4S, this later-generation version of the object that led
him astray, into the rough turbid water at the spot where his quest for
answers began and then he would be free. Able to begin his ascent into
heaven. This is what his head was telling him to do. But his gut told him

"No, no," and, thankfully, he listened. The gut, that second brain: closer to the heart, which must mean closer to the soul, too.

It's not the thing itself, but how you use it. The object did not lead him astray. In fact, an iPhone can be a very useful tool; it can do real good. But it's hard. In the same way that it's difficult to be a good person, it's hard. With it, you are easily susceptible to distraction, temptation, a spectrum of major and minor sins. They're mostly the same ones easily tied up with the internet in general—lust, sloth, envy, pride—but on a mobile device they're worse, more of an affront to God, because they tend to be committed at the expense of actual interaction with the world—the world He made, for you and for all.

So now Ray knows what to do. How he's supposed to make things right, his path to expiation. He must use his iPhone only for good. A smartphone allows you to choose your own adventure. So be a hero, not a villain. Don't be your own worst enemy. No wasting time… No training your brain not to remember things, losing the skills necessary to read a fucking map… No trolling. Don't make snarky remarks on comment threads or internet forums or social media. Just do good. Help others. If you're out in the world and bored, which you shouldn't be anyway, but still, if you feel like you need to get on your phone, be useful. Answer questions, offer advice. Look only for question marks when you scroll through your Facebook news feed. Log on to Reddit and comment on something you have firsthand knowledge of and real insight about. Give far more than you take. Never text and walk. And stop googling things as you think of them. Instead, write it down and look it up later. If you can't remember to do this, then you didn't deserve to know the answer. This will keep your mind active, agile; clear to really think. It will keep you sharp. Using the internet for information or socialization should be an activity, something you sit down for—it should not be used while out and about. You should not refuse the beauty of what's in front of you for mere pixels of red, green, blue on a 3.5-inch screen. Otherwise, you'll lose yourself. An abyss of ones and zeros will swallow you whole. Don't be a dumb motherfucker with a smartass phone.

This is the new outlook. It's part of what he's calling the Platinum Rule. Before, both in life and in the afterlife, aside from the recent short-lived demon phase, he more or less lived by the Golden Rule. But there's a problem with treating others as you'd like to be treated when you don't treat yourself all that well. And he sees that he didn't. Because it was okay to waste his own time with his phone, it was okay to waste others' time, too, by posting inane or churlish bullshit. It's not enough that he never really put anybody out in a major way; just because you don't do something all that wrong doesn't make the things you do right. Carrying on like that was enough to get himself killed and sent here to purgatory, after all. So the Golden Rule ain't all it's cracked up to be. The Platinum Rule is better. The rule is simple: Be good.

Like the Golden Rule, it's flexible. A matter of conscience. It starts from the baseline of morality—don't do harm to others—and then it's really up to you. Ray's involves a very, very loose interpretation of the Christian values he was brought up with as a heterodox Catholic. The Bible, in his view, was never meant to be taken literally; it is a book to be interpreted, personalized. A guide. Would he steal a loaf of bread to feed his family? Fuck yeah, if the person with the bread also had enough to feed theirs. Is it okay to lie? Yes, if it's not a lie that comes from a place of malice; all art, when you get down to it, is a lie. And art has been serving man's notion of God since there have been hands to make it. Plus, a lot of lies are really funny. Anything funny is good. Most jokes are really just lies that tell the truth, after all; they should be considered prayers, an invocation. Guys like Chris Rock and his fellow half-Mexican Louis C.K. are philosopher-saints as far as he's concerned. How about sex for pleasure? Anything wrong with that? No, not at all. In fact, as long as neither party isn't in it for more—and you can tell, you always can—it's one of the best ways to spread joy. Perhaps *the* best. And it is this, the spreading of joy, all that is good, which makes the Platinum Rule different.

Technically, under the Golden Rule, you wouldn't have to do anything for anybody and you would still be in the clear. But that merely stops the transference of evil with you. It's just indifference. If the evil stopped with you, and there was no good to push it out, then that evil is still inside you. Purgatory—where he is, not limbo, he now knows—is a perfect place for people like that, and that's why he's here. He mostly lived by a lazy Golden Rule. To get to heaven, you gotta do more. You gotta be good.

So that's what he'll do.

The major work will be done on the phone, since that was his biggest sin in life, but before getting too deep into that, he's starting with what's happened most recently off of it, trying to mitigate whatever damage he did to innocents during the whole demon thing. He's glad it happened, again—knows those two and a half days were an integral part of defeating Haruka—but it also resulted in more to atone for.

Brian went to his parents' place again this weekend—he usually spends about one weekend a month back there—and Ray's bought him a new toothbrush. It's a nice one, an Oral-B Pro-Health CrossAction. He's also cleaning the apartment, not only as part of his penance, but also so that he can tell Brian he knocked his toothbrush over while doing it, to give him a plausible reason for buying him a new one. A little white lie, not malicious, coming from a place that means well. And one that's kind of funny, too. He's already straightened up the living room and wiped down various surfaces in the kitchen. And now he's in the middle of the main event, the bathroom. On his knees he scrubs the tub.

As for the whiskey, fuck it. He didn't really drink that much, and plus, Brian doesn't need to be drinking whiskey. He's enough of an asshole already. Ray's still not sure if Brian's a demon or a projection, but whatever he is, replacing it would not be the right thing to do.

But there are other things Ray stole that should be replaced. Once he's done cleaning, he's going to ride over to 5 Pointz wearing a vizard— a Yankees cap and sunglasses under a hoodie, which not only makes him look incognito but like he's deep, deep undercover, very Puerto Rican— and return the spray paint he stole, leaving another white can he bought at the Home Depot on 59th and Third last night along with it. He's not going to try to track the guy he took it from down and apologize or anything. If he's there, great, he'll leave them in the bucket below and skedaddle, but if not, he'll just place them around the spot where he stole the one, and either hope the dude comes back or someone else will get good use out of them. Either way, the wrong will be righted.

Then there's the matter of the Naked Cowboy's hat. The day after becoming a demon, Ray, while biking through the crowds in Times Square at high speeds tormenting tourists, stole it for fun. He just rode up behind him, leaned over, plucked it off the man's head, and placed it on his own. The Cowboy gave immediate chase, but he was no match for Ray and Ghost Horse. After a madcap dash down Seventh Ave. to 39th Street, Ray veered right into Hell's Kitchen, where he removed his shirt and, putting the hat back on, spent the remainder of the afternoon riding up and down sidewalks spitting at people and evading the police who bore witness or responded to calls of these activities, lying doggo in or sneakily traversing sundry side streets and alleyways until nightfall.

Ray hopes the Cowboy will be there. That he had a reserve of white Stetsons—the words "NAKED COWBOY" handwritten on the front in big blue and red letters—and is currently strumming away. The plan is to toss it back to him in passing. That's all it really requires; he's not even sure whether the Cowboy is a being of good or evil—while he does spread joy to some, he does it in a way that's beyond irksome to others—but still, it would be a bit of a stretch to say what he did as a demon there was inadvertently good; he knows that, on a personal level, purloining this gimmicky man's fool's cap was wrong. If he's not there, he'll just toss it at the Times Square police substation on 43rd and Broadway instead and hope they get it back to him somehow. And if they don't, someone will at least get a nice souvenir. Like the spray paint, if the hat is paid forward it will still be another wrong righted.

Paying it forward is pretty much all he can do to take action with what happened in Hell's Kitchen. Since it would be impossible to track down the individuals he spat at, Ray's going to walk the streets after he returns the cowboy hat and drop the ten dollars in quarters he got from the bank for laundry recently as he goes along. What he can do, and already has done, for those individuals is say a prayer. He's wished that things go well for them—that if they are more than just projections from his mind and are fellow lost souls that they are happy and themselves good, the best versions of themselves they can be, like what he's striving for.

Lying prone in bed late last night, his head resting on folded knuckles, he said this prayer, as well as one for those people he antagonized in Times Square—especially the teenage boy with side-swept bangs he clipped from behind with his handlebars and the plump older Indian-looking woman who was so frightened at the sight of him riding toward her that she couldn't keep hold of her bag from the M&M's store, dropping it so fast it broke and spilled the candy-coated chocolates in a Cray-ola-rainbow ring around her. Then he said one for the thousands of people he hadn't done anything outward to but did have horrific thoughts about on that day, too. For while riding the streets believing he was a demon he saw everyone and everything as being like him. In hell. And so men, women, and children of every color and creed did what demons do—they fought each other, raped, pillaged, ran amok. The city was a free-for-all. Everywhere buildings burned. The streets opened up and cars fell through their jagged asphalt maws, especially the cabs that pissed him off by honking or driving too close. Things appeared normal, but Ray could see them for what they really were: evil.

Except they weren't, really. Sure, people are evil, but they're also good; it's a mixed bag. And once he found himself again, he knew these were sins of thought. He wouldn't have considered these sins had these scenes been thought of abstractly—the dark peregrinations of the mind are an essential part of understanding evil, and in turn understanding and doing and being good—but because he transmitted them onto others, fellow souls, he knew he had done wrong. Even if they were projections, it still would have been wrong. The people weren't abstract ideas of people. He saw them, physically, their bodies, their faces, do the things.

And where actions, good deeds, are impossible, words will have to do. So he'll continue to pray. Every night. And on top of specific people he thought bad things about, he'll do this for all souls, everyone living and dead. Is that too easy? Can such a blanket gesture really be considered good? Well, it can't hurt. And if his heart's in the right place, why wouldn't it? He's made up a prayer for everyone, which he plans to say nightly after everything personal and a Hail Mary and Our Father:

Sweet Jesus
Let us live
In love together
As love forever

Yes, tonight he'll pray. And this afternoon he'll continue doing his good deeds. He's even going to buy another helmet over on Vernon to make sure he can carry them out uninterrupted, with corporeal protection. But what of this evening? He'll atone for the very last of his demon offenses.

Before going to confront Haruka, Ray spent the day at home, on his laptop, doing demonic things there. The day before was about outward aggression, this day was about self-loathing. It seemed like a proper demon should have a healthy balance of both. He started out by sacrificing fifty of his Facebook friends at random, unfriending them, including really good friends from childhood and family members. Then he made a couple of throwaway YouTube and Twitter accounts to spout hate speech about Mexicans and other immigrants, until getting bored with that after a few hours and moving over to 4chan's /b/ board, where he hung out for pretty much the rest of the day—masturbating to pictures of anonymous users' ex-girlfriends, looking at horrible gore photos of people and animals; occasionally masturbating to those. He started numerous nonsensical greentext story threads using images vaguely related to anime, video games, drugs, and proceeded to argue with himself about politics and religion—ignoring anyone else who agreed or also argued with him—calling himself, in the parlance of the 4chan community, those guttural double-g-in-the-center racial and homophobic epithets as often as possible. He explored the very nadir of his soul there, digitally—as if, somehow, he already knew—biding his time until the big meeting.

And so this evening he will use his laptop to apply for jobs and broaden his mind, heart; build himself back up. He's only going to look at positions in journalism or writing—no more misadventures in alien industries like the courier business, only things similar to what he did before—and hopefully he'll get a job where he can make an impact, actually be useful. He'll read some articles about morality, ethics, philosophy. Find intellectual solace in the Platinum Rule. Then, as another part of his penance, he's going to try to use OkCupid in earnest. He hopes to find someone nice there, someone who could eventually be relationship material. He'll embarrass and disappoint the younger version of himself so that he can find someone for his next self, someone to be good with. To spread illimitable joy, love.

After tonight, he'll use his laptop as little as possible. Only when necessary for sending attachments and watching videos. Otherwise, his internet use needs to be all about the phone. The inconvenience of heavy browsing on it, the frustration that will ensue, will be a part of his expiation.

Yes, these are his plans. But in the meantime, on to the sink, the toilet, floor… Wipe, wash away the evil. Leave a pure, sparkling space. See the ceramic surfaces gleam pure and white. The chrome faucet and handles shine like platinum. See only what is good.

▲▽▲▽▽▲

Oh, dear, what a bad batch this one was. It actually took two full sessions—the second yesterday evening, also with wine—it was so dreadful, so hard to get through: high school level hermeneutical approaches to the *Odyssey*, analyses of Dante more torturous than the hell the man described, mediocre musings on *Hamlet*, and, of course, far too generous assessments of Kafka's genius. Most of the young women in the class wrote about *Madame Bovary*, none with anything interesting to say. The few students who tried *Gilgamesh* got it all wrong. Emerson's more conservative estimate ended up being correct. How many people joined him on that shore? One, only one. And even his final paper was just an A-. The lone male to write about *Madame Bovary*, the boy's—probably the redheaded one, but he honestly can't know—essay explained how emptiness, despair, and neurosis can only be accurately communicated through the realist style the book made famous; that it is widely considered a perfect novel because of its perfect aesthetic melding of form and content. Well, as the kids say, "Duh." But the paper was well-written enough, only briefly falling into bouts of circumlocution, and together with the student's anterior work from the term that did earn him solid A's, Emerson believes he could at least navigate a dinghy.

He's entering the grades on the computer now, making a list for the Registrar's Office to process into their system sometime during the coming week, his fat fingers smacking away. He'll have to hold on to these papers for a while, preparation for when the students complain. At least half of them always do. It'll be his responsibility, then, to mail the papers back to them so they can see their failings for themselves. Really, all the students should want to see his comments on their work, including those who do well, but people only ask "Why?" when they receive bad news.

Even after he sends their work back and they can read exactly where they went wrong, many of the students who got a B or C for their final grade in his course, and especially those who received an A-, still can't believe it. Or they choose not to. Some will harangue him until he just stops responding, then turn to the university and bother them. There was a time when, depending on who the student was, how important or prominent their family, the university would actually lean on Emerson for a grade change. The nerve! But now they know better. The students receive the grades they have earned, and that's that. Protesting only proves his point: had they correctly studied literature in his class, they'd already know that life isn't supposed to be easy.

Once he's finished with this, he'll write. His notepad has really been filling up these past few days… his brokenhearted prose having become only more powerful, moving… and before long he should be on to another one. And by then, hopefully, he'll have an assistant to begin the transcription.

Emerson was very confused earlier this morning: his job ad still hadn't appeared in *The Times*. Since asking his TA to run the ad, he had gone to great lengths to find it, searching the tiny type of the Jobs section with his magnifying glass on both Thursday, the first day it should have

appeared—job ads running on Tuesdays, Thursdays, and Sundays—
and in this morning's edition, going so far on both occasions as to look
over the postings in their entirety twice to make sure his wasn't placed
under the wrong subsection, all to no avail. So, about an hour ago, he
called Kevin to find out what exactly was going on. It turned out the
little ninnyhammer ran the ad as web-only. Emerson was assured, however, that he had already received interest from a great number of qualified candidates. As a punitive measure, and also because he's on such a
roll with his writing, Emerson asked him to screen the candidates for
him and arrange interviews with the six or seven best males from the
group to be conducted tomorrow or Tuesday. There were no questions
about why male-only, nor should there have been. With a short sigh, he
agreed, knowing his grade for the term and the exact phrasing of the
recommendation Emerson suggested would become available to him
were still very much up in the air.

The page remains stuck in the printer, awaiting its Arthur. Who will
he be? Emerson will know soon enough. For now, he need only concern
himself with his pen and notepad. His dear friend, the Culture, is dying.
Perhaps faster than he originally thought. This last class was yet more
incontrovertible proof that when he is gone, there will be no one left to
truly understand it, let alone contribute to it.

▲▽▲▽▲▽

A bite! The Platinum Rule's paying off already. That's not to say Ray
believes he's being rewarded, necessarily; bad things happen to good
people and vice versa all the time, of course. Or that simply following
the Platinum Rule shouldn't be enough reward in and of itself. But
there's something else going on here. Perhaps it just helps: attracts it. Be
good and goodness will follow. This time it just happened to be something like instant karma.

He had applied for the job last night, along with a dozen or so others
on Craigslist's writing/editing section. It read:

Editorial and Personal Assistant (Upper West Side)

Assistant for renowned literary critic and professor. Full-time for the summer transitioning to part-time in the fall. Requirements – excellent grammar and proofreading skills, computer savvy, fast typist, research experience, flexibility, thick skin. Degree from top college essential. Please apply with resume and cover letter. Immediate start.

Compensation: competitive hourly

Principals only. Recruiters, please don't contact this job poster. Do NOT contact us with unsolicited services or offers.

It didn't seem like it was the perfect fit for him, but there were enough things to like about it. The ideal, of course, would be writing gonzo-type stuff for a well-known news outlet—telling his truth, spreading what's good in him—yet aside from, like, *Vice*, which pays shit if at all, and which he'd already be writing for full-time if they were interested since he's freelanced for them, that probably won't be possible. The big magazines haven't really done that kind of thing since the nineties, and there wouldn't be advertising for it, anyway. So he applied for this assistant job knowing it seemed noble enough and like a good place to get back on track. You have to start, or in this case, restart, somewhere. He'd spend his days giving more than he was taking by virtue of the role being supportive, helping to preserve and promote literature—who reads literary shit anymore? Ray rarely reads books like that and has barely read any fiction published since the end of the last century, only, like, *White Teeth*, *Oscar Wao*, and regrettably, *Super Sad True Love Story*—and under conditions that come fall would allow him to have a stable income in a respectable field while also pursuing freelance stuff. And, of course, this would be a whole lot better than what he was doing before.

The reply:

Hi Ray,

Thanks for getting in touch regarding the Editorial and Personal Assistant position. The job would be supporting literary critic Emerson Towers at his home office while he works on his next book. If you're not familiar with him, I'd suggest looking him up at this time. I'm Emerson's current TA at NYU and can safely say that working closely with him, while always interesting, would not be for everyone.

If you're available and still interested, I'd like to schedule you for an interview with him tomorrow or Tuesday. He's looking to fill the position this week.

All the best,
Kevin Jameson

Ray knows he can't write back yet, even though he wants to badly. There doesn't need to be any investigation into this guy—he's been to hell and back, what's the worst this professor Emerson Towers could do?—to know he wants an interview for this job. But he's got to wait an hour or two at least; not appear so desperate. Then there's the whole do-I-pick-Monday-or-Tuesday? thing. Would Monday come across as overeager or proactive? It's only a day away. Shouldn't he seem like he has other important things to do, like he's wrapping up a freelance gig or something? But at the same time, he did apply for the job knowing it was an *immediate* start. They seem motivated to fill it… Monday it is, then. But not morning—that *would* look a little too desperate. When he writes back, he'll say: *Monday afternoon would be best, though I could also do Tuesday.*

In the meantime, he'll do his research. No, he doesn't need to google this Emerson Towers to know he wants this job, but he does to adequately prepare for meeting with him. He types e-m-e-r-s-o-n t-o-w-e-r-s into the search bar.

The first thing Ray's eyes go to are the photos of the man that load over to the right in the search results. He seems vaguely familiar; it could be because he looks like every stereotype of an old, rumpled English professor he's ever seen, except fat, or it could be that he's actually seen him before, the real him, on, like, an old *Charlie Rose* clip or something. He reads his Wikipedia and decides it was probably the latter. As for his TA's warning, what can be gleaned from this page is that Emerson's not all that politically correct and that he had several affairs a couple of decades ago. Ray can live with that. This Kevin dude's either super sensitive or maybe Emerson's sort of a dick in person. Ray will know the answer soon enough. In terms of what he was really after, Emerson Towers pretty much just seems like an old man who's perhaps a little too serious about a subject not too many people care all that much about anymore, something of a relict. Matching seriousness and subtle sympathy should be behind his interview answers; he should speak in his best General American, the one exercised most back at Columbia right after he lost his Texas twang and before the sort of affected flourishes of New York City street slang began creeping in—the one old white people love. Oh, an interview… for something he could write home about… He can't wait. But it's not time to respond yet. Only twenty minutes have passed.

So he digs deeper. Makes sure there's nothing he missed, no wild card up Kevin's sleeve that would validate him. And there isn't, really. He finds a .pdf of some twenty-year-old *Esquire* article profiling Emerson, painting a portrait of a brilliant academic revered and reviled in equal measure. Some find the way he expresses his opinions too forceful, while others see passion as part of the charm. Personality has always been the key to success in the U.S., whether people like you or not. The things Emerson likes, he knows well, apparently, and it's hard to find fault in his articulation as to why they're good, and the same for what he calls bad. That, as Ray sees it, is a man professing his truth. Gonzo at a blackboard. And as long as it's truth that's not really hurting anybody—and talking about fucking poetry and fiction surely isn't—then he is a man that does good. As for Emerson's personal life, the affairs, Ray's not in a position to judge. It seems these all took place with young ladies who were either students or assistants, which is pretty grimy, but still. He wasn't there and it takes two to tango, after all. Consenting adults are consenting adults. One of the young women interviewed for the piece was even quoted as saying, "I also gave Emerson sponge baths, but only because I wanted to. He so enjoyed his sponge baths." Ray feels sort of bad for the man's ex-wife, but that's about it. Though really, what happened was between them. The one thing this does tell him is why his current TA is male, and why he's probably in consideration for this. The man's learned from his mistakes. There's good in that as well.

Continuing on with his due diligence, Ray skims a few more articles about him. None are as juicy, but all are interesting enough; most focus on his opinions, the work. Back on Wikipedia, Ray familiarizes himself with the broad arguments of his nine books. They're relatively easy to follow, and more or less reinforce Ray's first impression. Would supporting such a man be good, then? Well, it would be good enough. There's room for it under the Platinum Rule. Emerson Towers seems like no saint, but few of us are. Ray would be doing good for himself and good for this man's cause, which appears to be virtuous: there would be worse things than helping out an old man who loves books.

An hour's gone by now. Ray's safe to draft his response. He does, then clicks send. He should probably do some laundry now, he thinks, at least iron a nice Oxford for the interview.

Ray's eyes shoot back to the message thread, still open on the screen. A response already: a yellow rectangle on the bottom reading "A new message from Kevin Jameson" along with options to "show" or "ignore." Ray clicks "show."

Hi Ray,

You're scheduled for tomorrow at 4:30 p.m. The address is 131 Riverside Drive, #8A.

Also, if Emerson asks, say you saw the posting for this job on The New York Times Job Board website. I don't want to bore you with the details as to why, but it'll just be easier for you this way.

All the best,
Kevin

What a delightfully odd last paragraph. But it's the first paragraph that matters—a bite becomes a tug. Hold the line till tomorrow then reel him in. Maybe he should wear his suit.

▲▽▲▽▲▲

Well, this is turning out to be quite the painful process. The first two just weren't any good, the maundering, jittery one this morning and the distractingly fey one that left only moments ago. Yes, they both went to Ivies—a Yalie and a Brown grad—but neither were particularly articulate; their tastes in literature were wretched, with one even admitting to liking Young Adult fiction; and their personalities dull. Perhaps he should've done the vetting himself.

It's not that Emerson wants a star. He is the star here. All he's asking for is someone competent, dutiful, and pleasant enough to be around. So far, little Kevin has demonstrated that finding anyone like that was too much to ask, a task far above him. It seems Emerson trusted a fool

to find the king who will serve him, and if Kevin ever requests that recommendation, he may say as much in so many words.

There's one more today, then tomorrow another four are scheduled.
He's stuck with the next candidate—he should be here any minute
now—but maybe he should cancel all of tomorrow's interviews. Combing through some résumés and corresponding with candidates himself
tonight, when he'll be too spent to write, anyway, could save him several
hours of work time tomorrow. Yes, maybe he should… Let's see how
this next one does, if he's any better. Frankly, he doesn't have high
hopes, judging by the résumé. The man has a Hispanic name, and while
that would be fine for the personal assistant aspects of this role, he's
afraid he won't be up to snuff in his editorial duties. That subpar intelligence issue… that which his students from the past few years have only
further proven. But who knows. Maybe he's an outlier, a secret genius.
Perhaps his immediate family has Spanish, not Central American origins: less savage, more Cervantes.

Emerson rises from his armchair and crosses over to the kitchen
counter. He eats an old-fashioned, then another—a little spike of sugar
and endorphins to help get him through this. They come from the bakery a few blocks away. He picked a half-dozen up this morning, thinking
they'd last these two days, that maybe he would have one to offer the
young man who would unjam his printer as a welcoming gesture. There
is only one left now.

The buzzer sounds. He crosses the room to the intercom by the front
door: "Hello?"

"Hi," the voice begins. "It's Ray Gonzales. I'm here for a three
o'clock meeting." It's lower-pitched and relaxed, unlike the last voice,
which seemed to practically snivel through the speaker. There's no trace
of an accent, thank God, and he says these things as they should be said,
as statements, unlike the first who replied, "I believe we have a meeting?" with the "-ing" on "meeting" lilting up like a distraught question—
a double dose of doubt in his voice. A better start than the rest, at least,
this one. Emerson buzzes him in.

While waiting, he pours himself a glass of water. His mouth is a little
gooey from the donuts. He drinks, guzzling quickly, but not with so
much celerity that he would risk spilling any down his face, chins, wetting his shirt or sweater vest, sullying himself. It's a shame to wash away
the sweet aftertaste of the old-fashioneds, but his voice must be clear and
strong for the interview. The interviewees aren't the only ones who need

to make an impression. This Ray must hear him as the stentorian authority he is; even if he turns out to be another dolt and they are never to meet again, he must go out into the world with proper reverence. He swallows the last gulp then moves into the living room, looking into the mirror and straightening his blazer and hair. He doesn't overdo it with the latter, finger-combing just enough to go from looking disheveled to intellectual. It must appear as though he simply doesn't have the time to do his hair, not that he only recently woke up. The doorbell rings. He mugs for the mirror and, after counting to five, steps over to the door. He opens it.

More Spanish-looking than Mexican, another good sign. Light skin, bright eyes, clean cut. His hair is so short it would seem prison- or military-mandated if not offset by the smart, slim-fitting suit; it comes together overall in a way that feels very *Gentleman's Quarterly*, a magazine which once wrote an article about Emerson, back when big national magazines still wrote profiles about literary figures. He's not wearing a tie, which is good, because neither is Emerson. The last one wore a tie, and it made him feel uncomfortable. An assistant should not wear a tie if the person he is supporting is not. Really, he should've taken it off. Like all of them, this one is shorter than he is—another prerequisite of any good assistant—but unlike the first one, he isn't too short. He's probably around six inches shorter at five-ten, five-eleven. Most short people tend to make Emerson uncomfortable as well, though not emotionally: physically. If he has to look too far down to speak to someone, his chins bunch up in a very unpleasant manner against his chest. Emerson extends his hand. "You must be Ray."

Ray accepts it. They shake. He has a firm enough grip; it does not get lost in Emerson's own meaty palm, but rather exhibits a certain strength that suggests an exercise regimen. "A pleasure to meet you, Emerson."

Releasing his hand, Emerson closes the door behind him. "I hope you found the place easily enough."

"Yes, of course," says Ray. "You're actually right by one of my favorite stretches of Riverside."

"Come, sit." Emerson leads him into the living room and gestures toward the sofa. After Ray lowers himself down, he settles in the chair perpendicular, a coffee table sharing the space in front of them both. It holds the remainder of Emerson's afternoon coffee resting atop a cork coaster, this morning's edition of *The Times*, and his interview notes, which he then grabs. "You're up here often?"

"Not as much as I'd like. But I've biked here quite a lot in the past." Ahhh, so there's the exercise. He's a bicyclist. That isn't good. Anyone who would willingly ride a bicycle through the frenzied streets of New York City could only have an I.Q. in the low double digits. That, or a death wish. Neither would be good in an assistant. "It's a very pretty part of town."

"Indeed. Thank you." Emerson smirks. "Do you happen to have a hard copy of your résumé?" Emerson doesn't, because of the printer. Obviously Ray should have at least one copy anyway as a matter of course, and if he doesn't, Emerson will know his worst fears of savagery have been justified.

"I certainly do." Ray reaches into the outside pocket of his briefcase, which is black leather and more utilitarian than handsome, and pulls out a black hard-shelled folder. He opens it and slides a copy of his résumé out, then into Emerson's hand.

The paper is not résumé paper, but it is a little heavier than your average sheet of printer paper. This bodes well for the youngish man. Résumé paper, with its cotton makeup and silly watermarks, means the candidate is trying too hard—the first one used it this morning—while the standard sheet—which the second used—is a little too flimsy to hold the name and accomplishments of anybody who is capable enough to work alongside someone of Emerson's caliber. He reads it over. "So you're a journalist, mostly?"

"That I am."

"A lot of web work, I see." This does not bode well for the youngish man; not only is his employment history almost exclusively comprised of jobs writing for websites, they're also sites Emerson has never heard of. Now he remembers: he tried visiting one called *Vice* last night upon receiving this Ray's résumé but the front page was so horrific, the headlines replete with references to drugs and genitalia, that he refused to look at anything else he was associated with—Emerson had his fill of genitals the other week at the museum, thank you—pretty much rejecting him in that moment, only going through with this interview because it had already been scheduled by that idiot Kevin. Oh well. While his mind is a trap, at this age it only holds on to the things he should care about, built with a wonderful mechanism to release and block out that which he has no use for. Regardless, he's here in front of him now: might as well go through the motions for a bit, like he did with the rest. What a painful process this is, indeed! Damn you, Kevin! "You'll have to forgive me, I'm not familiar with many of these publications."

"Most of them target millennials, so you're probably the better for it."

Emerson laughs. Could there possibly be room for a redemption story here? "Not a fan of your own generation?"

"I wouldn't say that." That's disappointing. "But the content isn't for everyone." That's even more disappointing. Yes, best to wrap this up as soon as decent manners would allow. But not before a light jab or two. The time Emerson's spending here shouldn't be completely wasted. A little fun:

"Content… now there's a term. They used to call it writing."

"I wouldn't want to call a listicle writing."

What's this, a sidestep? "Listicle?" asks Emerson.

"Yeah. You know, one of those lists like Eight Cats That Will Blow Your Mind or Ten Things Going on This Weekend You Can't Miss."

"Oh, those obnoxious things." Emerson's seen a few, unfortunately. Even Claire sent him one recently—Five Books Coming out This Summer That Everyone Needs to Read. No, actually, they don't. Everything on the list looked like pure dreck. Sadly, it seems that hyperbole is having another moment in popular discourse. The fast-talking young man this morning kept calling things "the greatest" and "the best" and "the worst." Many of his students last term, too, would exaggerate everything. Now he sees where they're getting it from. "They consider that journalism?"

"Sad to say, a lot of people do, yeah. They get the most clicks, so web publications continue to write them."

"And that's the kind of thing you wrote?"

"I've written some. But I've done a bit of long-form reporting, too. And everything in between."

"That is good to hear, the long-form experience." It is. Though his résumé claims as much, it's another thing to hear it spoken aloud. The first candidate seemed unsure of practically everything on his résumé. This is, of course, a role where oral communication will be crucial. This Ray is direct and self-aware, at least. Could he have just written for that trashy web rag to make a buck? The economic climate is still rather unforgiving; perhaps this Ray deserves some consideration, after all: the bit about those stupid lists, their raison d'être, was somewhat interesting. Emerson had a friend or two who wrote some articles for *Playboy* back in the day; maybe he's just being a prude. He scans the rest of the résumé. "Yes, I see. You wrote for the *Spectator*. I used to teach at Columbia, but I was a Harvard man myself."

"So I read."

Emerson comes to the education section. "Why did you choose to study anthropology?"

"Columbia doesn't have a journalism undergrad program. I figured that would be the next best thing."

"Not English?"

"Anthropology's a field that encourages you to see people for what they are, not what they aren't or what you want them to be. That seemed more useful than studying English, where there's a lot of judgment involved. It's hard not to read a book and ask yourself if you like it or not. That didn't happen to me when I was thinking about people, studying cultures, tribes. Liking them or otherwise seeking value in them didn't come into play; they just were. That, and my writing didn't seem like it needed too much honing for what I wanted to do. I thought it was good enough. As of course you know, most people who go to schools like the ones we went to or the one you now teach at have to be pretty decent writers to begin with."

"Oh, I wish that were true. But we'd be here all day if I got going on that one." Really, they would. And after such an idiotic explanation as to why he chose his major, he's again on thin ice, and Emerson wouldn't want to waste so much time. Journalism, like English, is about the pursuit of truth in storytelling, not presenting information with the absence of judgment—especially with regard to whatever forest-dwelling wildlings he was studying, those who definitively should be judged, and to their faces so that they might be guilted into joining civilization. Nothing just is. Every statement one makes is a judgment call, some are just more skillful about hiding this than others. But while his reasoning may be flawed, Emerson can't help but be impressed by the way he averred it: he's got a fine tone of voice and confident verbal manner. He's something of a charmer, this Ray. "Tell me, besides where I went to school and where I've taught, what else have you read about me?"

"Enough to know that I think we'd work well together." My word! And now we have outright salesmanship! A leap from charm, over cajolery, all the way to sleaziness! Did the Latin lover forget who he's talking to? This should be interesting. "I know about your reputation in academia and as a critic. I know how seriously you take your work. I'm not going to lie to you and tell you I've read any of your books; I haven't. I had less than twenty-four hours to prepare for this meeting, so that wasn't really possible." Less Latin lover than American bravado, then. It reeks of Hollywood schmaltz—some tired and unrealistic notion that gumption alone can get you the brass ring—but, still, it's not as bad as prevaricating about having read him. That's what the second interviewee did, clearly, claiming to have been a great admirer of Emerson's two most famous books but having very little to say about them besides the painfully obvious, that which can be learned with ten minutes and that ridiculous user-edited website masquerading as a resource they call Wikipedia. "But then again, if you just wanted to hire a fan, I probably wouldn't be here."

"Right. Fans don't make good assistants. What would make you, a journalist, a good assistant?"

"I've done a lot of research. Fact-checking. Technical writing. Copyediting. I've never formally worked doing transcription, but I can type fast enough and accurately. That's one nice thing about my generation, I suppose. We're all pretty good typists." Emerson could've done without the silly apologia. But aside from that, he is mildly impressed by this answer. Where is this Ray on the Cervantes-to-savage spectrum? Somewhere in the middle, it seems. But that is a good thing: not too smart, not too stupid. Honest and direct, Emerson wouldn't have to mince words with this one; he'd barely have to be polite. "But more than those things, I'm flexible. Open-minded. I'm a diligent, hard worker without an ego."

"You speak pretty confidently about yourself for someone without an ego."

"I came here to argue my case for the job I want. As far as I see it, I'm merely doing what I have to do. I'd say I've exercised my id here more than my ego." He hasn't, of course, but that was a decent attempt at a poetic turn of phrase to explain what he's doing here. Emerson chuckles. Ray smiles in return, probably not realizing he's laughing at and not with him. Clearly, he wants this job. He very well may be able to do it, too. But does he deserve it? Is this Hispanic writer of listicles really worthy of such an important role in this, Emerson's final ode to the Culture? If he weren't in such a rush, Emerson would say no, of course not. He doesn't look like much of an Arthur, the sartorial sensibilities aside. But he *is* in a rush, and this Ray *could* work. He has an agreeable enough personality, direct experience with many of the duties of the job, and he communicates clearly. Should that be enough?

Maybe. Let's find out more. Get to know *him*. Not what he wants, not what he can do, not the flannelmouthed American politician and salesman he's putting forth, but *him*. This Ray will either dig his own grave or prove himself actually worthy. Death and life are in the power of the tongue… 18:21, one of the best. Let him speak on.

▲▽▲▲▽▽

So far, so good, right? That ego thing just then was deflected pretty damn well. He's sort of guffawing now, bouncing around in that little chair, all kinds of jiggling going on. It's the second time Ray's made him laugh. He's counting.

Really, this Emerson guy isn't so bad. He's just kind of a dick, not an all-out dick. Most of these leather-on-the-elbow types are.

Still, though, how could someone grill a guy going out for an assistant job about having an ego? The whole job is to serve and support someone else, and in the past, it was almost exclusively done by women; and in Emerson's particular past, it was actually exclusively done by them. Progressive politics, the well-adjusted twenty-first-century male, and current economic environment aside, a guy who really had an ego would never want this. Especially not one with actual experience doing what he really wants to do. But he should check that. That sounds like ego. Does Ray actually have too much of an ego? No way; not compared to people like Emerson, at least. Maybe this guy is an all-out dick. Stop. The laughter's waning. He's just exhaled in a drawn-out way, and his rheumy old eyes are staring daggers again. No time for Freudian bullshit now. Just smile.

"So tell me, where did you grow up, Ray?"

"I'm from Texas. Just outside of Austin."

"I see. I've never been. But I hear it's nice. The cultural hub of the state."

"Yeah, it's a cool place. I don't get back much." It's been a year and a half, actually. Since the Christmas before last. He was dead then, he now realizes. But it was pretty much the same: still "weird," as it likes to be kept. He's only been back twice since he died, mostly because of recession-related financial constraints and having boomer parents, who instead of helping him out with a plane ticket on holidays or whatever let him spend them alone in New York for several years on end, probably as a result of some fatuous middle-American, middle-class logic that it would instill more responsibility in him or something. Fuckin' boomers... maybe that was a part of his penance in the afterlife, though, and not directly tied to the unique self-involved and self-righteous shittiness of his parents' money-obsessed generation. Could go either way. "But you know what they say, 'You can take the man out of Texas, but you can't take Texas out of the man.' "

"I've never heard that."

"Maybe it's just a saying back home." Whatever. While maybe he hasn't heard that exactly, he's got to be familiar with one of its variants: the farm, the country, the neighborhood, anything. He's just being difficult for the sake of being difficult... a half a chub getting harder. "Anyway, we all shoot pretty straight."

Emerson's looking out the window now, sort of rocking in his chair even though the chair itself doesn't rock. "When I think of Texas, I think, mostly, of *Blood Meridian*." He turns to Ray. "Have you read it?"

"Whoo—" Ray shakes his head. "Yeah, I read it. Toward the end of high school. Pretty gruesome, pretty wild. That's what you associate with Texas? I'm half Mexican and I don't even think it's that bad."

"Well, anymore. Right? But it was, once. Reading allows us to traverse time, space, one's own consciousness. It engages the mind like nothing else, stimulating every part of the brain and allowing the reader to experience everything as if they were truly there. *Blood Meridian* brought me to that Texas, that pivotal moment in Manifest Destiny, that horror, and it's left the longest-lasting impression."

"Right. I understand. It's a good book." *Blood Meridian* was a big deal with a lot of his more militant intellectual Mexican friends in high school. They'd all read it and be like, "This is why you gotta hate the gringos, man. This is what they did to us. This is what they took from us. Texas was born in our blood!" He's not sure if they forgot he was half white or what, but even if he weren't Ray wouldn't have really agreed. Obviously Manifest Destiny was terrible; the atrocities committed, those detailed in that novel, disgusting beyond belief—he understood why it *would* make them angry, especially at a time when there was so much anti-Mexican sentiment lingering in the United States and especially Texas—but he didn't understand how it could make them so upset they'd become bigots. Nor how they would think it was cool to enjoin him to be the same. Plus, if the shit dramatized in that book hadn't happened in real life, they themselves would have never existed; their families were what they were, like Texas, like Mexico, because of that history. It seems either shortsighted or willfully ignorant to be so pissed off at one of the key reasons for your own being, however horrific the circumstances around it were—unless you would have rather you'd never been born at all.

"Tell me about other good books. What else do you like to read?"

"A little bit of everything." That's not a real answer. Fuck. "I mostly read nonfiction these days, since it's the form of storytelling I practice. With fiction, I lean toward modernism and postmodernism: I like mid-twentieth-century work the best." Okay, better: it's shaping into something of a real answer. "With poetry, the older the better. Shakespeare, Dante, Homer." And that shape is a cone, pointing at a mirror, drawing the most attention to itself and how basic and bland it is. Oh well.

Emerson smirks, scratches the side of his face. "You can't go wrong with those guys. Who else?"

"Emily Dickinson's good."

"She's not old. She was writing less than two hundred years ago. It's an art form with roots that are around four thousand years old."

Fuck… yeah, he's right. Any way to spin this? "Right. She's an exception to that rule. I also like Pablo Neruda in terms of more recent stuff."

Emerson nods. "Okay." He taps the armrest of his chair with the index and middle fingers of his right hand. Ray's résumé's in his lap, his left hand holding it there on a tablet. It's just occurred to Ray that Emerson hasn't written anything down, while Ray's made a note of almost everything they've discussed: the last thing being "Bld Merid → Texas." The amount of time that's passed since anyone's said anything is now becoming awkward. That must be his cue.

"Other older poets I like are John Donne, Ovid."

The old man is nodding again, smiling to himself this time. Ray would like this part of the interview to be over. "Not quite as popular, but still very popular." Emerson stops tapping. His head tilts slightly. "Anyone more *obscure*?"

No, not really. Honesty would be the best policy to save face and, hopefully, move on. "Like I said, I'm a journalist. Unfortunately there aren't enough hours in the day. To be completely honest, I read a lot of that in school, not for pleasure."

"That's okay. They're famous for a reason." So that was all cat and mouse on a full stomach, apparently. "Plus, I'm not looking for someone who's a poetry scholar. Not all aspects of this job are so high-minded. You're comfortable with running errands?"

"Of course."

"Picking up groceries? Dry cleaning? Buying office supplies?"

If Emerson only knew the extent to which Ray will run an errand for pay. The last job, of course, has been omitted from his résumé—that umbrella term of "freelance" working its magic to tell the story of a steady, somewhat respectable job history. "Sure thing. Whatever you'd need."

"Do you cook?"

"Some." That wasn't in the job description, probably for a reason. Ray hopes he likes Mexican; he certainly looks like he's had more than his fair share of burritos. Really, who doesn't like Mexican, though?

"Can you make a sandwich?"

"I make a pretty damn good sandwich, actually." And not just tortas. People like to laugh when they hear employees at Subway being referred to as "sandwich artists," but Ray gets it. When done right, a sandwich can absolutely lead to transcendence: a lot of what he's made for himself has moved him more than most of the conceptual or performance art he's seen, for example.

"Would you feed it to me?"

Thinking about a BLT, Ray's stomach grumbles. Wait… the fuck? Did this motherfucker really just ask that? The tone's shifted, the air now heavy, constricting. Ray's head cants sharply. "Sorry?"

"If my hands were busy writing, would you physically bring a sandwich to my mouth so that I could eat it?"

Ray pauses… takes a moment… Feeding this man a sandwich would be even more humiliating than working as a bike messenger. While he *is* old, it's not like he'd be feeding him because he *couldn't* feed himself; he'd be feeding him because he *wouldn't want to* feed himself—one is an exercise in grace, the other a sacrifice of dignity for no real reason. Because his hands are busy writing? Who the fuck does he think he is, really? That would be a new low. Is this a put-on? A test? If he says, "No, I wouldn't," would he be rewarded like he was with his failure to identify recherché old poets? Or is this crazy fat old fuck for real? And if he is, would Ray do it? Would doing it be part of his penance? Does he deserve new lows now? Too much time is passing; his mouth answers before his head really ca—"I suppose I would."

"You suppose?"

"I would. Yes."

Emerson wiggles a little and smirks. "Good. Now, let me tell you a little bit about the project you'd be helping me with." Ray writes "May need to make, feed sandwich" in his notebook, then looks back up.

Hopefully that smirk was a sign he was just testing him. There's no way... "I've recently begun writing what is to be my final book. As you might imagine, this means a great deal to me."

"Of course."

"While I won't get into the details of the work right now, I will say that it's been a very free-flowing and emotional writing process thus far. I've been on a veritable roll, to tell the truth. Actually spellbound by the subject. Which, again, unfortunately, I can't divulge at this time."

"Naturally," Ray says, nodding along. What if that wasn't a test? What if he's really asked to bring a sandwich to this man's mouth and watch him bite, chew, and swallow it; witness the lump in his throat afterwards, the bits of mayo and mustard in the corners of his mouth, the smell of his breath; a smile, not at the taste, but at the demoralization he's causing? What if this willingness leads down a slippery slope that would end in wiping his ass for him? Again, not because he *needs* him to, but because he *wants* him to as part of a power play? Before the interview, Ray thought he'd been to hell and back, and nothing else could phase him. But he was wrong. He figured the worst he'd have to deal with here would be the smug personality of anyone who takes themselves too seriously, not someone who would fucking want to treat him like some sort of slave. Maybe it's God testing him, not Emerson. Is he supposed to get up and leave now? Not risk serving someone evil, most likely a demon? Or does he deserve to be someone's slave, since he's here now after becoming a slave to a device?

"I've chosen to write this one longhand. So that's where the transcribing comes in. Tell me, can you read this?" Emerson passes Ray a loose sheet of paper that had been tucked between his notepad and the tablet.

Ray clears his throat a little. Water would be nice in this moment. It occurs to him that he had not been offered any at the beginning of the interview. He probably didn't deserve any. He recites:

> *The last captain called to sea again*
> *Sails intrepid forward*
> *The waves they rock*
> *But he cares not*
> *He need only follow the stars*
>
> *Looking down at that compass*
> *Would just lead him astray*

His great old vessel
Done in by monsters, maelstroms,
Tidal waves
Foundering toward lost Atlantis

But by ancient stars
Burning oh so bright
And sails high and strong
He'll catch the gale
That will take him there
Out where he belongs

Not a distant shore
But heaven's door
One with the sublime
Another bright light
In the starry night
Shining with
True greatness

Looking back up, Ray passes the paper back to Emerson. It was a sign from God, that poem. He's with them here. Ray's been sinking in doubt. He need only look up: Be good.

"Thank you. That was a perfectly adequate reading."

"Who's that by?" Ray asks.

"Oh, that was just some silly thing I jotted down this morning to make sure candidates could decipher my chicken scratch." Yeah, with God guiding your hand, maybe. That's not to say Ray thinks it's an exceptionally good poem. It reminds him of some of the poetry he's written for fun, like the one about Fernanda's ass he wrote back in college—far from Nobel-worthy, but not without its moments. Mostly funny. But that would only make sense if God was trying to communicate with him. It required relatability, an appeal to his Truth.

"I liked it."

"It was nothing. But thank you." Ray nods and, still looking at him, writes "Remember the poem" in his notebook then underlines it. He smiles, knowingly. Emerson's posture shifts a little, but his eyes remain fixed and harrowing. "As for the research involved, I may just need help combing through old scholarly journals or texts to find some reference material. A lot of what I'm writing about I know inside and out, but of course fact-checking will still be necessary, which as a journalist I'm sure should come second nature to you. You know, make sure I haven't flubbed up the punctuation in a passage or quotation, that everything is perfect… Me and my old age."

"All information is guilty until proven innocent."

"Is it now?"

Ray said that without really thinking; it just seemed like a good rejoinder. And it was—a smart, sort of cryptic play on words. Now actually mulling it over, he still agrees. People deserve the benefit of the doubt, but information? Always hold it up to a cold white light. Misinformation is a tool of the Devil. Ray smiles, pleased with himself. It was like he was making up a proverb on the spot and expressing the journalistic code of honor deep within himself. So good. "I would say."

"That is a healthy attitude for a journalist and fact-checker." See? See? "I don't know about someone whose main role is supportive, however."

Hold on. What's with this ball-breaker? He's really going to grill him over shit that brilliant? Ray's a person, not information. Maybe Kevin was right. Maybe fuck this guy. Or, maybe, he should rise above it and keep to the Platinum Rule. "Sorry?"

"Well, if I adjure you to drop something off at the Post Office, is the information that is that request suspect? Or would you just do it?"

Okay, fair point—if he's this into semantics, fair point. "Don't get me wrong. I take direction well. I'm not resentful. I wouldn't overanalyze or fume during unglamorous tasks. Nothing would be disregarded."

"Good. Information is information." Yes, Emerson, Ray knows… hence what he just said. "It encompasses everything." Beat that dead horse, man; do something mean to it. "I'm looking for someone who understands the value of words and respects them. I can really only work with someone like that." Now that it's dead like three times over, sit on its neck. Cut out that limp curling tongue. Shit, no wonder this guy loves *Blood Meridian* so much. It's not the indictment, it's the violence.

But stop, man. Stop. Don't be bitter. Be good.

"I suppose I meant information on the page. How about this? All writing is guilty until proven innocent."

"Much better. In fact, I've built my career on that." Easy enough. Ray's learning how to deal with him; if they end up working together— which his gut is telling him he should still want—clarity trumps context. Simple. He writes "Be clear" and underlines it three times. "Let's see.

What else? You're aware that this position will become part-time once I start teaching classes again in the fall, correct?"

"Yes. Actually, that's perfect for me since I'd still like to balance some freelance work while doing this."

"But nothing that would interfere?"

"I wouldn't accept any gigs that would do that, no. Just projects with loose deadlines I could do in my spare time. As a professor, I'm sure you understand."

Emerson nods. He still hasn't written down a word Ray's said. What does that mean? Wouldn't he want to record these answers if he's taking Ray seriously as a candidate? Had he already decided he wouldn't hire him and now he's only going through this as a formality? Why bother? Emerson doesn't seem like the type who would waste his time. Who knows, though. Maybe he's just asking the "fuck you" questions for fun. He's already proven he would poke and prod to get off on exercising power. Like he literally did with those female assistants in the past. Old habits die hard, apparently. No, no. Be good. Give him the benefit of the doubt. Trust. "How do you feel about being on call should an emergency arise? About working the occasional night or weekend?"

"Whatever you'd need," Ray says. And he means it. He's here for a reason, God brought him here for a reason. Emerson isn't having fun with him; God is giving him an opportunity. So fuck your doubts, have faith... don't look down, look up. "Remember the poem," he tells himself. Emerson isn't a big fish to be caught, he's the captain to follow. Smiling, he keeps his eyes on Emerson's. They seemed so confrontational before. But there's no ice there now, only serenity; the blue of the ocean, the blue of the sky.

▲▽▲▲▽▲

The time has come for his least favorite question, but it's one that he's obligated, by basic decency, to ask. His shoulders slump. He folds his hands in his lap. "Now..." Emerson begins. "Do you have anything you'd like to ask me?"

"Sure..." He better keep this short and sweet. "What would the typical day be like?" Thankfully, he does. That's more like half a question. The information it's driving at, though, is a lot more important than anything the others asked; both mostly bothered him with inquests about his approach to critical theory, like he'd care or be impressed. An assistant is not a creative partner; an assistant is not tasked with keeping one on his toes—an assistant is an assistant.

This is what his will do: "I'd have you come in around 10:30 a.m. There will be fresh pages for you to transcribe then, the new ones I would have written the day before as well as marked-up printouts of what you would have transcribed previously. While you're busy with that, I'll be doing research or working on what will be your next day's pages. Then once you've finished transcribing, which shouldn't take too long—I typically average about fifteen hundred words a day, but that may go up to two thousand or even twenty-five hundred with this project—you'll either help me with that research or field incoming messages from my school email account, or both. My emails are not that interesting, so I'm inclined to trust you with them. Your main job as my assistant is to keep distractions away from me, which will keep me writing. I consider most emails terrible distractions. In the weeks ahead, they'll most likely be from my last term's students asking me, lugubriously, to change their grades. I have a form response to use for this. Everything else can be presented to me in summary later on during lunch unless I request it sooner. As for the repast itself, I'll either have you pick us up something from the neighborhood or make it for us, so I hope I can believe you when you say you make a good sandwich."

"You can."

"If there are any errands to run, right after lunch will be the time to do them, usually around 2:30 or 3:00. These can vary wildly, from going to the post office as mentioned before to picking up some confections down at the bakery a few blocks from here, stopping by the pharmacy for me, whatever I may ask. When you come back, I'll have you answer the emails from the morning and you can spend the rest of the afternoon fact-checking what you had last transcribed. The only thing you print out each afternoon is the completed, fact-checked transcription of that morning's longhand pages. I'll answer my own phone and read my own mail, but I'll have you go down to the lobby and get the mail for me. The very end of the day will be spent doing a light cleanup of the apartment. You said you'd feed me a sandwich, so I trust doing dishes wouldn't be a problem?"

"Dishes are fine." Well, that's wonderful to hear, because Emerson truly hates doing his dishes, and not just because of his minor arthritis. Anyone who went to an Ivy should find the notion of performing half of these tasks beyond galling, but he's not really evincing this; saying something is "fine" is giving that idea a C or C-, and that's what it deserved. Ray has not yet disproven himself. He's at least demonstrated that Emerson doesn't have to cancel tomorrow's interviews—if he's any indication of the quality of the candidates left to consider from Kevin's pool, then it should be okay; he's completely hirable. So should Emerson get it over with, see if he wants to take a crack at the printer? Or spend the day tomorrow carrying out those meetings to make damn well sure? It would be a shame to sacrifice another day of writing if he'd be left with Ray at the end of it all, anyway. Or to spite himself by not giving him the final test because he wouldn't want to feel he'd be wasting that time. As smart as Emerson is, he is only human, and the human mind has a fantastic ability to trick itself out of its own best interests when pride is involved. Hmmm… Let's listen to what else Ray asks; this will validate or shed what's left of Emerson's doubts. Since the most honest questions come out of people while they're relaxed, and he couldn't help but be secretly peeved by that last bit of interrogation, it's time to put him back at ease.

"It wouldn't be much more than that and a little tidying. Out here. My bedroom is off limits, of course."

Ray nods. "And when would the day end?"

Another half-question. Or, really, as a follow-up to the first one, more like a quarter-question. But still, perfectly valid: "I'd let you go around 7:00 most days, sometimes 8:00, depending on my needs. And, as we discussed, occasional night and weekend work may be required, but probably not till later on, more likely in the fall when my schedule isn't as open." There's one more question he'd of course want answered, so Emerson might as well get this over with now. "Pay is hourly. I can do twenty." He hates talking about pecuniary matters, even under these circumstances. A part of him's surprised he was willing to offer this so readily now.

"That would work for me." Ray smiles, scribbles what must be the figure in his notebook. He's been sedulously taking notes throughout. Like the struggling, hungry journalist he most certainly is; like the assistant, Emerson can't help but admit now, he wants him to be. That's why he didn't make him ask for that figure, that's why he just offered it— though he knows, if he had, he would've asked directly, this half-savage, half-Cervantes—it was a Freudian slip that proved what he really wants. So what if he rides a bicycle? So what if he doesn't really look much like an Arthur… if he's the wrong type of Hispanic? You would never know by speaking with him or how he dresses, the way he presents himself. More than good enough, he would make a splendid, stoic king.

"I'm going to be honest with you here, Ray. I don't want to hear any other questions you might have."

"Okay."

"I want to give you this job and I want to cancel the other interviews I have lined up. I like you. We did the dance. You understand the duties, you know the hours, you know the pay. Most importantly, you know this job isn't about you, that it's pretty much all about me, and you seem capable of doing well in accordance with that. I agree, as you suggested earlier, that we could work well together. That's a lot more than I can say for the others I've met so far. Do you still want to be my assistant?"

He's smiling big now, this Ray: even showing teeth. "Yes."

"Good. Then I only have one more question for you, and depending on your answer, the job's yours."

"Please."

Emerson moves the tablet and Ray's résumé from his lap to the coffee table. He folds his hands together, save the index fingers and thumbs, which come in line together in a little prayer before his lips. He takes a second and studies Ray: sitting there with an open, comfortable posture, wearing his dapper gray suit, the bright smile that remains. Is this his king, the man who will type his words, defeat his distractions, and help bring his message to the masses? The king who will serve his God dutifully and with exemplary grace? Emerson's wrists snap, his fingers pointing at him, the prayer a gun set to fire. "There is a page of my writing stuck in the printer. Can you get it out?"

▲ ▽ ▲ ▲ ▽

Everyone she's met has been so nice. They've all made Haruka feel so welcome on this, her first day. The office itself is beautiful, two floors of startup company wonderland—ultramodern iMac workstations, exposed brick walls with cool art everywhere, ping-pong, video games, areas to lounge around in with funky furniture. There's a dog running around, a Pomeranian, so cute it doesn't look real. And the work itself has been easy enough and fun, and she's getting paid well to do it.

But none of that matters now.

Right after eating lunch with the others on her team, before going back to the spreadsheet she began working on this morning, she logged into her NYUHome account. Her grades have been trickling in since late last week, and every time she's seen a new one, she's felt such immense satisfaction, so much happiness. It seemed like the perfect way to perk herself back up for the next phase of work, to counteract all that catered Korean barbecue she had just finished weighing heavy in her little stomach. After a big meal, more blood goes to the stomach, less to the brain. Last night, they had read:

PSYCH-UA 32: Social Psychology: A
MAP-UA 553 Cultures and Contexts: Pagan Europe: A
MATH-UA 122: Calculus II: A

But now they've been joined by:

MAP-UA 400 Texts and Ideas: Exploring the Western
Canon: B

She almost vomited when she first saw it. "No, no. It must be a mistake," she thought. There is no way she could get a B. She had had an A- in the class leading up to the final paper and that paper was perfect; she understood *The Metamorphosis* and its themes completely, expressed her thoughts with simple eloquence and irrefutable logic. It was an A paper all the way. But there is a possibility that Professor Towers couldn't see it. That he misinterpreted the objectively good essay before him through the lens of some stupid ugly old subjective reading glasses. Maybe he wanted her to write her final paper in bigger words, words that he might use. Most intelligent people know that actually isn't the best way to write: large and obscure words tax mental resources too much, interrupting you from making your point and disconnecting you from your audience. That's why simplicity in speech is valued and used by people in the most important fields, like tech and politics. To express things that really matter in this world. But maybe she wasn't supposed to write something objectively good for a broad audience like that. Maybe it was just for an audience of one: Emerson Towers. Did she misunderstand this, mess up the game? That there is a possibility of this literally makes today the worst day of her life. Way worse than a week ago when her old iPhone was smashed by that lunatic. Soon after that happened, she knew the phone could be replaced with something better, and it was the next day. If her GPA has actually been compromised, it cannot be replaced. Her perfect record will be gone forever. Growing up, she believed in the philosophy that anything lower than an A, including an A-, was an F. Even her parents thought she was too hard on herself. But the proof is in the pudding: she's had perfect grades her entire life. Until today. Right now, updating this list of musicians and record labels active on Tumblr, she wishes she was dead. Or that Emerson Towers was dead. Or the both of them and all of these stupid bands and label people and everyone on the planet Earth was dead. If she can't get this B changed, there isn't a point to anything. Seriously.

But she can't show it. The sorrow, the anger. The despair. These terrible feelings. She must save them for later. She will cry alone in her dorm room tonight. She will kick and scream and rage at the air. Not now. She must finish out the day pretending, going about her duties as the Communications Intern with a smile on her face and an upbeat attitude. This is the only way to behave in an office, especially a young, fun one like this. She must not let herself get too stressed out here. It would release an excess of cortisol, which is bad for cognitive functioning. You only get one first impression. You only get one first day.

But, but, but… if she really has a B, then who cares? Neither Facebook, Google, or Apple would hire her then. English is supposed to be easy! There would be no way to spin it; the pratfall effect does not apply in this situation. If this is really the first day of the rest of her life, then that life won't be worth living.

No. Keep it together. Block it out. It's a mistake. It has to be! Don't be sad yet. Being sad is such a waste. Being mad, too. It makes everyone's face red and puffy and nobody looks good with a red puffy face. There will be no sadness or madness tonight. Just think about something else and relax until all the info is in, until everything has been verified. Be productive tonight. Write him. Ask about the grade and the final. Then figure out what to do next. Haruka reaches for her phone and makes a move on Words With Friends. Her word is 'QI.'

Then a revelation: in the end, grades are just entered into a computer like everything else is entered into a computer. Computers can be hacked. So if it is an actual B, there is no need to get sad or mad—only even. Change the grade somehow. Sure, if the school found out, she would probably be expelled. But that won't happen. As it stands, her life would already be ruined. She'd have nothing to lose. If she really got a B, she'll have one of her hacker friends, one of the people she had planned on getting to hack that Ray, change it to the grade she really deserves: an A. Then she'll have them get Emerson back somehow too. Then that Ray, finally; she hasn't forgotten about him. But she must prioritize. With cold calculation she'll have her revenge. All of it. Not with the hot head she's still trying to dampen now. She'll get these awful men back by being herself. Who she really is: Smart.

All these people think they can mess with Haruka lately. No way. She's too smart for them. She's one of the youngest interns here at Tumblr, she's so smart. They have no idea who they're messing with.

Twenty bucks an hour is no great wage in New York, a city where the middle class starts somewhere in the six figures, but it is to Ray. Especially for doing what he's doing—which is to say: not much. The little work he has is done to the best of his ability, however, and to the satisfaction of his employer. This is all that really matters to him in fulfilling his role as an assistant. In the week since he's started, he's stolen no time, done nothing wrong; all duties have been carried out with complete probity.

He works from the living room on an old foldout card table against the window, having set up Emerson's desktop computer, monitor, and printer there to create his own little workspace, while the man himself toils away at his desk in the office. The editorial part of Ray's job basically just involves the transcription thing and spending about fifteen minutes a day going through the big guy's inbox, sending those form responses to the grade-grubbing students he mentioned during the interview. There hasn't been any research so far, probably because Emerson's still writing, as he says, "from the heart, pardon the cliché," and also because he seems to really know his shit.

All the pages Emerson hands over are perfect—the spelling, the grammar; there might be some lines crossed out or new ones written in the margins, but what's intended for inclusion is without flaw. As far as fact-checking is concerned, he needs none. Ray does it, but he never finds anything wrong: the Five W's always check out. Even subjective stuff like structure, tone, word choice, etcetera, he can't really find fault in—not that he'd overstep his role and suggest anything, anyway. But practically anyone who's ever written anything will read someone else's prose back and tell themselves they'd have at least done a thing or two differently, flipped this phrase, massaged that line. Not here. It might help that Ray's only familiar with about half of what Emerson's going on about, but that's not everything; you know good writing when you see it, and his stuff works.

It's the personal assistant duties that take up the bulk of the three to four hours of actual work Ray does a day: the cooking, cleaning, running around the neighborhood. But these aren't all that bad; the feeding him thing seems to have been a bluff or a test, and even if it turns out later that it wasn't, at this point Ray wouldn't really care. He feels like he's gotten that good of a deal with this so far.

To make the most of all his downtime, and feeling like it's there for a reason, he's going through with his plan of internet contrition—doing good deeds on platforms like Facebook and Reddit, answering questions and weighing in with thoughtful responses and unique insight when apposite; telling lighthearted jokes that spread joy here and there, too. He's done so much good already: for Emerson, for friends, for internet strangers, for himself.

He's transcribing now while the coffee's going—which is what he always does first thing—and while his fingers fly, he thinks about this: how happy he is to have this job. How well everything's going now. How since the moment at the end of the interview last week when he un-jammed Emerson's printer and was offered this job everything's seemed okay for the first time in a long time… It's still a little too soon to tell, and of course he wouldn't want to jinx it, but the thought that this job could be his real path out of purgatory, this peculiar academic Emerson his Virgil of sorts, has occurred to him now on more than one occasion.

The drip is done. He pours Emerson a cup—milk, two sugars—and brings it to him in the office. He doesn't say "Thank you." He doesn't say anything. But Ray doesn't mind. When he needs more coffee, he'll shout out "Coffee please!" and Ray'll heat up the pot or get another one going. The time they talk is at lunch, and only if they feel like it; forced conversation, it seems, is just as bad as forced writing to Emerson Towers. When he doesn't say anything, or when he's busy reading, Ray's happy to just eat and look at his phone to find more opportunities to help people.

Ray pours a cup for himself—black, easy—and continues transcribing. He finds he types faster when he lets his mind wander, that paying attention to the meaning of the words is not a good idea until the afternoon when he fact-checks. So now he thinks about others being happy for him. How thrilled the projection of his mother was that he had gotten something resembling a full-time job. How she googled Emerson and ordered his most famous book. How the projection of his dad, always so hard to please, seemed really glad for him, too, telling him it sounded like he was getting back on the right track then calling him "mijo" for the first time in years. He thinks about how even the projection of Brian has seemed cooler since he got this job. How they had a little toast over it, and he said, "Hey man—good for you. You're still a professional bitch, but at least you're not making your living doing what a child does for fun anymore," not even going near the Hispanic help stereotype of his domestic duties. How everything's coming up Ray. Then his fingers rest. The pages from yesterday are done. He scans the document quickly to make sure he didn't fuck anything up. He didn't, and the lack of squiggly red or green lines from the automatic spelling and grammar check is a testament to that. It's 11:15 and he's right on schedule.

Time to check the old inbox, his own. He opens up Chrome, which he installed on the first day to try to make his internet sessions a little faster. It worked kind of, but not as well as deleting all the malware off the computer itself and installing a few updates; the thing's still pretty slow—it's a PC from, like, the early aughts if not late nineties—but it's a lot better than it was. The first time Emerson used it after Ray made those changes he commented on its increased performance the next day. The cool thing about working with old people is they're bowled over by even the slightest of technological feats. Ray has five new emails since he last checked about two hours ago, right before leaving home:

> The New Yorker Store – Cover Spotlight: Spectrum of Light
> OkCupid! – rgonzo, New matches!
> Kmart – It's heating up, stay indoors: Save on an RCA
> HDTV + enter the TLC Extreme Sweepstakes
> Groupon – Brunch for Two or Four
> eBay – Ray: You have a special offer from eBay

He marks all of these as read without opening them. Unfortunately, after going on a couple of lousy dates this past week with ladies who outright lied about their appearance in their profile pics, specifically their weight, it seems OkCupid's a bit of a bust in terms of finding a nice girl. There's nothing wrong with having a plus-sized body type, but you can't start a romance off with dishonesty. Next, he logs into Emerson's account from the NYU portal. He has seven new messages. All have subjects like

"Grading question" or "Final paper grade." Scanning them, one of the sender's names sticks out in particular: Haruka Kidokoro.

No!! No, no, no, no, no, no, no!

It couldn't be the same Haruka. Could it?! She did go to NYU… but there's gotta be a decent number of Harukas there. Right? It's gotta be, like, the Japanese Stephanie. Ray clicks the message.

Hi Professor Towers,

The final grade I received in your class was not what I had expected. I was wondering if you could tell me my grade for the final paper I wrote about Kafka's "The Metamorphosis"? I had been keeping track of my overall grade based on your syllabus, and thought the paper I turned in was a very strong one. Please provide the grade so I might verify with my own records.

Thank you,
Haruka

It reads like a lot of the grade grubbers' emails, except a little more entitled. The tone is off, the ordering of the sentences more dickish than it needs to be; whatever is supposed to be polite is transparently not. Sounds like her. But could it really be?

A new tab. He googles the name: results from Facebook and LinkedIn. He clicks on Facebook. It's her. Holy shit. NYU, Class of '15. A different photo than anything she uses on OkCupid—an Instagrammed selfie of her looking away with a stretch of Midtown Manhattan skyline behind her. Most of her information is private. He goes back to Google, clicks on the LinkedIn URL. She's a communications intern at Tumblr right now. Just started. The profile is sparse; she's young. She was a social media intern somewhere else Ray's never heard of before that. NYU again under Education. The largest section is about her volunteer experience. Most of it took place in the Bay Area, which means that's indeed where she's from, like she had first said. Not heaven… Not hell. The Bay Area.

So what is all of this supposed to mean? Who's behind this one? God? Fate? Destiny? Why remind him of her? And why now, when things are finally settling down? He thought he defeated her. Whatever it is, Ray doesn't like it. Was he brought to Emerson, who's made things so much better, only to be brought back to her—she who had made things so much worse? Built up even higher to be knocked down even lower, like she said? Another circle of hell?

No. He defeated her, he recognized his death and sin and began his real atonement with the act of destroying her phone.

This is proof of that defeat.

Here she is, crushed, trying to start the process of raising her grade with her empty questions about verifying records—her perfect GPA, which she's currently lying about on LinkedIn, vitiated. Eighteen- and nineteen-year-olds think that shit is devastating, even though nobody really cares about or checks your GPA after college, except for, like, grad schools, who only barely do, taking a whole lot of other things into consideration. Haruka is a funny demon. A trivial, stupid thing that Ray can easily rise above.

So how should he? Let her wallow in her defeat? Make it seem like Emerson is ignoring her, just as she ignored him when he was at his lowest? No, no. Ray is better than that. Ray is good. He adheres to protocol. That which Emerson laid out. He looks up the grade she received on her final paper, a C+, and sends her the form response:

Dear Haruka,

You can be assured that the grade you received for the term is accurate. Your grade for the final was a C+.

If you would like, I can send your paper back to you through the mail so you can read my comments.

Regards,
Professor Towers

He sends similar responses to the others, then gets on Facebook. Scrolling down. No one's really asking for anything, and he can't think of any fun or witty comments to add to any of the posts showing up on his feed. Instead of forcing something, he just likes a bunch of mildly interesting things so those people feel good about what they posted. Being the answer to a question no one asked is not doing good, but offering positive vibes is. He logs on to Reddit to be of better use. "Coffee please!" shouts Emerson. "And a Danish!"

Late morning, when he gets his second cup of coffee, Emerson likes a snack. A donut. A Danish. Whatever was bought at the bakery in the days before. Ray heats up the pot, gets a Danish out of the box, puts it on a plate. There are only two left. He'll ask him if he wants him to get more at lunch. When the coffee's begun to steam, he goes into the office, grabs Emerson's mug, takes it back to the kitchen, pours some into it, then brings the coffee and the Danish to him. Emerson writes away, a copy of the *Iliad* open next to him. Ray returns to the living room. A guy on r/cycling is asking for input on whether he should try riding his bike to work. Ray offers him some:

Do a dry run on the weekend. That's really the best way to figure out what you're getting yourself into. Hope it works out, and have fun!

Over on r/diy, someone's posted a picture of an urban vegetable garden they built. He can tell it's not in Brooklyn, which would be too expected and precious to warrant any kind of encouragement, but rather some truly gray place like Detroit or Baltimore that could really use shit like that, so Ray offers them positive reinforcement:

Awesome project! There's nothing like eating food you've grown yourself.

When Ray was a kid, he'd help his mom with the garden in their backyard, growing tomatoes, carrots, parsnips, radishes, spinach. And there really isn't anything like eating from your own garden. He thinks about getting some seeds and cultivating little herbs or something in the windowsill at the apartment. Not the one in his room—not enough light—but the living room. Then he contemplates the view, looking out at the city from there. That's where he lost himself. That's where he found himself again, recently. That's where he is now. Rising. Above everything that had been bringing him down. No James Murphy over here. Not anymore. Rising. Above it all. Even above Haruka, now defeated. He got his proof today. He goes to YouTube, plugs in his earbuds, and puts on Ice Cube's *It Was A Good Day*. Although it's only late morning, he knows he can already make that call. Even if Emerson broke over the low volume he's playing this at and asked Ray to go and get then feed him a six-foot hoagie, it would still end up being a good day. Haruka has been defeated and he is moving the fuck on. Ray's rising, like one of those herbs he's planning on planting, among the skyscrapers from the perspective of his living room window, those very monuments to man, that man-made mountain range, over them, even, in that windowsill, as they lean toward the sun climbing up, up, up! Ice Cube gets it. A good day, indeed.

▲ ▲ ▽ ▽ ▽ ▽

The dog is staring at her again. His big brown eyes fixed on hers, feeling her pain. Dogs are supposed to be one of the most emotionally intelligent animals next to humans. Even more emotionally intelligent than chimps, despite the greater difference in DNA. Man's best friend, they call them. Makes sense. Haruka bets they might even have more emotional intelligence than humans. This dog knows what none of her colleagues do: that she is the saddest person alive.

But them not knowing is a good thing. They all think she's the same girl they met before the Big Moment, before her life was ruined by Emerson Towers; they think she is very upbeat and a very good communications intern. And they are right about the latter part. This job is pretty easy. She just makes spreadsheets and sends emails all day, and it only gets busy sometimes. As for the first part, she must wear a mask. Only the dog can see through it. Or maybe it smells it, this rank sadness within. Or maybe it's the sixth sense they talk about. Dogs know what's in the air; it could be sensing it there around her. Every time she exhales more of it expands out in front of her, the inhalations that follow sucking some back in, this then mixing with what was still inside her, becoming even greater, deeper: a constant, infinite sadness.

It's been a month since she got the bad news. And none of her hacker friends will help. Well, one said he'd be willing, but it would cost her 250,000 dollars. She thought he was joking. But apparently hacking into a school's system to change grades can lead to a pretty hefty fine and a jail sentence starting at two years. So now she doesn't know what she can do. She feels powerless. Even going on dates, which she's done a lot of this last month, trying to get over it, has done nothing to help make her feel more empowered. The B grade has corrupted her to the core.

While she'd rather right this wrong done to her, fix this profound mistake, she's doing what she can to get back at Emerson until she can figure out exactly how. She spends her downtime at work and some time at home in her dorm room leaving bad reviews for all of his books on

Amazon. This is done with several accounts, so as not to appear too suspicious. She also has found every positive review of his books unhelpful and is currently working on finding all of the negative reviews of his books helpful. Then after that she plans on leaving more bad reviews on this weird online community for losers who like books a lot called Goodreads. None of this has really made her feel any less upset about things, but it has made her feel like she's being proactive, which is something. Better than nothing. Amazon is a big deal to authors. Goodreads seems like it is, too. And her reviews will be online forever.

The dog runs away. Maybe it got bored. Or, more likely, scared. Something so cute shouldn't be in the presence of this awful sadness hanging about her. She hears a gchat alert through her headphones, interrupting the TED Talk she has on in the background, and looks back over at the screen. It's Ben, one of the interns on the community team. She suspects he has a crush on her.

> Ben: Hey Haruka – tickets just went on sale for the ps1 warm up parties. I'm going to the first one with some ppl on my team and others from the company on july 7th. R u interested?

Haruka doesn't know what "the ps1 warm up parties" are. She copies the phrase into Google.

She clicks the first result – MoMA PS1: Warm Up 2012. It looks like the official site. For whatever it is. She learns.

It's a daytime outdoor dance party. When she first saw it was affiliated with MoMA, she thought it must've been cool. But it looks like it's in Queens. Haruka's never been to Queens. Well once, the airport when she moved here, but that doesn't really count. She heard it wasn't cool. She's hung out in Brooklyn a decent number of times now; that's easy enough, it's off the L. But never Queens. Is Queens cool now? She thinks about googling that question, "Is Queens cool now?" but doesn't. Instead, she reads more. Tickets are fifteen bucks. A little too much for something she doesn't want to do. But if people from the company are going, she should go. It's a part of networking. She'll say she is interested, even though she isn't really. She's never heard of any of the people playing music and a mid-day dance party sounds weird. She prefers dancing after a couple of drinks, not to mention in a very dark place, but she's going to be with colleagues and she's underage. Also, Ben's crush on her creeps her out. He's very nice and he's white and sort of boring-looking. They also met at a place where they both work. Gross.

She begins to type. Her chat reads:

me: count me in! looks funnnn

The chat box says Ben is typing. Then:

Ben: awesome sauce!!

This pisses her off. Ben only started writing "awesome sauce" to her after she did to him one day. Haruka goes back to the search results for "the ps1 warm up parties." At least cool news outlets seem to write about it. She sees stuff from *Vice, Gothamist, Time Out*. Maybe it won't be so bad. Maybe she can drink a little something beforehand, discreetly. Dancing might do her some good.

Can someone as sad as she is still dance, though? Like, really dance? As if they mean it? She'll find out in a couple of weeks, she guesses.

The dog's come back. He's staring at her again, this time with a toy in his mouth. Is he trying to cheer her up? It's too cute for words. She reaches out to pet him, but he won't let her near. Another cute creature gone mean.

▲ ▲ ▽ ▽ ▲

Weekends now are almost exclusively reserved for folly; it's nice to get lost in *The Times*, watch a little television, catch up on his personal email inbox. Having no papers to grade or lectures to plan have made these days absolutely wonderful, and since he's having productive enough weeks, writing is not necessary. A little bit of rest can go a long way; sometimes the spell must temporarily be broken—even the most beautiful of eulogies benefits from the occasional dramatic pause, and of course the speaker must have a little time between words to catch his breath. He still reads the classics every day—that as necessary as food, water, air—but he does so only modestly: one- to two-hundred pages, mostly in English. Otherwise, everything Emerson does is just a bit of fun.

He orders his meals in, except for breakfast, which is easy enough to make, having grown accustomed to staying at home since hiring his weekday help. It's been nearly three weeks since he's left the apartment, in fact, save opening the front door to grab the paper. Though even if he didn't have his assistant, he probably wouldn't go out now, anyway. It's getting far too hot for such things. This summer is shaping up to be a real doozy, like many have been in recent years. New York used to have Edenlike summers. But now, because of Chinese capitalism and Indian overpopulation and those galoots out in Middle America driving their pick-up trucks and SUVs everywhere, Emerson can't even go down to the corner deli and pick up a pastrami sandwich without getting drenched in his own sweat. He should not have to feel like a dirty animal in order to eat a dead one. If only more people lived in cities with decent public transportation and intrinsically low carbon emissions per capita. If only more people were more civilized.

It's Sunday, 1:30. He's already been through *The Times*—a fairly boring edition—and is currently firing up the computer. Another nice thing about having hired Ray is now his computer is markedly faster. It's only of minor importance, speeding up his computer, but Emerson can't say he's not grateful for it.

Once the desktop loads and his machine settles down, ceasing to make the hellacious grinding noises it's liked to exasperate him with for the past five or so years, he clicks on the Internet Explorer icon and is directed to AOL. He logs into his email account.

A few days have passed since he's checked it and there are twenty-some new messages. He likes to look at them in the order they were received, so he scrolls down to the last mail he checked, making an effort not to read anything along the way. This is done by looking up over the monitor and watching the subject lines and senders go from bold to regularly weighted in his lower periphery. He sees Riverside Park across the street, the Hudson, the North Bergen basalt in warm summer light. It's nice because, even though his computer is now in the living room, the view has not really changed from that in his office. He imagines there is a setting he could adjust that would order his inbox in the way he prefers, but he does not care enough to try to figure this out, and worries it might transmute the entire inbox, not just the first page where his new mail would be. At any rate, his system works. This new batch of mail first seems unimportant—the New York Public Library is soliciting donations; the folks at Lincoln Center are letting him know it's the final week of an opera he's never cared for; a colleague whom he used to teach alongside at Harvard during the very start of his career, but never much liked, has sent over an article from a by and large sophistic literary journal he's sure must be pointless—but then, near the top, he spots a message from Claire, sent yesterday. The subject line reads "Checking in." He drags the arrow over from the scroll bar and clicks to open it.

Hi Daddy,

I wanted to write and say hello because I didn't get a chance to call before we left, and it's been a few weeks since we last spoke. The run-up to our trip was pretty hectic, as I'm sure you can imagine!

The trip! Emerson got so caught up with his writing that he completely forgot she would be gone already. So Claire is in Central America now! Oh dear... He wishes she wouldn't have sent this. Now he's going to be unbearably anxious until she gets back...

We made it here without incident, though—

Yes, but will you return without incident? It's occurred to him, on several occasions throughout all of this, that there is a good possibility she and the family will get kidnapped. Emerson knows Spanish, but it is Castilian Spanish, not whatever brutish Mexican or Central American dialect the kidnappers would be using, phoning him from their imbricated-red-roofed, weatherworn compound. Monday can't come fast enough now! At least if Ray were here he could help translate the ransom call.

—and we are having just a marvelous time. We landed in Cancun late Tuesday afternoon as planned. After spending the night getting pampered at a small boutique resort I'm sure even you would love—

Hardly.

—we got up early on Wednesday, rented a car, and began our adventure. So far we've seen Ek Balam, Chichen Itza, and Tulum. The kids have been great. Jonathan in particular is having

the time of his life, and not just when learning about the doomsday lore and human sacrifices at the temple sites.

Why does Claire seem to revel in her son showing such pellucid signs
of emotional disturbance? Emerson isn't bothered or surprised that he's
interested in death—most intelligent, sentient individuals are at a young
age, and anyone with his genes would be both—but the type of death he
finds so incredibly fascinating is deeply, deeply troubling. This violent,
backwards, savage sort of death. It spells out bad things, this fixation;
points to something profoundly wrong with the boy. They wouldn't be
there if not for him… Emerson wouldn't have to worry now if not for
him…

> In a little break from the ruins, today we went scuba diving, and
> we had to practically drag him out of the water. Kate seemed to
> really enjoy it also, but I could tell she was relieved to take the
> mask off in the end! I must admit I was, too.

Scuba diving? What's next, parachuting? Perhaps Jonathan isn't to
blame. Perhaps it's Marc, the good doctor. As the father, the patriarch
of the family, he is there to guide the way. They wouldn't go scuba diving
if he didn't think it was acceptable. They wouldn't be there if he didn't
think it was acceptable. You can have a respectable profession and a
good income and still lack common sense. Emerson's getting more and
more upset. And not just because of the danger involved—something as
ridiculous as a doctor taking his family to risk life and limb in a series of
otiose, as they say, "bucket list" experiences. No, it also has to do with
class. The daughter Emerson spent so much time and money and energy
culturing is enjoying a vacation that seems so utterly… pedestrian. This
would all be fine for a low I.Q. family of four from Indiana, but not
them, not people so closely related to Emerson Towers. It's just so terribly embarrassing.

> I'm writing you from the hotel in Tulum now, which thankfully,
> and somewhat surprisingly, has wifi. We leave for Belize tomor-
> row, stopping in Chacobben along the way. Marc's driving, of
> course, so don't worry. It's going to be a long ride—we probably
> won't cross the border until evening. I'd be in a swivet if not for
> Kate's phone and Marc's iPad, which Jonathan's been using a
> lot. On the plane and in the car so far, they've been a godsend.

Now it seems like this entire email has been specifically calculated to get at him. Claire knows exactly how he feels about those things. Of course the best option would be to give them a book, like he did with her. They're probably sitting there playing mindless games, watching silly cartoons. Flashing colors, noise, nonsense. What the hell is this? Emerson stands up.

He crosses the living room into the kitchen. Opening one of the cupboards, he reaches for a box of Entenmann's chocolate chip cookies. He carries them back over to the computer and, sitting down, pops one into his mouth. He chews. It's soft, sweet, delicious. He swallows, closes his eyes, and reaches for another to replace it, then another.

It's not Marc. It's not Jonathan. It's Claire.

He sees this for what it is now. A new form of rebellion. After her teens, she grew up, settled down, and twenty years later, she's gotten bored again. Not only this email but the entire trip was indeed carefully orchestrated to upset him. Her guile's gone above and beyond. This message could win a horror prize in literature, it's so unbelievably upsetting. As frightening as anything he's ever read: up there with The Book of Revelation, Dante, Poe, *The Picture of Dorian Gray*, Mary Shelley's *Frankenstein*.

A fourth cookie goes in. He opens his eyes. Let's get this over with—

We fly out of Belize Thursday morning. I'm unsure if I'll have internet access for the remainder of the trip, so no need to reply.

Of course there's no need to reply. The damage has been done; she did what she intended to do.

I'll give you a call shortly after we get back. In the meantime, attached is a picture of us in front of Chichen Itza's El Castillo, which, if you weren't already aware, was named as one of the seven wonders of the world in a web poll a few years ago.

All my love,
Claire

P.S. We've been covering up as much as possible and have used so much sunscreen these past four days, I should've told you to buy stock! Obviously, I'm getting quite jealous of Marc's tan.

Claire, Claire, Claire… Why torture your father so? This postscript being—what—a nictation to go along with the little smirk above, the bit about the Cancun resort even he would love? A callback to his original remonstrations more offensive than claiming he'd be comfortable in a place most famous as the site of the Great Annual Springtime Collegiate Orgy? If there had been any doubt about her aggression with all this before, it could only be quashed now. This last part was clearly meant to add insult to injury. Emerson swallows the last bit of cookie. He slides his tongue over his left bicuspid, where a smudge of chocolate remains. Just a little more to get him through this.

He knows sweets are bad for him. It's common knowledge, and his doctor has told him, personally, as much. Still, he considers them friends. The good outweighs the bad. They are there for him when everyone else lets him down—offering support, making him feel a little better. These are the chief functions of a friend, who otherwise take time away from more important things, like reading. And sweets, always there, ever faithful, never disappoint.

Is his daughter a friend? He used to think so. And he'd still like to. She's family, of course; he loves her very much, and will be worried sick until she comes back. But what, exactly, is she trying to do with all this? Has she maintained this semblance of closeness in their relationship for all these years just to get back at him now for what he did to her mother, the family?

Emerson looks out at the New Jersey cliffs and thinks of his son. Was he the more generous of the two in cutting him off completely? Is there more love there?

Another cookie goes into the mouth and Emerson clicks the button to download the photo attachment. The photo pops up on the screen, and there's the family, one of the new seven wonders of the world triumphant behind, the sun hitting everything at a harsh angle: Claire, in a verdigris dress, a large straw hat and sunglasses doing their damnedest to protect her; Marc, with similar glasses and no hat, wearing a short-sleeved button-up over linen pants; the kids between them: Kate wearing—good grief—a pink tank top and no hat and Jonathan a T-shirt, shorts, and Yankees cap, smiling so maniacally you can practically make out his uvula, even at such a distance.

"All my love," she wrote. Perhaps it's best not to reserve the weekends for folly. Perhaps he should just power through and write until the fall. Ray couldn't be here all the time for support, but he did agree to some weekend work. Some is better than none. Anything would be better than this. Emerson weeps.

▲ ▲ ▽ ▽ ▲ ▽

It's definitely some other level bullshit, having to come in on the Fourth of July working this type of gig. This is still an office job, even if it is a home office and a lot of his duties are more like those in the service industry. But whatever. The honeymoon phase couldn't last forever.

Emerson had broken the news Monday, at lunch. "Ray..." he began, "Since Fourth of July falls on a Wednesday this year and we're not looking at any sort of long weekend situation, I was wondering if you wouldn't mind coming in." Ray was chewing at the time and didn't want to answer with a mouth full of mushed-up fish tacos, so he didn't respond right away. This made him seem kind of cool to the idea, which he of course was, even though he wouldn't have wanted to give off that impression under normal circumstances, and that seemed to make Emerson uncomfortable. "And of course I'd let you leave an hour or two early, make sure you'd be able to fulfill any obligations you might have for the evening, watching Macy's fireworks or the like."

Ray swallowed. "Sure, whatever you need."

"Great."

And so here he is. Forty-five minutes into it and already not doing much. Just spreading good vibes on Facebook, liking quality patriotic posts as well as barely passable ones made by posters who would feel bad about themselves if no one liked them, which no one else yet had. Soon he'll pop over to Reddit and upvote and comment on similar items from strangers. There haven't been emails from grade-grubbing students to address lately; the time for that appears to have passed, and the NYU inbox has been otherwise quiescent. He's not really sure why Emerson needed him here today. Unless maybe it's not him, perhaps it's a part of his penance.

It's been weird: the big guy's game's a little off this week. He's not turning in quite as many pages, and there have even been a few typos. They've been easy enough to fix, but still... something's definitely amiss. Maybe it's the heat? Ray's primary task these past few days has just been to be at his beck and call to give him sweets. Monday he finished a box of cookies and asked Ray to go out and pick up some donuts, so he got a dozen, and they were gone the next day. He then bought a dozen more, and this morning could see there are now only five left. Is it good to help an old man consume this much sugar? It couldn't be, but there's not much he can really do about it. He wasn't hired to advise. He was hired to assist. He just hopes it's not on some Jack Kevorkian-type shit.

The one thing he can do to help ameliorate his diet is try to make more nutrient-dense lunches. Monday was tilapia tacos with whole wheat tortillas, salsa, and brown rice. Yesterday was a spinach salad and chicken soup—and while the soup did come from a can, Progresso, it was at least the low-sodium variety, which, additionally, doesn't have much of a calorie count. Emerson never really cares what they have for lunch; he'll eat anything. Or at least all of the things Ray knows how to make. They've been through his entire menu now. His only requests are about the baked goods before and after it.

Today Ray's gonna make hamburgers, even though it could hardly be considered healthy. It would just feel odd and sort of stilted not eating something like that on the Fourth, especially while everyone else is out there getting it in, and the emotional and perhaps spiritual benefits of celebrating the occasion would surely outweigh the negative effect of clogging Emerson's arteries with yet more deleterious shit. He'll make sure the ground beef he gets is lean, maybe he'll buy whole wheat buns. Use some of the leftover spinach from yesterday instead of lettuce. There.

Also strange this week: Emerson's been a lot more talkative at lunch, asking Ray all these questions about Mexico. Ray's only been there twice in his life, and nowhere near the Yucatan Peninsula, the area he's been inquiring about specifically, mostly in relation to its crime rates. They've all been questions way better suited for Google. Ray explained he wasn't that familiar with the area on Monday, and that his dad's side of the family is more of what they call Tejano or Texican, which Emerson just thought was cute. But because, as is the trend, he had even less to do that afternoon than usual, Ray took it upon himself to look up the crime rates for the Yucatan, then draft and print out a little report about it, leaving it with Emerson during his valediction that evening. So then yesterday at lunch, Emerson asked a few follow-up questions about everything, this time bringing up kidnapping there, which Ray not only couldn't really answer but also made him suspect Emerson might just be trying to make him feel weird about his heritage like Brian would for some reason, before he asked him to make a similar dossier for Belize, which sort of did away with that notion and left Ray not really knowing what to think. This is the closest thing he's had to a research assignment, and it's weird as hell.

But he did it, and left it with him prior to heading home yesterday, and suspects it's what they'll be talking about today at lunch over their marginally more nutritious hamburgers.

Is all of this indeed a part of his penance? It might make sense. Most of his Fourth of Julys since he's been dead have been fun—Bushwick barbecues, lackadaisical days at the Rockaways, Fireworks over the East River then Hudson from friends' and friends of friends' rooftops; burgers, hot dogs, bourbon, and beer, burgers, hot dogs, bourbon, and beer—of course after he recognized his great sin, he should have to report for duty on a day only the most unfortunate souls in America do—your food service folks, grocery store clerks, other low-wage employees attending to the more fortunate—made to come in without much real work to do, where at lunch he'll discuss something with discomfiting racial undertones, which could be designed to be as such, or which might be designed to mean nothing at all.

They still haven't called, which is good. Ray's here: also good. Emerson has sort of been counting on those horrible brigands making their call during regular business hours, when banks would be open. It's the Fourth today, but he very well couldn't expect such thugs to know it from the Sixteenth of September or even the Fifth of May; he couldn't expect them to realize that the banks are, in fact, closed for a holiday, so he had Ray come in just in case. Only one day to go until Claire flies back. Only one day until he can relax, breathe a bit more freely again.

Emerson didn't mind working today. Aside from enjoying the junk food of the occasion, he's never celebrated the Fourth of July like most Americans. Instead, he reads Whitman or Melville, recites *The Star-Spangled Banner* to himself, and contemplates the true meaning of what it is to be an American: a much better way to spend the day than the throngs of idiots causing or bearing witness to so many stupid explosions to the tune of the anthem. What a perversion… if Frances Scott Key would've only known, perhaps he would have never composed his marvelous poem, one of the finest ever by an amateur. No, Emerson is far from minding: Above anything else, on this day, he likes to do some work. Even during years when there wasn't a book in progress that required his full attention, he always found something to do—toyed with ideas for a *Times* article, tweaked his syllabi for the next year. For it is work that truly defines what it means to be an American, what separates and elevates its people above all others in the world today.

If only he weren't so distracted by all this Claire business, he would be doing better work. Or perhaps just more; his word count has been a little low, he can tell, but what's there is still good and he knows it. He watches the pen move across the page, each letter a drop of blood from his still gushing heart, every bit as rutilant as when he began. Oh! The Culture! Oh! His cynosure! Though he's not yet far enough along to discuss any American authors, and he wouldn't want to interrupt the flow of the text and jump to that point, it is still very much a celebration of Americanism: for it is with his own superlative American hand that he is writing something destined to join the Canon. He must keep going, even though that hand is beginning to cramp up.

"Ray! More coffee! Two donuts!" He hopes a part of Ray can appreciate working on a day like today, though he doubts it, and won't be the one to mention why he should. Really, it should go without saying. Here he is at his side right now, as Emerson continues on with more words, placing two donuts upon his desk, grabbing the coffee mug, forcing a smile. He seems to think Emerson can't see him out of the corner of his eye or in the reflection of the window in front of him, but he can. In his office, in his world, he knows everything. If only the one out there—out where his darling daughter, who may or may not hate him, and her family are—were so predictable.

▲ ▲ ▽ ▲ ▽ ▽

There's no point in going out tonight. All her friends from school are still gone for the summer and she hasn't been in the mood to make any new ones, so there would be no one to hang out with. Her only real friend right now is Siri, but she can't talk with her in public or people will think she's weird. Besides, she's always watched the fireworks on TV before. Why stop now? She'll watch them on the TV in one of the student lounges here in her building, or better yet on her computer, with a live feed streaming online somewhere. From bed. Where she is now, under the covers. Looking at her Instagram feed on her phone, scrolling through retro-style images of people she knows and people she doesn't enjoying the holiday with unhealthy food, sparklers, dumb grins. Haruka's bringing the world to her. No need to go out into it.

It's bad enough she's going out this weekend. To the daytime dance party with her coworkers. She's not in the mood to dance. At all. It was her birthday the other day and even then she didn't do anything to celebrate. She still doesn't feel any better about life in general. It's going to be terrible.

Everything is terrible still. Today is terrible. No work to distract her, and it seemed stupid to try to schedule a date. Who would have nothing better to do than go on an OkCupid date on a major holiday? Only a real dork for sure. It wouldn't have been a satisfying experience.

Nothing is anymore. Satisfying. Haruka wants to die. At the NYU dorms, they make it so you can't open the windows all the way and throw yourself out. She knows because she tried. Then looked up why the window wouldn't open and learned that.

Maybe she won't watch any fireworks, after all. Fireworks aren't even American. They're Chinese. It's kind of funny when you think about it, celebrating the birth of this country with something invented by the country it borrows the most money from, who basically owns it. Home of the free? Ha-ha. For a moment, Haruka is pleased about something for the first time in a long time: being half Chinese. But then she remembers she is also half Japanese and the two have warred a lot and also more importantly that she was born here and is really an American, and things go south again.

Maybe she'll just do nothing tonight. Go to sleep as early as she can. Dream of better days, when her life was good and fun. See if her neocortex will allow that. If only she could spend the rest of her life asleep, things might be okay.

▲ ▲ ▽ ▲ ▽ ▲

As the microwave clock switches from 8:34 to 8:35 p.m., he reaches over and picks up the receiver. He holds it out away from him, but can still hear the dial tone, warm and familiar. Will she be so warm? The pinky finger of his other hand, the only digit that fits, begins the business of dialing 2-0-3 in swift semi-circles, the rotary clicking, grinding as it returns to its resting position after each number meets the finger stop. Or will she be mechanical, cold? Going through the conversation as if by rote? All impersonal excuses like "Sorry, I should've called when we got in" or "I'm feeling a little jet-lagged?"

Will she even be at all? Was she able to escape that horrific place?

Emerson's waited long enough to find out. She didn't say they were flying out Thursday afternoon or evening. She said Thursday morning. It's only one time zone and about six or seven hours of travel time away—Emerson, lord help him, looked it up yesterday—so they should definitely be back by now. To subject him to such torture is completely unfair. The line begins to ring. One. A palpitation. Two. Perhaps someone captured them and didn't even bother to try for a ransom. Three. Perhaps they did but she had them call Diana instead, who, out of spite, would never let Emerson know, would rather he see it on the six o'clock news. The start of four…

"Hi Daddy." It's her. Emerson exhales. "You caught us just as we were walking in. Traffic coming out of JFK was a nightmare."

His free hand moves over his heart. "Then I won't keep you long. I only wanted to make sure you got in safely. You know how I worry."

"Oh, you're worse than the tour guides with all your gloom and doom." Emerson can detect the kids chattering in the background, what sounds like the plangent grind of suitcases rolling over hardwood. She probably isn't lying. That's good. "But yes, we're all here in one piece. There was a little turbulence on the flight, but that was the worst of it."

"Well, I'm very relieved to hear that. It seemed like you were having quite the time from your message. Give me a call back this weekend after you decompress and tell me all about Belize."

"Sounds good, Daddy. I will. Love you."

"Love you too, darling." He hangs up. There was warmth there, honesty. The kittenish teasing, by voice, with her particular cadence, actually charming. The love felt real. Perhaps he overreacted to her email last week. Maybe it was the coldness of the form that got to him; perhaps he misread by having to strain his eyes with that glaring, unforgiving monitor. Perhaps she really did go to Mexico for herself and her family, and not just to get at him. He could reread it. But no. If it fooled him once, it could fool him again. He'd rather speak to her on the phone. The love felt real, but was it? He will know this weekend.

▲ ▲ ▽ ▲ ▲ ▽

The apartment never smells like weed anymore, even when someone's getting high right in the middle of the living room. Like now. This is because of Brian's new toy, the Pax by Ploom, a portable vaporizer. It's pretty fucking cool—sleek, black, about the size and weight of an old iPod Nano or small remote, with this little light on it that goes from purple to green when it reaches the ideal temperature to take a hit. Ray's been slightly jealous since Brian received it in the mail this week. Though, now that he's really thinking about it, getting a little high off his third hit from the gadget on this Saturday afternoon, and probably his sixth or seventh since it's been around, he can appreciate that his own vape, the far less expensive and stationary Easy Vape Deluxe Digital Vaporizer that he got himself last Christmas, the one he keeps in his room and has never shared with Brian, does make the act of getting high seem more ritualistic and meaningful. Something about it being bound by its cord, stuck where it's been set up, making him come to it; Brian's is cold, clinical, all about mere convenience. Maybe Ray shouldn't be jealous at all. Nah, he really shouldn't.

That it doesn't really smell like weed anymore is mostly a positive thing. Ray likes that it no longer seems stuck in the couch, the paint on the walls. And he's especially happy that it's no longer in his clothes. This is particularly important with regard to his new job—wouldn't want history to repeat itself with that shit. Brian's solution for that problem always seemed to be massive amounts of cologne. Ray misses the vague nostalgia that the aroma of the smoke would conjure up—remembrances of all the good times that came before, especially those while he was alive, scent being the closest sense tied to memory and all—but that's about it.

"Any requests?" Brian's asking about the music, which he's just gotten up to change. He innately has shit taste and leans on Ray for stuff he thinks other people would think is cool, something oddly important to him: often he posts status updates about the bands or rappers or whoever Ray has them listen to and tries to pass them off as his own discoveries. These receive little fanfare. But that doesn't matter to Ray, even if it is sort of a reflection on him. For one: it's going through Brian, and nobody likes his posts. And two, which is sort of the main thing behind one: only lame people make status updates about music on Facebook after college. Unless you're actually a musician or music journalist or blogger or something, and have some direct involvement in what you're posting, nobody cares about what the fuck you're listening to or your thoughts on it. Why would they when they have Rolling Stone, Spin, Pitchfork, Brooklyn-Vegan, Consequence of Sound, Gorilla vs. Bear, /mu/, and a thousand other places telling them what's cool this hour, what they might be into, the same places that directly or indirectly exposed you to whatever it is you're referencing in the first place?

They're pre-gaming for the Warm Up party happening today, the first of the season. The doors opened about an hour and a half ago. Inside the apartment they can hear and feel traces of the bass from whatever electronica the museum's pumping out of the massive sound system in its courtyard, something even more abstruse than the abstruse first act who'll take the stage at 3:00. It's just loud enough to be noticeable, not loud enough to be distracting. Ray's a little anxious about competing with it with their own music, like he'll be listening to two things at once, but he'd still rather try than not. Brian's looking at him expectantly, standing across the room iPhone in hand, the phone connected to the speakers and most likely Spotify. Brian pays for the ad-free subscription.

"I don't care."

He puts on Death Grips. The second track off *The Money Store*—*The Fever (Aye Aye)*. Ray was listening to Death Grips a lot when he thought he was a demon over those few days a while back. This and their mixtape, *Exmilitary*. They're, in a word, intense. In more words, they make art/punk/noise rap that's both primal and ultramodern, violent expressions of conflict with the self and the world today mostly barked over hypnotic, glitchy beats. Visions from his demon days return: the time he spent in Times Square and Hell's Kitchen terrorizing people; shaving his head, which only now no longer resembles a cholo's; the plot against Haruka; manifold images of widespread disease, mutilation, and destruction similar to those that danced across his mind throughout the period: pedestrians with purulent and flayed flesh swarming the city streets, babies hanging in hypostasis from trees everywhere, all kinds of evil. Ray doesn't really want to listen to Death Grips right now.

Brian's nodding to the febrile beat, taking a sip of beer. Heineken.

Ray takes half a hit and, holding it, passes the vape to Brian as he crosses the room to join him on the couch. He doesn't want to hold it for too long because things just got way too heavy, and he only took the hit in the first place as a matter of decorum, to fulfill the obligation of a second puff in the puff-puff-pass ritual implicit with anyone getting high in a social setting, even one as loose as a Saturday afternoon pre-game with his roommate. He really, really doesn't want to listen to Death Grips right now. The East River running and eddying blood-red. Bodies falling from skyscrapers, joining the decomposing rats and birds littering the streets. "Ahh man, let's not listen to Death Grips." He exhales.

"Why?" Brian's eyes pull high and tight, his brow deeply corrugated. He seems genuinely concerned. Ray, sipping his own Heineken, can't tell if this is because he's worried Death Grips isn't supposed to be cool anymore, or if he thinks Ray's just being a bitch for not wanting to listen to something kind of abrasive, his expression evidence of how disapproving he'd be of that type of bitch-assedness. Ray can't tell him it's actually because it's making him have some kind of fucked up flashback, which maybe he'd still attribute to bitch-assedness, but he wouldn't want to play to Brian's insecurities, either: Death Grips is still cool. How to navigate this under the Platinum Rule?

A solution: "It's too good. Everything we hear at PS1 would pale in comparison." Ray passes him the vape.

Brian takes a hit and considers this for a moment, holding his breath for a good eight or so seconds while Ray takes another sip and does his best to block everything out: the music, the memories, visions… trying to meditate with his eyes open, while still looking like a normal person. Sometimes during meditation it's helpful to try to focus on one thing instead of nothing. After swallowing, as the last of the sip's bubbles tickle the back of his throat, he searches for the other beat, the bass from the museum—trying his best to connect with the Pied Piper that is PS1, the thing that will eventually, either way, take him away from this place— but it's not getting in anywhere with the discord of *The Fever* at the volume Brian's chosen to play it. Brian exhales and a light mist rises and dissipates in the air in front of him. "I guess that makes sense. But don't change it till this one's done." Brian nods along a little too emphatically, doing this little head shake thing when his nod reaches the nadir of its arc, and Ray's become embarrassed for him. "This shit is such fucking fire."

Now he's even more embarrassed. He tries not to laugh but can't help but smile. It's something a wack, affected white guy might have said in, like, 2004. He catches himself, and tries to see Brian not as a clown or figure deserving derision but as someone he should pity and pray for. Demons should be prayed for. The smile fades. Brian is still transfixed, so Ray hopes he didn't see it, and that if he did, he mistook it for assent or recognition or something else positive. The song's about halfway over. It's only around three minutes long, but given Ray's state, the last ninety seconds have seemed like an eternity. Ray pulls out his phone and opens up Songza, a different streaming service he heard about a few weeks ago and started using. It offers a concierge feature with playlists curated for the time of day and possible activities the user might be enjoying, which are accompanied by illustrations of street/bathroom-sign-style stick figures participating in the various activities. Right now it reads:

It's Saturday Afternoon
Play music for

Relaxing at Home
Doing Housework
Sitting on a Back Porch
Spending Time with Your Kids
Creating a Cool Atmosphere

Ray taps Relaxing at Home, the stick figure lying back and reading. A new screen loads:

We'll play you some easy-going music for relaxing at home. Just pick a genre.

Today's Relaxing Hits
Low-key Indie
Laid-back Acoustic
Mellow Reggae
Classic, Eclectic Mixes
Laid-back Country

He goes for "Classic, Eclectic Mixes," though he was briefly tempted by "Mellow Reggae." Reggae's actually really nice to listen to before electronic shows, but he would feel sort of cliché for playing it while the weed's still out; also, Brian probably wouldn't be too into it after he thought he was being so cool and cutting-edge with Death Grips. Another screen loads featuring three playlists:

Mellow Magic Carpet Ride
Ventura Highway: California Chill
Peaceful, Easy Feeling

The Fever is in its final throes. Ray rises and, once the song's last glitched-out beat lands then fades away, takes the speaker jack out of Brian's iPhone and pushes it into his own.

"I gotta get some Bluetooth speakers."

"Yeah?" Ray goes with "Mellow Magic Carpet Ride," a mix of classic rock and soul from the sixties and seventies. The first bars of *Dust in the Wind* drift from the speakers. This is so far away from cutting-edge, it's vaguely ironic, which should hopefully put Brian at ease. It doesn't really do much to block the bass from the museum, however. Ray turns it up.

"Nice. Old-school."

"A little old before the new, mang."

"Can you hand me my phone?" Ray grabs it from the entertainment stand and, moving back across the room, hands it to him. He sits down. Brian tries to pass him the vape, its little light glowing green, but he waves it away.

"Such a good scene."

"Huh?"

"You're my boy, Blue!" Brian takes another hit.

Ray thinks. Is he still talking about Bluetooth? A couple of seconds pass. "I still have no idea what you're talking about."

Brian exhales a little. "When Will Ferrell sings at Blue's funeral."

"Oh. Right." Now Ray gets it. He was confused from the start and, like, twice over—first he thought Brian was complimenting him on his playlist choice using some other lame circa 2000-2004 phrase like "old-school," but really, he was talking about the popular movie of that era, *Old School,* which, now that he's cogitating on it, still probably got its title or at least encouragement for it from the pretty lame and affected phrase, something that's sort of turning what happened into an Ouro-boros of a thing, which is frustrating, except, wait, wait, now he's realiz-ing he can prescind it from itself by telling himself that what he thought Brian meant was a compound adjective but it was really a proper noun; then he was confused by the disparate instances of the word "blue," which probably hasn't struck Brian as related or possibly confusing. Ei-ther the weed is very potent or this vape really sneaks up on you. Ray feels very, very high right now and is so glad Death Grips isn't playing anymore.

Brian exhales the rest of his hit. It's only just occurred to Ray that this is yet more music tied to mortality. Is he glad Kansas is playing? Like, is he not just anti-Death Grips, but pro-Kansas in this moment?

A couple of months ago, this song starting any playlist he chose would have creeped him the fuck out and made him consider everything about it at length. But now, with faith on his side, he knows to trust it. Yes, he's glad it's playing. This is a thumbs up from God, not a middle finger from Satan: this soothing cornball classic, the gentle plucking and lullaby vocals really saying the same thing that's in Genesis: *For dust thou art, and unto dust shalt thou return*. Ray reaches for his beer and takes a swig, tapping his toe ever so slightly.

"Anyway, yeah. They're just kind of expensive for the sound quality. But it would be so nice to just chill from the couch and do everything on your phone, you know?"

"I hear ya."

"In twenty years, I bet they'll have phones you can vape out of." Ray wonders when he'll truly turn into dust: when he'll transcend this con-sciousness that carried over from life and join God in heaven, as stardust. When he'll have put in all the work. He wonders when he won't have to listen to ridiculous and frustrating speculative bullshit like Brian is spew-ing right now, what must be a true mark of being in a purgatorial state, having to suffer through people going on about things that will not and would never be; that above all don't matter. "Shit, I should write that down. I should be the one to make it happen. With what's going on in Colorado and Washington State now, that could have mass appeal even sooner than twenty years. Ten. Five, even. Don't tell anybody about this, Ray."

"Don't worry, I won't." There's no one to tell, Projection of Brian. The bass from the museum seems to have gotten louder with a track change and is cutting through again. "You wanna go in, like, ten minutes? I wouldn't mind taking a look at some of the exhibitions while my high's still fresh."

"Yeah, fifteen-twenty. I'll be ready after one more beer." Brian sets the vape on the coffee table. "It might be fun to lay down some gallery game before the first real act. Is it a band or DJ?"

"Ahh, man. You're still gonna try that shit?" Every year Brian tries to pick up girls in the galleries at these things and every year he fails.

"I came real close last year."

"No you didn't." Not even remotely.

"And I have such a good opener."

"What was it again?"

"You just turn and say, 'So what do you think?' "

Ray remembers now. It's kind of funny, and in this moment he has an appreciation for Brian that reminds him of why he would have ever agreed to move in with him in the first place, rent break aside, but the Costanzan line isn't doing him any favors. It would be best not to encourage him. "That's not that good."

"Well, there's a little more to it. First you gotta stake a spot out. She has to come look at what you're already looking at, not the other way around. I agree, it wouldn't be a good idea to just wander up to a girl and say that."

"It's still not that good." Ray shakes his head.

"Yes it is. It's like asking them their major in college."

"Nobody wants to be bothered in a museum, man."

"It's not bothering." Brian takes a small sip of beer before he continues: "First of all, by staking out a spot, they're coming into my domain. If anyone's being bothered, they're bothering me."

"It's not your domain. It's the museum's. A space that's open to everybody there."

"But it's not. While I'm standing there, it's my space. I was there first. It's mine." Now this is getting stupid and too heavy on semantics, like most conversations between them do when they're both pretty high. Ray checks himself, tells himself to just let Brian talk, tells himself to do what he can to mitigate this; none of this is worth arguing about. At all. He listens for the violin in the song, its lift. "Second, the fucking thing's supposed to be a party. If I was at a house party staring at a picture or a vase or something in the hallway, and someone came up to me and looked at it, too, I would feel like it would be weird for me *not* to talk to them. It's great because they come into my domain and then think I'm just being friendly."

"Just don't do that shit when I'm around."

"What's French for 'walking distance?' "

"I don't know."

Brian takes another sip, a big one this time. Ray has about a third of his beer left. "How about in Spanish?"

" 'Podemos caminar.' We can walk."

"Podemos caminar. Podemos caminar. Podemos caminar." Brian's Spanish isn't half bad, actually. "All right. I'm gonna look it up in French." He brings his phone close to his face. Ray listens to the music: the long, violin-heavy bridge leading to the end of the threnody. " 'Distance de marche.' "

"That sounds more like 'distance of walk.' Translate 'we can walk.' "

Brian types away, most likely in Google Translate. The song winds down with faint, high cries in the distance. "Nous pouvons marcher. Hell yeah. Nous pouvons marcher... to my apartment... à mon appartement." The next song begins. It's a soul song—nice, easy bass; more strings—but one Ray can't identify yet. "What's 'to my apartment' in Spanish?"

"A mi apartamento."

"Fuckin' cake. It's true what they say. It's a lot like Italian, except less sophisticated." Ah, that's right… Brian took Italian because he's part Italian. That's why his Spanish is decent. Also, fuck him.

"What's 'I live in the neighborhood?' "

"Yo vivo en el barrio." Ray sips his beer.

"Wait, that's why they call Spanish Harlem 'El Barrio?' "

"Yeah."

"It just means 'the neighborhood?' "

"Yeah."

"That's fucking stupid." It's moments like these where he doesn't know what he's supposed to do with Brian under the Platinum Rule. He didn't say that because Spanish Harlem took over what was formerly known as Italian Harlem; he said it to get at him. The dig about "sophistication" was enough. Is Brian actually a demon he's supposed to defeat, too? "All right. Yo vivo en el barrio and… je vis dans le quartier. Yo vivo en el barrio. Podemos caminar. Je vis dans le quartier. Nous pouvons marcher à mon appartement. There we go. Gonna make a note"— Brian types some more on his phone—"in case I forget… along with… vape phone." He puts the phone down and looks to Ray, his bloodshot eyes terribly sincere: "Those are good closers, right? Speaking to them in their own language?" And it's with this that Ray understands: Brian's function is to help Ray become a better version of himself. All of the tests—of patience, prejudice, priorities—always leave him feeling more sorry for him than pissed and better about his own beliefs and ethics. Those questions, that look: they said it all. He's not to be defeated, Ray is to do the best he can with him. And that, in turn, will help him reaffirm his greatest attributes and bring out the best in himself. Something like an interdependent version of the Coué method.

"I mean, no? If you're able to sustain a conversation, then that means they know English, so just speak English. I don't believe in gimmicks. Just be yourself and try to make them laugh."

"Girls only think I'm funny when I'm being an asshole, and assholes use closers, Ray." Brian chugs his beer. They're almost a minute into this song and Ray still can't identify it—no chorus yet—but it does seem more and more familiar.

"Okay, man. Whatever you say. You asked me." Ray takes a sip. His bottle's about empty.

"I think I got this. You down for one more?"

"Nah, I'm good. I'll take another couple of hits from the vape right before we go, though."

"I'll let you do that by yourself. The Pax is on another level, man."

"Yeah, it sure is." Ray's high enough, so he's really only planning on taking, like, a half-hit to make up for the twenty minutes he's about to lose sitting here with Brian. This will probably be done over two quarter-hits. Here's the chorus. Ahh… *Just My Imagination* by The Temptations. So obvious now. Wait. Uh-oh. What?

The song is now making him very, very uncomfortable. Even more uncomfortable than when Death Grips was playing. And now that thought itself is adding another layer of discomfort because it seems vaguely racist. Like, why has he only been able to vibe out to the bland white guy band? But the two with black vocalists are somehow terrifying? Actually, he's not even close to racist. Racism's what you do, and barely what you say, not what you think or how you react to a fucking song. He's just high. This is stupid.

Ray reminds himself of his faith and everything is okay again. The song sounds good; he can groove along. It's a wonderful thing Ray has his faith. If he had any real doubt about his purpose or God's plan, what just happened would have been enough to make him second-guess something, maybe everything. Even though the lyrics seem to tell a story about infatuation with a beautiful stranger, which doesn't apply to him, not anymore, anyway, the simple recognition that it's a song called *Just My Imagination* was more than enough to stir something in him. But now, through faith, he knows better. This here, it's just another wink. The group is called The Temptations, after all. Another little test. God's just full of 'em.

▲ ▲ ▽ ▲ ▲ ▲

So hot. Even in the shade, or when a cloud passes over the sun, it's still too hot. She hates it. There's been a heat wave this week. How is she supposed to dance in this? If you dance in this, you will get sweaty. Gross. Her colleagues will see her sweaty and it will be embarrassing. She only met some of them ten minutes ago, and if that happens they might come to think of her as that one sweaty girl. Though they would probably be sweaty too. That's even worse. She might have to smell her coworkers' body odor. There are seven of them here with her. At least one is bound to sweat through their deodorant. If it's inappropriate in the office, it should be inappropriate out of the office. Yes, they have a cool, youthful company culture, but this is too much. As they walk deeper into the courtyard, she can actually smell body odor in the air from the crowd. It's not just because she was just thinking about it. This early in the event and it's already very noticeable. That and beer. Tiny molecules going up her nose. Everybody except her and Ben, who's also underage, just got some beer. They waited in line with them, forcing small talk. She has some citrus-flavored vodka in a flask inside the small purse she is carrying. Soon Haruka might have to sneak off and drink some to help her get through this.

The music is weird. She doesn't know what to make of it. All bleep bleep bloop blirp and stuff. Much weirder than the electronica she knows, less melodic. Like, she knows it's supposed to be cool, but does she like it? It's very loud. That's nice, at least. The loudness. Even if she doesn't know if she likes it. Now she won't have to talk to her colleagues so much. They're all right, the ones she knows, anyway, but it would be hard in this heat and with her bad mood. It will be more about communicating visually, with smiles and nods. Maybe she won't dance. Just sort of sway. Sway and smile.

It is a pretty crowd. She'll give them that. Mostly young, lean. On trend. Boys in cute tank tops and T-shirts. Girls in summer dresses, like her, and cut-off jean shorts. Lots of skin. Glowing skin, skin of every color. Her own skin glows, but naturally. She doesn't need a tan to bring it out. In fact, she hates getting a tan. When she is older she wants to be one of those middle-aged Asian women who walks around under an umbrella on a sunny day. She wishes she could get away with it now, but people would think it was too strange. Like talking to Siri in public. She is still too young for such things.

They find a spot on the dance floor. If only she could feel what she's supposed to be feeling: the celebratory mood of youth. If she felt it, she would overcome the heat. Like all these people here. She wouldn't care as much about getting sweaty or smelling smelly smells. She would want to bond with her coworkers and laugh and cheer. She would want to dance. She wouldn't want to just sway and smile while imagining herself as an older woman walking down the street under an umbrella on a sunny day talking to Siri. The only future she could imagine would be one of endless youth. So consuming is its effect, spirit: the time of life they call youth. Haruka knows because she used to feel it. That was the way it was… before the Big B.

She shudders.

It only lasted a couple of seconds. Did any of her colleagues see? Let's hope not. They're all standing in a circle now, looking around, and a few of them have begun to dance. Haruka smiles and sways. She wishes she had a prop, a plastic cup filled with something, like everyone else but Ben. She doesn't like having that in common with him. Maybe she'll get a water. Ben keeps looking over at her and smiling while nodding in time to the weird music. He probably saw her shudder. Stupid Ben. Why doesn't he get that she doesn't like him? At least he's just an intern, too. If he saw her shudder, it wouldn't have any potential repercussions on her career. And anyway, since he has a crush on her, he probably wouldn't care. Everything she does is great, including shuddering. That's the one nice thing about having an unrequited crush. You have someone who likes everything you do. But if anyone else saw it, they might not think she's a team player. They might not think she's a fun person. Right now she doesn't feel that fun, but she looks it enough, swaying. She raises her forearms and makes little moves with her shoulders, almost like she's dancing, her wrists limp and hands sort of pointing up and around at nothing in particular. Some might even confuse it with dancing. But it's not. Real dancing happens in the heart. The body only follows. Otherwise it's just movement. It should be enough to fool them, though. And make them forget about the shudder if they saw it. Not that she cares *that* much about what they'd think. It's not like she wants to work at Tumblr forever or anything. She still wants to work at Google, Facebook, or Apple when she graduates. If only that were still possible; if only she never got that B.

Yes, she really ought to have some vodka.

But first: she must fake dance for another minute or two before she makes her way inside. They haven't been here that long yet. Maybe it will help her connect again, the vodka. Maybe she'll learn she likes the weird music and she will dance for real. The mood of youth can return. A lighter head can help lift a heavy heart. She'll have a head so light it'll be like a balloon, carrying her up, up, away. So light it'll be in the clouds, dreaming she never got a B. Dreaming that life isn't terrible. Citrus-flavored vodka: take me away.

Bleep bleep blirp. Blirp bleep bloop… Her limbs, her hips, moving in sync with the beat… Bleep blirp bloop. Bloop bleep blop… The charade continues… Bleepy bleepy blirp blop. Bloopidy bleepidy blirp… And on and on until finally, enough time has passed. Thankfully, she did not get sweaty.

"I'm gonna run inside for a minute. Will you guys still be here?" She's addressing Ben. She's shouting to him over Amy, who works on the Brand Strategy team, dancing in the spot between them.

"You want me to come with you?" he asks.

So stupid, Ben. So pathetic. "Not unless you also need to use the ladies' room!"

"Ha-ha! No, I don't. Yeah, we should still be here!"

Haruka smiles, nods, and leaves. As she cuts through the crowd she's glad neither Amy or the other two girls in their group wanted to find the bathroom with her. Girls do that a lot. It's hella annoying and it would've made it harder for her to drink in private. It'll probably take a little time to get it all down; the vodka is harsh even with the citrus flavoring. They would've wondered why she was taking so long in the stall, and could have even thought she was pooping. Then they would have thought of her as that girl who likes to poop in public. Super gross! No way! If it were up to Haruka, she wouldn't poop at all. Her body would be so efficient, there would be no solid waste whatsoever. It would be more like her brain, which runs on only twelve watts of power and without any unnecessary material byproducts. But, anyway, now she can be anonymous. Now she can be alone.

She climbs a set of steps and makes her way through the doorway, inside the museum. It's very busy. More pretty people buzz about, others stand around, talking, probably trying to escape the heat. The room she entered has an information desk. She asks the bearded man sitting there where the bathrooms are. He gives her directions. She leaves, following them.

A line extending out into a hallway. It's not too long.

On her way to join it she peeks into some of the galleries. The art she can see looks weird, but no weirder than the type of stuff they have at the real MoMA—the two rooms she sees each feature one large, colorful sculpture. She'd like to look at them closer. See more. It would be way more fun than fake dancing in the hot courtyard. Maybe that's what she'll do while she waits for the alcohol to soak in. Look at some art. Yes. While waiting in the line, this is what she decides she'll do next. She also realizes, then, that it's a good thing she's here now because she actually does have to pee.

About a minute later she is inside a stall. She reaches into her purse, finds the flask, opens it, and drinks. Yikes. The citrus flavoring helps a little, but not much; it's even harsher than she remembered from the last time she drank it with Allison and Maeve during finals week. The vodka feels like it's burning a hole through the back of her throat. A swallow a second—one, two, three—each more painful than the last, new pain on top of the waning old. But she doesn't care. B students don't deserve mixers. Haruka hates herself in this moment. But she won't be herself when the vodka makes its way down into her stomach, into her small intestine, then through her bloodstream, up to her head. She'll only be part Haruka; the other part will be made of citrus-flavored vodka. Almost all gone. Nearly six ounces, four shots. But should she save a sip? Yes, okay. Just in case. Back in the purse it goes. A piece of gum comes out, then into her mouth. Time to pee. She hikes up her sundress, pulls her underwear down just below her knees, and hovers over the toilet. The stream flows. Relief. Less water, less waste: more room for vodka in the Haruka to vodka ratio. Blot, blot. Flush.

She washes her hands. She leaves the bathroom.

If she looks at the art for too long, some of her colleagues might think she's weird and antisocial. Soon they'll be wondering where she went. But does she really care? No. It doesn't matter. She knows she doesn't want a career at Tumblr; she shouldn't even be here right now. And besides, she can just lie later, say the bathroom had a long line, she got lost in the crazy crowd trying to make it back to them and then couldn't find them and went back inside, whatever. She's glad Ben doesn't have her number. Otherwise he could text her. Maybe they'll think she's a little stupid for not going to find another bathroom or not being able to make it back to their spot, but who cares? She knows they're the ones that are really stupid. They only work at Tumblr and they like to dance during a heat wave. If she were here with people from a better tech company, the kind she really belongs in, they would all be inside looking at the art because they'd be smarter. Haruka will take as much time as she pleases.

This experience will be on her terms, like everything should be. As the vodka makes its way through her body, she'll make her way through the museum's galleries. The citrus-flavored vodka and she will become one, and then the museum and she will become one, and then they'll all be one together. She'll take pictures with her phone. Haruka wanders.

▲ ▲ ▲ ▽ ▽ ▽

The video stuff they show here can be pretty hit and miss—bigger's usually better; the subtler pieces tend to rely too much on context, to the point that, without it, it'd be like watching paint dry, though sometimes the best bullshit from an artist statement can't save them, either. This one's big enough, not in terms of production values or having lots of fast cuts like you'd see on TV or in a movie or anything—it, like pretty much all contemporary video art, has its scenes carry out in one long take— but in terms of action, and it's pretty good. The title is *Efectos de Familia.* It's mostly a bunch of Mexican kids beating each other up. Ray stands with arms crossed, staring up at the screen, hanging toward the back of the cold dark room.

He came in somewhere in the middle, and is guilty of having read about it first. Usually he likes to save the context for after he's at least tried experiencing the thing on its own, be it a painting or something that takes more of a time commitment like this, so that it won't influence his gut response and he can try to figure it out by himself. But approaching the gallery he caught the info card in his periphery and saw the artist, a guy named Edgardo Aragón, was from Mexico and born in 1985, making them roughly the same age—Ray being a 1986 baby—and he couldn't resist. If not for the Platinum Rule, he might be jealous. Not because he's ever tried to become a video artist or anything. But because he used to be jealous of any coeval who was mildly successful doing something not-soul-crushing, and he especially would've been of a guy who shares the less advantaged half of his genetic makeup, actually coming from the fatherland itself, and who was able to overcome that to get his work in a museum like this. Instead, being good, Ray's happy for him. Even if this artist were actually alive and real, and not just some weird projection of his, he'd still be happy for him. He made some pretty damn cool art.

Had he not read what it was about first, Ray still would've appreciated it—the action goes far beyond horseplay; while sometimes funny, it's overall pretty disturbing—but the backstory does make a difference. Out in a dusty Mexican desert, the kids, who are all related to him, reenact fucked up shit that happened to older relatives of his: wrestling, pretending to shoot one another, holding a contest where they carry bricks; one kid digs his own grave. It's at once a comment on some intimate family matters—a plea to the next generation not to get caught up with the cartels and corruption like the relatives who came before them—as well as the state of Mexico on the whole. Or, rather, the projection of the increasingly violent and dangerous Mexico manifest in Ray's gestalt afterlife consciousness. Did Ray make this art? If this is a projection, wouldn't that mean he actually created it, like how people can make things up—abilities, languages—in a dream? Maybe. In life, he was a dabbler in several mediums: drawing, painting, and, as is the case with everybody since digital cameras came out, photography, which could translate to video art. But if not, if put here before him by God, it's still art with a sense of purpose. Ray likes art with purpose. Does it have a purpose for him, specifically, outside of appreciation of its concepts? It's here, he's here, for a reason, after all. What's it trying to say to him?

It sort of reminds him of playing with his siblings and cousins while growing up, and that's nice and all, but it's not striking any type of major chord. He's been at the museum for a little over an hour and he's still high enough, still wired into the deeper part of his consciousness, and nothing about his own family rings out as terribly important now. It wasn't the kid digging his own grave; Ray's already confronted his Death and defeated it. Now is about moving beyond that, recognition of sin, doing good works, making contributions larger than himself. Redemption, growth. The stuff he's doing over the internet, what he's been doing for Emerson. Emerson... Oh, Jesus, there it is! Ray told himself he wouldn't think about work or Emerson at all this weekend, considering how unpleasant it was to have to go in on the Fourth. This looks like a nightmare Emerson would have had this week: scenes of dirty Mexican children behaving like criminals, enacting violence. It's like it was pulled from the big guy's subconscious and made to play here on the wall in front of him! But why? Why did Emerson ask about all this shit this week? Is it some kind of clue? Is Ray supposed to figure something out involving Mexico? Everything is about the phone; everything is about the internet. Right? On the screen, a boy wearing a blanket over his head like it's a cloak approaches another boy on his knees, shirtless, wearing a blindfold, from behind. Ray's been here before. Standing here in this frigid dark room, staring at this horrific little scene. Another déjà vu! It's been a while… Ray falls back into his body, uncrosses his arms, and leaves.

He needs to isolate it, reflect on it, recuperate: Maybe he should text Brian. Welcome some distraction first. He left him in a gallery upstairs on the third floor when he started hitting on some girl, his second at-tempt, who had no ass and a sort of caprine face… not even a little cute. Nah, fuck it. Brian might, no, undoubtedly would, make things worse. He'll go downstairs. The sculptures and installations he caught passing glimpses of there when coming into the museum looked big, bright, fun. That gallery had more in common with the people dancing. The shiny, exuberant people sweating their asses off out there—the tribe of the happy ones.

Ray wends his way down the hallway, to the staircase. What could that have meant? Obviously it was about death, but hasn't that been squared away? Or is it possible that there's something he hasn't recog-nized in relation to his death? That he's the one with the blindfold? Does the extent of what he has to do to win God's favor not stop at 2007 and smartphones, but reach back further? All the way to his roots? Back be-fore he was born—not to Texas, but all the way to Mexico? But what about the other side of his family? The white mutt side: Scandinavian, English, German, whatever the fuck. If anywhere, that's where his in-born evil would be, right? No, that's stupid. People aren't born evil. White people innately aren't more evil, despite what his militant high school friends or radical leftist weirdos on the internet might say. Maybe it's not about the specifics. Maybe it's more about being aware of the general place you were before you were born. Where everyone was. It could have something to do with where you're ultimately supposed to go after you die. The return trip. He's seen his sin and is doing what he can to redress it, but he needs to see that other thing, too. To know it. See the unseeable, know the unknowable. *Efectos de Familia* was about looking at the past in order to move forward in peace; maybe that's why it was triggered. It could be that he's actually almost ready. As of Friday, he had racked up over 20,000 Reddit karma points. Maybe he received this sign as recognition he's on the right path, but he needs to see beyond his own sin, all the way to the origin of sin itself, evil itself, that which afflicts all mankind. This is what he must know and feel, and do his best to defeat. No, not defeat. Transcend. But how? Ray reaches the first floor.

It's busier down here, more people, louder. Doing well to distract. Soon he's at the start of the exhibition he had walked by earlier, in a room where the floor is completely covered by spongy earth. He bounces lightly on the balls of his feet. Then, tracking a little dirt in with him, he's looking at a lone green cube, a few feet by a few feet in dimension, in another room: simple, playful. A group moves into the gallery with him and obstructs his view, so he moves across the floor in a wide arc for a better one. From back here it looks like it's made of confetti, bits of it spilling out onto the floor at its base. He gets closer. Yup. Now that's what he's talking about. This disintegrating grass-green cube; maybe it's intended to be depressing, but it isn't. The object, its color's vivid saturation, is too reminiscent of a childhood plaything. Even if it's supposed to be about the death of childhood or something, it doesn't matter. It's as gentle and assuasive as *Dust in the Wind* was earlier.

Ray ambles through the galleries, tracking more dirt along with him, like everybody else. Not only are we dust in the wind, we're dirt on the floor. We break down and join something else: whether we're cremated or inhumed, eventually we all join the same thing. Something bigger than us. This is where we go, and where we came from. This is the place Ray needs to see, to know. Maybe it can't be seen. Just known. You can't see the air, but you know it's there. You can't see love. The place, wherever it is, cannot be seen…

What was happening upstairs was too much of a leap. This, this here is more his speed: a much better way to travel back in time; to get to the source, the bottom of everything. Baby steps. Movement and thanatopsis on his own terms. Through these rooms—another with confetti of every color getting blown around by fans, one with car wash brushes whirling against a steel plate; detritus, some type of disorder everywhere—he, like everything and everyone else, is leaving a messy trail.

It's both nice and strange how empty most of the rooms are for this exhibition. Nice because it makes access to the artwork pretty easy, no small feat considering all the hubbub everywhere else in the museum today; strange because he comes to this particular gallery often enough and the blankness of most walls along with the theme of impermanence prevalent in most of the work remind him of all the shows that came before. Feeling present, when Ray is fortunate enough to have that happen, is more like a spell than anything, and it can be easily broken.

Last year, down here, around this time, there was an exhibition called *Any Ever*. A hybrid video/installation thing, it consisted of cognate but nonsequential movies playing throughout a series of connected screening rooms. It was a prime exception to the "All video art must be shot in one long take" rule; maximalist through and through, the frenetic videos featured a cast where gender, race, age, and sexual orientation were nothing if not kaleidoscopic in scope and transmutability, everyone cartoon- or clown-like in candy-colored makeup, face paint, hair dye, and wigs. They mostly faced the camera and spoke to the viewer, in chipmunk tongues, about what seemed like everything and nothing, the profound and pointless juxtaposed in such a way that you couldn't know what's what, occasionally also jumping around and breaking shit. In addition to their voices, movements were sped up to come off as very unnatural while still being comprehensible. The camera moved a lot. Cuts were fast. Semi-cheesy eighties/nineties effects and text popped up and coruscated throughout. Disney, MTV, reality television, and old thirty-second advertisements seemed to define its aesthetic. It was like someone tapped into the collective subconscious of the twenty-first century, did a whole bunch of meth and a whole bunch of acid, and tried to teach themselves Windows Movie Maker or iMovie to show what the Western world had wrought. The viewing rooms boasted large screens and viewers listened through headphones, the furnishings comprised of everything from lawn furniture to airplane seats to conference room tables to suburban den couches with knockoff designer purses covering their legs. Nothing was normal, or as it should be in the real world, and the whole thing was completely terrifying.

It also made complete sense.

How could it not? It totally captured the feeling of what it's like to be alive today. Or, rather, it captured the feeling of what it was like for one guy to be dead. Ray now knows he's the one who created it—that it was his subconscious he was tapping into with it, one rooted in the eighties, nineties, and aughts, but not one connected to reality anymore, though it might have shared a lot with the collective subconscious of the Western world before he died in 2007. He made it up, just as he made up the white canvas covered in yarn he's currently staring at, the yarn fibers anything but fixed, the slightest movement of air through the room altering the piece in the subtlest of ways.

Of all the things he can't forget about his phantasmagoric work with *Any Ever*, what sticks out the most is the projection of one of the characters he invented, a white guy wearing brownface and a sort of auburn wig with reflective sport-style sunglasses balancing on top, some fingers atwirl in the wig, asking the camera, "Am I overexisting? Or am I over existing?" Then saying, "That's my inside joke."

Ray thought it was hilarious at the time, before he knew it was him. Now he doesn't know what to think. He'd like to take it seriously; get to the heart of his inner fucked up Hamlet's own inside joke. Staring through the yarn-covered canvas, he gives it a try and ponders for a moment...

The short answer: both. He would love nothing more than to transcend his post-death consciousness, this thing he's been stuck in now for around five years, and truly become like dust in the wind. The most he can do now is keep it moving. Keep letting the art offer up the clues he needs to know when he needs to know them.

He finds his way into another gallery. Here: a bookshelf.

This one reminds him, also, of Emerson. It's far less viscerally frightening than what was going on upstairs, and he's willing to think this through. He wonders, again, what is that man's role? Is it about servitude? Or is it about what he's about? Books? He's the Virgil to his Dante, that's for sure, but guiding him towards what, exactly? Is he supposed to read more? Probably. Everybody should. Well, Emerson's probably read enough. But wouldn't that take time away from the internet deeds? And what would Ray be reading? The books Emerson's writing about? He's only read a handful, mostly in school, and there are hundreds he's covered so far. Maybe he can ease up on the internet stuff and read a little more. He's racked up enough karma on Reddit and spends so much time liking things on Facebook that people probably think he's lonely or turning into a weirdo. Emerson, when he interviewed Ray, said, "Reading allows us to traverse time, space, one's own consciousness." This is just what Ray would like to do. Today has only reaffirmed that. Yes, the answer is here: in books.

But where to start? Well, the most famous book of all time, and the one that would probably apply to Ray the most, would be the Bible. Ray remembers bits and pieces from church growing up, and also in what he's transcribed recently for Emerson, who's written about it at length. How could he have not known that's where he was supposed to look for more clues before? It's pretty obvious. Was he so blinded by the internet thing?

Well, there's that. And also a salubrious skepticism of the Good Book. He got what he thought he needed to get out of it reading those sections while growing up—a decent spiritual blueprint, a healthy dose of guilt and fear, some good but imperfect ideas about morality—but he now knows there could be something else. His God has not been the God of the Bible since he was a child. And it probably won't be when he rereads it. But maybe there's something useful in there, something he hasn't seen, something he doesn't know. Through it, he can traverse his own consciousness. Yes! Ray will read the Bible. But not yet. Not now. Not while still a little high and leaving Brian in the lurch. He'll start tomorrow, on Sunday: the most important day it should be read! Yes, he's got a plan. Now it's time to celebrate the moment. Now it's time to dance.

Nodding to the bass from the courtyard beckoning him, he turns around in the gallery and starts toward the door. A small group is walking in—two men and two women, seem French or Italian or maybe a mix—to look at the bookshelf, followed by a lone young woman, Asian, who meets his eyes on the way in. He looks at her again, then stops dead. Haruka!

▲ ▲ ▲ ▽ ▽ ▲

No, it just can't be. Whyyyy? Just. Whyyyy? Don't let him see. Keep moving. Stay stoic. You've messed up once already today, Haruka.

He knows it's you. That's why he's still standing there, slowly shifting his stance and angling himself toward you inch by inch with every step you take. Don't pay it any mind. Let the alcohol do its thing. Be confident. So confident he will doubt himself. Make it so he doesn't know what he knows. Yes, just keep moving. Don't let him find your eyes. Keep them on the art. The bookshelf. All those dumb-looking books.

"Haruka!" She pretends she didn't hear, moving closer to the installation. He steps forward, at her. She doesn't stop. He touches her shoulder. "I defeated you. Why are you here?"

She turns toward him and looks startled, doing her best acting. "What?"

"When you emailed me you confirmed that I defeated you. Why are you here?"

When she what? She never—no. No time for that: "You must have me confused with someone else."

"You tried that the first time." She did. Dammit! The stupid depression she's been under lately has made her mind foggy, made only worse right now by the alcohol's increasing influence. Shit! What should she do? He continues, as if to himself: "This isn't good. You'll only complicate things. I defeated you. I came to terms with my death and recognized my great sin."

"I really don't know what you're talking about?" She says this with a sort of whiny, lilting voice, like a valley girl-space cadet. Lots of vocal fry.

"I just heard you speak. I know that's not your voice. Why are you here?"

"To look at some arrrrt?" She has committed to the voice. In situations like this, it is best to double down. Triple down if need be. She cocks her head. "Sorrrry man, I'm not whoever you think I ammmm! Byeeee now!" She turns and takes a step toward the bookshelf. People are grabbing, looking at, rearranging the books. There is a security guard here, so they must be allowed. It's that kind of art.

He calls after her: "That's not going to work, Haruka! You know me! We had weird sex once and later I destroyed your iPhone and source of power by throwing it on the floor and pouring coffee all over it." Embarrassed, then angry at what he just said, she stops walking and faces him again. "You shouldn't be here, but you are. I need to know why." He just had to remind her of the specifics. Like she had forgotten. What an asshole. But she cannot let on. Sound moves in circles, but light a straight line. No emotion. Not her face, not her feelings. Someone else's—the valley girl-space cadet's.

This is what the Haruka-citrus vodka hybrid brings out: a shapeshifter. It makes her mind a little less sharp, but allows her essence to become more fluid. Change form, execute function. She walks up to him. "Are you on drugs?"

"That's beside the point!" He scratches his head. His hair has grown back a little bit; he looks better with hair. "Now why are you here? I thought the bookshelf was supposed to bring me to the Bible. But instead, it first brought me to you. Is this a test?" His eyes grow big, mournful, like a puppy. It's cute. No! This guy is nothing but trouble and she hates him! He is an asshole! The worst person alive next to the Devil himself, Emerson Towers! No. Don't let the vodka make you emotional. Be in control. Know what to do. Calculate…

"I wish I could help you, mannnn. But I don't know youuuu." Yes, extracting herself from this really is the best thing to do. "Now please leave me alone!" She turns away again.

"Haruka…" He touches her arm.

"Get away from me! Freak!" she shouts loudly, cutting through the chatter of the gallery, the music coming from outside.

"Tell me why you're here! Were you sent by God? Satan?"

"I don't know you!" People in the gallery are staring at them. They have more of an audience than the bookshelf now.

"You're Haruka!"

Yes, she is; but he, he is no one. His strangeness, cuteness, and what he did to her in the past must be forgotten. Optimum functionality: "My name is Julie! Not allll Asians look the saaaame, asshole!"

"Hey! Don't you try to play any more games with me! Tell me why you're here, demon!"

"Excuse me, sir, is there a problem?" It's the security guard. Haruka can't believe it took her this long with all the commotion they've been making. She's Hispanic, stringy-haired, wide; probably dumb, definitely bad at her job.

"Yes, she's pretending not to be who she really is. Also, I already defeated her."

"Miss, is he bothering you?"

"Yes!"

"Come with me, sir."

"It's okay, we're just having a conversation."

"Now, sir." The security guard guides him toward the exit, her hand on the small of his back.

He peers over his shoulder as he moves forward, the stringy-haired woman in a blue blazer pushing him in step, then shouts, "I'm the one who responded to your email, Haruka! I read all about the B you got in Professor Towers' class!"

Huh?!?! What? Wait… Huh?!?!?! What. The. Fuck. What the actual fucking fuck?!?! Haruka's body goes stiff. He's smiling back. The security guard grabs onto his arm, reaching for her walkie-talkie with the other. "Quiet sir!"

"It was proof that you were no god, that you're just another grade-grubbing narcissist! And that I was the one with the power!"

"I have a situation on the first floor, leaving my room now. A guy that seems to be on drugs. I may need backup," the stringy-haired security guard says, speaking into the walkie-talkie. They're nearing the exit. Haruka remains in the middle of the gallery, breathless. More than confused, she is now completely mortified. What if one of the people here in the gallery with them works at Google? Or Facebook? Maybe hers isn't the only tech company that comes to things like this. Tech companies love things like this, she sees now, daytime parties, things with a vague Haight Street or Burning Man type of vibe. And if they're here, now they will know she got a B! If she ever had a remote shot of still getting a job at one of those places, it would be ruined for sure! Someone in this room could work in HR. They might remember her if she ever interviews with them. Everybody who works at those companies is very smart and would be beating the heat like her right now and would most likely have an excellent memory! Baaaahhhhh!!!

"It was validation for my recognition and good digital deeds!"

Haruka rushes forward. "Wait, wait. I was just kidding. I—we—we are in an improv class together." The security guard looks at her skeptically, her drawn-on eyebrows furrowed, her big lips pursed. "One of our assignments this week was to perform in public and cause a big scene. We are sorry for the disturbance." Haruka turns toward everybody in the gallery and takes a bow. One person claps. All others look confused, then away. The security guard shakes her head and starts across the room, calling off her backup into the walkie-talkie as she resumes her post. Haruka and Ray linger in the gallery entryway.

"Why did you toy with me?" he asks.

Haruka doesn't know what to do. She needed to deflect what just happened so nobody here would believe she ever got a bad grade, especially if any of them work where she wants to one day work, but beyond that, she has no idea where to go with this. He's employed by Professor Towers? What? How? And he reads his emails? This is obviously a conspiracy against her. He sounds like a lunatic half the time with his conspiracy theories, but now she can relate. The world hates her. Life is that unfair. One option is to rise above it: "Because I am God. I can take whatever form I choose. I chose not to be Haruka in that moment. I chose to be Julie. Just as online when you met me I chose to be missing pieces without any of the i's. I am what I am. And only that. At all times."

"You are not God. You are a demon."

"Only a fool would deny me." She slips back into playing God so effortlessly, like it was the role she was born to play. It has been too long.

A lot of acting this afternoon. For a moment, she feels like she's having fun, here now, playing God. She is nervous and anxious about everything, but it is also exciting. How is that possible? There has been no fun in the post-B world, only lighter shades of gray in a very dark existence. Then she realizes something that her subconscious must already know: it is entirely possible that she can use him.

"A demon who got a B."

"Fine. Fuck. You got me. Obviously you received the email for a reason. You—you're right. I was sent here. For you. You never defeated me, as you say. I am no demon, though. I want to talk to you about it. But we need to go somewhere quieter. All will be revealed there."

"I live close by," he says. "Just a couple of blocks."

"Perfect. Let's go."

They leave the gallery, wind down the hall, go out the door into the courtyard. Oh shit! Her colleagues. Things have happened so fast and with such intensity that she nearly forgot. They've probably been wondering where she's been all this time, perhaps even sent someone to find her. A half hour must've gone by, at least. She stops him on the steps as they're descending. "Meet me out front, I have to do something here first. I shouldn't be more than a minute or two," she says. He looks confused. It is very loud, but not loud enough that he can't hear. As a supernatural being who claims she was sent here for him, he probably thinks it's strange that she'd have any other business to attend to before running off with him. How vain. And he called *her* a narcissist... Haruka's plotting, but somewhere in the back of her mind. A background process. He doesn't ask her anything, only nods, and keeps going. She scans the crowd for her colleagues; there are more people here than before, but her group is not hard to find. Almost exactly where she left them.

At the bottom of the stairs, she cuts through the crowd. She knows how to handle this. All of the new people have made it feel even hotter down here, which she didn't think was possible. The air is still thicker than the crowd, the sun still brighter than the fashions, but they've made it worse: it's impossible to walk through and not get a stranger's sweat on you. So gross. So. Fucking. Gross. But she cannot scowl. She can, however, frown. It'll only help the acting she's about to do. The part: Sad Haruka. She sees her group in a little clearing. Almost there. They are all sweaty, the guys in their T-shirts and shorts, the girls in their summer dresses and shorts, all with such big smiles, all wearing sunglasses. She is not wearing hers. She didn't feel the need to put them back on when they stepped outside, and now, especially, it would seem inappropriate to wear them considering what she's about to say. Amy and this woman Karen, who is in accounting and who she just met, see her first and smile, then Josh, a programmer, she thinks, who she also just met, sees her too and smiles even bigger, his Ray-Bans lifting up on his face slightly. "We thought we lost you!" says Karen. It is obvious the beers have made them all feel good. Ben turns sharply when he realizes she is back.

"Yes, sorry, I had a family emergency."

Amy: "Oh no!"

"Is everything all right?" asks Ben. He is shouting. Actually, everyone's been shouting. The bleep bloop blirp music seems like it's getting even louder, or maybe it's the noise of the crowd.

"Not really! I just got off the phone with my mom! I think I have to go! My grandpa is in the hospital!"

Josh makes a face, pulling his lower lip wide and showing his teeth, as if to say, "Yikes." Everyone else nods sympathetically. She can't see their eyes behind their dark sunglasses, but their foreheads are a little scrunched as well. They're all worried for her.

"So sorry to hear that!" says Amy.

"I think I should still be able to come in Monday and everything! But I'm afraid it would feel weird to dance right now! Don't want to bring you guys down! I'm just going to go back to my place and try to FaceTime with my parents!"

"Sounds like a good plan!" says Karen.

"Sorry to be such a bummer!"

"Please! You're no bummer at all! Go, go!" says Amy.

"Let me know if you guys do this again!"

"Of course!" says Ben. "Hope everything gets better!"

"Me too! Bye!" Haruka waves at everyone, then leaves.

Her Chinese grandpa is of course alive and well, but back in China. Her Japanese one has been dead for years. Hiroshima. But that doesn't really matter in the scope of this.

All that matters is figuring out if this Ray is in a position to change her grade from a B to the A she really deserves. All that matters is if she can be repaired. Made to feel whole again. Herself. Perfect. Who she really is.

▲ ▲ ▲ ▽ ▲ ▽

A big lie that reveals an even bigger truth, like some of the better art they just left behind. The feeling is beyond strange, walking these streets with her, the same fake streets he roamed during those worst days, those restless, hagridden days of cathexis and powerlessness; the horror of that time has no emotional bearing on this moment—he is aware of it, but it's nothing more than an artifact, an unpleasant-looking clue—here with her now, not knowing what it all means, but having faith in her greater purpose in his spiritual journey, everything is good. He is doing the right thing, bringing this person who is no person at all back to his place, ready to hear the big reveal. Whatever else there is is just beautiful confusion as they walk together in silence. The path back to Ray's apartment is paved in gold.

They get there. She walks in like she knows the place, owns it, keeping ahead of him as they move through the living room then down the hallway, stopping only once she makes it to the kitchen. She doesn't look around, only at him, her eyes darting back and forth as she leans against the counter. She's wearing a white sundress, the first white item he's seen her in, though it seems significant to note that it's still a part of the grayscale. Is she a phone? Is she his first-generation iPhone? What color was it? He can't remember. Black and chrome probably. There is white in chrome when it's being reflected, though. He doesn't know what she is, really. But since seeing her again, her own phone has yet to make an appearance: this is also a significant thing to note.

Is it that he needed her on her phone then, so that he'd recognize his sin in her, and doesn't now, now that he's ready to move on to another phase? If Emerson is some sort of Virgil, what does that make her? Not Beatrice… Could she be Fate herself?! Is she everything she's supposed to be, or what he would need her to be, in any given moment?

Now, standing here at the kitchen counter, looking at him expectantly, when it is she who has something to say to him, the thing it seems she is supposed to be is thirsty. It is fucking hot today, like it's been every day this week. But would Fate actually need water? Why not? He's not really here, and he still requires certain creature comforts, after all. Ray wipes some sweat from his forehead. Bodily constraints are bodily constraints. Perhaps it is human connection he needs most now, about to hear her out. "Do you want any water or anything?"

"Sure," she says. He pours her a glass, then one for himself. He leads her into the living room.

"Have a seat." Ray gestures to both the couch and chair with a single guiding motion, then moves to open the room's two windows, the one that holds an AC in it from the top and the other one, the one with the better view, from the bottom. When he turns back around, she's chosen the couch. He positions a fan toward the seating area and turns it on, making sure it oscillates, while she settles in, sipping some water. Ray doesn't like to run the AC in the living room, acclimatized by years of being broke to exercise as much restraint with the things as possible, while also feeling compunction about carbon emissions and how bad folks have it in the Third World. He really only uses the one in his room if he has to in order to sleep.

He sits down in the chair, slaunchways across from her, and her eyes narrow in on him. Was he supposed to sit next to her? No, he needed her eyes to narrow in on him like that. Haruka reaches for the fabric of her sundress and moves it back and forth, causing it to billow at her chest, circulating small gusts of air up to her face. Maybe she's upset that it's still so hot in here, considering there's clearly an AC in the room. But that's okay. He apparently needs her to be upset, and plus, his own frugality aside, not running the AC really is the *good* thing to do, the right thing, those Third Worlders and the Platinum Rule and best intentions and all. He can see she's perspiring, but it's only minor. This is also something he needed her to do. She takes another, larger, sip of water and sets the glass down in front of her.

"You never defeated me. I am not to be defeated. There is no overcoming me." She says this quickly. "I am to be embraced…" Then, in a drawn-out breath… "loved." Ray is thinking hard. It's not a frightening or disempowering thought, but a comforting one, to love the idea of his own fate. If he were to trust in fate, then the madness of his quest, his part in it, would be over. But is she really Fate? Or is she simply Death? Death is a part of fate, the surest part, in fact. How would he feel about loving the idea of his death? Not great. What is she? "You must know me like you have known those who were closest to you. You are to love me more than any lover before. You are to think of me, to feel for me, as family."

"Right. Because you're…"

"I am not going to say it. It should go without saying. So powerful will be our intimacy, that words, mere words, would do it great injustice.

That is all I came to say. It is time now to stop telling, and to start showing." She rises, steps over to him, and lowers her head down to kiss him. Her mouth tastes a little like gum, but also, somewhere in there, vaguely like vodka. He wonders how his own breath tastes—like stale, two-hour-old beer and weed? Hopefully better than that. However it tastes, she doesn't seem to mind. Her tongue grazes his, their lips pressing together softly then hard then softly again. Is this his fate literally being sealed with a kiss? She withdraws from him, standing over him and staring down, the white dress clinging to her body in the heavy, viscid air. He stares back. The fan oscillates and blows her dress slightly. Then, lowering down to her knees, she undoes his belt, pulls down his pants, and begins to fellate him.

This is certainly interesting. Show don't tell, indeed. But shouldn't it be him bowed down before her? No. Fate does not require submission; it requires trust.

Still for the most part flaccid, he soon hardens to a full erection in her mouth. Can Fate suck a dick? Apparently so.

It's a weird thing, to fulfill Fate, literally, in the mouth. Whoa. He tries not to think about it. He tries, simply, to enjoy. He does. But not *too* much. Not so much that she can't look up at him after a few minutes and say, "Take me to your bedroom."

This is what he needs from himself. To take charge, to own his decision. To trust in Fate, all the way. He pulls his jeans completely off, leaving them there, and moves toward the ultimate fulfillment, taking her by the hand, bringing her to his room, shutting the door behind them.

Kissing her deeply, he backs her onto the bed, then lays her down. He unties the back of her dress with deft hands, and slips her out of it. Her skin is just as beautiful as he remembered. He kisses down her body. Does Fate want him to reciprocate? What are the other desiderata in this situation? He reaches her pelvis, still smooth.

"I don't want that," she says, stopping him. "Use your fingers."

Apparently he didn't need to do that. But a preference for fingers? Is she a phone? What is his Fate? How can you trust in something you don't really know? Well, this certainly feels good, this moment. He kisses back up, over her torso, then focuses on her breasts. He moves his hand down. She moans, a little wet, but not enough for sex. He touches her lightly. They kiss more; he continues rubbing her inner labia and clitoral hood with increasing pressure in precise strokes while she intermittently backs her head away so she can say, "Yes." A minute or two later she's become fully wet and says, "Now." He reaches over to his nightstand, opens the drawer, and pulls out a condom. "Not like that."

"I'm confused. I thought you wanted to…"

"I want you. Just you." She reaches out to him, takes his T-shirt off so he is fully naked. Then, lying back down, she grabs his member, still hard. Giving has always kept Ray aroused, something he believes speaks to a certain goodness in his nature. Wait! She's pulling him in! She wants to have unprotected sex!

He stops her, grabbing her hand and pulling it and his dick back so that the shaft is pressing against her inner lips, the head near her clitoris. He wants to mull this over, and maybe she'll confuse what he's doing with trying to tease her, buying him some time.

"It's time. I'm ready. And more importantly, you're ready."

"I don't know…" He really doesn't. Not because he's afraid of contracting any diseases or getting her pregnant; he's dead, of course, and she isn't real. It's more because he hasn't fully figured out just what she is. He thinks she's Fate… but it's still possible she could be a demon. But really? Sex is one thing. And he could have that with a demon as long as the demon were cool and attractive enough. But unprotected sex? That's something he only had with three girls in his lifetime, his one serious high school girlfriend then the two he had in college before he died. Would this be okay under the Platinum Rule? Surely this is a test, but of what? He doesn't want to do it. But maybe he needs to.

"I do." She grabs his member and puts it in. Or does she plug it in? What is she?

It doesn't matter. This feels fucking incredible.

Ray forgot how good it feels. Sex is always fun and all, but this, the raw kind, good God…

He goes with it.

Then… a problem: it's been so long since he's had sex that felt so good that he thinks he might come soon, and he's only been at it for like two minutes! The weed's all but worn off, and his buzz, too. He slows down. This, he remembers, can be an issue in missionary: it puts pressure on all the right places for an easy and early ejaculation.

"I want you to come in me. And when you do, I want you to tell me how you feel about me."

"Okay." Ray doesn't know what this means. But her talking about him coming has distracted him and made him self-conscious enough that he no longer feels like he could do it any second now, so that's a good thing. Now back to the topic at hand: he doesn't know how he really feels. Is he supposed to say, "You confuse me!?" Or, or what? She doesn't actually expect him to say he loves her, does she? She said he's supposed to love her like no other before, and that's one of the things that's made him so uncomfortable, that made him pause before they started. She surely couldn't expect that yet. Maybe, "You make me feel good?" He thrusts deeper. She moans. "Yes… yes," she says. She grabs onto his neck, pulls herself up, pushes him down, then grinds into him, slowly, before crashing down on him over and over again.

Their breath in tandem, the rhythmic squeak of the mattress springs, the bass from the museum through the windows, but no more words while she slides up and down on top of him. This is so different from their first time—no condom, at his place, no weird literature quotes—but like that time, it's also very intense, and seems very significant. She slows the pace, licks her lips, waits for him. He pulls himself up, then kisses her hard, brings her back down, moves one leg over the other so she's on her side, and lies there thrusting from behind. He reaches for her clit with his free hand.

"No, you'll make me come. I don't want to come."

"Why?"

"Last time you made me come and it created problems. For me and you. I—I'll explain later. Just you come. This is about you. Not me. Not us."

"Okay." He rotates around and lifts the other leg back so he's on top of her again, and kissing her once more, moves in and out of her with vigorous thrusts.

"Yes, yes," she says. "Give me all you've got."

He does. And soon, an explosion from deep within, unlike any he's felt in years, and as the ejaculate leaves him and enters her, he shouts: "I—I trust you!"

"Good." She kisses his cheek. "You'll need to. Because we are girlfriend and boyfriend now, Ray. And soon, you are going to love me." She reaches for tissues on the bedside table, wipes her vagina, throws them in the wastebasket. "You're going to love me so much you'd do anything for me. You thought that was good, just wait till then. The first time, we fucked. Today, we had sex. Just wait until we make love, Ray. Just wait. My pussy can be the gates of heaven or a portal to hell. It's been up to you this entire time." Ray is speechless. And what's more, in reverberating orgasmic bliss, thoughtless. There only to receive her words, to let them wash over him, soak all the way down into his soul. He believes every one of them. Rising, still nude, she leaves the room.

▲ ▲ ▲ ▽ ▲ ▲

Someone else is here now. She heard them come in a few seconds ago—the bolt of the door unlatched, then feet stepped fast and hard inside the apartment, the front door shutting loudly behind as the person moved. She's trying to figure out what to do. Haruka is very naked right now.

She could grab a towel, but she doesn't want to. The towels hanging from the rack on the door seem like they've all been recently used, all gray and green and dingy and sad-looking. After she washed, she just used toilet paper to dry Little Kaiju instead of a towel. Maybe she will just wait a minute and the person, probably a roommate, will go away to their room. Hopefully it won't take so long that Ray will think she is pooping. He needs to see her as a goddess or an angel, not someone who poops.

A voice, male, calls out: "Ray?! You here? Why are your pants in the middle of the living room?!"

Ray responds, but she can't hear what he says, only the muffled bass of his voice through the walls.

"You left me hanging, man! Wouldn't answer my texts, couldn't find you anywhere."

"Yeah, sorry. Something came up."

This is her cue. She is that something—she must not give him any time to try to explain who she is to this person, she must show him, and, at the same time, reinforce what she must be to Ray. Her hand turns then pulls the doorknob.

"Anyway, that girl you left me with ended up being a total bi—"

She is before them now: naked, glorious. They are awestruck, especially the roommate, a squat, generic-looking white guy.

Ray scratches the side of his face. "Uh…"

"No shit something came up."

"It's okay," she says. "I am a supernatural being."

"Brian, this is Haruka."

"Nice to meet you."

She looks them both in the eye, her face blank, then calmly walks around them and into Ray's room. She bets they looked at her backside. Climbing over the bed, she lies on top of the twisted covers. She didn't bother to close the door. They whisper, but she can still hear them:

Brian: "You use the line?"

Ray: "The line? Oh. No. We, uh, we already knew each other."

Brian: "The fuck's she on? Acid? Molly?"

Ray: "I have no clue. Probably nothing."

Brian: "C'mon. She's gotta be on something. Fuckin' angel dust?"

Ray: "Who knows. Maybe angel dust. Anyway, I should get back to her. Sorry I didn't find you back there."

Brian: "I get it, man. I actually came back to smoke a little more. Figured I'd face the stage and sort of vibe out. I wanna bring the Pax with me places, but I don't think it'd be that smart to hit it in broad daylight."

Ray: "Yeah."

Brian: "Goddam, Ray. You know, I never really caught that Yellow Fever thing, but give her a good pump for me. If she's that crazy out of bed, I can only imagine…"

Ray: "You don't know the half of it." Then one, two, three steps, and he's back in the room. He closes the door behind him.

"Are you ready to cuddle?" she asks.

"Sure, okay." He begins to disrobe again. "Sorry about Brian. I didn't think he'd be coming home."

"No need to apologize. I knew he was coming home. I know all about Brian."

"Right."

"I know everything. You need to remember that, Ray."

A smile of recognition from him. All of his clothes are off except for his underwear. He joins her on top of the bed.

"Yes, yes. I know it's hot, but it's time to spoon."

He gets behind her and holds her. Thankfully he didn't get all the way naked. This is gross and sticky enough as it is—she does not like anything about how it feels, physically. But it's what needs to be done. Soon, yet more endorphins and hopefully oxytocin will surge into his brain and he will be well on his way to loving her.

It's funny how life works out sometimes. It's funny how a terrible day can turn good, how hope can arise in the least expected of places. Like Queens. Now she has something to really live for again. He squeezes her tighter, holds her close. Disgusting. But even though she hates him, she can do this. Haruka is going for the win! Mind over matter, mind over matter… That's the business she's in, anyway. The brain isn't a muscle, it's stronger than that. And she knows just how to use hers.

▲ ▲ ▲ ▲ ▽ ▽

They're nearly fifteen minutes into this conversation and he still doesn't know what to think. Are his worst fears justified? "And there were these monkeys, black howler monkeys," she's saying now, "they claim they're endangered, but the funny little things were in no short supply where we were, especially around Lamanai." The statements keep getting stranger and stranger; hearing about the culture and customs and ruins left by all these backwards people was one thing, but now he must endure a report on the fauna? Emerson sighs, but it is a closed-mouth sigh, with the bottom of the receiver tilted outward, just in case. "The locals call them baboons for some reason." Yes, Claire, he's sure they do. Goodness.

He positions the phone back in front of his mouth, and his face comes alive—"Wild monkeys! What fun."

"Their cries sound more like barking or, really, broken-up bellowing than what you'd normally call a howl. You can hear them from two miles away."

"Well, I hope they didn't keep you up at night."

"We didn't hear any at the hotels where we stayed, thankfully. But as I understand it, they're loudest at dawn, so they would probably wake you up, not keep you up. Like a chorus of demonic roosters."

A chorus of demonic roosters? How bizarre is she going to get? Now he's had to imagine some type of monkey-rooster hybrid, a furry beast with claws and a beak making an awful sound, like something out of Dante. He does not like it one bit! That kind of imagery is only acceptable in literature, where it's there to make some profound statement, not in a phone call, during polite conversation! She is taking some liberties with her language! Painting some picture with these words! "Oh heavens. I think I'd rather be kept up—"

"Though they had roosters, too. Those and chickens. But more interestingly, we saw toucans, scarlet macaws, red-lored parrots..." And now we're on to birds, just birds... from people to monkeys to birds... fitting. This whole thing has been completely bird-brained. Actually, no, that's too generous—from its planning to execution and even this recap, ever lower on the evolutionary spectrum, the entire vacation has seemed to involve all the thought and brain power of an amoeba. His own daughter, as smart as a single-celled blob. How could it be?

Unless, again, it isn't. Perhaps it has something to do with her artistic temperament, a willful stupidity—some kind of hapless attempt to connect with her inner child. That would do well to explain the imagery of the rooster-monkey. "Wow, that sure is something," Emerson says, not quite certain what he's saying it to, or even if he's interrupting her while saying it. All he knows is that she's still talking about the birds.

The phone's receiver feels cold, even though the apartment is several degrees above what he'd consider comfortable room temperature. His old air conditioner can only do so much in this heat wave. Why does the receiver feel cold? It should be sticking to the flesh of his hands, ear, cheek. Because it hasn't been about stupidity, it hasn't been about entertaining her children, it hasn't been about her art—it actually has been a rebellion against him! A full-on assault!

He's known what to think all along, he just couldn't bring himself to wholly admit it… his daughter indeed hates him!

She must!

He tunes back in. She's still prattling on and on. Her voice sounds warm, but it's a lie. A terrible lie! The phone, the cold phone is telling the truth. His skin quivers then gives way to horripilation. "Especially with the macaw. It's not like in a zoo. Maybe it's because we were so much closer to the equator, but the way the sun hit its feathers, it produced some of the most brilliant…" And from the birds to their parts in this disquisition! Plumage! Oh, God. Emerson *must* shift the conversation… divert this terrible torrent! He's drowning! Absolutely drowning in her gobbledygook! Soon he'll be unable to speak! Breathe! Plumage!

"My, sweetie, it all sounds so lovely." If he is drowning, he must become Poseidon: absorb what she's using against him and blast it back at her. If she learned this kind of passive-aggression from anyone, it's him.

"Oh, listen to me, going on! But it really was, Daddy. We just might go back sometime before the kids are all grown up, and we'd love it if you'd join us."

She is relentless. She really must be stopped! How could his daughter try to hurt him so? And how best to mollify her? Forget Poseidon, now he must become Zeus: gain complete control. Yes, he is capable of great passive-aggression. Especially with his child. One of the first things a father must learn once his child is old enough to speak is exactly how to lie to it, both with bromides and more vulpine techniques. But he is painfully honest by default. The time has come: "I think I'm getting too old for such adventures."

"Surely you're not done traveling."

"Maybe another trip or two to Europe. I suppose I haven't said goodbye to the Louvre or Old Vic just yet." Emerson wistfully twists the cord of the phone with the pointer finger of his free hand, wrapping and unwrapping the smooth plastic coil, then wrapping it again.

"Then we'll all go together."

And what's this?! Enthusiasm about Europe, along with an invitation?! Could she really mean it? "My, Claire. I wouldn't want to be a fifth wheel…"

"Nonsense. Our trips abroad are some of my most cherished memories from childhood. And it's because of all you exposed me to, your guidance. I'd hate to deprive my own children of such an education. How about next summer?" She does! So what has all this been? Maybe it wasn't hatred, after all. He overthought it: hated himself through her. What a thing to do. It was really just a silly, small rebellion against nothing in particular. A reversion. Just trying to get his attention. Daughters don't want their daddies to be foxes, they want them to be lions. No Poseidons. Only Zeuses. Oh, he feels terrible.

"Well, I suppose I should be done with the book by then. Or at least the first draft…"

"Wait, you're working on something?"

"Oh, yes, I suppose I haven't mentioned it." She deserves to know now, after all that. Her daddy is indeed a Zeus. He is a great, important figure doing great, important work. She must be told. Assured.

"My, I feel horrid now! Going on about feathers and you're writing another book!" Oh, the self-awareness! Emerson has never been prouder of his daughter than in this moment. Smiling, eyes effulgent, he slowly shakes his head in surprise and gratification. To think, all that was running through his mind just moments ago! What a wonderful daughter he has. "Congrats, Daddy!"

"Not at all, darling, not at all. But yes, I've been at it for around two months now. It's been quite the undertaking."

"Oh my goodness, you've been keeping some secret! What's it about?"

"Not really keeping a secret, just trying to get to know the thing before I hazard talking about it." This is true. The only other person who knows anything about it, really, is Ray. Weisman doesn't even know he's actually begun writing yet. How much should he tell her? Too much time is passing… she may think there's something wrong with the line, or worse, that he's hesitant. He will tell her enough; no more, no less—"Speaking broadly, it's about the history of Western Culture, its very soul, which I believe is literature, and the fate of that soul. It is in a way a love letter and in a way a goodbye."

"Oh Daddy, I wish you wouldn't be so morbid. All of this talk of goodbyes…" She is at once warm and dismissive, a tone common among fools and mountebanks, rarely used by those who truly know. It's a tone he obviously does not care for, but he can forgive it here, now, even though his own mortality is nothing she could have any insight into that he would not. Because unlike a blithering imbecile or a charlatan, her use of it has taken at least some thought, and it is pure; it's a wish, something meant to reassure him, genuinely, something coming from a place of love. Her own attempt at being a lioness, he supposes. He respects her position, but still, he has not said all he needs to say. He has not said enough.

"Well… this book is to be my last."

"I see. Still, though. I don't like hearing it!"

"I don't think I'm going anywhere quite yet." He faces the window, those cliffs across the river. The sun has just begun its katabasis, the haze over the Hudson burning bright in ruby, coquelicot, gold. "But let's be realistic. It's about that time when one should be thinking of things in terms of finality. There's work to be done yet, and I don't think I could ever truly stop teaching, but soon I'd like to scale it back. Maybe go in once a week, do it as long as I'm able. But I'd like to spend the last chapter of my life largely reading and relaxing."

"And with family, of course."

"Of course."

"Then it's settled!" Claire is so loud and enthusiastic that it hurts his ear, forcing him to pull the receiver back. Everything is happening very fast. "We'll go to Europe next summer. For three weeks, or maybe even a month! Marc will probably only be able to do half of that, with the practice and everything, but I'm sure you'll help us manage without him."

Emerson truly doesn't know what to say. He would indeed love to go to Europe with Claire and her family; to show her kids what's what; ensure his legacy the best way he knows how: through himself. But what of his other legacy? The book? What if a draft is not yet complete? What if he'd have to rend himself away? "Yes, well, that sure would be something."

"*Would* be?" She has him there. It's something *he* would say to something so inconclusive, such a non-response. But it was the only one he had… Oh, what to do?! What to do?!

"Fine, yes—*will* be." He will be a lion! He will be Zeus! "We will go!"

"Oh, I can't wait!"

"What a time we'll have!" Emerson is very excited. As if he didn't have enough of an incentive to finish the book sooner rather than later, now this!

"Well, I should probably get going. Talk to Marc, iron out the details, then maybe even tell the kids! I want them to have what I had. To have their first trip to Europe be with you."

Emerson is blushing. He's short of breath, but not words: "You're too kind, darling. Have a wonderful Sunday. I'm glad you enjoyed yourself on the Yucatan." Of course he isn't, and almost kicks himself for bringing the matter back up again, especially at the end of what's turned into such a wonderful conversation, but something needed to be said that would make her feel good about everything, too, like he does now.

"It was quite the vacation. But I'm sure next year's will be even better!" Oh, atta girl, atta girl! Claire, Claire, Claire! "I love you, Daddy!"

"Love you, too, Claire."

She hangs up and then he does the same. Another trip to Europe, this time with Claire as an adult, with the grandkids. It will be the perfect way to begin his twilight years. Perhaps he shouldn't go back to school next year; perhaps he should tell them he's done. There are more important people to teach. His own family. Then, of course, the masses.

Emerson gets up from his seat at the kitchen counter and makes his way to the window, his eyes captivated by that brilliant sunset. All that color, all that beauty, blanketing the vista before him. There can be great joy before the night.

▲▲▲▲▽▲

Wednesday, Hump Day—this week's flying by, but not because it's been so much fun. It hasn't been. Just busy. Time also flies when you're really fuckin' busy. The stuff he's doing for Emerson is only part of it. While the domestic duties remain pretty much unchanged, the big guy's output has increased drastically and he's turning in more than when they first started out and nearly double, it seems, the pages he was producing last week—it's weird, Ray thought it might have been the heat that slowed him down then, but the temperature's the same now, so maybe it has something to do with the way he metabolizes a week's worth of a primarily sugar-based diet, like his body consists of so much mass that the sugar high takes longer to kick in or has an extra long half-life or something—which means there's twice as much to transcribe and also twice as much to proofread and fact-check. Even though Emerson's back on his A game, if not his A++ game, and it's all pretty polished, more is still more. But really, the main reason he's been so busy at work is that he's in effect taken on another job: Ray has a girlfriend now.

All day at work, every day, he receives a constant barrage of text messages—most inane, like:

> Hey!

> Hope you had a good commute.

> Thinking of you!

> How was your morning?

> What did you have for lunch?

> It's sooo hot out.

> Is it 6 o'clock yet? I can't even today.

Etcetera. Some of these are bookended by emojis of varying relevance, and there are also messages where they're in the text itself, forming cutesy rebus puzzles, and those composed entirely of emojis, which, while the most interesting of the bunch, are also the most bewildering, and those that take the longest to address. Then, around twice a day, usually within the first half hour he's at work and then again late in the afternoon, she'll also send him a listicle she'd like him to read, either via email or posted on his Timeline—she having found him on Facebook right after she spirited away from his apartment on Saturday, soon thereafter making their relationship Facebook Official, which, among other likes, prompted a passive-aggressive one from Emily, followed by something of a Dear John message in his inbox to the tune of *Hey, see you're in something serious now. Good for you! It's been fun.* These are mostly from BuzzFeed but sometimes from Cracked, with subject lines like *OMG –*

SO FUNNY! or *Whoa, this is crazy*. They don't really have anything specifically to do with him or any of what he's so far learned to be their shared interests, and are instead as broad and desultory a sampling of what he'd see posted on his news feed from the sum total of his over seven hundred other Facebook friends. They've included such topics as: two ingredient food recipes, images Ray wouldn't believe were Photoshopped, actors—namely Tom Hanks, Tom Cruise, Steven Seagal, Brad Pitt, and John Cusack—doing the same weird thing in every movie, cat gifs, life hacks, and, this morning, fifteen particularly "ninja" photobombs.

If he doesn't respond to these within twenty minutes or so, she'll then send him a follow-up message over gchat, and this is what's happening right now, even though he has the red circle with a dash through it up indicating that he is Busy.

Haruka: aren't those photobombs hilarious?

She never asks if he's read the thing she's following up on, be it a link, like it is on this occasion, or a text, instead always just taking the position that he has, which, if he's been out running an errand or cooking something, isn't always the case. It sort of feels like she's either trying to sell him something or is talking at him for the sake of talking at him, like he's not her boyfriend but just someone that's there. The whole thing has Ray pretty vexed, considering what she's like in person, but he hasn't really had the time to try to sort it out.

Sitting here now, fingers flapping away transcribing yesterday's pages, knowing he still has a good five to ten minutes that would be safe to ignore this message per gchat first-message etiquette, especially considering the Busy signal on display and how he's already responded to two of her text messages this morning, he decides to give it a go…

His gut instinct is that it's all meant to be putative and, of course, just what he needs. Messages marking the start of a romance used to require forethought and an effort to be at least somewhat charming; back when they were written in ink and delivered by horse or carrier pigeon or personally in the flesh, or even just the postal service last century, they were supposed to count. Now that they're delivered in more of a stream of consciousness than speech and at the speed of light to computers and phones where myriad other forms of communication are possible and likely taking place simultaneously, they're practically meaningless. And hers bring this to another level. Having to multitask and deal with all these annoying messages that aren't really saying anything would definitely go hand in hand with being in a twenty-first-century purgatorial state. If he is to trust her and eventually love her, then he needs to accept her completely, all of her, even the boring and the needy parts competing for his screen time. Can Fate be boring? Certainly; it sure was during life. Can it be needy, too? Yes; it's nothing if not that— its raison d'être is to make sure what is meant to happen does. This salvo from her is just getting the worst out of the way first, and surely it's a test.

Otherwise, this entire thing would be fucked.

Doubt has whispered in his ear that she could still be a demon, a trickster, here now to offer a different type of test. He told her he trusted her, but did he really mean it? So far he's held out on that whole reading the Bible thing so he could put all his trust in her, but was that the right move? Doubt, now, can't help but tell him the answer to both of these questions is "no." The main evidence it cites is that disparity in her personality, this problem of how different she is online and via text than in person; how when they're together she's totally cryptic and careful with her words and overall fascinating but through her other communications with him now she's as bland as they come: so basic she'd be a 14 on the pH scale. Ray recalls the OkCupid profile—it had been interesting enough to draw him in, what with her mysterious screen name, well-curated photos, and the handful of things they had in common, but weren't there some pretty basic things in there, too, including some of those things in common? As in, she liked coffee and museums and the only two good network sitcoms on the air right now? These questions are enough to slow then stop his fingers from doing what they were doing, and with a smidge of guilt, something of a slight sting now spreading in the side of his stomach, he reaches for the mouse.

Ray doesn't like disrupting the transcription process, knowing he does his best work all in one go, but he's simply too distracted to carry on. He'll just look for a minute or two. Emerson deserves his all, but clearly Haruka is a more significant figure in this whole thing, closer to God, and God must come before the job, yes, yes…

He opens Chrome, goes incognito, then types the address for her OkCupid profile into the search bar. The guilt, now in full bloom, quickly morphs into fear as he awaits the outcome—a fear of whatever's there. Obviously he wants her profile page to load, to get another look, learn what—if anything—he can figure out from it, but if it does, what the hell would that mean for their relationship? Like if she's as all-in as she's acting, then of course she would have deleted the thing by now, right?

The page loads. The profile is there.

It's there because it has to be. Their relationship isn't real; she isn't real. If she were, he might ask her about it, laugh it off with a "So what's the deal with this? I didn't know this was an open relationship—time to get me a hot date," and she might say, "Oh, I was just so swept up in us I completely forgot" or something. But, anyway, this is getting digressive. It's there because it has to be, like everything with her. That's all.

The profile is exactly the same, which is a relief. He can see it as it was when he first met her. And, indeed, except for the name and maybe her profile picture, it's pretty fucking basic, too. Coffee, museums, *Parks and Rec*, *The Office*, The Beatles, She & Him, deadmau5, *Pan's Labyrinth*, *The Breakfast Club*, *Catcher in the Rye*, *Emma*, exploring the city, going to school. The picture over the coffee mug, another on Minetta Lane—both with Instagram filters, but ones that aren't too aggressive. It's pretty much Freshman NYU Girl 101. Why did he feel he related to it so much the first time?

Maybe he didn't, really. Maybe it was the déjà vu. Gave it this false weight. Faith gone astray. That, or maybe Ray's basic, too. He does actually like a lot of the shit in that profile. The same as before, there's nothing wrong with museums, coffee, or those shows. Just because everybody loves The Beatles doesn't mean there's anything wrong with The Beatles. And, as a half-Mexican, *Pan's Labyrinth* will always have a special place in his heart. So what if it's a fairy tale for people too old for fairy tales? It's pretty damn good. Like enacting clichés, sometimes you just gotta be a little basic. Balance that fuckin' pH to a proper 7.

A-ha! And that's what she does. But she does it to the extreme. Online, and in text, she's a 13-14. In person, a 1-0. Like battery acid. Corrosive to the core. There to destroy him, eat through him, make him feel like nothing, powerless before her. He's more steady, stable throughout. In person, she is everything. Through a screen: barely anything; no, nothing. This only makes sense. When he's staring into a screen, he's staring into the abyss. That void of his own making. Of course the abyss would stare back at you.

He closes out the browser, looks back to Emerson's pages, and begins typing again. Letters form words, lines lengthen, paragraphs grow. Emerson's been writing about a novel called *The Prison of Love* by some Castilian guy named Diego de San Pedro. Obviously Ray's never read it, but in the bits and pieces of Emerson's analysis that he's absently caught while typing this morning, it seems like something he might like: an epistolary novel about messy and unrequited love that, because it was written in medieval times, comes across as being more interesting than gimmicky. Like *Super Sad True Love Story*, except good.

But there are more exigent matters than five-hundred-year-old fiction to consider right now: his very real situation, and where it's going. Yes, he got somewhere by looking at the profile. Gave Doubt a little less room to run its mouth, but between it and Faith, the jury is still hung. Tonight will help him make more sense of it. She's supposed to come over. Will she still be weird? Or more like the BuzzFeed-sending simpleton he's come to know? Will Hump Day live up to its second meaning? With spiritually heavy sex, perhaps punctuated by cryptic dirty talk? Or will she leave him wanting, his dick in his hand and brown balls turning blue as they watch Netflix or she shows him a dozen listicles on her phone, in person? Is she Fate? If so, what, exactly, does she have in store?

▲ ▲ ▲ ▲ ▲ ▽

This building is a little run-down. Not like the dorms. Everything there is renovated, nice. Here it looks old. So gross. Haruka hates it.

She's climbing the stairs now, up to his apartment. He lives almost at the top. She's getting a bit winded... so many steps. Also, the air is heavy and the heat still oppressive, even in this evening hour. New York is sweltering in the summertime. But it's okay. She's just doing what she has to do. There's been a lot of that lately.

So far this week she's had to put in quite a bit of effort to play the part of the girlfriend. She had all but forgotten how to do it. It's been two years since she had a boyfriend, the only real one she's ever had. Practically a lifetime for someone like her. Research was required. Sunday, the day after she made stupid Ray her boyfriend, she actually went back and read old gchat transcripts and Facebook messages from when that relationship began. Some were cringeworthy. But not on her part. On his.

She's basically interacting with Ray the same way she had with Kenji—sending him many messages designed to let him know she cares about him a great deal and is always thinking of him, as well as sharing web content with him that she finds funny or interesting. Of course with

Kenji those sentiments were true, and she very much wanted to know his opinion on the various things she shared. She liked Kenji. Eventually loved him. Not Ray. At all. This is why it feels like work. Because she actively dislikes him—no, hates him—and has to pretend so hard. It feels like doing a lot of homework for a boring class. Tedious. No fun. But even boring classes are ones you must get A's in. The stakes are too high, the payoff too important.

As long as he buys it—and she thinks he is—she knows she will get an A. In this class, his class, and the one that really matters: Professor Towers' class.

To do this, now she must play another part. The first part she played with him—that of God. The girlfriend is hot, God cold. Always. Never benevolent. An unforgiving, all-powerful God. The girlfriend asks for validation, the God asks for nothing. It doesn't need to ask.

This will do wonders. She will be both at once, a double agent for the greatest cause there is: herself. A girlfriend and God. It will confuse and frighten him, prime him to seek the simple answers that she will provide. He will become the most God-fearing man that ever has lived. And then he will do anything for her. He would kiss her feet. Cross the world for her. Getting her grade changed in Professor Towers' class will be a piece of cake.

She's at his door now. She knocks. Since she just rang the buzzer to get into the building, he should already be waiting nearby. He should've been waiting for her longer than she will have to wait for him. The lock clicks, the door opening within seconds. He was. Good boy.

Time to play. This will be the fun part. Pretending to be the girl-friend is hard, but this won't be. This is just sex. A small snack for Little Kaiju. And playing God. That's been really fun so far.

She doesn't say anything. No hello, no sweet salutations you would expect from a girlfriend. She simply grabs his hand and leads him to his room. She is in charge. Completely. The speaking only begins once they are doing it.

"I need you to… do something for me," Haruka says. They're a few minutes in. She is on top of him, facing his outstretched legs, giving him a view of her behind while she moves. It's the position commonly known as reverse cowgirl, but she doesn't like that term. It's vulgar. She only likes to think of it as the position where she is on top of him, facing his outstretched legs, giving him a view of her behind while she moves. Ha-ruka has just realized something.

"Yeah?" he replies. He is breathing heavily, like her.

"Tomorrow I need you to… take a picture of Professor Towers and… send it to me." The thing she has realized is that it's entirely possible this Ray is a hacker. That maybe he doesn't work for Professor Towers at all, but just hacked into her email and found her message in the Sent Mail folder. He has proven he's obsessed with her. If he had the capabilities, of course he would do something like this.

"Uh, okay."

"And it can't be… any picture. It needs to… show his face." This is essential. To really drive the point home, she twists around and looks at him. Seeing her face, he will know how serious she is about seeing Professor Towers'. His stupid, fat, ugly, old face.

"Okay." Ray is breathing even harder than her now. "I mostly only see him… hunched over his desk… But I'll try to sneak… something."

"No trying, only doing… It's part… of your pilgrimage."

"Okay."

"It will reveal… something to me, then more can be revealed… to you." It would reveal that he indeed has access to Professor Towers' NYU login, and could change her grade eventually. While it's also possible that he could do this if he has those suspected hacking abilities, it is not probable. If that is the case then he is lying to her. He is playing his own game. Maybe he derives some sick pleasure from this, the role-playing, and he is chasing that; he likes being humiliated like this. Perhaps he is naturally passive, a bottom among bottoms. A hacker would almost certainly be into that kind of thing. Most of them are completely fucked up. They hang out on gross websites, places like 4chan and LiveLeak. Weird IRCs. No, in order for this to work, in order for her grade to get changed, she will need to know he is telling the truth. That when he said he trusted her the other day, he meant it: Pics or it didn't happen.

"Okay."

"Ray, you cannot fail at this… You are nothing without me… You need me… more than you've ever… needed anything."

She waits for his response. She is riding up and down, up and down. Nothing.

"Without me… you are completely lost. I own… your soul." Up and down, up and down. She must admit, without a condom, this feels great. It's been a while for her like this, since Kenji. Maybe she should get a real boyfriend. On OkCupid. No. If this is to work, if her grade is to be changed, Ray will require her complete attention. Or at least most of it.

Still no words. He only looks at her, his eyes doleful.

"You are speechless because... you know it's true... You're not as dumb as... you look, Ray. That's good." Seriously, wow! The condom always hurts a little, but not this... It's a shame it's Ray making her feel this way. She doesn't like that. She wants to find something wrong with it. But she can't think of anything. But maybe it could feel better? There is always room for improvement. Everywhere. "I know you are... worshiping me now... I can feel it. But I need you... to worship me harder... Worship me harder, Ray."

He rises, still inside her, rotates her body, and lays her down in missionary. This is not what she meant. She just wanted him to take a more active role as he was, be less passive in his bottom position, hold on to her hips more firmly and pump into her hard instead of continuing to just let her ride him. But she'll take this. His worship. She's very glad to. He is literally on his knees now before her, his head bowed; he is thrusting hard, very hard, much like he did during their first encounter. It feels ah-maz-ing. He comes. This, too—his pelvis twitching and leading to all kinds of vibrations—feels ah-maz-ing... Ah. Maz. Ing.

Good boy, indeed. Little Kaiju eats well tonight. It's either a parting gift or, if he sends the picture tomorrow, the start of something she could definitely get used to. Sure, being his girlfriend sucks, but she can tone that down after a while. Everybody is probably like this during the first flush. And besides, what's a girlfriend to an almighty God?

It's not like it was before—no cramps, no fatigue. There's no need to tell himself to power through. Two months in and his hand is finally there: totally in shape, without a hint of pain or discomfort for a week, his askesis finally paying off. His fingers no longer seem fat, but like the brawny legs of a long-distance runner, there to power the pen, itself, now, the very extension of him. Each word is a footprint as it runs across the page, the distal phalanges of his right hand quick calves, the intermediate strong hamstrings, proximal puissant glutes, all working together in fluid, beautiful motion. He is more than possessed by passion, but now fully fit, able to continue this marathon with a body to match his mind. Every book is a marathon, but writing longhand, this is the way it's meant to be done! Barefoot. Like Pheidippides. Emerson can see that now, as crystalline as anything one would see at the peak of a runner's high.

And oh! How he's run! Starting with the Greeks, he described the childhood of the Culture, its strict religious upbringing through Homer, Hesiod, Aeschylus, Sophocles, Euripides, Aristophanes, Empedocles, Plato, Aristotle, Herodotus, and Thucydides, to name a few, beginning the story like any good biographer when the subject's personality had already been formed, its perfectionist tendencies there on full display, guiding it through a rigid period when aesthetics and order were of the utmost importance, a matter of serving the gods and the soul; then, his subject perfectly known to the reader, he brought it back to the actual beginning for some context; back to the Near East with *Gilgamesh*, then its toddling through the Book of the Dead, the major ancient religious Indian texts, showing that the priority the Greeks put on aesthetics is indeed half of what made the Culture truly what it was, that form was as important as function. From there: the Old Testament, then Rome, with Cicero, Ovid, Virgil, etc. and the remainder of its childhood spent roving the greater Mediterranean as the capable young nomad it was, with the New Testament, the writings of Saint Augustine, the Quran, and *One Thousand and One Nights*. Next it was off to something of an English boarding school for the Arthurian Romances and *Beowulf*, broken up by some jaunts here and there around other parts of Europe for *The Poetic Eddas*, *The Nibelungenlied*, *The Divine Comedy*, *The Poem of the Cid*, *The Book of the City of Ladies*, and *Prison of Love*, among others. Emerson began writing of this adolescence last week, jumping around as he's seen fit, and just started on Dante last night, what he considers the first real step in the Culture gaining a different level of maturity. It will continue its winding path across Europe for the rest of its teens, with its home base in England, the Culture soon to begin a youthful rebellion where God will lose some ground to man, to the self, especially in the self-actualization that came with Shakespeare, the Culture's true coming-of-age. Emerson loves Dante, but he can hardly wait for Shakespeare.

He reaches for his mug. It's light, his coffee nearly down to the dregs, and, when it slides onto his tongue, too cold.

"Ray! Coffee!"

And like a marathon runner needs water, Emerson needs coffee. It's not so much fuel as a matter of maintenance. How did the old masters get on without it? They just drank wine all day in ancient Greece and Rome. Should he have been drinking wine while writing about them, for authenticity's sake? No. He very well couldn't abandon all modern

conveniences, and everything that's been involved with his writing process to date. Giving up an assistant he can have sex with and writing
longhand are surely significant enough changes. Besides, many great
books have been written since the late 1500s when coffee was introduced
to Europe. Ray appears at his side and is gone just as fast, the large white
mug with him.

His hand is going now, and has since he set down the lukewarm
drink. It's sprinting across the page, gushing about the *Purgatorio*, a subject that only requires half of his attention he knows it so well. Or maybe
that's the coffee talking, so magical is the effect of the morning's first cup.
Right now Emerson feels he could write forever, as if his hand were being guided by a numinous force, the highest of powers. Is this what it
was like when the Bible was written? The Ramayana? The Greek dra-
mas? The Quran? Probably.

Coffee: just as good as religious fervor, the mild stimulant effects of
watered-down wine, anything else used to bring pen to page back then.
That is, unless it is true divine inspiration he's receiving. The coffee
could just be a delivery system for the words from on high; coffee did
come from the Middle East, originally, after all.

But Emerson can't go on like this forever. For one, school is going
to start up again in about a month. He would quit, as he had previously
considered, if not for the health insurance and the esteem of his departmental chair; he has a hard time imagining himself on some retiree Med-
icare plan and he is indeed an academic. He thinks of his post as a
lifetime appointment, similar to that of a Supreme Court justice, except,
as a guardian of the Culture, far, far more essential for society. That
doesn't mean he can't phone it in while working on the book, nor that
he can't cut his time teaching to one semester a year after this to enjoy
something of a retirement. Yes, that should be the plan going forward
after the next two terms. But one thing is certain: he should die at his
post.

Then there's the matter, more important, of the work itself. Though
his knowledge of the Canon is infinite, this book can't be. It must be
contained, stay true to this form of an elegy, hit the heart as much or
more than the head. And so far it has. His prose is so beautiful that it
reads more like poetry. To make it too long would eventually break one's
heart, so unbearably sad and gorgeous it could strike a reader dead.
Sometimes the effect is like listening to the song *Gloomy Sunday*. Emerson
isn't even quite sure he'll be able to read it all the way through once it's
done. His melancholy may be too profound. Oh, the Culture! Why?! It

must be just long enough to make the reader feel this incredible loss, not want to join in it.

And so he must continue to make the most of this time. As his hand moves across the page, Ray's delivers the refill, and while not a word is shared between them, they remain seamlessly flowing from Emerson's pen. The young man has come and gone again, the only evidence of his having been there the coffee with milk and two sugars currently steaming on the coaster beside him.

Uninterrupted, just as it should be, Emerson's hand goes and goes. Once the coffee cools enough, he drinks as needed with the free hand. Forget running, he's flying now. From Pheidippides to Pegasus. Yes, Emerson feels he could go on like this forever…

Until! Oh, goodness. A rumble in the belly. A feeling of unease, then substantial heaviness. He can't continue to fly toward the heavens with something in his gut weighing him down. Oh, coffee! Your laxative effect can pinion the alae you allow to grow and normally so gracefully flap and spread to soar.

Emerson rises. He shambles out of the office, down the hallway, and into the bathroom. Dante falls from his consciousness completely, and the entire time he can think of nothing but the matter at hand, the clarion call of nature. There to tell him, vociferously, that he is only a man. Nothing more. But then the noisome business is over with… yes, he is a man, but not *only* a man; he is an *important* man.

After washing his hands, Emerson lights a match. The wisp of smoke hardly clouds the room, but it does his consciousness enough that his work still is not allowed back into the picture; instead, he sorts through whether lighting a match is really the right thing to do.

There is the idea that it is common decency, something anyone who shares a bathroom should practice, especially if that bathroom is part of a home office. To not light a match would be uncivil.

Or would it?

This is the other argument: Lighting a match could very well be beneath him.

Emerson is not a common man, as is well known; he is a truly great and estimable man. So common decency need not apply to him—lighting a match actually denigrates his civility. When dining out, or enjoying the theater, the places people such as himself patronize often staff bathroom attendants. This should be no different. Ray smelling his personal stench wouldn't be the worst thing in the world; it need not be embarrassing. If he entered the bathroom so soon after Emerson left, wouldn't he deserve it? And, really, doesn't he deserve it regardless, to remind him of his place as a subaltern? Why should Emerson care so much about what his assistant *thinks*? He's not being paid to think. He's being paid to assist, to maximize efficiency around here so Emerson can do the thinking, so Emerson can get the very important task at hand done! He doesn't have time to light matches! If Ray should enter and find the smell offensive he can light his own damn match!

Emerson will cease this practice immediately. He pockets the matchbook from the medicine cabinet.

Has he been too easy on Ray? He asks himself this leaving the bathroom, moving down the hallway. The answer, upon reaching the living room and seeing the young man, is unequivocally yes. Ray is currently sitting sideways, facing him, in a sort of twisted, leaning, lounging pose, with his phone in front of his face. Everything about this—but especially the nonchalance with the gadget—is totally unacceptable. Even a pupil wouldn't be so bold. So for this to come from his own assistant?! And while he should be transcribing or proofreading his masterpiece, or beginning to prepare for lunch?! It is an outrage!

"Raaay?" Emerson doesn't let his emotions get the better of him. He addresses the young man while standing with his arms behind his back, hands folded, the quintessence of composure.

Ray lowers the phone, wincing ever so slightly. Emerson's eyes aren't so bad yet that he can't make out a wince. "Yes, Emerson?"

"What, exactly, are you doing?"

"Sorry, I was just… I received a text message from my mother."

His mother? How old would his mother be? He's somewhere between twenty-five and thirty, it seems, so she must be at least fifty, unless he's the product of something truly horrid. Do people that age actually text? Nobody should text, really, least of all anyone that old, but a mother texting with her son seems quite odd, almost lewd, especially on a weekday morning. But Emerson's mind need not go there. The bottom line is personal communications are not to take place during business hours. "I see…"

"So I was just taking a five-second break to text her back."

"I understand, Ray." Yes, Emerson understands. Ha! This generation, on top of completely living up to the "entitled" label it's best known for, also apparently thinks it invented the art of bullshitting, or at least can bring it to dazzling new heights. A five-second break? Psshaw! There's a good one! "So it wasn't an emergency. Correct?" Of course it wasn't. Nobody would text during an emergency, they would *call*. Otherwise it wouldn't be an emergency. Or it would be an emergency involving an idiot, whose life would be of little consequence, anyway, where the texting party would warrant anything that befell them.

"No, not an emergency. Again, I was just taking a little break." Ray turns the chair around so he can sit facing Emerson directly. He is careful to lift the legs off the floor so they don't drag, to his credit.

"A five-second one, to use your phrase."

"Yeah. It might have been ten, I don't know."

"These aren't real things, Ray." Emerson's hands unhinge behind him, then come together again in a soft clap at his chest. "A five-second break doesn't exist, nor a ten-second one. Not here or anywhere else. When you're an adult, there are bathroom breaks and then there is lunch." He looks into the young man's eyes. "That's it. I know you spend lunch with me, but if you choose to text then, I won't mind." And it's true. While it would seem somewhat ill-mannered, and Ray, for his own good, really should be attempting to pick Emerson's brain about literature and the arts—since not everyone gets to dine daily with a bona fide genius, the greatest reader of all time—if Ray chose to waste the opportunity and stare into his phone to text or surf the web, then he would be understanding of that. People treat breaks differently: some as opportunities for growth; others as a time for fun; and yet more, including Ray, it seems, treat it as an excuse to shut down their minds completely. Emerson, in a mixture of the growth and fun categories, sometimes does a bit of his pleasure reading over the meal—a book at the table, just as in all places, is never rude—and on these occasions, when Emerson has chosen to be unavailable, it would particularly make sense for Ray to do whatever it is he would like with his silly cell phone. "Or sometime around lunch, while you're running out to pick something up or as you're settling back in for the afternoon. If ever there was a time for personal communications, that would be it. Not during the morning."

"Sorry Emerson, I understand. Won't happen again."

"Good." This should be the end of the exchange. Emerson has what he needs, and there is work to be done. But it's been a while since he's lectured, and as an academic, the impulse to explicate and make damn sure his point has been made is hard to shake. "You know, in my classroom, I would confiscate it." No, no. There are more important things to do. He catches himself and offers padding: "But you're not a kid, and I know that won't be necessary. I'm glad we had this talk."

"Me too. You know, I didn't even notice I was doing it until you were there. I think it's a generational thing. Kind of stupid. Phone breaks are in a way the new smoke breaks."

Ah, Ray. There's that Latin charm again. The strange young man! Did he just push him away so he could pull him back in? Yes, there are more important things to do, but how often can he *truly* bond with the young man? "That's a very apt way to put it. Though, they're actually worse."

"Probably."

"Definitely. One degrades the lungs, the other the mind." Time for another lecture… but! He will keep this one short. "Our minds, Ray, our capacity for reason, are what make us human. Without them, we're nothing but animals. Beasts." Yes, yes. All of this is very good. Perhaps it can even be used somewhere in the book. "Our breath serves the mind, not the other way around." He must remember to make a note. Wait! Why should he make a note? This, if anything, would be a job for Ray. Why has Emerson been so easy on him? Why should he even want to bond with him? These interlarded flourishes of peculiar charm? Or has it been the spell of his writing this time around that has him all out of sorts? "Anyway, better get another pot of coffee going, I suspect my cup is now getting cold."

"Of course."

"And please write down what I just said, about what makes us human, about breathing and the mind. Just as a note. There might be a place for it in the book."

"You got it." Ray reaches for the pen and notepad resting atop his workstation. He turns back toward Emerson, writing. "Glad I was able to elicit a thought that might be book-worthy."

"Yes, well," Emerson laughs to himself. "Stranger things have happened!" After a moment of watching Ray's pen move, he scratches his head. "Read it back to me, please."

"Our minds make us human. We're like animals, beasts without them."

"It was, 'Without them, we're nothing but animals. Beasts.' "

"Sorry." He squiggles over his misprint. This is why Emerson's first impulse was to make his own note. The girls never got it right either, he remembers now. It must be perfect, not paraphrased; oh, the things that would be lost if he didn't have his own hands to write, if his genius were left up to real-time translation. "With-out them we're nothing but animals, beasts." Emerson listens, nods. "Our breath serves the mind, not the other way a-round."

"Hmmm…" says Emerson. "It's not quite as good without context. Write 'distracting technology' and draw a line connecting them."

"Okay, sure thing." The young man does what he says. "Do you, um, want this now?"

"Please," Emerson takes it, even though he was not quite sure if he actually wanted it. There are a few other random notes he's made to himself over the last two months back at his own desk that this can join. Really, though, Ray should be capable of holding on to these notes until he's asked for them. Emerson would certainly remember when to ask for it. And even if he didn't, Ray should be trusted to remind him after some time. But can he? "Actually, Ray, you hold on to this for now. And give it back to me one month from today. Can you do that?"

Ray sort of winces again, before his face resumes its usual, more phlegmatic disposition. Obviously he did not care for the request. The nerve! "Of course. I'll transcribe it and make a note to myself to deliver this to you on August…" He turns and opens up a calendar on the computer. "Twelfth. Oh, that's a Sunday. I'll give it to you on the tenth, then."

"That'll be fine, thank you. I've got some other notes you can transcribe and give to me then as well. And it would probably be a good idea to keep your notepad ready at all times in case I should say anything brilliant in passing or at lunch."

"You got it."

"Very well." Emerson turns and moves into the office. Seconds later, sitting down at his desk, he hears Ray putting on another pot of coffee, just as it should be. He sips from the cup too long neglected—interrupted by temperamental bowels and an insolent assistant. It's actually not as cool as expected, but not exactly at the proper warmth, either. He'll do well to wait for the new pot. Ray's not a bad assistant, really, not insolent in general, but Emerson *has* been too easy on him. Good grief, a five-second break! It's not only idle hands that do the Devil's work. Isn't that right, Dante? He reads the last paragraph back. Yes, of course. A little stretch then he's off again, somewhere in Italy, running up the Mount of Purgatory, faster and faster till he's taking both Virgil and Dante up in his arms, faster and faster still till his wings grow once more and he again takes flight. Except he's no Pegasus now. Much like how the Culture

morphed with Dante, he must morph again. Up, up, up they go. Onward to Paradise. Onward to Greatness. Emerson Towers: arbiter and
archangel of the sublime.

▲▽▽▽▽▽

Yay! It's him! Him!! Never has she been so excited to see a face she hates
so much. She actually, audibly squeals, she's so happy! Ray really *does*
work for Emerson! She has proof. Haruka has the proof she needs to
justify her hope!

"What is it Haruka?" her boss, Katherine, asks. She's sitting two
seats down the row at her own cool iMac station.

"Oh, it's… my grandpa!" She had to think for a split second, but it
still sounded okay. Like she was processing. Like she was so overcome
with emotion that it took that split second to complete the sentence. Haruka is acting again. Lately, she's been like a one-woman show. So many
roles. She is getting very good at it. "I just got a text. He's out of the
hospital now."

"That's great news! I'm so happy for you!"

"Thank you!" There's a bouquet of flowers on Haruka's desk, next
to her computer. Daisies, snapdragons, yellow button poms. Katherine
gave them to her when one of the higher-ups that was there at PS1 mentioned her grandpa was having health problems. They are very pretty.
Finally, Haruka can see that. Finally, Haruka can see nice things in the
world again.

She returns to her phone, the picture—the fatso standing in what
must be his kitchen with his mean and stupid-looking face as clear as
day, his hair like he just got out of bed, wearing a barely tucked button-
down and khakis. It's him! It's really, really him!

Ray's accompanying text reads: Here he is.

Yes, Ray, here he is. Here he is, indeed! She writes him back:

good boy.

Seconds later, a reply:

> He caught me on my phone while I
> was taking it. I told him I was texting a
> family member and he got pretty
> pissed. Does this have something to do
> with what will be revealed?

Oh, that's right, she forgot. A minor glitch in the hippocampus. Now Haruka must think of something. It shouldn't be too hard—he's practically doing it himself, finding something where there's nothing, for whatever the hell it is he's talking about. Whatever's wrong with him. It's like Haruka's his therapist. All she'll have to do is guide him with nonsense to make up his own reasons for why his life is messed up. Ray is stupid:

> Yes.

Then:

> Cool. Wanna go to the beach this
> weekend? It's supposed to be pretty hot
> Saturday.

No, she does not. Of course not. Haruka hates the heat and sun and even more than these things, she hates sand. In high school everybody always wanted to go to the beach… Ocean Beach, China Beach, Baker Beach. Not her. And it wasn't because the cooler climate in the Bay Area made it unnecessary. It was because of the sand. She'd go sometimes but was miserable. The thing about sand is that it gets everywhere. It would get on all her belongings: a blanket if she brought one, her backpack or purse, towel. And it also gets in everything. It would get inside her backpack or purse, not just on it. Practically every section. Crevices in her body. Between her toes, under her armpits, in her ears. Even inside Little Kaiju sometimes. Places where it had no business being. Though, really, it has no business being anywhere. Haruka would be happy if the world had no sand whatsoever. All of it should be gathered up today to make glass for cool devices for the rest of time; that would be the best use for it. Sand on its own is crude and stupid. The only way she could get it off was to go into the water, which was often too cold. She bets it is here, also. Being too cold is just as bad as being too hot. It sends a shock through the system, cold water like that. Then to get it off all her stuff, it required a lot of unpleasant work. And even then it wouldn't be all the way gone. There were always some grains left behind, found days or sometimes weeks later. There are usually annoying people around, too, on beaches. People playing sports and boomboxes. Everything about the beach is terrible.

But she will go. She will be the good, dutiful girlfriend. She will be fun! By texting him as God just then, she changed things. Made her two identities cross paths. A double helix. So now she must be a girlfriend, too, in real life.

It is a sacrifice worth making. Well worth it. She has her picture of Professor Towers! What a day! Proof! Real hope!! Haruka takes a moment to smell her bouquet. It's the first time she's done this. When they were presented, she faked it. But now she inhales deep. The scent is wonderful.

▲ ▽ ▽ ▽ ▽ ▲

Eventually the concrete ends and beach begins, but not quite yet; it's hard to tell exactly where. This stretch is longer than he remembered. The horizon line, hazy in the heat and wobbly in mirage, reads mostly as ocean, and the road has been roughly the same color as sand since the asphalt stopped at the motor blockade some dozen yards back, back when Beach 169th Street became a wide walkway for those on their way to New York City's very own little slice of paradise. But Ray can feel it, that it's coming; the air is different now, cooler with every step. And smell it, the mighty Atlantic's salty tickle, that sulfuric note that taps into past experience and tricks the brain into anticipating something nice and refreshing even though it, by itself, isn't all that pleasant—similar to the redolence of beer. Is that also sulfuric? He thinks it might be, and that maybe there's a correlation between how great beer is and how wonderful swimming in the ocean can be, though that's not really worth getting into right now. He should be thinking about Haruka. She's walking beside him, or somewhere between that and behind him. It's been a long journey since they met at Union Square around 11:30, a lengthy train and bumpy bus ride ago… about an hour and a half all told. Apparently, Fate doesn't like walking all that much. Or taking the bus. She seems to have lost something—besides what had been a pretty amiable and enthusiastic demeanor—about five minutes into the ride on the Q35. And while he's not a huge fan of taking the bus either, especially standing up like they were, this ride was full of other beachgoers, so it wasn't without a sense of occasion. Ray guesses this isn't so much a continuation of the hot and cold thing as it is simply what he needs her to be right now; he needs her to be more somber, restrained. It is, after all, serious business, what's to become of his very soul, they're going to talk about this afternoon. Maybe that's why he wanted her to reveal whatever it is she's going to reveal here. That in case it ended up being bad news, or more work than he anticipated, or whatever else on this wild ride he's been on, then at least he'd have a few good moments on a pleasant beach to savor beforehand, and hopefully remember afterwards. That is, if there will even be consciousness soon after this.

They make it to the end of the road, a wide, clear view of the sandy beach and cerulean ocean opening up in front of them. Ray, in swim trunks and a black-and-white-striped tank top, removes his Nikes while Haruka, wearing the same white sundress from before, keeps her sandals on, and they walk in a straight line toward the water. The sand is hot but not scorching. To their left is Jacob Riis Park—"The People's Beach"—populated by a crowd of mostly darker-skinned revelers, clusters of black and Hispanic families and friend groups having fun under the watchful eyes of mostly lighter-skinned lifeguards, the teen and college-aged kids of the high-ranking cops and firemen who themselves lounge on the other side of the fence at Beach 149th, over in the "locals" section, where these folks wouldn't have easy access or parking and definitely not much of a welcome. But, honestly, those beaches aren't any better. Ray's walked or hung out on the entirety of the Rockaways save Breezy Point over the years, in his freelance quasi-reverse retirement, and, for the most part, it's all the same: better than Coney and Brighton 'cause the waves break, just about as dirty. The only truly different stretch in terms of quality is the one to the right, the one they're going to: Fort Tilden.

"I'm so happy we're here," says Haruka.

"Yeah." Ray smiles. "Just about five more minutes."

"Seriously?"

Rounding a dune, they trek westward through the sand. "Like you don't know!" Another test, surely. She's supposed to know everything, so of course she'd know where the best part of Fort Tilden is. And the very beginning ain't it. Still too close to civilization. But it isn't far. Leaving "The People's Beach" behind, soon you will find yourself in more of a "Human Animal's Beach." Something raw, beautiful.

Fort Tilden, a former coastal Army base, is home to natural beaches, dunes, and a maritime forest shrouding a few decrepit military installations and buildings. There are no lifeguards, so no dumb motherfuckers who don't know how to swim making people nervous or splashing around obnoxiously in the shallows, and along with that no bothersome whistles blowing all the time. Since it's sort of hard to get to, the people around you tend to be those who are willing to put in a little work to earn a fun experience, which means they're for the most part pretty cool. Assholes either love convenience or things that require way too much effort, like extreme sports; this is somewhere in the middle. The closest thing it has to regulation is the sporadic National Park dude or lady zipping by on a four-wheeler and doing next to nothing about anything. A lot of people drink. Some smoke weed. Women go topless. Some completely nude. Men, too. Occasionally the folks doing this are old and a little in your face, weird New York naturalists who don't have the time or desire to find a proper nude beach or colony, but most aren't. It's got more of a European flair. A lot of the women who go topless are at least somewhat attractive, though that's beside the point; after you're, like, nineteen, boobs are pretty much just boobs. Ray's seen three pairs of them on their walk so far and it's not tantalizing at all—it's just a nice, natural extension of a nice, natural beach. Sort of like flipping through a *National Geographic* profile on the Tribe of the Tildens.

In the last couple of years, the place has been highlighted in some local trend pieces, *NY Mag*, *The Times*, some blogs, getting labeled "The Hipster Hamptons," since some of these people have tattoos and silly haircuts. But that's not really a fair title. Hipsters are clowns for the sake of being clowns—the old guys doing yoga naked would be closer to that—and these people are for the most part low-key; affiliating tattoos with hipsters would be giving hipsters too much credit. All are welcome here. He's amazed that more teenage boys haven't found out about it, but glad, since they'd surely fuck it all up. That nineteen-year-old thing again.

It's the weekend, so there are more folks here than usual. Sadly, this does take something away. The emphasis on nature is compromised: less beach to see and not everyone seems to get what the vibe of this place is supposed to be about. All are welcome, but that doesn't mean all know what they're doing. This sample doesn't yield a true sense of their ethology. Today there are more umbrellas, more Frisbees, more shit to take away from its realness. Also in the course of his reverse retirement, he's been here on more than his fair share of ninety-plus-degree weekdays, and those are truly glorious. But this will have to do.

"You weren't lying about the naked people," says Haruka. Of course he wasn't. But shouldn't she already know that? And why would she care, or even notice? She did, after all, parade through his own apartment completely nude, putting on a show for Brian. What, exactly, is going on with her? Is this another test? This pendulum swing of personality does not speak to her being something as solid as Fate. Is the thing to be revealed about her—about the ontology of Fate—or him? No use bothering himself with that now. These are supposed to be the pleasant moments. He sees another set of boobs, areola pointing skyward. For a moment, everything is better.

"No. No, I wasn't." The moment doesn't last long. They walk in silence, Ray leading them closer to the water till they're walking over tide-hardened, gray-fading sand. Again, he is troubled. Does he need her to be pendulous? Is Fate really fixed? Or can it change? He shouldn't ask himself these things, it's too complicated right now; he should ask her. A large wave rolls onto shore, water spreading over their feet. Cutting through the sound of the ocean, the beach, he can make out her flip-flops squishing with each step after the water flows back out to sea. Would Fate really wear plastic fucking flip-flops?

They march on. Almost. They're going back up a bit on the beach, about to pass the second rock jetty now. The area between the third and the fourth is usually pretty good.

"Hold on," she says. "My sandals." She takes them off, finally. They're able to move a little faster now. Another set of boobs. Not as nice as the others, but they're all nice, really. A welcome distraction until they're gone, until you're passing the person they're attached to and they could catch your gawking eyes through the sides of your sunglasses, your cheap knock-off Ray-Ban sunglasses. Wouldn't be cool. He turns his head to watch the water. Waves cristate then crashing. Looks good. No seaweed today, minimal spume. Human animals play in the surf. Or, rather, projections of human animals play in the projection of surf. He'd like to join them soon. But will Fate allow it?

Time to find out. They pass the third jetty. Here the waves tend to have a pretty decent roll, and he can see the crowd is more dispersed than in the areas they've passed. Now just to get far enough away from the rocks… Here's a spot, nobody in the immediate vicinity and it has a nice view of the water. "All right," says Ray. "Look good to you?"

"I thought you'd never ask." Another weird thing to say. Ray looks at her suspiciously, his glasses hiding his slitting eyes. She reaches into her backpack. Removing a rolled-up blanket, she hands him the loose end. "Will you help me spread this?"

He does.

They place their backpacks on opposite corners to weigh it down, then sit. He only brought a towel, one of his several-years-old, ratty shower ones, so this large, light cotton surface is pretty nice to have. If she is Fate, then this, at least, is a good sign. Unless she's setting him up to knock him down even further, again. He closes his eyes and inhales deep, bringing as much ocean air through his nose and into his lungs as possible. He listens to the surf, the ocean expanding and contracting; it's the closest thing he can think of to the sound of the Earth breathing. There really is nothing like it. A beautiful planet, it was. Okay. Showtime.

When he opens his eyes again, she's back in her bag. Out comes a beach towel. "I went to Kmart this morning and picked this up." She rises from her knees and unfurls it, revealing a Hello Kitty design. It waves gently in the sea breeze. "Like it?"

"Yeah," he says. And he really does. A wry smile, then, "If only I had one with Speedy Gonzales."

"Who's that?"

No. Not again. "I've been meaning to ask you Haruka..."

"JK! Of course I know who Speedy Gonzales is. I just wanted to make you feel old for a sec." She crinkles her nose, then smiles big. Now she's back to who she was earlier, during the first leg of the trip: the bubbly, personable Haruka he had initially met on their first date this spring. "But you're right, that would be perfect."

"I've always thought the best way to overcome a stereotype is to lean into it with, you know, self-awareness."

"Huh?" Fate, if anything, should never ask "Huh?"

"Wait, why do you think it would be perfect?"

"Because they're both really cute. They'd make a great couple, like us." She grabs his hand. It's a little sticky from the air, and very warm. But he doesn't mind. This is reassuring. "What did you mean?"

Until he's reminded why she's actually not being reassuring in the least: again, she should know. Really, anyone should know because of context, but she, as Fate, especially should know. He pulls his hand away. It's not her touch he's here for, it's her words. The right words. Meaningful words as far away from "Huh?" and "What did you mean?"

as you can get. Maybe she actually is a demon. No. He needs to trust in this. He needs to try. Have faith. But first, he'll need at least some clarification. He removes his sunglasses. "Shouldn't you know?"

"Why would I?"

"You told me you know everything. About me." For some reason, Ray thought she would remove her sunglasses, too, meet him eye to eye. Share a moment of intimacy. She hasn't and it's making him uncomfortable.

"I do. In any given moment I know all I need to know."

"In any given moment?" Ray really wishes she would take her sunglasses off, not only because it would make him feel closer to her but so he could better read her, too. But he can't just ask, that would be weird. "What's that supposed to mean?"

"Some moments I know everything. Like a god. Some moments I know very little, or next to nothing. In these I want you to tell me things. I'm excited for them, for you to share with me and show me things about yourself. Like anybody would be in a new relationship. I'll need you to tell me what I don't know. And it's very possible that I'll forget until I need to know again."

He takes some time to think. She is being very confusing and cryptic now, like a robot or something, and the sunglasses really aren't helping, giving her an even more unfair advantage. Ray would like to put his back on, but that would also be weird. Another few seconds at least— then it would seem like he naturally had decided against exposing his eyes to the glare of the mid-day beach sun. "This is how Fate works?" Okay, the sunglasses can go back on now. They do.

"You think I am Fate? No. I am not Fate. I'm way too young to be Fate, Ray! In classic mythology, Fate is actually made up of three women. Three old, ugly women." Holy shit, she's right. He remembers that now from like eighth-grade English. The argument could be made, however, that she's at least two women… and maybe there's a third in there, and they're all just hiding in this pretty little shell. Maybe instead of his Bible, he should start by reading more Greek and Roman mythology, sort of how Emerson begins his book…

But this is getting too convoluted. Let's get to the heart of the matter, why they're here: "I'd like you to reveal the thing you said you'd reveal to me now. What you said you'd tell me after I took a picture of Emerson."

"That's not how it works. One, I didn't tell you that. I told you after you took the picture that 'more can be revealed.' I never said I *would* reveal it to you just for taking the picture, or right after." Her sunglasses come off. She says she doesn't have to reveal anything, then shows him her eyes, finally. Is that supposed to mean something? "Have you ever played a video game, Ray?" No. It seems it was just for emphasis. But that was the question she wanted to give the sunglasses-removal emphasis to? Seriously, what the fuck?

"Yeah."

"All this means is you've leveled up. Two, I probably won't even tell you what the thing is. It'll more likely be something revealed through me, not from me directly. By being around me. Doing the right things. Learning. This is the only way to gain true understanding. I agree it is nice to just be told things. Facts. But this isn't about the facts. It's about truth. That is more elusive. There is more searching to be done." But there has been so much searching already! He's been through the levels; he thought she was the boss of the game. How long is this damn thing? Why did she have to come back? If she wasn't the boss, isn't his personification of Death, and she isn't Fate, what is she? The Riddler? The Joker? No, he's no Batman—no bored billionaire hero—and those guys would be more like demons. And she can't be that. He needs to trust in that, at least. Things were going so well until she reemerged. Or, at least, it seemed he was making progress, slowly but surely, putting in the work, for himself, for Emerson and the written word, for strangers on the internet, keeping the Platinum Rule and not her at the front of his mind; things were getting better. But if them's the breaks then them's the breaks. It is what it is.

"Okay."

"All that picture really meant is now you've earned my trust. I know I have yours." She reaches for his hand again. It's not as clammy as before. A little cooler, and just soft, delicate… "And you better not betray mine."

"I understand."

"Good! So today is really just about having a fun beach day." She squeezes, then pulls away and puts her sunglasses back on. "Thanks for bringing me here. Cool beach! What a fun activity!"

"Yeah, it's cool, right? Glad you like it." Is he really, though? A part of him knows he came here because he thought it was the end; he didn't anticipate she'd be in girlfriend mode for long if at all here… he wanted her to be the supernatural vessel that would take him away. He thought maybe this would be the place where this stream of consciousness would end—the one that began with his birth and has continued now five years into his death. That this is where his soul would finally leave the shackles of its human animal body, floating upward to heaven. That—

"Can I have some water?"

"Sure."

He reaches into his bag, grabs the Nalgene bottle they last drank from on the bus, the ice long melted, the outside of the bottle wet with condensation. She takes a sip. "So what did you mean by that, the towel thing?"

Who cares? That doesn't matter now. Ray wants to be alone to think; maybe he can make a break for the water soon. No. He should be with her now. Maybe he'll actually "learn" whatever the hell it is that she should have revealed. "Oh, just that, you know, it's, like, best to deal with unpleasant things like racism or whatever with humor. Use irony and exaggeration to strip it of its power."

"Oh. I don't believe that at all. Racism is not okay. Ever."

Well, that's not what he was saying. Taking ownership of something used to oppress you while leaning into a stereotype to make fun of it isn't the same as racism by a long shot. Is she supposed to function as a foil right now? Is that what he needs her to be? Kinda dumb? Or like Brian? What the hell would racism have to do with his death? Did the person who ran him over do it on purpose because he's Hispanic, or possibly because they couldn't see him walking there with his skin being as dark as it is? Wait, it's no longer about what he needs her to be at all times since she isn't Fate. Ray would really like to be alone to think right now. "I just meant—it's sort of like black people using the n-word. You know?"

"No, I don't. I don't know their struggles. I only know mine."

"Right." They could go on like this all day. Why would anybody want to talk about race and identity politics on the fucking beach? But he can't concede his point; that wouldn't be the right thing to do. Back to the Platinum Rule. Being right is good. Truth is good. "I just meant you can make something less offensive by taking it over."

"You find my towel offensive? And you think I bought it to be like a black person using the n-word?"

"Not exactly. I meant—"

"I don't think that kind of thing is funny or empowering. I bought this because I like Kitty White and thought it was cute. I believe I should be able to do whatever I want and not be judged for it."

"Hey, me too." And he does. Finally, a place where he doesn't have to be contrarian. "Everybody should."

"Well, that's not really true, either. White people, especially white men, should be judged for everything they do. They have all the power." Apparently, she does, however. Like one of those dudes in high school or the internet loonies. Surely this is a test. A test of patience! Maybe that's what she's supposed to reveal to him: that he still needs to be patient. Perhaps he was getting ahead of himself thinking that a couple months of stable, meaningful employment and a good karma score on Reddit were enough to allow him to ascend into heaven. This is purgatory we're talking about here. This shit's supposed to take a long-ass time. If she wants to go on like this all day, then he can. Maybe the day at the beach isn't supposed to be a day at the beach.

"You know I'm half white, right?"

"I do now. Guess that means I'll only judge you halfway!" She crinkles her nose again, leans over, and kisses his cheek. Perhaps they don't have to go on like that all day.

"Right!"

Giggling, she rubs his head and moves back to her side of the blanket. "I'm not so serious all the time. I like to have fun." She takes down the straps of her dress and wiggles out of it, revealing a light gray, almost silver-looking bikini, the top of which also then comes off. "It's so cool you can go topless here. I hate tan lines!"

"Yeah, I guess I'm pretty used to it. Must be nice for you."

"Did you know I'm half Chinese?"

"I do now." He smiles down at her. Her pale body shines in the sun as she leans back, broken up only by the skimpy silverish bikini bottoms. She's never looked more like a phone. But she isn't. She can't be, even if she has said things that sounded sort of robotic here. She has a human form with human needs; she just drank water, for crying out loud. Water would fuck up a phone-person. A celestial being wouldn't personify an inanimate, man-made object; that's just stupid. They could only take the form of an idea. And it couldn't be the idea of a phone. Fuck that. She really isn't Fate? Is she Death, like he thought before, the phone thing just leading up to it? His Death? An angel of death? And if so, is she more Michael or Samael? She's neither. She's female. Santa Muerte?! ¡Ay, caramba! That might make sense, especially because that figure isn't recognized by the Church. It's only a quasi-figure like he's only a quasi-Catholic. Maybe this is the healing process his family always told him about. But would a Mexican folk saint really inhabit the body of a young Asian woman? He realizes he's staring. Maybe she likes it, feels flattered; but all the same, he's not going to figure anything out this way. "I'm gonna go for a swim." Ray gets up.

"You're not going to invite me?"

Shit. That was pretty rude. He just really, really wants to be alone. "Sorry, wanna come?"

"No. I don't swim. You go ahead." Thank God. But what the hell? Why the games, constantly? "I always want to be invited though."

"Okay."

"To everything. Give me a kiss before you go. A real one." Ray lowers himself back down onto the blanket and leans over her. They kiss; their lips, then tongues, coming together. There is no discernible taste to her mouth or tongue… she tastes exactly like nothing. They come apart. "And when you are swimming think of me. You must always try to think of me," she says. She lies down. Removing her sunglasses, she turns her head to the side then covers her face with her bunched-up white dress. She looks strange like this, a slight, faceless, topless thing taking a nap. The dress covers her face like some kind of burial shroud. Maybe she is Santa Muerte. Ray rises, ditches his own sunglasses, and heads down to the water to see if he can find out.

Then—no, it can't be!—Fernanda from behind! A pang of something, a feeling of odd familiarity that is not quite like those other déjà vus, but certainly a form of recognition. His eyes must be playing tricks! They better be!

There are four bodies in the surf; three belong to a group of friends bobbing in the waves, what looks like a couple—a man with long hair, a woman with short—and their third-wheel friend with a beard, and the fourth, alone off to the side, belongs to maybe-Fernanda, a dark youngish female with black crinkled hair, standing in the shallows, her perfect caramel-colored ass barely covered by a bright green bikini bottom.

Green means go.

He walks into the surf, a few yards to her side. It's cold at first, but the ocean always is. He can't look yet. Too conspicuous. He moves farther into the water, a wave approaching fast. He meets it head on, diving into it—gelid, but in a good, bracing way, like the first gulp of ice water after a workout, except surrounding his entire body—and a dolphin kick down and up later, resurfaces. He turns and looks at the woman. It's not Fernanda, thank God.

It really is a marvel that there is another woman out there with as magnificent—as round, toned, and well-proportioned—a caudal region, and as lovely a spine leading down to it, but that's better than the marvel it would have been to run into her here. A city of nine million—it would be overwhelming, especially after bumping into Haruka the way he did before at the place he figured he might bump into Fernanda. Far too much cross-wiring. Another wave comes and he dives in, then down. Now he remembers why that was so painfully familiar. The vision he had the morning after the two of them agreed to stop hanging out! The one he had while watching Brian eat shitty sugar cereal in front of his cartoons, the one of her on a beach—starting with her, Brian, and their beige baby, himself then emerging as the result of Brian and the baby weirdly combining, playing with her in the water for a while, and then… what was it that happened afterwards? How did it end? Did she morph too at some point? He can't remember. He's still dolphin kicking and propelling forward, his arms pulling himself ahead laterally, moving farther out underwater. Dammit. It's probably for the best. Already too many tangles in this web as it is. And besides, it wasn't a real déjà vu, so it couldn't have meant anything that important. Not like the rest. That's not how this thing works. Right? He remembers: you can't will these things. What color was her bathing suit in the vision? Was it green? He's getting tired, and has been down here for almost a full minute.

He reemerges and breathes deep. His heart pounds. Turning back, he sees that he's pretty far from the shore, maybe thirty or so yards, way past everyone else. He treads water for a moment and stares at the girl. It's probably for the best that he can't remember those things from that strange daydream. Fernanda was never even a real girlfriend; it couldn't be that significant. But could she have been? Should she have been? She was a sweet girl, but no. He only had that reverie because of fucking Brian talking shit, making him feel more territorial over her than he really was. But how did it end? He swims in a side stroke, casually, then turns up the heat facing forward until he's closer to her, back to where his feet can touch. She walks away, up onto the beach. Probably back to her spot, her camp with her boyfriend or other attractive friends, creeped out by this weird guy swimming aggressively toward her while she was just trying to peacefully look out into the ocean. It's for the best.

He came out here to cogitate about Haruka, after all. Unless! Aha! Now he remembers! Or, like someone fighting consciousness during an unresolved dream, he's forced his mind into bringing himself where he really wants to go. Willed it into tapping his subconscious for what he thought she might turn into, which gave him the same answer it gave him then, triggering the remembrance: Fernanda *had* morphed, too! Except into nobody. A terrifying, no-faced, shorter and paler version of herself. Shorter and paler? Fuck! That wasn't nobody! It was Haruka!

Especially now, on the beach, her face covered with a shroud! Ray looks over in her direction, but can't see her, can only make out the top of his backpack sticking up on their blanket. It was a prophecy! Wasn't one of the first things Haruka said to him the first time they fucked something like "I am nobody?" Yes! What was it exactly? Ray never googled the quote. He remembers there was stuff from the *Odyssey*, Dante; maybe it's a line from one of those or another piece of literature, like most of the other crazy shit she was saying during that encounter. This is something he needs to investigate, something he needs to google. Along with Santa Muerte.

Ray floats on his back and looks up. The firmament is vast above him, a few swirling cirrus clouds, the erumpent sun shining bright over the world. He feels God watching him, watching out for him, smiling at him with a big, genuine smile. He's no closer to where he wants to be, up there, but cannot deny that, yes, something has been revealed.

▲ ▽ ▽ ▽ ▽ ▲ ▽

This time the phone didn't even ring, only the buzzer. What is wrong with her? He's never cared for surprises; few men do, even fewer smart men. And as one of the smartest alive, Emerson especially does not.

He knew it wasn't his assistant when the horrible sound first tore him from a beautiful meditation on later Shakespeare. Ray was himself hard at work in the next room, and every time he leaves the apartment to run an errand he'll take the spare set of keys. Was it a delivery lunch? No, the clock only read 11:30, and Ray would not be so stupid as to order something like that at 11:00 a.m., or really to order anything like that unbidden: Emerson pays for their lunches and they've only gotten delivery two or three times, on very stormy days, and at Emerson's insistence—a bit of charity so Ray wouldn't have to run around in a squall. So what was it? Emerson hoped a mistake. It was, but not in the way he thought it would be. The person buzzing had the correct address. It was Claire.

There are few things in life worse than a drop-in. The supposed whimsy and fun therein are fabrications only promulgated by uninspired situation comedies, pablum made for the enjoyment of fools. For individuals with actual things to do, it is no different than truncating that person's life by the duration of the visit. Especially one of his age. That it's his family member, his daughter, makes no difference: selfishness is selfishness; time is time. And to make matters worse, she's interrupted him while writing about the greatest master to ever live, and undoubtedly who ever shall. When will this horrible mid-life rebellion end? Oh, Claire.

She should be at the door any moment now. Emerson's been dawdling in the kitchen since he answered the buzzer a minute ago, keeping busy by sipping from his second cup of coffee and occasionally glancing over at Ray. He seems to be scanning the latest pages of the manuscript on the computer—proofreading before printing what will be waiting for Emerson's red pen later on. It's given him the collywobbles, being here to watch someone read back his unfinished work like this, even though he knows that the reader's opinion is of little consequence—if he has any opinion at all—and that he's been doing it for over two months now. Standing here, Emerson is very glad he does not usually bear witness to this, that he works in a different room. When it comes to feeling, out of sight really is out of mind.

A gentle rap at the door. What feelings will his daughter evoke when he answers it? As annoyed as he is, he hasn't seen her since the Great Central American Follies. Will his displeasure at her intrusion prevail or be replaced by the same relief he felt first hearing her voice upon her return, but heightened, because she will be here in the flesh? He turns the knob.

"Hi Daddy!" Stepping into the entryway, she drops her purse onto the floor and wraps her arms around him, reaching as far as she can. It squeezes some of the displeasure out, this celeritous act of love, but not all. Somewhere in the back of his mind Shakespeare is still whispering to him: *I would not wish any companion in the world but you.* But he must wait. Now that his daughter is here, he must make the best of it.

"Claire, my darling! What a surprise!"

"I had a meeting downtown this morning, and thought, what kind of a daughter would I be if I didn't stop by to say hello?"

"Come in, come in." She releases him, and he closes the door behind her. "Oh, well, you know me... I'm happy to see you, but you should never feel obligated."

She reaches for her bag and faces him. "Nonsense. So guess what?" He'd rather not… "Guess what?" He did not raise his daughter to say things like: "Guess what?" Oh, to go from the greatest master of language that ever was to that! "Lisa Cooley's decided to give me another show! It'll be this fall!"

"That's wonderful news!"

"Isn't it? Also, I brought some macarons to celebrate our trip." She canters over to the kitchen counter and, rummaging through her purse, pulls out a small box of the French cookie confections. This is an exciting development: an absolute best-case scenario for a drop-in. Emerson loves macarons. Across the room at his desk, Ray swivels his neck and smiles in their direction. Claire notices him for the first time. "Oh! Hello there," she says.

"Hi."

"Claire, this is Ray. He's helping out with that project I mentioned on the phone. Ray, this is Claire, my daughter." She glides across the room, and they shake hands.

"Nice to meet you," Ray says, still seated, twisted at the waist with his arm extended behind the chair. The disrespect! What is wrong with the youth of the day? Emerson must mention this to Claire in relation to her own children, neglecting to rise while meeting someone. It doesn't matter that she's dropped in and interrupted his work as well. Where are his manners? Not to mention, he very well might be getting a macaron out of it. Of all the times to be more savage than Cervantes, it's while meeting his precious daughter?

"You, too! Would you like a macaron?" Great, now he will get first pick! He doesn't rise and he gets his choice of these delicious, colorful treats. Such an injustice!

"I'd love one," he says.

She turns and grabs the box from the kitchen counter. Emerson watches with terrible envy as she opens it and Ray's undeserving brown fingers flit above in careful consideration. He wishes he would've intercepted it, tried some jocular, not-before-me incorrigible old man shtick. What flavor will Ray choose? Two fingers dive in, then dart out. The winner is… pistachio. No! That is the best, hands down! The green that was in Emerson's eyes is now even more present in Ray's hand. He will pay for this!

Claire meets Emerson in the vague place between the kitchen and living room. Now it's his turn. As his hand hovers, she says, in a hushed tone, "I didn't know anyone else would be here." He goes for the rose-flavored one, even though he doesn't like them that much. Ray's already gotten the spoils, really, and at least the rose reminded him of Shakespeare… with whom, now, considering how things are going, he would much rather be spending his time. "I'm not interrupting your work, am I?"

"No, of course not. You know it would be impossible for you to interrupt anything, darling." Emerson takes a bite. It's a little bland, but there's a subtle sweetness in the aftertaste that seems designed to appeal to a more sophisticated palate, which he likes. Perhaps it's best to start small, then move on to a bolder flavor. Emerson takes another bite. Oh, who is he kidding? Damn that Ray!

Claire reaches for one herself. Vanilla or almond, by the looks of it. "To be perfectly honest, Ray, I didn't even know my father was working with someone." She takes a bite.

"I didn't know he was going on a trip," Ray says, chewing, a hand covering his mouth. Emerson scans his desk, then finds the other hand: his macaron is already gone. He didn't even know how to eat it—what it meant to appreciate it, savor it—the brute!

"Then again, I didn't know he was even working on another book until last week."

Ray swallows. "I guess he's just full of secrets." Oh, what a thing to say… So winsome, so cute. Who does he think he is? Emerson is going to get Ray.

"Indeed. You are, aren't you, Daddy?"

"Yes, well, I suppose I've been keeping a few things close to the vest lately. But mostly because these items aren't really of anyone else's concern. Like I said before, I didn't want to discuss the book until I had truly known it. And Ray's no big secret. He's just my extra set of eyes and hands to help keep the project moving. Mostly with transcription, technical support, meals, other little things here and there." Another bite. He savors as much as he can, lets its flavor flower to full bloom. It helps.

"So you cook as well?"

"A bit."

"A man of many talents," says Claire. What are they, flirting? She's a married woman, and he's, what, probably fifteen years her junior! The last bite, then he signals for her to open the box. There are three left: one clearly chocolate, one yellow—no thanks—and the other a deeper-looking version of what he just ate, vermillion with a dark center.

"Is that raspberry?" he asks.

"I think so." He reaches for it. The rose fades. A bite, the burst of berries.

"I don't know about many," says Ray. Is this real modesty or false modesty? Both are good, Emerson supposes. And not really flirtatious. He's redeeming himself slightly, Ray, or maybe it's the vibrant deliciousness of this macaron that's swaying Emerson's thoughts. This might even be better than pistachio. Would he have even wanted that flavor at this hour? It's still morning—a strange time to taste pistachio, indeed. Rose and raspberry were much better choices, actually. All is forgiven. "More like a select few. Are you staying for lunch?"

"No, I'll have to get back home before long, but thank you." Claire smiles and turns to Emerson, "Daddy, would you be up for taking a little walk? A stroll down Riverside, maybe?"

Emerson hasn't left the apartment in ten days—too hot—but he can't let her know that. She would be concerned. He might as well go all the way with this interruption, get some fresh air and a small dose of summer. "Sure. How's the temperature today?" Another bite. Beautiful, beautiful berries. Raspberries are related to roses, actually, he remembers reading somewhere. The bush they grow from. Something that truly tastes like summer and that Shakespeare would approve of: he will make a note to have Ray buy him some raspberries. He eats the other half of the macaron. What a wonderful, wonderful flavor.

"Not too bad. You'll be fine in that."

"Let me just get my keys, then." He does, with a clumsy jangle, off the rack next to the door. Something occurs to him: perhaps Ray made the "secrets" comment out of fear. Should he let him fester in it? The pistachio faux pas is water under the bridge at this point, but what about the brief flirtation with his daughter? No, he was probably just being polite. And she was probably engaging with him like that because she was so pleased and surprised that Emerson would hire someone Hispanic; she must've been taking a cue from Emerson's own tremendous warmth and magnanimity. "Ray, in case you were concerned, you needn't worry about our schedule. I won't be going on that trip for a year or so."

"Oh, okay. That's reassuring. So, you're going to France?"

"Yes, along with a couple of other places. We haven't really worked out the details yet," says Emerson. This will be as good a time as any to do just that. Yes, Emerson really is making the best of a bad thing.

"Very cool," says Ray.

"Actually, I had some ideas I wanted to run by you," Claire says. "We can talk about it on our walk."

And they do.

Strolling under the nicely shaded canopy in the middle promenade of Riverside Park, she offers, "So I say we start in Italy."

But that's not how it will be done. This very well might be his last trip to Europe, and there are only two ways to do it: to retrace the flow of the Culture or to replicate it. To retrace would be the more clinical way to do it: a deconstruction. And that wouldn't exactly feel right. Not for the project he's working on, not for the way he wants to remember the thing when he comes back to America, where it will die with him. They will start from the beginning and walk in the Culture's shoes.

"The best way to do this, darling, is by beginning in Greece."

"Why?"

"This trip is about culture. That's where it began in Europe, where it spread into the Western world."

Then it is decided. They will begin in Greece, make their way to Italy, followed by France, and end the trip in England. A week or so will be spent in each, and it will be wonderful. They'll leave in June.

She walks him back to his building, leaving him with a goodbye kiss on the cheek. The entire interruption lasted about forty-five minutes.

Riding the elevator up to his apartment, he considers the episode's strengths: seeing his daughter whom he loves, eating macarons, and planning the trip. Then what was lost: his flow while writing about Shakespeare. What was lost was, of course, still greater than what could ever be gained. Who knows where his pen might have taken him were it left to ride along on that gale afflated by *The Tempest*?

Should he eat the remaining macarons now to cap it all off, a few moments of additional pleasure, one more distraction before he goes back to work? No. He'll wait till tonight. It'll be better to have the vestigial tang of raspberry on his tongue when he returns to his work; Shakespeare likely never tasted chocolate.

The elevator doors open and he steps out onto the floor. He walks down the hallway to his apartment, his steps the only noise audible on this very quiet early afternoon. Inside, he finds Ray at the kitchen counter, preparing a salad. "It was nice meeting your daughter."

"Yes, well, it seemed she liked you, too."

"I hope you don't mind, but I had one more of those macarons."

He... *what!?* The nerve! The entitlement! Only about nine weeks on the job and he should feel so comfortable? He's lucky to have gotten one! Especially pistachio! "They're just so good."

Yes, they are "so good"… that is the point! The point of the gift *his* daughter brought to *him* to celebrate *their* trip! What does *he* have to do with their trip? Nothing! Should he fire him here and now?

No, no. The book… they're in too deep. He's otherwise good at his job. But this… this really is strike two. If Emerson has to replace him, or even finish it on his own, he will… but not until after Shakespeare. In the interim: a phizog of stone. "No, of course not." Emerson peers into the box. And he ate the chocolate one! Oh, goddammit! Now all that's left is lemon?! Would this constitute a strike three? No, no. Still two, but what a strike, what a wild, flailing *failure*. Emerson's countenance belies what is burning inside him, his voice also—"Ray, can you make a note? Next time you go to the grocery store, would you please pick up some raspberries?"

"Yeah, you got it."

But there must be some form of restitution. "Oh, and I think I'm going to need you to work for me this weekend."

"All right," he says. "I had no big plans." Well, that wouldn't have mattered. If he had paid attention to Emerson's language, he would know that he wasn't asking, he was telling. This, too, should be punished.

"And maybe the one after that. We'll see." Ha-ha! Yes, yes, we will. Actually, it's already in plain sight… he sees them here then, too! Hopefully that was a good treat, Ray. Because now it is time to hunker down and work! "I'm just at a very important part of the book. I love Claire, but her intrusion today helped me realize I should keep what I have going as long as possible. I'll need you to be on your A game."

"Whatever you need." Ray is resigned, speaking into the salad. Good, good. But is this enough? No! It has just occurred to Emerson that after stealing the chocolate cookie he is now trying to feed him a salad! What is it, an attempt at helping him with his diet? Health consciousness should never be above actual consciousness, presence, doing what's right. And filching an old man's cookie, a gift from his only daughter, is not that!

"What else are we having for lunch?"

"I was thinking sandwiches." Good. A sandwich he will feed to him! No… not yet. He'll pace himself, wait until the middle of next week for a stunt like that. Break him down bit by bit. He might see it as too pugnacious, and he can't risk him quitting, though he'd probably never dream of it. Maybe after the feeding. One quit in the past after that. But that's neither here nor there.

"Very well. Thanks." Emerson pours himself a glass of water and brings it back to the office. He guzzles it, trying to calm down, trying to subdue all that is howling inside him, the great storm within.

Do not let a savage turn you into a savage, he tells himself. No stooping to another's level. The only storm he need concern himself with is the one on the page. He tries to read back a few of his lines, to see if he's able, to see if his head can manage it. The lines are wonderful. Then he's back where he belongs. He's back with Shakespeare.

▲▽▽▽▽▲ ▲

Ten down, two to go… or maybe it's nine to go; the big guy hasn't said yet. Lately he hasn't said much that would help Ray manage any sort of expectations. But it's cool, whatever's clever. Ray gets it.

Patience is what it's all about now. On the beach, Haruka had told him he had leveled up, then promptly began testing his with cryptic bullshit, silly comments about race relations, and insecure FOMO mind games. That was the introduction to this level. This is a time that will drag out more than anything had before; it will frustrate him, present him with both new and familiar, tedious challenges… there is no fast track to heaven.

And all of this is very palpable here on day ten as he transcribes, his eyes straining and red, enervated by too many days in a row spent staring at this shitty old monitor for hours on end. A lot of folks work every single day—immigrants, single moms juggling multiple jobs, finance fuckwads on the other end—but Ray in his off-and-on career never did—school doesn't count—and now he knows their struggle. After a while the extra money you're making doesn't matter. In addition to the physical shit like eye strain and his back hurting from sitting in a fucked up folding chair for a lot of the day every day, there's the emotional toll, in his case boredom and tetchiness, and the mental one: his work is sloppy as fuck now and takes a lot of double-checking, not to mention most of the time, right now excluded, he's not really sure what day it is.

But it's okay… he has patience.

It is indeed a virtue. Some might mistake it for inaction: but it's almost the complete opposite. Patience is constant internal action that allows you to remain calm and best handle whatever unpleasant thing you're faced with. The trick is to not let the negative feelings coming from that thing stay for too long—to reach down into the well that is patience, bring it up to the surface, and push it out around you, make it emit from you like a force field. That way, they can't really get to you. With enough patience, Ray is learning, you become sort of invincible.

Emerson sprung this whole extended work term thing on him a week ago today, last Wednesday, right before lunch—as close to the summit of the week's hump as you could get—saying, "I think I'm going to need you to work for me this weekend," instantly turning the hump's apex into a plateau. Ray had just eaten a macaron, one of the last from a small box of a half-dozen the big guy's daughter had brought over, thinking it might be a good deed under the Platinum Rule, that it was the right thing to keep as much unhealthy shit away from him as he could. There was no selfishness involved; Ray honestly didn't even really like the cookies. Rich people tend to have shit taste in sweets, and French macarons aren't half as tasty as the coconut type, the other one with the extra "o." But even if this were viewed as a crime, what came to follow would not have been a punishment that would fit it, and so Ray knew there was more at play, that Emerson was building upon what Haruka had revealed that Sunday on the beach.

And boy has he. He's made Ray carry out some pretty awful tasks, making good on the weird shit he suggested back during the interview while betraying promises about other things he said he wouldn't have to do.

Ray's now fed him twice, once a sandwich, once stew, and while ultimately pretty degrading, in the moment it wasn't so bad, really; it just made him feel kind of like a home health aide. He's also been charged with intercepting anything resembling junk mail prior to handing off the day's deliveries, a duty that would seem reasonable—despite Emerson saying he'd handle his own mail before—if Ray didn't then have to write hard-nosed individualized letters to the senders on Emerson's behalf demanding that they remove him from whatever list he's on, especially since Ray had told him on day two of this that he'd likely found the main list and would be happy to opt him out of everything all at once using the website for the Direct Marketing Association or by writing to their P.O. box, per the instructions posted by the FTC, a suggestion Emerson scoffed at, insisting it would probably result in even more junk mail.

Much worse than either of these, though, is that he had to deep clean the bathroom, which sucked not only because deep cleaning is only fun while high, and his job, again, is just supposed to involve tidying and light cleaning like dishes, but also because right before Emerson asked him to do it he had taken a shit and didn't flush, something that could have only been deliberate. At the end of day seven, Emerson had begun with one of his "Raaaay's," and so tired he could only be his real self, Ray responded with a "What's up?" prompting Emerson to make him handwrite, à la Bart Simpson, "I am an Ivy League graduate and understand the value of language" two hundred times before he could go home; and then Emerson never told him what he originally wanted, which was maddening in its own way afterwards. Ray's now gone to ten different grocery stores and farmers' markets in six neighborhoods as far away as Chinatown in search of the perfect raspberries, Emerson finding everything either too tart or too sweet, with plans to go out again today. And he's had to keep notes of every single thing Emerson says during lunch and print them out for him at the end of each day; this, while more wearying than abusive—he just runs the Voice Memos app on his iPhone while they eat and takes some time in the afternoon to transcribe it all, then prints—nevertheless really sucks.

There are still occasional moments of downtime. But at this point, they're not better than anything else, even all the fucked up stuff; they might actually be worse because the day goes by slower.

Maybe that's the point, though. It is, after all, about patience.

As he finishes up transcribing yesterday's pages, he decides to go to the Wikipedia entry for Santa Muerte. This is maybe the eighth or ninth time he's visited in the last week and a half. Even though he already knows all he needs to know now, he rereads. It's not knowledge he's looking for, it's comfort; the devout read their religious texts daily. Parts of this wiki now read back like prayer.

He had first visited the page the evening after going to the beach, and the evidence was pretty fucking conclusive that Haruka was Santa Muerte. Aside from being a folk saint—a figure tied to the Church but not recognized by it, subversive in the eyes of the Church but still loosely Catholic, a thing that would very much appeal to him—her patronage includes, among other things, love and bicycle messengers. The love thing was a little iffy: Did he love Haruka? Not yet… or at least, he was not *in* love. But they had shared the act of love. And they did so in a strange, intense, somewhat cold way. Death, it seems, would be those things; the body goes blue when it becomes a corpse. But the bike messenger aspect was just so oddly specific, and that sent him over the edge: proved to him beyond a reasonable doubt that Haruka was her. Afterwards, he found the exact quote he was trying to remember that day, the one from when they first fucked—"My name is Nobody." It was from the *Odyssey*. Odysseus uses it to cozen a cyclops, and while that didn't make much sense in terms of what was happening to him, the black and white of the quote as a standalone plus the notion of his own odyssey colored it with clear meaning. Maybe she's just his Death, but there really wouldn't be a difference. Death is death.

He is learning to love it, and knowing this has made things easier. Right now she is telling him to be patient. He reads again:

> Santa Muerte is associated with healing, protection, and safe passage to the afterlife.

It only makes sense that the day at the beach would be his last day off for what would seem like an eternity. It only makes sense that Emerson would turn into the sort of ogre he's turned into. And that Haruka herself wouldn't really try to help matters, would be so plaintive about him working this interminable schedule and not spending enough time with her, and would try to make him late last Saturday morning by keeping him home with marathon morning sex. She's not a literal guide, he knows. She's helping him by not helping him, by giving him another obstacle to overcome, by making him help himself. The Lord, after all, helps those who help themselves.

With the force field that patience creates, he can begin the process of truly healing himself… can be made ready for the journey ahead. A safe passage. After this, when he's ready, she will again show him the way. Ray has never been so happy to be so miserable.

▲ ▽ ▽ ▽ ▲ ▽ ▽

Here we go again. Hella annoying. On so many levels. God, this is stupid. God, he is stupid. "Ugh!" she says. Haruka just can't anymore.

His phone keeps ringing and he won't put it on silent. She's already asked him to at least twice since the movie started, and she shouldn't have to again. It's not okay. It's been almost a week since they've seen each other because of work and this is supposed to be their time. And worst of all, his ringtone is the marimba, the default ringtone. It's like, seriously? Get a personality.

Whenever he asks if he can pause the movie, she says no. It's one they've both seen before, *Akira*, but he's already given big fat dumb Emerson enough of his time. Worked something like twenty days straight. Without even making time-and-a-half after forty hours. She knows because she asked. He's just been making what he always makes. It sounds illegal. Maybe that's a good thing, now that she thinks of it; maybe that's something she can use as leverage somehow. Against Professor Towers if she needs to, or maybe Ray. At least something good might come out of all this disruption, these disturbances.

It's true what they say about men in New York. They all work too much. Devote too much time to their careers, not enough to love, to family. Of course she is not his real family, and their love is a farce—she still goes on OkCupid dates sometimes—but even so, she still needs him to see her that way. And to do that she is tricking herself into seeing him that way, too, as much as she can. Love appears as a reflection. The sex helps because of the chemicals, but only so much. Most of the time it takes a lot of convincing from herself. Still a lot of acting. The Method, they call it. Right now it's working. Right now she just wants to be loved, and to see her love in him.

"Haruka, something must be wrong." This has to be the fifth or sixth time Emerson has called since they started the movie a little over an hour ago. He's already left two voicemails. "I think I should take this."

"No. You've given him enough."

Every man loves it when a woman tells him "no." This is because hearing "no" releases stress hormones and men enjoy being stressed out. It makes them feel more important when they're stressed, like they matter more. Deep down all men know they are terrible and disgusting and for the most part worthless. They hate themselves, and so they like to be told "no." But you can't say "no" all the time. It's like sex; even though men like sex, they can't have sex all of the time. There have to be periods of non-sex where you do other things. Haruka is learning that in a relationship it is important to say "yes" just enough times to keep them around to tell them "no." This is the key to a happy, successful adult relationship. To balance and harmony. This is the key to cultivating real love.

"At least let me pause it so I can listen to his voicemails real quick. Just to make sure."

"Remember how mad you got at me for using my phone on our first date? And how I barely use it when we're together now?" It's more like she has PTSD whenever she takes it out in front of him, remembering the Big Incident. She wishes she could bring it out more often because it's like telling someone "no" without them even asking a question first.

"This is different. It's my job. Plus, you were just testing me then."

"Believe me when I say you don't need to worry about this."

"Should I though? Something in my gut is telling me you're testing me again now."

"No. I'm not," she says. "All that's happening is you're letting Professor Towers ruin the movie." The phone stops ringing, finally, and they are able to listen to *Akira* again. It's a very good part.

Ray interrupts it: "You keep watching. I'm gonna go listen in the living room."

"If you leave this room, I will too. I'll keep going until I'm all the way home."

"Haruka, come on."

"I'm serious," she says. "This is our time, Ray."

"Okay." They watch. Emerson does not call back.

Once the movie is over, they have sex. It's only okay. Ray is tired and distracted, doing his part without much gusto. But she makes it more fun by saying weird things to him. She's run out of fresh literature quotes, so now she cycles through whatever she's used before or she makes up new ones—"The human heart is a damnable thing"; "We are born every day and we die every day"; "To rise you must first fall"; "The truth you know has all been a lie"; "Before me all things crumble." It isn't hard. Saying strangely profound and cryptic things comes easy to her. They seem to simultaneously excite him and put him at ease, and for a few moments, before he orgasms, his movements actually feel very good. All in all, a 6/10.

She washes afterwards, like always. Then she brushes her teeth and performs her regular bedtime routine, having gotten into the habit of bringing her face wash and a few other supplies over to his place when she stays over. He better not be checking his phone, she thinks.

When she returns, he's still lying there. His eyes are closed, his fan on the nightstand blowing an oscillating breeze over his naked body. It seems his phone went untouched. That he fell into a sex-induced coma. This is good. She curls up next to him, grabbing his arm so that he will hold her. It's imperative that he holds her for some time now. To make sure his brain and hers get enough oxytocin. Tonight kind of sucked. But spooning will make everything all right.

Case in point: before long, she can feel some drops of post-orgasmic semen dripping on the back of her leg, near the crease of her buttocks. But she doesn't care. Normally this would gross her out immensely. She would thrash away from him, and maybe even shriek. It would be fucking disgusting. Fucking. Dis. Gus. Ting. But it isn't. It's just something that's happening. Like a gentle rain falling on her. Almost nice, in its way. The oxytocin is taking hold.

Haruka smiles. She beat Ray tonight. She beat Professor Towers. She beat both of them by beating Ray's phone. Checking her own, Ray snoring quietly beside her, she feels like she won an important minor victory.

She scrolls through her news feed on Facebook, seeing what all of her friends were up to tonight. It's Thursday, and a lot of people like to go out on Thursdays, so some of them seemed to have had more fun than her, but most didn't. She can tell by the pictures they're posting and what they choose to talk about. Just another night during the dog days of summer.

The thing that bothered her most about tonight was that it wasn't about her enough. It was mostly about Professor Towers. Hopefully Ray saw that. Tonight, if nothing else, should have proved to him how terrible Emerson is. Here Ray is, working for him like a slave, and then he harasses him when he finally gets off the clock? Interrupting him and his girlfriend when they're having their alone time? Interrupting him while watching a great, classic movie? Sure, the manga is better, but still. So wrong. Ray must see now. How she was right. How she's been right about him from the beginning, when he read that email she sent.

The weird thing is he doesn't complain about him. Or work. Ever. Sometimes she does about her own job and it feels pretty strange because he doesn't. But he must know. He must know how awful Emerson is now. Inside. And he wouldn't be able to deny it if she brought it up.

After the dust settles on this crazy stretch and his schedule becomes normal again, maybe he will admit to it. Some distance will help him gain perspective and he will see it for sure.

Then she'll do it. Then it will be time. She'll ask.

"We are born every day and we die every day." How did she come up with that one? It's actually pretty good. Sick of reading about her friends, she writes it as a status update. It instantly gets a like from an old friend she met in middle school, Jen. Then another like, and another.

Haruka is now her favorite writer in literature ever. All kinds of likes from all kinds of friends. We're up to seven now. "Where's that from?" one of them asks. What a moron. Why not just google it? You would see that it's not a famous quote and that she made it up. But oh well, not everyone can draw conclusions like that. Not everyone's so smart: "that's all me," replies Haruka. Then a different friend comments "brilliant," accompanied by a red heart emoji.

This further proves how wrong Professor Towers was to ever give her a B. She's so good at literature that she can make it up without really trying. But Haruka doesn't want to think about that now. It'll spoil her mood. She needs to relax now for bedtime. Another friend comments "mind = blown." She smiles at all the support she's getting, places her phone down on the nightstand next to Ray's, and closes her eyes. She inches away from Ray to be alone. Enough hormones for tonight. The whir of the fan lulls her. She drifts off into the day's death, into that void where we are all born again.

▲ ▽ ▽ ▽ ▲ ▽ ▲

Sleepless nights lead only to crazed mornings—oneiric images, emotions, stories, desires, sensations arise when they choose and stay according to their own codes. The subconscious will not be denied. Dreams that should have been morph and manifest themselves in tricks of the mind: minor hallucinations play out before the eyes in the harsh light of day, they enter the ears from the inside out; wild thoughts lead away from reason. Disassociated, unprotected, not itself or too much its most base, worst self, the mind cannot be trusted. Self-skullduggery. That's why Emerson must be careful now; there's no way of knowing what he's liable to do.

Ray should be here any second. It's the five-minute window between 9:57 and 10:02 when he usually arrives. The buzz, the steps, the knock, then it's typically right down to business. But not today. Today can only be a reckoning. Oh, oh! It's going to be something!

He must do his best to keep his cool, though, present himself as he would and should be, remember that one in his situation ought to seem more disappointed than upset. But, really, he's both in equal measure.

Ray, Ray, Ray… Oh, Ray!

Yesterday evening, he was bothered by an ever-present nagging feeling—the first-round edits to the section on Goethe he had composed the day before were troublingly extensive, and as he continued writing, moving deeper into what he considers the end of the Culture's middle age, something wasn't sitting right. He hadn't spent as much time looking back on any other section he'd written to that point, and so he decided then to reprint it with the edits Ray had transcribed that morning and give it another look, to make sure it was close to okay. He knew it wasn't just the Culture itself, the decline that gradually began in the mid-seventeenth century—Goethe, and particularly his *Faust*, had deserved more. It's such a fine work. Such a fine, fine work indeed, where reason so beautifully clashes with religion, both in full force, forging such stunning, resplendent truths. Yes, it certainly deserved more…

When he sat down at the computer, he thought that was it, he had finally reached his limit: that three weeks of ten- to twelve-hour days working at a fever pitch was just too much to retain quality. Perhaps it was his age, perhaps it was the fact that he had undertaken this project without an assistant he could also enjoy sexual intercourse with, one who could really help relax him, but in any case, Emerson had to put an end to the streak. He had planned to tell Ray he could take Monday off in addition to the weekend—Saturday and Sunday still up in the air before then, though Ray didn't know it—and he would do the same. It was time to catch a collective breath. They would resume work Tuesday after a nice, long weekend, then get back on a normal weekday schedule.

There would be no printing, however. And not because of his old nemesis, the printer. It was because of the computer itself! His computer, which had been fine for so many years, grinding aside, chose that as the moment it would like to die!

He booted the thing up, logged in, and was opening the Word document when it began making even more hideous noises than usual. Before he had the time to scroll down to the correct section, the screen started blinking, then went completely black. The monitor's power indicator light still shone its bright lime, but the tower's had been extinguished. He stooped down, an act of great labor, peeking under the card table to check and make sure he had not somehow accidentally kicked the plug out of the surge protector. It was fine. Catching his breath, he sat and attempted to turn it on again. Fruitless. What had happened? Was it too much use in this summer's sulfurous heat? Was it something Ray had done that caused this? Emerson, again, hadn't touched it in weeks! Of all the times for it to go kaput! Was there a way to bring it back to life?

He turned to his telephone, turned to Ray. This was, of course, his problem. Perhaps he would have answers. Perhaps he could help...

But no, he couldn't even be bothered to pick up the phone!

The computer was but a minor thing. He knew the work itself hadn't been lost; he still has the edited pages, filed, in order—his handwritten first pass typed out and marked up here and there with a bit of red ink. Simple enough. They'd merely have to be retranscribed. And nothing else saved on the machine was of real value. No, the incident with the computer was just symptomatic of the real problem: Ray.

The impudence!

As his assistant, he was to be on call at all times. This is what they had agreed to. It didn't matter that they had been working the way they had or that he hadn't needed him before on such short notice or at such an hour—the time would eventually come! And when it did, he was nowhere to be found! Such blatant disregard for his title, his responsibilities—the trust put in him! The utter boorishness! And not just toward Emerson himself, but toward the Culture! This is the most unforgivable of all. Ray is like a hospice nurse for Emerson's best friend! And he's treating him just horribly! He tossed and turned in bed thinking about it, all the disrespect. This was officially strike three.

But should he fire him? Or just scold him? The question has weighed heavily on him all morning, since the sun peeked through the bedroom blinds and the twittering birds outside let him know that in just a few short hours he would see the young man.

On the one hand, he would more than deserve termination for his attitude and the shirking of his duties. Ray was no Hispanic Arthur. Or he might have been at one point, but had now officially sullied the throne. He was not fit to serve Emerson or the Culture. Exile seems appropriate, yes.

But on the other, Emerson has done very good work with Ray around. Most of the time, he's a pretty good assistant, maintaining a nice environment, their process a well-oiled machine. If only his transgressions hadn't been so damn awful, and didn't speak so terribly of his character. It may be that he isn't fit to do this work, to be a part of this project, but that he's something of a good luck charm. Or that Emerson has subconsciously detected the mistake in allowing such riffraff to be a part of the Culture's last hours and legacy, and as a form of apologia to it, has risen to greater heights than would have been possible before in his own work. In either case, the output has been good. Their system works. Ray might not be worthy of the task at hand, but dammit, together they are getting results. Isn't that all that truly matters? Not to mention, if he fired him, he'd have to hire someone else, and that would be a major setback. But isn't today, also, a major setback? By keeping him up all night, he's effectively canceled out today; Emerson can't write like this, on no sleep, in such a state! And it's all Ray's fault! But no. They had hit a wall. Remember? Goethe? The Muses might be speaking to Emerson through Ray's actions, giving him a reason to slow down. It's not about them catching their breath, it's about *him* catching *his* breath. That would make sense. Emerson likes the sound of that. Yes, today will still be a reckoning. But it won't be a termination; it'll be a talking-to. The grandfather clock in the corner strikes 10:00, then chimes. Ray's officially late. It's never mattered before, this minute or two at the long end of the window, but it matters now. Oh, yes indeed. What are the Muses trying to tell him?

Then: a thought! What if he's dead?!

What if his foolish bicycling caught up with him and he's as dead as the desktop computer now taking up space on the card table? Emerson, sitting on the sofa, looks over at it for the first time this morning, something he couldn't bear to do before. He can't be dead!

Breathe, breathe, breathe… The Muses would of course do that for a good reason. But what would Emerson do then? It wouldn't be a complete loss, he supposes; it's more than possible, probable in fact, that the next assistant would be better. But, to maintain flow, he'd likely have to hire a flat-out transcriptionist temporarily in addition to another assistant. Interviews, training, time and money wasted. A major, major setback. And besides, weren't the Muses telling him just a second ago that he doesn't need an assistant who's worthier, he needs one who's just good enough to get the work done but flawed enough to make Emerson all the better to make up for it? Ray very well may be perfect for the job. No, let's hope he isn't dead.

The buzzer. He isn't! Emerson can't let on how much he feels he needs him now. Ray must think that he's messed up, gravely, and needs to change. And he has and does, Emerson believes that. The damage, that which needed to be done, has already occurred, and Emerson will write just as well to the project's end with the shameful knowledge he hired someone who didn't deserve to be here. Few kings are actually deserving of their crowns, but that doesn't mean they're incapable of greatness. He takes this knowledge and tucks it away, lets the emotions that were guiding him a moment ago break back through… Yes, Ray is not dead, but that doesn't mean Emerson still doesn't feel like he could kill him! He presses the DOOR button. Come up, Ray. Emerson lingers near the buzzer, staring across the room at the Hudson under a deeply furrowed brow. How should he begin? He'll know when he sees him. Steps down the hallway. A light knock. Emerson opens the door.

There he is, wearing a black polo shirt, untucked, over bituminous gray pants; an overstuffed backpack hangs over one shoulder, he holds his beat-up helmet in the opposite hand: a vision of insouciance. "Raaaay…"

"Hello, good morning." He steps inside.

"That's not possible at this point."

"Sorry. My phone died during the evening and I didn't finish charging it until it was too late to call you back." Oh, what an excuse! Of course Emerson's not buying it, but what is truly beyond belief is the boy's audacity! "I listened to your voicemails, though."

Emerson closes the door. "Perhaps you heard them, but you didn't, in fact, listen. I distinctly remember saying call me when you get this."

"I didn't think that meant after midnight."

"It did."

"My apologies."

"Go on," Emerson gestures to the living room workspace, the catalyst. "Take your seat, Ray."

He does, lazily dropping his accoutrements in a heap—the ruffian!—while Emerson settles into the far corner of the sofa. "So I'll take a look to see if I can fix this, but I have good news that might help ease some possible concerns in the meantime: I've been backing up the file, so nothing was actually lost, and I brought my laptop so I can use that today if your computer can't be saved."

Backing it up? What does he mean by that? While it's nice that there won't be any distraction or hullabaloo with retranscribing, this sounds strange: Emerson hasn't given him any floppy disks or anything. Did he take initiative and buy some? "So you have it on a floppy disk?"

He laughs. "No. Every day I save the document to Google Drive."

"What's that?"

"The cloud. I save it to the cloud," he says. "So, it's safe there."

"The cloud? What's the cloud?"

"Internet storage."

The internet?! Ray's been putting the unfinished manuscript some-where on the internet?! How dare he! And he had the nerve to chuckle just a moment ago? Really? Was that whole exchange an aural halluci-nation? "You've been putting my manuscript somewhere on the inter-net?!"

"Well, yes and no. I mean, it's not posted anywhere. It's not public." That's reassuring. Emerson's heart, breathing slow. "It's more, like, in it than on it. No one can see it but me. Just stored there in case of an emergency like this."

Emerson doesn't quite understand what any of this means, but how could he? The internet is nothing but a jumble of nonsense, an atrocious mixed metaphor. It's not meant to be understood. First and foremost, it's a web that you surf. What the hell does that even mean? It not only defies sense but the very laws of physics! And now, apparently, it also contains a cloud. And this is something that's supposed to be secure? That which looks solid but in fact is not, something literally as thin as air? Perfect! What a fine place for this incredibly important piece of writ-ing to be. In it, on it, either way: this is truly beyond the pale. Also, what if someone broke in and looked at it? Emerson's always reading and hearing stories about hackers doing this or that—sticking their noses where they don't belong. They could leak his work before it is ready! Emerson's enemies would just love that. "Ray, I need you to take it down at once. Delete any trace of it from the internet. You did not have my permission to do that."

"Ummm, okay. So you don't want me to back it up?"

"Not on the internet, no. But I like the idea of it being safe. I'll get us some floppy disks."

"If you end up needing a new computer, it likely won't accept floppy disks," Ray says. There's no laughter or attitude. Finally, he is being helpful.

"Why not?"

"They're phasing them out. The technology's a bit dated." Of course they are. Anything solid, simple, totally secure and private would be outdated!

"Is there another solution?"

"I guess I could put it on a thumb drive." What the? Who is in charge of naming these things? A floppy disk made sense; it was actually a disk that was somewhat floppy! Now we have storage solutions named after fingers? How could anything of importance be stored on something so small? And not only that but on the one finger which appears the most phallic and that is most famous for offering a cheap form of approbation or being involved in lurid activities like hitchhiking and hooking? "I could go out and buy one."

"Thumb drive? I don't like the sound of that. Is there anything else?"

"An external hard drive I guess, but that would be way too much space."

"That's fine."

"Okay. I'll go out and get a LaCie."

Oh, dear. Here we go again. "LaCie? That's what they're called?"

"It's a brand. They're pretty good."

"I don't like the sound of that, either. Lace is far too delicate."

"Okay. How about Western Digital?"

Now we're in business, finally. "Digital": honest, straight-forward, literal. Plus, the fact that it's preceded by "Western" is good, in the broad sense. Something called "Western Digital" would be fit to house a work about Western Culture. "That should work. Buy two."

"Great."

"So, I think now is the time to get down to brass tacks."

"Yes, of course." Ray turns and faces the computer. He presses the power button. "I'll see what I can do." He presses again, twice, harder, still to no avail.

"No, Ray. Not that. Not yet. Something more important."

He turns back. "Okay."

"You see, I'm very disappointed in you for what happened last night. So much so, in fact, that I considered letting you go this morning—"

"I'm very sorry, I—"

"Don't interrupt me. That's the last thing you want to do right now." Taking a deep breath, Emerson's elbows come to rest at his sides, while his fingers come together and form an arrow. He points the shape at the young man and speaks while it pulses. It is time for the show. "You see, to use the old baseball cliché, but one I suspect will resonate, I considered it strike three. Nobody is perfect, but you've made some monumental blunders that have made me question why I ever hired you. Your first was when I caught you on your phone sometime back, during your *five-second break*, as you liked to call it. I let you know about my displeasure then in no uncertain terms. The second was when you stole *my* macaron"—the finger arrow points back at Emerson now for emphasis—"a gift from *my daughter* to *me*"—then realigns itself with Ray. "I believe, over the last three weeks, that I've shown you my displeasure about that in no uncertain terms. I thought that if I showed you instead of told you, and had you complete a series of onerous tasks designed to prove your dedication to me and the project, that perhaps you would come out of it better, stronger, a paragon of discipline, and with some understanding: both of why it happened and how important the work we are doing here really is." Emerson shakes his head slightly, slides his fingers past one another; his folded hands come to rest on his belly. A different kind of emphasis. All significant action must be followed by inaction. "But it seems I might have pushed you too hard, all the way to the breaking point. Because last night, Ray, last night you proved to me that you are indeed broken." There. Now that's guilt! God, did that feel nice. God, did Ray deserve it. The reckoning has commenced!

"I'm very, very sorry."

"As you should be. But instead of firing you, I'm going to fix you, Ray. No more passive-aggressive toying. I may ask some questions along the way to help you understand, but if you don't, I will supply you with the answers you need." Yes, the Socratic method can only do so much for the dim-minded; sometimes all that's left is Emerson's final word. "So tell me, what was so offensive about you using your phone like that before?"

Ray wriggles in his seat; there are some glistening drops of perspiration marking his forehead, a few rivulets on either side of his face. Emerson hopes this is because of him and not the conditions outside from which he emerged. "I suppose that I was stealing time."

"Well, that is offensive, sure, but it was not the most offensive. The most offensive thing was your total lack of respect. From the act you were committing to your posture while committing it, you were a person that appeared to be, as they say, just hanging out." Emerson watches Ray carefully: upon saying this, the boy straightens up in his seat. Yes, this is going very well indeed. "You see, when I write, Ray, it is an act of devotion. I am submitting myself to thought, language, paying tribute to the greatest minds who ever lived, the utmost in beauty expressed by all of humanity throughout history. Your fingers are typing out my final ode to them, my lament, my love letter—so to catch them instead, all thumbs, banging away on your gadget exchanging some or the other banality, even if it is with a family member, it seems like sacrilege to me. Like you're socializing during a holy service. Do you understand?"

"Yes."

A perfect metaphor: something important, solemn, while still easy to understand. No use bothering him with the Arthur thing. It would enlarge his head to think he's some sort of king, and the notion of treating Emerson and not the work as the God to be served would probably seem less palatable; plus, it might confuse any Hispanic to think of himself as being like an Englishman. Now, as goes hand in hand with any good invocation of religion, a bit more guilt: "I can't make you care about what you're working on, but you at least need to pretend to. Be as deferential here as you would in any house of worship. Because even though you might think of this as your office, to me, while I'm working, it's much more than that, it's much more than my home, even. This is my temple."

"But I've been good since then, haven't I?"

"Well, I haven't caught you on your phone, but no, you've still been wildly disrespectful." Yes, lay it on thick. Make it soak through all the way down to the bone. "If not toward the work and process, then toward me. And while I wouldn't consider that worse, it's far from good…" Perfectly marinated, it's time to hold his feet to the next fire: "Why did you steal my chocolate macaron Ray?"

"I actually didn't think you'd mind." He rushed to say this.

"You didn't think I'd mind? My daughter comes bearing gifts, sweets no less, under the assumption that I'm alone, you take one without offer or permission after already receiving one, and you didn't think I would mind?" Emerson's hands jut out. "Of course I would mind!" He regains composure; the hands, the hands come back to their folded resting position, rising and falling with his uneven breath. This is actually good. A constructive conversation that might help him prepare for the upcoming term, set to begin in about a month: a reminder of and means to understand the twisted logic behind young entitlement. Practice. How could he have forgotten after such short a time? Because it's something he can't wait to forget. And he's been reading… so much beautiful work… yes, that's how.

"In all fairness, I thought it was more of a free-for-all since I was offered that first one."

"No, Ray, it certainly wasn't."

The boy's knee bounces—a hint of nerves—followed by, what's this? A smile in the eyes? "And to be perfectly honest, Emerson, since that's what you're being with me…" Oh, this should be good… the smile, was it a hint of happiness for that which is about to be said or more nerves? A mixture of both? "I also did it for the sake of your health." His wh-

what?! That's no good at all! Bastard! The hooligan! Emerson must be hallucinating!

"For my health!? Who are you, now, my doctor? That is ridiculous, Ray!"

And now he's wiping the sweat from his brow… as if he's actually turned the tables. The arrogance! "I was just trying to help."

"Do I seem like some do-nothing corporate C-suite oaf? An ignoramus? The type of guy who can't book his own plane tickets, who doesn't know shit from Shinola? I am not that, Ray, nor do I need the type of assistant someone like that would. I don't need you to decide anything for me."

"You don't seem to mind with lunch." Insanity! Pure insanity! Even if this were under the auspices of an open and honest dialogue, it would just be so smug. He truly is a savage! The boy must be checked, domesticated!

"Yes, because lunch is just fuel, Ray. I'll eat pretty much anything then! If I don't really like it, as is certainly the case with that slumgullion you call *cowboy stew* which you make on occasion, I'll just finish the meal off with cookies or a pastry. You see me do this all the time!"

"So that's why you do that."

"Yes. Now, back to you. I'm not the one on trial." This is a good place to remind him of that; Emerson may be honest with him, but Ray shouldn't feel so free. He is the help! Trying to play defense during his own reckoning… not with this guy, pal. Yes, he must be tamed. And he will be. With words. With beautifully moving words: "Whether it was a misunderstanding or an ill-conceived notion of performing a favor on your part, eating that macaron without inquiring about it demonstrates a level of comfort you should not have here. It was the same comfort I saw in your posture while texting that one day. The more comfortable you are, obviously the easier it is to be impertinent."

"Going forward, I will do my best to be more respectful around you. I work at a church. I get that now."

Aha! Now that's what Emerson was looking for! No excuses, reasons—but a promise. Men, especially crude men, tend to keep their promises. And that's what we need here: accountability. "I need you to do that not only here, Ray, but on your own time as well. Which brings us to last night. Now, I know we've been working a lot lately and I know it isn't as easy for you as it is for me. I wake up, I'm here. It's my book we're working on, and I thoroughly enjoy the work—" Yes, soften him, reason with him so effectively he won't see the point in trying to parry, as if he could. "Perhaps I burnt you out. But at the time of the interview, I let it be known that I'd need you for night and weekend work on occasion, so it shouldn't have come as a surprise, and you should've been prepared for it. But regardless if that was why you allowed your phone to die, I also told you during our interview that I'd need you to be on call, and the simple fact of the matter is last night, you weren't. You let me down. You really only have one job when you're not here, Ray, but it's a crucial one: just make sure your phone is on. You can even charge it here during the day if you'd like. That way, we can guarantee what happened last night will never happen again." Emerson takes a sip of water. He feels he lost it a bit back there—began to babble. Damn the lack of sleep! And damn Ray for it! But really, he should be able to express criticism concisely and effectively after any amount of sleep; this should come as second nature. Especially in front of someone like Ray. Why should he have spoken so inelegantly? He looks over at the boy; perspiration's visible on his face again. He hasn't consumed any water, which he brings in his own bottle, since he sat. Is this an act of penance on his part?

"I understand."

"Good. I believe you when you say that. I believe you understand that what we're doing is serious." Emerson does not want to risk speaking so much again. Let the boy figure it out now: "But do you understand why it is serious?"

"Because it's your life's work?"

"Have you understood what you've read so far, Ray? While transcribing and fact-checking? Have you really read it?"

"I mean, some books and writers I'm unfamiliar with, so parts have been a bit beyond me. But in general, yeah, I get it. You've taken literature and given it a sort of poeticized obituary." Of course a journalist would call it an "obituary" and try to jam it up against a word like "poeticized," preceded by "sort of." Oh, ye of limited minds! "The book is part biography and part lament." There we go. That's better!

"Very good! Yes, yes. That is correct, Ray. So this is not only about me and my legacy, it's about the legacy of literature, or really the Culture, its heart and soul." Emerson speaks with his hands; the lull is over, the right words will not escape him this time: "Literature is the spirit of the Culture, the lifeblood. They're one and the same. Words are everywhere. Storytelling is everywhere. Stories have been essential to human survival since prehistory: at their most base, they are how we communicate both threats and opportunities. They are how the subconscious sorts through problems as we rest; through the narratives that are dreams, we can go on and address life's travails. Literature refines these functions, elevates them to the spiritual realm. That's why words are so important, why literature is the highest art. Visual artworks, if not directly inspired by literature or telling their own stories, are still described in words. Dance is often performed as part of a story, and if not, is still described in words. The only thing that could conceivably rival it, as something unrelated, would be classical music, but even the masters in that field were often inspired by works in the Canon, and titled their compositions in words. Words give all things meaning. Stories are fundamental to the human experience. Which is why what is happening now is so, so tragic. For you see, Ray, the Culture, it's dying. We haven't gotten to that part of the book yet and I'm afraid if this spoils the ending for you, but the Culture is on its deathbed at this very moment, seconds away from the very end. My book is its last gasp—the final words it would like to be remembered by. And I know this because I know the Culture better than anyone alive. So what you're doing here, Ray, it should not only feel somber and religious but also deeply, deeply personal. Because it is. For me it is." Yes, yes: while guilt is great, reason is always better. Because… such a beautiful word; so marvelously effective, so persuasive. "The Culture, it's been my best friend since I was very young. I've read everything that matters, as you know, everything that's truly shaped and given meaning to the world throughout recorded history. Because that's what words do, Ray. At their best, there is nothing more powerful." Emerson's brow upturns; he's sure he's wowed him with his words, some actually brilliant—words truly at their best—some pure pap, but if not, there's always sotto voce conviction: "You've heard the adage, 'Actions speak louder than words'?"

"Of course."

"It's not true. They don't. The only reason anyone says that is because so few actually know how to put words to their full potential. The idiom that is in fact correct is, 'The pen is mightier than the sword.' As long as I'm alive, it will be. But then it won't. That will be it. Because Ray, because you see, language itself is under attack. And it's losing. Badly. The rise of television was one thing, but the internet has really escalated the assault. I'm afraid our military let loose a terrible evil when they invented it; worse, even, than the atomic bomb. Nobody will write anything of real value from here on out. Journalism—among the most basic forms of storytelling, the mere relaying of information—doesn't even stand a chance, has been reduced to those so-called 'listicles' or has reverted to sensationalism. Even *The Times* is riddled with silly teenage-speak and acronyms now, so forget actual literature. People don't know how to think anymore, Ray, let alone write. After one postmodern door-stopper, you've read them all. Pynchon got there first, really… and it was good… but most of the others have been pure drivel. Modern life is very complicated and overwhelming and it is advisable to be anxious about it all… Well, obviously! Do you know what the big literary event that has come to define the end of the twentieth century is, Ray? The biggest book of the nineties, and since?"

"Hmmm… Are you going to say *Infinite Jest?*"

"*Infi!*—yes, that is why the Culture doesn't stand a chance."

"I heard it was pretty good. I like his nonfiction."

"It isn't. It's not writing, just typing, as even a third-rate writer like Truman Capote would've surely agreed—and what's worse, the man tried to tie Shakespeare up in his mess." Normally Emerson wouldn't want to expound on this—it wouldn't be worth his time—but since Ray just said something positive about a hack, he must. No assistant of his can go on thinking that might be a book worth reading. This is, after all, about fixing Ray now. "It was a boring book because it said nothing new and did so in a way that was needlessly academic and gimmicky. He would have been better off writing a book called *Infinite Rest* that was just the letter 'z' ad nauseam for eleven hundred pages. And to top it off, the man himself was a clown, wearing his silly bandana everywhere as he did, even on television. I don't like to speak ill of the dead, Ray. I really don't. But it was just too much. Oh, so unique, such a genius. If he were my student, I would have kicked him out of my class wearing a thing like that. But that's what the Culture's been reduced to. Notable authors try-ing to carry on like they're rock stars of some sort instead of keepers of the Culture—writing for attention and not for its own sake. Any time I flip through a *New Yorker* and hazard a few lines of the fiction or poetry, it's utterly terrible. Everyone is still caught up in these postmodern gim-micks or they're just trying to rip off their favorite modernist from high school. For poetry, it's mostly the style made famous by T.S. Eliot. And fiction it's usually Faulkner or Hemingway, the latter of which was never that interesting to begin with. No offense, but he was just a journalist with only a tittle more imagination." That was nice. The bit at the end. Hopefully Ray has been put in his place in more ways than one… he heard *Infinite Jest* was "good." Ha! Now he knows better.

"If you hadn't led me down the postmodern road, I think I would have called *Harry Potter* the literary event that's come to define the nineties." It seems the dear boy now thinks they're friends again, that they've settled into a conversation. Why couldn't he see that that was all a part of his own rebuke? That Emerson's castigation of Mr. Wallace was a castigation of him, too, the type of person tasteless critics hoodwink into thinking that style of writing is good, who then perpetuate this notion without even reading it, degrading the Culture ever further. Like book reviewers skimming on a deadline. The dig at journalists couldn't have made it any clearer. Perhaps he doesn't care, and now he's just trying to charm him; maybe he views this discussion not as a part of the reckoning, but an opportunity to inveigle Emerson into thinking they're bonding. Who does he think he is?

It doesn't matter. Emerson can launch his own charm offensive. He told the boy no more games, but obviously that was just a part of his own game—"I'm not sure if that would be any worse, but I'm not talking about that. I'm talking literary. It's a tricky term, but it has to do with the academy and the Canon and critical theory, what those who know are supposed to call literature. But you're right, in a way: *Infinite Jest* is about as literary as *Harry Potter*. It could be a perfectly innocuous book in the sci-fi genre. Let's not confuse the issue. Let's stop the fuss."

"So what would you call it then? The true big book of the nineties?"

Emerson smiles. Now: a dilemma. Clearly Ray is wasting his time. There was no big book of the nineties. He takes a sip of water and stares at the boy, the sheen of his forehead, the ruddy color in his cheeks. Can he save Ray, and with him, the future of his own book? Then: a vision! Ray, denuded, sitting on the sofa next to him, leaning in and tenderly kissing him. Emerson turns from him afterwards, and finds that a chocolate macaron is now inside his mouth, melting on his tongue. Smiling, he chews then swallows, and a pistachio-flavored one instantly materializes on his palate to take its place. The whole thing lasts but a second. What in the hell? Oh, sleep deprivation! But alas, there is too much of a lag in the reckoning now. He must say something: "There was no great novel of the nineties. The last major books came out in the eighties, and they were *Blood Meridian* and then I'd say *White Noise* by Don DeLillo, who very well might have seen where everything was heading and whose work then articulated it all very well." What was that, though, really? Emerson's never had that sort of urge—a homoerotic one—before. Not even at boarding school, when practically everyone else not only had them but acted on them. "Have you read *White Noise*?"

"Yeah, actually."

"The Airborne Toxic Event has in fact occurred, and it's even worse than he imagined. Subtler, more insidious, its victims' deaths prolonged: resembling a normal *cloud* more than anything obviously virulent. And one of its first victims was the Culture. What it is now is a thing without reason." What would Freud say to such a daymare? Unless! No, it wasn't a daymare at all. But proof! It was indisputable proof that Emerson was never in the wrong before! Was never kidding himself about his motives. Take that, Diana! And it is proof as to why Ray at his core is such a lousy assistant, truthfully! "If long and meandering postmodern zaniness and stale, rip-off modernism are now the Culture, then it is not itself. It has been stricken by dementia. I'm here now to jog its memory one last time and then deliver it to a dignified death. This is, again, serious business. And I need your help with it. You will receive an acknowledgment in this book, Ray. You will forever be a part of the Culture's epitaph. Rise up to that. Earn it."

"I won't let you down again, Emerson." Oh, let's hope not. There is only one way to ensure that he indeed won't, but it will take some time, some planning, Emerson knows. What a revelation to have occurred just then! Sleep deprivation, it seems, can giveth as much as it taketh away!

The reckoning is over. It is time to move on, to rake the newly scorched earth until it is nice and loamy and sow some seeds. Ray searches his face for receipt, approval. He shall not be refused: "Good. I'm sorry if I've rambled. I haven't gotten much sleep. So, today: today I'd like you to see what you can do about my computer, and if it isn't working, then I suppose it's time to go out and get a new one."

"Okay, I'll see what else can be done. Maybe it's the outlet it's plugged into? But just in case, what would you want? A laptop? Another tower?"

"I'm an old man and I don't have the time or desire to learn a completely new computer. Another tower, please."

"All right, cool."

Emerson hates it when he talks like that. He really does. A shudder, visible he's sure, courses through his body. But he must rake now! Rake, rake, rake! No new damage to the ego, just stroke it! Without being obvious, without betraying the tone of today and this talk, make him feel better! Emerson smiles briefly, then nods. "Great. Once that's up and running, you can transcribe yesterday's pages and fact-check them. I won't be working today, so nothing else will be required by way of coffee, food, cleaning, the usual domestic duties." He should appreciate that!

"You'll probably be leaving early. Then you can take a long weekend through Monday." And especially that! But oh, oh, not too much, now… "I want you to think hard about what I've told you this morning, and we can resume a normal weekday schedule again on Tuesday."

"Sounds good."

Unless! Unless now is not the time to rake or sow at all. Perhaps it is best to save all that. Don't proffer such clemency—let the fuliginous earth remain! Scorch it further, in fact! Let him sit with his inadequacies a while, ruminate, add his own guilt to that which Emerson has brought down upon him! Oh, sleep deprivation! A gift and a curse indeed! Where, actually, is his mind? He must make up for this somehow. He must make things worse for the boy now to compensate for being somewhat agreeable moments before! They must get markedly worse before they get better! "Also, Ray, I think you need to start dressing more appropriately. And I would prefer it if you stopped riding your bicycle to work. Not only is it dangerous and a liability to the project, but now in the thick of the summer, occasionally I can pick up a bit of your scent." Very good. Very good indeed. All he needed to do was start speaking and it all flowed naturally. These were all things that had to be said at some point, anyway.

"Okay, Emerson. I've tried to mask it. I'm very sorry about that." There. Working already. Satisfied as well as truly tired now, Emerson feels like lying down. Time to wrap this up, once and for all.

"Very well then. How much would a new computer cost?"

"For what you're looking for? Probably around three or four hundred dollars, tops. Then maybe another hundred or so for those external hard drives."

"Okay, let me get you some cash." Emerson hurries into his bedroom. He looks across at his bed, unmade from last night, the place where he will soon claim real repose, finally, there to dream of Ray, as he should be, as he one day will be, with him, in love… willing to do anything and everything for him: just like all the others. Soon, soon… But first! Under the bed, he reaches for a shoebox containing a few thousand dollars in cash. He counts out five hundred fifty dollars, then returns to the living room. He hands Ray the money. "All right. I'm glad we are on the same page now, so to speak. I think I'm going to go take a nap. I should be awake by the time you leave for the day, but if not, leave the keys but trip the lock on your way out."

"Got it." One day Emerson will be able to trust him fully. The day when Ray is over the moon for him. Until then, the guard must stay up;

the keys with him. "Oh, and Emerson, thank you. Thank you for your honesty this morning, and for giving me another chance."

"Yes, well… don't blow it!" he says, smiling, as if he's kidding. Ray smiles back. It's a nice smile, yes—youthful, fresh. Full lips and white teeth. Almost feminine, like his eyes. Can Emerson learn to love him, too? He doesn't have to. Nor does he want to. That's not what it is to be about.

The answer, as it usually does, lies with the Greeks. How could he have not seen it before? Because of his mind. A mind like his, too bulwarked to listen to what Peitho might whisper in his ear. It needed to be out of itself for a while. Closer to the clouds, in range to receive a thunderbolt from Zeus himself.

Emerson goes into the cabinet before retiring. He brings with him a plate of chocolate chip cookies and pistachios, along with a glass of milk. They are consumed during various stages of undress.

His is a deep, dreamless sleep. And when he awakes he gives Ray a bonus: a crisp one-hundred-dollar bill from below his bed. He's sorry for his tone earlier, and appreciates all the hard work he's been doing, though, of course, he still expects his full effort. A new computer has been set up, same operating system as before, Windows XP, Ray tells him, so there will be no learning curve, the pages he wanted last night there in a neat stack. Two Western Digital hard drives rest beside it.

Everything is as it should be when the young man departs. And Emerson's soul swoons; perhaps getting ahead of himself, he leaves the door unlocked while he sits in his office and reads back his section on Goethe, just in case Ray should feel the impulse to return.

▲▽▽▽▲▲▽

Fuckin' hell, what a day… talk about a doozy! Though, really, it started last night, or maybe more like three weeks ago. They've tried to push and pull at him, like competing gusts of wind, but with the power of patience, he has prevailed. The last eighteen or so hours have proven this. Through the girlfriend/folk saint's unreasonable demands and fucked up ultimatums and weird sex, the berating from the boss in a culmination of unaired, unknown grievances followed by a strange bonus, Ray's remained unfazed by any of it. No: no one, nothing can get at him now. When even the good is bad, and everything seems ugly, that's the only recourse. Fuck the wind. As far as he's concerned, this level is over—he can make that call now; Emerson was the boss and he just beat the hell out of him, gained a patience badge and a hundred bucks, some of which is about to go to some motherfuckin' weed.

That's the plan, anyway. He's already asked Brian to text EJ and now he should be by in an hour or two. First stop when he gets home: the C-Town down the street for a six-pack. Something nice. Ray is going to chill so fucking hard when he gets home, oh man. Lately, he's been too tired to smoke, too tired to drink, too tired to do anything but zone out with TV or Netflix or Hulu and occasionally see Haruka. Time to change that. He knows that he's earned it; getting the next three days off was all the sign he needed. God is letting him off of this plateau. He just needs to get home now—Ray just needs to ride.

And that he does. Gliding down Central Park Drive, he passes Sheep Meadow, then Columbus Circle, boscages green and vibrant, almost oversaturated in the late afternoon sunlight, as *Power* from *My Beautiful Dark Twisted Fantasy* pumps through his headphones. Lots of people are out, lots of pedestrians and pedicabs and other cyclists, then cars, then horse-drawn landau carriages, but he hardly pays them any mind. They're just a part of the scenery. Outside of making sure they don't become more than that, he just needs to breathe and pedal, which really, to him, are the same thing; he and his bike are in perfect sync, everything streamlined. He's one with Ghost Horse: a man on a mission—to get home and kind of fucked up. Not so fucked up he wouldn't be able to help Emerson if he called, which is more than possible considering the new computer, but yeah, kind of fucked up.

In no time he's traversed the southern bend of the park's loop, and is going the wrong way down East Drive toward 60th and Fifth. He passes the blue-black West African pedicab drivers who bark at tourists along the drive's ingress, and then he's in real traffic. The sync is mostly maintained—he just, as always, has to make sure the immediate area around him is his; reaction is now as vital as determination, reflex is the modus operandi, even the propulsion forward is a reflex. Against all that is behind. He rides down 59th until he's parallel with the bridge, hanging a short left at First Ave. so he can go under it, then another a block later onto it at the joint bike/pedestrian path at 60th.

Winding up the incline, he leaves Manhattan, and that godawful stretch of work, to chase a bit of happiness. If Emerson had his way, this would be the last of Ray's post-work bike rides, but fuck that. Part of patience is knowing your truth and staying loyal to it; you just can't allow your face to betray what an attack on it actually makes you feel. Both Emerson and Haruka have shown him that, tested him to prove it to himself. Like last night, during Haruka's stupid petition: He just had to pretend to abide then wait for her to leave the room to listen to Emerson's messages. No looking back now, though. That level is over, and it's time for a little break before whatever the next will bring—a recharge of the batteries, re-up on good vibes. So enough about work. Let's just live in the moment for now.

The bridge is oddly empty for mid-afternoon on a summer Friday—no cyclists or pedestrians compete with him to get to Queens, only a few figures in the distance are moving opposite toward Manhattan. It's getting a bit cloudier, but as far as he knows, rain wasn't forecasted. Ray looks up, around. There *are* some pretty threatening patches coming from behind… Boy, wouldn't that just be his luck on a day like today, get caught in a cloudburst now in the ten or so minutes before he got home. Wet socks always suck. There he goes again. So much for the moment. Speculating as well as looking back, all laced with cynicism. Perhaps the moment can wait until home and beer and weed, perhaps he needs to work some stuff out first…

Like this whole biking thing with Emerson. Sure, he won't ride on days when it's way too hot or humid—the perspiration is gross for him as well; riding had just been one of the only available forms of exercise and stress release during this stretch, since sex with Haruka is actually more stress-inducing than relieving a lot of the time. It was essential to the maintenance of his form so he could continue through his three-week punishment—all prisoners need exercise, even dead ones—but under normal circumstances he knows there's nothing wrong with it, either, so he will continue to do it. Maybe he'll have to abnegate the helmet again in order to throw Emerson off; perhaps that's a part of the point: to offer absolute trust in God that nothing bad will happen to him, that He's helping him get to where he needs to be at all times. That trust in God is real freedom.

Ray continues up the slope, the back of his knees sweating, his polo clinging to the small of his back.

The patience badge has been earned. The skill can be tapped now when necessary. It doesn't have to be the default anymore—he can act from the heart instead of the head. God is watching, God is helping…

Up ahead a figure steps onto the outer guardrail. It appears to be a man. Is this what Ray looked like a few months ago, when he made his climb, contemplating a jump into the East River? Well, no, because this guy's already on the fence and moving at least twice as—wait, what's he doing? Hopefully he's not—he is!!

"No, don't!" Ray calls out.

But it's too late. He did!

Was he wearing a parachute? He didn't look like he was wearing a parachute. What was he wearing? From here, it appeared to be a hoodie and jeans. Wait, why would anybody wear a hoodie on a day like today, so hot and muggy?

Did that really just happen?

Ray keeps riding. Is there a net down there? Was this some stunt? Where are the cameras? This could be some fucked up prank; one of those dumb things you see on YouTube, usually made by some cadre of idiots in Southern California or Florida or maybe parts of Europe where people are as stupid as they are in Southern California or Florida. Ray pulls over to the side. No net as far as he can tell. Traffic's come to a standstill, though. Are there cameras anywhere? Who would have a camera? He's practically alone up here.

Did that really just happen?

Well, no. Of course not. He himself is dead. He forgot this for a second—seeing something horrific like that will force you to momentarily forget anything that should always be in the back of your mind, however important. But the fact that there are no cameras around doesn't mean there isn't Someone watching to see what Ray would do. He pulls out his phone. He's still above Manhattan, so best case scenario, the guy below is very, very badly injured. Ray shuts off Kanye and dials 9-1-1. He waits for the ring. Looks over again—cars still stationary. He continues to wait for the ring. It does not come. He presses the volume button on the side, looks at the phone. It still shows it's "calling..." It's not on mute, the call just didn't go through. He presses the red rectangle with the symbol of a phone inside it, dials again. Same thing.

"Fuck."

He hightails it up toward the closest emergency call box, passing a hard Dominican-looking girl who meets his glance and distraught expression with eyes that seem to say "Yeah-I-seen-that-shit-but-fuck-it-that's-his-bizness-and-I-just-gotta-worry-'bout-mine." Below the sign he opens the yellow case and grabs the phone. It dials out and connects as soon as his ear hits the receiver.

"Nine-one-one emergency," a woman's voice answers.

"I'm on the 59th Street Bridge and just witnessed a guy jump off."

"Where on the bridge?"

"Manhattan, north side." Ray hears sirens in the distance. "Over I think York Avenue."

"Can you describe the man?"

"Umm, I think he was wearing a hoodie and jeans."

"Age, ethnicity?"

"No idea. He was too far away."

"What's your name?"

"Raymond Gonzales."

"Thank you. Sending someone now." The sirens grow louder. Someone was already on their way, evidently. Maybe one of the motorists called before he could. A click, then the line goes quiet; Ray hangs up and closes the box.

Did that really just happen? He already knows the answer to this, but it's the feeling he can't shake. The question isn't just a question; it begs this feeling, this totally fucked up feeling, and it does it with constancy. He's asked himself this before since he's realized he's dead, but this is on an entirely new level.

The thing didn't happen. It wasn't real. But the feeling is…

He turns around and timorously rides back, stopping near where the jump took place. He looks over. A smooth stream of blood flows down the wide stretch of sidewalk on the eastern side of York leading to 60th. The man is out of sight, seems to have dropped too close to the bridge, but Ray's the better for that; he's seen enough. Traffic on York has only now begun to crawl again. The sirens wail, ever louder, and soon he sees the ambulance turning down York. Someone in their car must've gotten to 9-1-1 first. Someone, apparently, without AT&T. Ray rides away.

As he makes his way home, he replays the scene over and over again in his mind. Did he do the right thing? He did all he could do; that should be sufficient. The guy was too far away and too fast for him to have done anything more—a yank off the chain-link, an attempt at reasoning with him. The whole thing lasted only a few seconds. And, judging by where he landed, it was likely premeditated. No, he did all he could do. Hopefully this is what God was looking for from him.

When Ray was alive, he was ambivalent about suicide. Of course he got how it was a big insult to God, the giver of life, but he also empathized with the person, believed if they didn't feel like living, then they shouldn't necessarily have to. Life is difficult. For some people, excessively so. They had just returned the gift. God could be offended, sure, but He could also get over it. However, after seeing it—after actually watching it happen in real time—it's hard to be so tolerant or abstract. What he just witnessed now seems like a crime against the very idea of the world, not just a denunciation of the individual's world, his life, but the world at large: everybody and everything in it. When that man hit the pavement, it was as if he smashed through and created an abyss meant to suck in all that is and was and ever would be from here to the sidereal universe, a veritable all-consuming black hole. And it started with sucking in Ray's stomach. Yes, it's hard to see suicide as anything but ugly when you're given a front row seat to it.

Ray would've been the last person he saw. The last person he heard: "No, don't!" would have been the final words. Would he have considered it one more request he, literally, couldn't live up to? Or a comforting plea that he was indeed wanted, loved. Either way it doesn't matter. Either way he would have had the last laugh. "Why not?" he might have said to himself. Did he wear the hoodie as part of his rejection of the world? Rejection of his skin being exposed to the sun, the stifling summer heat, being told by God, nature what he should be doing? Wait, what was Ray wearing the day he climbed up the fence? Was it a hoodie? Was that guy actually Ray? A part of him, a splinter of his old psyche? He'll have to wait till he gets home to really think this through. It's too much now. Too distracting while on the bike. For now, he is still only "the man."

Be patient, he tells himself. The scene plays over and over again; his eyes help him to navigate the way home, but that's secondary to what he sees: the man climbs, he falls, the man climbs, he falls…

Ray gets home, finally—the minutes that passed feeling more like hours, days. He still wants to get fucked up, but for completely different reasons. Weed is off the table for the time being; that won't help until he can get a hold of himself. He is not himself yet: not Ray, just anxious, shocked, scared. Beer will help. Weed would enhance the reel playing and respooling—give it a blown-out sheen—beer will start fading it at the edges until he can lose sight of the action and focus on the why, not the what. Beer will help him listen to himself. He goes back out and walks to the C-Town and instead of getting something nice gets twice as much of something familiar, kind of cheap. No microbrew bullshit now, just a twelve pack of Corona. Comfort beer. Back at home, he drinks. He sticks a couple of bottles in the freezer but goes at the first one warm. It isn't perfect, though neither was he… But wait. He did the right thing: yelled "No, don't!," called 9-1-1 twice, rushed to a call box when that didn't work while a person closer to it didn't seem to give a shit at all. He tried.

He did the right thing. He was good. This warm beer is more of a reward than a punishment. A warm beer is still a good beer, despite what modern country singers say.

It wasn't real, he tells himself. None of this is. It's just a feeling he needs to shake. Maybe he doesn't have to consider why just yet. Maybe he just needs to drink. And take a shower. He does both at the same time.

The boozy ablution helps, and soon the reel indeed becomes unspooled and the man stops jumping. Ray can look at the scene from above. Somewhere between where he actually saw it and where God did, where He pulled the strings. Finishing the first beer, and taking his fully lathered loofah from his chest to armpits, he can finally bring himself to ask that difficult question: Why?

It was, as his instinct suggested, a test. It must have been. The man wasn't just a phantasm, nor a supernatural figure like Emerson or Haruka, though he could be as significant; he was either Ray himself or a specter of God's making, designed to see what Ray would do: how much would he do for a stranger or himself? Enough. That, as much, has been proven.

But to what end? Why there, where he almost jumped, where he felt that first déjà vu in the early spring, this bridge between Manhattan and Queens, spanning so much more at this point? Why now?

Let's start with the facts. A recounting of his experience:

He was riding his bike on the bridge listening to *My Beautiful Dark Twisted Fantasy*, excited to get home and sort of fucked up, after a long, strenuous stretch of work and a very strange performance review... Okay, there's a lot here already, some of it loaded, but perhaps not worth getting into just yet. Let's forget the backstory and focus on the event itself for a moment. Shouldn't be hard. He can still access it from that original vantage point, shift the camera from the overhead: a crane shot then a flashback... Going uphill on the Manhattan side, he saw a man about two hundred feet away climb onto the guardrail, continue up the fence, then over it, diving headfirst toward the street below. He couldn't believe it and hoped it was a stunt or prank, but soon realizing it wasn't, and that he was being watched and tested by God, stopped to call 9-1-1. His phone didn't work, so he then rode up to the closest call box, meeting a leaden stare from a Dominican girl along the way, and reported the event to a 9-1-1 dispatcher. After getting all the pertinents, she told him they were sending someone. It seemed emergency vehicles had already been on their way when he confirmed the worst, riding back near the spot where the guy jumped, seeing a steady stream of blood with several tributaries flowing down the York Avenue sidewalk. Okay, that was the moment itself. Then he left, upset—replaying it over and over again in his mind, disturbed not only by the obvious but also by several other perhaps unconscious layers of meaning he intended to work out later, which he is attempting now—but comforted with the knowledge that he had done his best. Right, so these are what he knows of the facts. That's what happened. Four of the Five W's, the who, what, when, where… but, now, again, why?

Thoroughly washed, Ray finds his hand reaching for his razor. He did not intend to shave but begins doing so anyway, sans cream, starting with the left side of his face. Perhaps he just needs more time in the shower. Things got a little better once he was in the shower…

But then! Another almost-déjà vu—triggered by memory, not outer body experience, a flash of something familiar, like on the beach when he thought he saw Fernanda, and that is: Didn't he shave after his own climb up the Queensboro Bridge fence? As a part of his demonic baptism? Yes, he did. But it was his entire body and his head, too. He hasn't gotten that far yet; he hasn't even gotten to the right side of his face. Also, he was taking a bath at the time, then. No, there's nothing to this; shaving is always cathartic, much like showering, changing out of clothes, anything where what once was carried during a moment or period of distress is purged.

A red herring. Nothing more.

Still, it might be best to exit this room before it seems like anything else might confuse him. After he finishes his neck, he puts the razor down. He leaves the rest of his body au naturel—the way God made him—then gets out of the shower. A thought: it could be a good idea to grow a beard now; having just shaved that experience, physically, off of himself, he should allow his corporeal form to remain as primitive as possible for a time—be the antithesis of what he was when he was a demon… see how that goes…

Drying off, he sees the man climb, then fall, climb, then fall. Dammit! He may have shaved, but he still can't lose him. He tries to find the other angle again, prevent this one from returning to the default. If he can work out anything, it won't be by rewatching it from here: it will be by viewing it from above. Ray goes into his room and gets dressed. It's been a little over an hour since he had Brian text EJ, and he might be here soon. Would weed really make things worse? He's made some progress, even if the scene keeps returning uninvited. Maybe he'd be all right if he only smoked a tiny bit, and the strain he got was straight-up sativa or a heavily weighted hybrid. As he's thinking this, the buzzer buzzes. He goes to it.

It's EJ. That's a sign. After their transaction—he asks for an eighth of Diesel—he smokes. Only two hits, from the vape. Then Corona number two, still a little warm, flows. Brian probably won't be home for another few hours still, that's good. A Spanish guitar Songza station plays from his laptop, and he opens a new Microsoft Word document in case anything important should occur to him. He sits on his bed in front of the fan. The bird's eye view returns. He thinks…

One thing that seems to have significance: Why didn't his phone work up on the bridge? With that kind of proximity to Midtown and all its towers, it's hardly the type of place where service should drop. Was it really an AT&T fuckup? Or more? Of course it wouldn't have made any difference—the "guy" would still be dead—but the fact that this happened *is* peculiar. Ray reaches for his phone. He dials out to Domino's, the Indian-owned franchise over on Jackson Ave., and gets an immediate "Heddo" from whoever's working the counter. He hangs up. An abnormality indeed. Ray takes a sip of beer. So… so far the event is telling him that he's a pretty good dude, and also that his phone sucks? Or maybe that it can't be trusted… Hmmm… he thought he had figured out that technology is just a tool, that it is incapable of being judged on those terms—something only as good or evil as the person using it. But now he's not so sure. It could actually be evil; in that moment, it totally tricked him, failed at the one thing it's really supposed to do: though it functions as a pocket computer, they call them phones, after all. That's what it's really supposed to be before anything else. But speaking of computers, Emerson's also let him down… Aha! Could this be the next level already?

There are no real breaks in video games—no rooms or lounges where the characters go to chill for a bit, reflect on the previous level, take a load off. Depending on the game, you might have to restock inventory, or there could be something text- or scene-based that suspends play to move the story along. But otherwise it's always a smash cut to the next challenge.

This sure seems like that. A crazy, chaotic new level. Perhaps intended to pit Ray against technology? Wouldn't that have been one of the earlier levels, too? Like, say, when he "defeated" Haruka? No, that level wasn't actually about technology. It was more about attraction, or maybe lust or pride. This morning's boss fight could have been at once the culmination of everything from the previous level and a tease of the next…

It would seem so. Since he wasn't able to figure it out based on his interaction with Emerson alone, God chose to hit him over the head with it—make him witness something abominable and also strangely personal to drive home the point that technology cannot be trusted! He was literally on his way home when it happened! Uh-hu. Then there's Haruka, who last night wouldn't let him answer the phone, who hasn't been playing with her own at all when they're together. Oh, Haruka! Always one step ahead of the game. What a girl, what a guide! Another thing revealed!

Ray knows what he must do now: he must give up his iPhone. Maybe that's what God was trying to tell him all along; he only went through months of mental gymnastics to convince himself otherwise. He actually thought he should be atoning on the thing. No way, José! Get rid of it!

Should he throw it off the bridge, maybe closer to the Queens side, to complete the set, the triad—his old helmet, the splintered version of himself, now the phone? Maybe. But not yet. He'll need a replacement first: both Emerson and Haruka need him to have a working line.

Clearly, another smartphone is out of the question. The iPhone got him into this mess in the first place, and an ersatz one will not get him out. What he needs is something simple, basic: all that there was when he was still alive. What he needs is a flip phone. Does AT&T even have flip phones? He doesn't know, so he asks Google.

He soon finds himself on AT&T's website, all white and orange and tacky, on a page for Basic Feature Phones. There's one for only twenty bucks, but it would require a contract renewal. Going over this with the projection of his mom and getting into the terms of their family plan would seem needlessly tedious now that he's out of the patience level, so he decides, instead, to tell her to take him off the family plan altogether. This should make everyone happy: Ray's supposed to be an adult, and this would be an adult thing to do. Something good. In keeping with the Platinum Rule. He just wants something rudimentary and cheap… a device that calls and texts alone, does the bare minimum. He's seen ads for both Virgin Mobile and MetroPCS here and there: online, on the subway, on TV. Virgin seems like it would be the better choice. The sound of it, "Virgin"—pure, innocent: the antipode to Apple and all its know-it-all evil. A company literally named after the birth of evil in man-kind, that celebrates it, the moment when Eve ate the forbidden fruit.

How could Ray have been so willfully ignorant before? Does this mean he'll have to give up his computer, too? Maybe, but not yet. Even though his mom could get him a cheap Dell, since she works for them, PCs and the latest versions of Windows suck, objectively, and it hasn't been revealed that his laptop is a part of this. If anything, it's been there for him through it all: a friend, assistant, and, several times a week, a lover. Maybe it, like a person, can overcome its base-level evil. Not like his phone, apparently. For now, he should just cover up that fucking symbol.

He orders the cheapest one he can find: a decently reviewed ten-buck Samsung. This is also good because Samsung is one of Apple's main competitors, meaning they're probably good guys. Then he picks the most basic plan, coming in at only twenty dollars a month, goes to Amazon and buys an inexpensive MP3 player—the SanDisk Sansa Clip+—so he can still listen to music while out and about, and begins shopping around for a Christian-themed laptop skin. Something to balance the Apple. He sees one for The Creation of Adam and is instantly sold.

Who was Steve Jobs, anyway? An adopted half-Arab on acid, really. Everything you need to know is right there. Close enough to Jesus to confuse some into thinking he might've been the second coming, but far enough, when you know the facts, like Ray does, to reveal himself for what he really was: the Antichrist.

No wonder Ray let him die last year. His work was already done… there taking over the world… devices aside, the pinche cabrón even invented must-see Super Bowl ads… fucking commercials people want to watch. Talk about enslavement…

Was it really Ray who jumped? He thinks so. To save himself. He searches some terms on Google News to see if anything pops up; nothing relevant does. Until: after some time, he eventually finds a Twitter account called NYC Scanner that reports what's coming in over the NYPD radio. It reads:

Jumper on 59th St. Bridge, DOA on York, Active crime scene.

Tweets, real ones, are meant to signal danger or find food for baby birds… Jumper. That's what they're calling him. But he didn't really jump, he sees now. He was sucked in. Thankfully, God's showing him the way out.

▲▽▽▽▲▲▲

Was she supposed to go over there tonight? She can't remember. It's been four or five days since they last saw each other, so probably. Otherwise, why would he be calling again? This is the second time. Once is too much, but twice, that must mean she's in trouble. Oh well. She'll smooth it over later. Technically he's still in trouble with her for not being available enough during their first month as a couple, when he was working all the time. So this could seem like payback for that. And besides, if he really wanted to get a hold of her, all he'd have to do is text. Haruka isn't that hard to get a hold of. He's just being a jerk.

It's hard to ignore her OkCupid date with all these interruptions. Every time Ray calls, his picture takes up the entire screen of her phone along with the words "Raymond Gonzales – mobile." Everyone on her phone has a last name. Except for Mom and Dad, of course. But anyway, when he calls it covers whatever app she's looking at, so that if she wanted to return to the app, she'd have to ignore the call, and then he'd know she did that because it wouldn't ring enough. So she just has to sit there and look at him calling. She doesn't mind that much—he's given her enough serotonin and dopamine and oxytocin at this point, so that when she sees his picture she thinks he's kind of cute—but she'd rather be looking at whatever it was she was looking at before. This time it was Instagram. The most recent posts under #cute. There are some really great puppies and kitties on there right now, enough to make it worth wading through all the selfies of strangers also using the hashtag. She likes Instagram a lot these days. It's, like, the new big thing. Ever since Facebook bought it out a few months ago. A billion dollars. Maybe Instagram's the future of Facebook. They say a picture's worth a thousand words, so it makes sense. Lately it's been a lot more fun to use than Facebook, a lot more positive feelings in less time. Pictures get a bigger reaction. Words are kinda dumb when you can use pictures.

Her date pulled out his phone, too, after she did, but she knows it's just because he's being petty. Occasionally he asks her about her meal and she offers a short reply but asks nothing back. He's in his early thirties, white, works in finance. She's going on dates with these types of guys again in addition to the more ideal candidates for ruin so she can have nice dinners sometimes. Ray doesn't treat her to those. He looks a little like Spencer Pratt from *The Hills*, which she used to watch in middle and high school. Lots of finance guys look like Spencer Pratt, no matter their ethnicity. Except when naked; some, the silly ones, also have tattoos. Like they're tough or something, but only off the clock.

Haruka takes a bite of her food—really good sushi, they're at this fancy place called Nobu—then it's back to Instagram. She looks at a picture of a bulldog. It's not that cute, really. Soon her phone dings then vibrates in the Heartbeat pattern. He left a voicemail. OMG, hella selfish! She's already had this talk with him. It was a big fight, actually. He says it's because he thinks hearing someone's voice on the phone is more intimate, that it's better. But it's neither. Voices are stupid. They influence how people perceive words, coloring them with unclear emotions, instead of letting the words stand on their own. Text messaging is much better. It allows people to be the idea they're expressing. If you want to express emotions, you should use emojis. It's what they're there for. That's one of the main reasons they got in such a big fight last week. Haruka was upset because when he got a flip phone and gave up his iPhone she could no longer send him emojis. She loves using emojis because they're clear and fun. They're the best way to tell someone how you're feeling. She told him that God wanted him to keep his iPhone, that it was a part of His plan. That the phone not working didn't have anything to do with the jumper. But Ray didn't believe her. He thought, like he does with most things, that when she said that she was trying to test him. He said his gut was telling him he was right, that his phone was evil. Such tired lines, all the stuff about "testing" and "his gut." He said all iPhones were evil and encouraged her to get a Samsung, or something else that used Android. Yeah, right. Only losers use those phones; texts should be blue, not green. That was another reason it was such a big fight. He was acting like a crazy person, he was saying crazy things. Only she should be able to say crazy things.

The jumper incident sounded awful, though. She couldn't believe it, a guy killing himself in front of Ray like that. That's just what an unstable guy like him needed, she thought. Another thing to obsess over—something to make him even weirder. She hates that it happened for her own sake, too, because it messed up her plan. Instead of realizing how terrible Emerson is once he finally got some time off, the incident made him appreciate the things he has more. How blessed he is—like one of those silly Facebook updates. And now it seems like he's becoming more like Emerson. He's reading more at home. Old, boring books. Last time she was over there it was something called *The Prison of Love*. She didn't like the title one bit, not for her purposes. Seemed bad for him to be aware

that love is in fact a prison. Before that it was Roman myths and trage-
dies, and before that Greek. It's very strange.

She deletes the voicemail and texts him:

> Can't talk on the phone right now.
> What's up?

She takes a bite of her food. It's good.
Ray writes back:

> Did you listen to my voicemail?

No, of course not:

> No. I told you I don't like them.

It's so rude. They say "Treat others as you'd like to be treated," but
that saying's messed up. It should be "Treat others as *they'd* like to be
treated." And Haruka does not want to be treated like the type of person
who listens to voicemails. Like some idiot.

> I thought you were coming over
> after work?

Oops. So she was supposed to go over. She writes back:

> Something is happening. It is not possible
> tonight. More will be revealed.

That's usually all she has to say when she does something like this,
when she forgets they were supposed to hang out. Something cryptic
then "More will be revealed."

> Okay.

OK Ray. That's her new nickname for him. Whenever she wins a
dispute, in person or over text or gchat or Facebook messenger, he always says, "Okay." He's also an OK person, Haruka thinks now, thanks
again to all the chemicals he's caused her to release in her brain. She

doesn't need to act at all with him anymore. Even though he did something terrible to her before, the past is the past. Of course she doesn't like him enough to truly commit to him, to be with him like she was with Kenji, anything more than an open relationship. Or, really, an "open on her end and closed on his" relationship. He still needs to be devoted to her in order for this to work. It wouldn't work if it were open on his end, too. She hopes he isn't secretly seeing anyone else, though she doubts he is. He's too much like a lost puppy when he's with her still. Like all lost puppies, he can be difficult, a handful. Especially when he brings up his little "tests." But for the most part, he's good. A good boy. But anyway, enough about Ray.

She takes a few more bites of her tasty sushi, then one of her date's. The name has been forgotten at this point.

"Hey!" He seems pissed, genuinely. Maybe he wrote her off, feels like the date has gone south. But she can fix that with a few choice words.

"Wanna get out of here and find someplace to fuck?"

He smiles, still chewing his food. He swirls his cocktail a few times then takes a big sip to wash it all down. Then he signals the waiter. "Check please," he says across the room.

See. So easy. Spoken words are really only worth something in real life, and barely then.

▲▽▽▲▽▽▽

Another day, another chance. Should he take it? "Ray, dear, more wine please!"

Time is truly of the essence now. Emerson will begin teaching classes again in less than two weeks, so their working conditions will change; going from full-time to part-time will only lower the intensity of their relationship and it will be harder to capitalize on it. Then there is the cardinal matter of the book itself—he is coming upon the most difficult part of the Culture's story to write: the end. The final flickers of genius in Proust, Woolf, Dickinson, Kafka, Melville, Yeats, and particularly Joyce will soon give way to the madness of postmodernism that they in part inspired, or rather that was a reaction to them. Emerson needs to be in tip-top shape to balance these things—getting through this last leg of the first draft and teaching—and he'll need Ray to be at his best, too.

Since the reckoning, Emerson's taken to calling the boy "dear" and "darling," and Ray has not asked him to stop or otherwise objected to it, not once. This is good. Soon he appears before him with a watered-down glass of merlot, the normally garnet-colored liquid turned cherry shimmering in the late-afternoon sun streaming through the window. Emerson takes a sip. This one is actually decent. The ratio, as he's instructed Ray, is one to one. It's a bit more alcohol content than the Greeks probably would have had, and of course they weren't drinking merlot, so Emerson likes to think of this concoction as a new spin on a very old classic: his own version of their nectar, much like his own writing. Honoring the Greeks is one of the principal reasons he recently started drinking a glass or two of watered-down wine in the afternoons, the other being the terrible sorrow he's felt as he's moved away from the Culture's peak and begun closing in on its rapid and tumultuous decline. It has only been four hundred years since Shakespeare, and this is the state of things? Insanity, complete insanity.

"Pour a glass for yourself and join me for a moment, why don't you?" Is this it? The moment, the big move? Even something as calculated as this should involve some spontaneity; the act of love requires it. It's the spark that ignites the flame, spontaneity. Ray leaves and comes back. Judging by the hue of his glass, he has opted not to prepare it Emerson's way, which is of course a pity.

Emerson smiles. "Cheers!" He extends his glass and it meets the boy's in a slight, dulcet clink. The boy also smiles before bringing the glass to his lips. Emerson watches him drink as he does the same.

Alas, it is not the moment.

This is not because the signs aren't there, the potential. Ray's decision to not follow Emerson's lead with the nectar mixture is only reasonable; this quasi-Greek potion is an acquired, sophisticated taste...

No, it is because of the beard.

Why, oh why, is he growing a beard? The sight of the patchy, scraggly, pathetic excuse of pogonotrophy shifting around his mouth as it broke into a toothy smile was just too much... the whole thing then seemed obscene. A real mood killer.

Trying this with a boy is one thing, but not a boy with a beard. Emerson needs an eromenos, not a pathikos, a kinaidoi. Some of the young ladies in the past had given him less to work with; Ray at least, generally speaking, maintains an air of good humor and alacrity. But as long as he has that thing on his face, it will be impossible to see him as ephebic, impossible to commit the act.

If anyone should be growing a beard, it's Emerson. He is the erastes here. Not to mention, so many important literary figures throughout history have worn them—not only the Greeks, but Shakespeare, Cervantes, Dickens, Chaucer, Joyce, Tolstoy, Dostoyevsky, Chekhov, Hugo, Conrad, Pound, Ibsen, D.H. Lawrence, Longfellow, Melville, and Whitman, to name a few. But Emerson never has, and it seems never will.

He was thirty during his first, and most likely last, attempt, teaching at Columbia. Around the one-and-a-half-week mark, the hairs poked through in such a way that was so uncomfortable he found himself unable to concentrate, especially while reading. It was terrible. He had heard this pain would only be temporary, but before two full weeks, he found himself reaching for the razor and shaving it all off, vowing never to try again. It just wasn't worth it.

But would it be now? Is he a stronger man after having lived and loved and lost as he has, and would it be wise in order to show Ray who's boss? He's sure he could grow a more impressive one than his. One fitting of a real erastes. No, no; he doesn't have the time. He must try to get the boy to shave.

He honestly has no business even attempting such a thing. Some of his TAs over the years have grown them as well, and of course, far too many of his undergrads; it's always such a joke, these boys with their beards. A male should wait until he has at least *done something* before growing one. Even though Emerson feels they're not really for him, he believes that a beard must be earned. "So I've been wondering, darling, what inspired the new look?" Oh, what a tactful way of doing this. Emerson is quite pleased with himself. It can be said that the first step to extirpate something you don't like is to ask it a good question.

"The new look?"

"The beard."

"Oh, there was no real inspiration." Ray is leaning against one of the bookshelves, a hand steadying himself in front of the section dedicated to Chaucer while the other holds his glass. If it weren't for the beard, he'd be a vision; at least half of Emerson's love affairs began with a similar pose. "Just switching things up I guess."

"I've never grown one."

"No?"

"I tried once—got as far as extended stubble. But as it was transitioning into a real beard, I just couldn't take it. It was too itchy and painful." Oh, heavens! That is not the statement to make, old man! Such a declaration of vulnerability may be appreciated by the twenty-year-old co-eds, half of whom were already gaga over you, but not this young man you hope to truly dominate! Emerson desperately wants to take a sup of his wine, though restrains himself, convinced the boy would pick up on his ignominity.

"Yeah, that happens. But only for about a week or two."

Great, now he is the one doling out assurances. Pull it together, Emerson! But carefully now, with grace: "So I've heard. I did want one back in my day, badly. As a young lad, I looked forward to a beard as a significant rite of passage. Then in the sixties and seventies they took on an entirely new, political meaning, and they became a way of identifying those in your tribe." That was good—evoke the romance of the sixties, free love, the good fight; everybody loves the sixties, especially those who weren't there. Ray nods. "Is that what you're doing now, dear, identifying yourself for your tribe?"

"No. I don't think I have a tribe." Ray takes a sip.

"Luckily for me, my wife—forgive me, my ex-wife, Claire's mother—fell for me even though I looked like a bit of a square. A fine mind, a quick tongue: they proved to be enough!" Emerson chuckles to himself. Ray offers a smile in return. It better not be a pity smile! Though, to hell with him if it is: this is the real Emerson. Grandiosity wrapped loosely, thinly, just enough in droll self-deprecation. Emerson sips his drink, the mixture hitting his tongue like sour grape juice. This whole thing would've been easier before he decided he should consummate their mentor-mentee relationship. He shouldn't concern himself with pity smiles, the boy's opinion of him! Oh, if only he had just tried then! Back before he cared, back before the beard. No, it was too risky. He, like always, was right. The aftertaste is pleasant, slightly sweet.

"Why do you ask? About my beard?" Ray shifts his weight. Aha! So that was what the smile was for; Emerson now has him feeling defensive about his beard! Good...

"Oh, no reason. Just making friendly conversation. I suppose this wine loosens me up some." Emerson sits back in his chair, an emphatic gesture, but one with the free feeling of a man enjoying his newly regained upper hand. He swirls the wine around in his glass. "That, and I thought we might benefit from a little break. The Culture's later years are so hard on me, darling."

"I guess so," Ray laughs. "If you need wine to get through it."

"Well, that's only half the reason I've added this to the routine. The other half has to do with the Greeks, whom I adore, and who, if you'll remember from the beginning of the project, laid the foundation for what we now call thought, critical thinking. They didn't have coffee, so they drank wine." Ray could only find this fascinating; if only he didn't have that damn thing on his face! "Alcohol acts as a mild stimulant in small doses, if you didn't know." Emerson sups.

"Yeah, I've heard that. It's a pretty interesting drug, alcohol."

"Isn't it?" Ah, perfection! They are truly bonding! If he can get him to shave that thing somehow, Emerson knows he can do what he needs to do; he can feel it. He is laying his own foundation, yes! "It's been number one over the ages for a reason, I suppose. Though caffeine might have eclipsed it by now, however minor a drug it may be."

"It's major enough. That's something, though." Yes, keep interested, keep engaged… "I wonder which is actually used more. But anyway, if caffeine were introduced today, the FDA wouldn't allow it. Or so I've heard."

"Yes, I've heard that as well. Caffeine and As—"

"—pirin."

They laugh. Emerson is beside himself, overwhelmed with joy—should he just try now? The act would be executed from behind, anyway; it's not like he'd even see the beard. "How wonderful! Listen to us, completing each other's sentences, unable to tell one another anything we don't already know. We've become two peas in a pod, haven't we?"

"There's a lot I could still learn from you."

And just like that, Ray extinguished whatever was alighting within Emerson. Such a stupid and painfully obvious statement: he would need some time before he could feel attracted enough to the boy to be able to do it. That, and perhaps the aid of a pharmaceutical, it was so bad. "Oh, of course, I didn't mean anything involving literature. I meant in casual conversation. Social trends, science—it's as effortless as talking about the weather for guys like us." It's probably for the best; all that about positioning was a cop-out. A beard is a beard. He *must* get him to shave it! But he can't just tell him to, like he did with the bicycling. The boy need not view him adversarially now. Maybe another question about it: "Isn't it uncomfortable, now, in the late summer's heat?"

"It's not so bad. I mean, as you can see, it doesn't really come in all the way. And because it's already hot, I don't really notice a difference." He takes the hand he was using to lean on the bookshelf and scratches it. Hopefully he's self-consciously questioning its existence and not just playing with it, doting. "The last time I had one was a couple of years ago, also in the summer. Maybe in the fall I'll be able to feel more of a difference. Maybe it'll keep me warm when it's cool out."

"Yes, well, one must do what one can to keep warm in the autumn months." Oh, Emerson, you old dog… But a little innuendo can go a long way. The autumn, now there's something to look forward to, unless he shaves sooner thanks to Emerson's prodding. "Especially the old. If only I weren't such a wimp." Emerson sips his wine.

"You should grow one. I think it'd look distinguished on you." What is he, now, actually openly flirting? Perhaps. Or maybe it's just that old Latin charm again; it's not like he perceived it as flirting before, just soft soap. Whatever the case, Emerson feels good about his prospects. Then: a notion! Perhaps he will grow a beard after all. As long as his is thicker and fuller than Ray's, he'll still feel like a proper erastes. And perhaps, just perhaps, on account of his growing one, Ray will not think it's quite as hip anymore. Emerson could run the risk of being perceived as imitating his subaltern by his own subaltern, but it is a risk worth taking!

"Well, anyway, this has been a nice chat, a nice break, but I suppose we should get back to it. You can finish your wine as you work if you'd like."

"I think I will. Thanks." Ray nods and leaves the room. Can Emerson stand to essay a bit of pogonotrophy himself again? Will it be as torturous as before? Or will his old, life-hardened skin put up more of a fight? Only time will tell—but not too much time. The process couldn't be more painful than writing about the Culture's last days, so he will do what he has to do! And the payoff! Oh, the payoff to come! It will be the perfect consummation as he reaches the finish line of this first draft, preparing himself mind, body, and soul for the next. He will truly be like one of the Greeks then, one of the greats!

▲▽▽▲▽▽▲

God this is taking forever. Maybe they should've just gone to the Botanical Garden, the last activity he had suggested before this one. The trip would have been long, too, but at least they would've been sitting down for most of it. Long walks are so dumb. It's not like a good cardio workout on a treadmill or elliptical machine or anything. You're not getting your blood pumping enough to reap actual health benefits, and you can't even watch or look at something worthwhile as you're doing it. Plus, it's really hot out today. Haruka is dying. Maybe she'll just dig a grave at the cemetery and get down into it. It will be nice and cool in there and then she won't have to walk anymore.

Really, though, she doesn't want to die. She wants to live. Flourish, actually: that's why she's doing this. Make him happy and he will make you happy. She tells herself this often.

It's hard, though. Especially today. This part of Long Island City is just so ugly. Very industrial, very dirty. Too many cars and not enough people. The cemetery better be good. He said it was, that it had some really interesting views of the Manhattan skyline behind rows and rows of graves. She's always liked a good cemetery. But his opinions can rarely be trusted.

"Just a few more blocks," he says. He must know, must be able to tell how unhappy she is. Nobody's said anything in a while. She's wearing sandals, and her feet are getting dirty. A layer of city on them. Also, few? What does that even mean? Give her a real number. This is now officially worse than trying to get to the beach.

"Okay."

The Bronx Zoo was actually his first choice for what they should do today. While Haruka loves animals, she can't go there. Ever. She heard about what they did. Read about it on mental_floss a little while back. She's been reading a lot of articles about offensive things lately. In 1906, they had an African man on display in a cage. A pygmy. They put him in the Monkey House with an orangutan and made him act like a savage. They sprinkled bones around the cage and told him to rush and bare his carved-down, sharp-looking teeth at the patrons on the other side of the cage. So fucked up. Even though it happened over a hundred years ago and the guy who was in charge then is long dead, that's still not a place Haruka wants to support. It doesn't matter how cute the animals are. Stuff like that can be understood as a byproduct of the times, but it can't really be forgiven. There are other zoos. She doubts there are many super-kawaii types of animals there that she hasn't already seen at the San Francisco Zoo, and couldn't see elsewhere.

After she told him about all this, he asked her what she wanted to do instead. She didn't have an answer. Really, she didn't want to do anything. She just wanted to stay in his room with the air conditioning on and beat the heat binge-watching something on Netflix. But he was cooped up at work so much earlier this summer that she knew he'd insist on doing something. Making the most of this Saturday.

Next he suggested the Natural History Museum, maybe a walk in Central Park afterwards. It was like he wasn't even listening to her. Here she was being very emotionally intelligent by acknowledging his desire to get out, holding her tongue about her own desire to stay in, and he was asking if she wanted to go to the Natural History Museum? It's another place that's very offensive. She went once, last fall. There were cool parts: the Planetarium, the dinosaur bones, the Hall of Human Origins, some of the dioramas of animals. But there were also dioramas of people. Like, fully evolved human beings, not cavemen, in recent enough settings. And surprise, surprise, mostly people of color. They say it's for education and to promote the various cultures, but it's not. It's just another place that makes white people—their repugnant children, mainly—feel superior.

"Oh, shit! We gotta hustle." Great! Now he's making her rush across the road! They started crossing this intersection when the hand was flashing orange and it just went solid. Where are they even? Some ugly road called Van Dam. Is this still Long Island City? How deep in dumb Queens is this place? "Sorry, sorry, sorry," he says.

They hotfoot it across the last of the lanes, to the gas station. A car tears down the road right behind them as they get there. Everybody in Queens drives too fast, like they're trying to kill someone. Don't they realize Haruka not only needs to live now, but flourish? And oh, what's this? Now he's making her walk up a hill?! There are hills in Queens? They really should have gone to the Botanical Garden.

"It's funny. The thing I think killed me, Haruka, was getting hit by a car. You'd think I wouldn't be so afraid, but I have no memory of what it was like, so I still don't want to get hit."

"Yes, Ray. It would hurt. You and me both. Don't put me in that kind of situation again."

"Right. I didn't mean to then. It's just up this hill and to the right," he says. It better be. They walk on, up the stupid hill.

After she explained that stuff about the Natural History Museum was when he asked her if she wanted to check out the Botanical Garden. But by then the Bronx was already tainted because of the zoo. And it seemed too far. Even the idea of looking at and smelling all the pretty, exotic flowers wasn't enough. She didn't want to recreate another beach situation, but it seems she has here. He said it would take fifteen to twenty minutes to get to the cemetery and they're easily already at twenty-five.

Still, she can't complain. Not vocally, anyway. Only with her silence. She's said "no" out loud enough times today. They were big "nos." And her agreement to do this was more of an "I guess." Also, she's said "no" a lot in general lately, since he's been using his dumb flip phone. It just really pisses her off. And also sometimes when he tries to kiss her because he's growing a beard and it is very scratchy. Some more "yeses" are in order. Or maybe just one really big one, something that makes all her "nos" seem trivial. Actually, maybe she'll give him more little "nos," so the "yes" seems even bigger. And that will prime him to say "yes" to her, when she asks her big question soon. Make him happy and he will make you happy. She tells herself this often.

▲▽▽▲▽▲▽

It's weird: what was once so infuriating is now, at least in this moment, totally reassuring. She didn't enjoy the walk here, that much was obvious, so this makes it seem worth it, offers a little bit of validation. Perhaps it's how she's using the thing. She just pulled it out and started taking pictures—no checking texts, social media, whatever. No distraction, just work; proper use: respect for the tool. It almost makes him miss his own. The iPhone actually takes pretty damn good photos—even Annie Leibovitz thinks so. But it's not for him. No. It can't be. The thing doesn't even reliably make calls; it's flawed at that most fundamental level. God doesn't want him to have one, these evil pocket computers calling themselves phones, these frauds… he saw the sign, figured it out. Yes, Ray's better off. He doesn't need that shit; his flip phone with its awful, awful camera will be enough to gather any more photographic evidence he might need on his quest. Shit ain't a vacation, nope, nope.

He has no idea why she's taking them. Maybe for pleasure, maybe to make some postcards for other sacrilegious folk saints to enjoy. He's just happy she seems okay. For a while there, she wasn't that cool to be around. The walk was one thing, but before all that she had shot down a bunch of other ideas about what they should do today—a trip to the Bronx Zoo, then the Natural History Museum, then the New York Botanical Garden—the first two for bogus reasons involving how offensive and racist they were. It's not like he invited her to see the Bodies exhibition… mad about shit that happened a long, long time ago and that had nothing to do with her or them. By virtue of simply being an American taxpayer, you're already supporting a place with a deeply unjust history, so shut the fuck up about peeping some cute little critters at the zoo, damn. It was like: if she's Death, even just some patron folk saint of it, it's the death of fun. But all seems good now. She points her phone away from Midtown and toward Lower Manhattan.

"Pretty cool, huh?"

"Yeah," she says. "Wish this had a better zoom, though."

"Trying to get the Freedom Tower?"

"Actually, yes."

"I don't know about that thing." And he really doesn't. Of course the site needs something, and it's long overdue, but it also seems to deserve much more than whatever that structure is they're putting up. So far it just looks like another big glass nothing, something resembling a large-scale residential tower or generic office building in Midtown not meant to compete with the more iconic surrounding skyscrapers, or something you'd see as the pride of another, far lesser city—hardly in or of NYC. The Twin Towers had grit and audacity; unless they build this thing twice as tall as he last heard they were planning to, the sorta corny 1776 feet high, and it became the tallest building in the world or whatever, it seems impossible that it could come close to carrying on that legacy.

"It's going to be even uglier than the Twin Towers."

"Never saw them in person, but I always thought they looked cool in pictures and on TV."

"I didn't mean in terms of looks. I like glass more than steel." No way, glass ain't shit when it comes to statement architecture. Fuck glass. Glass is only good for windows. Steel, brick, something solid and dense, that's what you want your building to be made out of. It seems the right thing would have been to remake the towers as they were, or maybe, like, a foot taller. That would've been a better way to show that America and New York can't be fucked with than whatever the hell this thing is that they're looking at. "I meant in terms of what it will represent. The arrogance. Using that word: 'Freedom.' Capitalism doesn't mean freedom." No, it doesn't. But that's not really the point—"It's only a matter of time before it goes down, too. An easy target. Nothing more." Wait, what? Yikes.

"Damn, Haruka."

She shrugs, snapping away in the camera app, her focus still downtown. "September 11th wasn't that bad. Two buildings on fire here, a small section of the Pentagon, a plane forced down in Middle of Nowhere, Pennsylvania. Three thousand lives lost, maybe double that injured. Big deal. A small price for all the war America has waged, all the lives we've taken, Ray. It was time someone gave it back. Around one hundred thousand people died in Hiroshima. Why did we think so little of their freedom? What have we done for the hibakusha since?" Oh man, she is going fucking hard. Making his militant high school friends seem minor league. "The only reason September 11th is such a big deal is because most of the people who died were white. America is a white supremacist bully, and you know what? Sometimes bullies get payback. And they fucking deserve it. Then you say 'Damn, Haruka,' like I'm being messed up, but I'm not."

He sort of gets what she's saying: the ethnocentrism, the delusional notion that no one would or could carry out an attack like that, but still… Damn. Geopolitics and modern warfare are complex and tricky and suffering is suffering; scale and stats shouldn't matter. Also, why always with the white people? "Not everything has to be about how evil white people are. Lives lost are lives lost. We're looking at the place where it happened, from a graveyard. Just seems disrespectful."

"Being critical isn't the same as being disrespectful."

"It's just cold."

"So what?" Now she's taking pictures of the graves, just graves; no Manhattan in the background. "The First Amendment is one of the things I like best about being American. It's okay to be critical of America. Americans are still critical of Japan, for example."

"I guess. But the popular opinion now just seems to be that the Japanese are sort of wacky, not evil."

"Yeah, but wacky as in can be easily dismissed or marginalized. If not sub-human then certainly sub-American."

"We think everybody's sub-American, though. That's American exceptionalism."

Crouching way down, Haruka captures several rows of graves with the skyline in the background, the graves almost as high in the foreground. Afterwards, she stands, sighs, and places her phone in the small purse she's brought along. She looks at him. "There was an episode of *South Park* when I was growing up, it was the sixth grade, where someone said, 'Japanese people don't have souls!' "—Ray remembers that line, from *Best Friends Forever*. That entire episode was fucking great, it might have even won an Emmy—"and then this group of boys started making fun of me saying I didn't have a soul. I laughed it off at first, you know, middle schoolers are so stupid. But they just kept going on and on for weeks with it. Until one day I was fed up and told them, 'You know I'm half Chinese right?' hoping they would stop, and this one boy says, 'Then I guess you just have half an evil soul.' "

He was wondering if she'd bring that into this, her Chinese side. It's a more convincing argument for what she's trying to say than decades-old, white picket-fenced hatred of Japan—even if that is a big part of America's history. A lot of the people she's lumping together do actually and actively hate China. Even in the oh-so-progressive Bay Area, apparently: "That's pretty fucked up."

"Then for the rest of the year they made fun of me for having half an evil soul."

"Don't blame *South Park*, though. It's a good show. Those kids were just idiots."

"No, it's not." She shakes her head. "It does more harm than good and it's not even that funny."

"I wouldn't say it does more harm than good. They make fun of everybody equally, you know? It's good satire. And it's really funny. Some people—"

"It's not real satire. It's"—she makes quotes with her fingers—" 'satire.' Just an excuse for jerks to get away with saying how they really feel, however ugly. Very lazy humor." That's not true at all. The more offensive aspects are mostly there to make a point, not just shock; it's way, way more sophisticated humor than the type of shit she sends him all the time. Internet humor. Dumb fucking memes about cats and whatnot. Those make the random zingers *Family Guy* throws out at you every twenty seconds seem artfully crafted and poignant by comparison. "But anyway, the point wasn't what they were saying, the boys in my school, but how they said it. Technically, they were right. In Buddhism, we don't believe in the soul. Only karma, deeds. The soul is more of a Western thing. The individual. I wasn't even sure I had one until recently. Professor Towers' class... Nevermind, I don't want to get into that..." Hmmm... is that when she discovered she was really Santa Muerte? Would make sense, especially since she just caught herself, doesn't want to talk about it now... Gotta maintain the mystique. But he's onto her. "It's just that white American arrogance. It's awful. And more than Japan, they all hate China." Yup, yup—now she's saying what he was just thinking. It's hard to argue with that one in 2012.

"Because we fear them."

"Do you know that twenty million Chinese people died in World War II? Of course you don't. Nobody does." Actually, he did know that. And that it was the Japanese who killed them. She probably wouldn't want to talk about that aspect of it. It would be weird to be half Japanese and half Chinese, Ray thinks. Well, no weirder than being half Mexican and half white, really. Everybody kills everybody, given the chance. "Talk about a people who deserve sympathy. But no, instead all Americans do is call to complain if they didn't get their General Tso's five minutes after ordering it. It's disgusting." But really, isn't she—more than Chinese or Japanese—American like him? And even more than that, per her soul, a Mexican folk saint? Sometimes it's hard to figure her out. Where she ends and Muerte begins, the different pieces of them. Like untangling wires. "I hope the Chinese take down that so-called 'Freedom Tower.' Just not while I'm here. I'm a New Yorker now, and that part's scary I guess. Not until after I graduate." This conversation is crazy on a number of levels. But then again so was all that shit about the zoo and museum.

"Do you like living here?"

"I do. It's fun. It's sort of like a real-life internet." Oh, shit. It is! It totally is. New York was like the internet before the internet. A densely populated, hectic, ever-evolving place that's always on, that you extract yourself from in order to rest, to catch your breath, and will be there in full force when you're ready for it again. The city that never sleeps. Interconnected in a grand plexus by a series of subnetworks and subsystems. Shiny parts and seedy parts. Covered in ads, understated and overstated. Multicultural. Everybody's here, every language is spoken. The anonymous mistaken for the rude: people here get away with saying how they feel, speaking their truths. Thank you Muerte, thank you God. Was Ray wrong in getting rid of his phone because it didn't work as a phone? If New York City's like the internet, then what's the difference? Even the hardware is the same as his old phone: while the vibe, what's in the air, here, is a lot like that of Web 2.0, the city itself, the physical thing, from its meticulous planning to stylish execution and the resultant great expense, is a lot like an Apple product. Aha! No wonder it's called the Big Apple! Does he need to give up the city like he gave up his phone? No, that's reaching. He can't completely disregard all the events and signs that came before this. If anything, she just provided him with a solid clue that he is meant to use the city as a real-life internet, not stare mesmerically at one in his palm. Ray strokes his slight beard, nodding.

That doesn't mean he can't miss it, though: the phone. For the convenience. For the fun. The mini-meta-New York City in your pocket. "Sometimes I miss my phone. For the photos, everything else."

"I would if I were you, too. You should reactive it." A little test. Nothing more.

"Nah."

"Then I guess I can share my pictures with you." He passed. She pulls out her phone, starts flipping through the photo roll. Ray smiles. "I'll send these over email. Documentation of the experience. Our nice Saturday activity. We should take a selfie."

Then they do. Neither of them smile.

They assess it. Them, graves, the city in late-August haze: a twenty-first-century *American Gothic.* "Nice. I'll post this one to Facebook." They hold hands and look out toward Manhattan.

Ray hears himself breathing over the industrial western Queens traffic beyond the cemetery fences—tires moving, starting, stopping. The place is practically empty. It's late enough in the day, a Saturday. More people probably come here on Sundays. He ponders for a moment about what he just participated in, a selfie in a cemetery: it doesn't seem entirely age-appropriate, or maybe nothing about it was appropriate. But it's the age thing he gets hung up on. He squeezes her hand then lets go. "Why do people your age take pictures and shoot videos when professional crews are present at, like, concerts and sporting events and stuff? When the experience is already being documented with way better production values and you could be there totally in the moment? Like, I have a camera on my flip phone: I just don't want to use it because it sucks and it's kind of nice to be fully here with you. The benefit is much smaller than the cost."

"That's a stupid question, Ray. Especially after we just took a selfie."

"I don't think so."

"Make no mistake: when I send these to you, it won't be documenting your experience, or even our experience. It's not called an *usie.* I'll be sharing *my* experience with you. That's why. Anything shot for TV or magazines or a web article is fine for the general public, the people who weren't there, but what I capture with my phone, that's mine. When I look at it again later, I am looking at something that exists as a reflection of me and my experiences. When I share it with others, I am sharing me. We are not sharing the event."

"Got it," he says. And he did.

"Thank you for bringing me here, Ray."

"You're welcome."

"I really mean it. It's beautiful."

She reaches for his hand again and, after receiving it, begins to pull. Guiding him, they move silently down a little declivity, weaving through and between rows of graves, occasionally stalling at taller ones, then across a walking path to another section of the cemetery, the closest to the southernmost perimeter fence. They pass by more graves, saying nothing, seeing no one. Some burial sites seem recently visited, marked with flowers, mementos, other tokens. Then, coming up to a bush, large and the lone one in the row, she stops.

"Sit," she says.

He does. She curls up before him, on the low-lying grass, and reaches for his lap. Her fingers come to grip the outline of his genitalia.

"What are you doing?"

"Thanking you." She unzips his pants, pulls his member out, and, lowering her head down, takes it into her mouth. This seems profoundly fucked up. But his body disagrees, allowing himself to grow in her mouth until he's fully erect. Maybe it's okay?

She's supposed to know best, after all. If this is where he's meant to be, what he's supposed to be doing, then this can't be wrong.

Thankfully, they're not actually on someone's grave. He shouldn't and hopefully wouldn't have been able to get hard then—he's not a horny teenager with nowhere else to go, not that he ever hooked up in a graveyard while living. But they're close enough to a few graves that, instinctively, this still feels pretty weird and wrong. He makes it a point not to read any of the names, just fixes his eyes on her bobbing head.

Maybe it's not disrespectful. First of all, these dead people aren't real. These are, at best, cenotaphs. And even if they were real, they probably wouldn't mind. It's not like it's personal, not like the idea of pissing or dancing on someone's grave. And plus, Ray's heard old people in retirement homes fuck like rabbits; they're closer to death than he would be if he were still alive. Also, don't the French call orgasms "the little death" or something like that? This has gotta be above board. In fact, more than that, it could even be thought of as good. Cyclical. Where life comes to an end, more should begin. Very Buddhist, actually, carrying out a sex act in a cemetery.

Unless! She might just be doing this to prove a point. Show him how weak and dissolute he is, how easily he and all men can be manipulated through their dicks. He had just been chastising her for her lack of deference in the graveyard, about all that September 11th stuff—could it be that?

No, he already sorted it out. The dead probably wouldn't care and so he shouldn't, either. The only people who would care would be the relatives coming to pay their respects or those at the Archdiocese of New York who run this thing. But they've barely seen anybody here and they're concealed behind a pretty big bush. Not to mention, none of those people would be real, anyway. Getting caught isn't an issue, even in broad daylight.

But why, exactly, is this her way of thanking him for taking her here? Was that his downfall? Maybe he had been texting with a girl he was hoping to get a blowjob from or have sex with when he was hit crossing the street back in 2007?

Maybe. Or maybe fellatio is just a nice way to say thank you. Something that shouldn't be overthought, even in the strangest of circumstances. Ray lays back and tries to give himself fully to it, there in his makeshift plot behind the bush. He does, eyes fluttering, then all the way shut. And soon enough the little death overcomes him.

▲▽▽▲▲▽▲▲

Last days are always the same. One part sadness, two parts excitement. It was the case in grade school, middle school, high school. It was the case with her first job, at the ice cream shop. Then the next at Starbucks. All the places she ever volunteered growing up—the SPCA, the Boys & Girls Club, the old folks' homes. It was the case at the internship she had last summer at her friend's startup. And it is the case here at Tumblr.

Haruka looks around, soaks it all in. This is how she wants to remember it. The young, hip people. The cool iMac stations they, like her, are sitting at. The exposed brick and weird art and furniture everywhere, all under such great lighting. Just as it was on the first day, except now hers. The dog runs between two rows close by. He's so cute; she'll miss him most of all. She breathes in the air around her desk, no discernible scent, so perfect for getting work done. She takes a bite of the red velvet mini cupcake she picked out from the box HR got her and the other interns whose last day is today. The light, fluffy cake and yummy, sweet frosting melt on her tongue, soon inundating her brain with dopamine and endorphins. She has Little Dragon playing on Spotify through her earbuds and her final spreadsheet open on Google Docs with only a few more fields to fill out and more than enough time to complete it.

She will think back on this place fondly; it has been good to her. Made her bank account nice and full, provided good professional experience and a welcome distraction during the days she was suffering from the worst thing that ever happened to her. But she won't be looking back too much. She's too pumped up about what's to come.

Tumblr was just a stepping stone. Katherine has suggested she could come back next summer, but Haruka knows that won't be happening. She'll be on to bigger, better things then. Yes, her time here was nice, but it is over now.

Google, Facebook, and Apple are still calling out to her, and now Twitter, too. Google runs the world, Facebook runs the life, Apple provides the best tools for people to use these things. And Twitter begins revolutions, sparks real change. Tumblr is fun, and can help people with their feelings, but it doesn't do what they do. It won't change the world.

All she needs to do now is ask Ray. Getting perfect grades next semester shouldn't be that hard; she's not taking any stupid English class this time around, nope. Mostly math and science, where there are just right and wrong answers—easy peasy. And, really, asking Ray shouldn't pose any issues now that they're as far along as they are. It seemed like he wanted to say "I love you" the other day after the blowjob in the cemetery, but stopped himself. Should be a piece of cake. Like the last little bit in front of her. She pops it into her mouth, reactivates the dopamine receptors. The wonderful chemical floods her nucleus accumbens. Oh my God, she can't wait. She just can't. She'll be a sophomore with a perfect GPA and two internships under her belt already, one at a trendy and growing company—an obvious choice for next summer's programs.

Bloonk: a gchat alert has cut through her song. She goes to her Gmail tab and looks in the lower-right corner. There were three conversations open already—one with Maeve, who's excited to come back to New York this week, one with Sukhpreet, one of her best friends from high school, and the other with Katherine, who's in a meeting somewhere else in the office. They're joined by a new window showing it's Ben.

Ben: Hey how's it going over there? You get a cupcake?

Stupid Ben. He thinks he still has a chance. She's been able to avoid him for the most part since PS1, but he still messages her sometimes. In the beginning he'd ask how her grandpa was doing, like she wouldn't see the ploy. Now it's just boring everyday things. She starts writing him back. The chat box reads:

me: hey! good, good. and yup! red velvet.

Then:

Ben: red velvet! mmmm.
Ben: the chocolate's good too.

Now he's writing like her. In all lowercase. He still copies her sometimes and it's annoying. One time he started a chat in lowercase then Haruka deviated from her normal all lowercase and responded using proper grammar and punctuation to see what he'd do, and he switched. That's more how he usually types, how he typed in his first chats with her, in this weird hybrid of proper punctuation and shortened netspeak terms. He's such a loser.

me: yeah, it was really sweet. i'm happy with my choice.
Ben: i feel like this summer just flew by.

Haruka doesn't. While better during the second half, her summer also started off really sad. Time feels slower when you're really stressed out and depressed. A very irritating trait of psychological time, one of the worst. If only humans could just keep clock time no matter what. She types, responding:

me: i know! i've never had such a fun work environment.
Ben: think you're coming back next summer?
me: you never know. we'll see!
me: you?

A little giggle to herself. It's amusing to toy with Ben, even if it is sort of a waste of time.

Ben: same as you. you never know what tomorrow will bring!

me: right
Ben: well i hope we can still hang out even though we won't
be working at the same office now.

And there it is. Ben has more nerve than Haruka thought. He pretty much just asked her out. And it's not exactly like she led him on or anything, she's just been relatively nice to him. Some balls. It's funny. Ben should do stand-up comedy maybe. Or at least improv. Why would he think she would ever date a guy like him? Aside from being too nice and kind of ugly, he also only goes to the New School. She goes to a better school. That's not really how the world works, Ben. She is very young and smarter and much more attractive and she can do better than that. In fact, she is. Ray's at least kind of hot, and he went to Columbia—an Ivy. It doesn't matter that he's also kind of a loser, an assistant and a "freelancer" without any freelance work to speak of. That he sucks at life. It's not like their relationship is real, anyway. Yes, she likes him but she still cheats on him all the time. Not that this matters. The point is that Ben is being very unprofessional right now. And her spending time talking to him is no longer amusing. This could be time spent scrolling through Facebook or browsing Twitter or Reddit or looking at funny things on 9GAG or doing anything else. She could be finishing her spreadsheet right now. Or setting up an OkCupid date. Instead she's wasting her time chatting with a joke like Ben. Ben, this will hurt:

me: I don't know how much my boyfriend would like that,
but maybe I'll see you around the neighborhood.
Ben: I meant as friends of course!

No he didn't. Ben is not as brave as she just thought; he's a coward. It's funny how she used capitalization to show him how serious she was and then he immediately used it back. How pathetic. Haruka hates Ben. Unfortunately, they do live in the same general area, the Villages, so it's entirely possible that she will run into him again. But she hopes not. And she wants him to not want to see her, either. Hopefully now he'll be too embarrassed to say hi in public. But if not, maybe she can scare him:

me: Oh, I know. But still. He's the jealous type.
me: Latin… lol

There. Take that, stupid Ben.

Ben: Well sometimes me and my friends throw little parties
in our dorms. Maybe you could bring him along!

Ugh! This guy just won't take a hint. How about this?!

   me: he's a little older, might not be that into it. but maybe!
   Ben: An older man, huh?

Finally. It shouldn't have taken all that for you to see that you're not
in Haruka's league, stupid Ben! Fool… She hopes he thinks he's some
kind of gangster or jet-setter or something. Someone powerful. If he only
knew… well, Ray *is* nuts. He has that going for him, Haruka guesses.
He probably would try to beat someone like Ben up if he hit on her at a
party. Considering what he did to her iPhone… Haruka stops. She's
bringing up bad memories to herself. She doesn't want to think about it.

   me: ha! yeah…
   Ben: either way we'll always have tumblr.
   me: yes, we always will! speaking of!! i should probably get
   back to work. my last spreadsheet!
   Ben: lol. me too. Talk to you later.
   me: bye ben

Haruka wishes that this were the last goodbye she ever had to send
to him and that she could block him right now. Not only on gchat, but
on Facebook, too, and Tumblr. But she can't. Yes, she hates him and
he's hella stupid and too nice and ugly, and he goes to a worse school
than her, and he's wasted a lot of her time, but it would not be a wise
business move. The tech community is a small one. Especially in NYC.
But maybe by this time next year she'll be able to. When she's interning
at Google. Or maybe Facebook, working on projects for the main site or
Instagram or some other cool new thing they buy. When she won't need
anyone anymore, when she'll really have made it.

▲▽▽▲▲▽▽

Eyes closed, the smell of old wood, mostly. Faint traces of frankincense and candle smoke occasionally add their own passing flourishes. He's surrounded by the low echo of the organ and the slight movements of the people and His words, not comfortable on the knees, but happy. Good to be here, as always. That familiar current has begun quivering within, that pulsing Something Wonderful, coursing through the body from down deep, below the nervous system, deep, deeper down still, emanating all the way from Ray's soul—light cleansing his entire being from the inside out. It's been too long, since the Easter before last. In moments like this it's insane that he wouldn't come every week. It seems more like a need than a want, a matter of maintenance: like a shower for the spirit, something crucial to get rid of the muck and stink of the world, not only his world but any world. How can he stand them for so long? The moldering muck and the stink? There are always reasons, never enough time; an all-too-short memory.

To the Catholic, including the quasi-Catholic and twice-a-year Catholic, all manner of actual and heterodox and lapsed Catholics, a church service is really about ritual. This transcendent feeling Ray's currently experiencing comes from that. Mass is pretty much the same everywhere, and this soterial sensation can be attained as long as you're open to it, not only in as beautiful an environment as St. Patrick's, like here now, but in as bland a one as his old church back in Austin, or one in a foreign country where you don't even understand the language. That's why some people like to go to Mass in Latin. The cues are enough, this feeling's there, maybe even stronger. Because much of the power of the words is held in the act of saying or hearing them. Whatever meaning they carry is secondary. That is not to say that these things are done by rote in Mass—rather, it's more of an incantation.

For to try to understand the words, first and foremost, is a fool's errand. That's why everyone thinks Christian fundamentalists, or really any kind of religious fundamentalists, are wackjobs or idiots or both. What most Catholics understand, it seems intuitively, or perhaps because they were baptized as babies and already put on their path without much of a say, is that they are supposed to behave like actors; it's about learning the lines, the cues, then feeling them, there in the church and also out in the world. That's it. That's how Christianity is supposed to work; it is based on feeling, not knowledge. That's what it means to be a follower. And that's why it's pretty ridiculous that they switched up the script, that "one in being with the Father" is now "consubstantial with the Father," that "And also with you" became "And with your spirit." It really doesn't matter. To contrast that with most Protestants, too many think they're supposed to be like directors, like they can unpack the multivalence behind every line of the script, and that it all needs to make complete sense. But the thing is, it doesn't. And can't. Ignoratio elenchi. These folks are obsessed with trying to find a reason for everything, and that's why they're doomed. Good luck trying to really understand the words of a book full of contradictions and nutty claptrap about things like shellfish and slavery and homosexuality. Concepts quite removed from the simple unconditional love of God… No, no, no… Hell no.

Yes, the Bible is indeed infallible, they're right about that, but its infallibility is in its inability to be truly understood. It's a paradox. As messy and monotonous and sometimes gorgeous and sometimes horrendous as existence itself. Jesus' message, that God is love, is the only real takeaway. The Devil, as always, is in the details. The Bible is infallible. The Bible contradicts itself. Therefore, that which contradicts itself is infallible. That's the only way it makes sense. Otherwise it's just a Choose Your Own Adventure book used to justify what you already believe, or the morality you strive for but know you'll never actually attain. Most people are hypocrites. The vast majority would say they are good, or are trying to be good, but are in fact pretty bad.

This is why a Catholic church is the best place to receive it, to read it and hear it—the Bible. The Church is as corrupt as, or more corrupt than, most people. Between the Crusades, the sex scandals over the last few decades, and everything in between, who are they to judge? That's right: no one. They are far from perfect. Like us. But they keep trying. And they do it in a way that is simple, dependable. Familiar. And that should be worth something to someone who says they are good or are trying to be but who is in actuality bad.

So today, on this Twenty-second Sunday in Ordinary Time, Ray is feeling it. God. The Holy Spirit. Coursing through him, all of him. That feeling.

He is one with the people, the priest, everything, God. It doesn't matter that half of the others here are awful—that tourists still mill about the side aisles of the church taking pictures even now during the holiest part of Mass; that lots of folks chose to sit at the very end of their pews so that others would be discouraged from sitting by them; that people showed up incredibly late and with shopping bags from garish Fifth Avenue stores thriving on sweatshop labor; that parents don't check their kids when they act out or excuse themselves to the back when their babies cry. Or that the priest's homily invoked bullshit about the evils of abortion. Or that the Church will soon take up a second collection even though it, through the Vatican, has its own bank that launders money for the Mafia. They are all one and the same. Imperfect; flawed, but trying. Trying something. Even the building, such a marvel of architecture and atmosphere, is trying. It, like Ray, is undergoing a renovation. Outside it was ugly scaffolding, not smooth neo-Gothic stone spires adorned with grand finials, reaching towards the heavens; inside there's more scaffolding, dull metal in the midst of dark wood, stone, stained glass, back near the western end of the nave, inside the big bronze doors of the Fifth Avenue entrance… the church seems to be making its transformation from the outside in, while Ray's is, again, coming from the inside out. They are complementary. Two parts of one body—the body of Christ. Ray opens his eyes. He looks toward the high altar. An interesting thing about St. Patrick's compared to most any other church he's ever attended is how small the crucifix is. In most places, Christ is a wood-carved giant. Here, though made of gold, he's tiny, hanging on a thin cross that couldn't be more than a couple of feet long, lost in the grandeur of the sanctuary, not the focus of it. You have to find him. But when you do, you are rewarded. Past the parishioners lining up ahead for communion, past the priest and the deacons and the lay helpers handing it out, Ray's eyes fix in on this hidden treasure. He can't make out Christ's features, but he knows what's there, and that he's looking more and more like him these days. That's another confusing thing about Protestants: they ask "What would Jesus do?" then they give themselves Lego man haircuts and vote Republican and avoid the wrong side of town. Jesus was a bearded, long-haired socialist who hung out with lepers; someone those prigs would call a wild man. Ray sees Him and he knows He sees Ray. And he is forgiven. By Him. The priest probably wouldn't want him taking communion—would say he isn't ready after having premarital sex, after using intoxicants, exploring the sinful thoughts he has. But that doesn't matter. If Ray or everyone else cared as much about this institution's secrets, they wouldn't be here. They need each other. And Jesus' perfect love accepts them all. He rises and follows the others in his pew up the nave toward the altar, ready to receive communion.

▲▽▽▲▲▽▲

It's time. He's staring at her lovingly, into her eyes, her head rising and falling with his breath as it rests on his chest. They've just had sex, good sex, where she said nothing. She's been doing that more often lately, saying nothing during sex instead of strange things. This isn't only because she ran out of things to say, the recycled and original, but also because she knew it would be more effective. It would mess with him. "Why did she stop saying those things?" he would think. He would view it as a part of his journey, confuse it for progress. Sometimes what you don't say is more powerful than anything you could say. By saying nothing these past few weeks, Haruka has primed him.

Another reason it's time is because classes have started up again. She's gotten all her books, her syllabi, has the expectations for the semester laid out before her. But it's been hard to concentrate. Adjusting from work life, which is easy by comparison, is only a little bit of it. The main thing is that it's hard to perform as a perfect student when right now she is not a perfect student. She needs the grade changed before it gets any worse; there is inertia in the negative. He, an outside force, must stop it. Set it right for her. Yes, it's time.

"Ray," she says.

"Hi."

She sits up. "I need to talk to you about something."

"Okay…" he says, straightening himself up. They both come to lean against the wall his bed is pressed up against. Most good conversations don't begin the way she began it. She has already made a mistake. Should she stop and try again later? No, she must continue… It's time. This is it.

"Don't worry, it's nothing serious. Just a small favor."

"Okay, good. Usually conversations that begin with 'we need to talk' are bad news."

"No, this is good. An opportunity, really. I misspoke."

"Okay, great." He smiles. That's good; maybe it was smart to make him a little nervous first. Maybe she knew without knowing. When he hears what it is, he'll probably be relieved. "Oh, is that it?" he'll think. "That's all?" He'll jump to help her. Maybe they can even do it together now in bed, on his laptop.

"This will be a positive conversation. You should be happy to help me. It should be a pleasure."

He smiles again, scratches his head. "All right then. Well, shoot."

"Ray, I need you to change my grade in Professor Towers' class."

The smile fades, but the hand stays in his hair. He cocks his head to the side like a dog. "Huh?" This isn't good. When he says "Huh?" it means he is confused. And when he is confused, things get complicated, and not long after that very, very stupid. She must make it simple.

"That's the favor. I need you to change my grade."

"I thought the grade change email was just to bring you back to me. So you could help guide me."

Uh-oh. Here we go. Remain calm. She reaches for his free hand and holds it. "Ray, to help yourself, sometimes you must help me, too." A good line. This will take playing into his absurdity, using his own delusions and vanity to trick him.

"I don't get it."

"I need you to change the grade to what you think of me as a girlfriend." That's good, too: guilt. He went to church on Sunday so he should be very responsive to that. "This has been one of your most important tests, and you haven't done it yet. Do you think of me as a B grade girlfriend?"

"I need to think about this." The other hand goes from his hair to his beard, stroking the longer whiskers on his chin.

"What's to think about? So you do think I'm a B grade girlfriend?"

"I understand this is a test, but I don't know if I can believe you in saying the test is how I would grade you based on your performance as a girlfriend."

"Remember what I said on the beach?"

"Yeah."

"I said most of the time I would guide you without telling you. This time I'm just telling you." She makes sure her eyes plead with him: "I had hoped that you would just do it on your own, out of love, but since you haven't done it yet, I have to tell you."

"I don't know, Haruka." He lets go of her hand and reaches for the covers, pulling them over his genitals, even though it's pretty warm in the room. Not good. "Let me get back to you. I need time to think about this."

"No, there is no time."

"But you could still just be trying to guide me by telling me one thing, instead of actually telling me—like the thing you're telling me is supposed to guide me to do something different. Reverse or sideways psychology. I need to figure that out. It's never been that easy with you."

"No, Ray. This is no trick. No riddle, no koan, no double-cross. I simply need you to change the grade."

"But why in the hell would you, Santa Muerte, need your grade changed? You're not even a real student." Ray thinks that she's Santa Muerte, this weird saint recognized by Mexicans but not by the Catholic Church: a fake, blasphemous saint. Back when he thought she was Fate, she instead wanted him to think of her as Love incarnate. But she likes this. She likes being Santa Muerte, and has tried to make it work. It might have been too ambitious for her to expect him to see her as Love. But she's still somewhere between human and a manifestation of God to him, which is enough. She's tried to embrace this role. Santa Muerte seems like a badass, a feminist role model. Very powerful.

"Because you see, Ray, it's not about me. As always, it's about you." This is what the idiot must think. "You're the one who made me a student and so I must play by the rules of a student."

"But you would've gotten the grade you earned."

"No, I was cheated," she says. And she was. "You know Professor Towers. He has mood swings. Some days he's good, some days he's bad. He must've graded me on a bad day."

"He does have his days…" he agrees. Deep down he knows how bad Professor Towers is; everybody who's spent enough time with him does. She feels close, but he's still teetering on the edge. If he wants a little guidance, she will give him a little guidance. Haruka grabs his hand again.

"Now tell me, what do you think heaven is, Ray?"

"I don't know. The closest I can think of is a feeling. Or an energy. It's probably love. You just join love. They say you see your grandparents again or whatever, but it won't be like that. You don't see, but you feel them. You join their love and everyone else's love who ever lived." This is an interesting answer. Of course there is no such thing as heaven. There is only the reality of one's perception and the planet Earth and that is where the human story ends. If there is a soul, it only exists during life: it's more like a person's brand. And as for love, it is nothing more than chemicals in the brain. But still, this is an interesting answer. It is pretty. If Haruka could bring herself to believe in God or heaven, it might be something like that. A feeling. An endless stream of dopamine and serotonin and endorphins and oxytocin as warmth and positivity. That would be nice. But she knows when she dies, she will be gone. Nothing. That is why it's important to live a good life. To get the most out of it. And that is why she must exploit his naïve, pretty little answer.

"Then love me, Ray, by doing this. It will get you closer to heaven."

"I do love you." This is great! "I mean, I have love for you." Even with the cop-out correction, it's still great. He has never said "I love you" before. She must exploit this, too! Exploit it, exploit it!

"Then help me, Ray." She says his name very clearly this time. This will light up his middle frontal cortex, middle temporal cortex, superior temporal cortex, and cuneus, subconsciously persuading him to do her bidding. Then she quickly kisses his hand. "This is the most important test of your faith, yet." She kisses it again, twice. "If you make me perfect, I can help make you perfect. Ready for heaven."

He yanks it away and pulls the covers up farther, past his belly button halfway up his torso. Uh-oh, why?! "Aha! I knew it. So you want me to make it worse?"

"What?! No!" What in the actual fuck is he talking about? If he did that! Oh my God! It would, it would! Ahhhh!!

▲▽▽▲▲▲▽

Finally, something to hold on to—something there, clear, in the foreground! Visible through the chaos spilling out from this conversation. He's typically not fully aware of both of her identities in real time, seeing her mostly as just Haruka, his girlfriend, in her presence and Santa Muerte while they're apart, but questions like the one she's asked here can't help but tangle them and obfuscate what he thought was the truth. But now Ray knows! Now he gets it—"I think I see what you need me to do now. You must've known. Of course! It's about love. It's one of the main things you're a patron of, right? This has to be the last step. The last level, you might call it, in the video game analogy you've used, that you thought would speak to me. And it has! Oh, it has, Haruka! But, anyway, it's about love. Plain and simple. That's God: love. And it transcends mere goodness. I've been trying to be good for what's seemed like so long. Be good. The Platinum Rule, I call it. But it hasn't worked. It was a moral thing, not a spiritual one. For a while things even got worse.

So then I had to master patience as a skill. This is purgatory, I thought, of course there would be waiting. You helped me do that, and especially Emerson. But it's not about being good or keeping patient. It's about loving. And in order to achieve that perfect love, obstacles need to be there. God's love is unconditional love. Love despite our faults. Lucky for us, we're bad, Haruka. All of us are bad. Every one of us is far, far from perfect. And that's why it works. We're supposed to be ourselves, a mixture of the good and the bad. But mostly the bad. Those are our best parts to God. Opposites attract. We were made in His image, but from His bad side. And He made us that way so that His love, which is really all love, can course through us, can lift us up. It's so much stronger when people aren't perfect. Demands more from us, requires more love. We love each other to heal each other and ourselves through the very substance of God."

"Yes, Ray. I understand." She reaches for his hand, strokes it lightly. She keeps doing this and he doesn't like it; he needs his hands free. All of him needs to be free right now, to think. "You are right about this, just not about what you need to do. To love me, to lift me up, you must change the grade."

"But why?" He lets his hand stay with her, for now. This is an easy enough point to address by the logic he just laid out. "Your grades wouldn't matter to those who loved you enough."

"Ray, it's about the gesture. The kindness."

"Kindness isn't the same as love."

"It's a form of it." Now she's massaging his hand. It feels very good, but he can't allow her to continue. She's not trying to keep things level and calm, she's not trying to create a space where he's all right; she's trying to coax him. But into what? Towards what she's saying or what he thinks what she's saying is actually saying? He squeezes back hard then lets her go, bringing his hand to wander in his beard: freedom.

"Sure, it's a form of it. But a very minor form. Exponentially smaller than what I'm talking about here. Agape. Everlasting and unconditional love. Compared to agape, kindness is shit. I think really it's just because you're trying to trick me."

"Ray, I'm not."

"I believe what I just said. This is my truth. And maybe you're not trying to trick me, but it wouldn't matter. I would just be wrong. In need of your understanding, your love. I'm still right about the nature of love and the nature of us." He shifts his focus from her eyes, which, clearly pained under a pulled brow, have been looking into his own, to her body. She's still nude, on top of the covers, unlike him; her torso, long in proportion to her legs and without much fat, still folds in an unflattering way with several ventral creases. He's hidden his own stomach, but imagines it's folded in a similar way, even though he also doesn't have much fat, actually has quite a bit of muscle definition. This enshrouding wasn't done out of shame. It was out of some kind of want for protection, security. His reaction is the natural one; she's just reinforcing his intuition, showing him what he needs to see. "Nobody's perfect, Haruka. Nothing's perfect. My belly is imperfect, your belly is imperfect. The Bible's imperfect, every religious text is imperfect. And that's why they lead us closer to God. They make something simple complicated to keep our rapt attention. Like a puzzle to be worked out. Faith is a puzzle meant to take someone's entire life to complete. But really, it doesn't have to. It can be as easy as understanding love. That easy. Don't just 'be good.' Love. Love as hard and as much as you can, especially with those who need it most. Take only what you need and give back far, far more. Love. Give love and give it without condition."

"Ray, you're everywhere. You're not making any sense."

"It's about embracing our imperfections, Haruka." He pulls the bedding from his lap with a sudden jerk. "I catch myself being afraid even though I don't need to be. Like during this conversation, at some point I covered my shrinking dick and ugly, wrinkled balls, all the way up past my imperfect belly. I gave myself a safety blanket, literally: a physical comfort to make me feel better about an uncomfortable conversation. But with your love, I can be nude; I can be myself. Like you are with me right now. We can be ourselves through and through. With the love I'm giving you, maybe you could do that as a student."

"Ray—"

"So what should I give you, an F? The farthest from perfect there is? Your parents and whoever else you're worried about in your form would have to give you even more love."

"No! Ray, you can't!"

"You're showing me one thing and telling me another."

She gets out of bed, puts her panties and T-shirt on. She stands between the bed and the television. "Happy now?"

"Not really, just sorta confused again."

"Let me be perfectly clear then…" Climbing back on top of the bed, she grabs both sides of his face at the cheeks using one hand, gripping tight: "If you give me an F, I will take you straight down to hell and then murder your entire family. They're still alive, remember. I can ensure they join you there. Nuclear *and* extended. This is not a test." Her eyes scan back and forth across his, searching for some confirmation he's not sure he can provide or feign. She finally lets go and sits back in her spot against the wall. Her hand comes to stroke her leg as she looks away from him.

Ray is perplexed. Her actions and words and tone and everything seem to be saying the same thing now, and it's very much at odds with where he was sure she was guiding him before. But his belief in the imperfect is too strong to be swayed. What, exactly, is going on? The best he can come up with: "Then I guess I'm just not supposed to change it? The B is imperfect enough?"

"Ray, I need an A."

"So an A-."

"Stop trying to frustrate me. No, just an A. I have to have a 4.0."

"But why?"

"You are wrong about how God works. How to get into heaven. You're just looking for shortcuts." She's still facing away, addressing the air, not him. He doesn't like what she's saying because his old friend Doubt is whispering that she could be right. Could God be in the room with them, nodding in concordance with her? Unless Ray's actually right and looking for shortcuts is a part of his imperfection? "Yes, God is about love. But it is a perfect, pure love. There must be some justice in that. Order. We're supposed to do right, not wrong. Like you said, we are made bad, Ray. And that is why it is so important to be good. At all times. Being good requires sacrifice. People can't just do what they want all the time, occasionally do some nice things for others on their own terms, call themselves loving, and still join God in heaven. You don't get to make up the rules. I need the 4.0 in order to better receive God's love. So be good, already: do what's right and help me."

Ray scratches his beard, looks away from her. Maybe he can find God in his room, too. "It's not just calling yourself loving, though. It's about actually being loving. You can't fake that. And it's impossible to be good all the time. To sacrifice all the time. Or be perfect all the time, whatever the metric. It just is. That's why your orderly love sounds like an oxymoron to me. Justice is a moral issue, love a spiritual one." Yes, she must just be trying to bewilder him. To metagrobolize him as part of her guidance. She's showing him tough love. It was a smoke bomb, her outburst of anger. If not God, he is finding truth in the room. But really, truth—something between fact and faith—leads to God. "Love isn't about rules. It's a feeling. You know when it's there and when it's not, and it can be brought on by different things for different people. That, that's truth. One's truth leads to God. Some people see it in kindness, others in tough love, like you're showing me. Someone's truth is in what they love."

"Good! So you see. My truth is telling me I need the grade changed."

"But mine isn't. It's not a real wrong you've suffered, Haruka." He looks over at her; a luminous smile fades fast. "You'll be the better for your B. B is for better. My gut is telling me that the best thing for you, and I guess me, is to make sure you keep the grade you have."

She shakes her head. "No, Ray. You're wrong. You're being stubborn and very cruel." He can make out his reflection ever so slightly in her increasingly glassy eyes. Are the inside corners wetting? Can Santa Muerte cry? Of course. Saints are, by nature, particularly lachrymal creatures—even Billy Joel knew that. But over something like this? Maybe it's a part of the trick. It must be. Stay strong.

"No, I'm not. At worst, if you're not trying to trick me, this is righteous indignation."

"Then don't be so righteous or so indignant." A single tear falls. "What I need isn't for you to say. But I can tell you that God needs this from you." Her voice strains: "He needs me to have an A in Professor Towers' class." A second tear, from the other eye, rolls down a now flush cheek. Ray wants to laugh. That last sentence, in that histrionic cadence, with that tear… it was just too much. If there was any doubt before, now he knows. The smoke has fully cleared; he sees the way.

"I don't believe you."

"You should. I'm trying to help you, but you won't listen. You still have real work to do, Ray. This isn't Mario. You don't just get to warp through worlds and get to the end in half the time. Love doesn't lead to a warp zone." But it does. Of course it does. "So if I'm to help get you where you need to be, I need you to do this for me. I need to be perfect by the terms I've described. According to my truth. Once I am perfect, I can help you be perfect. Love is very much a part of this, the most important part. But there are still rules to follow. Love is like the sun. We can harness its power, but we still revolve around it. Not the other way around. There is an order to things. Perfection requires order, not messy, careless love." That second to last bit, that thing about the sun: that was good. How does Ray reconcile that? Well, the sun—the sun will one day die. But love cannot die. God cannot die… It was just a metaphor, though. Not literal. Don't be so dense… So what then? Well, it can be said that the sun shines for us. That it and everything else were made by God for us.

Really, though, they could go back and forth on this all night, like she's the Grand Inquisitor or some shit. Just trust the gut and speak from it. Hell, the gut and reason are in agreement on this one. "But what you're asking for almost objectively doesn't make sense. Grades don't matter Haruka. If I helped you with this, that would feel careless to me. Because nobody should care that you got a B. Nobody ever asked to see my grades after college. No one will ask to see yours. What would any of this have to do with anything?"

"You say this because you never made it out of college. Remember? You were already dead."

"Yeah, but you're not alive either."

"It's a complicated thing, this form, Ray." She wipes her eyes. "I am a person. Flesh and blood. I am two in one. You just had my flesh. You should know this." Her voice has returned to normal, is stronger even. She did not say "You just had my flesh" in a way that suggested she was trying to guilt him, that sex should be viewed as capital. Everything was said as fact. And it is. Her form *is* a tricky thing—she *is* a tricky thing. He is having a romantic and sexual relationship with a girl who is a little too young for him and who he also views as a saint. It's all a bit fucked up. But she's not a real saint; she's a folk saint. Believing in her is blasphemous, and that's why this makes sense. He was never a great Catholic. And she's not so much younger than him that this would be illegal or gross if he were still alive; some people just might view it as sort of strange, a twenty-six-year-old with a nineteen-year-old. Just a little strange—not even Woody Allen strange, their age gap is such that it would just be a little... off. These are two wrongs that make a right, and it makes sense. Of course. He's always been a tad hedonistic, a tad grimy, but with a good heart. His faith journey has always been on his terms; it would be for everyone. It is a Choose Your Own Adventure. And he's just now starting to choose wisely.

Ray's glad he was able to buy into her emotion, that he recognized it. It rang through as the truth. He's no longer compelled to laugh—this is serious, and it should be handled as such. Even if what she claims she wants is stupid, he should treat her with respect. "I know, I know. You're not just a projection, you're much more important than that. But even if you were alive, and you weren't Santa Muerte, you were just a nineteen-year-old girl named Haruka Kidokoro, your grades wouldn't matter. Even when I was alive I knew nobody would look at them once I got out. That's what everyone always said. Unless you were going to grad school, nobody cared. And even then it didn't really matter as long as your overall GPA was decent and you could demonstrate your seriousness in other ways."

"Ray..." She shakes her head slowly, then, a moment later, the tears return. This is very odd. Can he believe her crying now? They are quiet tears, tears of frustration, it seems. She covers her face. Now a few sounds... They've become tears of desperation. "I worked... so hard for this... you can't even know."

Oh, boy. Ray is in a bind. She's not crying for any remotely good reason, but they're not crocodile tears, either. He can tell she really, really means them. Is it possible that she does have her own journey to go on? That she's not just here to help him with his? And that getting an A in Emerson's class would—whatever the rationale—do her some good? That they in fact need each other? Like he just said, she's not merely a projection. And also like he just said, her grades don't matter. So why not just change it? If they don't matter and it's that easy? For her? She'd still be imperfect, she'd still play into his narrative in a way that he needs her to. Except instead of her parents or whoever having to love her more, he'd have to love her more: remembering this fight, how unreasoned the request was, the trouble this episode had put him through. Is there something to any of this? "Hmmm. Maybe you're right. Maybe if you had perfect grades you'd be a worse person? Most people who care this much about their GPAs are assholes, kind of soulless."

She sniffles, uncovers her face. She wipes her eyes. Ray's feeling kind of shitty about his frostiness throughout this conversation now. Especially that last part, now that he remembers what those kids had said to her growing up. Fuck. Has he been too selfish, too harsh to his guide? "Yes, Ray. It's because I need to be more of a soulless asshole. It's not my parents as Haruka I'd need more love from. It's you. I know you don't care about my grades, and that doing this would make you lose respect for me. It would mean you would have to love me more. You see, it's about you. It's always about you."

But, but, but... then that last hypothesis wouldn't make any sense. "This is pretty confusing, Haruka." Ray searches the room again for truth—his dresser, his walls, his blank, black television. If she has her own journey, then how could it all be about him? It couldn't. So either she's not on her own journey or she is indeed trying to deceive him— but to what end? Was all that stuff about hell and murder and his family a bluff, a part of the test? To see how strong his faith in the imperfect is?

But she would still be more flawed in his eyes if he gave her an A; she's right about that... That form of imperfection would be worse than changing the grade to an F, which would matter more to her and her family. What would matter to *him* would be the respect thing. So he should change it to an A! Unless she just wants him to think he should do that for some reason? It couldn't be as easy as the thing she originally asked. Maybe she told him that it was about him as another form of guiding him and that it isn't really. Has he been selective about what he's been told and takes at face value and what he's been told as some strange test this entire time? Where is the truth? "I think I'll need a couple of days to think about this."

"No, Ray. Just do it now. Let's get your computer."

She leans forward, toward it—another hand fast approaching Adam's and God's. No. He puts his hand on hers before it can make it. "Haruka, even if I wanted to, I'd have to wait until I was on Emerson's computer. I'm sure they can trace IP addresses and all that shit."

"IP addresses don't matter in the afterlife, Ray. Trust me."

"But grades do?" No, of course not. But then there's her form and her own possible journey and who knows what else? Right?

"Just do it and see what happens. Wonderful things will happen for you. You say you trust me, so trust me."

"I do trust you. But I have to read between the lines with you a lot, I know this. That's what I trust."

"Not right now, Ray."

"Just let me think a minute."

"Okay." And he does. They sit there in silence, him naked, her in her T-shirt and underpants, fingers stroking her hair. He goes back over everything. And it pretty much all conflicts. There are several cases to be made either way. A complicated puzzle with a simple solution. Like life, like faith. It doesn't matter what he does, as long as he does it with love.

▲▽▽▲▲▲▲

Oh, please, please, please, please! Please let this idiot do the right thing! Wait, who is she praying to? She almost sounds like him. Oh, God. There she goes again! Spending time with him is toxic. She meant it before, when she was crying. She's been through so much, having to deal with him! But it could end here! As long as he does the right thing, the reasonable thing! The only thing! He's just been staring at the wall in his small, stupid room for almost five minutes. People into religious things are terrifying, really! The bizarre laptop skin was one thing, but now this?! What the hell is he looking at? She must remain calm. Logic will lead him to the correct choice. It must. Out of her peripheral vision, Haruka sees him swallow. It looks like he is about to speak. She turns to him and he does—"I feel like you're really trying to guide me away from doing what you're telling me to do. That's the thing my gut is telling me, and that's also the thing that would make the most sense."

"Gaaaah!" she groans, pulling at her hair. She has been so good during this whole ridiculous conversation. Agreeing with him, playing into his nonsense. But every time she does, he just flips it back, contradicts himself and her. There is no reasoning with him! She can only yell now and pull her hair! "This is so stupid!"

"Haruka, just relax."

No. She doesn't have to relax. She had been relaxed for the last half hour going back an eternity! "Ray! You must! If you don't, I'll break up with you!"

He flinches, scratches his head. Sometimes it takes a big threat like this to get things done. Now he'll see! How important this is, just what's at stake. Hopefully, that is what it—"Okay." What?

He couldn't be so nonchalant about this. He just said he loved her, how could he have such a reaction? Be so blasé? And more importantly, if he accepts the breakup, what has all this been for?! It would be a waste! "No, it's not okay!"

"If you broke up with me, then I would be sad. But I'd still love you. And maybe that would be better. Our relationship would be broken, but the love I have for you would still be there, as strong as ever. Maybe even stronger. And of course I'd be hurt, so I'd need even more of my own love." There he goes again—talking crazy! People need to be together to be in love. They need the exchange of endorphins and oxytocin, duh!

She breathes deep, does her best: "No, Ray. That is not how love works. It thrives on inertia. We would be much happier together, there would be so much more love between us."

"Love doesn't thrive on inertia. There's a reason why the divorce rate is what it is in this country. But look at people in arranged marriages in other cultures. They often have great bonds." What. The. Fuck. What in the actual fuck is this dumb motherfucker talking about? Arranged marriages?! What does that have to do with anything?! "It's because of all the obstacles they had to overcome to fall in love in the first place. Their relationships don't start out as storybooks, but they always end happily. They're fundamentally flawed, so they require more love."

Haruka is done. She just can't. This is now officially a giant waste of her time. And if she's not leaving here with her grade changed, she's still leaving here with something. Some form of satisfaction. She will tell him what he is! At least that might make her feel a little better! "You! You are an idiot!"

He smiles and just sort of shrugs. "In some ways, yeah. We all are."

Crying, bawling… she can't believe this is happening. It was all for nothing! Nothing! All the time she spent… and actually falling for him a little! Stupid chemicals! Talk about an arranged marriage, this was just like that, Ray… Oh! Maybe he'll still help her, maybe she only needs to say it one more time—"Change my grade, Ray! Please!"

"I now know I can't. It's not the right thing to do. I'm sad to see you go, but I get it."

Haruka wipes her eyes. How could she let herself show so much in front of him? Another thing to be sad about, this great shame. But instead of more tears, she redirects it. What she's feeling needs to go out, not in. "I never liked you Ray. I never loved you. This was all a trick to get my grade changed."

"Oh, come on Haruka."

"And I saw other men constantly. I cheated on you constantly."

"You did?" Of course he'd ask about that one, he wouldn't be so blasé about that one. For such a difficult person deep down he's rather simple: like all of them. Vain and stupid.

"Yes."

"I guess I must've needed that for some reason."

Oh, goodness. Enough! Enough of this insanity! She will tell him. This will feel the best of all! "This isn't the afterlife, Ray. Here's the big news, which I'm sure you've known all along: you're not dead, you're just nuts."

"Now I know that's not true."

"It is."

"I love you, Haruka. But I won't miss all the games. I know my truth. That's not true." And she won't miss anything about him! His ugly face, the dumb things he says, like just then… his stupid run-down room and apartment. Good riddance! Moron! She scurries out of his bed, puts her shorts on in a frenzy. Finds her bag. Does she have everything? Her phone? It's in the bag. Everything she needs… except the one thing she needed most! Her grade! Oh, why?!?! There will be another way. There has to be. Time to get out of here and find it; she's misused enough of her time here with him.

"You deserve to be the loser that you are, Ray. Goodbye forever!"

"Come here, Haruka."

"No." She steps forward and reaches for the doorknob.

"One last kiss! That's how everyone should say goodbye."

She turns to him. He gets out of bed, still fully nude, something she's only noticing again now that she's no longer blinded by anticipation or sadness or anger. It's no use indulging any of those things now. He looks weird. Especially his penis retreating into itself like a turtle, the testicles hanging asymmetrically. He pulls her close, looks into her eyes. Haruka allows him to kiss her, but she keeps her eyes open. He does not. Was there anything nice about this relationship? Not really. His tongue slips past her lips, caresses hers. It feels nice, normal, comforting. She can't believe what's happened. The relationship did give her hope for a while, she supposes. That was something. Got her through her internship with a happy enough demeanor. And she also came a few times, which was fun. It hasn't been a complete loss. But it's been mostly a loss. And fuck him for kissing her one last time like he means it, like he really loves her. She bites down hard on his lip.

"Ahhhh!" he screams, pulling away. His lip is bloody.

"That's how everyone should say goodbye, Ray."

He holds it, tries to suppress the blood flow. "Okay, I understand. And I love you still. Goodbye, Haruka."

"What the fuck. Such a fucktard." He is. He really, really is. She leaves the room, Ray naked and bleeding and putting tissues on his lip. They come from the same tissue box they usually use to clean up after sex. She wishes she had instead given him a goodbye blowjob and had done that. Oh well. That might've been too gross, anyway. The room-mate is standing in the hallway, seemingly eavesdropping. She didn't bother to close the door. "Go ahead and take a look."

"Nah, I'm good."

She approaches him. He sort of flinches, and she smiles, reaches for his shoulders. She whispers in his ear, "Me and Ray are broken up now. Find me on OkCupid if you ever wanna fuck. Missing pieces, no i's." Then she turns sharply, steps quickly. The brain is attracted to fast-moving objects. Hopefully he'll find her. Ray would deserve that, too. She intentionally doesn't look back into his room as she rounds the corner. On her way out, she leaves the apartment door open, too.

Sometimes plans don't come together. It's okay. The important thing is to remain optimistic. And adaptable. To pay attention to what's here, now, while always keeping a bright and happy future in the back of your mind and at the finish line somewhere in front of your eyes. Another opportunity will show itself.

▲▽▲▽▽▽

Positive vibes radiate all around, everything here is wonderful. When people speak of quality of life, when cities promote theirs, this is what they're talking about, this is the quintessential image: people enjoying recreational activities on a sunny day near a body of water. The same can be said of the afterlife, Ray supposes. And New York City's quality of afterlife is so fucking on point this Sunday afternoon as he glides down this Midtown stretch of Hudson River Park.

The other cyclists, the pedestrians, even the rollerbladers, who are normally oh so silly—he's got nothing but love for them, and it seems they him. He's approaching the Intrepid as part of a little pack of other individual cyclists who've found themselves riding together for the last minute or two as they've carefully navigated around the slower folks on this somewhat-congested portion of the path. Usually riding like this with other people would annoy him greatly, but not today. The sun's high, humidity's low, the air clean and crisp; the few clouds are pure white and fluffy in the azure September sky; the temperature's in the low-mid seventies with a cool breeze coming off the water, and it's impossible to get mad about anything.

When they pass the Intrepid, they are greeted with a heroes' welcome. A covey of children in matching chartreuse T-shirts, probably members of some weekend youth program, line the pathway, clapping and cheering with huge smiles on their little faces at the sight of the cyclists. One of them has a bubble gun and shoots a flurry of large bubbles at them. A few hit Ray, one even on his freshly shaved cheek. Did they think they were a part of a bike race that might be happening? Or were they just on their way to the ship and got excited at seeing Ray and his new pathway friends looking cool on their bikes? It doesn't matter. All that matters is that moment was glorious.

The little cavalcade Ray's found himself in disperses when they get to Pier 83 and the cabs dropping people off for Circle Line tours complicate things, disrupting their path, some cyclists rushing to beat them, some riding alongside them, some stopping, like Ray. He's back to not wearing a helmet again, and though he feels like it's for a good reason—a form of kenosis: without cephalic protection, he must place his full trust in God—he's still going to do his best to avoid unnecessary trouble. Ray was glad to ride with those guys for a while, but their stint as a unit is over now. Time to ride as he usually does, alone, but today not against everyone, just on his own, a solitary figure on a shared path paved with peace and love and unity. When the cabs stop coming, he resumes his ride.

The mind does some of its best wandering when the body's moving forward. This is true on a bike, or on foot, or on a plane, train, or in an automobile, anything. There's just something about steady onward motion that's uniquely conducive to shedding any hang-ups and inviting real mental latitude. And, it seems, conversely, the mind is best at plunging forward, at submitting itself to something and following a fixed path, when the body is stationary. In a quiet room between sixty-eight and seventy-four degrees, wearing clothes that are snug but comfortable, sitting upright. Free of any distraction. Unlike out here, the room has no exigencies, so the mind makes up its own. Work, it says. Or watch, read. Dedicate me to something specific. A mind narrows in on that thing then moves resolutely toward it, doing its best to ward off anything that might interrupt or alter its course; thought is a train, consciousness a stream...

It's kind of crazy to think that he did this for work for a while. What could be better? But then again, it wasn't exactly this. It wasn't seventy-three and sunny; it was cold, brutal, the last leg of a terrible winter then the thaw of spring, and he was hardly ever able to move in one long, fluvial line. He had to move everywhere, all around Midtown and the lower island, and wherever it was, he was late, always. That's no way to do work. Good work is done with dignity, and there is no dignity in rushing. And plus, the money was shit.

Passing an old shipping complex on his right and the Javits Center on his left, the sky opens up along with the river at this part of the greenway. Any Midtown skyscrapers in view are deeply recessed, Jersey seems like a faraway land, on some *Game of Thrones* shit. He pedals ahead into the panorama.

For as strange as his current job is, he's never really had to rush, not like while a bike messenger. Even when he worked that marathon, or now only going in part-time, with Emerson back teaching classes. The workflow has always been smooth, steady; there's never been a notion of doing things to alleviate anxiety. And that system seems to be paying off. From what he can tell, the first draft of the book is almost complete. They're "nearing the end of the carnage" now, as the big guy describes it. The Culture, according to Emerson, does not die a dignified death. It's been stricken by madness, bombarded by strange forces, many of its own making, now out of its control, and it's started to cannibalize itself. Ray wouldn't be surprised if the thing ends with some sort of horrific suicide, like setting itself on fire, a burning limb dangling from its mouth.

And as his writing's grown more violent, Emerson's never been easier to deal with. Though, they're probably not related. Really, he's been sort of a pussycat ever since Ray defeated him. Which would only make sense. But it's not only that he made him more agreeable that day; he's earned more than just his respect. Now Emerson calls him "dear" and "darling" all the time. It was a little weird at first, but something he soon surmised was a mark of familiarity in its strictest sense: like Ray's family now. Like Emerson loves him. It's sort of sad. His daughter only came around that one day, and Ray learned he also has a son, but they haven't spoken in decades. That's actually a part of the reason Ray shaved; in addition to it being kind of cathartic after the whole Haruka situation, he feels he can fill in that role for him a little better clean-shaven. Having this kind of presence in his life makes Ray feel good. He's been told that once he's gotten through a third or fourth draft, something fitting for his editor, which would likely be in another six months or so at their current rate, but maybe sooner, that he'd like to keep Ray on to continue assisting him with this and that, still come in a couple of times a week and help him go over his lecture notes, or cook for him and straighten up, then eventually manage any print, television, or radio interview requests he's sent. Ray sees it as him looking for excuses to have him around, basically paying for his companionship. But he's cool with that, especially since Emerson's also suggested he could hook him up with some freelance work once this first draft is done, mentioning by name *The New Yorker, New York Times, Harper's,* and *The Atlantic.* A fucking dream come true, any of those would be. Sure, he probably wouldn't be able to do his thing at full gonzo, but a part of journalism's perversion and the rise of infotainment is that voice is very important these days, and compared to the type of stuff he used to work on? Compared to fucking listicles for fucking nonsense blogs? Shit… if only he were alive so he could really enjoy it.

But he's not, and he has to remind himself of that sometimes. Ever since Haruka said what she said.

Ray passes the Frying Pan, this weird old boat they turned into a bar on Pier 66. He went there once for someone's birthday party or something and was amazed, at the time, at how they let a bunch of people who had been drinking run around the decks and inside of this rickety timeworn ship, with multiple levels and low guardrails and rusty shit everywhere—like, for insurance reasons. But now that he knows he's dead it totally makes sense. It's because they weren't allowed to do that, the people weren't real. It was a sign that he was dead. Something absolutely absurd to let him know he wasn't alive anymore and that it couldn't have been actually happening. Otherwise, people would be getting injured all the time, or worse. Now, as he understands it, mostly douchebags go there and it's a place to be avoided. A defense mechanism he created, perhaps, to keep him on a forward-looking path and not go searching for clues at irrelevant blasts from the past. He tries not to think about that, invites back only the good vibes, takes in what's around him and ahead. The leaves on the trees lining the strip to his left show the first pale yellow traces of turning. Time moves on and so must he.

It's hard, though. To move on right now. Perhaps the key concept there was relevance; the Frying Pan doesn't matter, but there are things in the past that do, especially the recent past. Maybe he's supposed to reflect a little right now. Let the mind do its thing… look back for a bit and feel confused or hurt or weird if he needs to. Inside doesn't need to be as pretty as the outside. Because a part of the reason he embarked on this excursion—his Bible in tow inside his backpack—down to Battery Park for a little recharging, then on to service at St. Patrick's, is because of how badly he misses Haruka. The important thing is to not dwell; it's okay to stop by, but don't stay for long. Honor the pain briefly, give it the deference it deserves, tell it you love it, then it will let you go. Set you free. Yes, there are enough adages to support this. No pain, no gain. If you love something, set it free… For pain to love you back, then set you free, you must first learn to love it.

Like he learned to love Haruka. It's strange. They never really got along all that well outside of the bedroom. Like, they never became real friends. Didn't have that much in common, their personalities clashed, minds didn't really meet. But he did love her eventually. And no matter what she said, he knows she loved him. They became lovers. Real lovers. Not in the way creepy old people use that term; it wasn't just about the physical—the sex *plus* the strange things she said during it was what made their relationship seem so meaningful… Haruka's body and the spirit of Santa Muerte coming together with him, his body filling hers and her words filling his soul… until she didn't have to say anything at all. Until the act felt just as meaningful without the words, until they were no longer needed. And by that point, they still weren't really friends? Did he love her all the more because of this, to make up for it, physically? Perhaps. Their loving was about creating an experience, and it seems that they were both almost compulsively drawn to it.

He still beats off to her. But now when he does it, Haruka's body is absent and it's just to the part of her that's Santa Muerte. He masturbates to the words that she had said, not the words themselves, the words of literary titans, but the act of her having said the words: her lips parting, breath pushing them out, the distinct sounds made by her strong little voice, how they entered the air then his ears then his brain and settled in there, getting warped by memory… but not really because he doesn't have a brain and whatever words were spoken weren't really, and if they exist anywhere now, it's in his very soul. Words. These words you can rarely remember verbatim but that you can't forget because of how they made you feel. It is this feeling that he thinks of most. Sometimes after he comes, he's so taken with the beauty of it, he tears up a little. Yes, he misses Haruka, but he is still very much in an active relationship with Santa Muerte. She's still his guide, his love. And she's doing a damn good job.

Just look at him now, flying down the path, nothing but positivity directed at everyone around. All of these people here rambling about Chelsea Piers are beautiful, even the ugly ones.

Now that Haruka's gone, Ray's been reading the Bible from start to finish, out loud, quietly, hoping for a certain rapture. A search for the right spell—the right words that hold the key. And Santa Muerte has led him here. It's not blasphemous if you truly believe; the only real blasphemy is not believing in anything.

▲▽▲▽▽▽▲

The usual buzz then the usual knock at the usual time… he takes the chain from the top, unbolts the latch, and opens the door—to a most *unusual* development! Emerson is elated! The beard! Ray's beard is finally gone! Oh, what a day! What a welcome surprise!

"My goodness! And who are you, stranger?" He laughs to himself as the boy—and oh, now isn't he just the very image of that?—enters the apartment, even wearing his backpack on this day!

Ray scratches his head. "Yeah, switching it up again I guess. Summer's pretty much over, the leaves will fall soon, so I figured my facial hair should, too."

"That's quite lovely, dear. It's like your face is a piece of performance art." Emerson, of course, hates performance art—art is always recorded while performance is just that, performance… something fleeting, ephemeral. But he figured Ray might have some appreciation for it, like many young ignoramuses.

"I don't know about that, but yeah." He drops his bag at his workstation, rests one hand on his chair. "So I suppose I should get to the new pages?" Apparently the boy is in no mood to talk about the latest look, like he was in no mood the day Emerson brought up the beard. But no matter. The main thing is that today is the day; that is certain. Not just yet, Emerson still must plot, he must think, but all of the conditions are in place: he has his own beard now, grown to a respectable enough length, and the first draft of the book is nearly complete. "Yes, of course. Don't want to hold you up. And I'll take my coffee now too, please."

"You got it." He still says things like this—but not for long. No, soon such hard-edged street slang will no longer be an issue, will no longer pollute the air here. Not after Emerson tames him. Then he will speak with perfect grammar at all times and will himself be perfect, and he must be. For in a short while Emerson will begin work on the second draft of the elegy. As impassioned and enthralling and beautiful as his from-the-heart, off-the-cuff prose has been, the real art of writing is, of course, in rewriting. So far what he's done has been little more than mere performance; soon it will be time to find the sublime in it, to eliminate all else, then write around it, repeating the process until all that's left is the truly magnificent—until all that's left is the highest of art, perfection. In order to do that, though, in order to really live through those words, in their meaning and in their rhythm, there must be no disturbances in his life whatsoever, especially here at work. There can be no more alarms going off like "You got it," but he also can't be bothered to make his own coffee, cook his own food, or order takeout. Only by domesticating Ray can he get there.

"Sorry, I know you're ready to move on from this, but I really must say I forgot how fresh-faced you were. If you don't mind me asking, how old, exactly, are you?"

"Twenty-six," Ray says. Just about what Emerson thought. A little old, but still but a boy by today's standards. He's facing away from him, turning on the computer, his hair, an inch or two longer since he hired him, and more prominent now that he's shaved the beard, awkwardly poking out over his ears.

"Twenty-six, my word. What an age, especially now. In my day, you'd likely be married, perhaps with a little one already. I was thirty when I had my son. But my how times have changed. Look at you, you're still the epitome of youth."

Ray turns, smiling as he crosses the room toward the kitchen, and replies, "Yeah, I don't know too many people like that. Only a few of my friends back in Texas." Now that the focus is off of him and his beard, he seems to be loosening up. He opens the cabinet to get the coffee grounds.

"No, no, it's a good thing. Youth—it's so beautiful, so magical. I'm glad your generation's extended it. You should enjoy it as long as possible. And you really are the beau ideal, the very image of it without the beard." Is he laying it on too thick? No, he couldn't with this one. "I'll miss having my beard buddy, but I understand, Ray, I understand."

"It's a good look on you, Emerson. Glad you're having fun with it."

Fun… heretofore it's been quite the opposite of that—itchy, then hot, far too irritating throughout, even if it's now given him the appearance of having one instead of several chins—but it seems like some *fun* is finally in store, oh yes! "Thank you, yes indeed. Well, I better get back to work now." As Ray continues to measure out the coffee into the filter with precise sifting motions, Emerson returns to his office.

He's so excited, he can't even bring himself to wrap up his brief coverage of Hemingway—such a simple, surface-level wordsmith he could normally write about him in his sleep, though it would probably lead to a nightmare: the man was a bastard, a devil whose celebrated adventure club, glamour-filled lifestyle and slapdash, no-frills prose led far too many a loutish idiot to think they could and should write, too. He was someone who relied almost solely on emotion and very little on expanding thought or the immense pleasures of pulling out the dictionary, whose place really should have been with the rest of the hacks in the twentieth century writing for the movies. The man had more in common with his excessive drinking and fighting and hunting and fishing with the average Red State imbecile than he did with his good friend the genius James Joyce, and his influence, not Joyce's, is still the predominant one today. Pure madness, the Culture more animal than man now, as if stricken by rabies. But he can't even articulate that on the page.

It's not fair. He already knows what he's going to do, how to initiate it, what to say—has fantasized about this day for almost six weeks now. Perhaps it would help if he saw *it* on the page.

Perhaps once it's real there, he can move on…

Flipping through his notepad, Emerson reaches the very last piece of paper and rips it out. He writes down his plan, frantically, his hand in a dead sprint. He sees it, smells it, tastes it, hears it, and he feels it; oh, how he feels it!

And just as Emerson is ready to get back to work, the boy himself stands in front of him with what will be his first cup of coffee of the day, and he again becomes flushed. The wait… waiting really is the worst. But he can't. Not yet. The scene he limned on the page, that's the way it should transpire.

But what of spontaneity? Hasn't he conceded that romance requires it? Love is not an art, it is a force, and the act of love is one that must be put into motion. It is a performance! Needing natural, impulsive brio! To hell with the plan! To hell with the wine and the onset of dusk and currying his favor with a takeout lunch of his choosing. Let the affair begin this morning, in a new dawn! And anyway, the move might benefit from the circumstances around it seeming less contrived; Ray is dumb but not that dumb. Oh no! This is now sounding, too, like a plan—do it now, just do it! Ray sets the coffee down on the desk and Emerson gently places his hand upon his wrist before he can turn away. "Ray, what would you say if I asked you to sit on my lap?" he asks.

▲▽▲▽▽▲▽

Wait, what? He couldn't have really just said that. Right? No, no… Ray must've simply heard him wrong; it's early, after all—not all of his faculties work so well until he himself has some coffee. Fuckin' ears. But then… why is Emerson's hand still on his wrist? "Sorry?"

"What would you say if I asked you to sit on my lap?" Holy shit, that *is* what he actually said. Ray reaches over with his other hand and removes Emerson's from his wrist.

"Are you feeling okay?"

"Come on, darling. Don't answer my question with one of your own. If there's a Socrates here, it's me. That's one of the reasons I can no longer see a shrink. Why I haven't in years. The question thing is sort of mine. Some personal traits one holds dear just can't be co-opted."

Ray backs away, knocking into the bookshelf. The old man is smiling at him, his eyes like the center of a flame burning blue-white. Ray knows he doesn't have Alzheimer's or anything; he's way too sharp for that. Something's up. "What… the hell is going on?"

"I'm sorry you're having this reaction. I figured you might, but hoped not. It is a pity."

"So you're serious right now."

"No inflection, but that still seemed very much like a question. You've asked three now and haven't even answered my one." And he's being a dick about it, to boot? It's way too fucking early for this shit.

Unless it isn't. Could this be happening, right now, for a reason?

This, like so many strange incidents before, is surely a test from God. So Ray asks himself to what extent is he willing to suffer? How imperfect is he supposed to become? Does he need to compromise that much of himself, break himself in that particular way so he can love himself more? Because there isn't anyone else here who's supposed to supply love to him now. No Haruka… and Emerson, he's no paternal figure… That's the most fucked up part about this. Ray thought all this "dear" and "darling" shit was out of some sort of fatherly affection. But it was far from that, he now sees. If Emerson was any kind of guide before, he is no longer: his role has been clearly defined, and it's one of betrayal. Ray is supposed to hurt, is supposed to need more of God's love, that much is true, but he's not supposed to endure the unique physical pain Emerson has in mind, or the resultant emotional trauma. No. He will not sit on his lap. He will not let his Santa Claus-looking Moloch of a boss butt-fuck him. That is no way into heaven; he is supposed to feel heartsick, and he does. "I'm not sitting on your lap."

"Ray, I'd like to talk to you for a moment about the Greeks and how they relate to the next phase of our project."

"Oh, *Sweet Jesus...*"

"You see, in ancient Greece, in many arrangements such as ours, the mentor and the mentee, or the erastes and the eromenos as they were called, would have a physical component to their relationship..." Emerson's hands come to fold on his large stomach. He couldn't be more casual about this, and it would seem truly bizarre if Ray didn't now understand he's supposed to be more Judas, Brutus, or Cassius than Virgil, or if he hadn't been aware of his past. Should he have known all along? No. They were all women before, he had read... he couldn't have seen this coming... "strengthening their bond and thus the work they completed together, as well as lifting their individual spirits through pleasurable sensat—"

"I'm aware of the pederasty practices in ancient Greece, Emerson."

"Good! Then you're aware that the bond between the erastes and the eromenos was one of the most sacred, beautiful bonds there could be—stronger, even, than that between a man and his wife. For you see, that was for mere procreation. This other bond was for education, citizenry, the soul! The stuff that makes life worth living, not just the animalistic creation of yet more meaningless life—"

"That's all well and good for them but we're not in ancient Greece."

"Oh, if only." When Ray said "*Sweet Jesus*" before it was not saying the Lord's name in vain, it was a prayer. The start of the prayer he made up earlier this year and has been saying nightly since. He finishes it now, subvocally:

> *Let us live*
> *In love together*
> *As love forever*

He needs His help, His love, and limitless patience to withstand listening to this shit. Did Emerson feed the young women the same lines in decades past, tweaked with some perverse rhetoric about feminism and the history of educational systems in order to get beyond the same-sex part? How long has he been planning this with him? From the very beginning or only recently? And wait, is that what all that shit with his beard was about?! Oh, God. And he fell for it! All of those ridiculous questions and comments… ¡Diantre! Now he wishes he never would have shaved. Something is beginning to coalesce from the confusion, fast becoming hot and dense deep in Ray's abdomen. "I'm also aware of your history with assistants and students. Why you're no longer at Columbia."

"That nonsense. All a terrible misunderstanding."

"The answer, again, is no, Emerson. I'm not going to sit on your lap."

Emerson simpers. "Ray! I don't think you fully comprehend what this invitation means. The work we're doing here, the importance of it. The book needs—" Oh, man. Ray can't listen to this shit anymore. He really can't.

It's time to flip the script, time for Emerson to listen to him for a fucking change! The thing in his stomach knows what to say: "No, you're the one having trouble with comprehension. This isn't ancient fucking Greece and I'm not your eromenos!" The old man's mouth droops, his hands unfold and come to grasp the armrests of his chair; that oh-so-smug disposition has died a hard death. "Even if I were homosexual, this would be wildly inappropriate. I'm like fifty years younger than you and your fucking employee!"

"Ray!" Now red and shaking, Emerson stands tall. He spits his words—"You do not speak to me this way! Silence that vulgar tongue, you savage!" Savage? Oh, what the fuck? "I am Emerson Towers!" He's moving forward, one of his chubby fucking fingers advancing closer and closer to Ray's face. Nu-uh. No fucking way. "I demand respect! You, you are nothing! The only way you will ever matter is by association with me!" Ray's backed up all the way to the bookshelf now, and Emerson pushes forward still. "So let me do what I need to do!" The finger-wagging hand dives down and grabs at his polo, like he's trying to consume him, like he's trying to take him by force. Ray punches him hard in the gut and he quickly releases him, then falls over, knocking down some books with a flailing arm. "Ahhhh!"

"I used to think you were like Virgil, man. A good dude and a good guide, delivering me from something. I thought the weird shit you'd ask me to do sometimes was making me better, stronger. But this is something else completely. Now I see you're more like the judge in *Blood Meridian*. The only difference is I'm no savage and I'm no kid. Try to touch me again and I'll really fuck you up."

"Go! Get out of here you ingrate! You're fired, Ray! Fired!"

"You can't fire someone who clearly just quit."

Emerson tries to get up amidst the books, but slips. "You would say that, you fool!" His breathing stertorous, he comes to rest on his side, holding on to a shelf for support. "You were a terrible assistant! One of the worst I've ever had!"

Even though Ray knows he was a damn good assistant and that less egomaniacal employers often feel their employees would be nothing without them, these invectives still cut. But why? Why should any of this barking matter, these minor insults on top of such a major injury? Because Ray needs to continue fighting. Needs to pursue all that is right in this moment. Emerson is no guide, Ray only has God now. "Just pay me what you owe me and I'll be on my way."

"You expect me to pay you after that? You just clouted me, you brute!"

"Are you a demon, Emerson?" Yes, Ray is shining a light on him. Asking him a question to tell him something about himself, like he might try to do, this wannabe Socrates, stealing his powers to expose him to himself and Ray's knowledge of his true essence to God.

"If anyone is the demon here, it's you!"

"That won't work, Emerson. I hold the light here, and the mirror. Not you."

"Oh, Raymond Gonzales. The great poet. It's"—Emerson lifts himself up, spluttering—"been an honor, but I'm afraid all good things must come to an end. Now go!"

"You owe me a week's pay. I'm not leaving till I get it."

"Ray, I could sue you for far more than you're worth. It's entirely possible I just bruised my hip and will need an operation. We'll call it even. You're getting a tremendous bargain here."

"I just want what's rightfully mine, Emerson. Please don't make me hurt you again." Is this still righteous indignation or is it verging on wrath? The threat itself isn't wrath. It's just that, a threat. He doesn't really want to punch him again.

"Oh, haven't you done enough? What kind of way is this to treat an old man?!" Emerson, still breathing heavily, retucks his shirt.

No, Ray doesn't actually want to hit him again—at all. It was effective then; he became physical after Emerson became physical, but here it wouldn't be. Ray knows what this motherfucker needs now, what he deserves. Words: "You're hardly some helpless old man. You're an abusive blowhard, a bully. And you fooled me for long enough. So you're going to get me my money now or me hitting you again will be the least of your worries. I'll delete the file. Throw the backup hard drives out the fucking window. Start tearing up pages."

"You really are a mongrel, an implacable fiend. I don't know how I could have been so reckless to let you in." Emerson shakes his head. "Fine. I'll get you some cash." Ray backs away, lets him pass. Good. It's almost over...

Unless! He follows him out of the office, down the hall. Emerson turns around. "What are you doing?"

"I'm following you to make sure you don't try any bullshit before I get my money."

"Oh, this really is beyond the pale!" But it isn't. He could try to call the cops, grab a weapon, do any number of things to thwart Ray's triumphant moment, deny him before God. They enter the room together. It's the first time Ray's ever been in here... it's dark and dirty, with clothes strewn about, snack food wrappers littering the nightstand, a dresser that hasn't been dusted in months if not years. It's stranger still to be here now—to see his bed, which he's currently crouched under, retrieving money from a shoe box—considering what he had proposed. But Ray's gotta do what Ray's gotta do. Emerson stands up, rubs the money between his fingers. "Ray, you know actual penetration isn't involved, right? The Greeks only had intercrural sex. The erastes just rubs it between the eromenos's thighs."

Good Lord. Sweet Jesus. Mother Mary. Santa Muerte. All the angels and saints and powers that be. Dear, dear God. What a test indeed. This has been the hardest boss fight he's had to go through. Emerson is like a pedophile priest and Bowser in one. "So it's not just food, then? You're a glutton for punishment as well? Say one more fucked up thing to me, man."

"Oh, here." Emerson extends the small stack of bills, a corner of the bed between them. "Take it and go."

Ray reaches out and snatches the money. He counts it. The math seems right. He puts it in his pocket, then starts down the hallway, happy, victorious, his mind set on grabbing his backpack and leaving.

But then: "Enjoy your life of utter mediocrity, you *internet journalist*."

He stops. That was a very strange thing to hear him say. The word "life" referring to his own is always jarring when it lands between the ears now... especially when spoken by a figure Ray knows not to be a projection. Sort of like with Haruka upon their goodbye telling him he's not dead, just nuts. So what is Emerson, exactly? He would ask that of Haruka all the time, but seemed to accept Emerson straightaway in his role as a guide, this guy bringing him toward better books and out of poverty. It was almost as if he were an incarnation of the knowledge Ray had taken for granted and ignored—all the great old texts he had overlooked during his life in favor of reading magazine articles and blog posts and more relatable novels and watching TV and movies and playing video games. Here was a man so interested in thought, the mind, that he had let his body go to shit: there was no need for a normally functioning form, his was all swollen mass of brain, while Ray was slim and trim upon his death. Yes, Emerson was knowledge, and in some ways reason, and with the betrayal, it's now more like he's supposed to represent the limitations of that, of what can be learned through epistemological methods alone. Books will only get you so far; it's vital to trust in what's there outside of your comprehension, that which you can't really know: God. Even the books about Him don't come close. So maybe it's really Him that's been saying these things. While it wouldn't be completely out of Emerson's character to come at him with something like that—of course he'd want the last word—the thing he said is just too perfect. Something that, were Ray alive, would play into too many of his insecurities. These figures have seemed to try to goad him into thinking he's still living, but that would be impossible. It's a test of faith. In Ray's conviction that he's dead, and the heavenward path that he's currently on. Yes, he needs to forget the mind, forget reason, and trust only in God. God, who last he checked wants him to be imperfect; God, who wants there to be more to fix. He should trust only his impulses now—forsake reason, embrace the id, the way God made him, all of us—and his impulses say fuck this fat fuck for talking all this shit—especially after Ray had warned him not to say anything else to get at him—and fuck God for making him say it, for making him feel bad and belittled and confused. "I warned you!" Ray turns around, rushing back into the room, and punches him again, this time in the temple.

"Ahhhh!" Emerson falls down onto the bed, clutching the left side of his face.

It's strange to see Emerson rolling around on his bed, writhing in pain. But better than it being the other way around. Then Ray has another idea… He'll fuck up some pages after all! Those are the real source of his power, where he produces the most his intellect has to offer. It'll be like the phone with Haruka. "I told you not to say any more fucked up shit, Emerson! I know you know the value of words." Ray turns and leaves the bedroom. "I guess you'll only learn if I ruin some pages!"

"Ray! No!"

Back in the office, Ray starts ripping up clusters of sheets in his note-pad.

Emerson appears in the doorway, steadying himself with it, the other hand still covering the side of his face. "What are you doing? No! You have your money, you've assaulted me, now twice. You've proven your point, now go!"

Ray pours coffee all over Emerson's pages.

"No! You bastard!" Emerson rushes forward and Ray backs off. He still holds the coffee in one hand and considers splashing what's left on Emerson, too, but decides against it at the sight of the old man beginning to weep over his coffee-soaked fragments of torn-up notepad.

"I didn't even realize until after I did it... but coffee's always in-volved."

Hunched over the desk, Emerson sobs. "Please go now, Ray."

"Seriously, what the fuck does that mean?"

"I don't know what you're talking about. You... you belong in an insane asylum. Bellevue... not here." He sounds in every sense defeated. "You've done enough."

Ray agrees. "You know, I think you're right." He places the mug down next to him and leaves the office.

In the living room, he grabs his backpack and hears Emerson quietly say, "I always am," between short sniffles. Damn. This guy really was a trip. Ray shakes his head, smiles. He moves briskly over to the door then watches Emerson, broken, cry for a moment.

"For what it's worth, I learned a lot being here. Some of the books I've read after transcribing what you wrote about them have been abso-lutely fantastic. But more important than any of that, today you really taught me a lesson: The Greeks had it wrong, man. All good teachers are more like good parents. I thought of you like that in a strange way. So now I know I can't really trust anyone. Only God and myself. Peace, Emerson." He opens the door and leaves.

▲▽▲▽▽▲▲

Oh, goodness... such a speech, such a ridiculous nightmare. Worse than any sanctimonious after-school special Diana would force the kids to watch decades ago. Yes, let's have a nice summation of what you've learned here along your journey before you leave. Because obviously this has all revolved around you. And what is the moral of the story? Books good, trust bad. And I've confused you for a parent because I've spent all of my twenty-six years as a child. Oh, dear God. "Goodbye Ray," Emerson says, long after the door has slammed shut, and with a certain ambivalent pity. Some for the boy, but most for himself.

So much for spontaneity, so much for romance. How could that have gone so terribly? Anything can happen given the Latin lover's mercurial constitution, it seems; there really was no way of anticipating all that.

Emerson peels his face from the desk. He stands up, composes himself, makes his way to the bathroom. A minor cut near the eye, some slight swelling—nothing more. If any of the students ask, which they would have no right doing, anyway, he fell. No, what's physically reflected in the mirror has precious little to do with why he doesn't like what he sees. The man in the mirror has poor judgment; he should have known better. Emerson can't fathom what he ever saw in Ray—he was desperate, confused, or perhaps presbyopic. He shanghaied himself into something horrible. Ray was never worthy. Of any of it. In the end he revealed his true colors, all that sub-human jargon, all the "mans" and "dudes." And to cap off their time together with something as atrocious as "Peace"? My goodness, Ray, we agreed you had done enough.

And really he has. Oh, has he. It would have been better if the young man just went all the way with it, just killed him then and there. Looking into the mirror, Emerson feels worse than dead.

To be rejected by someone so truly awful: the deep injuries this has caused will be hardest to fix. The pages should be easy enough.

Emerson returns to the office, begins piecing together the coffee-colored jigsaw laid forth—what Ray did, he did quickly, haphazardly, without any real care, leaving large chunks—a job so simple a child could do it. Before long he has the fifteen or so handwritten pages Ray ripped up fitting together and back in order, ready for the tape.

It will not be so easy to repair his life, to keep the book coming along, nor his heart after all he's endured this morning. This he knows. If only… yes, if only the boy could have just killed him then.

▲▽▲▽▲▽▽

So many hearts already, almost twenty likes. Another great post. The new blog is really starting to pick up steam, she thinks. It's only been a few weeks and it already has close to 50 followers. Soon it'll probably be 100, 200. Then 1,000. How many people has he hurt over the years? Well, that number would correlate to the number of people he's taught. Probably over 10,000. Not all of those people are going to be on Tumblr, though; many are way too old. Still. Who knows how big the blog could get. He is still teaching and the guy is also sort of famous outside of NYU. Anyway, Haruka is very happy with her new hobby.

She works on it on the evenings she doesn't go out on OkCupid dates. Since breaking up with stupid Ray, she's going on a lot more of those again. For a while immediately following the breakup it was with girls, too. But after going to bed with two or three, she discovered she wasn't bisexual, just bored. So now it's just men, like before: the ones who really deserve it. Her truth bombs. She's gotten back into talking during sex. Except this time she tells them scary science facts on top of saying cryptic literature quotes. Like: Dark matter and dark energy make up 96 percent of the universe. And: The sun doesn't rise, the Earth just spins. And: When we breathe, we are breathing in the very same molecules our dead ancestors did. And: One day the sun will obliterate the Earth and all life here will be gone forever. And: Everything you know and will ever know is housed in three pounds of tissue, isolated from the world. And: Color doesn't even really exist, it's just how you perceive wavelengths of light; color is all in your head. Or: There are more atoms in my eye than there are stars in the known universe. The science ones are better. Stupid old made up stories have nothing on cold, hard science.

It's nice to get back into the swing of things with her sex life, but this blog is fun too, in a different way. A more relaxing kind of fun.

In the Kübler-Ross model, there are five stages of grief: denial, anger, bargaining, depression, and acceptance. The model is supposed to apply to most major losses. Stuff like death, breakups, dealing with your parents' divorce, overcoming addiction. In general, it works. But for Haruka, and she imagines most others like her, the smart ones, the brave ones, there is another stage: revenge.

That's not the same as anger, revenge. No. Anger is a much simpler concept. An easy emotion to tap into. Primitive. It's rooted in the limbic system, the amygdala. A banging of the fists and stomping of the feet and overall feeling of "I'm mad!" Anger can be reduced to an emoji, or several with slight variations. Although, they're usually a little too cute for what's at the core of that actual emotion, anger. It can be very scary when witnessed.

Revenge is more complicated. More sophisticated. It's also less scary-looking, almost clinical when carried out. It would take at least two distinct emojis to express properly. More like three. Something to depict a wrongdoing, something to show contemplation, then lastly the victim committing an evil act with a calm, satisfied smile. That's what Haruka's doing with this blog, smiling like that as she watches her dashboard fill up with even more hearts and like notifications. Yes, she is getting her revenge on Emerson Towers now. Her new blog is called *Guarding the Ivory Tower: Academia's Biggest Troll.*

Only after she gets her revenge, and the wrong is righted, will she be capable of acceptance. People who eventually accept something terrible done to them without seeking payback are just lazy. The Kübler-Ross model is for them, the complicit. Not Haruka. The Kidokoro-Kübler-Ross model, on the other hand, is one that is much better to follow and is much better for the world. It creates justice. Balance. Deaths can be avenged. The Kübler-Ross model would just have you accept someone dying of cancer. But under the Kidokoro-Kübler-Ross model, cancer would be cured. Parents would have to answer to their children for their divorces, give them whatever they want all the time to fill them with more happy hormones for the sadness they created. The drug addict would kill his dealer, or at least get him locked away forever. And the scorned lover in a breakup would move on to someone twice as hot as their ex, then rub it in the exes face over social media. Rational, intuitive things like this. In keeping with the greater good and what's right. This is the Kidokoro-Kübler-Ross model.

Back in the summer, when she'd spend some time on Amazon and Goodreads giving Emerson's books bad reviews and finding similar ones helpful and all the good reviews unhelpful, she thought she was carrying out revenge. But it wasn't really. It was still just anger. Back then, the people who saw her work were already interested in Emerson. They were seeking him out, had already met him in some form. Probably as the brilliant but difficult literary critic. By giving him bad reviews, she was merely chipping away at a statue. Saying "I'm mad!" with a red face and frantic arms and hands working small tools going chip-chip-chip.

But by discrediting him on Tumblr, she can create the original figure. A new statue. He'll no longer be lauded or controversial. The people who find her blog might not even know who he is. Through the use of attention-grabbing adjectives in the post titles like 'racist,' 'sexist,' 'misogynist,' 'terrifying,' and 'shocking,' etc. along with hashtags at the end of the posts like #feminism #racialjustice #equality #endallracism #endacademicoppression #academiccolonialism #ipaytuitionforthis etc. she can reach all kinds of people who have never heard of him and present her version of him first. And she is, more and more. These people care less about Emerson Towers than the things she's making him stand for, mainly sexism and racism and an ignorant blind promotion of white men in literature while overlooking women and writers of color. She is defining him first. He is no longer principally known as brilliant but difficult. According to her, the first impression is that he is just an asshole. A sexist, racist piece of shit that actually doesn't know what he's talking about, and who has thrived in a system—academia—that has deep roots in racism and sexism. If someone happens to go to his Amazon or Wikipedia page after that, they will be looking at what's there through that lens. Anybody praising him will be a part of the problem. They will either be against equality or ignorant, simply caught up in old thinking. Like those who did not stick up for black people during the civil rights movement. Then Haruka's audience, en masse, can take him down. No more chipping. There will be complete destruction through revolt. The mob will take the original statue down using chains and ropes and sledgehammers, the smart and effective way. Eventually more of his reviews will be bad than good, and his Wikipedia page will mostly be about what a bad guy he is instead of all the work he has done with the books he has written. His scandals and reputation as a terrible person will become the main part of his story.

Then, when this happens, she can take her complaints about him to the school and they will seem legitimate. She can present her case: that she is a woman and a person of color and as such Emerson had a clear twofold bias against her, which was reflected in her B grade. They will of course believe her because the evidence will be conclusive. The board need merely look at Wikipedia to see as much. Maybe that won't be until she is a senior. But she has a feeling it can happen way before that.

This is because Haruka believes. It is not in anything she can't identify through her senses, not an unknowable something in the air. Mainly, it is a belief in herself. Because now, just now, she came up with a plan to get the ball rolling even faster than it already is. To push the blog forward with incredible force.

You see, Emerson hates phones, technology, basically anything that's actually useful in this day and age. And she's going to use her phone to get him. Or, rather, she'll simply use it as the beautiful tool it is and he will get himself. With it, she can easily share his true nature with the rest of the world. In his own words, with his own voice, speaking now. And the rest of the world—the people who matter, the people who use the internet a lot—will hate him like she does. She can barely wait. In a couple of weeks, yes, that's when she'll do it. She just needs to let the blog gain a little bit more momentum. And, of course, look up his class schedule and make sure it doesn't conflict with anything too important concerning her own, like a midterm or something. But if she has to miss a lecture or two to do this, so be it.

Until then, she'll continue to enjoy what she's been doing and the modestly impressive growth she's had. Oh! There's another like! And now a reblog!

She's averaging about two posts a week on *Guarding the Ivory Tower: Academia's Biggest Troll*. Tonight was post seven. She writes them before she starts her real homework, a little something to get the productivity juices flowing after hanging out and doing college things and dinner. The first step is to take an Adderall. Then she goes online and finds old newspaper and magazine articles about Emerson's controversies written in the eighties and nineties—back when he was mildly relevant—and basically she just copies those. But she gives credit, so it's not really plagiarism. Also, since it's on Tumblr, it's always an act of creation. Like covering a song and giving it to her fanbase, with her spin. By using her font of choice under her theme as part of her unique blog, she's presenting something totally different. And especially since the audience is new, it's definitely fresh and original to them.

She keeps the posts short, limiting it to one or two items that show how sexist or racist he is, with a little bit of commentary about how and why it's so problematic that he's allowed to continue teaching, told in a pissed-off, snarky voice that's still fun enough and action-oriented. Sort of like Jezebel or The XX Factor, but with even more outrage. Before publishing what she's written she'll step away for a moment, check her phone and social media profiles, texting back whatever friends had texted her during the time she was working on the blog or liking a few items on her news feed or Instagram or favoriting a thing or two on

Twitter. This gives her brain a little break and distance from the post for ten or so minutes, before she reads it back to make sure it's good and tweaks as necessary until she can click the "Create post" button. After she's done, she'll eat a cookie or another tasty treat—even though Adderall generally keeps her from getting too hungry—because she has earned it, and usually before she's swallowed the last bite she'll have at least two or three hearts accompanied by likes appearing down her dashboard. Love and validation, what she deserves. Then many more follow.

One thing that might get her in trouble with her base is using the phrase "Academia's Biggest Troll" in the title. She conceived of it as a hella funny play on words because Emerson is not only terrible and extremely frustrating, a classic troll, but he is also super fat. Haruka doesn't really like fat people. They gross her out. It might be an Asian thing, because Asian people, especially women, aren't too fat very often. So fat people seem disgusting to a lot of them, like her. And untrustworthy. Disgust influences trust. But most of her fanbase, people interested in feminism and social justice, they call it, wouldn't appreciate the double entendre. They would view it as fat-shaming, a buzzy topic right now within their greater online community.

If she's ever called out or asked about it, she'll pretend she had no idea and she'll say that such accusations are hurtful. But inside she'll giggle. Fuck Emerson's stupid fat ass!

Because the difference, really, is that fat people are not like women or people of color. Women and people of color are born into a position of immense disadvantage. Most fat people are born normal, like everyone else. Ones with glandular problems and similar health conditions are very few and far between. The thing that most fat people feel makes them a target of oppression, they do to themselves. So they are oppressing themselves, really. There are such things as underweight and overweight because each individual has a healthy weight range that's been proven by science. Haruka has a healthy weight, but it's on the lower end of the scale for her height. Tee-hee! On the other side of the coin, there's the actual oppression of women and people of color and those are completely wrong.

Fat people should just get revenge on their weight by killing it. Losing pounds. Too many of them are caught up in the Kübler-Ross model when they really should be using the Kidokoro-Kübler-Ross model. They shouldn't accept that they are fat, they should become a healthy weight instead and live longer and happier lives. It's simple.

Haruka smiles to herself. She very much wants to open up Facebook and write "Fat people should just get revenge on their weight by killing it" as a status update, but she knows it wouldn't go over well. Too many of her friends are into blind, Kübler-Ross-style acceptance; they are not as smart and brave as her. No, it is not safe. Maybe she could put it on Twitter? No, a lot of her followers on Twitter are also her friends on Facebook. She wants to post something now, though. She opens a new tab, goes to Facebook, and types:

Write on adderall, edit on adderall.

It's a pretty good update. Actually, it's more than that. Another example of great literature. Wonderful parody of that old quote they say is Hemingway's but actually isn't Hemingway's, and also very meta. Take that, Emerson. It's one of those things she'd say she had no idea where it came from if she weren't on an amphetamine right now, but she does know where it came from: Adderall. She wonders if it makes your neurons transmit even faster than the 268 miles per hour they say is the maximum, if that's why they call it speed. Sure feels like it right now. Haruka laughs.

"What's so funny?" That's Allison. She's in the room with her now because she is her roommate this year. They live in University Hall.

"Oh, nothing."

"Good status update."

"Thanks."

"Is that what you were laughing at?" Allison is sitting on her bed reading her phone, while Haruka is at her desk.

"Fine! You caught me." And soon Haruka is going to catch Emerson Towers!

"It's okay, it's good. You should be happy about it. I almost lol'd too when I read it."

"What can I say, I'm a genius!"

Allison lowers her phone a little, peeking over it at Haruka. "Aren't we all when on Adderall?"

"Awww, so good too!" Haruka is very pleased with their exchange. She likes Allison a lot in this moment. She has an idea, hopefully Allison will go for it. "Would it be weird if we recreated this in the comments?"

"Ha! I was just thinking I wish I would've written that in the comments instead of saying it. I don't think it would be weird at all. Let's do it!"

"Okay, write 'lol' or 'dying' or something, then I'll write my genius line and we can take it from there."

They do, and everybody loves it.

Now likes are pouring in on Facebook, over twenty already for her original update and five apiece for their Adderall-genius exchange. It's amazing how self-worth is actually quantitative now. Oh! There's another one for her "What can I say..." line. This makes Haruka very happy because she knows Allison's comment is actually better than hers, but she still has one more like. It's from Lucien, a friend from home. What a good friend. She'll have to like one of his status updates or comments sometime soon. So much dopamine right now, Haruka can barely handle it. Is it possible to get hungover from too much online love? She clicks back over to Tumblr. Two more likes and another reblog! Now she looks at her phone to see what's going on there. She has four new OkCupid messages since she last checked after chemistry a couple of hours ago. My goodness, this is what people mean when they say you have the time of your life in college!

Haruka wouldn't have thought that at the start of the term, but through revenge, anything is possible. Especially hope. The road to deliverance is wide open. Acceptance awaits at the very end, bright and warm and wonderful.

Two of the guys are cute, one is old, the last is ugly. She writes back the ugly one and sets up a date for tomorrow. Now she mostly likes going on dates with ugly white guys because she knows that after they fuck they for sure fall in love with her and have a greater chance of killing themselves once she ignores them. Most ugly white guys still feel quite entitled and almost all of them also have ugly souls. For a while, when she realized there was the revenge stage in her grieving process, she thought maybe her activity on OkCupid all this time might have had something to do with that. That she was getting back at Kenji somehow for breaking her heart in high school, or maybe even her dad in a way, though she doesn't know for what. But it's not true. It's just fun to make men fall in love with you, and there's nothing wrong with what she's doing, because men are evil and they deserve to be unhappy. And besides, she doesn't really put that much thought or effort into it.

Not like all the planning and blogging that's going on with Emerson. It's work, but enjoyable, rewarding work. Revenge requires work.

Once she's through with him, she'll get Ray back, too. She doesn't know how yet, but she's really hoping that that guy, his roommate, finds her online. That would be perfect. She'd make sure they'd do it at his place, make sure they got caught together. It would ruin Ray probably. He'd probably have to move out. Maybe he'd want to kill himself, too, die for real. Otherwise, perhaps her success will be enough. She heard somewhere that the best revenge is a well-lived life. Once she exacts hers on Emerson, her life will pretty much be perfect and she will someday run one of the best companies in the world. Like Google or Apple. The first female person of color CEO of a premier tech company. Knowing that would definitely make a pathetic loser like Ray kill himself then. She giggles again. Allison doesn't ask why this time and Haruka's glad. She didn't want to have to explain.

Some things should be kept to yourself. Stuff like that, and apparently stuff about fat people. Allison would appreciate Haruka's stance on them, though. Maybe she'll share it at a party this weekend and they can laugh together.

But that's neither here nor there. It's time to get the most out of this pill and do some homework. The hearts and likes will still flood her feeds, even when she isn't watching.

▲▽▲▽▲▽▲

One two, one two, one two—the arm goes out, the hand spreads for the grab, then bam! Yes! Another one! Ray slips it into his hoodie pocket, rounds the corner, and rides. That clown-looking culero barely knew what hit him. He might even still be looking down, in mid-drag of his cigarette, wondering if he's in a dream. For Ray it's bam!, but for them it's gotta be poof! Too stunned at first to ask what, how… who? That's the real question, who.

A fuckin' demon, that's who. But a demon for God. He'll find out what exactly he has later. After he gets out of here, closer to Greenpoint at least, more metal and fences and sky than claustrophobic nonsensical blocks where every other structure is fronted with variegated brick or shitty pastel siding. Between then and now, maybe he can snatch another one. He zigzags through Williamsburg blocks: down Driggs, across S. 2nd, skipping Bedford, then up Berry to Grand, hanging left, wending his way toward the water, then north.

Finding the mark, going in for it, then the escape: chasing being chased, the constancy of outpacing, outwitting. A rush like no other. The hits are loop-de-loops leading into the next, over and over again on an all-day thrill ride. Tons of ghost bikes here, and once he even saw a Google Street View vehicle coming at him until he changed course. Each time must be without error and as discreet as possible and so fast it doesn't matter if they run after you on the spot or not. Some do, ask what, how, who? quicker than others. Especially if they were wearing headphones that got ripped out of their ears, which that guy wasn't. Ray gives a quick glance over his shoulder: nothing, nobody. Just more Midwesterners, probably, some Eurotrash, and one old Dominican lady. The trends are lamer than usual this fall. Dudes with *Mad Men* haircuts but lumberjack beards and shirts, ladies like they're coming off the set of *Twin Peaks* except with Beats headphones the size of earmuffs.

Ray picks up the pace again. That guy, cigarette guy, will be coming either way: if he's not currently running after him—panting, tobacco-scarred lungs a-heaving, long beard a-swaying, empty-handed index finger a-pointing to anyone who'll listen while he cries about it in his undoubtedly high-pitched, effete NPR-host-sounding voice—then he'll try to come through the cops. "Whatever, spic bastard. I got a tracker and insurance," he might sneer before he borrows a loftmate's phone and dials the closest precinct. But maybe not if he's actually from the Midwest, Ray guesses. Those people are mad polite. If he's from someplace like New England, or Texas, like him, or the South, or the West Coast, or even the Off-West Coast like Idaho or Nevada, then most definitely.

The bottom line is: they're always looking for you. They've got to be. You could even be on the news by now, in the papers. Who knows. Five days of this shit would be enough to make NY1 take notice or at least DNAinfo or something. A serial offender. Although, you do wear the hood and look like lots of other brown people here on bikes. Just another spic bastard motherfucker. Not that it would matter. If shit hit the fan, it would most likely expedite things. It would be for a reason. But it won't, and it wouldn't. Because this is what God wants you to do right now, as long as He'll keep letting you do it.

The sport of it, that pure thing, is for Him more than you, always. Isn't that how it actually is with every game? When athletes go for the glory, they're really going for God. It's not just adrenaline you're after with this; it's the mind and body working in perfect accord for the spirit. The Spirit. That thing on loan from God, that thing He'll eventually want back. Each get should be better than the last. This is the only way the spirit can advance. This is how you will save your soul, return it to Him. Ray knows this now.

He's very grateful to God for bringing him here. It never felt so good, in life, to be so bad.

Stealing is bad. The act itself, that is. To take from someone else. No está bien. But God likes it when you steal for a good reason. He must. If Robin Hood was real, then he's definitely in heaven. Dude wasn't an antihero, but a regular hero. It's not only stealing, though. Any bad act for a good reason is especially nice in His eyes. Like, again, the whole righteous indignation thing with Jesus where he got all pissed and drove out the moneylenders from the temple. That's why God gave us tempers.

See, it's about balance. There is no good without bad. No love without hate. If God wanted us to be perfect, incapable of sin, He would have made Adam perfect, incapable of sin, not with a rib that would eventually turn into a helpmeet capable of sin. Of eating the apple. You see, Eve wasn't evil. Like a lot of women in history, she just gets a bad rap. She was just doing what she was supposed to do during all that lapsarian business. And we're all the better for it. Without Eve, there would have been no sin, and thus no need for Jesus. Without Jesus, God would be incomplete. And we wouldn't know that He is really just a synonym for love. That was the only way we could ever hope to know Him, and know how much we truly need Him. God made us with balance in mind, both good and evil. In His image. God's version of evil, though, that's tough love… Could all evil really be tough love? Maybe. Is there anything in life that isn't love? Is that what Bjork was singing about? Is she a prophet? Probably. Would make sense: she's always seemed nuts, never even tried to hide it.

Ray calls what he's doing scalping. It sounds so fuckin' badass. The news would call it apple picking, but that limits what he's really doing. A demon does not pick apples: a demon fucks shit up. Honestly, he has Emerson to thank. During their fight a couple weeks back, Emerson kept calling him a savage. He thought about that for a while afterwards. It wasn't just some racist bullshit—it was a cue, a hint from God about what he should do next.

He's been at it since Monday, going after iPhones in Williamsburg, Greenpoint, and Bushwick. Occasionally he also ends up with an old iPod Touch or some other smartphone that vaguely resembled an iPhone from a few yards away, but this being North Brooklyn, he usually gets the real deal, the latest and greatest from the desperately hip.

And he knows this will please the Lord. While others target Apple products because they're the most expensive, Ray does it because they're the most depraved. They're an affront to God. Flagrantly. He suspected as much before, but now it's been confirmed. A symbol of humanity obsessed with evil, lost in a cult whose emblem is literally a celebration of the moment it was brought into the world. While of course evil is necessary for there to be good, to celebrate it like that is too much. Like proudly calling yourself a Satanist instead of just living as a hedonist. Anyone buying into it is without balance. He already sold both of his Apple products over the weekend. That's a big part of how he got started with this. Posted his old iPhone bundled with his MacBook on Craigslist and found a buyer in ten minutes. A dude in Chinatown, brought him to the back of his trinket shop: "You have more, I buy. Good price. No questions." The buyout wasn't that great, really, only decent, but that didn't matter. Ray's next move revealed itself.

Scalping: since so much of these people's intelligence and ability to function are inextricably linked to their smartphones, stealing them is like cutting a part of their heads off. Half of the inventory he sells, half he throws away. A guy's still gotta eat and pay off the loans, but the point of this is to rid the world, his world, of these things... even if it is one at a time. Like that story about that guy "making a difference" by throwing starfish back into the sea. Except half of the starfish Ray eats. Balance.

The best targets are hipsters. Now Ray has nothing against them per se, but if anybody deserves to have their shit jacked in this city, it's probably trust fund kids or idiots who spend over half their restaurant or media job incomes on rent to just make some rich Hasidic guys even richer, always more interested in style than substance. Those who can't wait to trade in their old iPhones and stand on some line for ten hours the second a new one comes out. Of course they're all just projections, basically only here so Ray can steal from them, a strange descendant of the type of folks he knew while alive and in college who liked to hang out around the East Village and LES. The fact that rents are priced higher in this part of Brooklyn than in those Manhattan hoods now is only further proof that he's dead and none of this is really happening. That'd be the day... Almost as crazy as having a black president... He's spent the bulk of his time scalping here in Williamsburg, occasionally also going over to Bushwick and always hitting at least one person along the Williamsburg/Greenpoint border. He doesn't want to do it too far into Greenpoint, risk robbing someone who might frequently make the walk over the Pulaski. Or mistakenly rob the projection of a Polish immigrant, someone who worked hard for their device in this simulation.

Others with ties to Europe are more than fair game, though. His second favorite target is European tourists. There are also more than enough of those here on these motley blocks, easily spotted by their DSLR cameras, affinity for gaudy graffiti, and strange designer jeans and shoes. It's fun to rob them because Ray never liked them while living. They were the absolute worst while he was in college, back when the euro was still really strong and they treated New York like it was their playground. The rudest motherfuckers alive, honestly. Didn't know how to use a sidewalk and still acted like they owned them. See them in a bar or restaurant and they were never tippin' even though they knew better. Fuckin' assholes would try to talk straight through movies at the AMC, try and pull that shit nonstop until they were yelled at or shushed by more than one person. No decorum, no compunction, just total arrogance. Really, really fuckin' bad.

As Kent turns into Franklin around 14th, Ray spots another one. Hipster, woman, young: wearing a floppy hat, circular sunglasses, some kind of jean shirt, bleach blonde. The phone is in her left hand. Especially sinister. She's lost in it, probably trying to pick which Grimes song is gonna give her the best 2:37 p.m. vibes. He passes her, then caracoles, popping Ghost Horse onto the sidewalk. Ray doesn't discriminate: steals from men and women alike, every race. One two, one two, the right arm goes out then the hand grabs onto it. The headphones jerk her forward slightly before they come out of the jack as he wrests it away. These ones are never as clean, always less of a bam! "Hey! Fucking asshole! Get back here!" She gives chase immediately. Ray breaks left for 13th, rounds the next block up Wythe, left again, against traffic, not that there really is any, then it's a right at 15th, a left on Nassau, and another right on Lorimer, where he can cut through McCarren Park on his way to Bushwick.

Across the street from the entrance to that pool where they used to have those concerts, he bivouacs under a goldenrain tree next to the running track, trying to seem inconspicuous as he takes inventory of his new stock. The beardo's phone was a 5, the newest model, released just last month. Hers was actually some LG thing that looked like an iPhone by dint of its case; it'll go for about fifty bucks less. Ray tucks them under a blanket in his old messenger backpack, where they join two 4S's and a 4. Next, he unclips his MP3 player from his belt loop and connects his headphones, so any of the people hanging out around here would just think he had stopped to safely put on some music. Finding *Hail to the*

Thief, he goes with *Myxomatosis*. Then he pulls out the second sandwich he made that morning from his bag and takes off, eating as he goes. The post-apocalyptic cuboid hellscape that is Bushwick, his old neighborhood, awaits—usually good for a phone or two with less stress from the possibility of there being cameras or cops who would give a shit close by—then it'll be time to ride over to the Williamsburg Bridge, throw a couple of them into the East River, drop the rest off with his dude in Chinatown, and carefully make his way to the Queensboro, then home. They're always watching now, they have to be.

▲▽▲▽▲▲▽

Stick to the plan. It's a good plan, it will get you far. Forget all these feelings you're having right now. They are useless. Ignore the walls as they bend in, how the students buzzing by you look the same as they did last term, but slightly off, like they're wearing makeup, wigs. How everything is like that. The same, but off. Like you're on a drug. Just focus on the good plan. Not how he is here right now as he was then, except even older, uglier: reading notes before class at his podium, terrible lips pursed, the Devil in his den. The students continue to swarm past as Haruka steadies herself on the back of a seat at the end of the last row. She breathes deep. Now move in a little, sit down, settle in. It'll be okay. Just stick to the plan. She pulls out her phone, slowly, then opens the Voice Memos app, presses the red record button, watches the timer count up. That part's done. Now place your notebook carefully atop the phone, obscuring it just so. There's no way he could still see it. Is there? No. This room is here to serve you now, not him.

And does it ever.

Any lasting negative emotions completely subside, her nerves totally calm about ten minutes in when Professor Towers, pressing a Hispanic girl near the front for an answer to one of his dumb open-ended questions, gets the following response:

Girl: Sorry, I don't have a reference for that. I didn't read that part.

Professor Towers: Excuse me? You didn't read it?

Girl: No. I had to stop after the Persephone myth. This text was just too upsetting.

Then after a little more back and forth other students chimed in and began talking about how uncomfortable it made them, too!

The book they are discussing is the *Metamorphoses*. Haruka was confused when Professor Towers first started talking about it because it's pretty early in the semester and her class didn't read Kafka until the end. Except it isn't Kafka. It's one of those dumb old Roman or Greek things. Some guy named Ovid was the author, apparently. Emerson must've switched up the syllabus or something this term.

These students aren't like those from last semester at all, Haruka realizes. Pretty much everybody in her class was quiet, but this group is more like the way people are on the internet right now: very opinionated, outspoken, riled up. Or maybe this book really is just that bad? No, it couldn't be. It's too old to be that crazy. Half of the people complaining are probably only doing it because they didn't read all of the book and think they have an opportunity to get away with not completing their homework. Haruka knows how students operate. But it doesn't matter. All that matters is their outrage. And that he's saying dismissive things back to them and she's getting it all on record! Oh, what a difference a few months can make! They are really going off on him, they are telling him why what he's saying and making them read is not okay!

"There's a blog about you, you know." What?! Haruka can hardly believe her ears. It came from a skinny white guy with cool, blue-dyed hair. "And it's right." Oh, what a day to come! She is famous! WOWOWOW!!!

"What?" Professor Towers asks.

"A Tumblr. It's about how problematic you and your teaching are. Has anybody else read it?"

"I have," says the Hispanic girl from before.

"Me too," adds an Asian girl. Haruka thinks Korean. "I knew this class would be problematic when we got the syllabus and it was all books by dead white men."

Now Professor Towers is shaking his head. "I don't know what a Tumblr is, and thankfully, I don't care. If you're finding problems with my teaching style, it's too late now to drop the course, but you are more than welcome to leave and accept an incomplete for the semester. Would anybody like to go at this time?" He scans the class, his eyes passing over all of them in an evil death stare. She meets his with her own, feeling empowered by the way everything's gone so far. Was that too bold? Are his eyes even good enough to see her eyes? Will he realize who she is? That she's not supposed to be here, and perhaps look closer, discovering the phone after all? No, no... of course not. He never cared about any of the students in her class, why would he now? If they looked the same to her, they must look the same to him, including she herself, even though she's actually very interesting and unique. "Didn't think so."

"We shouldn't have to accept an incomplete," says the blue-haired boy. "You should have to change what you teach and how you teach it. And you can start by providing a few trigger warnings on any bullshit like the thing we just had to read." My, this boy is brave! Also, trigger warning? What is that? Haruka has never heard of it.

"Get out of my class now, you! Go!"

"He shouldn't have to leave," says the probably-Korean. "He's right. Some of the myths were very violent and several, not just the Persephone myth, even had rape in them. It's not fair to anyone in the class to have to read something like that without a warning first if they've dealt with similar issues." So that's what it is. Makes sense. Trigger warning! What a cool term, a lot of things in life should come with one. Anything unpleasant. That blue-haired boy and this girl are so cool. Why didn't she know what a trigger warning was already like them? Is she going on too many OkCupid dates? Not spending enough time online, neglecting new trends? Between that, blogging, and all the school work, it's hard to keep up these days. Internet culture can change so quickly, but she must do her best. She's feeling a little out of touch all of a sudden.

Professor Towers' hand goes to his forehead. Many people in the class look to each other and nod in agreement about trigger warnings, Haruka included with her neighbor, some sad-looking white girl four seats away. Then Professor Towers sighs a long sigh and speaks, staring at the probably-Korean: "Now for you: The reason we are discussing books by dead white men is because this course is called Exploring the Western Canon. I don't have the time or the spirit to tell you why the thing we call the Western Canon is mostly comprised of works of literature written by dead white men, but perhaps if you paid any attention to even elementary school history, you'd have a notion as to the answer. Trust me when I say that something far more problematic is that a person such as yourself should make it all the way to this university, let alone my classroom."

"That's a really fucked up thing to say," says the blue-haired boy. Haruka wonders if he and the Korean girl are in love, or if they even know each other. She hopes not. It would be like they were commenting anonymously in a thread somewhere: something pure, magical. "We're here for an education. Not abuse. It's a part of your job to make this a safe space."

"You have the gall to tell me what my job is? And continue to use language like that in my classroom? Wait, why are you still here? I told you to get out!"

"You can't kick me out. I'm paying for this. We pay your salary."

"I'm sorry," says the probably-Korean to the blue-haired boy. "But I didn't appreciate you speaking for me right then. I can speak for myself."

"I understand. I was just trying to stick up for you."

"I know you're an ally, but I can stick up for myself, thanks." And now, to Professor Towers: "But he's right. I agree with everything he said." Then, back to the blue-haired boy: "Just not that he was the one to say it instead of me." She smiles and he smiles back. These two people are wonderful and Haruka wishes all three of them were best friends together.

Several pockets of students, the ones nodding before, mainly, begin talking to each other throughout the room. A low growl, getting increasingly louder. Then the class seems like they are on the verge of a riot.

"Enough!" Professor Towers shouts. His voice cuts through the chatter like thunder, silencing everyone. It is frightening. Haruka knows this is going to be good. Really good. Dare she? Yes. She already has enough on him, enough to do what she came to do. It's exceeded her wildest dreams, how lucky she is to be here today of all days. But it could be even better. The internet is, like most things that matter these days, a mostly visual medium. A third of the human brain is dedicated to processing vision. What she's about to do just didn't seem possible before. But now his hands are quite full.

She reaches for her phone, ends the recording in Voice Memos, and opens up the Camera app. Selecting the camcorder function, she begins filming Professor Towers as he rants and raves: "I have been a teacher for almost fifty years, and I can easily say you are the most ridiculous group I have ever had the displeasure of endeavoring to enlighten! Or perhaps there are some serious students here, I don't know. The few quiet ones. I haven't read any of your papers yet. But you, all of you hugger-mugger agitators and those buying into this rabble-rousing, you think literature is supposed to make you feel safe?! It's supposed to do quite the opposite of that, believe you me! Ovid hardly glorified that rape, you idiots! It's a very sympathetic portrait. You think upsetting scenes should require warnings, or that you might have the option to skip reading them in my class? What warnings has life given you in your darkest of times? Does it give anybody? The best works disturb, challenge, inspire. They expand your mind, help you grow. They make you stronger! Help you get through life's worst moments when they actually come. A book is not a binky!"

The Hispanic girl is shaking her head. "You're treating these books like a binky yourself. I feel like we should be reading more contemporary work, dealing with the more challenging issues of today. Like race, like sexism, poverty. Most of us already read at least two of the books on your syllabus in high school—"

"Trust me, what you received in high school is not the same as what I am teaching you."

"Says you."

"Yes, because I'm the professor! Not to mention the most important critic of our time! Of perhaps all time! This is not a democracy. I can't believe I'm wasting my breath right now on this, this complete nonsense. The bottom line is I'm teaching you the classics, not leading a student-suggested multicultural book club. There are other places to read the most minor contemporary writers of immediately forgettable talent who can only see between the page and what color their skin is or what's lacking between their legs!"

People gasp, then resume their chatter. Some address Professor Towers:

"Wow," says a black guy, who begins to pack his things.

"Lacking?!" says the Hispanic girl.

"So messed up," says some random white girl.

"That blog is sooo right," says the probably-Korean.

"I can't believe he just said that. My ears are, like, literally bleeding. Fuck this racist, misogynistic fuck," says the blue-haired boy, Haruka's favorite. Haruka imagines everything he's said as tweets and she stars all of them.

Professor Towers laughs. "If you don't like what I'm saying, then, for the love of God, and hopefully the last time, leave." His laughter waning, his hands come together. "Those who are interested in an education in the sublime, please stay. Ovid has waited for us long enough."

"Nobody go anywhere," the blue-haired boy looks around the class, arms spread out, urging everyone to remain calm. "Darnell, you gotta stay, man." The black guy, his bag packed, was standing up to go but sits back down. He looks confused. "We're paying for this time and this space and what's supposed to be a quality education, and we need to figure out as a group what to do about him." Now, to Professor Towers: "You're completely out of line. I think you should go, Professor Towers."

Professor Towers laughs again, louder than last time. "This is my classroom and I'm not going anywhere. But you, if you're not out of here in fifteen seconds, I'm calling Public Safety." He ends his statement with a horrible glare dead set on the boy, a wretched smile.

"Go ahead. I don't care." The boy looks like he's crossing his arms, but Haruka can't really tell from here. She hopes so; it would be very defiant. Brave to endure such a mean-looking stare. "You have no idea what we can do to you. You're the threat to public safety here, you racist old coot. That Tumblr is soooo right."

"That was a little ageist," says the Hispanic girl.

"I'll let it slide." The probably Korean one is now sticking up for the blue-haired boy. Haruka wonders if he will get mad like she did. Probably not. White people usually get really excited when a person of color likes them at all, so her sticking up for him is probably making him very, very happy.

"We have to fight for what's right, always," says the Hispanic girl. "He has a lot of problems. His age shouldn't be seen as one of them."

"Get out of here. All of you! Class dismissed." Emerson waves his hand in a grand motion. "Those who are serious students, I'll see you next session. But the rest! You're vermin. And I will no longer let you spread your plague of ignorance. Leave from my sight at once! Especially you three—" He singles out the blue-haired boy, the Hispanic girl who started it all, the probably Korean catalyst. "Anyone who believes a word these imbeciles have to say, follow your blue-haired freak of a leader and discuss how you'll annoy the administration somewhere else. And never come back!"

"Freak?!" snickers the blue-haired boy.

"You realize that I am Jewish and that you calling me a rat is very, very offensive, right?" says some random apparently Jewish girl.

"Oh, don't try that with me, missy." Professor Towers is shaking his head quite emphatically. "I've got some Jewish blood in me as well. Don't you try to take me out of context."

"My parents are big donors here. I hope you enjoy teaching your last semester," says the girl.

"We'll see about that. I've weathered greater storms than this. Money people do not frighten me. And you, you back there!" Now he is pointing at her! He is pointing at Haruka! Oh, no! Heads swivel. "What are you doing? No phones in this classroom!"

"She's recording him!" the Hispanic girl shouts.

The blue-haired boy whips out his phone. "Whoa, what a good idea!"

"Everybody start filming him!" says the Jewish one.

Emerson crosses his arms. "Yes, everybody please start filming me. With your telephones that contain no film. You can immortalize me calling Public Safety to escort all of you away and then you can find my good side as I read one of these upsetting myths. You like warnings? These are your last, you babies."

"We're gonna make this go viral," the probably-Korean suggests.

"Matthew, get Public Safety on the line!" Emerson shouts this at his TA, who is sitting at the end of the first row, where the TA from her class had sat.

"On my phone?"

"Of course. I don't have one, and they've removed all the landlines here, the fools."

"Hold on, let me look it up."

"This is crazy," someone says. Haruka doesn't know who. The voice was deep. Maybe the black guy, Darrell. Or was his name Darnell? It doesn't matter. This moment actually isn't that crazy. It's kind of a lull in the action, to be honest. Haruka hopes people keep filming.

Emerson walks over to his TA. She follows him, a little more action. The TA must've nodded at him or something because Haruka didn't hear anyone say anything. "Yes, hello. I've got a group of unruly students here. I've asked them several times to leave and need assistance promptly in order to make them exit my classroom."

"We should come up with a hashtag," says the Hispanic girl.

"Yes, I would suggest several officers."

"We should tip off that Tumblr," says the Jewish one.

"Yeah, if that person isn't already here right now." The blue-haired boy, the smartest, counters: "They've got to be."

Professor Towers hangs up the phone. Haruka giggles. These people love her and don't even know who she is, have no idea she's inspired them in more ways than one today. An anonymous goddess. Her phone is both a video camera and the sharpest pitchfork in the room, shoeing away the big monster. Professor Towers walks over to the podium and begins to read: "Not far from the walls of Enna, there is a deep pool. Pergus is its name. Caÿster does not hear more songs than rise from the swans on its gliding waves. A wood encircles the waters, surrounds them on every side, and its leaves act as a veil, dispelling…" Haruka stops listening. This poem or whatever it's supposed to be is stupid and boring, but being in this mob is fun, so she thinks about that instead. More people raise their phones because apparently what he's doing is really fucked up, this myth being about a rape or something. This class is amazing. Like the comments section on a blog, but in real life. A great example of the wisdom-of-the-crowds principle. Maybe humanities classes aren't so bad to take anymore. Maybe Haruka doesn't have to be wary of other stupid artsy-fartsy classes she'll have to take to fulfill her core requirements when this is the new way to behave in a humanities class. More and more phones go up. Public Safety will be here any second, so they're trying to join the side of good. The right side of history. She wonders if this is actually what it was like to march for civil rights in the sixties. Enjoy these last moments, here, now, as much as you can, she tells herself. The party is almost over. What an experience. This has been beautiful, one of the best half hours of Haruka's life. But the afterparty, the one online, the one that can really count, will be even better. And it, like all things on the internet, will be stored somewhere on a server for all time, will go on forever. There's nothing like a plan that goes even better than expected. Revenge with extra credit.

▲▽▲▽▲▲▲

For the first time in ages, it aches. It's not because it has worked for the better part of the afternoon, through the evening, and well into the night. Nor because it did as much clenching as it did this afternoon, in tandem with the other one, jaw, and teeth. No, the muscles so strained today are only superficial to the ache; what he's feeling now runs far, far deeper, an ache that can be sourced all the way to the soul. The long months, not hours, of work. All it's been through, all it's held up. His bleeding heart and the Culture it bleeds for, and more recently his own great mass after the crushing blow from his ex-assistant. Emerson wrote tonight until it was done, until it was time to stop. Until what will likely be the last word of the Western Canon was written. His hand aches now because it has earned it.

The events that transpired this afternoon were, more than anything, proof that he's been wasting his time in the classroom this term. So when he got home, he went to his true purpose. He didn't plan on finishing it. Around four thousand words in the last sentence just presented itself. When the pen left the page, he knew it was right. Reading it back now, it still feels right. He looks over at the clock: 12:39. What a wonderful time. Even the time feels right: 12:39 a.m. on October 16, 2012, the moment the Culture spoke its last words.

In the coming days, weeks, and months, Emerson will have to revive it and kill it all over again many times over. Part necromancer, part caretaker, part garroter. Starting tomorrow, when he transcribes the words he just wrote, as he's had to do since Ray left. Like always, he'll read them on the page and correct them until they're good enough, then make the alterations in the manuscript. This will be the second death, and the birth of the real first draft.

Oh, the first draft!

Emerson rises from his desk, pours himself a little glass of his finest Bordeaux. He takes a sip. Absolutely delicious. He's had a bit of his half and half concoction tonight, for the stimulation, and to wash down the takeout Reuben he ate in a rush for dinner, but it was of course with a cheap wine, nothing like this. This is good enough to reward himself for writing a masterpiece.

But has he? Only time will tell. Time, time, time…

How will he protect his time in the coming days, weeks, months, to ensure this book lives up to its full potential, and now, along with that, its beautiful, certainly Canon-ready last sentence? The problem created by his inability to tame Ray is still alive and well. He was just lucky to be writing about the Culture's final, tumultuous days when it hit. The process could welcome chaos because it's been a chaotic time for the Culture. But what about reading back the sections on the Greeks, on Dante, on Shakespeare? Surely they deserve more. He can't bother himself to go through his collection of takeout menus, call this or that diner, and receive delivery Reubens then. He'll, again, need assistance.

One thing Ray demonstrated, and that his class this afternoon proved beyond any reasonable doubt, is that young people today are universally terrible. He can't hire anyone under thirty. Completely out of the question. But assistants over thirty would most likely be too dim, since that's no title to have at that age, and he needs an assistant who can look up to him, who can love him. That is the only way to make this work. So what to do? Standing now, in the kitchen, looking out over the

Hudson, into the dark, into the vast world outside, the answer is clear. He needs Claire.

She's very bright and already loves him… is the only person on the planet who does, in fact. His concerns over the summer have since ablated; foolhardiness shouldn't be confused for animus. Her love for him is stronger than anything he could have hoped for from a protégé. It's storge, not eros, he needs in order to see this through. Perhaps it's always been. She should be his assistant! Oh, it's so painfully obvious. Yes, that boy… that vile, misbegotten mongrel boy was never right. She'll be a much better assistant, anticipating his every need, cooking foods she knows he likes, cleaning up the Towers way, doing everything right to a T! It won't be the disaster it was with Diana. The love of a significant other is simply far too involuted; that of a daughter is pure, innocent, wonderful. Emerson is becoming overly excited. He wants to call her this very instant!

But that's impossible.

Or is it?

Yes. It's late, she and Marc must be in bed, the phone would surely wake the children, etcetera, etcetera. Unless… well, unless it just makes more sense to call now…

Unless all those reasons not to are actually reasons why he should.

What if he called her tomorrow and she wouldn't want to do it? What if she's reluctant, too protective of her own time, work, life? Emerson will be asking for a commitment of at least six months. A three-day-per-week commute to come here to the city and serve him. She has her painting, social calendar, the kids and their schedules. She barely comes now, why would she say yes?

The only way she will is if she feels he really needs her! Which he does. And which, more importantly, the Culture does! They need her more than her conjugal family ever could right now. But she might not understand the actual paramountcy of finishing the book, knowing it's his last, yet still not believing it would be worth all that. She may only be willing to come here if it seems like more of a health concern. That's why he needs to call her now.

She will think he's losing it. Dementia. Alzheimer's. Something of that sort. People only call past 9:00 p.m. when there's an emergency. She'll want to come here to take care of him. Check in, see how he's doing. It's been months since the macaron fiasco. Yes. Don't overthink it now, old man. Call! He must!

Whistling the melody of *Twinkle, Twinkle Little Star*, her favorite song as a tot, Emerson dodders around the counter and reaches for the telephone receiver. He begins dialing her number, the thick gears of the rotary grinding over his strained tune through the late-night air. The line rings; he goes quiet. Oh, goodness! He's actually doing it! He lowers himself onto the closest stool, struggles to get another sip of wine down before someone—

"Hello?" It's Marc. Of course! He's probably used to getting calls from patients or whichever hospital he's affiliated with at this time of night. Best to play it cool.

Emerson swallows the rest of his sip in a rush. "Hello Marc. Could I please speak with my daughter?"

"Emerson! Is everything okay?"

"Oh, yes." Why couldn't he have just checked the ID? Or, really, shouldn't he have some mobile phone dedicated to on-call issues? What the hell are these devices actually good for if not to prevent awkward interactions such as this? Of course things aren't okay! That's why he's calling so goddam late! "My apologies for calling at this hour. But I was hoping, if possible, to speak with Claire?"

"Yes, of course."

Marc withdraws, then a muffled exchange on the line. That went better than Emerson could have hoped. One nice thing about Marc is that he's pretty succinct. Then, after the handover, her: "Daddy? What's wrong?" She's so solicitous, so kindhearted.

"Darling, I didn't wake you did I?"

"In fact you did."

"Oh, I'm sorry," he says. Yes, act as if it's not that strange that you should be calling after midnight. That it's more like a quarter to nine instead of a quarter to one. Signs of a mind starting to go, as if he's operating from another time zone or believes being awake now to be a part of her schedule. Something he would never do if he had all his wits about him, or was indeed okay...

"What's the matter?"

But! Oh, how does he get into it? The form, yes, the form should be off, but the function still fairly intact. Be as honest as you can be: two parts lion for every part fox. Either way, she'll think this is strange: "Is Marc still in the room?"

"Yes, we're in bed."

"Would you mind going downstairs? I was hoping for a bit of... privacy."

He hears her getting up, various bits of rustling. "Okay. I'm making my way there now." She cuts in and out slightly, on the move. Emerson waits a moment, takes another sip. "So what's wrong?" she asks.

"Claire, I'm not well."

"Okay… what does that mean?"

"I haven't been feeling myself lately." He rotates on his stool, catches his reflection in the darkness of the window across the room. Who is this man? He failed himself with Ray, failed himself with his students. But is he any different? No, it's people who have changed, not him. His only hope, to protect himself from this world, is his book. "I need help."

"But nothing is wrong right this instant? This isn't an emergency?"

"Well, something is wrong, but no, this is not an emergency."

"Oh, you scared me half to death! I thought something had happened!"

Emerson turns back around. "But something has happened, my dear."

"Please stop being so cryptic! What is it? Why couldn't it wait until the morning?"

"I just felt like I had to call." He twists the cord of the phone in his fingers, his old habit. "I'm not well. I've spent all night… all night in a bad state. It's felt like the world is out to get me lately. My students revolted during my lecture this afternoon, darling. Tried to diabolize me, stage a coup, and take over my class. They recorded me with their cellular telephones because they were offended by a poem." Emerson shakes his head. "A two-thousand-year-old poem. I had to call Public Safety and have half of them removed. Then there's the matter of my assistant quitting last month. Oh, how my project has suffered." It hasn't, actually. But this is what she needs to hear, a little something from the old fox within! "The book, you know. My last. The thing I told you about."

"Yes, how could I forget."

"That, that was the real blow. I feel myself unraveling at the seams."

"Are you still seeing Dr. Horovitz?" She's softened, thankfully, since her "cryptic" comment. The adrenaline has worn off, the jolt of being woken up at such an hour by the sharp ring of the phone. All that's left is a somnolent sweetness.

"No, I'm not seeing anybody. It's been a couple of years, in fact."

"You should see somebody, Daddy. Even I'm seeing somebody."

"That won't help. I've spent enough of my life in those chairs to know." And he has. Sometimes if he happens by a furniture store and catches a chaise longue in the display window, he shudders. The damn things aren't even comfortable; how do the doctors expect people to really open up? Let their subconsciouses be known? Sessions should take place with the patient in a large, warm tub of some kind. Decent, of course, or obscured. The chairs are enough to require treatment in and of themselves! It's all a vicious cycle. "My needs are more of the day-to-day variety." Yes, lead her there, slowly. Easy, now… "I was wondering, Claire. I was wondering if you could help me."

"Help you what?"

"With the book."

"I don't understand."

"I'd like you to be…" No, no, easier still… "I'd like you to assist me."

"You want me to be your assistant?" She sounds more confused than excited. He didn't help matters with his awkward phrasing, but he suspects she knows exactly what he's asking.

Emerson turns back around. Looks past himself, through the window. Out into the night air, the same blackness hopefully she can see through her kitchen window. He'll spell it out, frame it. Show her it won't be the end of the world—"Most of the heavy lifting has already taken place. I just thought it would be nice if you could come down a few times a week for the next five or six months and take care of some small odds and ends for me. You know, help me with grocery shopping, general errands, meals. All the little things that add up and take away from my ability to focus." Yes, very good, old man! No objections yet. It would be no big thing at all. Now put some icing on this cake: "And it could also be an opportunity to spend more time together, you know."

"But Daddy, I've got the kids. Dropping them off at school, picking them up. Their activities." Uh-oh. Not so sleepy or sweet anymore… but exhausted, terse. "And then there's the new series I'm working on, all the preparation for next month's show. The holidays coming up. I've been feeling stretched thin as it is, I'm afraid I wouldn't have the time."

"What if I paid for a nanny?"

"You know how I feel about the idea of a nanny raising my children. I've told you before." She has, and she's wrong about them. They don't actually raise the kids, they just help the parents by pitching in with the less glamorous bits. If Emerson could have afforded it back when he was raising her and her brother, he certainly would have brought one on, especially when he had to work from home on his eighth book. Not to mention, they're a wonderful sign of status. All truly civilized people should want to hire a nanny.

"It wouldn't be for that long."

"No, Daddy. I'm afraid it's out of the question."

"I see." Has he made a mistake in calling now? Should he turn up the zaniness to drive home how strange the act of contacting her at this hour really is, start calling her by her mother's name? No. He shouldn't have to. And also, she might not totally buy it: he can't be both suffering from dementia and in need of succor at home for the purpose of finishing a masterpiece. If he is losing his mind, it should be to madness, not senescence. Much like the Culture. He is mad for calling her this late, yes, that is enough. The rest should be an appeal to some logic borne of that simple fact. "It's just that I'm at a critical juncture, dear. The first draft is almost ready, and in order for the thing to really take shape, I'm going to need someone here with me taking care of these things. Someone I trust."

"There's no one else you trust? No students from recent years?"

"No, no students. I can't work with young people anymore, Claire. Not after today. That's why I've called you. It's quite serious."

"It sounds more like you just need someone there with you. A home health aide does all the things you described." Oh my God, she must be kidding… A nurse? She wants him to hire a nurse! A nanny isn't good enough for her but a nurse is what he requires?! Maybe he's been wrong. Maybe he was right this summer—she really does hate him! "I could ask Marc if he could recommend someone from—"

"No!"

"Oh, I'm—"

"I don't want a nurse, Claire. I don't want any more strangers in my home, anyone who wouldn't see the importance of what I'm doing. That's why it didn't work out with my last assistant. A nurse would just be another distraction, and I need someone who can eliminate all distractions." He taps twice on the kitchen counter. His eyes pull up, a slowly growing smile. If only she could see him, his pleading, the heartfelt sincerity! "I need you."

"I'm sorry, Daddy. I just don't see how it's possible."

Oh, how awful. The betrayal! But! Perhaps… perhaps it's not a totally lost cause. It'll work if he can ease her into it, if they start small. "What about… what about just helping me on the weekends. Could you do the weekends?"

"I don't know. Maybe some?" Oh, what the hell!? She is treating him just horribly! It was a mistake to call this late. She is an out-and-out terror in the middle of the night! "A day here and there. Most Saturdays are very busy. You know, Jonathan's soccer games and Kate's riding lessons. I could come maybe one or two Sundays a month."

"Oh, Claire."

"Daddy, you're not being fair. You know how busy Marc is. Sunday's really the only day we can spend together as a family."

Easy, old man, easy. Reason… suasion. Thought! As always, the answer is in an appeal to rationality! "Then why not bring them all down on Sundays? Have Marc take the kids out while we work?"

"Marc hates the city, you know that."

"Well, we all must do things we don't like. Don't we? I'm currently teaching a class that apparently would rather I were dead so they could study contemporary flapdoodle written by nobodies, where the only requirement is that the author is something like a deaf-mute Muslim lesbian or bisexual Pygmy teenage runaway or dyslexic zombie Aborigine! Oh no, anything but Ovid!"

She's quiet. Did Emerson go too far? No, no. She should feel his passion. Mistake it for madness! Aha! Plus, it felt good to vent. "What?"

"No matter. The point is I think it would be more than fair to propose to Marc. The kids should see more of the city. In fact, I don't know why we'd go all the way to Europe before they'd spent any real time in Manhattan. Why travel four thousand miles if they haven't even appreciated what's forty miles away. He could take them to the museums, the zoos…"

"Don't be like this, Daddy. Don't try to use our trip against me this way…"

"Claire, I'm being reasonable. I'm not asking for much. Only a day or two a week."

"Daddy, I can't," she says. No, darling. It's *won't*. You just *won't*. Such a disappointment! His own daughter, now?! How could she? "I'm sorry. The timing just isn't good."

"Oh, you! You're just as selfish as your mother!"

"Daddy…" And now it's Daddy, Daddy, Daddy! A term that's supposed to convey affection. But the last few times she's said it, all he's heard is a spoiled little girl trying to get out of doing what's right. That's the Daddy she's using! The spoiled girl version!

"I'm an old man! Here all alone! You're refusing what is essentially my last wish!"

"The reason you're alone is because of what you did to Mom!" Aha, now the truth comes out! Soccer games, riding lessons! Psshaw! "With your assistants!" Uh-oh. Wait… he didn't know she was aware of the specifics. "You think I haven't read the articles? You think I don't remember what it was like at the time? I'm good to you Daddy, I'm the only one!" No, he didn't anticipate this, and… and she's right. Oh, God, she's right. How awkward would it be for her in that position? That which broke her home? "It's not a fair request!"

"Forgive me, darling. Like I said, I, I'm not well."

"This is a bit much for me right now," she says, trailing off into a whimper. Oh, his poor little girl! "I think I need to get back to bed."

"All right, then. I'm sorry."

"And do think about seeing someone, Daddy. I agree, you don't sound well." Should he? Is it not them, not the world—is it really him? No, no, no. He can't. No more alienists. If he's indeed going mad, he deserves it…

"Claire…"

"Yes?"

"I love you."

Quiet. Then: "I love you, too." She doesn't say it with any real gusto, doesn't seem to mean it as much as she's merely conceding the point. "I'm sorry I can't be of more help. Goodnight." She hangs up.

"Goodnight," he says, though he knows she's no longer there. He hangs up as well. First Ray, then his class, now her. Emerson has no one. Just Weisman. And only eventually. For now, no one but himself… a certain piece of knowledge he's gained through this conversation… a certain loneliness confirmed: that which probably drove him to books in the first place.

He must not be meant to concentrate fully. He must be meant to go it alone. On the page, as in life. How will he hold up? He's about to find out. He downs the rest of the wine, then reads back his four thousand words from today. They're breathtakingly beautiful in the night, but tomorrow may tell a different story.

▲▽▲▲▽▽▽

It's not that scary, not that big of a deal. Who cares if the power went out? They both have their phones; they have all kinds of non-perishable food items—Lunchables, Pop-Tarts, dried fruits, nuts—and over eighty bottles of water between the two of them. They lit a sweet-smelling candle and even have an old-school flashlight so they can make it to the bathroom and back. That way they don't have to use the flashlight app on their phones, don't have to drain their batteries without good reason. Stupid Allison. She doesn't need to be freaking out like this, crying under the covers like she is. That's no way to spend a stormy night in bed. This is actually pretty fun. Hearing the rain, the wind. Catching occasional flashes of light on the walls and out the window on 14th Street. Not to mention, classes have been canceled for tomorrow, and could possibly be for the rest of the week. Maybe Allison's phone doesn't have a full enough charge or something. Haruka's is at 97 percent: more than enough to last her until the morning, when this will all be over. The storm is spiraling along up above, and this little princess is as happy as can be.

That's how she feels right now—like a princess. Not yet a queen, but almost. And one who isn't just waiting for someone to step aside, but is actively chasing her destiny. A warrior princess about to take what's hers. She's made amazing progress recently in killing the main, big thing standing in her way. The giant troll under the bridge blocking her on the way to her kingdom: Emerson Towers.

Maybe that's why she feels so good. How couldn't she, now, after all that's happened? Allison could possibly be right... this should be scarier than it is. Haruka's just riding high. Until a few hours ago, they were actually calling it a hurricane, not the superstorm they're labeling it as now. Lots of other people have been freaking out about it over Facebook, too, and judging by all the movement she hears in the hallways outside their suite, in her dorm as well.

Haruka looks away from her Tumblr dashboard and over at Allison: a lumpy mass hiding under the covers in the flashing white-blue light of their dorm room, weeping quietly, sniffling from time to time. She probably thinks Haruka can't hear her. But she can. Nope—Allison isn't right. Allison's just weak, a girl who puts on a show on the weekends, that of the invincible party girl. But living with her now, Haruka knows the real her. Someone who during the week cries under the covers when there's a storm she thinks is too scary or if some boy doesn't text her back fast enough. A weak little white girl. Most of the other people freaking out over Facebook are white, too, and they also include boys. It's because white people don't really know struggles, so when any type of disaster strikes, they don't know how to cope. Haruka looks away.

She has more notes since the moment she decided to look at Allison: three more likes, three more hearts. Her Tumblr is now a bona fide sensation, and it's only been two weeks since she carried out her plan.

While putting together her post covering "The Craziness in the Classroom," as she calls it, she received tips and footage from several of the other people there. She published her take that afternoon then posted two follow-ups that evening using the additional footage, and the contributors linked their blogs to hers. This made her followers go from 800 to 2,500 overnight. Then one of her followers asked if they could get the raw video files of all the footage she had because they knew how to use Final Cut and were also good with music production and wanted to make a mashup out of it. A few days later, they sent back a really great music video of Emerson saying terrible things in Auto-Tune to a snazzy beat, which she also posted. Then early last week NYU Local wrote a story about it, making the video go somewhat viral on Reddit, and now her followers are up to 5,000. It's crazy. So many followers! And the video has, like, almost 20,000 views. But best of all, today NYU Local put out a follow-up story that claimed Emerson was brought in by university higher-ups on Friday in light of this scandal, and the buzz is that he's facing major disciplinary action, despite his tenure! He may have even gotten fired or asked to resign! He's going to have to leave the university in disgrace! She can just feel it! All because of her! Bwah-ha-ha-ha-ha-ha-ha-ha-ha!! Haruka is so happy. Everything is going her way now.

And this storm, the storm is even for her. It's washing the city down. Cleansing it, making it better. All for her. New York: the capital of the world, the center of the universe. And right now it's getting nice and clean. All for her. Maybe it actually does make sense that Allison's so afraid. Maybe everyone should be.

▲▽▲▲▽▽▲

Zone A, they were calling it; evacuate, they said. Hell nah. Evacuate eshmacuate. The A must stand for *all right*, 'cause this storm ain't shit.

Right now is supposed to be the worst of it, but it really isn't much. Ray's weathered way worse this year: working that fucking bike messaging job, confirming he was dead, falling for Haruka, getting fired from that fucking bike messaging job, becoming a demon for the first time, working for an old fat guy who wanted to fuck him, figuring out Haruka's identity then losing her to save his soul, becoming a demon for the second time. Real storms. Shitstorms. Real shit. Sandy's just Irene's slightly more pissed sister. When she leaves, she'll probably also paint the sky all pretty in lilac and lavender over soft grays, offering a little apology, an adieu suffused with contrition. Real storms never apologize.

Their power's on; they're fine, just kickin' it. Ray was hoping Brian would go back for this one, like he did during Irene, but it looks like he needs him here for some reason. That is, if he's even a phantasm. Ray still doesn't know. If he's a demon doing his own thing, then he probably just wised up and realized they're at a high enough elevation up in this apartment, and storm provisions cost a lot fucking less than train tickets to and from Long Island, so might as well just stick it out at home. Keep things as close as you can to business as usual.

And they are: a little bud, a little drink, some obnoxious debate about nothing every now and again. Ray on his new laptop—a Dell picked up on the cheap with an assist from the Moms's employee discount—Brian on his phone. CNN's on mute while a jazz playlist streams from Songza, Brian's iPad connected to the speakers. The storm's so unimposing that they can still see the Empire State Building through the window, which they can't even make out on some standard low-pressure system nights. The only thing that's different is the wind, which, sure, seems to be battering all the trees in the area pretty fierce.

"Such bullshit, man," says Brian.

"What's that?"

"That I gotta fuckin' work from home tomorrow. It's like the world's ending out there and I can't even enjoy my last night alive." This is an absurd statement on a number of levels. The weather's far from apocalyptic, and Brian seems to be enjoying himself just fine. The fucking thing isn't even being classified as a hurricane anymore.

"It's not that bad."

"It's pretty bad."

"Nah."

"Tell that to the people downtown." Brian's staring into his phone, a pale blue glow shining on his visage in the otherwise warm room. "A transistor just blew in the East Village and now it's pretty much dark everywhere below 39th."

"Really?"

"Yeah, man. Check Twitter."

"I'm good." Ray gets up. He isn't checking Twitter anymore these days; really, he's been pretty averse to it ever since the whole jumper thing, when he saw that DOA tweet from the scanner account, the same point in time he abandoned his iPhone. Using Twitter on a laptop is just kind of strange. Instead, he looks out the window, out toward Midtown Manhattan. Fuck, Brian's right. Between the condos on the LIC waterfront, he can see the Empire State Building towering above darkness stretching south as far as his vantage point allows and also some ways north, ending near the cluster of buildings that Ray knows mark the beginning of the East 40s. Not bad for a sub-hurricane. He stays by the window.

"All my broworkers got a good excuse, but not me." It's kind of funny, Ray thinks: all those dumb motherfuckers who say shit like "I never go above 14th Street" are pretty fucked right now. Except... she, she must be down there somewhere. Down in all that nothingness. "Our fuckin' boss knows where we all live, you know." But she's all right. She's gotta be; the Empire State is telling him so. He used to look out at it and think of her. It helped him come that one time, and since then, it's hard to disassociate it from her. It's still lit up, shining with hope, a physical manifestation of hope just for him: he can't be with her, but he's glad she's all right. No, wait. Maybe it's for *them*, not *him*. Maybe she's looking at it, too, this lodestar, and thinking of him, comforted in the dark. *Somewhere Out There* Fievel/Tanya-style. "You think they're trying to be cool with you when they ask you shit like that but they just use it against you."

"Yeah."

"Damn. I bet they're all getting really fucked up."

Ray turns. "In the dark?" He sits back down. Who is he kidding? Haruka's probably staring at her phone, like Brian. That, or fucking some dude who lives above 39th Street or out in Brooklyn or wherever. Someplace well above sea level. She probably took the zoning shit seriously, planned ahead. Fuck. Whatever. Haruka doesn't matter. Santa

Muerte's who really matters. And she's here with him; for better or worse, she's always there with him now.

"All you need are good hurrication supplies and your phone, maybe some candles." What the fuck is Brian talking about again? Envisioning Haruka fucking some other dude made him forget. That, and being kind of high. Oh, yeah—how he isn't fucked up enough or something. Idiot. "I know these guys. They're smart. Probably planned ahead and scored some coke or molly. Still fun by flashlight. I'd be so much happier right now even if the lights went out if I was twice as fucked up."

"That's kinda sad, man."

"You wouldn't understand, Ray. I work hard for a living. My job is stressful." Brian continues to say things like this occasionally. He's still under the impression that Ray works for Emerson, and that his job involves little more than the chores people do at home as part of their personal lives, after real work: "I get it. You're like the guy's mom. You make him food and check his homework. Cool job. Fuckin' academia, man. Even the professors are babies," he remarked a few weeks into it, after the honeymoon period of being cool and supportive. Letting Brian know that Emerson tried to fuck him and that he's now purloining iPhones to make ends meet is just a bad idea. Brian would never let him live it down. That a rotund elderly guy thought he might have a chance at fucking him would be the subject of daily ridicule for years, open to callback contumely likely for as long as he continued to communicate with him. And he'd probably be too paranoid about the idea of some authority possibly tracking Ray down to this apartment to arrest him and also finding Brian packing his Pax or something, leading to disbarment. But this is beside the point. Brian's being a dick, and deserves no response. Ray says nothing. Scenes of water rising in Battery Park play out on the television… It's actually pretty bad. The Seaport must be even worse. Maybe there's flooding all through the Financial District, Tribeca. Maybe this is God's way of showing His displeasure with Wall Street and celebrity culture, and those seemingly insane evangelicals are actually onto something when they say God uses natural disasters as punishments. Except it's not for shit like abortion or gay marriage or whatever. Katrina hit New Orleans because it's pretty much just a vice den, and those people are too into Voodoo and Hoodoo and all that black magic shit. Japan gets earthquakes all the time probably because they create and sell a lot of fucked up technology that enslaves people the world over; California, too. That makes sense… Mene, Mene, Tekel, Upharsin. The only ones that aren't that fair are, like, the ones that hit

Third World island nations. But then again, who knows. Most people are assholes. In the world. Thailand's also sort of a vice den, apparently—underage prostitutes and shit—and anybody Ray's interacted with from Indonesia or Sri Lanka or whatever while out in Jackson Heights has been pretty rude. His people close by in Corona are way cooler. Eventually: "They probably won't have to do work all week, those lucky bastards."

It would only make sense if their power went out, too: another test. Brian is probably just foreshadowing this. "Maybe our power will go out, too."

"I don't know. Probably not."

"We are in Zone A."

"We're too close to the main station." Huh? Oh, yeah. Ravenswood. That's what he means. The power station across from Roosevelt Island with the red and white striped smokestacks, the biggest in NYC. Provides about 20 percent of the city's entire power supply. You only see plumes of steam or smoke or whatever rising from it on cloudy days, like they're trying to be sneaky about it or something.

Ray feels like he should speak now, but doesn't really have anything to say. So he says this: "It's kinda crazy how much those people pay in rent, and how better off everyone has it in the outer boroughs right now."

"Better off? Have you been listening to a word I've said?"

"I meant people who aren't sad and desperate."

"Fuck you, sad and desperate."

"Like, normal people who don't hate their jobs as much as you."

"Touché, I guess. Who knows if they have power everywhere, though. Or if there aren't other places getting fucked in different ways by falling trees and shit. They're just focusing on this in the news because it's the most important part of Manhattan for commerce. I mean, if Wall Street doesn't get power back soon, that'll have severe repercussions on everyone, not only in New York, but America, the world." Brian's right about this, and it's pretty fucking shitty. Or at least it would be if any of this were real. Ray reminds himself it's not. Did he create this storm? And Irene? Or did God, for him? And why? "I bet the beaches around here are really getting fucked up. Coney. The Rockaways."

Ray can't cogitate on that right now. "Yeah, probably." Or can he? Brian's just staring down, still looking at his phone, reading Twitter or whatever; the TV's showing some poor asshole standing out in the rain, getting blown around, like it always does when these tropical weather systems get big enough—why not think this through? If these storms were supposed to set the scene for some act of heroism, then he's fucked that up these past couple of years by basically staying in throughout their duration and getting sort of buzzed and a little high and watching TV and movies and, at least last year with Irene, reading everybody overreact to it on social media. Hmmm... There could be something there. That he's not on Twitter or Facebook or anything right now, reading or liking anyone's statuses about this. This is the heroic act: non-participation. This second storm here, among other things, shows how much progress he's made. Sandy is here to prove—

"Damn. If only Robert Moses were still around to see this."

"Huh?"

"It's pretty much his cream dream. Robert Moses built the projects on Coney Island and the Rockaways because he figured eventually hurricanes would come and kill all the poor people."

"Oh, shit. That's right. I remember hearing something like that." And he does, now. Just hearing the name "Robert Moses" in that moment out of nowhere was a little jarring. Apparently the guy had like twelve jobs at once or something and did evil shit in at least half of them. He was responsible for some cool stuff, like the world's fairs and getting the UN to set up shop here and developing some of the parks and whatnot, but overall the dude seemed like a total fucking asshole, some tyrant who played the fuck out of every system he could and tried to fuck with the disenfranchised any chance he'd get.

"Watch, man. Deaths will be reported."

"Probably. But mostly just old people who don't have anyone watching out for them." Ray is bumming himself out now. He knows he's a demon and all, and that he was just thinking some pretty fucked up shit about people in the South and Japan and Third World countries, but that was all fairly abstract, and this feels overwhelmingly real. He can look out at the very storm that's currently probably drowning some poor old people, and that sucks. But they're not real. He tells himself that again. But if this were real, those people would die, since they did in similar situations while he was alive, and that makes it feel real. He's done smoking for the night. Smoke less, drink more. The only old person he can think of who would probably deserve to drown in an almost-hurricane would be Emerson, but he knows he's gonna be safe there high in his eighth-floor apartment on the Upper West. Even if it were really, really bad, fucker'd probably float anyway. Ray reaches for his beer, takes a sip.

"I don't know. Look at Manhattan. Look at the news."

"I mean, I get it. But look out the window. It's really not that bad. And besides, most of those people probably went inland, with friends and relatives or to a shelter."

"Yeah, but not all." Brian looks up. "And Robert Moses was counting on that. Laziness and stupidity. If the next one's bad enough, like really bad, you'll hear about all kinds of ten-person families dying out there. Trust me."

"Oh, Jesus."

"All good things must come to an end."

"Yeah, good things. Living in the projects. Living the dream." Ray's spent an increasing amount of time near housing projects lately, having moved his scalping operation from North Brooklyn to Harlem two weeks ago after he saw an NYPD Crime Stoppers flyer with his blurry, hooded likeness taped to a Bedford Avenue telephone pole. During some subsequent sleuthing, he discovered several Brooklyn online news sources including DNAinfo referring to him as the North Brooklyn Bandit. It seemed like a sign from God that he should move on. Astoria would be a little too close to home, he thought, and the authorities may trace him back to somewhere between there and his original stomping grounds, which is exactly where he resides, so he figured the Manhattan side of the Triborough might actually be best, remembering that people like Jill lived there as well as other folks he knew from college, and that *The New York Times* among other outlets had in recent years written a lot about how hot the neighborhood was becoming in terms of real estate and dining. So far, it hasn't disappointed. In addition to the clueless kids who emigrate out of Columbia and think that gentrification is bad except for when it applies to them, there are quite a lot of tourists running around west of Lenox. Especially French people. French people fucking love Harlem for some reason. There aren't too many cameras around and/or cops that do shit, so even though the commute's considerably longer, he feels pretty good about it. But anyway, in pockets around all these bougie new places catering to white post-grads and Europeans, there are tons of projects, and he can tell that living in one would fucking suck. None of the people hanging out around them seem happy at all; anyone who doesn't look completely crestfallen usually just looks pissed. Except the little kids. They don't know enough to be that sad or mad yet.

"They are, though. For real. If I'm good in this life, my reward in the next would be to come back as some muli living in the projects."

This is upsetting on many levels: the casual use of "muli" is of course the most obvious, but then there's the talk about lives… the present and the next, the possibility of past. It's sort of overwhelming right now, considering everything Ray's been thinking about in the last few minutes. He turns away, toward the window. "If I'm really good, it'll be by the beach. You know how fuckin' awesome that would be? To be our age, living like that." And now bringing up the beach… how nice it would be to exist as one of the poor people he was just slamming, to live among families of folks he was smiling about dying tonight in the perfect world he shares with Robert Moses; how awesome it would be to trade places and live like them when he, at his age, is luckier than anyone Ray knows to live like he does in his uncle's building and save the money he does… it's just getting worse and worse… "Living in the projects has got to be like just staying in fucking college forever."

Until it doesn't. Something has just dawned on Ray… All the inflammatory speech, the ridiculousness, the contradictions. Brian isn't just supposed to be an object of pity. He looks back at him. "Oh, God."

"No, no, man. Think about it. You don't have a job or really any responsibilities and you're just living in these giant fuckin' dorms where you know everybody." Ray can see it now, maybe because he hasn't really been using social media. He can see Brian's true role, his function for what it is, with perfect clarity, finally. "Nobody has to work, so you could just spend your days hanging out with your friends, by the fucking beach, and at night you would just be hooking up." Part projection, part demon: Brian is meant to push him with ludicrous bullshit, and he always has been. Brian does what a certain person does on the internet all the time, for fun, except in real life. "Now, I personally don't find that many black women attractive, but if I were black, too, I'm sure I would. So after ten to fifteen years living there as an adult, you'd probably have fucked, like, everybody hot in your building and all the adjoining ones." Brian's a troll, plain and simple. Just a fucking troll! "Everything's fucking paid for. It's like college forever on a full-ride scholarship." Shit, it's even in his last name. He's just realized this. Does everybody's fucking name mean something? Everybody he's spent time with lately seems to have some loaded goddam name.

But really, this is a good thing. A great thing, even. What a relief! He's dealt with him throughout most of their time knowing each other the way one should, no must, deal with a troll. Avoidance when possible, dismissal and lighthearted counter-trolling when not! They only feed off of self-righteous rhetorical argument, trolls—even plain old reason doesn't stand a chance; Ray, in this moment, is very pleased. Sandy has removed a layer of sediment that had been covering this truth!

"Yeah, so Robert Moses was probably just jealous."

"Something like that."

You gotta troll a troll, my dude. Those who use force only respond to greater force. Might makes right: "And what are some of the other reasons, man? You just want a bigger dick?"

"Fuck you. You don't know shit about my dick. You wish you knew shit about my dick."

"Curse of the Irish."

"That's just some bullshit somebody made up to try to keep the Irish from getting all the pussy, man. Not only are the Irish some of the prettiest and most eloquent people alive, but they also know how to have fun better than pretty much anyone on the planet." That's not true. Mexicans are capable of way more fucking fun; Irish people just drink a lot, in a sloppy way, and it usually gets ugly. St. Patrick's Day always involves fighting, public urination, vomit. While Mexicans drink a lot, too, they at least eat while they're doing it. Ask a random focus group which is better—Cinco de Mayo or St. Patrick's—and overwhelmingly, unless they're made up of people who are at least part Irish, they're gonna go for Cinco de Mayo. Though to a certain extent he's right about the pretty part; a lot of girls with that emerald blood are indeed quite attractive. Soft features, well-balanced faces. Still, Ray's very happy about invoking the Curse of the Irish and deriding him over his dick size. The content, tone, brevity seemed very baseline troll, with a hint of something spicy—the delivery quintessentially Mexican, like it should've been accompanied by an *¡Ay puta?!* and a chuckle to himself. "And anyway, even if it were true, which again, it's not, I've still got the Italian side. Sausage for days, kid." So if Brian is meant to be a real-life troll, what is he guarding? Internet trolls get in the way of a popular opinion or a person's good argument or take some aggressive action toward the general peace. Is Brian blocking Ray's peace? Yes. Is Ray meant to move? And if so, where? An image of Haruka's face flashes in his mind. Why? He could never live with her, no. Their time is over. Isn't it? Was that actually Haruka, or Santa Muerte in her form? He looks over to the window, out toward the Empire State.

"Hey, if everything below 39th doesn't have power, how come she's still all lit up?"

"Huh?"

"The Empire State."

Brian shakes his head. "What the fuck are you talking about? That's obviously a phallus, bro."

"No way. Empire State's feminine. You just got dick on the mind." This last bit feels almost too trolly-Mexican. Like he's playing a part and Brian knows it, or will soon. Ray's slightly ashamed and decides to tone it down.

"Look at that fuckin' thing. How is that feminine? It's a giant, thick fuckin' dick."

This is not true; the Empire State Building is feminine, and not just because it's reminding him of Haruka right now. It's always seemed that way. A strong, beautiful woman. "The Chrysler Building is masculine. Empire State's feminine."

"How?"

"Cause the Empire State's always lit up in different colors, man. It pretties itself up. Shows off. Like a lady." And this is the reason. The Empire State is always switching up its look; it doesn't just run with the same thing night in, night out. Like the same business suit or business casual duds a dude would wear. The big beauty gets bored with classic white, goes all out with different colors for different occasions. The Chrysler Building on the other hand... "Chrysler Building just stays the same. It's consistent. You know what to expect. Understated. Elegant, sure, but conservative." Yup, yup. "They're a couple and the Empire State is the woman."

"The fuck outta here. Both of those buildings are just monuments to the architects' dicks. If anything, following your argument, the Empire State Building is just gay." Brian might be onto something there with the first part, but while the building may have been conceived of as masculine, since then, it's proved to be anything but. The architect may have been hoping for a boy, but he got a girl. Even if it's some kind of transgender person, it's a girl; though Ray doesn't really think it's a transgender person. He once watched a documentary about the Empire State Building—or maybe it was an episode of like *Modern Marvels* or some shit—and in it, the guys who built the thing, now old, and quite straight, would refer to the Empire State Building as "she" all the time, speaking of it like it was this great past lover. It killed some men, its construction, and the guys who built it were the type that would only let a great love for a great woman do that.

But Brian, like all trolls, wouldn't respond to such romanticism. Just more hyperbole and a play on common masculine insecurity tropes made personal: "So the building most emblematic of your city is a gay dude? The one all the tourists come to see, the one on all the postcards. The one we look at through this window and say, yup, we're in New York, couldn't be anywhere else. You should tell all the people from Middle America. I don't think motherfuckers from Missouri would pay thirty bucks to go up to hang out on the tip of a gay dude's dick." That should be enough; now to save face for his own sake, get further away from the troll within and closer to himself. "I mean, I personally don't think there would be anything wrong with that"—the old *Seinfeld* caveat, still good—"but New York City isn't just a haven for gay people."

"It kind of is, though. I'm glad to be from Long Island and can't wait till I've saved enough to buy a decent house there. Shit's gayer here than pretty much anywhere in America. Everything that makes New York New York is extremely gay. Broadway, gay. Fine dining, gay. The fashion and art industries, gay. Liberal Jew media, gay. Pushy, entitled mindset, gay. Our football teams don't even play here, gay. And all the tall buildings, again, are just monuments to dicks. Because this city is gay. Even Manhattan Island is sort of shaped like a penis."

"So you're saying it's just gay dicks on dicks on dicks on dicks."

"Pretty much. It's exponentially gay. The only non-gay big industry here is finance. But it's not enough to balance out everything else that's gay. That's why they call it Wall Street: they give the whole industry its own geographical name because it's sort of its own thing."

"Whatever, man." Ray's frustrated because, even though ridiculous, Brian's fucked up logic is flowing pretty hard right now. Maybe it's 'cause he's still too high. He wonders: Is this what it's like to read *Mein Kampf?* Like, in order to finish it, you'd sort of have to just buy into its flow. That's neither here nor there. What matters is his own original argument, which is pretty solid. It's his truth: "The Empire State Building is a lady. She's like the queen in chess, the most powerful piece. She's like America."

"Now I know you really don't know what the fuck you're talking about. America is the most masculine nation-state that's ever existed. America is more like Wall Street. Mean as hell, straight, big dick swinging, winner-takes-all mindset. You're from the west, man. You should know this. For Christ's sake, we stole half of Mexico."

"If it were masculine, it would be called Americo."

"Semantics…" Brian looks down at his phone. Ray got him good with that one. Retreating with some *Big Lebowski* line, that's what's up.

Unless it isn't. Unless he wasn't. Maybe that's Ray's baggage, since watching that as a teen, that was the first time he heard the word "semantics." Maybe Brian really meant that as a rhetorical defense and wasn't withdrawing into his phone but rather felt so comfortable with his place in this argument that he could now multitask. Fuck him. References, though, when they're not cheap and transparent, they're effective: "You ever see *Sex and the City*, man?"

"No."

"Well in it, the main girl, Carrie, she tells the main guy, Big, that he can't leave New York 'cause he's like the Chrysler Building." Hopefully this reference is weird enough to work. *Sex and the City* is another thing Ray watched as a teen, after getting accepted into Columbia, curious about the lay of the land with getting laid in New York. It didn't really prepare him for dating as an undergrad, but the show was entertaining enough. Better than that goofy half-baked shit HBO put out this year to try to finally replace it, *Girls*. "That's 'cause she's the Empire State."

"So your argument is from *Sex and the City*?"

"No. I made up Carrie being the Empire State part. I've just always seen the building as a showy woman. Someone who likes to get dressed up. It makes sense if you think about it."

Brian looks up. "You're just confirming what I said about everything in New York being gay. You're a straight dude, Ray, citing *Sex and the City* to make your case. Do you know how gay you sound?"

"It's 2012, man. The world's different." And it is. Brian's going on like it's 1998, gay this, gay that. At this point his use of that word seems less descriptive of the New York "fabulous" thing and more like a flat-out pejorative.

"No, the goddam world's ending. And I'm not nearly fucked up enough!" Brian reaches out to the coffee table and then takes a hit from his Pax, the little indicator light having glowed green for some time. Exhaling, he continues, "Like I said, they're all dudes. They're all dicks. Fuck Sarah Jessica Parker. *Family Guy* said it best, man. Bitch looks like a foot. Anyway, I don't know why it's still lit up. Shit has its own zip code. They probably have their own generators, too."

"Word." Ray takes a sip of his beer. "Sounds about right." Brian takes another hit, then looks down at his phone again while he holds it. There's nothing really more to be said in this argument. Ray doesn't know if he won, but he does know, either way, that Brian lost.

Ray gets up, makes his way to the window. The Empire State Building. What is it, now? Not a stand-in for Haruka, but maybe a beacon connecting them, like he thought before. Some *Gatsby* lighthouse shit, perhaps. That didn't end well, though, and this probably won't either. Is that real hope or false hope?

"And I bet they're gonna cancel all the Halloween parties, too. One of the funnest weekends of the year. Fuck Sandy. Goddammit."

"Who knows. Again, look outside, man. It's really not so bad."

"I don't have to look outside to know, I got it all here. Fuck. The world's actually fucking ending."

Ray crosses the room, sits back down. He wasn't lying about the way it looked outside, but more shit *is* flooding on the TV. He can only imagine what it's like on Brian's phone. Ray takes another sip of his beer. He really should move out, first chance he gets. Away from Brian, away from this view of that edifice. A place without any view. Somewhere simple but nice. Or maybe he should just get the fuck out of New York altogether.

▲▽▲▲▽▲▽

It's terrible, what's happening out there. The storm rages on, winds ululant, rain spraying every which way… Tree limbs over in Riverside Park thrash about, the mid-autumn leaves clinging for dear life with most losing. Inside this apartment, however, it's okay—finally, it feels okay to be here. His sight beholds something awful, and what can't be seen, what surrounds his home is that same something awful, but Emerson is safe and sound. Yes, safe and sound. As it will be from now on.

He listens to the news about it on the radio. Downtown has it the worst, sounds the most harrowing; it's gone dark and the water is apparently rising so high in parts that the streets have begun to flood. Good. The school and those idiot kids, that's where they are: in that warren of lunacy and depravity. He takes a sup of his syrah.

How is it in rural Connecticut, he wonders? Will any oaks from the surrounding grove crash down upon Claire's house? Give her a real project that would keep her home? And how is it in Queens, in whichever godforsaken neighborhood Ray lives? His situation seemed so dire Emerson wouldn't be surprised if he resided in a basement dwelling somewhere. Perhaps it flooded and he is now dead. Wouldn't that be nice!

Of course, Emerson could never know for sure. And really, it doesn't matter. Ray is already dead to him. As is anyone younger, anyone who is college-aged. And the administration of New York University, who fired him last week, using the finest rhetorical and legal acrobatics to get around his tenure status. He would contest it if he actually cared, but he doesn't. The only thing of any real consequence will be the change in his health plan, but he'll manage. It's a complete waste of time trying to teach the dead. Emerson takes another sup, smiles to himself.

So what of Claire, then? Oh, Claire. He couldn't wish anything so devastating upon her, just the property damage. Major property damage. But he wonders what she wishes upon him…

For she didn't call—everybody on the East Coast has known for days now that this storm was coming, and she did not call. Nor did she write one of her emails: the slightest, most impersonal gesture she could have offered. He's checked, twice, once yesterday and once this evening. And no word at all, even as the storm set in. Nothing. Her poor, old father here all alone, in what would seem a tremendous time of need, just two weeks after his desperate late-night call to her, facing this monster storm when she knew he didn't have anybody—and nothing. No word since that night. And so he is here: alone.

Alone, but safe and sound. This storm has demonstrated that the apartment isn't beset against him anymore; it's a haven. The lingering stench of the Ray fiasco lifted when he opened the window one last time before the rain began and he understood it was much, much better to be in here than out there. He doesn't need anyone else. With books, you're never lonely. Your friends are the best minds who have ever lived. And today, having twice read the complete first draft of his elegy, he knows he will be among them.

It's that good. Not perfect, not sublime, yet, but still… it's very, very good for a first draft. His book kept him wonderful company today.

And he will make it absolutely glorious without an assistant. After all, he knows now he is the only person he could ever fully trust again. He doesn't need Claire. He doesn't need Ray. He doesn't need anybody. The work to be done will be that of a true author, a true artist. It will be done alone. It will be so exceptional that Weisman will likely not want to change a thing.

The rest: be damned.

If the book is good enough, he won't need coffee. He won't even need to eat. The book will be what keeps him going, the book is what will nourish him. He has spent his life accumulating the wisdom and the fat stores to make the most of this very moment, to take care of what's coming next and reach his true apotheosis. The subsequent drafts will be the culmination of his life's work. To be done here, alone, after the storm and all its noise passes and the floods wash the rest away.

▲▽▲▲▽▲▲

Oh my God!! Oh my God, oh my God, oh my God!!! This is such good news!! And she… she just can't even!! Oh God!! It's so amazing!!! Haruka squeals with pleasure, actually has to sit down. She does, on the curb, just like that. Still staring into her phone, barely noticing the cars whizzing by. The words:

> Miss Kidokoro demonstrated, in no uncertain terms, a masterful understanding of Franz Kafka's "The Metamorphosis." This is graduate student-level writing—a pleasure to read.

> We have weighed this according to the rest of the items on Professor Towers' syllabus and have decided to amend her grade in this course to an A. It is well deserved.

What a week! Since Sandy, she learned she got A's back on all her midterms, she heard Professor Towers indeed got fired, and now this!!! A small committee from the English department had been assigned to reevaluate her final in that class after all that had happened and she just got this email with the result. She can hardly believe it!! She got an A on the final paper so now she has an A for the entire class!!! Professor Towers' class! She did it! She got her 4.0 back!!! Without the help of a hacker, Ray, or anyone else! And now she is whole again on paper. Perfect! Literally perfect!! Something that makes her totally Google, Facebook, or Apple ready!!!

Haruka almost cries, she is so happy. She takes a moment before posting the same update on both Facebook and Twitter:

> there must be a storm before the rainbow. remember that.

People will think it's about Sandy, very topical, but she'll know the truth. When she rises and moves on, she practically skips. Her steps have become lighter than air.

▲▽▲▲▲▽▽

Holy hell, he's actually closing in on him—this guy can really run! "Heiy yooou! Thieeev! Yooou couume beck heeaare wivth ma phuooone!" Maybe he was a track star back in high school. Wait, is there such a thing? Track in France? Seems like if there was, they'd just stand around in little uniforms smoking cigarettes, but this guy can move. Wait, is there even high school in France? What would they call it? It's gotta have some pretentious bullshit name that's its own; most if not all European countries have some silly designation for their secondary schooling to make them seem less like high school and more like some form of junior college. France's would naturally be insanely silly. The guy's yelling after him like anybody around would give a shit, would try to help him. Dude doesn't know Harlem. Pasty-ass motherfucker's gonna have to fend for himself. Like Ray is right now, raising a little hell to get closer to heaven. Carrying out one of his own 400 Blows on this fuckin' guy. Zig around this lady, zag around that dude. Curvet down the curb, past the ghost bike. Lean left, weave into traffic, into the next lane, and hug the median. Cut across 126th, between the Range Rover that just hurtled by and whatever's next, which turns out to be a sedan that's seemingly accelerating at him on purpose but he's made it. No way this guy's gonna run into the street after him with all that shit. Then pump-pump-pump to pick up speed and cross 125th just as the light turns green so you're ahead of the cars sharing Lenox/Malcolm X with you which have yet to hit the gas. By the time you cross all four lanes they're close and honking so it's a hard left onto 124th, beating the pack of cars traveling north up Lenox/Malcolm X, then you're in oncoming traffic but more or less not, because there is no traffic right now on 124th, just that one crappy hatchback that was waiting at the light. Now you're good. Three today: that'll be enough. It's Día de Muertos, and he wants to cut work short so he can celebrate.

He makes his way to Marcus Garvey, which, like all city parks, is still closed because of the storm. Along its perimeter about halfway down to

123rd he assesses his stash. Two iPhones and a Samsung. He'll throw out one of the iPhones later on, crossing the Triborough, sell the newer iPhone and the Samsung now.

Even though he'd have to go completely out of his way, he was riding down to Chinatown and selling to his guy there during the first two weeks of hitting this area. Seemed like the right thing to do, an apposite gesture of loyalty to the guy who got him into this game, as well as a sort of penitent act, all that biking that wasn't absolutely necessary. Being a demon works both ways, even a demon doing what you do for love, for God. You gotta commit hateful acts unto yourself as much as others. But the day after Sandy, he went down there and the guy's shop was closed. Trees had fallen all around in the neighborhood, some traffic lights and power lines had collapsed. Downtown in general was a shitshow, with copious pockets blighted by wind or flood, while uptown it was as if nothing had happened. When he thought about it, standing there shut out of the dude's shop, it seemed like a sign from God that he could make a clean break; he was ready to receive a little of God's love after over a week of riding an extra fifteen or so miles a day out of deference for some shady Chinese guy. The man had served his purpose. Maybe Manhattan is purgatory and the higher up on the island you hang out the closer you get to heaven, he thought. You are closer to a lot more poor people up there, after all, so that would make sense, considering what Jesus said about a rich man getting into heaven being harder than a camel walking through the eye of a needle and whatnot. Also, it would be a helluva lot more convenient to sell up there. There are tons of pawn shops and sketchy electronics stores, everywhere from El Barrio to Washington Heights. It was decided. He's been selling up here for the past two days, since Wednesday.

Today he'll sell to the pawn shop near the Metro-North station, which is the closest to where he is now. It'll be his first time working with them. He hugs the outline of the park, careful not to agitate others on the sidewalk, mostly black men standing around in small groups, chatting, probably wishing they could go back to doing their thing, whatever that is, in the park; others of both sexes and varying races walk purposefully past them, small kids in tow, or big dogs, or nothing but their fear. Marcus Garvey: Ray doesn't know much about the man. Just that he was important enough to warrant renaming this park, which had gone by Mount Morris before, after the asperous mound of mica schist at its center. Soon he's where Fifth terminates at the northern border of the park, where he can get back onto 124th and flow with the west-east traffic that comes from those making a left instead of a right off Fifth. Even Malcolm X still has to share his shit with Lenox, some old white guy. Marcus must've been a pretty big deal. But who the fuck was Morris, anyway? Probably also just some rich old white dude. Really, who cares, though? Fuck anybody who'd call a hill a mountain and name it after themselves.

Beyond Madison Ray passes a bodega, then a restaurant, followed by what appears to be the New York College of Podiatric Medicine. Weird. Not just because feet in general are weird but because a foot college being based in Harlem seems especially strange, albeit for no good, immediately placeable reason. A man who is homeless or mentally ill or likely both stares at him on the other side of the street as he nears the end of the block. What does he know? What do they all know? At Park, he crosses under the above-ground train tracks and hangs left. The scene starts to get much starker much faster here; east of Park around 125th is a part of Harlem that the Europeans and Columbia kids rarely tread. Only the daring and the sad walk these dog shit-mottled, garbage-strewn sidewalks, this little slice of the seventies/eighties New York everybody fetishizes and thinks they're experiencing down in Alphabet City or out in Bushwick or whatever, but that's really only here, in East Harlem. Well, here and the South Bronx, probably. But even as a demon, Ray has little interest in fucking with that part of town… It's supposed to be the area that gives most credence to The Bronx's borough motto, something in Latin that literally translates to "Do Not Yield to Evil." A right on 125th and he's pretty much at the spot. In front of the place there's a light pole next to a bus stop. He pulls out the chain from his bag, careful not to hurt the merchandise, and stepping over a tumbleweave, locks it up.

The air smells weird, different from the grit and gas emissions common along major drags in the city. He's ridden by the Popeyes across the street enough times at this point to know it isn't the fetid fried chicken exhaust they pump out—sort of like Subway with their bread but much, much meaner… This smell is even more offensive than that, something akin to burning plastic. Ray looks around. It's not like there's a factory or something on this block, just a couple of bodegas near him and the pawn shop. The nail place down a ways is closed, probably out of business, otherwise that would be the prime suspect. Makes sense that it's closed, though: what woman in her right mind would pay to get her nails done on this block? Everybody here looks either deranged or completely miserable; even the business people coming and going between the Metro-North station and 4/5/6 line at Lexington usually look somewhat unhinged. Then he sees it, a group of three: two dudes, both black, and a lady, probably Dominican or Puerto Rican; they're standing by a chain link fence in front of an open lot next to a bodega. Is that PCP? Or crack? Maybe it doesn't just *look* like seventies/eighties New York up here, maybe it really *is* fuckin' seventies/eighties New York up here. Has he just secondhand smoked crack? But hold on. It looks like they're just passing around a joint. No metal pipes or anything. Ray's too curious not to ask, and plus he's dead anyway, so it doesn't really matter, nothing to lose: "What's that, man?" He addresses the closest guy, the one who's currently holding the joint.

"Nothin'."

Well, that certainly isn't true. "Smells interesting." He nods, trying hard to look interested… trying to make it seem like his "interesting" isn't simply a euphemism for "bad."

"Mind your own fuckin' business."

Normally, that would be that. Touché. But again, Ray's never smelled anything quite this horrendous, and he wants to know what he's already inhaled. "Okay. But I'm not a cop or nothin'." He licks his lips for good measure. Disenfranchised black and Latino people seem to be more comfortable around you when you lick your lips a lot.

"Be nice," the lady says to the dude. Then, to Ray: "This just a little Spice, sweetie."

"Spice?"

"Spice, K2. It's legal. The A-rabs inside sell it. It's like weed, but you can still pass your drug test. Cheap, too!" Oh, shit. Ray's heard of this: basically, it's made up of herbs or potpourri or whatever sprayed with Chinese chemicals that are supposed to mimic THC. It was in some article about the rise of legal synthetic drugs, mentioned alongside Bath Salts, that crazy-sounding shit that the authorities suspect made some guy down in Florida bite off a homeless man's face earlier this year.

"Oh, nice," Ray says. Of course nothing about this actually sounds nice, but it's better if they think it does, and the information *was* appreciated. "Thanks."

"Wanna hit? Try it out?" the first guy asks. The other one still hasn't said anything; he's just kind of leaning against the fence, completely out of it. Weed doesn't do that shit to you. The fuck kind of chemicals are these people honestly smoking?

"No, I'm good right now."

"So you just tryna flirt wif my girl then?"

"No."

"That's right, no. Fuckin' faggot."

"Stop it, Mike! He was just aksin' a question. You don't gotta always fuckin'—" And he'll take that as his cue. Ray walks away, toward the pawn shop. Hopefully they don't fuck with his bike. The other guy shouldn't; he's too fucked up, and it seems like the pissed-off one would be too busy trying to calm his bitch, that is unless he can't and he takes his frustration out on Ghost Horse. Anyway, this should be quick.

And it is.

The manager, stationed behind bulletproof glass, tries to lowball him but Ray tells him he knows they'll pay one-fifty for the iPhone elsewhere and a hundred for the other—which is roughly what the Chinese guy would've paid. And he gets that: two-fifty. The whole thing takes about two minutes. Questions about their origins aren't asked, and he's sent off with a "Come back anytime," which is pretty much what happened at the place yesterday and the one before it. Hitting the same one up once or twice a week on inconsistent days seems like the best plan.

Back outside the couple's still arguing, the other guy stuck in his trance. Ray's quick to unlock his bike and ride away. He keeps with traffic down 125th and takes a sharp right at Lexington where the Pathmark sign looms large. El Barrio, ho.

It's kind of crazy. He's making more money now than he ever made before, living or dead, doing this phone thing. And he could be making even more if he didn't throw out half of what he snatches. Sure, what he's doing is totally fucking illegal and he's had news stories written about him or whatever, but the amount of paper he's stacking right now is pretty considerable. If he wanted, he could easily move out of Brian's. Today. The problem is he doesn't have a very clear idea of where he's supposed to go next. He'd like to go to heaven, obviously, but despite putting forth all his might and main, he still can't figure out how to get there. And the thought of leaving New York seems ill-conceived the more he mulls it over—his entire quest has taken place here, it should end here. Notions of moving back to Austin or going on some pilgrimage to Mexico or the Vatican or Middle East just don't sit right. They don't make sense for his story. Is he supposed to, like, move here to East Harlem or something? Is that why God and Sandy led him here for work? Put his money where his mouth is about this area being closer to heaven? One plus is he could wander the streets of the island until he found the exact place where he died: keep this shit self-contained. You would just know it when you saw it, wouldn't you? Or is it the opposite? Is he supposed to put in more penitent outer borough time, but somewhere worse, like East New York or an industrial hood in the Bronx, which five minutes ago he thought was still too scary, or some other shithole area like Brownsville or South Jamaica? Is he supposed to live like a New York Jesus among its poorest and most downtrodden? He just rubbed elbows with some pretty sickly-lookin' folks, maybe some prostitutes should be next, befriend his own Maria Magdalene? Nah. The closest thing to prostitutes he could find would merely be the ladies who work the strip club circuit. New York doesn't really have street prostitutes anymore, probably not even in a place like Hunt's Point, where that one fucking great HBO late night documentary took place that he watched in his youth. Since Giuliani and shit most if not all the hookers, it seems, have migrated to the internet. And God doesn't want him on the internet more than he has to be. Right? Right. He's supposed to be free. He's supposed to be himself, do what he wants, but in the actual world. New York City: the original internet. That's why he's here… that's why he can act like a demon again. Nobody's authentic on the internet-internet, really; they're just a calculated representation of themselves, even when anonymous. And he probably doesn't need to move to a place like Hunt's Point or Jamaica. But maybe here. This is nice, El Barrio. Not Long Island City nice, but nice: eclectic like the best parts of Queens but with more storefronts arrayed in primary colors. Not having to spend time with Brian would undoubtedly give it the edge over Long Island City. If he was supposed to be somewhere shittier, he'd be in jail now. That's where God would've led him… manacled, dragging his feet. Rikers or whatever. Instead he's here, feeling pretty good. Ray hits the light at 117th, the first time he's had to stop since 125th. Such smooth fuckin' sailing these past eight blocks it's gotta mean something.

Maybe he'll move here if he's not in heaven by New Year's. Then, a thought: it's possible there won't be a New Year's. Next month, isn't that when they say the world's supposed to end? According to the Mayans? Like the 20th or 21st, right? Most people who've looked into it know it's bullshit, that the end of the calendar just denotes the end of a cycle. But maybe it's not. Maybe that cycle is this mode of existence for him. Maybe the Mayan prophecy and the doomsday thing he heard about all his life were just for him. Maybe that's when it'll finally happen! That's when he'll finally be called up to heaven! A blaring string of honk-honk-honks behind him. Oh, shit! The light's green. He crosses 117th and rides up onto the sidewalk, past two pawn shops right next to each other. Does this mean anything? Obviously if he lived here, he couldn't sell to them. They'd be too close to home. Maybe if he lived here and were still doing this they would help protect him; the police wouldn't finger him as a suspect when there'd be so many other closer pawn shops like these to sell to. But hopefully he won't have to live here because he'll be in heaven by then! Also, police at this point could be thought of as angels. They'd just play a role to get him where he needs to go, a superficially antagonistic force that's actually facilitating the process, fulfilling the prophecy, like Judas Iscariot or something. That is, unless they're demons.

Ray locks his bike at a parking station in front of the second pawn shop. He rounds the corner at 116th, past the subway entrance and Mexican restaurant and myriad black, brown, beige bodies coexisting with a bit more equanimity than they do up on 125th, toward the Associated. Outside there's a flower stand, a stocky Central American-looking dude manning it. Ray picks a bouquet of marigolds, looks like a dozen, half yellow, half orange.

"Hola," he says to the man.

"Hola.

"¿Cuánto cuesta?"

"Diez."

Ray hands him twelve.

"Gracias."

Then he's off again, carefully holding the marigolds between his right bicep and ribs as he rides west on 116th. This is one of the few occasions where a basket on a bicycle would actually be helpful. He doesn't want to put them inside his messenger backpack for fear they might get squished, and leaving it open at the top would run the same risk should one fall inside, or an even worse fate should they all come tumbling down into the Spanish Harlem streets. But, whatever, this system is working so far. Baskets on bikes are pretty inefficient, and overall pretty stupid… for show, for women and dandies who want to use them as transportation to and from picnics. He just has to take it sort of slow.

And he does. The pace matches his mood, which has gone from manic to wistful. Another nice thing about working this neighborhood as opposed to North Brooklyn is that the cops here always have their hands pretty full, and so while he still has to be quick and careful, he doesn't really feel like he's constantly being followed. Skirling sirens won't precede anything. If he got caught, it would be in the act. Dudes ride around on motocross bikes and ATVs up here sometimes, getting up on the sidewalks, doing wheelies, being general terrors, and the cops do nothing, so his little hustle is pretty unlikely to gain their attention on these streets. He knows nobody's gonna ask the guy who looks like a flower delivery man right now if he has any stolen phones on his person. He'd probably have to snatch something from a plainclothes cop he mistook for a Frenchman in order to get caught.

Reaching the top of a slight hill at Park, Ray recrosses under the Metro-North tracks. There's a little garden center to the right holding all kinds of plants and planting supplies, an interesting use of the space between here and 117th, with a wide variety of palms outside seemingly unfazed by the storm: either they were brought inside somewhere during, or they weren't. They wouldn't have had to have been. A big storm wouldn't be a big storm without some palm trees blowing around. Now there's a notion: Maybe Katrina is concatenated to all the imported palms in New Orleans. Maybe these storms are hitting because of palms imported here. There are those huge palm trees down in that weird Trade Center building on the Battery, after all, the one by all those yachts. And that area got hit hardest. Maybe they act like magnets. These ones are small, these plants trying to beckon those El Barrio denizens not too far removed from their tropical origins, so they probably don't have as much of a pull. In footage of big storms, you never see palm trees getting terribly damaged. They just sort of flap in the wind, their fronds whipping but holding. Maybe they summon the storms, these palms. Or they're a vessel, something that a voodoo master uses to conjure the squalls. Yeah, that might make sense… New Orleans, now here. Something to do with Africans, the slave trade…

But probably not. While the residents of Harlem didn't particularly get fucked up by Sandy or Irene, those in the more impoverished parts of New Orleans did. These storms aren't an act of voodoo. They're an act of God. Of course. Like the palms of Palm Sunday, these mark the return of Christ. He's here among us now, has been for a little while, and the end is nigh…

Unless it isn't. Unless palm trees aren't magic, they're just resilient. The trees are only trees, sea levels are only sea levels. God made them and walked away and now they simply do what they do…

Right? Ray doesn't really know.

He crosses Madison, then Fifth, doing his best not to think about it. Not to think about anything. To just concentrate on the movement of his body and the road, the increasingly blander buildings here on the right side of the tracks passing by in a blur. Until…

Sometimes he wonders if Haruka was right, if he really just lost his mind at some point. It wouldn't be so bad, to actually be living; it would be pretty nice. The world was okay while he was in it. He had fun, a decent childhood, a bright future. But he knows he's not. This isn't a life, this thing he has; no, it's not a real fucking life. The way he's behaved, the prolonged adolescence, especially the strange adventure that has been his quest this year. What kind of life would it be? It wouldn't be much of one. And that's why he's doing this now, today. On this Day of the Dead he is honoring himself.

Hanging left on Lenox, he finds he can do it again. This meditation while riding. The streets will let you do that until they won't. Soon enough he's down on 110th, then heading north up Broadway. It isn't until he's stuck in the median at 114th, waiting for the light to change, that the spell is broken. He's about to go against traffic or up on the sidewalk to get to his last known residence down the declivity of this street. Here, between his old school and his old home, he feels quite literally stuck in the past. He's about to go the wrong way. This is enough to fuck with him.

In matters of pilgrimage, should you be more like a shark? Just keep moving forward, never back? Would his time be better spent on the hunt, doing the thing he's actually up here to do? How vain it is to celebrate! This can't be what he's supposed to do. But why not? As a demon, he's just supposed to do what he feels like he's supposed to do. And this felt right. It was a part of the plan for this day. There's nothing wrong with a celebration. The Eucharist is a celebration. And it's a look back. We look back to Jesus' Mass to help us look forward to heaven. No, there's nothing wrong with a celebration.

The light turns, and he keeps to the street, going against traffic. Sharks are not creatures of God. Noah did not bring any fucking sharks along on his ark; sea creatures have to be more the Devil's. Thriving there in the low, cold, dark depths. That's why Jesus was a fisherman. He killed fish. Yes, this all makes sense.

Is he ready to lay them down? Is he adequately feeling the spirit of the day? Yes, for the most part. Then why does he have to ask? Now, twice, he's questioned what he's doing here.

He looks up at what was his window, standing there with the marigolds now gripped in his hand. Maybe he should just do it: "For you, sweet prince," he says. Then in Spanish: "Para ti, dulce príncipe." He inhales, takes in the moment, then lays them down. It feels right, but not complete. Then it occurs to him: the phone, the phone he still has. He wasn't supposed to have the phone while he did this. The doubt was his subconscious telling him. He wasn't supposed to wait to throw it away in the East River today; he was supposed to destroy it in the East Harlem streets or feed it to the sewer or some shit. Right? He looks at the phone. Holy shit, it's an old one. He knew it wasn't one of the newer ones when he was figuring out what to sell, but he didn't know just how old it really was. A first-generation. Then he knows what he's supposed to do: he lays it down, too, next to the flowers.

Something warm, starting in the back of the neck, tingling up and over toward his forehead, then back down to his eyes, cheeks, lips, then all the way down through his entire body, absolutely heavenly, washes over him. It carries something away: a burden. The feeling, it's like the opposite of one of the déjà vus he'd have before. Nothing to do with the mind, no coming out of yourself to go back into yourself. It's all body, all heart. Pure bliss. Something like aftersex, but tingling all the way through to his very soul. He stands there, immobile, letting it run its course, letting his being vibrate until it can no more. But it won't stop. Is this heaven? It's a new morning this afternoon in Morningside Heights.

▲ ▽ ▲ ▲ ▲ ▽ ▲

Jackrabbit sex: pretty much the worst there is. She figured it would be bad, but not this bad. At least he has a small dick. That's the difference between jackrabbit sex and jackhammer sex, the actual worst. The only way a guy can get away with either is after some truly amazing foreplay. A delicious appetizer for Little Kaiju that's as satisfying as a meal in and of itself, something so tasty it doesn't matter what comes next. But that didn't happen here. Nope, not in the least. Oh well. It still sort of photographs well, this thing that they're doing. Or well enough for Haruka's purposes. And it's making a loud sound that should drive Ray nuts. Hopefully the microphone is picking all this up. Not that there are many nuances. It's mainly just whap!-whap!-whap! That's the noise. Pelvises and lower abdomens smacking. Oh, if only Ray were here and she hadn't had to suggest they make a sex tape. Now she must really ham it up. "Yes! Yes, Brian. Fuck me!"

"You like! That! Big dick!"

"Fuck! Yeah! Oooo! I feel! So! Full!" But she doesn't.

Brian reached out this afternoon. He found her on OkCupid and wrote to her asking if she'd heard from Ray. Apparently he hasn't been home in a couple of days and isn't answering his stupid flip phone either. It seemed like a ploy, and it probably was. When she told Brian she hadn't spoken to Ray since the last time she was over there and asked him if he wanted to take her up on the offer she had extended, with a winky face emoji, he jumped on it.

"Take it! Take it, bitch!"

Oh, what the fuck? Now she has to lie here while he calls her sexist names? This is ridiculous. She might barf. On him. And he'd deserve it! But that wouldn't be good for the tape. Ray clearly hates himself, but he's probably not into puke porn. Maybe he's actually helping out, Brian, by acting this way. Ray would've never gotten away with saying something like that to her, and the fact that Brian did will drive him wild. No, vomit does not come out of her mouth. Instead: "Oh God! Yes! I think I'm gonna cooooooommmmmmmmee!" Hopefully this will really get to Ray. And maybe inspire Brian, too: make him want to come at the same time as her. A lot of guys are into that. Either way he better finish soon. She tilts her iPhone in and makes a sexy face at it, eyes open only just so, in major contrast to her wide ecstatic mouth. This has to be the best acting she's ever done in her life. It has to be the best acting anyone's ever done period. She deserves all the acting awards that have ever existed for this performance, to be honest. It would only be fair. The major ones have mostly gone to white women, anyway. And they usually just get them for pretending to be crazy. Not much acting there really for white lady actresses. Halle Berry could keep her awards but that's pretty much it. She points the phone at Brian who looks into it and smiles, then grunts. He keeps going. Even faster, if that was possible.

Finish up now! Okay?! Finish up you moron!! She wants to say that to him. Among other things, very mean things like she does everyone else. She wants to make up more literature quotes. She wants to tell him in very serious terms that he is nothing: a nobody, a loser. That he is boring and pathetic, the kind of guy who would fuck his friend-and-roommate's ex-girlfriend because she's probably one of the only females he has not in some form or another paid to speak to him in the last six months. And then she wants to end it by telling him some of her science facts. Stuff that's really, really scary. Facts about the universe to really make him feel insignificant. She wants to tell him all of these things that are true. This is the only way she ever has any fun with guys who fuck like he does. But no. The fun must come later.

For now, she must make sexy faces and bear it, the bad sex. Oh, good. He's putting her in doggy: the beginning of the end for many guys. Should she just prop the phone up on the pillow in front of them so she can work some of her magic, make sure he comes? No, it's been a good distraction. She'll take all of the distraction she can get. "Here," he says, reaching for the phone.

Well dammit. Now she doesn't even have that. It makes sense, though, that he'd want to record them from his perspective now. His small dick going inside of her from behind, resuming in this new position. Maybe it'll make him slow down. Wait... nope.

This experience has been so unpleasant that she almost forgot about all the nice things that have happened to her in the past week. It's pretty much all she's been able to think about until now. Reminding herself will help her get through this...

It's like Sandy swept through last week and made right everything that was wrong in her life, all the big things. Haruka knows really that it was all her, her intelligence and effort, but sometimes it's nice to assign something external with meaning that marks it as a big turning point. Something poetic, like a storm. Last Tuesday people in her dorm got evacuated and she had to stay in the Kimmel Center on a cot, but she didn't care at all. She was loving Sandy. Because earlier Tuesday is when she heard Emerson had been fired. Plus, classes had been canceled and she had her computer and phone and chargers and everything, so she got to catch up on a lot of web stuff she had been missing out on by going on too many OkCupid dates. Then for fun, even though she already got what she wanted, she posted stories she received from some of Professor Towers' students over the years on the Tumblr. Really drove the nail in his big, fat coffin. She and all these students and really anyone dealing with unfairness in academia created quite the support network. Oh! And she got to meet Alec Baldwin! He came down to Kimmel to talk with the students during the evacuation. He was tall and very handsome, unlike Brian.

This stupid guy... Brian. Overeager idiot trying to use her as a Fleshlight. So gross. But it'll be okay. Because she's really the one using him. And now she'll not only get revenge on Ray when she sends this tape to him, but stupid Brian, too. Knowing how crazy Ray is, he'll probably try to fight him. Or destroy his phone. Or dick. He's lasting longer in doggy than Haruka had expected. What the fuck? More time passes. "I'm gonna come," he says, finally.

"Do it! On my! Face!"

"Oh, sweet!"

She turns around, shuffling on her knees. He pulls his condom off with one hand then grips himself, pulling up and down, the other holding the iPhone, and ejaculates towards her. Some lands on her face, but most her neck. This is the clip that would play on the big screen when her name was announced among the other nominees before getting her Oscar, Golden Globe, whatever else—her very best acting in under ten seconds. "Mmmm," she says, taking it from her neck and smearing it all over and eventually into her mouth, mugging for the phone.

"I wish I had clones so we could bukkake."

Of course he does, the fucking pig. "That'd be so fucking hot." She licks her lips, still staring into the iPhone. "But you're all I need big boy. I haven't been fucked like that in a long, long time." Brian takes his pointer finger and brings it to the side of her face, which is wet and sticky and gross. The touch of his hand feels even more revolting, though. Like he's actually intimate with her. He gathers some semen onto his fingertip and moves it into her mouth. Also disgusting. The salty taste, his pudgy little finger. She swallows, opens wide. Like she's seen in the videos. Then she giggles.

He brings the phone down. "And that's how you fuckin' do it!" She rises out of bed, quickly. "Oh, shit! I'm still recording," he says. But she's already out of the room. She heard him while walking through the living room toward the hallway.

In the bathroom, she washes. Not enough to really feel clean. It'll probably take a full shower once she gets home. Maybe two. Thankfully her dorm is open again today. Fuck, that was sickening. How do hookers do it? Drugs, definitely drugs. Haruka thinks about scouring the kitchen for some vodka, but decides against it.

She goes back to his room to get dressed, gather her things. Brian's room is bigger than Ray's, but more poorly decorated. There are flags for the Giants and Yankees sports teams on the walls. He's one of those guys. Now would be a really great time for Ray to come home, almost as good as while they were doing it. Who knows. It could happen. Unless he's dead. Actually fucking dead, not just the silliness that goes on in his mind. Could he be? Haruka hopes, even after what she just went through. Brian is fumbling with her phone still. Gross! With his semen fingers! "I kinda fucked up the end there, wish I knew how to fix it."

"I can probably figure it out." She snatches it away from him. Now she's gonna have to use a screen cleaner and some Purell. Maybe twice. The thought of Brian's sperm on her beloved phone almost makes her shudder, but she's done enough acting tonight that she can handle it. She reminds herself of the nice things. That she is a 4.0 student again. Little Miss Perfect.

"Yeah?"

"Yeah. I'll just transfer the file to my computer. Do something really quick in iMovie."

He's still naked, his gross little dick flopped over while he lies on his side in his dumb bed under sports flags. She's halfway dressed already. "Damn, you're a talented girl, Haruka."

"It's not hard." She pulls her sweater, gray, over her head. Now she is fully dressed.

"I just mean you got a lot of talents."

What she's proposing really isn't that hard. Anyone who went to college should be able to figure out iMovie, but maybe it's just people her age. Brian is older. A 4.0 at NYU is probably way better than whatever he got at Columbia. He doesn't seem very smart. How did this asshole get into an Ivy? Between him and Ray, maybe it's that Columbia simply has bad taste. But she'll take his compliment. "That's true."

He finally puts his underwear on. "Remember, under no circumstances can Ray find out about this."

"Duh. That's what I said…"

"I know, but I mean, really. I'm not an idiot. I'm sure that at first you probably just wanted to do this out of spite or something. I don't know what went on between you two, but he's my boy, you know?"

"He won't find out. You're right. Just us. Who knows. Nobody can find him. Maybe he's dead."

"Shit, maybe." Brian produces three awkward little heh sounds, a weird, gross laugh. "Nah, don't say that. When will I see you again?"

Haruka grabs her purse. "I don't know. Message me." She's still figuring out what to do with her phone now. Does she contaminate her purse with it? No. Tuck it in the front pocket of her pants, even though it's too big for that? Yes, that's all she can do. It's not worth it to ask him for Purell. She slips it into her pocket, the top sticking out.

"Can you send me the raw file now?"

"I'll send you the finished product."

"Yeah, but I wanna jerk off to it later tonight."

Hella gross. Fuck Brian. She wishes the video didn't need any tweaking, that she could just send it to Ray right this instant. But Brian's right: it will have a better ending if she cuts out the part with him trying to figure out how to stop the recording. Maybe she'll make other edits, too, ones that make her look better. No, that would take away from the authenticity. This shouldn't seem forced—it should feel like real revenge. A pure act. Because it is.

She actually wasn't planning on sending Brian anything at all, but maybe now she will. Another bit of revenge just for him. Maybe she'll cover the frame with text that tells him what a shitty lay and person he is, juxtaposed with literature quotes and science facts. All of that over her faking it with him for ten stupid minutes. That seems fun. But does she have time? Today's Monday and she did get a lot of homework assigned today. The professor in her experimental physics class is really trying to make up for the lost time from the canceled sessions last week. But she should do it eventually. Maybe this weekend. That's what 4.0 students do, they take on other projects. Things that seem like homework but are also fun. Because they are capable of that. They are capable of more than others. "That's hot, but no. Be patient. You'll have it soon enough."

"All right, but you better color correct it too or some shit. Give me more of a tan or something. Make it worth the wait." He had the same thought as her. Funny. It must be the Instagram Effect. Oh jeez. Instagram Effect? That's something Ray might say. What a regrettable thing, faking that relationship. It didn't even work to get her what she wanted and now here she is with evidence of him having rubbed off on her months later. Relationships are the worst. Haruka can't wait until she sends this and gets her closure.

"Bye." She says this to Brian, but really she means to all of it. He follows her to the door as she leaves. That familiar click, the lock going into place. A comforting sound, something that usually came right after a tender kiss… Uh-oh. Why did she care enough to do this, what honestly was the point? She already had everything she wanted. Isn't the best revenge a well-lived life?

No. This will be so much better. The ending be damned… Haruka opens up the video gallery and clicks the file. She doesn't need to watch it back to know its power. She chooses Ray as the recipient and writes "thinking of you" in the subject line. She hits send. The attachment fails, Gmail says it's too large. Fuck. Guess she'll have to wait after all.

But not long. It's a quick commute back to her dorm room and as soon as she's there she connects her phone to the computer and uploads the file to Google Drive. Then she copies the shareable link and chooses him as a recipient and sends it with the same subject line as before. There.

This upcoming weekend, she'll get Brian. Oh, will she ever. But Ray couldn't wait. Now it's finally over, now she's done with him forever, and it feels fantastic. Haruka puts on a Spotify-curated indie dance party playlist and dances around her room. But only for a few songs, maybe ten or so minutes. A celebration is deserved, but there is homework to do, then a shower, maybe two, three, to take. Then she'll see if her computer needs any updates, her phone, too. It would be nice if there were entirely new versions of the OS software available. That's how good she feels, like a phoenix.

▲▽▲▲▲▽

A ring, then another. He was in so deep, and it was oh so good, that he was actually able to block out the first. As if in a dream too wonderful to depart. But the second crept through to successfully announce the call, and now the third is too sharp to ignore. Emerson nearly jumps out of his office chair. He must end it, this maddening, ringing noise. This tyrannical tintinnabulation. An alarum for waking life, the telephone. It's the trustiest tool to yank someone away from actual productivity. Weeks have passed since the thing's rang its strident ring, since whatever foolish telemarketer dared to dial him. Surely it's not one of those again. He gave the last such a stern talking-to that he's undoubtedly on the Do Not Call list for life. So that leaves two probable options: It was a week ago today that Claire should have called to check in on him anterior to the storm, so maybe this is that overdue propriety. A call from Guilt, really, more than Claire. Or it's the university, on the horn to grovel, to admit their grave error, and ask for him back. Still Guilt, of course—simply in another form. Both would receive a chilly reception! Well, let's see which manifestation it's chosen here. Emerson picks up the phone: "Hello."

"Good morning, Emerson. It's Morty." Morton Bernstein! Now this is a surprise. His agent! Did Weisman sell him out, tell him about their meeting earlier in the year? Tell him about the project out of impatience?

He must act dumb. "Morty! My, it's been ages. To what do I owe the pleasure?"

"Well, Emerson, I heard the bad news." A long pause. Then, with tenderness: "How are you holding up?" The bad news? What the? Oh! The school! Weisman didn't sell him out; one of the ne'er-do-wells in the department must have, and not about his book—no, they're all in the dark about that, obviously—about his dismissal. They all know everybody, they all publish. Oh, the fiends! Cui bono? Well, isn't this just embarrassing…

"You know, Morton, it's a blessing in disguise, really."

Emerson is met with silence. The line isn't dead—he would hear a tone. What's the matter? Is it the connection? These damn things! They distract then don't work, they're altogether terrible! Phones! He should disconnect it and the computer, make everyone contact him exclusively through the mail!

"Hello?"

"Yes, sorry." Morton clears his throat a little. "I'm just a bit shocked is all. That's not the reaction I expected."

Of what interest is it to Morton Bernstein whether he goes on teaching, especially at his age? If anything, he should understand that he would have more time to dedicate to his writing now! Isn't that what he wants? The bloodsucker! This call is outright bizarre and uncouth. So what if they can't put his teaching title on the back flap anymore?! "How the hell was I supposed to take it, Morton? A bunch of petulant miscreants aren't interested in reading the classics, and I'm supposed to hold their hands through some silly book club, some—"

"Oh, goodness. There's been a misunderstanding."

"A misunderstanding?"

"I'm talking about Bob…" he trails off in a way that's very serious, a bit forlorn. This isn't good.

"Bob? What about him?"

"You haven't heard?"

Oh, no. Please no. "No, I haven't heard." It just couldn't be!

"Oh, I had figured… Emerson, Bob passed away last week."

No! No, no, no, no! It just can't be! Emerson loses his balance, falls against the wall. He steadies himself with a stool. It just can't! "Weisman? Bob Weisman is dead?"

"I'm afraid so." And there it is. Oh, heavens! When he suggested such a thing back in the spring, he was really only teasing! And now here it is, a nightmare come true! Did he create some sort of self-fulfilling prophecy with all that "Don't die on me" business? A suggestion to rival those made in *Oedipus Rex, One Thousand and One Nights, the Mahabharata, Macbeth*? My goodness. Retain composure now...

"Oh, my. No. No, I hadn't heard."

"I figured somebody at the publisher's office would have reached out."

"Nobody had, no."

"Well, anyway, my condolences." Morton is certainly earning his commission with this call. Oh, his reaction a few moments ago must have seemed so callous! So terrible! Thankfully, that miscommunication didn't last long... he can still hardly believe it. Robert is dead!? "He was a good man," Morton says.

"What happened? Do you know?"

"I heard through the grapevine it was cancer. Apparently, he had been battling it for quite some time—" So that's what their vernal check-in was about. He knew! Robert knew! Oh, the poor man. Perhaps he thought he would still be here to edit it, to bask and share in its greatness, but he knew the clock was ticking. Above all he just wanted Emerson to write! "But Bob being Bob, he kept it close to the vest. They say it had been in remission, but it came back this summer and took a sharp turn for the worse last month."

"Poor man. What a way to go."

"I understand there will be a funeral in a few days. Thursday. Will I see you there?"

No, that's not how he'll bid farewell to his dear friend Robert. He will do it by reading the edits he made to his old manuscripts! That is the way the man should be remembered, the purest respect he could pay him: "No, I'm afraid I couldn't bear it."

"I'm sorry, Emerson. I hate to be the messenger here, I honestly thought you knew already."

"No, I'm glad it came from you."

"I appreciate that." That was the least he could give Morton for this, now. He can just picture the old fellow: sitting in his office, working in shirtsleeves, somewhat wan, this difficult call to a star client made even more difficult by having to break such dolorous news. A drooping plant against a white wall. When you break the news of death, you become

Death, and there's always a sickle somewhere. "Is everything else all right?"

"Yes, yes. Sorry… before… I've just stopped teaching, that's all."

"You have?"

"Only recently. The youth these days are no longer interested in receiving a proper education and there was an incident at the university, but I'd rather not get into it." Emerson sits down, finally.

"Sure."

"Anyway, it may come as a surprise that I've been writing again. I'm fairly deep into something, in fact."

"It does."

Should he tell him? Yes, he should: "I had actually met with Bob this spring, following that little book review I did for *The Times*." Morton deserves this. And it is only in Emerson's best interests as well. For if this chef-d'oeuvre that he was just in the midst of reading back for the seventh time, making only minor edits to the prose, is to become canonical, it must be placed with a properly enthusiastic publisher. It must make as large an impact as it can in this strange, ever-vicissitudinous publishing landscape! And Morton should start considering this now. "What I'm working on is my last book, Morty. It was to be my and Bob's final project."

"Oh, I'm sorry Emerson. While I know it could never be the same, we'll do our best to get it into the right hands when the time comes." Good old Morton. Another of the few direct people in the book business. Now if he were gone, too, Emerson really wouldn't know where to turn.

"Thank you for calling, Morton."

"Of course. Let me know if there's anything we can do for you."

Emerson thinks. It would be nice if they could send a card or some similar token of remembrance to the widow on his behalf, or a stately floral arrangement for the funeral service, but that would be poor form. Something he'll have to do himself. "I'll be all right. Still a little thunderstruck is all."

"As we all are."

"I imagine it will just take some time."

"He was a giant."

"That he was indeed." Yes. Because only a giant could stand tall enough to bend the ear of a god. Poor Robert. In his final moments, did he think of Emerson? The beautiful book he will now never read? He will be missed. "Goodbye."

"Goodbye." Morton hangs up, then after a few seconds, Emerson does, too. He sits there for a moment on the stool, staring at the phone...

Robert Weisman is dead.

He's lost friends before, and of course family, but never a collaborator of such importance. It's like losing a piece of yourself. It's almost enough to reach for the wine, even at this early hour. But instead, he reaches for the phone jack. There will be no more interruptions today. To hell with Claire, to hell with the school. To hell with Guilt's potential call. He will finish reading back his elegy today, just as Weisman would've wanted it, then tonight will belong to the two of them. Old friends and the nine marvelous manuscripts they worked on together. Should he dedicate the final book to him? No, that might be a bit much. But a hearty acknowledgment is certainly in order somewhere in the back.

It must've happened around the time of the storm. He wonders, did Robert see it? From a hospital bed, or in his bedroom, surrounded by loved ones? Another in the string of the gods' cues. You can rely only on yourself. Yes, the book needs a properly enthusiastic publisher. But not an editor. Now he knows, undoubtedly, that he is the only human being alive qualified to make any adjustments to it.

Using the counter to steady himself, Emerson steps down from his perch, then makes his way back to the office, back to his desk. Who should the book be dedicated to, though? Really no one, but these things ought to have dedications; that, too, would be poor form. Hmmm... The only men truly worthy are the ones he's writing about. Perhaps, perhaps he will say, simply: "To my forebearers." That should be sufficient. He sits down, reaches for the manuscript, takes up his red pen, and reads.

Thank the Lord for this seat, for the absence of too many people interested in going to Queens at this hour save the creatives working in loft offices around his neighborhood and the film and TV folks en route to Silvercup or Kaufman Astoria and the lawyers on their reverse commutes to Court Square or Kew Gardens or whatever other courthouses and the spraddle-legged immigrants and ex-convicts coming off the graveyard shift and the unfortunate souls too broke for a cab to JFK. Wait... the unfortunate souls? More like the sensible. From here, Midtown East, it would take, what, forty-five minutes for a cab to get out there—and that's only if traffic was being cooperative—while the subway to AirTrain would clock in at around an hour? That's a savings of fifty or sixty bucks between the fare and tolls and a decent tip: the difference a cab could potentially make, under the very best circumstances, would be a very expensive fifteen minutes. The only real pain in the ass with what they're doing is carting luggage through the subway, but it's not that bad. He himself had hauled all of his belongings through the subway during one particularly broke-ass move right after college, the one to Bushwick, using just luggage. How could he have mistaken these wise folks for unfortunate souls? Because he's been run the fuck ragged, that's how. Ray's slipping, barely able to catch himself, because he has been a very, very busy pilgrim.

How long has it actually been? Does it matter? Not really. But let's figure it out. Tuesday morning now, a little after 8:00 a.m. He rode on up to Harlem Friday mid-morning. Ninety-three or -four hours, thereabouts. Should he make it an even hundred—follow the wise ones out to JFK, poke around there? Could there be anything to that big, even 1-0-0 number? He already swung by LGA over the weekend, maybe he should follow these sensible souls to Jamaica then the AirTrain then the terminals. Become sensible in his own right... by booking a trip, literally soaring up above the clouds in that all-important hundredth hour. *The Divine Comedy* had 100 cantos. Maybe each hour of this trip was supposed to represent something like that. Is this the way to get to heaven, finally? He'd get a one-way ticket for Austin or maybe Jerusalem and the plane would just never stop its ascent until he finally saw God welcoming him. No, not today. Ray's spent enough time on trains in the last four days, not to mention buses... and foot. Fuck a plane. We're not making this a planes, trains, and automobiles thing. Fuck Steve Martin and John Candy. The ending to that movie was super weird, totally saccharine with the strange introduction to the wife and that odd hazy backlighting. Fuck *The Divine Comedy*, too. Fuck everyone and everything. Also, didn't he already decide this was a New York-only adventure? Slipping, slipping... harder to steady himself by the second. A warm meal, his bed: These are the only things that sound good right now. It's time to go home. Yes, home. Actually, now that he thinks of it, that sounds like heaven.

Maybe it is. In another five minutes, he'll know. Maybe he'll emerge from the subway and finally recapture it.

It's been a long ninety-some hours. Feels more like nine hundred, really…

The E pulls into Lexington Avenue-53rd Street. More airport travelers will surely get on here. But will any old people? Pregnant women? Best not to risk it: Ray closes his eyes, pretends to sleep…

The dull reddish-black inside his eyelids is pretty foreboding, but not as unpleasant as the reality that he'd have to let yet another old person or pregnant lady have his seat. Of course it's the right thing to do. But you can't do the right thing if you don't know about it. And he's done more than enough of that during these last four days, trying to do the right thing or what he thinks would be best in every situation, trying to recapture *that* feeling. The doors open; he hears the people come in, luggage roll. He tries to recap it all, see if he can before reaching Court Square… do some self-imposed flashing-before-the-eyes hyperspeed montage thing here in this, the last of many legs of transit during this long weekend: It started, of course, on the Day of the Dead, with the ride out to Harlem, his work, then the short celebration. That's when he felt it, that feeling. Oh, man. What a fucking feeling! Where, how, why did it fade? He'll get there… unfortunately. So when it set in, he thought that was it. That soon he'd be floating skyward, seeing the street then city from above, then North America, the planet Earth, solar system, galaxy, the entire universe, until he was up there, up there on high in the white light with God, feeling that feeling forever, surrounded by the opalescent positive energy of everyone he ever loved who had passed on, his abuelita and abuelito, his grandpa on his mom's side, the first of the gang to die right after high school, everyone; he was to be a part of that: love, agape. But that didn't happen. Instead, after a moment, maybe ten or so seconds, the tingles started to fade. But a funny thing happened when he took a step forward, toward the door of his old building. It got stronger again. It was the type of shit the saints might write about. First he walked to the front door, thinking that perhaps the feeling was guiding him up to the old apartment itself, but that door of course being locked, and the tingles fading ever so slightly with every second he just stood there, he could only move away. Going back toward his bike made the feeling fade twice as fast as it had when he was just standing, so he decided, instead, to move the other way, down the hill at 114th toward Riverside. And the feeling, again, became stronger. This is when he got the hang of the thing, understood its rules and mechanics. And so it guided him, through trial and error, up Riverside for a bit, then over a fence into the park it shared its name with—also closed down due to Sandy, just like Marcus Garvey had been—where he thought it might be bringing him down to the water. He figured it would perhaps drown him in the Hudson in some last, bloated baptism… this positive feeling in direct contrast to the uneasy one he'd come to associate with the East River earlier in the year. But then it required he veer right around 120th Street, over a different fence and out of the park eventually all the way back onto Broadway, which he took up to Hamilton Heights, then Washington Heights. He rarely had to wait at prohibitive traffic signals throughout, and when he did, the feeling maintained until the light changed, when its degradation would snap him out of whatever slavering rhapsodic state he might have been enjoying just standing there. God, or an angel, was watching. Somewhere in the lower 160s, it had him hang right until he got to Amsterdam, which he walked up until he was hugging High Bridge Park in the 170s. He wondered if here, too, the feeling would guide him into the closed park and down to the water, the Harlem River this time, which he couldn't see from his vantage but knew would be much more difficult to get to through this park, a park he'd been to before exactly once during his lifetime for reasons he couldn't remember, and knew would involve, Sandy damage notwithstanding, neglected overgrown woodland paths and a trip down large rocky overhangs and athwart lanes of busy parkway traffic below—if he would be baptized here, he would be tripped into it, so to speak—but fortunately it eventually had him cut back across somewhere in the upper 170s. On St. Nick, he turned right again and this leg was also weird and short-lived, a tease of something beyond his grasp. In the lower 180s, he found himself cutting left for a couple of blocks, until he was back again on Broadway. He passed Fort Tryon Park, then Dyckman, and made it all the way through Inwood, all the way to the top of Manhattan Island. He thought for sure he would be made to stop here, and this would be the moment of ascent, God pulling him up by the scruff of his neck or the hood of his hoodie or his messenger backpack at this spot north of 220th, that there was something to his earlier supposition about Manhattan being structured like Mount Purgatory and the higher up in street number you went the closer you were to heaven, but no. When he stopped, forcibly, at the entrance to Broadway Bridge, the feeling began to fade, and he found himself resuming and being led across the bridge and into Marble Hill. Then he remembered this neighborhood was ac-tually technically a part of the borough of Manhattan, even though it wasn't on the island itself, instead sharing the same land mass as the Bronx, and figured the ascent would happen once he eventually reached the top of it. But it didn't, then, either. He didn't know where Marble Hill ended, just kept walking under the above-ground 1 train tracks as per the dictates of the feeling, and soon enough found himself near Van Cortlandt Park, which he knew for a fact was a part of the Bronx, and which hadn't been closed down, the storm sparing it and its plentiful trees from much damage. Inside the park, he moved beyond the play-fields, around a golf course, and into some thick woods where only crit-ters and the occasional lone creep seemed to tread. It was late afternoon and the light was failing at this point and the whole thing would have seemed quite ominous were it not for the feeling which he trusted com-pletely. That is, until it was no longer there. It went away somewhere in those woods, and no matter which direction he stepped when it began to fade—north, south, east, west—it just kept on waning and waning until it had gone entirely, as if it flitted away in the mild autumn breeze now turning cooler, and he was left in those woods alone save the birds and squirrels and the eyes of men that he could no longer see but was sure could see him. He made an X at the exact location he felt he finally lost it by dragging the toe of his shoe through dead palmate leaves in lines a few feet long, and then decided to keep going. Because he'd been venturing north more than any other direction for the last two or three hours, he figured this was the way he should still move, until he saw a sign that said "WELCOME TO YONKERS" and he knew this was too far. Van Cortlandt Park ended in Yonkers? Apparently so. He had left New York City for the first time in a long time and while relieved noth-ing terrible had happened he was sure he wouldn't find what he was looking for in fucking Yonkers. So he retraced his steps, tracked down the X, and thought maybe he should stay the night there. That he need only fall asleep at this spot and the feeling would return. The light was all but gone then, and actually staying the night seemed like a horrifying prospect as he stopped moving and it got colder and colder, so Ray re-solved to see if he could cut to the chase, if he could take a little nap then after his long day of cycling and walking. It would be enough to test his hypothesis, surely. And it was. He was able to fall asleep for about twenty minutes, which was enough to dream in that self-conscious-travel-dreaming-type way that usually happens on the subway or other lulling forms of transportation like a long bus or plane ride, that sleep that starts with plans to sleep since sleep would be better than being awake during the ride as a means to effectively teleport to where you're trying to go.

But when Ray opened his eyes after that, after little hallucinations of patterns and shapes and voices making random sounds, some words, most not, he had not been transposed to heaven; he was still in the septentrional Bronx backwoods, except now surrounded by scarier-sounding critters, the crepuscular and nocturnal—swirling bats and scrambling raccoons having pushed out the chirping birds and squirrels—and perhaps the eyes of even creepier men, though he did not really fear them. In sleeping in those woods Ray understood he looked crazy, and the one thing that will help in almost any New York City situation is to simply appear crazier than anyone else around. He would not have been ripe for raping or killing; his body seemed already discarded lying there in the woods, and as long as he wasn't stumbled upon by bored teenagers with big sticks, he would be safe. When he rose he brushed the leaves from his hair and clothing and headed back in the direction he originally came from when he entered the park, guided by distant light radiation and whirring cars through the woods and the now officially cold-ass air, until he found the fence surrounding the golf course, then the opening of the park into the playfields, and the way back to the 1 train, which he gladly took after grabbing some food at the Burger King across the street. While in his trance before, he hadn't experienced hunger, but in the time that had passed since he awoke from his nap, it became practically overwhelming. He ate his food on the train, checked his phone, which was absent of any new text messages or voicemail, and thought about what had just happened, how it related to his journey so far, in total, and where to go next. The obvious answer of course was back to the old place in Morningside Heights. He hadn't realized he left Ghost Horse there, so taken before with that oh-so-nice feeling that the thought of his having a neglected unlocked bicycle never even crossed his mind. The rapture apparently cares not for bicycles. When he arrived the bike was gone, and soon enough with it any notion of recapturing those tingles simply by returning to the spot where they first washed over him. Maybe it was never a bike, but a bier, he thought then, or hoped. His memorial was still intact, iPhone and all, which seemed somewhat miraculous until he realized the kids milling about this neighborhood would have no use for a five-year-old first-generation iPhone. He then roved Columbia's campus for a while, stood outside his earlier places of residence, then other buildings where he'd spend a lot of time—the library, dining hall, assorted school and departmental buildings—followed by area bars and restaurants, some of which had changed, but nothing. He bought more marigolds at the Westside Market near 110th Street to see if they would conjure anything if he laid them down at any of these places, going back and trying them at all the points where he had just stood by laying them down along with his childhood crucifix, which he had recently started wearing again for protection while scalping, figuring that would be just as effective as a stranger's old iPhone, if not more effective, but, again, nothing. The stares of bewildered students and strangers he could deal with, but the frustration was mounting, so he decided it would be best to get the fuck out of Columbia territory. He thought, maybe, he should go back to Van Cortlandt Park, which is actually in a pretty nice part of the Bronx, and lay his marigolds and necklace down back at the X, the spot precisely where the feeling had died, before realizing that idea sounded pretty stupid, since he'd never been there while alive, and instead he should concentrate on hitting up other neighborhoods he used to frequent between 2004 and 2007, other notable places that might carry some significance from his three or so years in New York where he could try the memorial. It would only be the Day of the Dead for another couple of hours, but, he thought, if he stayed up long enough, it would still be the same day to him. Plus, because of the storm and all the disrupted and limited train and bus routes, all public transit was free today courtesy of the MTA. First he went down to the Upper West, the AMC movie theater by Lincoln Center he always used to go to, but nothing happened, so he then moved into the park, hopping a fence then another into Sheep Meadow, where he and his friends would get together during the first days of fall semesters, still warm and before real responsibilities surfaced, or at the end of spring semesters, when the sun and skin used to come out following long New York winters—but, again, nothing. After quickly trying the Bethesda Fountain, where he used to sit and think sometimes, he left the park and found his way to the subway at 72nd Street. Next he went to Times Square, the final stop for many downtown trains, everything south of it still a little too fucked up. While he wasn't interested in the hellhole itself, he was in the surrounding theaters, where he'd catch shows as part of organized school trips at deep discounts, but even off-off-Broadway as far as the New World Stages on 50th and Ninth proved fruitless. As did St. Patrick's across town. Subsequent to venturing west yet again, regretting not trying Times Square itself for the hell of it, he went via bus to 23rd Street, where they kicked everyone off due to their limited routes, and then he walked to the Meatpacking District, an area he never liked but whose chichi clubs he had occasionally been dragged

to, followed by the West Village, then over to the East, trying the marigolds and crucifix mostly at bars, music venues, then certain NYU dorms
where he vaguely remembered partying and hooking up with a few
NYU friends of friends over those years, but again, nothing. Cheap pizza
and bodega coffee from a steaming Anthora helped perk him up at three
in the morning, when he started, again on foot, heading south, passing
through the LES and trying more music venues and bars where he may
have celebrated sundry birthdays, then through Chinatown, where he
had tried this or that dim sum spot and had sporadically bought a few
doodads, then west again, finding himself in SoHo, which isn't a place
he'd really hang out, then down into Tribeca, which wasn't either. He
could see more signs of damage than he could before on the bike earlier
in the week, which added a heavy atmosphere to the pretty dead streets
and seemed eerily reflective of what he could only admit then was his
pretty damaged mind. He didn't really know where he was going for a
while, before deciding, fuck it, he should just walk to the Staten Island
Ferry because at least he'd been there once or twice while in college for
the free views of the Statue of Liberty, and maybe they had resumed
service since he hadn't heard of it getting flooded, and at least the termi-
nal would be warm, not to mention there was a bathroom. They had
and it was and there was, but the marigolds and necklace unfortunately
didn't have any effect. After taking a coffee-pizza-burger-brewed shit, he
got on the 5:00 a.m. ferry, and unfortunately they didn't do anything on
the Staten Island side, either. Ray realized he was reaching at this point,
and that any other places would be a real leap of faith, having hit most
of the major ones he would have had the time to visit while balancing
an Ivy League workload. But still, he wanted to try. He napped on the
5:30 return trip, deciding twenty-minute naps here and there wouldn't
really count to make it a new day, and was awoken from a deep dreamless sleep by one of the ferry mates on the other side after everyone else
had gotten off. Next he found his way to the totally ravaged area around
the South Street Seaport, where the memorial wouldn't take either, then
up to the Brooklyn Bridge pedestrian promenade, nope, then back over
to Manhattan across the Manhattan Bridge, also nope, then breakfast at
the Canal Street McDonald's before heading down into the subway,
which was open and now cost money to ride again. Buying an unlimited
weekly he rode the 6 all the way up to 125th Street, where he woke up,
and decided to get on an express train to the Bronx Zoo, also open and
also nope, then down to Yankee Stadium, another nope, before going
back down to 125th and getting on the M60 to LaGuardia, the airport

he flew out of most given the straight shot to Columbia, nope, then a bus down to Corona and a ride on the 7 out to Citi Field and the former site of Shea Stadium, nope, then lunch at a pretty dope food cart back again in Corona, then back on the 7 to 42nd Street and the main branch library on Fifth, nope, then the F all the way to Coney Island, nope, and so on and so on to other far-flung corners of the city and many places in between for another three days of naps and getting up for old people and pregnant ladies on a transit system slowly regaining normalcy while he had lost any semblance of it with delirious walking and trying his makeshift memorial in front of familiar structures and eventually avoiding texts and calls from Brian and fast food and fast food shits, going really to any place he remembered visiting in the last three years he knew for certain he had been living and then places he had been during death for good measure until this very moment and the robotic female voice on the E train saying: "This is Court Square, 23rd Street. Transfer is available to the 7 and G trains."

Ray opens his eyes and slinks out of the subway car, past an old woman who was standing over him… Oh well…

When he emerges from the station, it's not God's smiling face and open arms he sees, just Queens. Will he catch Brian on his way to work?

The apartment is quiet enough for Ray to hear his own mendaciously beating heart. Nope. Good.

He makes himself some scrambled eggs with spinach and a little ketchup, eats them, and decides to take a shower before lying down. For the last day or two, maybe longer, he's been stinkin' pretty bad, mitigated only by rubbing a little soap in his pits and down his pants in this or that public restroom stall. Afterwards, he puts clean underwear and some pajama pants on and gets into bed…

When he wakes up, it's almost dark out. He checks his phone. Daylight saving time ended at some point over the weekend and it's only four o'clock. He got that solid seven or so hours that had been eluding him for three days and is surprised it was not more. Unless it's four o'clock the next day? Nope, still Tuesday, says the phone. For the first time in what seems like a very long time he opens up his laptop and checks his email.

Promos, Facebook notifications about birthdays—how the fuck do you turn those off?—nothing of real consequence… until: a message from Haruka. Oh boy. Subject line: thinking of you. This should be rich.

Ray opens the message. It's a link to a video file uploaded to Drive, the text of the link in standard blue up top, a preview of what looks like a close-up of Haruka's bare shoulder and head in profile in the footer of the message, a white play icon partially obscuring her in the middle of the letterboxed rectangle. He brings the cursor to hover over it revealing the title "haha.mov." He clicks it, and the box pops out in a half-screen theatrical presentation of the video, the sides of the browser going a semiopaque gray over his inbox. The video then plays by itself.

It isn't long, maybe a second or two, before he realizes it's a video of Haruka having sex. He doesn't really know what to think about it besides the obvious regarding her motives in sending it to him, what's communicated in the subject of the message and title of the video. Haruka's fucking someone else. Okay. He believed her when she told him while they were breaking up; he didn't need proof two months later. But out of some form of morbid curiosity—mainly a nagging disgust with her, himself, and pretty much everything else in that moment, he decides— he can't bring himself to stop watching. And it's then, about twenty seconds later, in what was surely also twined up in that curiosity, that he sees *who* she's fucking: Brian.

Okay! Now this means something. Like, important. Okay. We've got Haruka, both his ex-girlfriend and someone whose form is ingrained in his mind as the, or at least his, embodiment of Santa Muerte, a figure he considers himself still romantically involved with through memory and masturbation, fucking Brian, his roommate for the last couple of years and a troll and foil in the narrative of his afterlife. What they're doing is entirely in keeping with both of their personalities, and in Haruka's case, both of hers. The important thing to discern, Ray resolves, as they switch positions and she starts riding him, moaning for Brian like he himself rarely heard her moan, is which one she is supposed to be in that moment: if she is fucking him as herself or Santa Muerte. Like, she isn't real, she isn't actually in front of him, so while this seems *more* like a thing Haruka would do, is it actually Santa Muerte working through her? If he had walked in on it, that would be one thing… but the simulacrum, the transmission of it over the internet, would suggest it's Santa Muerte, and that she's trying to tell him something, or perhaps God is sending him a sign through her. He looks on intently—the two bodies crashing together in shakily shot footage, the streaming properties of the YouTube player without the branding Drive uses making them blur so it's hard to tell where one ends and the other begins—and perhaps more significantly he listens closely: more moaning, weird words of encouragement she would have never offered him, the whap-whap-whap-whap and more whap-whap-whap. Ray's soul aches watching this, whoever she is in it... it's really not fun. But he knows he needs to. Brian ups the ante, calls her a bitch; she seems to love it, he fucks her in doggy, she asks him to come on her face. Then after some awkward fumbling it's finally over.

Well, that was devastating. And Ray's glad for it. The devastation. It would have been truly horrible if he got hard or something while watching Haruka fuck Brian. But he didn't. At all. If anything, right now he wishes he didn't have a dick. He wishes he didn't have anything and wasn't anything, that he was in fact still sleeping and what he had just witnessed hadn't happened, no matter the actual nature of existence in death. And this is a testament to something. Ray cares. He really does. He feels like a good dude with a good conscience. A demon no longer... just a very unfortunate soul.

Then, a thought: Is that why he was sent on his fruitless chase? To get him out of the apartment? The video was clearly shot in Brian's room. When did it happen? He moves the cursor over to the upper right corner X then clicks, the theater mode player flashing away back to the message—yesterday, 9:13 p.m. Good thing it wasn't another 9:11. That would've really been too much. There was that period earlier in the year, back when he had just realized he was dead and was working as a bike messenger and then met Haruka, that he'd look over at a clock shortly after the nine o'clock hour, a.m. or p.m., and it would always fucking read 9:11. The implications of that freaked him out so much that he'd often force himself to find a clock around 11:09, thinking it would reverse it... Anyway, so that means it most likely happened yesterday evening or over the weekend. When he was gone, chasing heaven around the city. A diversion!

Unless... the two were interdependent. It wasn't a diversion. The experiences needed each other. Ray needed to be gone so this could happen and this happened because Ray was gone. Brian would've never been so bold if he were around.

Brian. Brian, Brian, Brian... Ray could kill him. Lay in wait in his bedroom, in the very spot that this occurred, and stab that little puto in the neck, watch him bleed out over that fuckin' bed where he fucked his ex-girl. Should he? Is that his ultimate function, someone so odious Ray is supposed to literally murder him? Would it be a righteous killing?

No. Not only because there probably isn't such a thing, but also because that's not what this is telling him to do. This is telling him to leave, telling him that he's been right. He needs to leave this place. Brian's place. It was a heavy-handed way of confirming that he's meant to be alone now, live alone. Perhaps to heal. To get right so he can get to heaven. But where? And how? Living alone is so fucking expensive in New York. He'll have to overpay, that's a given, but maybe he can make it work in a shitty neighborhood. Somewhere dangerous, where it wouldn't matter; perhaps where he thought before, Friday, East Harlem. Ray opens a new tab, goes to Craigslist.

So that's Brian's real role. What he has to tell him. And Haruka? Santa Muerte?

Well, it seems they are saying the same thing as Brian: Go. Quit. Give up the ghost, motherfucker. Quit thinking about me and jerking off to me. I am disgusting. A perfidious bitch. And I hate you. That's Haruka's bit. And Santa Muerte's: I'm not her. I can't be anymore. Because you probably won't be able to get hard by thinking of that face. It'll probably just make you really, really sad. I have moved on. Your last memories of it in the physical throes of love are not to be with you but with someone who has betrayed you. You need to believe in me in a new form.

He needs to find another face, another body for Santa Muerte. Jerking off to a skeleton won't work. Ain't nobody like a bone but a dog. But in due course…

First things first: He needs to get the fuck out of here. On Craigslist, surprise, surprise, everything looks pretty insane for East Harlem. Fifteen hundred for a studio? A fuckin' studio?! No thanks. ¡Que chingados! Half the asshole landlords and real estate snakes are trying to call it SpaHa. The other half call it a continuation of the Upper East Side. Same shit on StreetEasy. This isn't going well. But it's the place, he knows it. That's where he should go…

So he will, physically, to find his apartment. God will not reward him on the internet-internet, only by walking around there. Ray is highly motivated. He's not gonna stay another night in Brian's den of misery. He's gonna find his own space, among folks who share his roots, or at least half of them, Casa del Ray. And if not in the next few hours, then what's another night sleeping on the trains?

At least he never gave Brian rent this month. It was usually cool—and it *is* a *was*, now—to settle up by the end of the weekend following the first before he started bitching about it. And so since he was gone this weekend, he didn't pay. Motherfucker could try to take him to civil court for that shit when he discovers Ray's empty room later this week, if he has the balls, but Ray's got a solid case. Photographic/pornographic evidence of the source of his woes, in fact. Judge Judy, Brown, Mathis, and whoever not on TV would know what's up.

He packs some cash with him saved from stealing phones, around four grand he's kept in a box under his bed, along with his laptop, pen and pad, his Bible, and a change of clothes. Then he's gone. Back to the city for yet another search.

▲ ▲ ▽▽▽▽▽

It's happened in the past. A similar sentiment. Not just from her roommates last year—they don't even really count—but other guys.

> You could charge for that, you know. There are enough guys out there who are into this sort of thing. And you should. Cuz you're a fuckin whore.

Her cut of their sex tape with the text overlay evidently really got to him. Haruka smirks. Silly Brian, trying to react to this as if he were a tough guy. But she knows what he really is. The same as so many others: a hurt, scared little boy. Just mad that she never really liked him. Haruka's reading this message and it's like every other sentence is just WAAAH, WAAAH, WAAAH. Ha-ha.

She never got a reply back from Ray, which kind of sucks. But it seems the message was received loud and clear:

> And I can only assume you sent a version of this to Ray as well since he moved out this week while I was at work and also blocked me on Facebook.

She was hoping to learn of a confrontation between the two of them, but apparently that's it. Pretty passive-aggressive. Unless he's planning some surprise revenge for him like he did with her before. Or maybe he's planning one for the both of them. Whatever, she'd be ready. Guess she'll never be certain until it happens. At least she knows that he knows. That's all that really matters.

Anyway, he has a point, Brian. She went on a couple of other OkCupid dates last week and they just weren't the same. The thing she did with Brian, then sending it to Ray, how mean it was, the high she felt from it—it can't really be topped. Having sex with people and telling them what losers they are is like nothing now, like drinking decaf coffee or sugary soda, a humdrum, only mildly pleasant experience without any real kick. And it seems it won't be the same again. So she might as well make money doing what she's doing, take it beyond using men for nice dinners occasionally. But she's not going to become a prostitute, oh no no. There's nothing wrong with that, if that's your choice, but it's not for her. No. She is going to be a dominatrix.

It'll be nice. People will pay her to show them what losers they are, how insignificant and stupid. All without feeling like they got anything from her. Because with sex the other person feels like they get something. They feel like they get a lot. That used to be a part of the fun, because she would give them this thing they really wanted then take it away. The making them be in love with her aspect. But now she sees that it'll be fun to deny them anything at all from her. There will still be love, but it will be self-contained. Her job is to make them fall in love with their own self-hatred. Haruka will be a conduit for them to explore their true nature. Like an app: this thing with a specific form of power over them, the thing they will become addicted to.

She does a Google search on how to become a dominatrix in NYC. Various old articles come up, mostly confessional pieces from current and past dommes, links to dungeons she might work at, outfits and tools she could buy, etc. She soaks it all in, eager to start this new adventure. What a fantastic idea. So much right brain activity right now, so many neurons coming together to form new network pathways in this amazing eureka moment!

▲ ▲ ▽ ▽ ▽ ▲

Settling in is something strange, the shift to nesting after all that's involved with a move… the flurry of activity, that motion, lost to a conscious decision to finally just chill and try and enjoy it. There's always more you could do, always something else—scrub the baseboards, burn some sage—but after a time enough is enough. Today he got a new bike, currently leaning against the wall under some of his paintings of video game characters populating mountainous and sylvan landscapes, and that was his enough. Ray's got the foundation in place for his new life. He looks around. Home sweet home, baby.

Sure, it's a home that looks sort of like De Niro's in *Taxi Driver*, except even shittier because he does not yet own a chair, but whatever. He crosses the room to grab a beer from the fridge. Well, maybe it's not that much shittier. There *is* grime on the walls but not *as much* grime as T-Bickle's spot, if memory serves correct. Plus he owns a high-definition widescreen TV; that character probably woulda killed for some shit like that. Ray remembers him hanging out at home a lot, sitting in front of his TV watching this and that while he thought about shit or whatever. Right? Ray opens it, takes a sip. Hmmm… *Taxi Driver*. It's been a while since he's seen that; perhaps there could be something of relevance in there, otherwise why is he feeling such a connection with it right now as he finally settles into his new home? And why did he choose to live in one of the last areas that could still pass for seventies/eighties New York? Ray torrents it, watches it. Still good. But no clear signs.

He snagged this studio for twelve-fifty. It's on the top floor of a walk-up, across the street from some projects on 108th. He got it the day after he decided to leave Brian's: that night, quite alert quite late due to waking up at four in the afternoon earlier that day, he wandered a lot of El Barrio in a back and forth up and down matrix writing down the addresses and phone numbers of buildings with "RENT NOW" or "APARTMENT AVAILABLE" signs. This building was one of those, had a Puerto Rican landlord who liked him well enough, despite his being a little loopy from yet another night of weird half-sleep. He had only caught about three hours in the Metro-North station on 125th before calling up folks the next morning. This apartment was the third one he saw.

"You're what? Mexican?" the landlord had asked, in English, while showing the place. He fit the bill as an older semi-successful Puerto Rican landlord type—just as much property owner as he was DIY super—wearing a little straw hat, glasses, and thin mustache, but over a sweat-stained plain white T-shirt: almost like a stock photo.

"Yeah."

"I like your people. They get a bad rap around here but I like them. Hard workers. What do you do?"

At this point Ray knew he wanted the place. It had a certain old New York charm he appreciated—unlike the first he saw, which was renovated and too sterile, not to mention way too pricey at fourteen-fifty, or the second, which was a basement unit and next to the building's laundry room. This one had that seventies/eighties shit going for it, seemed nice and quiet, warm, with south-facing windows, a bodega next door. So here, after a little hesitation, Ray figured he could get on the guy's good side by affecting a bit of a Mexican-lost-in-Nueva York thing, complete with a hint of an accent, barely there, like it was coming out of him now only because he was more comfortable, but not pronounced enough to make any of their interaction before seem strange, though he hadn't said much: "Restaurants."

"Right."

"Can you do twelve?" The apartment was going for thirteen hundred, which he'd pay. But people from Latin America are prone to haggle. "I can pay cash."

"No, too low."

"But the floors are…" Ray made a slant out of his right hand.

"What? You gonna bring in a pool table?"

Ray laughed. "And the paint's peeling in spots."

"You sure you want it?" He seemed genuinely rankled, his eyes turning into hard slits peeking over the glasses resting low on his nose. The radiator in the corner of the room hissed and Ray tried to diffuse the situation with another little laugh. It did not work.

So, an appeal to emotion, and to that most basic bond among men: "Look, I like the place. But thirteen is a little high. I, you know, I send money home."

"La familia?"

"La familia."

"Bien." The landlord nodded solemnly. "You have papers? You're not gonna get me in no trouble?"

"Yes, I'm legal. Here's my ID." Ray handed his Driver's License to him. He looked it over and handed it back.

"Okay, but lowest I can go is twelve-fifty. And I need first, last, and security."

"Okay. I have that."

"On you?"

Ray reached into his bag, took the envelope that had been in the box under his bed out, counted the cash, mostly in twenties. It took a while. The landlord just stood there. Then Ray passed it over, and the landlord counted, too, faster, his fingers flying through the stippled Jacksons, Grants, Franklins.

"You can pay cash every month?"

"Yeah."

He finished counting. "Then it's yours. Let me go draw up a lease and get you your keys."

And then he did.

Ray's on a one-year lease, though with any luck, he won't be here that long. He won't be anywhere. He'll be energy, the energy of that tingle.

When he got the keys, he actually felt something like it again, the warmth and the vibration, but not for very long, and not half as intensely, fading almost as soon as it started no matter what direction he moved. But it was definitely some kind of sign, he knew. The landlord asked him what was wrong. He said he was just doing a dance because he was happy.

That was four days ago. Now he's unsure of where else to go, what else to do besides continue to snatch phones so he can feed himself and keep paying for this place and his student loans. That's what the new bike is for. Is he supposed to pay off all of his loans now? Then maybe God will let him into heaven? No, that seems too stupid. Higher education is kind of a racket; that is not the debt he's required to pay, though he'll continue paying it down since it's the right thing to do. So what is the new apartment for? Besides just not living with Brian? This is the new level. What's it about?

Sitting on his bed, Ray looks around. What has he done so far while being here? He's moved his stuff in, cleaned, set up Time Warner, bought a bike off Craigslist today, and watched some shit, most recently *Taxi Driver*.

Perhaps what he's been doing is what it's about: nesting. Perhaps there's nothing out there after all—his wild goose chase around the city a week ago yielded nothing but proof that he needed to get his own place, and so maybe it's all in here. At home.

Home: a loaded term. What is it? They say home is where the heart is; it's sweet, where we go for Christmas, if only in our dreams. Christmas? Heart? Maybe that's what the slight tingle was telling him. By being here, he can actualize his heart, the source of love, and commune with Christ. It's time to look inward, into his own heart. The walls of this studio are a reflection of what's inside. He looks them over.

What does he see? He doesn't know.

And soon he's bored, and wants to do something else. Watch something else on his TV, poke around the internet for a bit, whatever. Then perhaps his first impulse was the correct one, the first after settling in: He is to consume media. That's what people really do at home, right?

A lot of folks tend to tie the word home up with family. But most of the time family members living under the same roof will ignore each other for media. If home is about love, much of that love is focused on the web, television, movies, music, books… Love is in action, it's in what you spend your time doing. That could be hanging out with members of your family, or taking in media. So what does he want to do now?

Well, he's all caught up on *The Daily Show* and *Colbert* and *Parks and Rec* and shit, the shows he missed out on before the internet had been set up in here. He just watched a movie. Read a book? No, too tired now. A little Skyrim or Mass Effect? It's been a while since he's played a game, but nah. Maybe some music…

But first, he'll smoke a little. Aside from reading—like real reading, not skimming—smoking makes the consumption of almost all media at least a smidge better. He packs a small bowl, takes a hit, then another, and one last one. Now what to put on?

Ray's been listening to Death Grips a lot again lately, but it's too late for that, and listening to them while high regardless can be a bit much. Last month they released another album: *No Love Deep Web*. It's darker than *The Money Store* or *Exmilitary*, by turns despairing and combative, in fact fucking brutal sometimes, a clangor of primal drums, unearthly electronics, yelping vocals. Controlled chaos pushed to new limits. Music for a modern demon on the run for sure, oh man. Ray knows, since Death Grips didn't exist while he was alive, that he's the one who came up with them, and he doesn't really know how. So good, so groundbreaking, especially this last album: perfect not only for his scalping operation, but also for what he's been going through mentally since Haruka and Emerson. Cryptic lyrics about alienation, mental illness, ego, drugs, impending doom, misanthropy, the internet. Goddam. Fuck it, one song. But a mellower one. While he figures out something else to listen to. He opts for *Artificial Death in the West*, then opens up Firefox.

Where to? Consequence of Sound? /mu/? Pitchfork? Reverberating synths fill his ears, the start of that fantastic fucking song.

Pitchfork would be the obvious choice while listening to this. Not only because that's how he found out about Death Grips in the first place, and it may push him toward making up something of similar quality that better matches his mood and the hour, but because of its name:

Pitchfork. He considers this for a moment. It's one of those things that he's never really questioned until now, its name, just seeing it as its own thing, a brand. Obviously it's some Devil thing, a harbinger back to the good ol' days of rock being subversive, scary.

But what are its specific origins? For good measure he looks it up on Wikipedia.

Apparently this blog is much older than he thought it was: it's been around since the nineties, and the founder used to call it Turntable. Pretty wack name. Duh, duh, duh… Ray skims. Oh, okay. He renamed it Pitchfork when it became a daily blog, after a tattoo Tony Montana had in *Scarface*? That's pretty funny. Nothing to do with the sex/drugs/rock and roll Satan-scare angle, or pointing people toward shit; it's actually just another dude a little too into *Scarface*. Who would have thought something so snobby would be so basic and douchey in origin? Whoa. Hold on. Those same people, the dorm room dons, are usually also a little too into De Niro and Scorsese. It's always, like, *Scarface* at the top, then *The Godfather, Godfather II, GoodFellas*, and then, like, *Taxi Driver* or whatever. Does this mean he should watch *Scarface* now, see if there are any clues there? No. It's almost three in the morning. Too late for a double feature, too tired. Moving takes a lot out of you. But it's that inertia, even deciding to chill should feel hectic, like work. No. Music… he's supposed to turn to music, then sleep. This is a red herring.

By the time he's figured all this out, the song's over, and he still doesn't know what new shit he's supposed to listen to. He listens to *Artificial Death in the West* again.

Fuck Pitchfork. He considers looking up the Consequence of Sound wiki page but doesn't. The Pitchfork thing has been too debilitating, too distracting. It has nothing to do with his spiritual journey. God doesn't hate good music any more than He hates sex or drugs. All are paths to transcendence. We're all perfect creatures of God, figuring out our own way back to Him. The Devil didn't even have a pitchfork. And even if the Tony Montana tattoo was itself pointing to the Devil and Pitchfork co-opted that, it still wouldn't matter. That shit's not anywhere in the Bible; it's just medieval scaremongering. Not like the Apple thing. Ray smiles at his Dell, that replacement computer meant to help him be better. The apple is actually in the Bible.

His song is over again. More quiet, then sibilance from the radiator. New York's starting to get cold now, but not in here. Nope. One more time.

He finds himself looking up Consequence of Sound anyway. Another blog based in Chicago. What the fuck? Is that all people do in Chicago? Listen to music? Probably. Ray's never been, but he hears it can get really fucking cold. A lot worse than here. The haves stay in and argue about music, or blog about it, and the have-nots murder each other on the South Side. Right? At least he's not in Chicago. The have-not neighborhood he now calls home isn't like theirs. If he were in Chicago, he'd be one of the dickheads writing about music instead. At least the name "Consequence of Sound" isn't so multivalent, is self-explanatory with no silly origins. But he doesn't remember reading anything on there recently that led him to that great of music. Should he go to /mu/?

Fuck, the song's about to end again. He doesn't really want to go to /mu/. The dumb shit people argue about on there is too frustrating and message board culture is largely stupid. This is too complicated. Fuck Chicago, fuck music blogs, fuck message boards, fuck being a little too high a little too late. Music's still where it's at, but now he wants to watch something also. He needs to occupy himself visually so he doesn't cogitate on the iconography associated with fucking music blogs. He goes to YouTube. They'll have videos queued up for him. Something there, in his face, that he can just click on. Who cares if it's supposed to be good? At this point, all that matters is if it's better than nothing. The first thing he sees is a recommendation to watch a video by Lana Del Rey called *Ride*. Weird. How'd they get that in their "Recommended for You" algorithm? He's only seen one video by her—that *Video Games* thing from like a year ago—which, while decent, didn't convert him into a fan or anything. She was just some kind of mystifying blog darling last fall, and otherwise all he remembers about her is that she apparently bombed horribly on SNL earlier this year, though he never cared enough to look that up and see it for himself. Just saw Gawker's coverage of it for some reason. A regrettable reason. Any time spent on fucking Gawker is regrettable. Anyway, should he click? Watching shit that's supposed to be so bad it's good sort of loses its luster after you turn twenty-five. Time seems too valuable. But he never turned twenty-five… and often his time doesn't seem very valuable at all… So, should he watch this? Or maybe look up the SNL thing? No, watch this one, definitely. It's what YouTube is telling him to check out. What it told him to look at after he said to himself: Just fuckin' go to YouTube. Also, the song's called *Ride*. That's the frontman of Death Grips' name. Maybe that's the connection. Or maybe that's why the algorithm got confused. Should he really

watch this shit? In the rectangle with the video title, she's in profile, holding a rope or something, a cerulean sky behind, like the image has some
corny Instagram filter over it. Wait, in profile?! ¡Caramba! The last time
he saw a woman in profile in a YouTube-looking box it was… it was
her! He clicks.

Warmth washes over him immediately as the word RIDE fills the
player, then the tingle in the back of the neck. It's back! In full force! He
makes the video full screen and the tingle pulsates everywhere through
his being, down the neck, down the arms, then his torso, his legs, moving
into the feet then right into the toes, every inch of flesh, then deeper,
spreading throughout his nervous system, and finally soul. The letters,
white on black, fade one by one, then an exterior shot of a desert, Lana
swirling in and out of frame in slow motion as she rides a tire swing, her
hair long and wavy, flying in the wind, her neck craning back in what
looks like a form of subdued rapture. A spoken word narrative begins,
strings lifting behind it. Images of Lana as a biker bitch, a streetwalker,
a lounge singer, a young lost soul accompany her breathy words. She
speaks of seeking comfort in the company of strange men, finding her
place in the world, living her crazy life as she sees fit. The song itself
starts about three and a half minutes in. It's an orchestral dream
rock/pop number about escaping the war within by living life on the
open road, a song about freedom. Scenes of the different Lanas from
before crosscut, but with added flourishes, vivid new details: Lana
draped in an American flag with her bikers in the desert dusk, Lana
dancing slowly with a man in a motel room while wearing a big red bow
and bedazzled earrings in the shape of the cross, Lana in an Indian head-
dress playing with guns by firelight. Live fast, die young American grandeur. When the song's over, her monologue resumes. More about her
journey, more about deliverance. Then the credits and the warmth, the
vibrations fade.

Whoa. That was fuckin' something. He wouldn't have been that into
it if not for the feeling; the song was just okay, and while her monologue
was occasionally pretty in terms of word sounds—alliteration and asso-
nance and consonance and whatnot—the sad girl tropes in what she was
saying weren't really for him. The thing was shot and edited like it was
being marketed to froward fifteen-year-old girls, which it most likely was,
like Lana in general most likely is. The type of teenage girls who watch
Gossip Girl and were assumably the only audience for that botched U.S.
version of *Skins* that was so heavily ballyhooed on the subway last year,
who can't wait to move out of the suburbs to the big city, who try coke

the very first time they see it cut up on someone's vacationing parents' coffee table: basically NYU girls in three years. Aha! NYU girls, like Haruka. Is that the connection? Why were they both in profile?

He looks Lana Del Rey up. Her name as listed on Wikipedia is actually Lizzy Grant, and she didn't go to NYU, she went to Fordham. That's intriguing. A broken Catholic, like him. Is she what some on the blogosphere condemned her for, what he just thought of her as: a product? Baseless indie nostalgia dressed up for the mass market? Or is she something more authentic? Her debut album was called *Born to Die*. That's loaded. He watches the video again. The feeling doesn't take hold, though he doubted it would, and he's sort of glad because he's able to look more closely. He decides, soon, that she's not a product. It's in the nails. Her long nails, her manicure. They're very strange for the type of thing the Illuminati would be trying to sell—almost Jersey, these nails. This is an individual. A very Lynchian individual.

A bit more research, trying to get the whole skinny. He finds pictures of her before she was famous and with his first peek of Lizzy there's something even more interesting: the understanding that she isn't real. While her retroussé nose indeed seems genetic, the person she was before was a sportive blonde with thin lips, not this sultry brunette, this pouty lost girl singing of life and death, of profound matters of the soul.

Her face is not real. She's not real. She was perhaps invented by Lizzy Grant, or perhaps by God, for him. Del Rey? Of Ray. Through her, he can ascend to that heavenly realm.

Ray watches the video one more time, and before long, a tingle does come over him, but not *the* tingle. This one's in his pants, and it demands action. Santa Muerte has a face again.

▲ ▲ ▽ ▽ ▽ ▲ ▽

If it hasn't come by now, it won't. He knows this. It's far, far too late, beyond anything remotely acceptable, even as empty a gesture as it would be. So why does he keep glancing over at the phone, wondering? Why did he begin checking his infernal email twice a day rather than his old custom of only twice a week? Because an empty gesture is still a gesture, but much more than this, it's better than dealing with the truth. The truth has been having its way with Emerson lately, has been tearing him apart inside, and he's just sick of it. Just absolutely sick of it. That's why he keeps looking over at the phone. That's why he'll probably log back on to the computer in an hour, before he orders takeout for the eleventh time this week. Because any distraction at this point is better than his reality.

The truth can have a funny way of revealing itself. One would like to think, in all its undeniable power, it would always be obvious. Either golden, a glorious beam that parts the clouds and lights the way, or totally hideous, a nasty pit that opens up in the earth, completely dark save the theroid eyes and teeth of those terrible monsters that reside there. But it can be sneakier than these. It can be pernicious. It can creep in like smoke, slowly but unwavering, until all that's left is that blackness that one would expect in the pit, but instead of the monsters, it's the thing itself that begins to kill you, only from the inside out. And this is the type of ineluctable truth that he's had to deal with these last two weeks, since learning of Weisman's death.

The truth is that Emerson's alone. Utterly. And unlike what he maybe thought before, there is absolutely no virtue in it. It's only horrible. Abject sadness. He was simply in denial then; no man is an island... or, at least, he shouldn't be. Donne was right. England, after all, has Ireland right there. As much as they've feuded over the years, they still have something in each other. A bond. All islands need some sort of connection, even the great ones. Crete is still in the Aegean Sea—is one of many Aegean Islands, part of that archipelago. Emerson not only has no surrounding islands, but no islets either. If the food delivery men count, perhaps they could qualify as offshore rocks, but this might be a little too generous.

Should he go out? Take a walk around the block? It's been weeks since he's left, maybe over a month. No. There's nothing for him out there. There's nothing for him anywhere...

Oh, what a terrible feeling this is! Why couldn't Claire have just done the right thing? Why didn't she call and invite him to Thanksgiving, extend the olive branch, be the good child and overcome that little bit of unpleasantness after his request? And now it's only three days away. Is she really expecting him to make the next move? She couldn't. Oh, if only. If only...

Emerson sighs.

Yes, if only. Then he wouldn't feel like this. But she didn't; and now here he is, sitting on the sofa, reading back his awful manuscript—that's right, awful!—sneaking peeks at the phone after every other paragraph.

That little bitch! No, no that isn't any way to think of your daughter, your own flesh and blood...

And honestly, it isn't her fault that the new book just isn't that good.

He learned this after Weisman's passing. Oh, Emerson's been such a fool. Hornswoggled not by some incarnation of Nemesis, no, no, only himself. Vanity of the highest order. A dupe worse than Narcissus. To think: he could tell the Culture's story as one would a person's? Delineate the phases of something so complex and significant, so far above man, as he would some mere individual's? The closest attempt there was at something like this was the New Testament, and it's hardly the best part of the Bible. And the Bible, really, is just one of the many, many texts that make up the Culture. That's what he signed himself up for. Bedlamite! An impossible task! Sure, the thing is readable, but it's readable precisely because it's all wrong, all false! Nonsense! Forced stultiloquence from a man who long ago lost his touch, hardly deserving of the subject at hand!

That's what reading back all his old work revealed to him in his mourning of Weisman. It showed him that he himself *had been* a genius. No longer! Those books, those books were so perspicuous and stirring and logical and good. What the hell has he been wasting his time doing? Indulging his insanity, that's what.

Just like the Culture itself, he has gone absolutely mad. He might as well have written his own damn autobiography. Because that's what the thing reads back like now. It doesn't read like the sterling criticism he wrote in the twentieth century. No. It reads more like an utterly second-rate autobiographical novel: just an exaggerated, idealized version of his own life story with the occasional passage of poetic élan, trying to coast by on pretty but quite meaningless prose, purple to the core. This book isn't even remotely like his others. How could he consider it his tenth work? Critical theory can't be presented as artfully as poetry or fiction! A fool's errand. Totally. Capote could barely get away with writing like this in his narrative nonfiction, let alone... No. No need to drag Capote into this. Why does he keep thinking about Capote? He wasn't even that good... The point is, the point is the whole thing is a bust; it's either back to the drawing board or a complete overhaul of this atrocious stack of paper here. Otherwise he'll leave this planet having only written nine books, and that would be unacceptable. Nine? There is no authority to that number! It must be ten!

How is he to do it? Weisman would know. Yes, he would. Perhaps Emerson made other missteps like this in the past, and Weisman was his saving grace. He can't remember. It was so long ago… But it doesn't matter. Because he's gone now. Even though Weisman would probably know, Emerson won't. Because he is all alone.

It also doesn't help that this week would have been his and Diana's forty-fifth wedding anniversary. Wednesday. She looked so beautiful that cloudless, crisp fall day…

Claire was the only thing Emerson had left from that union, but now she, too, seems to be gone.

Alone, alone. All alone. Alone. Alone, alone, alone…

How can he cope? How can he fix his final book? He can't do it completely on his own. It's always required an assistant, an editor. The process. He cannot trust himself. If he is an island, he is a volcanic one. Alone in a troubled sea. Alone…

Alone, alone, alone, alone…

Emerson rises, crosses over to the kitchen. He pours a nice, full glass of cabernet. He sits back down. He thinks.

But how can one who has been abandoned—truly, no one left in sight—be less alone?

Before, his answer would have been "books," but now he can't bring himself to believe it. It was a taradiddle wrapped up in weltschmerz, just some defense mechanism to feel better about being an unpopular youth, about being as lonely as he was. No. The last of his real friends is dead. He says a little prayer, and he hears his old, rasping voice reassure him: "I've done my part."

"Is that all, Weisman? Am I supposed to be here alone?" he asks. There's no response.

But then: his old, fake friends chime in.

"Knowing yourself is the beginning of wisdom," says Aristotle. A smile from Emerson, a sip. Then: "What is a friend? A single soul dwelling in two bodies."

Next it's Dante. "The path to Paradise begins in hell." My word! It certainly does! "Remember tonight… for it is the beginning of always." Cryptic, strange. Oh, Dante… he could have done without that last one! Someone, please, say something a bit more cheerful.

"Words are easy, like the wind." It's Shakespeare to the rescue, of course. "Faithful friends are hard to find." Emerson nods knowingly. Oh, goodness, are they ever. A beat, then: "Be not afraid of greatness, Emerson." Shakespeare addresses him personally, just like he would.

The next and last voice, strangely, belongs to Yeats. "What can be explained is not poetry." Yeats is good, but not nearly as good as those who spoke before him. Nevertheless it is he Emerson hears. And it is that which he says.

Then all is quiet.

Emerson sups, thinks more. Poetry, huh? Isn't that what the very best writing is, in some way or another? Aristotle laid it out in his *Poetics*, poetic in itself. Dante, first and foremost a poet, invented a language for heaven's sake. Then there's Shakespeare, every bit the poet that he was dramatist. And of course Yeats. And now… and now he himself? Is that what they're telling him? That his writing doesn't have to be like the pellucid academic work he produced in the last century? Has he been too hard on himself these past few weeks? Were they reassuring him?

Emerson can't know because he doesn't know, and nobody else is here to tell him. His fake friends are gone; nobody alive could tell him. He considers, again, what it was they said.

He needs his soul in someone else's body; he needs that friend. Right now the closest thing he has is this wine. He drinks it all down. Makes them really join forces. He withdraws the glass from his lips and places it down on the coffee table before him, catching his warped reflection in the wide bowl as he leans back. Then: an epiphany.

Emerson knows just what to do. He looks first at his manuscript, neatly resting atop the coffee table beside the wine glass, then over, past the phone, to his set of kitchen knives, their handles sticking out of a bamboo block, and lastly, toward his open bottle of wine. Yes, yes. There's an answer indeed.

Taking one last disapproving look at the manuscript, well illumed by the room's harsh overhead light, he stands up and quickly crosses into the kitchen, where he removes a small knife from the wooden holder with a jerk and shing, then, using his other hand, snatches up the bottle, a rivulet twirling out in a ruby ribbon as he hastily rounds the corner. Moving down the hallway, he drinks. He enters the bathroom and places the knife beside the tub before leaning over it and turning the H faucet handle and the C one ever just so. After opening the closet, he retrieves a handheld mirror, which he lays down next to the knife. Another swig and he places the wine down, too. He undresses. He takes a long look at his strange, bearded face and bare, corpulent torso in the bathroom's vanity and sees a man with a story, in the end a very tragic one. There is no denial, no anger, no depression, no bargaining, only acceptance. It's in the eyes. He lowers himself into the tub, which is now quite full and, as usual, just a little too hot, and after cooling the stream for a few moments turns off the faucet.

For minutes, he just sits there, his large, pale body bunched up in manifold mounds, bony at the joints, otherwise very round and dimpled. Reclining a bit more, head still above water, he breathes deeply. He tries not to think about anything during this, does his best to merely feel the warm water, watch the steam rise, appreciate everything here as much as he can as the simplest of pleasures.

Then it's time. The first thing he reaches for is the wine bottle. Glug, glug… glug, glug… soon it's gone. He wipes his mouth and folds his hands over his colloped belly. Another deep breath as the last of it slides down his throat. Next he leans over and carefully grasps the handle of the mirror. He balances it atop the faucet, the broad side down and handle resting precariously up against the shower pipe, giving himself one last look into his eyes before the big moment. A little rheumy, but wow… such a deep, beautiful blue. Deeper than the sea, than the color of the very planet we inhabit, those wonderful eyes of his! Narcissistic through to the very end, isn't that right old chap?! he thinks. One's final moments shouldn't be without a little humor. This thing isn't so serious, life. The greatest moments of tragedy are lost without a bit of levity. It's okay that it's come to this. Somehow he always knew it would. He winks.

Reaching over again, he goes for the knife. And now, the coup de grâce: careful to avoid another look into the eyes, he reaches for the mirror and directs it at his genitals. It's the first time he's seen them in quite a long while, years maybe, and it's a very strange sight indeed. His penis has collapsed into itself and appears at least twice as wrinkled as any other part of him, more wrinkled than he thought was possible; the hair around everything is a lighter shade than it could have been before, the scrotum darker than he remembered. It's altogether hideous. And that's fine, because it's not going to be like this soon. Yeats. Yeats, Yeats, Yeats… Emerson asks him to guide him through this. To hold his hand, as it were, through the process. He doesn't hear the man, as he did before; instead, Emerson hears his own voice speaking Yeats' words:

> *Picture and book remain,*
> *An acre of green grass*
> *For air and exercise,*
> *Now strength of body goes;*
> *Midnight, an old house*
> *Where nothing stirs but a mouse.*

My temptation is quiet.
Here at life's end
Neither loose imagination,
Nor the mill of the mind
Consuming its rag and bone,
Can make the truth known.

Grant me an old man's frenzy,
Myself must I remake
Till I am Timon and Lear
Or that William Blake
Who beat upon the wall
Till Truth obeyed his call;

A mind Michael Angelo knew
That can pierce the clouds,
Or inspired by frenzy
Shake the dead in their shrouds;
Forgotten else by mankind,
An old man's eagle mind.

And just like that, the hand is held, guided to do the deed. The knife goes in, the blood comes out. He creates an incision through the base of his penis where it meets the scrotum, penetrating the urethra to the bulbocavernosus urethra, just as he remembers from Forrest Bess's drawings. In this slit he's created, essentially, and just like Bess, a small vagina between his penis and testicles. Soon he is surrounded by red. But this matters not, because he has been born again in the water—his own mother and father, his own friend and lover, capable of anything and everything. And there his penis is, remade. There his vagina is. He's pleased to meet it. The pain is excruciating but he's still so, so pleased. Emerson tilts his head back and submerges himself fully, careful to exhale while underwater, and only briefly. He needs to get out of the tub now. Can't risk falling unconscious. Things are getting a little hazy… Losing blood… But it matters not… matters not…

He gets out of the tub, carefully but quickly, and realizes he didn't set… himself out a towel. The old him was… such a fool. Worse than Falstaff… He grabs the hand towel to stop the blood flow, then gets himself a proper towel… from the closet. As he steps out of the bathroom and into the hallway, he… wraps himself up in the thing, a clean white bath towel over the white hand… towel he's still using to apply pressure to the new source of… his powers. It is not his far-gone mind that will do the thinking now… it is this, this, this! This! He unlocks his front door… gets it ready for them. Then… with the… last remaining bit of… strength he can… muster… he dials… 9-1-…1…

Sometimes the sessions can get a little boring. Like right now. Nothing's really going on. Nobody's posting to Instagram. Facebook's pretty quiet. Nothing interesting is trending on Twitter, nobody's arguing about anything. And Tumblr on the phone isn't really the same. You don't get the full experience that you would on a larger screen, unfortunately. She's already read a couple of HuffPo and BuzzFeed articles, but they weren't that good. Slow news day, both personally and in the actual news. So she's mostly left with what's right in front of her. It's moments like this where what she's doing actually feels like work. Thankfully, his time is almost up. Haruka pulls the chain. Her sub yaps.

It's a muffled yap, but a yap is a yap. She knows the abrupt squeal well now that she's been at this for a couple of weeks. What sounds so terrible from a dog or small child is just wonderful coming from a grown man. A little dopamine surges, and now she doesn't feel so listless.

But it's still good that his session's almost over. Who knows how long the dopamine will last. Plus Allison should be back soon.

Her phone vibrates. A text from some guy. That's nice. She's always happy when she can set up other appointments during an appointment. Keep the "non-billable hours," as they say, to a minimum. It's a lot like how she used to set up dates on OkCupid while on other OkCupid dates, maximizing her time. Some habits just translate well to other undertakings. Some things are just in one's nature. Efficiency, multitasking, being forward-looking in general: these are in hers.

The text is from a new number, which is even more exciting. Third new number this week. Word is spreading. It looks like Empress H, the Dorm Room Dominatrix, is really starting to make a name for herself.

That's how she's known on the web, on Backpage and the other SW sites where she advertises. She offers a unique experience. While everybody else is basically still doing the same thing from the last century, abusing people while dressed up in leather and stilettos, she's tweaked it for modern times, made it better. She doesn't need a costume or dungeon, some other stark environment. That tired aesthetic. No. Only her room at NYU, dressed as herself. It's completely innovative. And effective. Her clients cry sometimes, thank her profusely, give her more money than the five hundred per hour she had originally quoted them. They say they've been looking everywhere for someone like her. She currently enjoys a perfect 10 rating on The Erotic Review.

When a potential client contacts her, first she has him fill out a form on Google Docs asking him to tell her about himself. She requires some broad strokes about them: their name, contact info, line of work, if they're married, if they have a family, what they're looking for from this. All with complete confidentiality of course. Then there are some optional questions about their upbringing and fears. In doing her research, she was surprised to learn that a lot of dungeons and escort services require quite a bit of personal information from their clients. So she's following suit. It makes it seem like she is doing some very careful vetting, taking this very seriously, and they like that. Everybody wants to be a part of something exclusive.

Once they've filled her form out, she'll wait a day or two then say they've qualified. She'll ask if they want to make an appointment. Offer some times when she's available, then see what works for them. Right now it's only lunchtime and weekends. Then after making the appointment, she'll actually take the time to look over what they've written. Get to know what she can use against them. And during the sessions, she does.

A typical first-time session begins when she goes down to sign them in with security, where she acts nice, engaged, asking them a few questions about how their day is going as they make their way back to her room. What a perfect college girl. What a charmer. Then when she shuts the door behind them, she'll ask for her money. After counting it she'll spit in their face and tell them that she doesn't actually care about what they were just saying. She'll tell them that other dominatrices are liars, that they're just acting when they're being mean to them. But that she is acting when she's nice. That this is the real her and the person they deserve in their lives to be brutally honest with them for a change. And then she'll go on to insult them about their problems, or their appearance, or whatever.

This will last for about ten to fifteen minutes. For the rest of the hour, she simply puts them in timeout.

Timeout involves a bit of a throwback to the old dungeon sensibility, but little else is borrowed from that. She makes the men strip naked and wear a gimp mask linked to a leash, then kneel facing the corner. It's sort of by the wastebasket in her room. The mask has no eyeholes. Just a zippered mouth, so they can breathe. Poorly. She tells them to think about what she's said.

It's kind of like therapy, but instead of trying to help people work through their problems she uses them to hurt them even further. She validates the problems, which validates the person and what they're doing seeing a dominatrix, and helps them live in a world of their own shit. Most people will live in their own shit if they have enough time or money. These rich, old white men not only live there already, but want to add onto it. A man is little more than his problems. The men love this because they hate themselves, and even more than this they love to hate themselves.

While she tells them to think about what she's said, she just sits on her bed and does homework or plays around on her phone for the next forty-five minutes or so, occasionally tugging on the leash. Not too hard, just to remind them she's there. A little way of showing them that what they're going through in their own heads isn't really their doing, but hers. It's very clever. Much better than all the abuse other dommes usually have to dish out, as she understands it. That would take too much effort. All the whips and stuff. Timeout, like with kids, is a way more effective punishment than spanking. They do the work, she gets the credit.

She imagines the experience for them is sort of like what's supposed to go on in a sensory deprivation tank, except they're primed to only have a bad trip. When she tugs, some of the idiots probably think they're experiencing some sort of breakthrough, something very profound. She bets a lot of them must have been teenagers or in their twenties during the seventies, when *The Dark Side of the Moon* and *Wizard of Oz* mashup thing was big. A friend of hers with a dad about their age had her do that in high school. They ate pot brownies and watched. It was kind of stupid. She thinks it must be sort of like that for them. False meaning in coincidence. They either really enjoy that aspect or the fact that being a sub in a dorm room is even more humiliating than in a dungeon. Especially with the lady calling the shots being so young and also a minority. For many of these guys, it has to be a fucking nightmare. She can only imagine. But it's what they want and what they pay her well for. It can't

just be the discomfort they feel from the mask and leash and being naked, the pain that shoots through their aging arthritic knees.

She has two steady clients already, executive types who like to see
her a few times a week, including this one here. He's the quieter of the
two. The other moans sometimes while in timeout without her even tugging on his chain. So she says, "Shut up!" This guy makes no noises
while in timeout unless she tugs, as it should be.

With them, she builds on the insults from the first session or creates
new ones, which isn't hard. Both of them are not only old but ugly and
have wives and kids and work in finance. There's a lot to play with there.
Many ways to make them feel shitty and guilty, including simply for being there with her. "What would your kids think if they could see you
like this?" she might say at the top of the session. "Scum!"

One thing she won't do, though, is overtly talk about systemic issues
they're complicit in. She learned that in her research. Nobody wants to
talk about feminism or racism or anything like that. No big societal problems where they're made out to be the passive bad guy. Everything must
be on a micro level, specific to them, not macro. Because she looks the
way she does, they're buying into her identity politics anyway. Her other
steady client actually admitted to seeking her out because he works a lot
with the Chinese markets. China scares him, he says. They're making
bad investments and building entire cities on spec and America owes
them so much money and they have a decent military and many, many
people. The opening of the Olympics in 2008 was genuinely frightening,
he believes. Nightmares from the drums. By coming to her, he can face
his fears in a safe environment.

She said many mean things to him for this. Not only about being a
racist, but about being weak, about being too pathetic to really enjoy his
privilege. It's okay that she calls him a racist because he's admitted to
being as much. But it wouldn't be okay to talk about racism in general,
bring up black people or another race. She spoke of his specific privilege,
not white privilege as a sweeping concept. That's the difference. Again,
Haruka knows that he's not really facing his fears, but wallowing in
them. She doesn't care though. Money's money. It also doesn't matter
that she's only half Chinese. He obviously doesn't know the difference,
can't recognize the features on her face that are clearly Japanese. Stupidity goes hand in hand with racism. It's not a surprise, she knows this
all too well already.

The timer on Haruka's phone goes off, interrupting her as she absently scrolls through her Instagram feed for the second time in five

minutes. The session is complete. She pulls hard on the leash and says, "Time's up."

He remains on his knees, which they're instructed to do because she's so short and it makes the next part easier. After walking over and removing the leash, she helps him take the mask off. He breathes deep. She turns around and places both objects neatly on her desk, then returns to her phone while he dresses.

"Thank you, Empress H," he says. He wipes his face, which has gotten quite sweaty from being confined in the leather for so long. Gross. "That was a very intense session. I thought a lot about my adolescence, my mother, what brought me to—"

"I don't care. Save it for next time. I don't want to hear about your stupid mom or about what it was like growing up in the 1800s right now. Your session is over."

"Right." He fixes his hair, salt and pepper and a little shaggy.

"Now GTFO."

"Huh?"

"Get the fuck out, you dinosaur."

He smiles, pulls out a few more bills for her as a tip, then leaves. Haruka hears the door to her suite shut behind him. Allison should be back any minute. Haruka wonders if she ever sees them coming down the hall or out of the building. Other students must, probably think there's a prostitute among them like her old suitemates did. But maybe not. These guys also look like they could be students' dads.

Haruka tries her best to schedule appointments for when Allison's in class, but as business grows, it's getting harder. That was their agreement. But now she's going to have to start scheduling some evening sessions, not just lunchtime. She hopes she'll be cool with this; that after a little more talk about smashing the patriarchy, Allison can maybe spend more time in the library. That is, if she doesn't go for what Haruka actually has in mind.

That other client, the openly racist one, sort of got her thinking. To him, and everyone else, though more subtly, she's their own Chinese boogeywoman. Some strange, small dragon lady meant to represent personal, work-related, or geopolitical fears. While her unique, innovative approach is what's getting these guys to leave good reviews and come back, it's her looks that first get them through the door. Men are visual creatures, everyone knows this.

Not everybody into this type of thing likes Chinese or Asian girls, though. A lot just stick to their own kind, to white girls. But pretty ones, like Allison. So if she were able to do it, too, while Haruka was in class, and Haruka could take a little cut, then she could really multitask. It would be a win-win. Prosperity and happiness for the both of them. Allison, like her, loves good food. Haruka is making so much money that she hasn't been to the cafeteria since she started, instead ordering Seamless from all the best restaurants offering their food on there. She can see the jealousy in Allison's eyes when she's eating it.

Haruka is thinking about asking her soon. Grow the business like a real entrepreneur by scaling out. Maybe she can secretly record one of her own sessions so she can show her just how easy it honestly is. That might be good.

But first things first: she'll tell Allison she can stay anonymous and safe, like her. In fact, the idea she had for her plays right into that. Sort of inspired by her other client, Haruka thinks she should pretend to be a Russian girl. Put on a little accent. That's usually the type of white girl that finds themselves in the greater sex work industry now, Russian or similar. It'll feel authentic. And with Haruka's new approach, all the men will love her, Allison.

China is the new enemy of the straight, white American male. China and the Arabs. But growing up, for them, it was Russia. The Red Scare, duck and cover. Allison can tell them she knows all about it. She could terrify them. It would be incredible. Haruka laughs to herself loudly, she's so excited. She's been standing for a while, daydreaming like this, and sits down.

Another thought: if this worked out with Allison, if the system really proved itself, she could expand even further. Get an Arab. Or an Indian girl, it would be the same to these rich asshole idiots. Then Hispanic, black, everything. There is a fear out there for everyone. She could potentially have the most successful NYU dorm room startup since Def Jam. Any girl at this college or really any progressive school could and should want to be a part of something like this. It would be completely legal and badass. The rhetorical defense is ironclad. Haruka shakes her head, she's so blown away by her brilliance.

Are there any problems with her ideas? Of course the university doesn't like businesses being run out of the dorms, and expanding would make things harder to manage discreetly. But if they ever caught wind, she could just move out. By then, she'll be rich. Two hours of her time could cover the monthly cost of a room in an apartment now. Four hours her own apartment. She'd just have to make it look like a dorm room, or otherwise kind of embarrassing and strange, no place a rich man should want to be, in order to maintain her brand.

A brand. Haruka's really building one, now. But aren't we all? Aren't we all? Hers is just smarter than most. First an empress, then an empire.

▲ ▲ ▽ ▽ ▲ ▽ ▽

Time to pull the trigger, time to make it official. The finger glides and the arrow moves in a sharp line, morphing into that weird gloved hand as it hovers over the PURCHASE button, but only briefly, because just as soon as it takes shape the thumb drops and smacks the plastic below then bang! It is decided. Ray's heading to Austin for Christmas in two weeks.

He leans back, sort of pushing the laptop away from him at the same time, and stares at the order confirmation page. White light from a glass screen—colors, symbols, words, a simple presentation that belies something pretty complex: that he is going to be there. When he really thinks about it, booking this trip is almost as hallucinatory as anything else he's experienced lately. Not just because it's actually fucking weird that an arrow should morph into a hand, or that by submitting numerical data meant to represent little pieces of paper, he'll be able to board a flying aluminum tube, but also, and primarily because, it's been two years since he's seen his family. Lots has happened since then, most importantly the realization of his own death.

But now more than ever it seems like he needs to go there and be with them and love them. Even though he's working off a whisper, galvanized by something that could have been little more than a trick of the mind, it feels like it's the right thing to do. He's looked out there, looked within, and now the signs are pointing toward bringing it all back home, back to the start. Austin—the grasslands. It sort of makes sense. He's thought it before, just didn't do anything about it. But now, during the holidays, the timing couldn't be better. Maybe this is the culmination of everything. Home should feel like heaven. Didn't someone once say, "Death is a homecoming"?

If not, they should have. Ray looks this phrase up. Searching for the term between quotation marks, getting only exact results from Google, he learns that apparently someone did, back in the eighties. It was expressed in those precise terms by some rabbi he's never heard of in an essay he's never read. Something titled "Death as Homecoming." Great minds… He has no interest in reading the rest of this dude's piece, however.

Was it another, similar quote he might have been paraphrasing when he asked that question? Or was it actually his own original thought? He searches again, this time without the quotation marks, modifying it to the phrase *death going home*. He finds several similar sentiments. A Chinese proverb suggests, "Life is a dream walking. Death is going home." That's one he'd rather not contemplate. It preys on past fears a bit too much, could put a damper on his high hopes. But Mother Teresa said, or maybe wrote, "Death is nothing else but going home to God, the bond of love will be unbroken for all eternity." More positive and matter-of-fact, that one he likes; maybe that's where he got his quote from. His mom is a pretty big Mother Teresa fan. She could've shared it with him when his grandpa died or something, trying to console a distraught teenage Ray. He especially likes this variant because it implies that there is no such thing as hell, that all there is is heaven, and the heaven of his imagining: that oh-so-good feeling of endless love.

But how could that be? He's dead, and this isn't heaven… He closes out Firefox, lowers the lid of the computer. Content not to confuse himself further. He thought he sorta had things figured out, and he wants to hold on to that; not divagate. Ignorance really can be bliss.

Will this be it? Or lead to it? The real homecoming? he wonders. Unfortunately, the "going" part in Mother Teresa's thing is taking quite a long time. Maybe that's it. The "going" part can encompass being stuck like he's been. Perhaps that's all that purgatory is—prolonged death throes. It's entirely possible that it's still 2007 and he's lying in the street, struck by that car only seconds ago. Trapped dreaming through his last seconds of life, a sleep paralysis episode lasting years and years. Uh-oh. Now he's letting the Chinese thing get to him. Why did he have to read that shit? Because maybe he was supposed to, and maybe they're right.

Consciousness is a tricky thing. It's something he's known before, but sort of forgot. The last few weeks fucking with some pretty serious hallucinogens have more than reminded him, though:

It started about a week after he discovered Santa Muerte's new face. He was glad she chose Lana Del Rey as the vessel with which to reintroduce herself, and that week he got to know the new persona that went with the makeover very well through her music, words, videos. She seemed ideal for him in a more obvious way than Haruka had been. It was in the broad strokes: how he'd never actually met her or would meet her, how she was someone he could only know through a device—their relationship completely postmodern. She was physically attractive, but contrived, presenting herself with something of an integument, so she was little more than an idea—and that made her seem vulnerable, attainable. Like if he knew this strange girl with the gaudy nails and fake lips in real life, he might have a shot. But he wouldn't meet her; she was designed for him, clearly, but only as an object of media. One perfectly suited for his unique case.

There was, of course, the *Born to Die* aspect... and the EP that followed being called *Paradise*... As someone who died young, Ray was indeed born to die, and the thing he had been striving for since the discovery of his death was paradise. These characteristics made it seem acutely evident, almost too good to be true.

The music itself was only so-so at first, but after listening to her and nothing else, at home, or out while stealing phones, it felt greatly rewarding with enough repetition. The main draw was the videos, though. Beginning with the experience that first night, he masturbated to them regularly over the next couple of days, and by the end of the week, these acts were carried out with almost religious fervor. She had begun to interfere with his work, insomuch as he stopped doing it, stopped stealing phones altogether. Her music had grown on him, literally; now with the sense memory of watching her videos and masturbating, when he'd listen to her songs, riding his bike while scalping, he'd get erections. It was totally distracting. He had let her consume him.

And while jerking off to Lana Del Rey videos did indeed bring him closer to God, it only did momentarily, like with all orgasms. The actual feeling he was chasing, the warmth starting in his neck and coursing through his entire being, not just his member, never returned. Though their love was still very strong, he decided the honeymoon was over. He wondered what next.

It was remarkably similar, he thought, to what had happened with his wild goose chase around the city. One nice, seemingly important experience followed by an obsession with repeating it, executed through flawed means to no avail. In that case its purpose revealed itself not in some active discovery, but in the passive experience of not being somewhere. It was while he was gone that Haruka and Brian fucked in his old apartment, after all.

Perhaps he got so caught up with Lana because he wasn't supposed to steal phones anymore, he told himself. That there was something bad out there. The temperature, rapidly dropping now as they entered the shitty side of autumn, could only reassure him of this. Between what he had saved working for Emerson over the summer and made stealing phones in the early fall, he had enough money to live here for almost half a year—or until he figured something else out or it got warm enough to start scalping again pleasantly—even with paying off loans. There wasn't anything for him out there.

But was the thing he was truly looking for in here, as he thought? In his new home? Or further, in his old heart? He leveled with Lana, asked her why she, too, was a dead end, and again listened to her album and EP, this time back to back and very closely, for a response. The lyrics were confusing, sometimes contradictory. She seemed to speak to herself more than him. But this is the strength of any good mystic.

For in this, he found what he had been seeking. That refusal led him to the line of questioning that gets at the bottom of everything, and with that of course inevitably back to the beginning, right where he started with her: to the video for the song *Ride*, the first song off the *Paradise* EP. He watched the video while blocking out all amatory urges, trying to take it in with a stricter, more traditional form of holy reverence, and as a result the fog in his mind lifted and he saw something clearly. The word at the top of the video. RIDE, on black. The letters fading one by one, and out of order: I-E-R-D. The last letter to linger… D.

D… it wasn't for his dick. He was not meant to ride his hand, as he had been doing. Nor was he meant to ride a bike anymore; that part of his journey was over, too. He wasn't meant to ride the subway or buses, either, as he had during those wearying days after Sandy. No.

That's when he remembered the connection, the thing that had finally convinced him to click on that video that night in the first place. He was supposed to go back even further, to what brought him to Lana. It was the notion that perhaps his previous musical obsession, Death Grips, had somehow confused YouTube into leading him to her with their frontman MC Ride. Ray hadn't listened to Death Grips since that night; he hadn't listened to anything but Lana. But he saw, then, that they were of the same essence, Lana Del Rey and Death Grips. The angel is nothing without the demon. Opposite sides of the same coin. The coins they lay on the eyes and mouths of the dead.

Together, there was balance. Breathy whispers and violent outcries. One too quiet, the other too loud, both saying the same thing: ride. They

required his own voice to tell it to himself in a measured tone and cadence.

For the first time, Ray pored over all of Death Grips' lyrics, not just
the songs he liked, on Rap Genius. There, he found the path forward,
the inspiration he needed. There was a lot to pick and choose from under the umbrella of that word, ride, but the most salient thing for intro-
spection, the real deep diving shit his situation seemed to necessitate, and
one that Lana shared in her lyrics, was in drugs.

And he knew just how to get what he really required. It was in the
title of Death Grips' last album, and in one of its songs: the deep web.

Of course. All of this shit started with the internet, with that addiction. Surfing the web instead of paying attention to the world around
him… that's how he died. But in death, there should be no more surfing.
No skimming the superficial. He needed to go deep. Deep, deep, deeper
than he'd gone yet with weed and drinking. The answer was indeed right
there in front of him: in that album *No Love Deep Web*. There could be no
love, no communion with God, until he went to the deep web, then all
the way inside himself to really understand and ready his soul. Then it
could radiate through his body; he could reemerge prepared, his soul
expanding until it was boundless, a part of the force called love. He
needed to travel all the way down through the deep web, down to the
bottom, the dark web, and buy some serious fucking drugs in order to
do this. He needed medicine to make himself better. Hallucinogens were
the way. This is what he needed to do.

So he did. He got a VPN, downloaded Tor, picked up some bitcoins,
did a little research, and went to town via the Silk Road. A few days later
the vacuum-sealed packages started coming in the mail.

Ray was meant to ride. But unlike with his hand or on the bike or
the subway or buses, he wasn't meant to have as much control. He had
to strap himself into something he couldn't get out of until it was through
with him. This is, after all, the nature of life. Life goes until it ends. Even
sleep isn't a real break; it's more like the blinking of an eye. It was time
to submit to the most unknowable and unpredictable forces within, become a psychonaut and search for his soul. As they say: buy the ticket,
go for the ride.

The first thing he took was LSD. It was between that and shrooms,
those being the two hallucinogens he knew he had tried while still living,
but acid got the edge because it's synthetic. It seemed to make more
sense to do a man-made drug considering the heavenly warmth had
come upon him when he placed that phone in front of the old dorm and

when he met his new lover, Lana, digitally. Also, he knew based on his prior experiences that it was more intense, so he thought it might act as something of a shortcut. He took it in the early afternoon on a Sunday, and kept a notepad handy to jot down any important impressions.

The trip was good and bad. He intended on sticking to his apartment, really own the home as a reflection of the heart thing, explore it as himself, but after five or so hours it didn't work out that way.

In the beginning he just sort of hung out appreciating cool visuals around the apartment—heightened colors, morphing objects, all the trailing and afterimages, his own face and body generating new features and limbs in the mirror—and listening to a long, long playlist he had made of some of his favorite music from when he had been alive: a mixture of classic rock, alternative, some hip-hop, and a decent dose of electronica, heavy on synths. He wrote down:

Things look cool, things sound good.

He had had moments of deeper insight, but not really about his spirituality or his quest—it would mostly be about his living situation, about being in an inner-city apartment and how that relates to nature.

He wrote only one of these down, and it was:

I have my own apartment now and there is wood on the floor made from trees that used to stand vertically but now they're horizontal and in a parquet pattern and there's electricity that is powering my speakers providing this beautiful music I loved while living generated probably from natural gas but wouldn't it be nice if it was wind or solar instead and I would have that except that costs more money and isn't that a car going by outside running on oil, and another one, and another one?

This was accompanied by visions of himself where he was a tree growing for hundreds of years, then was natural gas flowing around for millions of years, then a buried organism becoming fossil fuel over hundreds of millions of years, all going through the process of getting from nature to his apartment and then to him, when he would become himself again and notice the next thing then become that. This went on for a while, though he wouldn't remember everything else he became.

Eventually he had decided he didn't like the apartment anymore because of the peeling paint and cracking walls and ceiling, and that it wasn't an accurate representation of his inner life at all; that his heart or soul or whatever was perhaps an old one but not in the way this looked, like some seventies or eighties throwback shit except with his weird paintings featuring video game characters and modern appurtenances everywhere—like a normal twenty-something's studio apartment through a fucking Instagram filter—and that if he did have an old soul this place should look more like the inside of a pueblo or temple or something, and while he probably couldn't decorate it like that he should at least repaint to make it look cleaner or brighter and less derelict. He wrote:

Apartment: kill instagram, build pueblo.

Then he tried standing on furniture to look at it from unusual angles or tilting his head to try to modify weird visuals and cover up blemishes for a quick fix, but it didn't work—the patterns just played out as they pleased—and he still thought his new place sucked.

After this, he tried going online briefly to read old emails from around the suspected time of his death, to see if that would lead to anything, but the screen was too bright and blurry and the letters seemed to either bounce around or fuse together, making it impossible to pay attention. Writing was different because he didn't have to read it back; muscle memory really was a marvel, he thought.

Next he lied down in bed, attempting to make peace and learn to love the ceiling cracks, and noticed a cluster that looked like the wrinkles in an old person's smiling eyes, but he did not know the old person, just saw an unfamiliar old face, and wished it looked more like one of his deceased grandparents, but in the end was glad it didn't because that would've been a lie… he would've forced it, and at least the old eyes didn't look like fucking Emerson's, that scumbag.

Ceiling cracks. he wrote.

He wondered if he could actually commune with his grandparents then by going outside and looking up at the clouds, and that's what brought him outside.

The sun was setting and the last light of day was dancing off the city scenery wonderfully, gilding everything, but his grandparents weren't anywhere, and that was okay. Walking through fresh air at dusk and seeing all the other people around strolling down the sidewalks looking beautiful in that golden light helped him become happier and more lucid again, and he thought it might be a good idea to go to the nearby waterfront and look at the river. See where water, land, and sky met and what secrets their meeting might share.

So he went up First Ave., then across 111th hugging Thomas Jefferson Park, then crossed the overpass above the FDR to the esplanade, and at the railing stared into the East River. The water was cool-looking, moving in really fun patterns that radiated and twinkled, but when he moved his eyes up and followed the water across the river to see where it met the land and sky he was then faced with the gigantic main building on Ward's Island and he felt it staring at him like it knew something he didn't, and before long a terrible feeling of dread took over. He looked away and down the river instead, and was eventually caught by the monolithic Citi tower in his old neighborhood, which was much, much worse, screaming "Heyo fuck you, pal!" at him in an old, Archie Bunkerish Queens accent, immediately making him think of Brian and Haruka fucking again, those images playing out on a projector over the water like a cruel riverfront drive-in IMAX porno. He thought fuck this and fuck the East River, and before he left he wrote that down:

Fuck this and fuck the east river.

He didn't want to go back home, though, so he sat in Thomas Jefferson Park with his back to the river. The people milling about made him feel better about being outside, so he decided he'd stay out but move around because it was too cold to stay sitting. It seemed wise to go to the Hudson River, like it would restore balance after staring out at that vile East River, and that maybe he should look at his old dorm again along the way, like it would tell him what exactly had happened when he placed the phone there before, and a plan was made to walk west.

He got up and ventured out. The walk was going well until he almost got hit by a car crossing Second Ave., when he got confused as to whether the hand signal was actually flashing or if it was solid—it was solid—determining then to make his way down to 110th, aka Tito Puente Way, which was busier than 111th and allowed him to flow with a crowd. He felt like a red blood cell traveling among other blood cells in Tito Puente's body, and it was nice. Eventually Tito Puente Way became Frawley Circle and he thought he was being transfused into some guy named Frawley, that Tito had donated him to a blood bank, but then the road turned into Central Park North and he didn't know what he was anymore. Shortly after that, before even walking a block along the park, this ran its course and he decided he was even smaller than a cell, smaller than a molecule or atom, and he experienced full ego death and realized he didn't need to go to the Hudson anymore because he was the Hudson, nor the dorm because he was the dorm; he was the East River, too, as well as everyone out in the city this evening, and everything else, everything that ever was or would be, anywhere. And while this might seem like it was what he had been looking for, what his definition of God was, it wasn't. Because it was absent of love. There was no warm feeling to accompany this; it was just information. Such is the nature of most things synthetic. It was connectivity that was only connectivity, a noun, no other binding.

I am everything – information, a noun.

He turned around, went home, and, now starting to come down, decided to watch computer-animated cartoons on Netflix, which were fun, occasionally pausing to eat cheese, cold cuts, and peanuts when he got hungry. Another two or so hours passed and he knew the trip would be over soon, so a little pissed that nothing that revelatory happened in terms of his quest, he put on alternating Lana Del Rey and Death Grips songs and closed his eyes in a last-ditch, kind of desperate effort to see if they'd show him anything, but they didn't, and instead, to accompany their music, he had visuals of 3D animated dragons and penguins and other shit probably entrained over from the cartoons dancing to whatever was playing among a background of swirling fractals, which while also fun didn't really mean anything, so he decided to get ready for bed and try and fall asleep, and after a while, he did.

A week later he went for the shrooms. It seemed prudent to give himself some time between trips, recuperate a bit after the ride, spend his days rereading his Bible and good metaphysical poetry—Donne, of course, along with George Herbert, Pita Amor, Anne Bradstreet, Martin Adan, a few others—and eating well and exercising and meditating about his quest to get his body, mind, and day-to-day emotional well-being in a good place. It also seemed wise to do them on Sundays.

This time he decided to take them closer to dusk so he could trip into the night, like the Mexican Indians would. He would just stay home, make it a rule, not run around all pell-mell as he had last week.

The experience started out fine enough. More cool visuals, slower than while on acid, not quite as crisp, everything moving in an organic

rhythm. Objects around the apartment would morph subtly, some surfaces adopting strange patterns; larger things would breathe. The fridge,
the television, the bed. They breathed in and out like him and he felt
renewed goodwill toward his apartment in general.

During the preceding week, he decided against painting or redeco-
rating, that it was an impossible and silly task to try to make the place
look like some sort of pueblo or whatever, not to mention inauthentic to
him as a person. He thought that the apartment didn't have to reflect
what was in his heart in that type of way; by virtue of having his things
there, that was enough. It was okay that the shell was kind of ugly. A
heart, a real heart is pretty fucking ugly—a lumpy, asymmetrical mass
of muscle, varicolored vessels sticking out like rusty old plumbing. It was
what was inside that mattered. So he just resolved to clean his space
more and keep it tidier, and that would be doing his part.

But even with scrubbed-down baseboards, he still knew this was an
intellectual defense; these things were decisions he had made. He still
didn't feel like he liked the place. He had told himself he should and
why, and hoped that, with enough convincing, he would soon enough.
Optimistic but still skeptical.

An hour into the trip, though, *Psilocybe cubensis* did the convincing.
The apartment was wonderful, it was a nice enough space and he was
lucky to have it. Above all, it had been there for him in a time of need.
He felt very grateful. And in addition to these things, the shell was in fact
of his heart.

He wrote this down:

The shell, the apartment, is of my heart.

The walls looked like they hadn't been painted since the eighties because Ray was born in the eighties. That's when his heart began to beat.

Walls – 80s. Heartbeat – 80s.

It wasn't an Instagram filter of an apartment, it was the real fucking
deal.

Au-then-tic.

Ray was humbled. This, this was authentic afterlife living: he imagined a brochure describing his apartment as such, showing off its incredible qualities, his portly Puerto Rican landlord standing on the cover, beaming with pride in a gold chain and wifebeater as he guided the viewer's eye to the room with an open-palmed hand, the other leaning on a cane. What a great, friendly place. The walls, too, began to breathe.

Having sorted out the apartment, he turned off all the lights, lit a dollar store Jesus candle, and laid down on the floor. A modified version of how the Mexican Indians did it, he thought. He wanted to summon God, his God, or at least find the knowledge within himself that would lead to Him. He knew it had to be there, he knew he'd been given enough clues.

This was a lot better than acid, he thought: with shrooms he could keep it mellow and really look within. He was lying there musing over how misleading LSD was and how wrong he'd been about his apartment before and how pleased he was with the shrooms for showing him the truth about it, how excited he was for the next little phase of his evening where he'd discover the truth in himself, when something that seemed like an ugly truth surfaced and stared him down: He thought that since he had been wrong about his apartment then that must have meant he was wrong about everything. He had been lying to himself all year.

A chorus of echoing voices, masculine and feminine, shouted "Liar!" He didn't like them at all. They persisted, called him "Liar!" again. He wanted to block them out.

He looked at the candle of Jesus. He thought about Jesus, and asked him to show him his love. The voices now called him "Fool!" Ray shook his head, no, no. Then they called him "Fool!" again, but it was in a language he had never heard before. Could it be an ancient tribal Central American tongue? Or Aramaic? He didn't know. Only that they were calling him a fool, this was very clear. As if they mistook his head shaking for a language preference. He looked closer at Jesus, the flame flickering inside the glass. The painted image wobbled and wavered, like a mirage.

Jesus on the cross… it wasn't real, either. He had been wrong about that, too. The New Testament was apocryphal. Jesus was a mirage. He probably never even existed, the man. Was probably made up by the Church. That, or greatly embellished. For control. Power. Money. The sweet asses of little boys. Ray shivered. There was no God. He knew it but he dared not write it down.

Ray blew out the candle and felt his way around the apartment for the light. When he turned it on, he picked up the candle and stared at it, the smoke still rising… He followed a wisp toward the ceiling then looked back down once it had completely vanished.

Jesus' image swirling like smoke… no matter the state, lights on or off, it told him the same thing. "Goodness," he said. "Shrooms giveth and taketh away."

He decided to try to keep the mood lighter and put on the same Spotify playlist from last week. The Mexican-inspired shroom ceremony he was having had gotten a little too heavy, and in the wrong way. He needed some time to process what they had just told him.

It seemed like a good idea to distract himself and ride out this trip by playing some Super Mario emulators online—Mario loved shrooms, and it would make this thing seem less intense. How powerful could they be if they were used by a video game plumber for the amusement of children? Well, they had convinced him there was no God, so pretty fucking powerful. LSD and its wackiness and main lesson about sterile connectivity were a pleasure cruise compared to that revelation and the idea that he wasn't in fact dead. That he was probably just severely mentally ill. Hadn't Haruka said something to that effect? Could she have been right? No, no. Don't go down that path, he told himself.

Mario's got better paths, better portals. He fired up Super Mario World, his favorite as a kid, and started playing. But not for long. "Child!" the voices called out. Then: "Puta!" They ruined it for him.

He closed his laptop and looked in the bathroom mirror. He began crying hysterically, but then his face, body began to morph. He was a lie, too. That wasn't how he really looked. He knew this. And if that was the case, then maybe the shrooms were wrong about God. Of course they also could have been wrong about his apartment, it could have actually sucked, but that would be better than God not existing and his journey being a lie.

He got it. Shrooms are full of shit. That's the whole story. Grown in shit, it's their essence: they try to humble you in these ways that bring you down to their level, but it wasn't going to work anymore.

Ray brushed his teeth, drank some water, and went to bed. Visions and desultory voices persisted, but he told the ones he didn't like to fuck off and embraced the nice ones, and eventually drifted off to sleep.

The week that followed had Ray doing some damage control. He expanded on his notes, which, pointedly, seemed a bit more crabbed this time around, and wrote down what he couldn't bring himself to during the trip, figuring out what was what: mainly that he liked what the drug had said about his apartment, disagreed with what it said about his death and God, sort of agreed with what it had to say about being an adult and playing Mario—so much so that he took his paintings with video game characters down—and ultimately decided that shrooms were just like anything and anyone else: imperfect. Capable of great truth and great falsehoods.

Next up: mescaline.

It was the last of the three drugs he had picked out, and he was excited to try it since he never had while living. He had bought it in crystalline form because it seemed like a happy medium between the lab-created LSD and the earth-grown shrooms, and also because processing it himself from a peyote cactus into a tea or other ingestible form seemed like sort of a pain in the ass. Since neither LSD nor shrooms had done much to help him figure out what was really going on, he hoped it would hit him just right, like he was Goldilocks and they were his Three Dancing Bears. LSD danced too fast, shrooms too slow, not to mention creepily, trying to cop a feel while susurrating fucked up shit in his ear, and he wanted mescaline to sway in time with him; he wanted to look into its eyes and find love: God's love.

The seller had an excellent rating on Silk Road and it was supposed to be pure, really good shit. Also, the Mexican connection seemed even more on point than with the shrooms, since there was no real accounting for where they had been grown, but peyote is really only native to Texas and Mexico.

He took it in two doses, swallowing capsules he had packed it in, each dose separated by about a half hour to make it easier on his stomach. This time he opted for starting his trip in the morning. When night fails you, look toward the morning.

It was an unseasonably warm early December day. The sun was nice and bright through the windows, heating the wood of the floor, heating his skin, and it didn't take long to think it would be nice to be out there with it, covered in that warmth. An hour in and he wasn't that high yet: if anything, at that point he had only seen a few things around the apartment shift slightly, breathing again, but with slower and shallower breaths than they had while on shrooms. Weird visuals in his apartment had been well covered by psilocybin and LSD, he thought, so why not take the show outside? Sure, the point of these experiments was to explore his home as himself in addition to his actual self, but where did the definition of home end? Certainly his neighborhood could be considered home... otherwise he would be more or less immured. Perhaps that was why he hadn't had any real, positive breakthrough about himself yet; he had been limiting himself and his definition of home, and connecting with God would require openness. His soul would need to expand outside of his body. While wandering his neighborhood on acid, he hadn't really been thinking of the area around his apartment as home, but rather "outside" or "the area around my apartment" until it wasn't, until it was Tito Puente's blood vessels, then that guy Frawley's, then everywhere and nowhere, en route to a place that was an older version of home. That wasn't home. Today, outside could be home.

The day was nice but not quite as warm as it had seemed feeling it from inside. Luckily he had a jacket on over his hoodie. Windows can play tricks, he thought, and he was glad to be rid of them. The sun shone directly on him now. He wrote down:

Windows can play tricks.

But weren't his eyes windows, too? And didn't they do little but play tricks while under the influence of these things? Maybe.

They were different in that they were lying from the inside out, because he had asked them to lie. Lie to me, baby, he had said. You lie and I'll figure out the truth. Ray couldn't get mad at his eyes—he liked them too much, what they did for him, even if they were liars—and soon enough he couldn't get mad at anything. Even the idea of his windows. They lied for a good reason because they had brought him out there...

But not all tricks are bad.

They had lied to help him get at this truth: that everything was absolutely beautiful on this sunny December day. What a home he had.

Before long he found himself in the Conservatory Garden. It was intricately textured and lovely, this place, this garden. The lawn at the Fifth Avenue entrance was still pretty lush and verdant, despite how far along they were in the fall. The perennial hedges and shrubs that lined it and the other paths of the north and south sections maintained their quiet dignity in their deeper, duller hues. The guiding force, the ushers of the garden, they asked not for attention—they want that for the fountains, for the dancing nymphs, for the flowers—only that the viewer find their way.

On this occasion they were leading towards death. Beautiful, beautiful death. It was everywhere. Some things were already gone. Many of the larger trees and shrubs had lost all their leaves, naked branches twisting gnarled into the firmament. Others were still in transition, patches of leaves crying out with their coruscating yellows, oranges, reds. Hallelujah! they seemed to say. We will not leave without a fight! We will burst, first! You will see us! Hear us! Burning trees, burning bushes. We speak God's words!

And Ray listened. He peered beyond them and saw the sunlight through their thinning branches and listened. I am that I am indeed. Life and death, alpha and omega. Nothing without the other, both beautiful.

Death is beautiful, he knew it. His own death must have been beautiful—perhaps it still is if, in actuality, he's remained there in that moment, lying on the ground in 2007, like everything moribund here.

The trees further along in their transition, where only a few dull ochre-colored leaves barely clung on, were also beautiful.

The few extant flowers—mostly winter carnations and pink heirloom roses—shrinking, withering, content to go gently, were beautiful.

Every death is different, unique, but they are bound together by the common destination. Other plants in their sundry patches around the English section were dense, dark, drooping. A growth cycle well lived. A life is little different, and we could all only hope for as much.

Before leaving, Ray stared into the eyes of two stone sculptures, characters from *The Secret Garden*. Was this the secret? That he needed to learn to love his death, this state? That whatever it was, there was no use in fighting, in searching like he's been? That he could just be? He jotted this down:

Death is okay. Maybe I can just be. They told me this as a secret.

Mescaline was good, mescaline was progress. He wrote this down, too:

Mescaline is good. Mescaline is progress.

But why would he need progress if he could just be? It didn't matter.

He decided to keep wayfaring through the park. Over concrete paths and steps and dying grass covering rolling hills tufted with more fading trees of varying foliage he made his way south. Everything was beautiful here in Central Park, especially this part. Few tourists. But even if there were tourists, they too would be beautiful. What a wonderful thing to have as part of his home. His yard. His Eden? Perhaps.

More steps, great steps. He kept moving until he made it to the Met. There he donated two dollars and wandered through the Egyptian galleries, staring at artifacts thousands of years old. He went through the American Wing and became immersed in strange rooms that once belonged to rich people. He hustled through the Medieval galleries and realized how blessed he was not to have lived then. How violent a time it seemed; it was hard not to see blood smearing the swords, guts sliding out of the armor, flames reflecting from it all. But it was short-lived. He smiled at European sculptures of hypermasculine figures Emerson must've masturbated to. He imagined Emerson's version of porn, that he might go to the Met's website and masturbate to digital images of these very statues on that old monitor of his, that coming here might give him an erection like he himself would get listening to Lana Del Rey while riding his bike. He giggled uncontrollably and thought Emerson deserved this, he deserved to masturbate just like anyone else. What happened between them was water under the bridge. He wished him the best. He thought of his own, real father and thought he deserved to masturbate also, that everyone deserved to masturbate as much as they wanted because it made their lives better. Then he was in a modern and contemporary gallery and one of the first things he saw made his mouth drop: a painting of Adam and Eve embracing one another that looked like him with Lana Del Rey. Eve's hair was strawberry like it was on the cover of *Born to Die*. Maybe Santa Muerte was also the modern embodiment of Eve. Zombie Eve. He read the info card: William Zorach. Spring in Central Park. These things were in bold, so they were easy to discern, and he jotted them down:

William Zorach. Spring in Central Park.

Otherwise the info was hard to read. Trying to get through the description with the letters sort of swirling, Ray felt nauseous, so much so that he went to a nearby bathroom and threw up. Luckily, it was empty, and it didn't attract any attention. He decided to get out of the Met. What he had seen and read was enough and well worth two bucks. He got what he came for. He also got those tourists he had wanted, throngs of them. On his way out he passed a gallery filled with Mesoamerican artifacts. A mask seemed to whisper, "Go see your parents. They miss you, mijo." He saw its lips move and agreed with it. He felt better after throwing up and agreed with everything, everything he didn't have to read, and everything agreed with him.

Walking down the Met's grand steps, it felt really good to be outside again, back in his yard. It was warmer now that it was afternoon. He thought of the Met as being sort of like his garage back in Texas, where he had kept really cool shit he liked to use only occasionally. He made his way back to his apartment through the park then city blocks, surrounded by beautiful life and beautiful death. He spent the rest of the afternoon watching Lana Del Rey music videos feeling tremendous love and affection for her while intermittently eating Mexican food and drinking apple juice until the evening when he was no longer high.

In the days that followed he wrote down his impressions and thought more about all three trips, the lessons learned, the nudges they seemed to give him, and expounded on everything in his writings.

He was supposed to love both his apartment and his death, his current state, whatever his existence had become, along with all existence. Now more than ever it was important. Love and be loved in return, but don't make your love conditional on being loved back. The cold rain and wind, the short days and long nights, all the time spent indoors: the things that normally suck so much about the end of this season will help you do this. A positive outlook in hard times: difficult to cultivate but crucial.

But this did not mean he should become passive in this state. Yes, it was okay to just be as he was, but there should also be a goal in mind. The Garden of Eden/Lana Del Rey thing on mescaline was proof of that, how pissed the shrooms got at him for playing a mindless nostalgic video game. It was more about having resolve and putting in effort, but accepting the outcome either way. An idea presented itself for the next step of his quest. He studied the painting *Spring in Central Park*, looking at pictures of it online, and decided to try something out.

He ordered a used first-generation iPhone off eBay for about fifty bucks, ripped some Lana videos off of YouTube using KeepVid, then downloaded them onto the phone, which took up most of its paltry 8GB memory. He went to Central Park and watched the videos, embracing the phone and Lana in his hands, firmly but gently. He looked into her eyes and gave her love.

When Eve ate the apple, the apple went inside her. Now Eve was inside of the apple.

Ray had righted the wrong, reversed the course of evil in this world. It was his gift to all of mankind. But when he did this, nothing happened. The earth did not shake, no rainbow appeared, he was not called up to heaven. And evil did not instantly vanish.

But it was okay.

He buried the iPhone somewhere in the Ramble and knew something would grow from it in the spring.

Perhaps the tree of life, the tree of love. The thing that would suck up all the evil from the air, release it back as love.

Perhaps something he could climb in a hundred years to get to heaven along with all of humanity.

Maybe that's why he thought of himself as a tree during his acid trip, he thought. Maybe that was a clue, too. Maybe Ray was sent here to do this. Maybe he is the second coming of Christ. Maybe we all are. There could be clues without feeling. He had already spent hundreds of millions of years waiting during that trip, what was another fifty, hundred?

Was he actually supposed to wait until the springtime to watch the videos? To have embraced the phone and Lana and Eve then? No, because that's not what he did. There are no such things as mistakes, not in this universe. Maybe he really was the second coming of Christ, yes, yes, maybe we all are. Whatever happens does for a reason, and that reason is the teleological order of all things, the rhythm of the universe.

So now all there's left to do is go see his parents. Listen to the mask. They say if you want the truth, give someone a mask. Hopefully whatever spirit speaking to him through it then was right. But if it's not, oh well. It'll be nice to see his parents, regardless. His old home is a home away from home. The same as his dorm rooms were in college. Everywhere on this earth is a home away from home now on the grander scale. Heaven: that's his real home, and he knows he'll be there soon enough.

▲ ▲ ▽ ▽ ▲ ▽ ▲

Ahhh, now that's better—soft but supportive, placidly cool to the touch. The body without wants, leaving the mind to do exactly as it pleases. There's nothing quite like a properly fluffed pillow. Especially when someone else is doing the fluffing, someone who should have been doing the fluffing for months now not weeks, someone who truly deserves to be doing the fluffing. "Thank you, dear," Emerson says.

"You're welcome, Daddy." Claire smiles. "Can I get you anything else?"

Of course she can. How otherwise do you make up for so much lost time? "Oh, I don't know. I suppose I could do with another sandwich."

"You must have quite the appetite today! I'm so pleased it's returned."

"Yes, I wondered if it ever would!" And it's true. He practically wasted away during his first two weeks here at Claire's house, losing all of nineteen pounds. He was, of course, in shock after the episode, not to mention those three ghastly days spent at St. Luke's following it. But there was also the terrifying notion, when he arrived, of defecating in the bedpan they set him up with in the guest bedroom. Micturating in it was fine—and actually quite enjoyable through his new orifice, hearing the pleasant tinkle rather than that old sporadic pressurized stream—no, he didn't mind them emptying that out; he knew his urine was sterile and had no overwhelming smell, but having his daughter or her husband clean out his excrement was simply out of the question. He thought it better, then, not to move his bowels at all, despite Dr. Marc's protests, which were then followed by the idiotic suggestion that he wear a diaper and they just not look at it. This, too, helped him suppress his appetite. The subsequent week, last week, marked a bit of a return to form once he was able to get out of bed again and defecate in the bathroom, and now, finally, after enough days of moving around a bit per his doctor's instructions so as to regain strength, his appetite is back with a vengeance. He's also working on the manuscript again—he made Claire go to his apartment over the weekend and get the last printout of it that he had left in clear view on the coffee table—and needs all the glucose he can get for his brilliantly burning mind. "Isn't it something?"

She smiles, without eyes, betraying any attempt to suppress frustration, and starts toward the door.

"Claire?" He catches her before she's gone.

"Yes, Daddy."

"A little less mustard this time. Please."

"Of course, Daddy."

It's been fun toying with Claire these past few weeks. One of the great highlights of his convalescence, in fact. She felt just awful for what had happened, blaming herself for taking him to the Whitney and ex-

posing him to the Forrest Bess exhibition earlier in the year, and for refusing his request that she assist him, especially since he had bargained
her down to coming in only once or twice a week, and also for not inviting him to Thanksgiving. She knew he wasn't well, but didn't know exactly how unstable he was, she told the doctors; she could have
prevented all this, perhaps, if she had just come down and helped out a
little as he had asked. As it was, her father mutilated himself and almost
died, Thanksgiving had been ruined, and it was all her fault.

Emerson smirks, proud of himself, and looks around the room. Her
art hangs on the walls here, gauche little pieces for her; the newer works,
he's asked. Things that didn't sell from last month's show. No wonder.
They're all that really stick out in this sparse, modest chamber, aside
from the nice view of the backyard. Birds and gray squirrels busy themselves among the oaks, trying to keep warm in the cool country air. The
air Emerson himself walks in twice daily, alone in the morning, then with
the children mid-afternoon, the only occasions where he changes out of
his pajamas. There isn't a bookshelf in the room, which is a pity, generally speaking, or really more as a comment on her poor taste and skewed
priorities, but he doesn't really mind for his own day-to-day purposes.
He made do before she went down and retrieved his pages by reading
whatever back issues of *The New Yorker* they had lying around the house
and the daily editions of *The New York Times*, along with his regular dose
of canonical books with what his daughter keeps in the living room—
Poetics, the Bible, some Shakespeare, Proust, Emily Dickinson, Yeats, of
course, Kafka for a self-deprecating afternoon laugh—and also, for some
fun with the children in the evenings, a wonderful volume entitled *A Little
History of the World*. He didn't want to look at his own work while still on
too many pain pills, while not yet fully comfortable in his head or new
skin. But this week, he's been both, not to mention off of the medication
completely, against his doctor's orders, and the thing is really coming
along. Speaking of, time to get back to it! Enough looking around hither
and thither, daydreaming. Claire should be back in just another minute
with that third sandwich and he must appear busy.

Emerson leans over and picks up the manuscript from the
nightstand, resting it on his lap, then extracts the pen he had placed behind his ear before his second lunch. He reads.

The thing really isn't all that bad, not as bad as he had convinced
himself it was after Weisman's death. A major loss can suck everything
else in with it. Amidst the renewed vivacity he now feels—the operation's
goals fulfilled, Yeats and to a lesser extent Forrest Bess vindicated—he

can see it's actually quite good. Especially after reading so much of what passes for literary criticism in *The Times* and *New Yorker* recently, he knows the book will stand as a monumental achievement in the end. In its purest sense. A mausoleum for the Culture, his old identity, his new dual one, all of them.

It's an easy fix, actually. Instead of carrying on as he had before, he simply needs to take out all the "I's" and "me's" and "our's" and general impassioned lamentations, and just describe the Culture's story in more pragmatic terms. A bit like *A Little History of the World*. The poetry he had breathed into it can remain, the exquisite metaphors and similes for the stages it went through, but now it won't really read as some sort of personification of the Culture itself, but the story of the idea, the movement it had been, a beautiful thing that was and is no longer, and these words will read back as if they were spoken from on high. Emerson Towers does not mourn the Culture; God does, and you should, too. He himself is merely God's mouthpiece now. The pen crosses out some effusive blathering about the moral authority of George Eliot. There can be only one moral authority here. He reads the paragraph back—yes, yes, much better. It is becoming truly sublime!

Claire appears in the doorway, a turkey sandwich on a thick, pale amaranth plate extended before her. She moves to set it on the nightstand, next to the half-full glass of water remaining from the previous lunch an hour ago. Emerson looks back to his pages. "Claire…"

"Yes?" She places the plate down.

"I'm sorry, but this is a particularly important section… I'm still very hungry, but would hate to lose momentum. Would you mind feeding me?"

A brief moment of silence, then: "I'd be happy to."

His eyes still gliding over his words, his right hand ready with the pen and the other propping up the manuscript, the sandwich floats in front of his mouth. He takes a bite.

It's very good—the smoked turkey, swiss cheese, tomato, lettuce, mayo, and most importantly, mustard coming together in splendid harmony between the slices of multigrain bread. The old sandwich bit, one of his favorites. His assistants over the years all got it in some form or another; he had to do it one last time before he becomes his own this coming weekend. More chewing, then he swallows; the pen moves, the page turns.

That John Montagu, he sure was onto something. Everybody likes to disparage English food, but they forget that their culinary history contributed something as fantastic as this. Of course there was room for improvement in terms of the manner with which to eat it—to leave one's hands not only free from the grease of meat, but both to do exactly as they were doing before, whether that's playing cards as he had been or toiling away at a masterpiece—which is why Emerson just loves doing this.

Another bite. He chews, he swallows. Then a tickle in the throat. "A little water, please."

Claire places the sandwich back on the plate while Emerson reads on. The glass appears in front of him, but does not get closer.

"While I continue to read, if you don't mind." It comes toward his mouth and he receives it between his lips. He slowly tilts his head back, raising his pages so he can continue. A little difficult to make it work, but totally worth it. He succeeds, not really skipping a beat, and after a few gulps, begins moving both his head and the manuscript forward, and she takes the hint and the glass away. "Oh, thank you, thank you." The sandwich then returns. Emerson continues to eat and read.

He doesn't know what exact expression Claire is wearing, but imagines it's either something like bemusement or that of a perturbed cat. Out goes some long-winded digression about Tolstoy and his solipsism, and finding himself increasingly distracted by the uncertainty, and with the sandwich now almost gone, he decides to have a look and see how she's actually taking this.

Biting down again, he turns to her and smiles as he chews. Perturbed cat. It's the more aggressive of the phizes he had imagined, and that just won't do.

He swallows and smiles again, then takes the last bite, messily. She forces a smile back. Oh, Claire. What if he were actually sick? As in, he couldn't, physically, feed himself? If this were his deathbed? Would it be so different? Would you still look at him so? It's enough to make him wish he *had* defecated in that bedpan, even with his embarrassment, just to spite her, if this is her attitude! He lets some crumbs fall from his mouth. "Uh-oh. There are crumbs in the bed! You do know how I hate crumbs in the bed!"

"I'll get those right out." She brushes them to the edge, then into the waiting palm of her other hand. Emerson shifts his weight over to face the window so she might get anything that could have made its way under him. She folds his covers back and does. "There we go…" she says.

Like a nurse. The job she suggested he fill with a stranger before! Now, that's justice. He shifts his weight back and smirks at her, knowingly. This has been marvelous. He picks up his masterpiece and continues reading while she tucks him back in.

"All right, Daddy. I have to go pick the kids up from school. Will you be all right for a while?"

The pen strikes out some more "I's" and "me's" in another gushing bit about Tolstoy. "Yes, I think I can manage." He waits a few seconds, when he figures she's about out of the room, then says, "Just a little more water before you go, please."

His eyes still on his work, Emerson laughs. It's a slight laugh, short, but audible all the same. If she were to ask, he could claim he had been reading something terribly witty in his manuscript. But she doesn't ask. He catches her shadow in his periphery and soon the water is gone. More words about Tolstoy and family and death and heroics. The glass returns, now full. "Thank you," he says. Should he ask for a refluff of the pillow? No, it would be too much, too captious; he's reached his limit. Besides, he'll be getting up soon after she goes. All that water has begun to overburden his bladder.

"All right, Daddy. See you in a bit."

He says nothing, just reads on. The start of the ignition, tires crunching over gravel, then rapid acceleration. Outside, the birds, startled, fly away from the thicket, wheeling across the sky. Emerson leaves the bed.

He shuffles down the hall to the saffron-scented bathroom. More of Claire's pieces hang here: older, better ones. He must sit to urinate now. But he doesn't mind; he prefers it, in fact—it's more dignified. He's always enjoyed a good sit. After the trickle comes to an end, he blots, flushes, and makes his way back to the bedroom.

All of this with Claire has been an act of petty revenge on Emerson's part, a trifle. He did it because he could. It's been fun, but he'll be more pleased to get out of her hair now, and on to better things. Leave her and her family to their Christmas season while he starts his new life. He spots his reflection in the window: the yard, the dreary nemoral scenery filling out his semitransparent form. The birds have returned to the trees, happily chirruping and trilling. There are no squirrels in sight. This country air, it really is for them, the birds.

Emerson gets back into bed and back to his editing. He'll be through marking up this draft soon, then it'll be back to New York City, a new beginning back in civilization.

▲ ▲ △ ▽ ▲ ▲ ▽

Clouds are very pretty from above. You can really appreciate their unique shapes, consistencies, the different colors they reflect. And that they're a part of a system. If they were to turn gray and break, water would fall onto the mountains and flow down streams to lakes and rivers and eventually the sea. The water would support the cities and suburbs and the rural towns and farmland you can also see up here, down through them, the clouds. Haruka has a view of it all.

A window seat on a long flight can help you to see the broader order of life. People feel like they get a God's eye view, like they're very powerful. It offers that kind of perspective and scope. That's why everyone wants the window seat. They want this view. At least for a little bit, even if they also want to read or watch stuff for the majority of the flight.

But most of them, they don't deserve this seat at all. Even for a little bit. They just have their heads in the clouds. Their heads pass through them, unaware that they're aerosol masses of water droplets or ice crystals, and they actually get high. On false power. They experience a bogus reality that is just in their heads.

In this reality they're very, very special. But in real life they're not. Not like her, anyway. Most of the people, even those with her here in first class, aren't the least bit extraordinary. She looks across the aisle, then ahead of her. No. These people aren't anything. Just rich. She can tell. They barely deserve the plush leather seats they're sitting in, the service from their first-class-only flight attendant, so forget about the type of view this offers.

She's contemptuous of them, the others with their window shades up. Those who, just like her a moment ago, have taken some time to look out.

Then there are those in this section who frighten her. They're the ones who have been asleep in their seats since right after they boarded, or who, like the guy directly behind her, the stewardess had to yell at to put their devices away before the plane could taxi out to the runway back at JFK. They seem above this view.

This is a flight to SFO and they very well might be. Gods and goddesses of Silicon Valley, they already know what's there. They don't need a reminder of what the clouds look like from above. They've seen it enough times and they're doing something better. Sleeping or working on the thing that made them deserve their seats.

That's why, even though she likes the view from above, she prefers the view from below. Like they must. She sees all the psychological issues people face when they look up at them, the clouds: good and bad, how little things can become big deals. From below, clouds lie. And if you understand them, if you understand the lies, then you can harness their power.

To most people down there, they seem like everything. Clouds. They seem mystical and very important. As if they carry out God's will. They change moods, plans, whole lives. People modify what they're do-ing on any given day based on whether they're parting for the sun, gath-ering for snow or rain or lightning, in the midst of actually doing those things. They are both where people place their hopes and dreams and how hopes and dreams get ruined. Like recently in New York, with Sandy. Just ask anyone who lost power or their business or home. Or anyone who might have been desperately searching for the rainbow af-ter.

Haruka didn't look for any rainbows after Sandy, no. They found her. She just looked for understanding. Sandy ruined many lives, even took some. But it put hers back together. They don't have storms like that back in the Bay Area. She saw the clouds and understood them not only as you can clearly from up here, on a scientific level, but for what they were to people down there. How their power could most effectively be utilized. She saw God and it looked like her.

That's how she decided she could really hurt Ray. That's how she came up with her idea to become a dominatrix. And that's how she's taking things even further, with her app. All by looking at the clouds and seeing what they are. Seeing how other people see them. And seeing where they go. In America, because of the jet stream, it's usually east. Toward the next day, the direction the Earth rotates. Toward the future. Potential isn't in a limitless sky. It's in the clouds. And it's online.

The internet is like everything that came before it, but so much more. More powerful than the greatest words ever written or spoken in any language, more powerful than any image or symbol ever seen, more powerful than hope or fear, more powerful than religion, faith itself, the totality of the human spirit. The invisible infinite that rules over our lives whether we want it to or not. But really, who doesn't? Everyone wants a master, everyone needs some version of God.

Okay, enough of that. Time to get to work, like the other winners here.

She closes the window shade with a sharp tug then reaches for her laptop. It's a new MacBook Air, the 13.3-inch model MD23LL/A. Not only a wonderful status symbol, but perfect for business meetings and for use on planes with its small size. She pulls her seat's tray out and places it carefully on its surface.

The screen glows. Bonobo. That's the app. Free love. That's the slogan.

She's got her business plan open and is looking it over. Thankfully the person sitting next to her is busy with their own screen, watching some dumb movie. Otherwise, he would get to see the future of love, and he wouldn't be ready for that. Again, too much truth.

She just landed a major investment. One of her clients. He's in love with her and when he heard she wanted to create an app, he offered to help. A hedge fund guy. Very, very successful. Practically a billionaire. He gave her two weeks to come up with a business plan. She took a bunch of Adderall and gave it to him in two days. He was very impressed.

There were only a few special conditions before he cut her a check. One was that she start sending him mean text messages throughout the week. At least one every other business day to keep him going. That's been easy, though she's had to set a reminder. The next was that they could do a couple of FaceTime sessions while she was away for the holidays. All of her clients knew she was going away for a couple of weeks and most were pretty upset about it. Rich guys are spoiled like that. With the rest of them she didn't care and told them, "So what?" That made them like her more, but it wasn't the same with this client. He really needed it. So now she has to do that, too, while at her parents' house. And the last thing was that she also start kicking him in the balls at the start of their sessions. She normally wouldn't want to deviate too much from her program, but since so much was at stake with working with him, doing that seemed like a no-brainer. Plus, it didn't require that much time or effort and she knew it would cause him a lot of physical pain. A nice crushed-sperm icing on top of the emotional shit cake they had been making together. Anyway, she kicked him in the balls at the start of that last session and after the hour was complete they drew up a little contract and he cut her a five-million-dollar check. It was a win-win.

Now that money's in the LLC she set up last week. He also helped her to land some meetings with a couple of venture capital firms he has relationships with in Silicon Valley. That's how taken he was with her idea. The meetings are in two days, the Friday before Christmas. She could potentially get another fifteen million in investments during this trip, maybe even more, you never know.

So what's Bonobo? Bonobo is sort of like Tinder, but better. Just because you get there first doesn't mean you're the best. This app is going to be another thing like that; it'll be to Tinder what Google is to Yahoo.

Of course, now Haruka doesn't want to work for Google anymore. Or Facebook or Apple or Twitter. Ever. Why would she? Now she has her own thing. The future of love. The future of life. And she's the big boss of it all. Not to mention, well on her way to becoming quite wealthy.

She's also planning on dropping out of school. It's pretty funny. She lols. Shakes her head. The guy sitting next to her must think she's crazy. But to think! All the trouble she went through to get that stupid grade changed! Well, to be fair, it sort of makes sense. We hate to lose more than we love to win. It's more natural to avoid pain than to seek extra happiness, and there's no way she could have known before how things were going to develop this fall. Really, the main difference is that what she's doing now is on her own terms.

Before, it felt like the end of the world because she wasn't in control. And now she's going to drop out of NYU with a 4.0. In full control. That's a more impressive GPA than Steve Jobs or Bill Gates or Mark Zuckerberg probably had when they dropped out of their schools. She has no way of knowing, but she bets they didn't have perfect GPAs. Even if Bill Gates and Mark Zuckerberg did go to a better school, it's doubtful they had that. It's nice. She's going to join their ranks, and likely on even better footing.

Her parents don't know she's dropping out yet, but it doesn't matter. Besides Bonobo, she's got her dorm room dominatrix business, and it's flourishing. She could probably buy their house from them in another six months, she's making so much money. And that's all that really matters to them. That she is a success. She'll explain everything to them this week. They're not going to care that she's a dominatrix; even if the men she works with get some kind of sexual satisfaction, it's completely self-contained. And what she does is totally legal. Plus, they're pretty open-minded and progressive. "So what are you doing exactly?" they might ask. "Oh, just smashing the white supremacist patriarchy," she might answer. "And getting rich in the process." They'll be very pleased.

Her plan with Allison and her other friends around school worked out wonderfully. She's got all of the major races and nationalities represented, something for everybody. Even with the white girls. Maeve's pretending to be British, for example, to capitalize on old colonial fears and the feeling of inadequacy some guys feel when spoken to with their sophisticated-sounding accents. They've already expanded to Columbia and the New School, and Allison's looking at getting her friends at fancy Boston-area colleges involved. Haruka, too, with her old friends now at Stanford and USC. A nice little expansion. Allison, or Madame A, as she has come to be known—though her clients think that A stands for Anastasia or something similar—is running the day-to-day of the business now while Haruka focuses on Bonobo. But she gets a nice little cut of everything. Combining that with what she is poised to make from her app, she could honestly become a billionaire within the next five or so years.

When she gets back, she's going to get her own apartment. A loft somewhere downtown she thinks, close enough to NYU and her operation. The only thing she'll have to do is outfit a little corner of it to look like a dorm room. Shouldn't be hard. There's the Kmart in the East Village for odds and ends, but mostly she'll just have things delivered from online, probably Target or IKEA if not some dorm-specific site. As long as she keeps her aesthetic, keeps her brand, her clients won't be able to complain. And if they do, she'll just tell them to shut up. Or she'll just stop seeing them altogether and focus solely on Bonobo. Though really, thinking about it, that wouldn't make that much sense. The last few sessions, when she wasn't studying for finals to ensure her 4.0, she was working on Bonobo anyway. It's such simple multitasking, very easy money, and a lot of fun, these sessions most of the time.

Anyway, back to Bonobo. The idea. When Haruka first heard of Tinder back in September, she was very jealous. She wished she had thought of it. Of course it was sort of a rip-off of Grindr—the app where gay guys find and have sex with one another—but by successfully repackaging it for everybody, it seemed revolutionary. They said it was for "dating" and "making friends," though everybody knew it was basically for sex. It was very visual, like Instagram, which she loves, and very fast and easy to use. It made love and sex into a video game, pretty much. Brilliant. So much better than stupid OkCupid with its extensive profiles and all the effort needed to set up dates and make things work. Here was an app that let you ask: "Are you hot? Are you near me? Wanna fuck?" And it made it socially permissible and easy to do that. The team behind it targeted NYU and other college campuses in their initial launch and Haruka's been keeping an eye on it ever since.

They also have good branding. A good slogan. A good logo. A little thing that starts a fire. Very nice. Aside from the whole obvious part about the heart in the throes of passion, or a burning love, there are also a lot of "hot" people you can find on it for sex. People come together with a "match." But what kind of fire does that match really start? It isn't the flame of an endless love. Haruka knows that. Ha-ha. It's hellfire. And that's why she wants in.

Bonobo is branded in a similarly deceptive way. It's named after a very cute primate, looks sort of like a chimp. And all they do is fuck. They fuck as a greeting, they fuck as a form of general bonding, they fuck for food and while trading other little things, they fuck to resolve conflicts. And they fuck their own genders as well as the opposite. Pretty much all of them. They're very sex-positive. Some people even look up to bonobos because their societies are so peaceful, they think we can learn from them. And that has a little something to do with her slogan. By making her slogan "Free love" she can tap into that, the notion of peaceful living. It's also sort of a double entendre that functions like Instagram. It harkens back to a bygone, romantic time. The sixties. And it's also a giant fucking lie. It's all pretty genius. People are going to eat it up. And that's what she's counting on.

Because while bonobos are very peaceful and pretty happy, they're also very gross. As a society. They engage in incest. And not just cousins or brothers and sisters. Absolutely anything goes, including parents with their children, with the exception sometimes of mother and adult son. The most heinous of human crimes is normal for them. And none of them ever settle down. They don't ever practice monogamy. It isn't a phase, it's just how sex works in their society.

And Haruka is counting on this as the future of sex for humans and, in a way, love. Because if everybody can just fuck for fun using an unending pool of high-quality partners, whenever they want, like they're ordering takeout, why ever settle down? Sure, some young people won't participate. Religious types and losers. And of course there will be those who want kids eventually. But if this trend catches on from colleges and becomes the normal routine, then that will have profound effects on intimacy throughout the world. Divorce rates will be insane in twenty years. It'll be like Facebook. Started in colleges, now everybody uses it.

Over one billion people and growing. And just as Facebook has eroded attention spans, Bonobo will erode intimacy. If love is free, it will be of very, very little value. Beautiful! That is what she was trying to do to all of those guys this year, feeding her Little Kaiju, and now she can do it to the entire world!

The love will be free, but little else. There will be ads. User information will be sold to marketers. And eventually, she thinks it'll break out beyond being a dating app. They'll, again, be like Facebook. Facebook started out as a social network, but now it's so much more. A marketplace. A news and media platform. Control communication and you control the people communicating. People could exchange sex for all kinds of things. Pilates or yoga classes. Oil changes. Rent. Utilities. Furniture delivery. Guitar lessons. Homework. Like a skill swap. Bonobo will go so far beyond Tinder it'll be ridiculous. Her primate will stomp the Tinder out, make it go the way of Betamax and LaserDisc and AOL. But the flames will be kept alive, burning the world down, destroying everything. Especially love. Everything but money.

That's what she and her client want. See, the thing about the men she sees is that they hate themselves, but they hate everyone else just a little bit more. That's how they make their money. Exploiting honest, good people and spreading something evil. Google tracks their users even though their motto is "Don't be evil." That's how a lot of successful people make their money.

The plan is to hire a team and roll out the app in eight U.S. markets within the next six months. It'll be a lot of work! But she is ready. Then after that, the rest of the country, then world. She'll be based out of New York, but will really be bicoastal. Two teams. The product team in San Fran, sales and executives in New York. Lots of time on planes, up here with the clouds.

She proofreads the business plan one last time. It's ready. She's ready.

Might as well look out the window again… before it gets dark, before all you can see are the towns like circuit boards. She wonders: were there clouds in the sky on the day of Hiroshima? There certainly was one afterwards. Hers will be bigger.

The screen on the seat in front of her is showing that they're flying over what looks like the exact middle of the country at this very moment. Kansas, she guesses. She laughs. Something very, very funny. And it's not simply her imagination; there's a cloud outside that looks just like two bonobos fucking, some oblivious small town beneath it.

▲ ▲ ▽ ▽ ▲ ▲ ▲

Whoa, whoa, whoa… is he back? Wowee, wowee, wow, wow. Oh my God! He's back? He's back. It's good to be back, it took a while to get back. Hello! It was good to be there, too, though. More than good. Oh man… was that it? That was it! So thankful. So joyful! So intense. Wait, but he's back? Why is he back? Because he's supposed to be. Not ready for that yet. Must be it. Fuckin' bonkers. That's what that was. But fun! So much fun. Whoa, whoa, whoa, whoa. Yaho, wah, wowee, wowee, yah, weh, wowwee, wowee, yaho, wah, wowee, wow. Ray just met God.

Or, at least, that's what it seemed like. Did he really just meet God? It's hard to put into words what the fuck that was. There aren't words for what the fuck that was. Few could come close. But that would be God, right? Something ineffable? So was it the real deal? An event beyond, not just a chemical reaction in his head?

That's the real question. Perhaps there's another way of supplicating for the truth. That place… did it look like home? Really, this looks more like home. The old home he knows. His childhood bedroom, everything pretty much the way he left it. That just looked like energy. In the end, that's all that was left. After the most intense come-up he could have ever imagined. The rocket blast through the atmosphere, his body a loose vibration of screaming atoms. His consciousness spread between them, still able to see and feel. And, oh did they… The geometry of things, sacred symbols, a kaleidoscope of all he's ever known. Going, going still up through the cosmos. Through astral systems he hasn't known and couldn't have known. The stars streaming past until there was just the light from them left, prismatic trails widening and then all-consuming. Beautiful white light, the warmth of the womb, undulating waves of goodness everywhere. The circumfluent warmth he felt with the tingles before, the warmth he'd been chasing. More than feeling sunshine, or light, it was like he was sunshine, light. Just beautiful energy all around. Love. Then yes, that was home. Real home. Where everyone's heart is, or should be. That was God. Yes, he joined it.

Enter the Void didn't have shit on that. Hell, even *2001* couldn't really prepare you for that. Holy fucking shit! Wow, wow, wow, wow!!

So what does this mean? That experience he just had, what he'd expected of death but had never actually gone through? It must mean he… it must mean…

If he were actually in purgatory, wouldn't he have experienced something similar? Like, gone to the halfway point on the way to heaven? Stuck there in the atmosphere of everything he had known for a time? Wouldn't there have been some introduction, some set of rules, some set of challenges laid out? That would only be fair. Purgatory should be nothing if not fair. It's supposed to be about justice, right? How unjust would purgatory be without some terms? He hasn't been in purgatory at all. If anything, this "afterlife" he's been living is more like a version of hell. A slow-burning hell. Maybe just the edge of it, maybe it's been limbo all along after all. But not purgatory. He just saw the light. Fuckin' A. The shrooms all those weeks ago were really only trying to help. He simply didn't want to believe them. LSD gave him the information, he just couldn't capture the feeling he needed, couldn't follow the blueprint. And mescaline only hinted at the beginning of this feeling, largely forgetting the blueprint. DMT, fuck. DMT is the truth, the whole truth, and nothing but the fuckin' truth. And it's in us. It's in us all, naturally. Every living organism. No wonder they call it the spirit molecule.

Holy shit. He isn't dead at all. That was it, that was the real deal. The feeling of dying. The white light. Heaven. The journey Mother Teresa spoke of. It lasts only a few minutes, then you're there.

And you only get a peek. He's glad he understands as much as he does about what he just experienced. Obviously he isn't ready. God doesn't want him yet. There's still more to do here. He's alive! It's December 21st, just in time for Christmas, and Ray's alive again!

Leaning forward, he removes the blindfold he had been wearing. What he was told to wear for the best results. D-Motherfuckin'-T! Wow!

So what was all that, then? The whole journey? The déjà vus and love gained and lost and the tingles and love gained again in other, aberrant forms? What? Divine intervention? An impetus to get him here, so that he'll live his life with a bit more verve, stop wasting so much time treading water in New York? Keeping his head just above the surface with temporary jobs and solutions? Perhaps. Ray wasn't worthy of whatever that was, but a life actually well lived can make him so. He needs to snap out of it. Act his fuckin' age. Stop carrying on like a pelado, stealing shit from people. Stop drinking and smoking so much. And he needs to stop with the bullshit jobs. The quick fixes. He needs to work. Contribute to the order of the universe in some meaningful way, something truly positive. Good is still open to interpretation, of course. Everything is everything. He'll get back to that place eventually. But when he's on the verge, he wants to feel like he's earned it.

And he can start by burning some incense. Do a solid for everyone else in the house. His parents and brother and sister will be back from Christmas shopping in a couple of hours and now it smells like burning fucking plastic and mothballs in here. Felix, his high school friend and the guy who hooked him up with the stuff yesterday, didn't tell him about the smell. Nor did he mention all the hooting and hollering he'd do. It's a good thing he didn't wait until the middle of the night, his original plan. That woulda been bad. But worth it! Fuck! It stinks terribly but is so, so wonderful.

Honestly, the only reason he didn't do DMT back in New York is because he was scared. He had read about it during his initial research for his psychonautic experiments and it just seemed like too much, like what he might experience would be big, but terrifying and false. Forced. This drug people say helps you experience death without actually experiencing it. Others mentioned the God thing, had similar takeaways. But he wanted to meet God through himself, with a nudge. Not through a chemical. When he got back into town and ran into Felix, though, at the bar where everybody from high school meets up each year in the days leading up to Christmas, and they got to talking and he mentioned he had some DMT, it seemed right. Organic. Like it was all coming together. And it did. Now he gets it: Everything.

The ride's over. He can go back to normal, back to his old self. Whatever he feels he left behind around twenty-one, twenty-two. A dude with potential, a dude with something to give…

Ray pulls out some of his old incense from his nightstand drawer, Nag Champa. Still in there from when he used to mask the smell of smoking weed. He wonders if they'll even burn anymore. He pulls one out, sets it up, lights it. Still does.

▲▲▽▲▽▽▽

Then there they were… the last words. A tear. But only one. Emerson is finally finished. He wouldn't change a thing, not one word, a single punctuation mark. He's read the thing back now ten times in a row. Ten times for his tenth book, that was the test. Before this draft he got to eight times, but had to start over when he caught a comma that really should have been a semicolon, somewhere in the middle, a section about Chaucer. But now here it is. He's read it back those ten times and it's still perfect. More than perfect, in fact—transcendent, sublime, a truly sacrosanct text. The only fitting afterword to the Culture itself, a tome that shall echo in eternity.

Though in his editing he successfully altered the book to describe the Culture as a subject, he can't help in this moment to think of it, again, as an old friend. A very close, lifelong friend now gone for good, its ashes blowing in the wind. He allows himself a few private lamentations…

As with any story worth telling, it was, in the end, a tragic one. What do we say of those who burn too brightly? Do we shield our eyes or turn our heads when the glare makes us uncomfortable? No, we cannot. We must watch the explosion without movement or blinking, all the way through the afterglow. Take with us the memory of what once was. In all its glory and intensity. Emerson's magnum opus is that afterglow: an outline, a trace memory of the thing he held so dear, the entire Canon. Still visible, but only just; something crucial for all the eyes have seen. For we are nothing without our memories, without our proof of them. The present is ephemeral. The memory is what lasts; history is written as substantiation.

Goodbye! Goodbye, old friend! It came together so beautifully. Another tear. He just can't help it!

It's okay. He's earned this moment, a little bit of emotion. In fact, both of his identities have. Though the assistant in him would likely only shed a tear of pride.

He performed very well this last week in that role. Much better than Claire, that bastard Ray, any of his past assistants. He kept himself on track and focused, stocking the apartment with plenty of premade food, coffee, paper for the printer. He unplugged the phone, unplugged the computer when not in use. None of his assistants ever did that! And if they knew him well enough, they certainly should have! That is how you really read. With no distractions whatsoever, he read and read and read and read. While eating, while drinking, even while going to the bathroom, he read. He couldn't do it in the shower, so he simply did not shower. Fifteen hours a day until this very moment.

Now, it is finished. And now, in many ways, so is he. A writer no more. A teacher no more. Yes, there will probably be some promotional appearances and tasks that he'll have to endure for the book, but aside from those, he's free to live out the rest of his days doing whatever he'd like. Reading and relaxing, mostly. But there may be time for other pleasures as well.

Mainly, to embrace himself, as it were, in his duality. Since he's been assisting himself, he has also begun that process. Late at night, after his meal, to blow off some steam. He's starting to get the hang of it, the rather specific mechanics of his new equipment. Truly elevating the art of self-love. Forrest Bess's idea was to receive another male organ inside of the orifice he created. Not Emerson. He is all he needs. But he has yet to achieve orgasm.

It is a marvel of the male anatomy that orgasm can be attained without tumescence. The proper touch is really all that's required; that and a vivid imagination. Last night, folding himself into himself, he came very, very close. He certainly understands that particular feminine frustration now! Goodness! And that it can still feel nice, something like a massage. But climax is of course the goal.

Feeling emotional and, well, deserving, right now seems like the perfect time to try again. He pats the manuscript not once, not twice, but thrice, and moves into the bedroom.

He undresses and gets into bed. Under the covers, his mind and hand wander... until they both become very focused. He recites, in his head, some of the best lines from his work. His hand responds, in kind, by moving to the rhythm of those words. Yes, yes! It is rhapsody and ecstasy like nothing else! More and more, please! Genius proclamations! Lyrical odes! He's really giving himself the business now! More! Yes, that one about Aristotle! Then Socrates and Plato! This one on Shakespeare! And that on Chaucer, now with perfect grammar! Cicero! Virgil! Ovid! Dante, Dante, Dante! Such brilliant words about Dante! Troyes! Pizan! Bunyan! Borges! Austen! Proust! Oh, he's really working up to a fever pitch! San Pedro! Cervantes! Dickens! Donne! Dryden! Shelley! And the other! Fielding! Scott! Gay! Blake! Coleridge! Swift! But not too swift! Keats! Dickinson! Tee-hee, tee-hee! Milton, Molière, Montaigne! Marlowe! Goethe! Tennyson! Eliot! And the other! Kafka! Hugo! Woolf! Joyce! Oh, Joyce! Yeats! Yeats, Yeats, Yeats! My man! Melville! Whitman! Flaubert! Rimbaud! Joyce again! Ibsen! Ibsen, Ibsen, Ibsen! Scott! Wilde! Byron! Oh, you devil, Byron! Brontë! And the others! Tolstoy! Dostoevsky! Chekhov! Poe! James! Twain! Calvino! Céline! Now we're getting dirty! Camus! Sartre! Shaw! Conrad! Lawrence! Pessoa! Beckett! Thomas! Neruda! Lowry! Wharton! Pound! Yes! Pound, Pound, Pound! Elliot! Cummings? Not yet, but almost! Oh, you! Faulkner! Oh, goodness! Faulkner! Bellow! Nabokov! Mailer! Williams! Wordsworth,

Wordsworth, Wordsworth! Yes, almost! Almost! Gaddis! Roth! Carver! Pynchon! McCarthy! DeLillo! And more on the Greeks! Back to the Greeks! Aristotle again! Plato again! Homer! Aristophanes! Euripides! Herodotus! Sophocles! Another on Shakespeare! Oh, William! Shakespeare, Shakespeare, Shakespeare! Shakespeare, Shakespeare, Shakespeare, Shakespeare! And Towers! Towers, Towers, Towers! Towers, Towers, Towers, Towers, Towers, Towers, Towers, Towers, Tow—

Ughghuhghguhwguhug! Ahahshhahahwhofgdwhah! Yes! Yes, yes, yes! He can feel it, the rush! It's coming! He's coming! But… Why? Why is his arm?! The other one? The left? Oh, no! Oh dear! He! He, he! Well if this is it, then this is it! What a world! What a life! At least he, at least he… Yes! There it is! He can see it coming! Clear and white! Pure white! And more white every—Auhguhauahuduf! Gwahuruhgusurhuiuguhgeh… Ahduuahduijhwiu… auhfguer—

▲ ▲ ▽ ▲ ▽ ▽ ▲

No way. What?! As if things could get any better. Closing on the fifteen million dollars then another ten of seed money yesterday was one thing, but this. This! This is more than Haruka could have ever asked for this Christmas! This! She can still barely believe her eyes. Maybe because she's smiling so big her vision's actually getting blurry. She relaxes her face, reads it again. It's true! It's true all right. Emerson Towers is dead!

She still had a Google Alert set for him, from back when she was doing the blog. Something she forgot about because after her nobody really wrote about him. And it just notified her. Emerson Towers, Renowned Literary Critic, Dies at 73. That's the headline. From *The New York Times*. She clicks on the article.

She doesn't read *The New York Times* that much because it's very boring, so she has more than enough free articles left this month. It opens up. She skims it. Losers read, winners skim.

It's sort of a puff piece. Seems rushed, really. Talking about his life and writing career for the most part, with a tone that's a bit too favorable for her liking. Yes, there are words like "controversial" and "pugnacious"—negative words—but also stuff like "acclaimed," "brilliant," "significant." No mention of his firing. They say he was "a man who lived up to his oversized name." Dumb. Also pretty sexist, if you ask her.

No real details about the death itself, either, just broad strokes. It says he was "found dead in his home on the Upper West Side Saturday" and that his daughter is the one who found him "after being unable to reach him for a few days." They point to "natural causes."

But it wasn't. It was Haruka who killed him. A heart attack, maybe. Or perhaps suicide. She wouldn't be surprised. But she knows the death that took him. And it was her. Ha-ha. She finds her reflection in the glass of her phone. So cute, this death. The only thing that could make this better is if she gloated to Ray a little bit. Now he won't have a job. Hilarious! All because of her! Is this enough revenge? It is for Professor Towers! Her recording him and getting him fired and all stressed out must've ruined him. And now he's dead! She eviscerated him. Like, literally. Bye-bye, motherfucker! Zot! LOL! Good luck giving good students B's now from hell! Hee-hee-hee! Now he is nothing and Haruka is everything. That's what it feels like. Everything is going her way, absolutely everything. Merry, merry Christmas indeed!

She pulls out her phone and texts Ray: heard about your boss. sorry. ☹

Another irony. Like "thinking of you" on the amateur porno she sent him. Ray liked irony, she remembers. Like racism could be ironic and you could strip it of its power by appropriating it, pointing to the n-word being used by black culture and stuff like that. Like irony is a tool or something. See how he likes it when she does an irony at him. It doesn't seem like it was very funny the last time, since he moved out and all. Idiot. Maybe he'll kill himself, too, now. That would be nice. Though she'd have no way of knowing. He isn't important enough to get written about by *The New York Times* when he dies. But Haruka will be. Way more than Professor Towers, she'll be a multibillionaire when she dies. That is, if she ever dies at all. Who knows. Maybe soon you'll be able to upload your consciousness to the cloud somewhere, hopefully put it on your phone. Is anybody working on that? Hmmm… maybe that can be her next project after Bonobo. Someone's going to get there, might as well be her. It's only a matter of time.

▲▲▽▲▽▲▽

A tug of war, pitting the old head against the new heart. The original plan was to ignore it. And so far he has. It's not smart to engage; he knows this. The tone was, after all, pretty weird—could go one of two ways, but both bad. Was she being antagonistic, like with the "thinking of you" thing? Or did she mean it, which would still make her, like, crazy, totally bipolar? You can't offer genuine sympathy, kindness, for something unrelated and heavy after doing what she did: the dog you smacked is gonna think you're just petting it so you can smack it again. Also, all lowercase? What the fuck? Real condolences would've deserved a bit more gravitas. Unless she really is that chiflada, that much in her own world. Best not to engage, that's what the head says. It pulls Ray away from his phone.

But not the new heart. It's a very, very strong muscle. Since going to Mass with his family on Christmas morning, he's trying to exist in a more pure, Christlike way as he forges ahead in his recently rediscovered life. To carry out the rebirth in Jesus' image. His heart taking in blood tinged with trials and evils and, bonifying them, pumping out unconditional love. He is meant to be like the reverse-evil apple tree he planted in Central Park; we all are. That's what Jesus was. God planted him in Mary to right wrongs and to preach magnanimity. So what would Jesus do? Ray's not gonna wear a bracelet now or anything—he's not some jerk in 2002; not to mention, more importantly, Jesus wouldn't have worn a bracelet like that himself—but it's a question worth asking. His heart would say the only question worth asking. And the answer is simple and obvious: turn the other cheek.

If you're the dog, allow yourself to get hit again. Then lick the hand that deals the blow.

But the head counters: it's possible, no probable, that Haruka is just a conduit for evil. She wasn't ever Fate or Santa Muerte, obviously... only a strange young woman, flawed like all of us, with her own issues, and also like all of us, though perhaps even more so, susceptible to the Devil working through her. That's who Ray had danced with there on the edge of hell this year. In the Bible, Jesus, after listening to and rebutting Satan a few times, eventually casts him away. Ray's tolerated enough of Haruka's games. Shouldn't it be time he cast her away for good?

But what is she tempting him with here? Condolences? This text isn't very Satan-like. Sure, she could be trying to set him up for something. But this message in and of itself isn't evil. If and when that time comes, the time she's trying to bamboozle him again, he can cast her away for good. Delete her phone number or make Virgin block her. Easy. She'll be out of his life once and for all. Leaving him for angels or whatever to come around.

So: fine! He can rise above it, be pleasant. That's what Jesus would do. Until he's pushed to the edge, one last time. Then it'll be away with you, Devil! He replies:

> Yeah, sad news. He hasn't been my boss for a while, though, so I had no idea his health was failing. Hope he's in a better place.

And Ray does, really. He forgives Emerson for what he tried to pull, the peculiarity of their working relationship, his rudeness and generally volatile nature. All of it. All the shitty things that Ray thought were tests but were nothing more than this guy acting out. Because at the core, it mostly seemed like Emerson was just profoundly lonely. And above all, those people need love. There was decency in him—he paid well enough, valued something non-evil in this world with all those books he'd go on about. So hopefully now there are traces of him in that energy, in the love Ray just tapped into with that text. Maybe he helped make him more eloquent then. Hopefully Emerson's just gone home, where we'll all be someday, a part of all that's good.

It was a pretty big shock to learn he had died. Especially from Haruka. That was a lot all at once—the news, having her as the reporting source. Ray hasn't really been going online while here with his family, not since the DMT breakthrough, anyway, trying to maximize his time with them. Cooking and eating meals, watching movies together, playing games, all that good holiday stuff. Participating in familial love, the real, face-to-face kind. There has been little room or desire to see what's up on the web, and Emerson's death wouldn't exactly interrupt prime-time programming. After she sent that, he confirmed it, read the *New York Times* article she must have caught. Pretty wild. Good ol' Emerson, he'll have to get the book when it comes out.

The phone vibrates. Haruka's written him back:

> how r u?

Then another text:

like, in general these days?

Perhaps she is building towards some final temptation. That, or an apology: trying to pave the road to redemption through some let's-bury-the-hatchet, pre-New Year's texting. Lowercase texting. That's weird; doesn't the iPhone just automatically use proper capitalization? She must have changed the settings to make it all lowercase. He can't help but think this would be better in person, the forgiveness or the casting away, whichever it will be. Ray'll be back in New York tomorrow, a couple of days before New Year's Eve. That would be a nice way to end this year and go into the next with a truly clean slate, really put his new-found Christlike M.O. to the test. Forgive her in the flesh. Maybe they can get together. Would Jesus forgive someone over text? Not if he could help it. What would Jesus actually do? Try to arrange a meeting.

Ray: I'm okay. You?

He's still with his family, so he can't stay on his phone like this too much longer—even if they are just watching *It's a Wonderful Life* for the tenth time in about as many years—but he has to ease his way into it a little bit. No more than what's necessary, though. Jesus would probably be pretty direct over text.

▲ ▲ ▽ ▲ ▽ ▲ ▲

Lol nice. That was a close one. It seemed like he wouldn't ever respond, but then he did. Now Haruka's getting him where she wants him. In-volved, with her. The right kind of user engagement.

She wonders why he wasn't working for Professor Towers anymore. Maybe when he got fired, he couldn't afford to pay Ray's pitiful salary. Ha-ha. Talk about killing two birds with one stone. Now to stand over one of those birds as it twitches, taking its final breaths, and sing because it can't. Ray was just as bad as Emerson with the power he held over her. Who owns the air now? Who do you see when you stare up into the clouds? Her fingers fly:

> i'm good. really busy.
> actually, i've got some big news.

Yeah?

> you'll probably think i'm crazy. i dropped
> out of school.

Oh wow. How come?

> i'm starting a company, building an
> app. just closed on major seed money
> from investors.

Congratulations. That's pretty exciting.

Stupid Ray. "Congratulations. That's pretty exciting." If it's so damn exciting, where's his exclamation point?! He's hella lame. Derp, derp, derp, I'm Ray. Haruka herself is in a lowercase mood now, it seems more cas, like: "ya know, just out here in silicon valley makin millions, burying my enemies, nbd." Ha-ha. There's a difference between keeping it casual and being a downer, though. Ray and all of his stupid periods and his general tone are annoying her. But two can play at this game.

> thanks.

> Are you in NY for the holidays? I'm in
> Texas now but will be back in town
> tomorrow. There are a few things I was
> hoping to talk about in person with you.

This is even better than she could have imagined. Oh, goodness, Ray! You get a little attention and you want to meet again?! He must still be in love. So nice!

> what's so good about talking in person?
> ppl are more honest in writing.

Some things are better said in the flesh.

> idk about that. but anyway, i'm away
> right now.
> won't be back for another week.

Oh, okay. Want to meet then?

Haruka thinks for a moment. Hmmm. Does she want to meet then? No, no she does not. While yes, it would be nice to actually see Ray cry while he complains at her about how she fucked his friend and sent him a video of it, or about their failed relationship, she doesn't want to risk anything bad happening. Lately, she's been having nightmares about the time Ray destroyed her phone and about how he made a scene in the museum. She doesn't want to deal with anything traumatic or awkward. No, not worth it. She's a CEO now and will be a public figure probably soon. She'll just have to imagine his face.

> i don't like suspense with people. what is
> it? tell me.

Not a huge deal, just wanted to go
over some stuff. For closure.

Closure: Now there's a silly idea. Nothing ever gets closure, the only real closure is death. That's why she's still having nightmares. Even remembering those incidents now, she's getting goosebumps. A little sweat building in the palms. Her phone covered in coffee! People looking at her at PS1, people who might have had really good jobs at premier tech companies when she did not, making her feel like a loser! It's terrible. Terrible to think about! Why does Ray get to have power over her again right now? This is not why she contacted him! She contacted him to gloat! Maybe it's not a good idea to stare a dying bird in the eye. It might reflect something back at you that you don't want to see. It might be better just to step on its head:

> is it about the video? that was nothing.
> just fun.

Good luck coming back from that one, Ray! She knows how you men are! So territorial about love and sex.

That was a part of it, but I guess it's okay.
Nevermind. Have a good New Year's.

And there it is, the face she's been hoping for. Except she can't really see it. Just sees the concept of a sad face, like an emoji. Only brownish. He's brownish, right? She's sort of forgotten what Ray looked like. She remembers he had a nice body, good abs, but that's about it. Maybe, maybe she can look him up on Facebook real quick. She does. Unfortunately, his profile pic is a faraway shot and he's looking off to the side. Oh, Ray. What an ironic way to use Facebook. Not even really showing your face! So smart, so cool. Hmmm. His profile settings are pretty strict and she can't see any other photos. It's times like this she wishes she hadn't unfriended him after their breakup. She really wants to see that face, sad, as it should be:

we could facetime if you want.

Yes, FaceTime. Best of both worlds. He'll get his talky meeting and she'll get to see him when he gets sad and emotional without actually being there in person!

Still got a flip phone.

Oh, no! She forgot that too. Though, how could she? That was such a big deal in their relationship. Because: Because she has to worry about much better things now, like running two businesses. She can't keep track of her ex's phone model. Also, he really should have come back to the twenty-first century by now. Another opportunity to be mean to him. A consolation prize:

oh i forgot. then sorry. i don't like skype
very much or google hangouts. too
formal.

All right, Haruka. No worries. Good luck
with your company and take care.

Shit. That wasn't as satisfying as she had hoped. It's like the bird's gotten up, singing, and taken flight again. He's acting like he doesn't need her anymore, or care that much since he couldn't get what he wanted. Has he moved on? Does he have another girlfriend? Did he really just want closure? Wait. Why does she care? She doesn't still have feelings for him. Right? Oh fuck! This is terrible. It's because of the sex. The sex they had, it was good. Too many pleasurable chemicals in the brain. Too many associations between the neurons. That, or she's believing too much in her process. She might be dominatrixing herself with this. She did, after all, bring this on herself. A glutton for punishment. No! She can't be distracted by this. Sex, hate, attraction, dopamine, serotonin, endorphins, oxytocin, too much intertwined. She must put Ray in his place. Of course he likes her still, no loves her. Right?

She reads back their conversation. Yes, there is something there. Something still for her. He shouldn't be anyone else's boyfriend. He should be hers! It wouldn't be so bad to have someone around for good sex in the coming months. They will be stressful. They can get beyond what happened. Right?

Is this why she reached out to him, not to gloat, but to rekindle the flame? Rekindle! No! Don't give that to the competition. If anything, she reached out for free love. If they were to have a relationship again, it would have to be an open one. That's her brand. She must take a chance here:

> i miss you sometimes, Ray. i think
> i might be in love with you.

Heaven, hell, purgatory: they're not just for the dead, they are very much a part of living. The three primary modes of life—winning, losing, and waiting. Everything else we do falls on the spectrum between these three big ones. Right now Ray doesn't know exactly what he's doing. He's staring at the message again, sitting on his bed, his back to the wall. Over the last few days, he's looked at it dozens of times. Is this indeed hell, dragging him back? The last temptation, and the one where he fails for good, falls into Satan's awaiting claws? Or is it actually heaven, calling him forward, up? When he highlights the text, it appears with black lettering over a white background, the sender's name in a nice, bright blue. Like the azure sky in the heaven of fluffy clouds. There is a case to be made that she's calling him up there. Really, though, more than anything, this is feeling an awful lot like limbo again, whatever it was. Uneasily waiting. Who knows. He's alive now, but no better off.

He closes the phone. The front of his Samsung Entro reads: 5:33, Mon Dec 31.

So what now? It's not as simple as figuring out what Jesus would do, then doing that. Too glib. No, there are no fail-safe ways of being, he's realized that. Any man who thinks he has it all figured out is a fool and cannot be trusted. Greater men have tried to mimic Jesus before and failed miserably. Everyone who tries does, in fact. Those men could only be those men. Jesus could only be Jesus. Ray can only be Ray.

That text shocked him out of all that thinking, back into himself. His actual self. Fully realized incrementally after he landed, took the AirTrain, then the E train from Jamaica, then the 6 back to his apartment. Where he's spent nearly all of his time since, thinking, only going out once, to the grocery store for a few comforting staples. No aspiring king of kings here, just another prince of pause, or duke of doubt, shilly-shallying.

Wait, wasn't that, like, a Burger King character? Ray laughs.

He reaches for the Dell, googles it. It was. That's right—he had learned about the greater Burger King Kingdom at some point during the mid-aughts, after seeing enough memes featuring the rebooted King character from the seventies/eighties, the dude in all their ads with that menacing mask. The Duke was apparently a Hamburglar copycat or something back in the day. A bigger laugh, a shake of the head. At least he can still make himself laugh right now. At least he won't spend New Year's Eve with total analysis paralysis, brooding over a flip phone. He puts the laptop down, looks toward the front door. Maybe he should, like, go somewhere.

Wait, didn't one of those memes have something to do with God? Also why the seventies/eighties again, now that he's back in this apartment?

He picks the laptop back up, looks up the meme on Know Your Meme. Under "Spread": the Burger King standing in front of some guy, the caption WHERE IS YOUR GOD NOW? Some shit from Something Awful. Sounds about right.

He thought he had stumbled onto a minor distraction, an amusing coincidence, and yet it was just more reinforcement that he is as lost as ever.

Because he is. When that text hit, when he read it, it felt like love. It coursed through him as warm and vivid as he'd ever felt it, including while on DMT. His heart didn't have to process anything; the love had already been there. A big, mysterious love mainlined through his eyes straight to the soul: unlocking all that was there in his heart, pushing it into his blood then his entire body. Oh man, did he feel it! Full swoon. He wanted to write her back, to tell her he loved her, too, in that instant, to share the wonderful thing he was feeling, but he couldn't.

His head wouldn't let him.

It told him: Hold on, dude. You don't realize this, but you just won. Ignore this and the quest will be over. You can go on with your life, really build something. Like a normal person. She's been the primary source of grief and confusion throughout all of this, and her admission of being in love is an admission of defeat; it is the key to your personal victory. Not that you should need a reminder, but it's probably just been Satan working through her, anyway. Satan is in love with all humans and it's our job to reject that love. This is your chance to cast her away. The girl openly gloated about fucking your then-roommate a mere four texts before—"just fun." Remember? Remember that shit?

And he has. But he doesn't want to! He goes back and forth between those two texts—an admission of love and an admission of hate. And he's in effect been turned into a pillar of salt. Sitting here in bed barely doing anything, just trying to figure this out, again poring over the case files, considering buying more psychedelics, more drugs in general… thinking maybe he's too dumb to see it for what it is and that he needs coke or meth or Adderall. Or maybe he should just say fuck it and go the heroin route. Try to force a constant state of peace with that. Or love, with more DMT or MDMA. Lana didn't work for that long, but maybe he could trade in Haruka for Molly. Or live out the rest of his days fucking up his dopamine and serotonin receptors, not to mention body, on a cocktail of everything. Turn his brains to mush and organs to shit to feel all there is to feel until he ODs for real. But deep down he knows it won't compare. Sinead and Prince are right. Nothing, absolutely nothing can compare to the real stuff.

The heart wants what it wants! The head is all wrong: Life isn't a game meant to be won, and ignoring her won't be ignoring his problems. So far it's just made things shitty again. This still isn't a life. No, this still isn't a life… And besides, how fucked up is it to think Satan's working through her? That's some bullshit; it's not like they were together when she fucked Brian anyway. The rules of modern romance call it fair play… And so what if she claimed to have fucked other guys while *they were* an item? That was then, this is now! You're in love! Real love! Tell her! Have a conversation about it, clear the air. There could be a future together… a bright, shiny, beautiful future.

Yes, there could… Or a deep, dark, despairing one. Winter's only just started… you wanna drag old baggage into it, and into the new year? Really, man? You reap what you sow, made this shitty bed you're literally currently stuck in. Go out! Get some pussy, dammit, it's fuckin' New Year's. Forget about her.

Ray's head has a point. Maybe it isn't real love he's feeling. Maybe it was all the crazy sex, that it seemed to mean something more because she'd say all that weird shit at a time when he was very susceptible to it, and that they were doing it without protection. Do that last bit enough times and it'll feel like love, just ask any high school kid. That's the crux of what it means to be a high school lover, after all. Oh shit. Has he been tested since her? Now that he's alive, maybe he should, if she really did cheat on him as much as she claims. His dick feels fine, but obviously that ain't everything, and better safe than sorry… On the to-do list for next year.

At any rate, the head might be right. He should get out of here, go out and try to get lucky. Safely, of course. See how he feels after he sleeps with someone else. He hasn't had sex since her, not real sex; jerking off to Lana Del Rey doesn't count. That was just another strange celebrity crush, like he had on Megan Fox a few years ago, before he learned she had a brachydactyly type D. If it feels empty, he'll know. His head deserves that before he lets his heart run the show completely.

It's New Year's, a good time to get it done. Single women are looking for that kind of thing tonight, and besides, he can't sit on this text for too much longer.

Has he been invited to any parties? He logs on to Facebook and checks. Nope. But it makes sense. He's been pretty incommunicado for most of this year, not really responding to any of the shit that he was invited to. Then there were all the friends he sacrificed back in the spring. It seems like people have probably given up on him. Fuck. He could text around, but that might seem a little desperate. It's almost six. His old friends from college who've crewed up probably feel good about their respective crews, plus he hasn't seen most of those guys in a pretty long-ass time. Would seem weird…

Should he fire up the old OkCupid account? While also a desperate move, there would only be desperate girls on there, too. Hmmm. Nah… seems a bit contrived. If there's a chance of testing his connection with Haruka, it'd have to be with someone he actually liked and who actually liked him. That's why it's nice to meet people through friends; at least at parties everybody knows somebody, there's a semblance of vetting and community, friendship. It's not just about coming. He needs that damn party, a place where conversation and feeling people out can be carried out casually and efficiently. Should he actually text around? Hmmm… Nah, if it doesn't work out and he can't drum anything up he'll feel like a loser, and that's no way to start a new year. So what then? Well, there are also bars, which are sort of like parties but with strangers…

He'll go to one of those. Yeah, that'll work.

Ray showers, gets dressed; makes sure to put on a nice shirt. He decides to eat a little something, but nothing that'll fuck up his breath, no onions, no garlic. Just a simple quesadilla—ham, four cheese blend, spinach, sour cream, no salsa. Brushes his teeth. Flosses. Maybe the sour cream was a bad idea. Gargles some mouthwash. There's a bar in the neighborhood pretty close by he's been meaning to try out, The Duck. He goes there.

It's a pretty weird spot. He had learned about it after moving to the area, looking up bars on Yelp, and one of the pictures on the page was of a toilet. In person, this seems about right. Not that it's a complete dump. The place is clean for a dive; there's a certain finicky pride at play in the lowbrow aesthetic, like a really clean Airstream trailer—after the big bouncer lets you in, you walk into a dark, empty room lined with some arcade games, then around the corner into the space with the actual bar, a back bar, brighter, old country playing from the jukebox over strained speakers, Christmas lights and beer signs and license plates and other tesserae denoting old Americana all over the walls. It doesn't really feel like you're in New York anymore, and especially not East Harlem. The bartender, white, with ample cleavage busting out of a low-cut shirt, has a small-town pretty face with high cheekbones, flashing a bright but snaggle-toothed smile as you come in. A few bras hang from the ceiling for some reason. There's a pool table farther in the back, two guys who could be drug dealers or biker gang members or both, one black, one Hispanic, playing a friendly-looking game with two sort of chubby but still cute Hispanic girls. The other customers, mostly men, sit around looking at their phones or the flat-screen televisions behind the bar, the only real twenty-first-century touches. It's a place where the patrons are well aware that they are creatures who piss and shit and occasionally vomit and wipe away blood and, if they're lucky, like Ray's hoping to be, fuck. They appreciate a good, clean toilet. Nice job, guy on Yelp.

But enough thinking about the internet. How the place lives up to what he saw there. Ray's actually here now, and he should think about being *here*, in the moment. Unfortunately, it's pretty slim pickins currently in terms of the fairer sex. There are the two in the back playing pool, spoken for, then another one sitting at the bar, who also might be on a date, and isn't even remotely attractive, anyway. Otherwise, just the bartender, who, while decent-looking, will surely factor flirting into how she makes her tips in a place like this, so anything he gets from her is gonna be a lie, purely transactional. Ray sits down on a stool and hangs his coat on a hook under the bar.

"Starting early, huh?" she asks.

"Yeah, guess so."

"My kinda guy." Already at it… That shit where the dark, dashing stranger comes in and charms the pants off a bartender, literally, and fucks her at break time in the bathroom or in a back alley or closet? Only happens in the movies, or on cable TV. In real life, it takes months and an actual friendship to be able to fuck your bartender, and even then it'll have to be done on the sly. Shit's bad for business. He knows because he did it once, right after college. When he was living in Bushwick. And the bartender told him he probably shouldn't come to the bar anymore. Anyway, bartender's out. "What can I get you?"

"I'll take a shot of well tequila and…" He looks over the menu. The beer prices in this place are absofuckinglutely amazing for NYC, meaning pretty average anywhere else. Not really anything over five bucks, PBRs are only two. There are even pitchers for, like, six-fifty. Cheaper than a single draft in most places here. But he can't drink a pitcher by himself, as much as he sort of wants to right now. Not a good look for whatever ladies that might walk in… though he could possibly parlay it into a "My date didn't show up, wanna help with this?" kinda thing. No, no. Too cynical, not enough yourself; you won't get over someone by living a lie. "A Lone Star," he answers. That'll be nice, a little taste of home. Honestly, he feels like he's back in Texas right now. There's even racist shit on the walls—permissible here because it's about Indians. "No serving Indians after dark," a sign says. Kinda fucked up, but it's not like too many are gonna be coming in here. In a way, this sign is invaluable, that they can get away with shit like that, even if it is meant to be tongue-in-cheek. Haruka would hate it. The bras too, though maybe she'd find something empowering and feminist in that. Who knows. You never can anymore. The drinks come and Ray pays the bartender with a ten, leaving a buck for tip on the counter. It's cheap enough and her *Coyote Ugly* ploys are transparent enough that he feels okay breaking the dollar-a-drink rule.

He sits and sips—tequila first, then beer—stares vacantly at the closest TV. College basketball. It would be better if it were a movie, anything. Or one of those year-end recap specials or some kind of *Rockin' Eve* pre-show. That would be fun, listening to old country while reading closed captions depicting what television producers think Middle America would want to hear to best remember the year that was. Such a fucked up year that was: 2012, the year he thought he was dead. Some people thought the world would end, he did them one better by thinking his already had… He wonders what Haruka's doing right now. Probably hanging out with her family, or solidifying plans with old friends for tonight. Maybe an old flame. No. No more ruminating about Haruka. He came here to see if he can get over her, not do the same shit he was doing at home but in public.

Maybe to kill time he should try to make a friend with another guy sitting here alone. That way if some single ladies roll through, he'll have a wingman. He doesn't want to spend New Year's Eve watching a game he cares nothing about. He evaluates his potential new compadres: eyes still on phones and TVs, or the bartender's tits. Nah, pass. These dudes don't seem like they'd do him any favors. Either too old or too weird. This place is definitely wild for Harlem. Somewhere between Texas and New York for sure. Like Memphis. Hmmm… maybe this is what bars are like in Memphis? Johnny Cash is playing on the jukebox now. No, Nashville, then. Really, though, how the fuck would he know? He's never been to either. Let's just say this is in New York, but not. A dream version of it, but with some twang. Like *Eyes Wide Shut* remade by Tarantino or Robert Rodriguez. Except less bloody, true to the suspense of the original. Those are his vibes tonight. He's cruising like a Texican Cruise, trying to fuck to forget, but with even grimmer prospects in this veritably strange honky-tonk bar.

Dammit, now he's thinking about her again, even if it is in a roundabout way. He shifts his focus back to the TV, tries to get into the game. He fails. Maybe he should get out of here after these drinks, go to a neighborhood where more young people like to hang out, the East Village or Williamsburg, or even just over to the old Columbia bars. Walk a half hour over to 1020 or whatever. A little bleak, but not totally. Grad students hang out there, people around his age—locals, too, to play pool—some of the students might even be older than he is; hitting on them wouldn't be bad at all, actually. Interesting international types, unable to afford the trip home, lonely. They'd already have shit in common with the Columbia thing. Maybe he could meet someone he really likes.

He pulls out his phone, checks the time. It's 7:05. People with bigger plans might pre-game at 1020 in another hour or so. So what to do until then? He can't just sit here watching fucking college basketball. Maybe it would be okay to think about her, to look at the text again, see if this change in environment was what he actually needed. If it leads to any epiphanies. He can't just not think about Haruka if he wants to think about Haruka. That would be dishonest; while it's okay that he's out in order to test his true feelings for her with someone else, to deny her his thought wouldn't be fair. To her or himself. And besides, it's not like he even has the opportunity to strike up a conversation with someone right now. Nobody's here. And if someone comes in, it would probably be better if he looked busy, involved. Like he was on his phone texting someone. He reads the text:

> i miss you sometimes, Ray. i think
> i might be in love with you.

Love. Love, love, love. Staring past it, it echoes back, in her voice. He takes a big sip of the tequila. He stares still.

"Whoa, is that a flip phone?" It's the guy closest to him, two seats down. Black guy, early to mid-forties maybe, wearing a beanie and a workman's jacket. He'd had his nose in an LG or something before this.

"Yeah."

"Damn, man!"

"I like to keep it simple," Ray says.

"I'll say. Shit's thick as hell, too! Not even a Razr!" Others around the bar take notice, looking over at the two while grinning or trying to suppress grins. "Partying like it's 1999 up in here tonight! Whooo!" The man laughs to himself, heartily. That's interesting, another Prince reference. Must be the law of attraction. Ray joins in the laughter, half to ease any tension the others might be looking for, half because he thinks getting called out on the type of phone he has is genuinely funny. Especially by a black guy. It's not only for Indians: having a flip phone is grounds for a little acceptable prejudice at The Duck. At least there's honesty in this, though. It would probably be a good idea not to break out his phone at 1020 unless absolutely necessary. They'll definitely be more subtle about it, the co-eds, which would be a lot worse.

"Yeah, well. I thought the world might end this year. So I downgraded."

"Oh, man! You know I'm just playin'."

The bartender approaches. "Whoa, can I see it?" She leans over, her crossed forearms pushing her chest forward so it's even more pronounced, presumably on tippy-toes. It's a choice view for Ray, but he can only take it in briefly. He meets her eyes when he hands the phone over. She handles it for a moment. "Wow! Talk about a throwback!"

"It's nice, you know. Just calls and texts. I don't really like being connected to the internet all the time."

"Is that what you tell people?!" The guy chimes in. He laughs again, even more heartily. "Nah, seriously, though. You know I'm just playin' witchu." Ahhhh... Now this guy's actually starting to suck. The Razr comment was good, the Prince one even better, but all the "You know I'm just playin' " shit when you're really not is insufferable. Like he's trying to have it both ways. Ray's a lover not a fighter for the most part though, isn't interested in trouble tonight at all, so the best he can do is dodge and feint.

"I can respect that," says the bartender. Or get in the good graces of the girl every straight male here, which seems to be all of them, probably wishes they could fuck. She continues, "We're too plugged in. I just deleted Facebook from my phone. I went home for Christmas and spent half my time looking at *this thing*!" She waves her phone in front of him. Probably a newer iPhone, judging by the shape, but it's moving too fast to know for sure. "I was like, 'Whaaat? I thought I came back to see my family, not look at pictures of everyone else's!' It was so dumb."

"Where's home?"

"North Carolina."

"Where's your accent?" There's that old Gonzales charm... She seems like she actually likes him; maybe, just maybe, he can fuck her tonight after all. No! The tequila's hitting too quick. He should've had more of a dinner, a side with that quesadilla. This is, again, purely transactional; he knows this. Keep her at a distance. The tip he left before probably just made him a challenge, which, because not too many people are here right now, she's accepted.

"Only comes out when I'm drunk or mad." Oh, man! That was such a good answer! Who knows… maybe Ray can make history and have sex with this bartender on her break tonight, if she gets a break. She walks away. One of the biker/drug dealers from the pool table's come over for another round. Ray watches them. The Doors are now playing on the jukebox, *Alabama Song.*

"This right here—this is knowledge." Ray turns. Is this guy drunk? It's a little early, but maybe. That or just one of those guys who really likes to run his mouth once he's found some dumb thing to glom onto. "This is power. Sure, you can look at it how you want. For some people, it might be too strong. Like crack. Always gotta have it, can't look away. Candy Crush! Candy Motherfuckin' Crush, baby! I don't know if that's your problem, young man, but it isn't mine. For me, it's like a weapon. You just have to know how to wield it. No disrespect, I'm just sayin'." Of course he'd eventually actually say "I'm just sayin' " on top of "I'm just playin'." And "No disrespect," that other unbearable non-apology, is always a welcome addition. Goddam. This dude seems sorta sad, though. Like he just got his first fuckin' smartphone or something and can't wait to brag about it.

"Is it, though?"

"Yeah. Like right now, I'm watchin' this game, and I can check out stats at the same time. See how my fantasy team's doin'. That kind of thing." Oh, man! Ray smiles. He really, really wants to laugh right now. This is the weapon this motherfucker's wielding? That's his katana? The power is in reading stats about twenty-year-old student athletes in the Midwest for his fucking fantasy college basketball team?! Oh, fuck! And Ray thought he wasted time this year. But all he can do is nod. It's a good idea in Harlem—East Harlem, particularly, given its crime stats— to do everything you can to keep the peace. Sure, Hispanics got it bad in this country. But nobody's got it as bad as black people. American Indians, but that's it. He reminds himself of this. Rich people in America look at Hispanics like sub-human help. But they look at black people like monsters; in short, worse than animals. This dude wants to gloat because he's got something nicer than the vaguely handsome youngish mixed-race man Ray is, even though he's sort of an idiot? Sure, why not. No skin off his back. Fuck! That was racist—unintentionally, but still! Wait, is it really? Where'd that idiom come from? He'll have to look it up later. Either way, he can't be thinking shit like that! Ray just nods. Maybe the guy will think he's fucked up and leave him alone if he nods slowly enough, and he can go back to talking to the bartender. She's about done getting drinks for that other guy now. "You know what I'm sayin'?" Nope.

"Yeah, totally. I guess I just don't have the same discipline." Two young women walk in, one Asian, one white, neither bad-looking. That was a good line for them to walk in on, a nice way to set the tone for a potential one-night stand. Ray: so wild and free, such a rake. "Gotta do what works for you." They settle in on the two stools on the other side of him.

"Right. Just gotta do you. Always. If you can't handle the power, you can't handle the power. What's your name?"

"Ray."

"I'm Smoke."

They lean in and shake hands. "It's not that I can't handle it, Smoke. I just don't like it. Sort of like math. You can be good at math in school and still hate it." Ray's pretty happy with this interaction, even if this guy is an attention hog and sort of a time burglar; the addition of the two ladies flipped the script, and now he feels okay pushing back a little bit more. If they're listening in now, they probably feel like they walked in on some type of sitcom. "My thing is, really, I don't like being that available. For the man, you know?" Behind him, the girls put in drink orders, a whiskey-coke and a rum and coke. Nice. They came to party. "When you got a phone like that and your boss knows it, he'll send you emails all the time, day and night, and expect an immediate response. Weekends, too. That ever happen to you?"

"Yeah, but you got a thing like this"—he holds up his LG or whatever, the cool white light of some NCAA basketball stats page or fantasy sports site glaring outward—"and you can fuck around at work, too. It all evens out." His gaze goes from Ray back to the game.

"I'd rather compartmentalize my time. Be at work when I'm at work. Stay chillin' when I'm chillin'."

"I feel you, I feel you. Guess that's you doin' you." He looks back at him. "What'd you say your name was again?"

"Ray."

"No it's not. I'ma call you 1999 instead." Then towards the game again. Of course Smoke is trying to be condescending, but Ray actually likes the cognomen. 1999 was a good year; pre-9/11, pre-Bush, bangin' economy, the send-off to a pretty amazing decade and century—he can't remember what he was doing then exactly, but probably little more than going to school, gadding about with friends, playing PlayStation and after-school sports… Plus, getting any kind of nickname from a black guy, even one meant to be rude, is an honor. "Ahhh shit!" he says. Now he's going back and forth between the screens of the television and his beloved phone. "C'mon. Rebound! Shit!"

Ray sips. The tequila's now gone, Lone Star's got a decent dent in it. Because his own eyes have nowhere else to go, they too drift toward the game. In his periphery, he sees the two girls hunched over their phones, occasionally sipping on their drinks. Another Doors song comes on, *The End*. Are they even together? Or did they just happen to come in at the same time? He commits, looks over at them, smiling, though no one's there to see it. The bartender, too, is now staring at her phone. Hypocrite. The crush he had on her decompresses. The girls are slightly oriented toward one another, their legs angled in, so they most likely do know each other. He's been looking over at them for long enough and decides to just go for it: "Hi, sorry to interrupt. Are you guys together?"

The white one, who's closest, turns. "Yeah…" She's pretty gussied up, wearing glittery multi-toned eyeshadow and oxblood lipstick.

"Me and my friend Smoke over here were just having a discussion about smartphones, and I couldn't help but notice you—"

"Damn, 1999! You botherin' them girls? Don't bother them girls. He botherin' you, girls?"

"No, we're okay," she says.

"Yeah, it's fine," the Asian one follows.

"I couldn't help but notice you weren't talking to each other because you were too busy on those things." That didn't come out exactly as he had hoped, so Ray turns toward the bartender, seeing an opportunity to take some of the heat off of them by putting it on her, the heartbreaker. "And I see you're on your phone now, too! I thought you were in my corner!"

She looks up. "I know! I'm so bad! Ever since I deleted Facebook now I can't get off Instagram."

"You young ones need more willpower," says Smoke. Maybe he's a recovering drug addict or something. Seems to have a hang-up about self-control, probably on some insecure he-who-smelt-it-dealt-it kick. The name is also telling, Smoke. Ray's figured him out.

"Well, if you have to know…" she's smiling, more flirtatious than hostile—"I got a message from someone on Tinder. That's all." She looks over to her friend. "And she wasn't just gonna sit there and not look at her phone while I was on mine."

"Yeah, that would be weird. Like eating in front of someone not eating," the other girl says.

"Totally." They laugh.

Ray has no idea what Tinder is. Some new platform where you talk to friends? Did she just mispronounce Twitter or something, was responding to a DM? "What's Tinder exactly?"

"You haven't heard of Tinder?" the Asian one asks. Her lipstick is also red, less bold but still festive; her eyes are done up with wings in pretty heavy black. The dress she's wearing shines gold.

"Nuh-uh."

"Wait, how old are you?" she asks, sort of jumping over the white one, who looked like she was about to speak. That's unfortunate. Although she looks nothing like Haruka, the farther girl's ethnicity is still a problem. Since she's also Asian, and Haruka's the only Asian Ray's been with, he'd definitely be conscious of it if they ended up having sex. Fucked up, but it is what it is. He needs someone completely different to try to get over her. Why couldn't she have been black or Hispanic or anything else?

"Almost twenty-seven."

"Maybe that's why." The white one says. He's glad to have her back. "It's a dating app. Came out earlier this year, a lot of people in college are starting to use it."

"Oh, there she is!" Smoke again, booming. Dude could give Deion a run for his money. Ray looks over. Another bartender—black, pretty, also with an ample bust in a low-cut shirt—makes her way behind the bar. "There's my New Year's date! Ha-ha!" This explains why there's a decent number of black guys in a bar with a sort of redneck aesthetic.

"Hi sweetie," she says to Smoke. She and the other bartender exchange greetings while Ray shifts his focus back to the girls sitting next to him. Jim Morrison's still just getting started with this long-ass song. It's pretty good, though.

"Where do you go?"

"Hunter," says the white girl. The Asian one has since returned to her phone, thankfully. "The social work school close by."

"It's kind of crazy how fast online dating is shedding its stigma." And it is. That also came out kind of rude, though, so he tries to smooth it over, show them he's with them: "I mean, I just set up an OkCupid account this year and that was a pretty big step for me. In high school, me and my friends used to make fun of all that stuff, Match, eHarmony."

"There is no stigma anymore. Not for people our age, anyway, a few years younger. We don't even call it online dating, we just call it dating."

"Yeah, grandpa…" the Asian one says, not looking up. Didn't Haruka call him that once before?

"Hey, just because I have a flip phone doesn't make me a grandpa."

"I think it totally does, actually," she says, still not looking up. "Like the dictionary definition. The first definition is using a flip phone. The secondary one is having grandchildren." She clearly likes him more than her friend. Which makes sense. Her friend's apparently working out the details of a date; any kind of charm offensive he could mount would be lost on her tonight. So would it really be so bad to try to take the Asian one home? Wouldn't that actually be the ultimate test to see if he's over Haruka? To be conscious of it throughout, and still go through with it? She certainly had to be conscious of him while she was with Brian. Brian… fuck. That whole thing. Her motives were definitely different though, not a test of love, but hate. Does she actually hate Ray? Yes! So why would she say she loves him now? And why does he think he's in love with her? That was such a fucked up thing to do. He'll let that fuel him as he focuses on the Asian girl, who still hasn't looked up.

"So how's Tinder work? Why's it so good compared to, say, meeting someone in class or, you know, at a bar?"

"It's not an either-or thing," the white one says. "Just another option. Have you heard of Grindr?"

"The gay hookup app?"

"It's sort of like that. It's location-based. You see pictures and a brief description of people. Swipe right for yes, left for no. If they also swipe right it's a match and then you can message each other."

This sounds fucking wild. Basically a digital meat market, where people are judged on nothing more than their looks or deceptive photography skills and the few words they'd use as a sales pitch. Like that old website Hot or Not except you actually get to fuck the hot person. It made sense for gay guys, because they're men, and pretty much all men are trying to fuck all of or at least most of the time, but women? "Holy shit. And this has appeal for women?"

"Lots." The Asian girl finally looks up as she says this. "That's some double standard you got there, mister. We mostly want the same things as guys, believe it or not. But you can use it in different ways if you want. Some people want something more serious, some actually just go on there to meet new people, make purely platonic friends."

"You're on it, too?"

"Of course. What do you think I've been doing while we've been sitting here? Can't let her have all the fun. Most of our guy friends from the program are out of town for break and I need a date for tonight."

Ray could be that date, Ray would like to be that date. He's sitting right in front of her. They've engaged in some flirtatiously antagonistic repartee. Why not invite him? Maybe because she doesn't even know his name yet. "What are your names, by the way?"

"Caitlin," says the white one. Ray shakes her hand, lightly, thumb over the back of it.

"Gracie," says hopefully his lover for tonight, moving her phone into the other hand as she accepts his. Maybe this time it actually is a sign… Grace. This divine thing in front of him, meant to carry him away…

"Ray," he says, shaking. She's got a nice, soft hand, if a little cold. He lets go. "You can order up a date for New Year's using GPS. Damn. There really is an app for everything now." He takes a long swig.

"Ha-ha. Yeah."

"I think it's a really interesting time to be alive, especially young," says Caitlin. "I mean, I love my phone. I came here because of Yelp. Made my way from our apartment with Google Maps. After this, we're gonna take an Uber downtown…" Uber, that's right, he's heard of that one. A cab alternative that picks you up curbside wherever you are. God bless 'em. Anybody who's ridden a bike through the streets of New York City knows yellow cabs deserve every bit of badness that comes their way, especially undercutting competition. He hopes they become the new standard. "Then meet this hot guy I started messaging with on Tinder yesterday and a hot guy Gracie hopefully finds on Tinder tonight at a cocktail bar I found on Foursquare and verified through Yelp. Seriously, I don't know how I'd function without it. I don't know if I'd even want to. It would be like using a torch to find your way around after electricity was invented."

Goddam, she sounds sort of like Haruka, too—except she isn't eighteen or nineteen. And she wants to be a fucking social worker. It's a bit scary, actually. "I guess I believe in the torch. I like figuring out how to get around…"

"Well that's because you're a guy. Guys love that shit. You'd all rather walk in circles than ask for directions. Sorry, I got shit to do!"

"Oh my God! Yes!" The bartender comes over and high-fives Caitlin, using her phone-free hand. They both smile big. The other bartender's been chatting with Smoke, which Ray's overheard behind him here and there, when Jim isn't going too hard, Smoke favoring a more hushed tone with her.

"Hey, now who's generalizing?" All three of them still seem too busy smiling at one another and exchanging knowing eye contact about men and directions to react in any way to this. "And besides, it's not the destination, it's the journey."

"Now there's a line if I've ever heard one," Caitlin says, laughing.

"You could put it on Tinder. You're kinda cute, you'd probably get lots of right swipes," says Gracie. Ray smiles. The bartender leaves, goes over to the unattractive lady and her dude who must seem ready for another round. "Oh, I forgot. Flip phone."

"Seriously, though, there's virtue in just being in the moment, letting stuff happen."

"Who said we're not? You can do both at once. This just lets me curate my future moments better." Caitlin taps on her phone, which she's placed facing up on the bar next to her drink. "Go places I wouldn't otherwise know about. It's just another form of word of mouth, that's all."

"Yeah, but you can't really have it both ways. There's no multitasking with the moment. Just a few minutes ago you were sacrificing being here because of it. You looked it up on Yelp earlier and now that you're here you're on to the next thing. If you do that, you're never really anywhere. There is no moment. No present, only the future. You know?"

"Not really. It seriously is just a little multitasking. You're still breathing right now, aren't you?"

"It's not the same."

"Guess you're carrying the torch for all of us, then," says Gracie. She turns to her phone after this. "Oh, nice, look!" she holds her phone out for Caitlin.

"You still at it 1999? You don't have to hide behind all that Zen-type bullshit!" Smoke shouts over. The other bartender's now helping some new arrivals. "If you're too broke for a nice phone, you're too broke for a nice phone. This The Duck, man. No judgments here."

"That sounded a lot like judgment, Smoke."

"No, no! No judgment. Just real talk."

"Well cheers to that, cheers to real talk in the coming year." Ray raises his Lone Star. Smoke raises his PBR. They both take long sips.

It's the last of Ray's bottle, and as it goes down, he wonders if Smoke's provocations are all in fun, or if he's actually been trying to pick a fight with him. Either way, it doesn't matter. He's gotta get out of here.

This song's getting too intense as it reaches its climax and these girls aren't gonna invite him out, not when there's a buffet of "hot" men to choose from on their phones. Maybe if he had met one of them on Tinder. And if he drinks more and keeps at it with Smoke, he may offer his own real talk, which would involve how silly it is to play fantasy sports, let alone college fantasy sports, or jabs about how he seems to be using this place as some type of budget strip club, and it may end up being that true, bloody Rodriguez or Tarantino remake after all. He'd rather keep this what it is: more of a long-form version of the video for Drake's *Marvins Room,* but over different music. You can't even go to a bar anymore, meet strangers that become friends or women who become lovers. You need the extra step of finding them through an app or bonding over an app, that or the make and model of your fucking phone, which you must display as much as possible.

"Another round?" The white bartender's swooped in, seeing Ray's now empty.

"No, I think I'm all set. What was your name?"

"Lana." That's funny. They shake hands. If Ray still thought he was dead, this would seem loaded. Especially with all the Americana shit everywhere. But he doesn't and it's not—just another stupid coincidence, like so many other things this year. Probably isn't even her real name, not that it is with Ms. Del Rey, either. No. Just another meaningless coincidence.

"Ray. Nice meeting you, Lana from North Carolina."

"For what it's worth, I think what you're doing is brave. I'd do it if I could."

"Thanks." He smiles at her, then turns to the other girls. "Nice meeting you two as well. Happy New Year."

"Happy New Year." Caitlin simpers, then returns to her phone.

"Bye torchbearer," says Gracie, not looking up.

Ray steps down from his stool and puts on his coat. "I'm outta here, Smoke. Have a good night now."

"Good meeting you 1999. You keep that party going for us, now. New year, old you."

Upon standing Ray noticed he really had to piss. He does, into the famous toilet from Yelp. His first impressions were wrong; this place actually is a dump—a dump for all humanity. He flushes all the same, even though none of these people would know the difference. Because all places are now, and they will be, until some start adopting a policy where smartphone use is not permitted. Like those supposed movie theaters in

Paris that don't even sell food, attenuating as many distractions as possible from the experience of cinema. But that probably won't happen for a long, long time, and when it does, likely wouldn't catch on. He'd be the only guy in there. Ray leaves the bathroom, some indistinct new song playing, then the bar.

Where to next? He doesn't know. It would be too pathetic to go home, to spend the evening staying in watching some Ryan Seacrest thing alone, doing nothing. Inevitably going over his Haruka text messages again… New year, old you indeed.

Oh, Haruka. Haruka, Haruka, Haruka. What's the point of trying to get over you when everyone, now, is you? Forget the social workers, or the bartender… even guys like Smoke are you. It's the world now. There's no point in trying to love someone else—they're all just iterations of you. He should be more excited—the head has caught up with the heart. But it doesn't feel that good. He's sure the fervor from before, when the heart was challenged, will return, but for the moment, the head's earned a little mourning…

The first stop: the liquor store on 111th and Third for a half pint of whiskey. Then, a bodega for a coke. He drinks half the coke down, adds the Evan Williams discreetly around the corner outside. He sips. A little something for his loss. Then he walks, just one more for the road.

Then he's on it, or, rather, under it. Ray gets on a downtown 6 at 110th. Too busy for a seat, but not to lean against the door. A good spot. He looks at the people, all but a few brown or black. Those in groups, most probably half-drunk, revel. They wear coats and party accessories: hats, glasses, things that glow and blink. Items to complement all the talking and shouting and laughing. They are here, even if their accessories read 2013. And those alone, who wear nothing like that, but still glow, from their palms, like *her*, are there. That somewhere else, that nowhere and everywhere, beyond, in the future. Ray's somewhere between them all. But not lost, found. Happily in this liminal flux as he stares and sips. A little bite at the end; Evan's always been a bit harsh. But he wouldn't have it any other way. A subway preacher gets on at 103rd, an old black man in a rumpled suit and hat who warns that the end is near. He's late to the party. The hooting and cachinnating drown him out; the others, by themselves, were way ahead of them. Probably didn't even notice him. Blocked out by earbuds and a bright graphic interface. He moves into another car before they reach 96th. Mostly white people and some Asians get on here and join the others, roistering or staring, depending on if they're in groups or not, just a little more subtly dressed. The dress is refined, but little else. They're every bit as loud or preoccupied depending on if they're here or there. An increasingly white demographic gets on at every stop after this. The rich, but not rich enough for a cab tonight. Or even—what is it?—an Uber. Ray just stares and sips. The only person without a group not looking down since the preacher. He gets off at 59th Street.

Outside, he looks up into the night air, the tall specular buildings on the cusp of Midtown East and the UES, the passing clouds, the plume of his breath. He finishes his bourbon-coke and pops a mint. He heads west.

Before long he's there. The Apple Store. Their flagship location in the city, open twenty-four hours a day. One of the most photographed places in NYC. Last year it was number one. More than the Empire State, the Statue of Liberty, the Chrysler Building. The Apple Store. Up five spots from 2010. There were no articles about it this year, at least none that he saw, but it's probably still number one.

He enters the cube and descends the winding staircase. People buzz around, various races, ages. A clamorous whirlwind interrupted only by those in the blue shirts. Ray speaks to one of them near the iPhone table. They get him the latest model, then someone else in a blue shirt helps him pick out a plan, transfer his number over. Personal Setup they call it. Now Ray is a person again, like all the rest. He reemerges.

There are still a few hours to pass. But they'll be easy. He moves across Central Park South to the Seventh Avenue entrance. This is the closest he could get to where he really wants to be and still feel comfortable. There are other people here, smart ones who've figured it out. That, or those who were turned away from the real place and asked the right questions. Probably of their phones. Like he can now. He walks a little ways into the park, and he can still see it: Times Square. The ball. The Crossroads of the World, the Great White Way shining with New Year's spectacle and fulgurant advertisements. Two hours to go. He spends them downloading all kinds of cool apps: Google, Gmail, Facebook, Instagram, Twitter, Wikipedia, Uber, Google Maps, Yelp, Seamless, Spotify, Songza... everything except Tinder. He downloads and plays a few games. Looks up a few things, skims some year-end lists. They fly by, the hours.

Then it's time. The countdown: 10-9-8-7-6-5-4-3-2...1!!! Happy New Year! The ball has dropped. *Auld Lang Syne* just started playing somewhere in the distance. And he knows who he wants to kiss.

He opens the FaceTime app and selects Haruka from his contacts list. It rings. Then there she is.

"Ray! You have FaceTime now!"

"I love you, too, Haruka," he says. And he does. All of him. Not like before, now he's really in love. There's a difference. He would die for her. He loves her with the head and the heart, with enthusiasm. It returned once the phone was in his hand. The God within meeting the God without. Ray's home now. Where he belongs. With God, in love.

It's beautiful. She's seen the future. In the present. 2013. Should be a good year. Lucky '13. It'll have a hard time beating this one. So much happened, so much that changed the course of things. It's still 2012 here, they've got a little bit of time to go. She's enjoying what's left of it. The Year of the Dragon. Ha-ha. She is the dragon. More than anyone she knows, it was her year. Next year should be good too, though. Dragons and snakes aren't so different. The terms have been set. They will fuck sometimes because he knows how to please her and that is valuable. Good for stress relief. To feed Little Kaiju, recharge. They are free to see other people. Just not through Tinder, she told him. That's the competition. He's even going to work for her. Help her with branding: logo design, press releases, marketing, ad copy. Small picture creative tasks. Mostly word stuff. On a freelance basis, of course. Little gigs here and there more than it would be a job. But steady and paid well enough that he won't have to leave New York. He understood, said it sounded great. Times Square looked beautiful in the background. Maybe one day they'll run an ad there. But just for fun. The most effective ads are online, of course. The most effective everything is online. She's so glad she has him now. The future is nothing without the present. It depends on it. And now her present is perfect. He's hers, she has him now. There's nothing he can do about it. Actually, they're all hers. The whole world is hers now. There's nothing anybody can do about it. Nope. It's hers. All of it. Not just now, but forever and ever. This is everything. Lol. Haruka is literally dying. Lololo101o11100010 10001000 10011110…

▲▲▽▲▲▲▽

```
11100010   10001000   10011110   11100010   10001000   10011110
11100010   10001000   10011110   11100010   10001000   10011110
11100010   10001000   10011110   11100010   10001000   10011110
11100010   10001000   10011110   11100010   10001000   10011110
11100010   10001000   10011110   11100010   10001000   10011110
11100010   10001000   10011110   11100010   10001000   10011110
11100010   10001000   10011110   11100010   10001000   10011110
11100010   10001000   10011110   11100010   10001000   10011110
11100010   10001000   10011110   11100010   10001000   10011110
11100010   10001000   10011110   11100010   10001000   10011110
11100010   10001000   10011110   11100010   10001000   10011110
11100010   10001000   10011110   11100010   10001000   10011110
11100010   10001000   10011110   11100010   10001000   10011110
11100010   10001000   10011110   11100010   10001000   10011110
11100010   10001000   10011110   11100010   10001000   10011110
11100010   10001000   10011110   11100010   10001000   10011110
11100010   10001000   10011110   11100010   10001000   10011110
11100010   10001000   10011110   11100010   10001000   10011110
11100010   10001000   10011110   11100010   10001000   10011110
11100010   10001000   10011110   11100010   10001000   10011110
11100010   10001000   10011110   11100010   10001000   10011110
11100010   10001000   10011110   11100010   10001000   10011110
11100010   10001000   10011110   11100010   10001000   10011110
11100010   10001000   10011110   11100010   10001000   10011110
11100010   10001000   10011110   11100010   10001000   10011110
11100010   10001000   10011110   11100010   10001000   10011110
11100010   10001000   10011110   11100010   10001000   10011110
11100010   10001000   10011110   11100010   10001000   10011110
11100010   10001000   10011110   11100010   10001000   10011110
11100010   10001000   10011110   11100010   10001000   10011110
11100010   10001000   10011110   11100010   10001000   10011110
11100010   10001000   10011110   11100010   10001000   10011110
11100010   10001000   10011110   11100010   10001000   10011110
11100010   10001000   10011110   11100010   10001000   10011110
11100010   10001000   10011110   11100010   10001000   10011110
11100010   10001000   10011110   11100010   10001000   10011110
11100010   10001000   10011110   11100010   10001000   10011110
11100010   10001000   10011110   11100010   10001000   10011110
```

```
11100010  10001000  10011110  11100010  10001000  10011110
11100010  10001000  10011110  11100010  10001000  10011110
11100010  10001000  10011110  11100010  10001000  10011110
11100010  10001000  10011110  11100010  10001000  10011110
11100010  10001000  10011110  11100010  10001000  10011110
11100010  10001000  10011110  11100010  10001000  10011110
11100010  10001000  10011110  11100010  10001000  10011110
11100010  10001000  10011110  11100010  10001000  10011110
11100010  10001000  10011110  11100010  10001000  10011110...
```

ABOUT THE AUTHOR

A.D. ALIWAT was born in the United States of America in 1985. His literary debut, *Alpha*, was published in 2013. He lives in New York City.

www.ingramcontent.com/pod-product-compliance
Lightning Source LLC
Chambersburg PA
CBHW020856130726

47900CB00014B/799